"I hate my mother so much. I know hating's bad, but it does me good to hate her. Sometimes, I don't think I'll ever live long enough to hate her and Grandma and the rest of them enough for taking me away from Daddy."

CHARLOTTE CULIN lives with her family in Rancho Palos Verdes, California. Trained as an archaeologist, she has only recently begun writing. *Cages of Glass, Flowers of Time* is her first novel.

Cages of Glass, Flowers of Time

Charlotte Culin

LAUREL-LEAF BOOKS bring together under a single imprint outstanding works of fiction and nonfiction particularly suitable for young adult readers, both in and out of the classroom. Charles F. Reasoner, Professor Emeritus of Children's Literature and Reading, New York University, is consultant to this series.

For my sister

Published by
Dell Publishing Co., Inc.
1 Dag Hammarskjold Plaza
NewYork, New York 10017

ISBN: 0-440-91319-5

RL: 5.1
Reprinted by arrangement with Bradbury Press, Inc.
Printed in the United States of America
December 1982

10 9 8 7 6 5 4 3

Chapter One

*Mom said an hour . . . go look in the stores an hour
. . . then meet her at the grocery.*
I can't get caught breaking in!
I'll never get my chalk if I do.

I made myself stop running. I walked hurriedly instead, trying to keep from looking at the cars passing
me. I hoped I looked as if I still belonged there, was
just going somewhere on a Saturday morning—the
same as anyone else.

Only no one must see me.

I longed to look at the beautiful, familiar old houses
I was passing, but I didn't let myself look at their
white-columned porches, shaded by magnolias' glistening black-green leaves. As I hurried past, I
watched the patterns in the brick sidewalk.

One more lawn to the corner. One past that to the
alley. I ran for the alley.

Inside it, I could see the high stone wall around my
house. I ran toward the battered old green door in the
wall, grabbed the latch, pushed against it.

It wouldn't open. They'd locked it. I leaned against
it, hating them.

An hour.
If I'm late she'll see the chalk!

Quickly, I climbed the wall. On top, terrified the
neighbors would see me, I pushed myself off. I fell
into long, uncut grass. I didn't have to look up. I knew
I couldn't be seen from the houses on either side anymore. The walls and trees were hiding me from them.

I wanted to just lie there believing I was home
again—safe with no neighbors meddling. I just wanted

to look at Galway Hall, the oldest house in Galway Fields, my home.

I ran toward the back of my house. I knew there was no use trying the back door. They'd said in court they'd put new locks on to keep Daddy out. They couldn't keep me out! They couldn't keep Daddy out either, if he'd come back!

I pulled the nail file I'd stolen from Mom out of my pocket. I crouched down in front of the cellar window near the back stairs. It was easy to slip the file between the shutters and raise the latch inside.

Then I heard the neighbor's door slam. I froze, terrified. I crouched lower, shaking, hating her, praying she hadn't seen me climbing the back wall. I could still hear her voice from a month ago—out on the front porch with the sheriff—telling him, "I know she's in there. I saw her coming home from the store not half an hour past. That's why I called you again. Poor child. Lugging all those groceries. No one to take care of her."

I heard a car door slam and then another. I stayed frozen until I heard the engine start. I waited until I heard the car going away down the driveway on the other side of the wall.

I let out my breath, shuddering.

This time she didn't see me.

This time she can't feel sorry for me.

This time she can't take everything I love away from me.

Hating her, hating the lawyers, the court, and hating Mom, I jiggled the window until the lock slipped open. Then I let myself down through the opening into the cool, dark cellar. I closed and latched the shutters behind me.

In the dark, I walked across the cellar floor. Knowing where everything was, I wasn't scared I'd fall. I ran up the stairs counting the fourteen steps.

My age now.

I pushed open the door at the top, stepped into the beautiful, walnut-paneled hall.

I was safe here.

I ran down the hall to the studio. My other box of chalk was still on the table by my easel. I leaned down to smell the chalk. I pushed my fingers into the multicolored fragments in the tray. I smeared my fingers across the rough, naked paper pinned to the easel, waiting for me.

Then I saw the sores on my arm and remembered. Quickly, I found a paper bag in one of the cabinets along the wall. I took three new drawing pads out and stuffed them in with my chalk. I got a handful of charcoal sticks and dropped them in, too. Hesitating, I took more and put those in my pocket with the nail file.

Even if Mom catches me and takes my chalk again, I'll have some charcoal.

I looked around the studio, at the glass doors all down one wall facing Grandmother Burden's beautiful garden, at the brick floor, at the fireplace, at Daddy's easels—abandoned.

When they made me leave him, he ran away.

I saw a pile of his drawing pads on a table by the fireplace. I began looking through the one on top. It was almost filled with his sketches.

An hour!

I made myself let the cover fall closed. I put it in the bag, too.

Then I ran through the house. I was too scared I'd be late to stop and look at the portraits of me. I just counted them till I knew I'd touched them all. I had to stop at the door of my room.

Everything's the same.

Everything's just as Grandmother Burden left it long ago. Just as I left it.

I wanted to go in. I wanted to touch the carved headboard on my four-poster bed. I wanted to stretch out there and feel safe again—remembering how every morning the headboard's deeply cut flower petals were the first thing I touched . . . and the last at night.

Grandmother loved me.

I looked at the painting above my bed, the only one in the house Daddy hadn't done. I smiled back at the young woman in it.

Grandmother loved you, too. She named me Claire after you. Told me I should be good, gentle, and kind like you . . .

I turned away feeling cold inside.

"Gone and dead when I was nine" was almost the only other thing Grandmother Burden ever told me about the Claire in the painting. "My beautiful sister, gone and dead."

Grandmother was dead and gone when I was seven. It was just Daddy and I, then.

I can't cry. Mom'll know where I've been if I cry.

Back outside, I hesitated by an old dead tree in Grandmother's garden. With me beside her, watching, she'd planted vines around it. After she'd died, the vines had kept growing and growing. They'd engulfed the tree. Now they cascaded free from its broken limbs in waterfalls of white blossoms high above me.

I looked back at the house. Daddy'd painted the tree last summer. I hadn't looked at the painting in the studio.

I can't go back. It has to be an hour.

I stopped running in the park across the street from the grocery store. Mom's ancient, beat-up car was parked near the front of the lot. Praying she wouldn't come out and catch me, I ran to the car.

Inside it, I crammed the bag of drawing things under the front seat. When I looked up and saw she still wasn't coming after me, I rested my head against the seat and closed my eyes. My heart was pounding in my ears.

She said meet her in the store.

I took a deep breath and made myself go inside. Mom was standing in front of the beer display.

Even after a month, the fact that she was my mother and I had to live with her still shocked me. Over the years, I'd seen her in town a few times. I'd found out who she was, known why she'd stared at me so, but I'd never spoken to her. I'd always been too shocked. I never wanted her for a mother.

I looked down at the round, white marks and red scabs on my arms. When I looked back up, Mom was staring at me, angrily.

"What the hell you want?" she snapped, slinging another six-pack into the grocery cart. I backed away.

"Nothing."

I'll never want anything from you . . .

"And that's all you're gettin'! Go wait in the car like I told you, till I'm done."

I saw there was hardly any food in the cart. Just a few things and beer. If I did what she said maybe she'd get more food. Maybe she'd come back next week. Maybe she wouldn't wait three weeks again.

Hungry, I went back outside. I climbed in the back seat of the car where I'd be out of her reach. I put my hand down to touch the edge of the bag that had my things inside, pushed aside the empty beer cans I felt instead. *I hate her . . . I hate her . . .* I kept my eyes closed, touched the bag of my things, until I could see Daddy's face and the beautiful studio behind him.

I have my chalk now.

I can draw again.

I can look at Daddy's sketches . . .

I heard Mom bang the cart against the car. Hoping all three bags weren't beer, I got out to put them in the trunk.

She grabbed one of the bags and got into the front seat. By the time I'd put the others in and pushed the cart back, she'd already started drinking beer and smoking a cigarette. Watching the red, burning end of it, I got into the back seat on the far side. She ignored me and started the car.

Relieved, I leaned my head against the vibrating window.

I could just barely see the purplish-blue mountains in the distance. It was the same section I'd always seen from my room at home. I watched them until the trees had hidden them.

Then I saw Mom was leaving Galway Fields a different way. Instead of going the easiest way, past the university and the huge, old houses between it and Galway Hall, she'd turned down side streets. Those still had brick sidewalks, but the houses were smaller, closer to the street, and ugly. They needed paint and repair.

There are no gardens here.

When Mom finally reached the highway, I looked out across a field at the Carolina mountains I loved. In the fields, the wind was dancing through the long brown summer grass.

Can I ever catch movement like that on paper with chalk?

I squinted, trying to see the way the grass stems were bending. The car was going too fast. I was too far away.

She'd never stop to look at anything!

When we passed a small, ugly unpainted house, I looked away. I didn't want to see the broken-down cars standing in the yard with hoods up, doors open— abandoned to chickens and filthy, ragged small children that were running and screaming in the August morning sun.

Is that how children play?

Mom turned off the highway onto a narrower country road. There were more houses then—standing nakedly by the road. All the trees had been cut down around them to clear space for nothing—no grass, no flowers. One had a vegetable garden between it and the road. The house peeked out over the rows of corn with ugly eyes. Its broken window panes had no curtains behind them.

The countryside's beautiful. People make it ugly.

When we'd passed the small country store and gas station, I closed my eyes. I didn't want to see anymore until I had to. I braced myself for the bump I knew would come when we turned off onto the dirt road.

Once the car jolted to a stop, Mom yanked the keys out and threw them at me.

"Put the stuff away. Damn fools! Saddlin' me with you! Tellin' me I got to see to you! I'd like to know when someone's goin' to see to me!"

I kept quiet. She'd started to the house with her beer.

Drink it fast.

Pass out soon.

So I can sneak my things upstairs and hide them . . .

I didn't want to get out and go into the ugly, little two-story tenant house Mom called home. But I was too hungry to wait. I got the two bags out of the trunk and hurried inside with them.

In the kitchen, I grabbed a loaf of bread out of the top of one bag. I didn't see anything down in there to put on it. I tore open the loaf and stuffed slices into my mouth.

Food. Two days since I've had food.

I heard Mom walk back across the floor upstairs and start back down the stairs along the kitchen wall. I tried to close the loaf, tried to choke down the bread, tried to get out of her way.

She laughed and picked up her bag of beer.

"Eatin' like a pig!" she said. "I knowed you would! Sure couldn't take no pig by the restaurant. Knowed

I'd be 'shamed by your eatin'." She laughed and went outside.

I stood still, hating her, crushing the loaf of bread against me. As I ate more of it, I watched her through the window spreading a blanket out in the sun.

She can't see the car from there.

Last weekend she stayed out there drunk till after dark.

I turned back to the groceries. She'd just bought junk. A few cans of soup, some dry cereal. Some cans of spaghetti, a box of crackers. There wasn't anything to put on the bread. Nothing I could cook. Nothing that would last more than a few days. There wasn't even any milk for the cereal.

Sick inside, I opened one of the cans of spaghetti. I ate it cold out of the can, too hungry to heat it or put it on a plate.

I made myself put the rest of the junk away in the empty cabinets. Then I looked out the window again. Two beer cans were turned over on the ground near Mom. I watched until she'd picked up another can and awkwardly opened it.

I slipped through the ugly front room and outside. Carefully, I opened the car door. I got my bag out from under the seat.

Inside again, I crept upstairs with it, through Mom's small room to the door of my smaller one. I closed the door behind me and leaned against it wishing it locked.

I stared at the small bed, at the small bookcase filled with the few books they'd let me bring from home, at the beat-up old table. I'd pushed it under the window—used it as an easel—till Mom caught me with my other box of chalk and destroyed it.

This time she won't catch me.

The sketch pads just fit into the bottom drawer of the big, ugly old dresser. I put the chalk and charcoal in there, too, and covered them up with my clothes. I left the other charcoal sticks in my pocket. Then I took Daddy's drawing pad over to the narrow bed.

I closed my eyes against the room and opened the pad. When I opened my eyes, Daddy's sketches were all I could see. They surprised me.

It always took Daddy just a few lines to catch anything beautiful on paper.

I turned the pages slowly, studying each one, trying to hear his voice again telling me how he'd made them.

Some were so familiar—my hand holding a flower he'd found. The same flower lying on one of the tables. I started feeling good inside again. I turned another page and found part of the living room at home. He'd drawn me leaning over something the same way I was now—so my long hair piled up on the book and its blackness caught the light. I smiled and pushed my hair away from my face and back over my shoulder so it wouldn't mess up his sketches.

I wish I was home . . . with Daddy.

I wish he could have stayed there after they made me leave.

I didn't hear Mom till she'd thrust the door open so hard it slammed against the wall. Frantically, I tried to throw the covers over the sketches.

She laughed. "Think I'm a fool!" she cried, coming at me, slapping me. "You're the fool! I knowed you'd go runnin' there! Knowed you would! What've you got?" She ripped the bed covers out of my hands.

For an instant, we both stayed frozen as she saw Daddy's drawings. She sucked in her breath, shocked.

Then she started screaming, "I brung you here! I kept you from Momma!" She ripped the drawing pad away from me, knocked me off the bed. I got downstairs in time to see her grab the matches off the stove and run outside. I went after her. She was already ripping pages out of the pad.

"No!"

"I told you!" she screamed. "I told you no drawin'! I told you I'd kill you for bringin' his dirty stuff here!"

"No! I'll take them back! Don't burn them! No! I won't draw!"

She was striking matches and letting them fall on his sketches. I tried to push her aside. She grabbed a handful of my hair and held out a flaming match.

"Drop 'em!" she screamed.

Her eyes were glittering. I dropped the shreds of paper. She knocked me sprawling and started striking matches again. "I told you stay away from there!"

"I hate you!" I yelled, too scared to go near her.

She wasn't listening, didn't hear me. The paper'd caught fire. She was staring at it, smiling at the sight of Daddy's drawings burning.

"I hate you!" I screamed again.

She half turned, stared at me, and smiled.

I hate myself for crying!

"You got work to do. They make me take care of you, you're goin' to work for it."

"You don't take care of me! You never have!"

"Did he?" She nodded at the drawings, laughed at them burning and curling at her feet. "Was he takin' care of you? Sheriff told the court he found him passed out drunk! Said you was takin' care of him! Wasn't no food in the house! Principal said you wasn't in school the last month!"

I ran from her . . .

"You want to eat, you're workin' for it!" she yelled, laughing . . . I ran till I couldn't hear her anymore. I kept running.

Liars! Liars! All of them!

Nobody! Nobody ever understood. Daddy just had to draw. Painting was his life. They wouldn't listen. When I tried to tell them I had to be there . . . they wouldn't listen! They wouldn't let us be. They just kept poking . . .

I stopped running and looked at the woods around me.

Nobody ever understood . . . what it was like . . . watching him smile . . . when he got a drawing right . . . listening to him talk . . . about finding beauty everywhere . . . if you know how to look.

I collapsed in a heap, looked up through pine branches at bits of blue framed by moving limbs.

So many shades of green . . . I could never count them . . . but I could draw them.

I closed my eyes. I listened till I saw Daddy's face . . . heard his voice at home . . . saw his narrow hands as he sketched something on the linen tablecloth.

I was never hungry then.

I was happy.

No one ever hurt me.

I looked around the woods again at browning needles under pines and starkly green cedar running across the forest floor. Near an old dead tree I saw something white. I crawled over and found pale, low, fleshy flowers. Their white nodding heads were nearly like tulips with smaller, narrower, overlapping leaves. Beautiful, pale green stems poked out of dead wood ground.

Even here something's beautiful.

Maybe the way I feel now . . . inside . . . is how Daddy felt . . . when he saw something and had to paint it.

Maybe I can pretend . . . I'm still with Daddy . . . drawing . . . here.

Chapter Two

Wishing I had my chalk and could draw, I looked at the woods around me. I wasn't far from the river. I could hear water in the distance. I started toward it.

The woods ran right down to the bank. The river was much narrower than upstream. The water sounds were louder.

I hurried through the woods until I saw a building. Afraid it was someone's house, I ducked down and listened.

When I didn't hear any people sounds, I stood back up. The building had a slate roof.

Only old places have those. Daddy loved to draw them. He always had to see old places up close.

Still scared I'd find people, I slipped from tree to tree until I saw the building was an old abandoned mill. It had to be ancient. The lower part of its walls were rock with logs above. In a few places, I could see the ax marks on the logs.

I dashed across the empty clearing to the open doorway. It was half dark inside and bare, but one of the millstones was still in place. There was just a hole in the far wall where the shaft should have come in from the waterwheel. Carefully, I crossed the old floor to the window at the upstream end.

The waterwheel was completely gone, but the dam was still blocking the river. Someone had filled in the hole where the sluice had fed the wheel. The water flowing to the dam was as smooth as glass—then broke and disappeared into the roaring I heard. I stayed still trying to fix in my mind how, mirrorlike, the water caught the trees and sky.

The windowsill under my hands had square iron nails holding it in place. They'd nearly rusted away into the wood. As I reached out to touch the dark stains around them, I heard someone yelling.

Someone's coming! I'm trapped in here!

There was a dark space in the corner. I fled into it and stayed frozen as the voices came nearer, yelling and laughing.

Kids. It has to be kids.

The voices went past the open doorway at the upstream end of the building and into the river. I stayed still listening. When no one came in, and the noise stayed in the river, I moved enough to see out the window.

Several boys were swimming in the deep pool. They seemed to be playing some game. They'd climb up on the dam and dive off—yelling as they tried to catch and dunk each other.

They mustn't see me. Kids always hate me. They make fun of me. Mom said boys . . .

The upstream doorway was closer to the woods. I slipped toward it trying to hear if the boys were still near the dam.

The doorway opened on to a stone platform. Hesitating, listening and ready to run, I stepped out into the bright sunlight. Blinded, I looked toward the river and saw black curly hair.

A boy was climbing up out of the water on to the platform. Before I could run, he looked up, saw me, and froze.

Startled, I froze too. His face had gone white. He looked even more terrified than I felt.

He's beautiful!

He's . . . he's older than me . . .

I fled toward the woods. When he didn't yell, when I didn't hear him after me, I looked back. He hadn't moved. He was still clinging to the platform, was still staring at me, looking scared.

Shocked, I slowed down . . . stopped.

Why does he look scared?

Still staring at me, he started climbing out of the water.

I ran and ran till I was sure he hadn't followed me. Far upstream, I came to a huge, flat rock that jutted out into the water. I climbed down the bank and up onto the rock. The trees on the far side of the river were leaning out over the water. In the deep shadows and reflected sunlight under them, the air was green. The branches of one tree curved beautifully.

I remembered the charcoal in my pocket, dug it out, and started drawing the tree on the rock. I had half of it right when I saw the sores on my arm. I tried to see the green under the trees again. Tried to shut her out.

I hate her! I hate her! At least . . . at least . . . she can't get in my house. In her will, Grandmother Burden left Galway Hall to me. She made it so Mom can never live there . . . can never get her money.

But Daddy!

I looked away from the river remembering how I'd found out about Grandmother Burden's will. I hadn't known about it until I was in court. After the judge had said Daddy was unfit and I couldn't live with him anymore, he told me the will said if I wasn't living at Galway Hall, Daddy couldn't either. . . . If he wasn't taking care of me, he couldn't use Grandmother Burden's money anymore either. I tried to make the judge see I had to stay with Daddy, that Grandmother'd wanted me to, had expected me to.

My face burned as I remembered the judge just interrupting me and saying, "No, it's obvious Mrs. Burden hoped to force him to take care of you."

He hadn't given me a chance to say anything else. He'd turned away to tell Grandmother's lawyers they should have gotten Grandmother to set money aside for my care and education.

For a moment, I'd thought the lawyers would tell him what Grandmother'd wanted, but they'd just looked away, said that she was only interested in keeping the will from being broken.

"You did a good job of that," the judge had said. He'd read the rest of her will out loud then, sounding mad. It said if Mom or any of her family got me, they couldn't have any of the money or live in Galway Hall, and I couldn't either until I was twenty-one. It also said if I died before that neither Daddy nor Mom nor any of Mom's family would get anything. Galway Hall would go to the city, to be an art museum kept up by Grandmother's money.

I'd quit listening then, relieved Daddy hadn't been in court to hear it. At least when the sheriff took me home afterward to get my clothes, Daddy'd already gone.

If they'd just put him out in the street . . . with people standing around watching . . . the way they watched me . . . I'd have died.

I looked down at the burns on my arm remembering how the sheriff had kept telling me they were doing it for me . . . they were making me leave Daddy for me . . . that I'd be with my mom now the way children were supposed to be.

She said she didn't want me!

She'd yelled it out in court . . . and her mother . . .

I tried to remember what Mom's mother looked like. I'd never seen her before. I hadn't even known I had another grandmother alive until she'd said, "Her Grandma Simmons'll take her!"

I'd looked at her then, shocked inside. She'd smiled at me, but I'd looked away again, startled because Mom yelled out, "No, you won't! I'll take her!"

I looked back at the green air under the trees wondering why Mom'd changed her mind. If she didn't want me, why didn't she let her mother have me? Why did she rent this ugly little place and bring me out here?

Because she hates me . . . hates Daddy . . . wants to get back at us.

Suddenly, I wished I'd looked at Grandma Simmons longer in court.

If her eyes were gentle . . .

I looked down at my arm wondering what the judge would say if he knew about Mom's drinking and burning me with her cigarettes. If he'd send me to Grandma Simmons. He'd said they had to see that someone was taking care of me.

They all said that! But they'd just dumped me. I hadn't seen any of them since. None of them cared what I wanted. None of them listened to anything I tried to tell them.

The judge just wanted the school and the neighbors to shut up. The neighbors didn't even care. They just hated Daddy. They just wanted to get rid of him.

Hating them for making me leave Daddy, for driving him away, I looked down at my drawing and the few sticks of charcoal lying beside it. I closed my eyes and saw Daddy's face.

They can't take that. No one can.

When I opened my eyes again, the green air was gone from under the trees across the river. It was beginning to get dark. I was cold, tired, and hungry.

I can't just stay here.

Mom must be passed out by now. Maybe she hasn't found my chalk. Maybe she thinks his sketches are all I got.

She'll go back to work Monday. If my chalk's still there . . . I can draw then.

I put the charcoal back in my pocket, washed the black off my hands in the river, and started back up the hill to the house.

I stopped at the edge of the woods. The house was

quiet. No lights were on, but the car was still in the yard.

She said I have to work . . . if I want to eat, I have to work.

I'll have to be careful . . . not care . . . not let her trick me.

Slowly, I went over to the living room window and looked inside. She was lying on the old sofa. Beer cans were on the floor beside it. I watched her for a long time. She didn't move.

Quietly, I slipped around to the back door and went in through the small, enclosed back porch to the kitchen.

The food she'd just gotten was all over the floor. The rest of the bread. The cereal. Everything. Even the cans had been opened and dumped.

I turned on the light. There was no chalk, no paper in the mess.

She didn't find it.

Trying to be quiet, I got the dishpan, filled it with water, and put in the soap that was left. The broom didn't clean up much of the mess. On my knees, scrubbing the worn floor, I closed my eyes, saw Daddy's face.

She didn't find my chalk. She'll go back to work Monday. I can draw then.

I didn't look up or open my eyes when I heard Mom get up and stagger to the door. Somehow, I was almost sure if I didn't look up, didn't say anything, just kept scrubbing, she wouldn't hurt me.

Chapter Three

I woke up and lay still in bed, listening. The house was quiet. I half remembered hearing Mom's alarm earlier and her noise downstairs.

Tuesday . . . it has to be Tuesday . . . she's at work again.

I slipped over to the window and peeked out to make sure her car was gone. Then I opened the curtains, wishing the sun came in the window in the morning instead of afternoon.

Quickly, I got my chalk and drawing pads out from their hiding place. At the small, old table under the window, I laid the chalk sticks out so their colors made a rainbow—the same way they do in a box when it's new.

I sat down and looked at the things I'd drawn yesterday. Then I turned to a fresh page and closed my eyes.

When I saw Daddy's face, he looked the way he did when he was working. Smiling, I opened my eyes and looked out the window. There were some willow trees in the distance. In a group . . . they were . . . bowing gracefully . . . like dancers holding hands.

I started catching them on my paper—drew them in a circle, holding hands, with their green dresses sweeping the ground.

The chalk slid easily over the paper. It left a trail of tiny crumbles. Carefully, I held the pad up to blow them away so they wouldn't smear the page. Under my hand, the trees grew, dancing.

I'd just started trying to draw some squirrels hunting food in the yard, when the sunlight began falling

on the page and distracted me. I moved the drawing
pad and studied it. I hadn't gotten the squirrels right.
I was startled to see I'd started drawing the ugly, little
shed in the yard.

I ripped the page out of the book. The shed was
ugly, just like the house and Mom. I wouldn't draw
anything ugly, ever.

I looked down at the clean white paper and my
hand. It was trembling. I closed my eyes and tried to
see Daddy's face again, tried to feel good inside again.

Instead I felt sick. I opened my eyes and stared out
at the shed.

*I have to find something to eat. If I don't, I can't
even draw.*

I got up and looked for some clothes to put on. The
ones I'd been wearing since Saturday were piled on
the floor. I was too hungry to care if they were dirty
or rumpled. I pulled them back on.

Downstairs, the refrigerator was empty. There
wasn't even any beer in it. The cabinets were empty,
too.

I started cleaning up the empty beer cans on the
table.

*She said she'd get food. When I begged her last
night . . . she said she'd get food.*

There was a nickel lying on the table. I remembered hearing more change fall when she'd gotten out
her cigarettes.

The change was still on the floor. I found fifty
cents, searched for more. When I was sure I had it all,
I ran outside.

When I could see the little country store and gas
station, I stopped running and looked down at myself.
I'd forgotten my shoes and my feet were dirty. I
couldn't remember if I'd brushed my hair. When I
tried to feel if I had, I felt a tangled mess.

They'll ask questions. They'll feel sorry for me.

I felt ashamed, but I was too hungry to go back.

The parking lot outside the store was empty. There was only one car at the gas station.

When the screen door banged shut behind me, the woman at the counter looked up and frowned. I hurried to the food cooler, found a package of cheese for fifty cents and took it to the counter. As I put the change down, I stuck out my chin and stared at her the way I'd learned to so she'd look irritated instead of sorry for me.

She took the money and put the cheese in a bag.

I didn't run till I got to the door. Then, I dashed out without looking.

No!

I crashed into a man. His arms shot out around me to keep me from falling or knocking him down. I pushed at him, looked up, and froze.

The boy! The boy from the mill!

He was huge, much taller than Daddy, much taller than anyone I'd ever seen, and beautiful. I stared into his scared green eyes feeling strange inside. The skin of his bare arms was touching the skin of mine.

No one's touched me since . . .

Laughing and yelling exploded all around me. Two shorter, ugly boys were peering around him. Their faces were red and twisted up with their noise.

"Yaaaaaaa! Clyde caught a freak!"

I pounded my fists against the boy's chest. He jumped back into the others. I fled past them, past the car in the gas station, out into the road.

An old black man had started across the road. When I saw he was carrying a guitar and wearing an old tuxedo and looked terrified, I stumbled. He put his hand out toward me. I veered away from him and ran into the woods.

I didn't stop running till I got to the ugly, little house. I stopped then and stood still, ashamed, trying to ignore how much my chest hurt from running so hard.

Freak! Freak!

My face turned red remembering how stupidly I'd just stood there staring up at the boy. But my arms still felt strange where his had been touching mine. I still felt strange inside, remembering.

His eyes. I stayed there because of his eyes. They're the same color green as the air . . . under the trees at the river.

I closed my eyes trying to see his face. He hadn't laughed or yelled . . . he hadn't moved either . . . he'd just stood there, too, staring at me and looking scared, the way he did at the mill. Clyde. They called him Clyde. An ugly, stupid name.

I looked down at my dirty rumpled clothes.

A freak . . . that's why he just stood there . . . that's why he looked scared . . . I am a freak!

The bag of cheese was still in my hand. I went inside, climbed on my bed. When the cheese was gone, I just sat staring at the willow trees outside the window . . . almost not hungry anymore.

Chapter Four

The next morning, I was too hungry to draw. After I heard Mom leave for work, I got up and sat at the window staring out, wondering what to do.

I'd seen a pay phone outside the store. I wondered what would happen if I called the sheriff the way the neighbors had. Would he come get me if I told him there was no food and Mom was hurting me? Would they let me go back to Daddy?

He didn't listen when I tried to tell him Daddy needed me. None of them listened.

School . . . school was what started it before. It has to be almost time for school to start. If I don't go, they'll have to find out why . . . They'll see she won't feed me . . . hurts me. They'd have to do something, then, they'd have to.

I tried to count up days. School usually started the last week of August. I knew it must be the middle.

I wished we had a phone, or I had some money for the one at the store. There were a couple of men Daddy knew in town—men he used to stop to talk to sometimes, when we were out shopping. They might know where he'd gone. They might help me find him, help me get him to come back.

Maybe Mom dropped more change . . .

Downstairs there were just beer cans on the table. I sat down knowing Daddy'd hate my calling them anyway. One of the men ran a pool hall. The other had the newsstand where Daddy got his magazines. They weren't his friends. They wouldn't know where he was. I was just being stupid.

I saw a loaf of bread on the counter and opened it.

Automatically, I looked in the refrigerator for something to put on it.

Food. She's gotten food.

I can draw, now.

Quickly, I stuffed myself. Then I ran back upstairs, got my chalk and paper. I took them out in the woods to draw—away from her mess, away from the ugly, little house.

The rest of the week, I didn't see Mom. At night, after I ate, I went up to my room to draw. I set her alarm for the time she got off work. When it rang, I hurriedly cleaned up from drawing and hid my things. Then I cleaned up her last night's mess in the kitchen, made her bed, put her alarm back, and went to bed.

Mornings, I got up after she went to work. I spent the days in the woods drawing—with Daddy in my mind.

Saturday morning, I stayed in bed a long time wishing it was a weekday and Mom would go to work. I knew I couldn't risk drawing with her home.

Finally, hungry, but still not hearing her, I got up and looked outside. Her car was in the yard. I crept to the door and carefully opened it. Her bed was still made up.

I wanted to climb back in bed and stay there until Monday.

She'll come after me if I do.

I got dressed and crept downstairs as quietly as I could. She was asleep on the sofa with beer cans on the floor beside her. The front door was standing open.

I went back to the refrigerator. She hadn't been to the store. I ate the last of the food quickly, scared she'd wake up.

When I wasn't hungry anymore and the kitchen was clean, I slipped out the back door. I went around to the front porch and sat down on the steps. When she woke up, she'd see me there through the screen. I could run if I had to. Hating her, I closed my eyes and concentrated until I could see Daddy's face.

Sometime later a car coming down the road made me open my eyes. I got up wondering who it was—if someone was coming from the court.

When I saw it was an old car, I began to feel scared. The first day I was there, Mom'd said awful things about boys, that they'd hurt me, that she'd kill me if they came to the house. I went to the screen door.

"Mom! Someone's coming!"

She didn't move. The car was pulling up in the yard. A woman was driving. She'd seen me, started rolling down the window. I made myself walk to the car.

Grandma Simmons! I'd forgotten about her.

She finished rolling down the car window and smiled at me.

"Come to see my grandbaby," she said.

I tried to nod, tried to smile back, walked toward her.

Her eyes are mean.

Frightened suddenly, I put my hands on the car door.

"Lemme open th' door, honey."

Her voice is mean, too.

I couldn't look up from my hands on the door.

"Where's your momma?"

I made myself look up. Her eyes got smaller and meaner. Her smile faded.

"Inside," I heard myself say.

She pushed at the door. I backed away. As she got out of the car, she handed an old cardboard box to me. I took it and looked down at a homemade cake. My name was scrawled across the top in a garish red—*Clare.*

Startled, I looked back up at her.

She doesn't even know how to spell my name.

"Made it for my grandbaby," she said, smiling again and reaching out toward me. "Let's go see your momma."

I moved so she couldn't touch me. She set off for the house. Suddenly, not understanding why, I ran past her to the door and yelled through the screen.

"Mom! Grandma's here!"

Mom sat up. "What?"

"Grandma's here! Grandma Simmons!"

I saw terror on Mom's face. Then Grandma Simmons pushed me aside, yanked the screen door open, and ran into the room.

"I knowed it!" Grandma screamed. "I knowed if I didn't watch you, you wouldn't take care of her!"

Mom's arms shot up in front of her face as Grandma struck out at her.

"No, Momma! Listen, Momma!"

"Fool!" Grandma screamed, pounding on her. "Always playin' the fool. Thinkin' you could get that money if you took her!"

I backed away, turned, stumbled down off the porch. Behind me, I heard blows and Mom screaming, "No, Momma! I don't want Mrs. Burden's money! Lemme be!"

I looked down at the cake, tried to keep walking— scared I'd throw up. I tried to shut out the sounds, tried to fill my head with the times Mom'd hurt me. I wanted to be glad someone was hurting her. I couldn't. I felt too sick inside.

I stopped by a tree, leaned up against it scared I'd fall.

Finally, it got quiet in the house. When Grandma came back outside, she was smiling. I couldn't look away from her or move.

"Git upstairs and git your stuff! I'm takin' you with me. They got to see this ain't no fit place. They got to see your momma's no good!"

Numbly, I shook my head.

"Don't shake your head at me," she screamed. "You want to live with 'nother animal? You done it already. Go look what he done to my girl. I had me a good child till that no-count come and took her from me! Look at her! Drunk as a pig! Same as him!"

I shook my head again, terrified.

"Come on or I'll pull you upstairs myself! We're goin' to town!"

"No," I whispered. "No. I won't go with you."

"I thought you had some sense! Well, you'll git some! I started beatin' your momma too late! I'm not makin' the same mistake with you! I'll beat sense into you if it's the last thing I do!"

"No! You ruined her! You did it, not Daddy! I won't go with you! The court gave me to Mom!"

She rushed at me. I threw the cake at her. It hit her. She stopped and looked at it all down the front of her. I ran.

"You run off," she screamed, "and I'll get the sheriff! I seen there's no food!"

I stopped running. "Get him!" I screamed. "Let him see what you did to Mom! I'll tell him you did it!"

"He won't believe you," she yelled, starting after me. "You seen how much they listened to you in court. They know you're a liar, tellin' them your daddy was takin' care of you! He never took care of nobody!"

I started running again, knowing the court sent me to Mom, knowing Grandma wouldn't get the sheriff now. She was the one wanting Grandmother Burden's money, not Mom.

I kept running, blindly, lost.

Chapter Five

I stopped running at the top of a hill and numbly looked around, unsure of where I was. There weren't any houses in sight. Below me in the woods, trapped between my hill and the next, a small pond caught golden sunlight. I rushed down toward it until I saw trees were growing up close around the pond, crowding, threatening to choke it out.

I turned away, stumbled back up the hill, sank down next to a huge pine tree.

Grandma wasn't drunk. She beat Mom like that and she wasn't even drunk. She wants Grandmother Burden's money. My money when I'm twenty-one. She'd have to keep me till then to get it. She heard the judge say they couldn't give her or Mom any of it. . . . not even if I died! If Daddy doesn't come back . . . if she got me away from Mom . . .

I closed my eyes, tried to see Daddy. Instead, I saw the terror on Mom's face when Grandma Simmons ran at her. I shuddered, opened my eyes, saw the tree beside me. I stared at its bark until each indentation grew larger, distorted, moved, changed color.

Bach. That's Grandmother's favorite piece by Bach.

I sighed and let the music wash over me. The hair along my arms and up my neck tingled, rose up the way it always had when I heard it. Something was wrong. I moved slightly, wondering why the music didn't sound right.

Something hard was under me. I opened my eyes.

The woods . . . why am I in the woods?

Bewildered, I looked around wondering where I was and how I got there. The air was still alive with

the Bach. I turned, looked around the old pine beside
me.

Below me, down the hill, an old black man was sitting by a pond playing a huge guitar, and nodding his
head in time to the music.

I must be dreaming.

I crept closer. When I could see the old man's profile, I stopped. I'd seen him before as I ran from the
store. I'd seen the pond somewhere, too.

When the old man finished the song, he moved the
guitar back and forth, tuning it. The front seemed to
be covered with mirrors that caught and refracted the
light into glistening rainbows.

I held my breath, hoping the dream wouldn't end.
The old man bent his head back over the strings and
started playing music I'd never heard before. I slid
down next to a tree and leaned against it, listening.

He played one song after another. At first the songs
were gentle and beautiful. After a while they began to
be loud. He laughed as he shouted out the words and
slapped his guitar in rhythm to the music. Then the
songs lost their laughter. His deep, rich voice became
harsh. Just as I began to be afraid, the song changed.

"Ease my mind," he sang, "tell me when you're
comin' home. Been waitin' here, Lord, seems like since
I was born."

He stopped playing and just stared out over the
pond.

Suddenly, I was scared it was just a dream, that
he'd go, and I'd never hear his music again. I'd started
toward him when he began fingering the Bach melody again, gently.

I stopped, closed my eyes. I saw him putting out his
hand when I'd run past him at the store. Grandmother
Burden had put out her hand that way once when I
was little and fell while running toward her.

She always tried to keep me from being hurt.

I felt strange inside. At the store, the boy had put

his arms out the same way. He'd caught me. He'd kept me from falling.

I realized the music had stopped and looked back at the old man. He was staring at me, looking terrified, the way he had at the store.

"Seen you up there," he said. "Watchin'. What you watchin' an old man for?"

I made myself keep looking at him and answer. "I like your music. It's beautiful. You were playing Bach."

"How'd you know the name of that song?"

"It was on a record I had . . . when I lived in town . . . with my father."

"You play the piano?"

Puzzled, I shook my head. No one in my dreams ever asked questions. "No. I don't even have the record anymore. I don't even live . . . with my father . . . anymore."

He stopped looking scared. "You livin' somewhere around here?"

"In the tenant house—over there." I leaned my head toward it. "Hearing the Bach again was nice."

He smiled. His face was gentle. As gentle as Grandmother Burden's.

His eyes aren't mean.

"You know more Bach?" I asked, uncertainly.

"Naw. Can't bring no more to mind." Still smiling, he fingered the opening melody. "I ain't even got this one right yet."

I felt puzzled again. Almost always in my dreams things happened the way I wanted them to.

"Are you real?" I asked, scared he'd look scared again, but having to know. "If I wake up will you still be there?"

He laughed. "Lord, child. I been flesh and blood all my livin' days! What's makin' you think you're dreamin'?"

I felt stupid and ready to run. He started picking at the Bach melody again, still smiling but not meanly.

"I woke up and didn't know where I was. You looked scared. No one's ever looked scared of me before."

He looked startled. "Don't go worryin' your mind, child! I ain't scared no more. You just got the same face as the lady that used to play me that song. Seein' you down to the store, I thought I was seein' her. It got me to thinkin' on her. She treated me good when I was half the size of you."

"I look like someone who was kind to you?" I asked, confused.

"Yes," he said, gently. "She's been gone a long time. Seein' you sittin' up there lookin' just like her scared me half to death, till I seen you don't talk like her at all. 'Sides, when she was livin' they didn't have no records."

He was smiling. I felt relieved suddenly and almost safe.

He thought I was a ghost. I thought he was a dream.

I tried to smile back, but his was fading.

"Who's been seein' to you, child? What you been doin' sleepin' in the woods?"

"I live with my mom," I said, looking away as the reason why I'd run into the woods crashed down on me.

"Your momma don't want you down here. She wants you home," he said firmly.

"No!" I screamed. "No! She doesn't care where I am! She—" I shut up, scared, remembering the neighbors at home, remembering Grandma talking about getting the sheriff.

"She's just mad with you now?" he asked gently. "Maybe she's out lookin' for you. Maybe she's already feelin' sorry she's been mad with her baby."

I shook my head wishing I'd kept quiet, scared he'd

feel sorry for me and call the sheriff. "No! No! She's at work! It's . . . it's all right. Don't feel sorry for me!"

He looked surprised. "Why ain't you playin' with the other young folks? There's lots of 'em livin' right along the road."

"You don't want me listening to you!" I turned away as I burst into tears. "I wouldn't bother you!"

"Hush that," he said. "You hush that cryin'."

I wiped at my eyes and desperately tried to stop.

"Where's your kerchief?"

I looked back and saw he was leaning toward me, studying me and shaking his head.

"Ain't nobody seein' to you while your momma's workin'?"

I remembered Grandma and couldn't answer.

"Sure looks like nobody. Children got to have somebody seein' to 'em! Look at yourself. Dir-ty! When's the last time them clothes seen soap and water?"

I looked down at myself. I still had on the same clothes I'd worn to town the week before. "It doesn't matter," I said, desperately.

"Don't give me no stuff!" he said angrily. "That sounds like white trash talkin'! There ain't no white trash knows playin' like I been doin'!"

I nodded, struggling not to cry anymore.

"Lord, child." He bent over his guitar and played the Bach again.

When he finished, I'd quit crying. I tried to smile back, find words.

"Your guitar's . . . beautiful. It's . . . different."

"Yes. This is a twelve-string. Only somebody knows what he's doin' is goin' to get himself a box like this here. Leadbelly, Blind Cat, my daddy. This here was my daddy's. He got it for himself down there in Galveston. Was mine when he died."

He turned the guitar from side to side. The sunlight caught in the wide inlay around the opening in the front and threw more rainbows at me. The old man shook his head and smiled. "Real mother-of-pearl! My momma's name was Pearl. That's why my daddy got himself this box."

"Your daddy taught you . . . to play?"

"Yes. When I was knee-high to a grasshopper. I learned some songs from my momma, too. The one I played you is all I 'member from Mrs. Adair. It's been out of my mind till I seen you the other day. Listenin' on it again makes me feel good."

I nodded. That's how I'd always felt hearing it.

"School's goin' to be startin' next week. That's good, child. You ought to be with young folks like yourself, not out in the woods listenin' on an old man."

His smile still made me want Grandmother Burden. "I hate school!"

"Get along now!" he said, drawing back. "You can't mean that."

I couldn't shut up. "I do! I'm not like other kids. They hate me!" I tried to keep from crying again and wished I'd stop babbling at him. "I don't care!" I said desperately. "It doesn't matter."

He shook his head. "Not bein' like other folks ain't always bad. Sometimes it's right good. But you got to smile at people, child. You got to know lots of 'em is just as scared as you if you're goin' to like 'em."

"I didn't say I was scared!"

"Naw," he agreed. "Only the people I know that carries on nobody likes 'em has got scared of tryin' to find out. Unless they're mean. You don't look so mean to me, child. And that's the truth."

I looked away from him so I wouldn't tell him what scared me.

"You got yourself a good head on your shoulders," he said. "That's good. You've been listenin' and thinkin'." He put his guitar in its case and got to his feet. "Think on yourself, child. Somebody's got to."

Chapter Six

Once the old man had disappeared over the far hill, I went down to the place where he'd been sitting. An old stone wall was built into the bank a few feet from the pond's edge. The path leading away from the pond was well worn. I thought he must come there often.

I sat down on his wall and stared at his pond. He'd said he wasn't a dream. Yet he'd played the Bach piece. It was almost the only music that Grandmother Burden had ever listened to. He'd played it wrong, but he was more like her than he was like other people.

Only he was like the neighbors at Galway Hall, too, asking questions.

He said I was dirty. He said I looked like white trash. I felt myself turn red and looked down. I was a mess. Daddy'd be angry if he saw me.

I shuddered remembering. Daddy won't see me. He's gone. I wasn't dreaming. I live with Mom now.

Mom!

I started running back toward the house. If Mom wasn't all right, if Grandma'd killed her, if Grandma'd gotten the sheriff!

They'd never believe me. They'd make me go with Grandma the same way they'd made me go with Mom. I felt cold inside and had to stop.

Mom doesn't care about me.

Maybe Grandma was waiting for me to come back. Maybe Mom'd said she could have me.

I looked back the way I'd come, wishing I'd told the old man what had happened. He wasn't like the others. He'd cared when I cried instead of getting mad. He'd played the Bach so I'd stop crying. . . . He'd also said I needed someone to see to me.

Mom. When we came back from town, Mom said something about someone seeing to her.

I started running again. When I got near the edge of the woods, I slowed up and crept from tree to tree. If Grandma's car was still at the house, I couldn't go back.

Mom's old car was the only one there. Relieved, I ran to the house.

When I got to the door, Mom was still lying on the sofa. For a moment I was terrified. I'd been gone a long time. Finally, I saw she was breathing. I slipped inside, past her to the bathroom, and got a wet towel.

I made myself take it back in the living room, go to her.

Grandma's worse. Grandma's worse.

"Mom?" Scared, I held the cold wet towel near her head.

She moaned. "Wanna die," she said. She raised up a little.

I braced myself to run and moved the towel so it barely touched her. She buried her face against it and started sobbing as if she were a small child. Then suddenly, both her arms clamped around my legs. She buried her face against me and screamed and cried and clung to me. I struggled to stay still as inside me terror and hate and fear and revulsion and pity boiled up and made me want to run.

Finally her sobs eased. "I hate Momma!" she wailed. "I never want to see her again!"

I'm safe now.

"Go get in bed," I said. "I'll bring you some ice."

Mom nodded dumbly and tried to get up. I reached out to help her but jerked my hands away when I saw the black-and-blue marks all over her arms. For a moment we stared at each other. Her face was red and puffy from crying, but it wasn't bruised. I felt cold inside.

If her arms were covered no one would know the way Grandma pounded on her.

"Are you all right?"

She nodded and took the wet towel. "I got to get you some food," she said. "Tomorrow. I can't go nowhere today." She shuffled away from me.

I listened to her fumble her way upstairs. I closed my eyes and tried to see Daddy. I couldn't. All I could see was Mom's bruised arms.

I opened my eyes, looked around me, saw my dirty clothes and the beer cans on the floor. If the sheriff saw them or me he'd never hear anything I said.

I can't go to Grandma. Grandma's worse.

I gathered up the beer cans, took them out to the trash heap. I covered them and the others with brush. Back inside, I crept upstairs to get clean clothes. For a moment, in my room, I stood touching the edge of the drawing paper hidden in the bottom of the drawer.

I have to see to her. If I want to be safe, if I want to draw, I have to take care of her.

Mom woke me up early the next day. I was scared till I saw she was sober, dressed, and wearing a sweater to cover her arms.

"Get up," she said. "We got to go to town. School starts tomorrow. We ain't got food neither."

She went to my closet and yanked the door open. "Any of this stuff fit you?"

"Not much," I said, getting up, scared she'd go over to the dresser and start looking in it, too.

"Hurry up." She went out the door without looking at me.

We went to a place in Galway Fields called Encore, a fancy name for used clothes. I was surprised it was open on Sundays. I hadn't seen it before. The sign outside said it was run by a group of doctors' wives.

When we first got inside, Mom stood over me grabbing anything that might fit and holding it up in front of me. The things were awful. I was glad no one else was in the place except two women behind a counter. They were staring at us and whispering.

Mom finally noticed it too and started calling names loud enough for them to hear.

I turned away embarrassed and terrified she'd make a scene, but she only snapped "Hurry up" at me and walked away to the far side of the store.

I began finding some nice things on the rack. The women were still whispering. I tried to ignore them and remember going shopping with Daddy instead.

I couldn't find him in my mind. The places we'd gone were too different. He'd always picked beautiful things. It had been too long ago. I picked out a bunch of the nicer things hoping Mom would buy a couple of them.

I looked up. Mom was just standing by the window. It was too warm to be wearing a sweater. I looked down at the scars on my arms. Hurriedly, I put the short-sleeved things back and found others with long sleeves.

When I took them over to Mom, all she looked at was the tags.

"All right, darling. You want them, we'll get 'em."

Her voice was so artificial I wanted to die. I couldn't look at her or the women while she paid. Mom went out in front of me. When I caught up with her near the car, she half turned and slapped me.

"Blackmail," she said. "That's what it is."

I put my head down and kept quiet. I had to have shoes for school, too.

At the shoe store, Mom told me as we went in how much she'd spend. I soon saw there wasn't anything nice for that. I waited, trying to decide what to do.

"Will you quit messing around?" Mom snapped. "I want to get goin'!"

One of the clerks hurried over. He grinned at Mom.

She grinned back and indicated me. "School shoes," she said.

He took one of the display shoes off the nearest table and held it out.

"We've almost sold all of these." His smile widened.

Mom smiled back. She didn't even look at the shoe.

"All the best-dressed girls are going to be wearing them."

I felt sick. The shoes were half again as much as Mom had said she'd pay and they were awful, too. Nobody with any sense would be caught dead in them.

"We'll try 'em," she told his smile.

I couldn't decide whether I wanted to keep wearing my old shoes which were so small they hurt or the horrible things he was pulling out of a box. It didn't matter what I wanted. They hardly knew I was there trying them on.

When we were finally outside with the box under my arm, Mom looked at her reflection in the window next door and patted at her hair. Her eyes met mine and the smile disappeared.

"What else do you need, brat?"

"Underwear . . . and school supplies."

"Well, I'm tired of draggin' you around. You go get 'em and meet me at the store. Don't get lost. I'm not goin' to wait no more." She dug into her purse and gave me some money. "I don't get paid till Friday. I can't give you no more if I'm goin' to get food."

I knew that meant beer, too. Watching her walk away, I wondered if she knew Grandma had tried to take me to town, if I'd find myself there if Mom got mad at me.

I can't make her mad. No matter what.

But when I got school supplies, I bought a drawing pad small enough to fit in my notebook. I was sure Mom would be too busy thinking about getting her

beer to care what I'd bought. If I'd had more money,
I would have gotten watercolors, too. I wished I'd
brought the change with me that I'd been finding
cleaning up after her. I'd hidden it in my room in case
she stopped getting food again. I hadn't counted it. I'd
just added it to the sock.

When we got home she took her beer in and left the
rest for me.

Upstairs, finally, I smoothed out and put away my
new things. I felt pretty good about them. Except for
the shoes—I'd never feel all right in them.

I hoped desperately the clothes had belonged to
town girls that I wouldn't see again. I suddenly
wanted to stay at the tenant house and not go to
school at all.

Late that night, I woke up to a horrible sound. At
first, I was scared I was caught in a nightmare and
couldn't get out. Then I knew it was Mom crying. It
sounded the same as an animal dying.

I hated her so much, but the sound was awful. I'd
die if I hurt that much inside. I've never cried that
way. Even in court when I found out Grandmother
Burden's will wouldn't let Daddy live at Galway Hall
without me there, too, I didn't cry that way. Even
when Grandmother died, I didn't. I tried to shut out
the sound.

*It must be awful to be Mom. Nobody cares about
her. Grandma doesn't. I don't. Nobody. She's stuck
here forever.*

I couldn't bear listening to her. I held my pillow
over my head, but I couldn't stop thinking.

*When I grow up, I'll go to college the way Daddy
said. I'll be an artist like him. I can draw. Mom can't.*

Nothing could be worse than being stuck like Mom.
I'd die if I was stuck the way she is. I'd die.

Chapter Seven

When Mom's alarm went off the next morning, I remembered hearing her cry. I thought about all the things she'd gotten me for school and got up.

She was already downstairs in the bathroom, so I hurriedly dressed and brushed my hair. Then I went down to the kitchen and started fixing her breakfast. I meant to get it ready and get out of her way, but she came out before I had finished.

"Stop houndin' me!" she yelled. "Lookin' at you makes me sick! Every time I see you, you look more like your filthy father!"

She grabbed at the skillet.

"No!" I yelled, running to the stairs. "No. I have to go to school!"

"Then get your stuff!" She threw the skillet at the sink. "I got to get to work!"

Sitting in the back seat of the car, as far as I could get from Mom, I stared at the back of her head.

I hate school, but I have to go. If I don't, they'll start asking questions. They'll make trouble. I'll be at Grandma's.

I tried to push Grandma out of my mind. At least I wasn't going back to my old school. The kids and teachers would be different. I stared out the car window, remembering. The old man at the pond had said other people were scared, too. According to him, I just had to smile and things would be different.

I'd never seen the county high school before. As Mom drove down the hill toward it, at least a dozen yellow buses were already there. Swarms of kids were pouring out of them. Watching them, I felt sick inside.

The school was huge. The junior high school I'd gone to in town was small.

I made myself look down and smooth my skirt out over my knees. Knowing I was dressed all right wasn't helping. My hair was too long, my shoes were awful. Suddenly, I was sure everyone would know my daddy'd run off and left me and my mom hates me.

Mom was saying something. I shook myself awake.

"You stayin' there all day?"

She'd parked the car and was waiting for me to get out.

I hurried after her. As I came up to the crowds of kids, I clutched my notebook as close against me as I could.

A wall of glass doors opened into the lobby. Straight in front of them were double rows of doors with *Auditorium* in huge letters above. I nearly had to run to keep up with Mom. The hall and office were mobbed.

Mom pushed her way through to the office counter and looked mad. A secretary was with us in a minute.

In another minute, the secretary was mad, too. Mom didn't know anything at all about my last school, what shots I'd had, nothing. I looked away embarrassed as the secretary went on and on, being superior to Mom.

When she asked my birthday, I interrupted and told her. I didn't look at Mom. I'd known from her sudden silence she didn't remember when it was.

"Are you going to college?" the secretary asked. She held up two lists of classes.

I nodded, sick inside.

"College!" Mom yelled.

Every single head in the office turned toward us. I wanted to die.

"Please, Mom!" I begged. "Please!"

I was bewildered by the change in her expression

until I saw a man had joined the secretary at the counter.

"Hi," he said, smiling. "I'm Fred Fader, one of the counselors. I'm sorry I couldn't get over to help you sooner. You can see we're really busy."

Mom just smiled. I tried to calm down. Mom was almost nice when men were around.

"They didn't bring any records. She's a transfer from town," the secretary said.

"That's all right. We'll send for them if you'll just sign this." He pushed a form toward Mom. Then he started circling the college prep courses open to me.

I watched, glad he didn't have my grades. Mom moved impatiently beside me. Almost stammering, I babbled the classes I wanted: "French, algebra, world history, English, and biology."

"That's a heavy load," he said. "Do you think she'll be able to handle them, Mrs. Burden?"

Mom looked uncertain and didn't answer.

"She can try them. If they're too difficult, let me know. She can drop either biology or French and try it again next year." He smiled at me. "How does that sound to you?"

I nodded and frantically tried to smile back.

"Fine, then we're all set?" he asked Mom.

She nodded at his smile. He got several forms and rapidly filled them out. I stood there dazed as he chattered about schedules, teachers' names, and had Mom sign the forms.

Then he pushed one into my hand.

"This is your bus number at the top." He tapped it with his pencil. "You keep the top copy of this and your last teacher will take the bottom one. First you'll need to take it to the bookstore. They'll give you your texts since you just moved and your teachers aren't expecting you."

He turned back to Mom. "She'll need lunch money

today. We have milk and a few other drinks for sale if she wants to bring her own after this."

While Mom dug into her purse, he turned back to me. "The bookstore's around the corner from the auditorium. They have school supplies for sale too, if you need any."

Mom pressed two dollars into my hand. "Get anything you need," she said.

I took the money, sure she was trying to impress him. I wondered what she'd do if I kept it.

"We hope you'll enjoy Chatham High," Mr. Fader was saying.

Mom was still smiling at him.

Somehow, I found the line for the bookstore. A few people were ahead of me. I got in line and stared at the floor.

Daddy always said I'd go to college. I've always known I would. He's even picked the school. I have to go. I . . .

"Hey, wake up!" Someone shoved me from behind. I lurched forward, bumped into the bottom half of a Dutch door with a counterlike shelf.

The kid behind the door looked irritated. Behind him I saw the school store.

I held out my class list, tried to speak. He grabbed it and turned away. I felt myself go red, and tried to look at the store. It was only an oversized closet with shelves, but the ones on the far wall were filled with art supplies. Watercolors, paints, brushes, chalks, and various kinds of paper.

The kid put my books down on the counter.

"You want anything else?"

I shook my head "no" asking, "How much are the watercolors?"

"Which ones?"

"The cheapest."

He went over to the shelves. "The cheapest are a

dollar-fifty. The most expensive are six dollars." He held up the largest box.

I stared at them, wanting them.

"Do you want any or not?"

I jumped, startled. I'd forgotten him. "What?"

He and the girl behind me burst into laughter. I grabbed my books and fled.

By the time I found my French class, the bell had already rung. The kids were sitting at long tables arranged in a large square. They stared at me when I came in. Most of them looked older than me.

Then the teacher smiled, told me she was Mrs. Lively, and asked my name. She was tiny, with white hair. She seemed nice. When she started class, I tried to listen to her, but I was too upset.

Daddy has to come back. If he doesn't, there won't be any money for college. Grandmother Burden's will says if I'm with Mom or Grandma I have to be twenty-one before I can have any of her money. That's too old for college.

Mom will never send me. Even if she has the money, she'll never spend it on that. Daddy has to come back!

"Claire!" Someone touched my arm.

I jumped and saw the class was staring at me and pin-dropping quiet. For a moment, I was scared I'd talked out loud. Then I saw Mrs. Lively, looking worried instead of angry.

"Don't you feel well, dear?" she asked. "You look very pale."

Don't feel sorry for me! Don't ask questions!

"I'm fine, thanks," I forced out.

She smiled and asked someone else the question she must have asked me.

I can't get in trouble in school again! I can't!

I didn't let myself look away from Mrs. Lively anymore. I stared at her and tried to listen, tried to write down what she said.

When the bell finally rang, I was scared to take time to look for my locker. It took me almost the whole break to find my next class, English. Everyone was still standing around in there, so I stayed by the door and waited, unable to look at anyone.

When the teacher came in and started assigning seats, I concentrated on the wall and listened to the names so I wouldn't miss the place I was supposed to be.

"Clyde Bowman," the teacher called.

I made myself go up to her desk and hold out my class card.

"Claire Burden," she read off it. "Yes, you're next."

She put my name down in her attendance book and sent me to the next empty seat. Just in front of it, a boy's legs were blocking the aisle. When he didn't move, I looked up.

It was the boy from the mill, and the store, staring up at me, looking shocked.

I dropped my huge pile of books. They mostly landed on his legs.

"That's the freak?" someone asked, loudly.

I looked up and saw his fat, ugly friend behind him again, staring at me wide-eyed.

"Shut up, Jimmy!" Clyde said, turning toward him.

As the class laughed, I gathered up my books and sat down behind Clyde, wanting to disappear, knowing my face was still burning.

I made myself look at the teacher, stare at her. When she looked at me and smiled, I looked away. Teachers had smiled at me and felt sorry for me before. They were why I was with Mom.

I can't think about Mom. I'll forget to listen if I do.

I opened my notebook, made myself copy down the teacher's name, Mrs. Morgan, from the blackboard. Then I made myself listen to her, write down what she said till class was over.

I was glad to escape to gym. That, at least, would

be all girls. They might tease me and pull my hair or call me "Clairely A. Burden" if I got put on their team, the way girls had in town, but I'd almost learned to ignore them.

Instead no one noticed me. They were all too busy trying to listen to Miss Jameson's shouted instructions. She thought we were all burdens. By the time class was over, I'd almost calmed down.

It wasn't hard to find the biology class. The room was next door to English. The teacher's desk was just inside. She was already there and looked up and smiled.

I held out my class list. She told me her name was Mrs. Carter. After she put my name in her book she said she'd assign places when everyone had arrived. She suggested I look around until they did.

I tried. There were glass cabinets down one wall with displays inside. I'd started toward them when I saw the room. It didn't have desks like the other classes. Instead there were many small built-in tables. Each had a sink in the top. Two adjustable stools were behind each unit. I turned away to the glass cabinets wishing my last name was Zachariah or Zud so I wouldn't have to share a table with someone.

The someone I shared with turned out to be Clyde. When I heard my name after his and went to the table, he was busy lowering the stool so his knees would fit under. I sat down and half turned my back to him. I watched Mrs. Carter assign seats to the others. After she'd finished and gone back to the front of the room, it was impossible to ignore him. He was too large. If I moved, I'd touch him. I didn't move or look away from Mrs. Carter the rest of class.

His ugly friend wasn't in the class, at least.

I was starving when lunchtime came. I almost ran out of class. When I found the cafeteria, there was already a line. I got in it, looked at the floor, listened to the noise, tried not to think.

Someone tugged at my hair. I jumped, looked around. The boy behind me was smiling and leaning toward me.

"You're in my French class." He reached out toward my hair again.

"Don't touch me!" I snapped, jerking away.

"Jeez! A townie snot! 'Don't touch me!' " he echoed, leaning toward me to mutter four-letter words.

I was too hungry to run. As kids laughed I stared at the floor, kept moving when the person in front of me did, wished I was home or dead.

Finally, the boy got tired of making noise and stopped.

I still had all my books. I balanced the tray on top and turned to look for the nearest empty table.

The cafeteria was huge and crowded. All the tables near the counters already had people at them. The only empty ones were at the far end.

I'd started that way when I heard someone laugh and couldn't keep from looking up. It was Jimmy, Clyde's ugly friend. He and Clyde were sitting with a table full of girls. The girls were giggling and staring at Clyde as Jimmy laughed and talked.

I turned away and kept going to the empty tables in the far corner of the room. As I put down my books and moved my tray, I saw the edge of the sketch pad I'd gotten to keep in my notebook. Wishing I could draw, I stared at the black edge of it as I started eating.

I remembered the watercolors in the school store. Maybe I'd have enough of Mom's tips for the small box.

There were windows along one of the walls near me. The purplish-blue mountains were just barely visible behind the pine woods surrounding the school. I finished eating, pulled my notebook to me.

I hadn't brought any charcoal with me, but one of

my pencils was soft enough for drawing. I started sketching the mountains, protected them with a wall of tall, slender pines.

The bell ringing startled me. I looked up, saw the cafeteria was empty. Frantically, I grabbed my books and ran.

I got to history class the same time as the teacher. "Almost didn't make it," he said, smiling.

"New," I said, trying to smile and holding out my class card.

He took it. "Burden. That's an old name around here. You've moved from town?"

I nodded and tried not to see the kids turning around.

"Interested in local history?"

I started shaking my head, thought better of it, and tried to nod instead.

When he laughed, the class did, too. I looked down at the floor wishing he'd leave me be.

"I'm Mr. Allen and I'll be assigning seats," he said, walking away, "so everybody up against the wall."

The rest of my teachers assigned seats, too. Bowman was sitting in front of Burden in all of them. He didn't look at me anymore as I passed him going to my seat.

I spent the classes trying to listen, trying not to think about Mom or Grandma.

In the last class, I sat trying not to stare at Clyde's black curly hair. He and everyone else were still working on the review test that Mr. Davis, the algebra teacher, had handed out. I'd started it, didn't know how to do too many problems, quit. I wanted to put my head down on my desk, but I knew I'd start crying.

The old man was wrong. I'm not scared people won't like me. I'm just scared.

He'd been right about one thing. It was different

from town. One or two girls had smiled. They'd said
"Hi" and stopped to talk. I'd just looked away, unable
to speak or smile back.

*I hate school. I can't let them talk to me. If I do,
they'll ask questions. They'll find out about Mom.
They'll make me go to Grandma's.*

*I hate school. I hate having to come here so I can
stay with Mom.*

Chapter Eight

Somehow, after school, I found my bus. One of the seats near the front was still empty. I sat down as close to the window as I could get and piled my books up so no one could sit beside me.

The noise on the bus was incredible. I wondered if it was always that way. I'd never ridden one to school before.

We hadn't gone far before I heard yelling and looked up in the driver's rearview mirror. Jimmy was half standing up. The kids around him were laughing. Clyde, too.

I looked away out the window, saw myself reflected in the rearview mirror outside. At school most of the girls' hair had been short or barely touching their shoulders. Mine had never been cut. Daddy'd wanted it long for his paintings.

I put my hands up to my hair to see if I'd look the same as the other girls with mine cut short, too. I looked away. It wouldn't help. I'd still be different.

Besides . . . if I cut my hair and Daddy came back . . . he might not want to paint me anymore.

I closed my eyes to keep from crying. Daddy'd already quit painting me. When I'd gotten worried about school, the neighbors, and his drinking, he'd told me I was ugly and quit.

He has to come back. If he doesn't . . .

I opened my eyes, saw the store go by.

Frantically, I grabbed my books and yelled at the driver. There was so much noise he didn't hear me till I got to the front. He was irritated that I hadn't told him when I got on where my stop was.

Somehow, I got off without dropping any of my books. My arms were ready to break before I got back to the dirt road, much less down it to the ugly, little house.

The squirrels I'd tried to draw were playing in the yard. They ran when they saw me coming.

I didn't watch them go. I went inside, dumped my books on the ugly, worn sofa, and ran upstairs. I climbed in bed in my clothes and bawled, wanting Daddy and Grandmother Burden.

Then I remembered the old black man. I ran all the way to the pond.

Seeing him sitting on the wall playing his guitar, I was overwhelmed. I sat down a few feet from him and just started bawling.

"What's this?" he asked. "What you hollerin' like that for?"

Trying to stop crying, I told him the whole day. He sat shaking his head and listening until I'd run out of things to say. Then he took out a handkerchief and wiped his forehead.

"Uh, uh," he said. "Don't go takin' life so hard. You got to let life slide a little bit, child. Don't go around 'spectin' every little move is the last one you got. First thing goes wrong you're ready for everythin' else to be goin' wrong, too. You got to take your time. You got to take it easy. Now, 'stead of thinkin' on yourself, look at somebody else. See if you can't figure out how they feel. You watch 'em good enough, you're goin' to see lots of folks just as ready to jump scared as you. There's lots needin' friends, child. Just like you."

I looked away, ashamed I'd come.

I can't have any friends with Mom. He just doesn't understand. He's . . .

"You got yourself some schoolwork for tomorrow?"

I nodded.

"All right. Now you listen on this, then you get on home and get to work on school."

He started playing the Bach. I let the music wash over me, began to relax, began to watch him playing.

I wish I could draw him.

When he finished, he smiled. I tried to smile back.

"That's better," he said. "Now you get on home and do your work."

"I hate it!" I said. "It doesn't matter anyway."

"Who says?"

"Me. Nobody cares what I do! Why should I work!"

"Whoo-whee!" he said. "Now I'm gettin' mad. You come down here hollerin' things is bad, but you ain't willin' to do nothin' to fix it. Well, I ain't playin' for nobody that won't do nothin' to fix things for themself. You want to listen on ol' Daniel Beasley's playin' you got to show me some work!" He started putting his guitar in the case.

"What?" I asked, startled. "How can I show you my work?"

"You just bring it down here, after your teacher's seen to it." He nodded to himself and snapped the guitar case shut. "Yes, when I see her marks I'll know if you been foolin' around or workin' like you're 'sposed to." He got up and started away down the path.

"You just don't want me to bother you," I said.

He stopped and half turned. "What you're goin' to do is up to you, child. I don't have nothin' to do with it. You got to do most things for yourself, 'cause there ain't nobody else who's goin' to. I was a whole lot littler child than you when I learned that for myself."

I looked away, feeling ashamed.

"I'm comin' down here tomorrow," he said, gently. "You got yourself some good work from school everythin's goin' to be just fine."

I watched him go on down the path.

He's right. If I get bad grades in school, I'll be in trouble. They'll start asking questions . . .

*   *   *

Back at the house, I carried my books upstairs and spread them out on the table under the window. I opened my notebook and started trying to read the things I'd written down in French class while Mrs. Lively was talking.

I couldn't read any of it. There was just a jumbled-up mess of words. I turned over to the English notes, the history. They were all the same. I couldn't read them.

I threw my French book across the room.

Mr. Beasley's words seemed to jump back into my head. "First thing goes wrong," he'd said, "you're ready for everythin' else to be goin' wrong, too."

I crawled under my bed after my French book and dusted it off.

He said he'd play if I showed him my work.

I opened my book to the beginning and started reading, trying to make sense of it.

It was dark when I got hungry and quit. Downstairs, eating a cold can of spaghetti, I looked at the mess from Mom's having thrown the skillet that morning. All my good resolutions disappeared. I didn't even know what time the bus would come by in the morning.

I was ready to start crying again when I remembered I wasn't going to go getting into any more panics. All I had to do was set the clock an hour earlier than it had been today. I could go early and wait until the bus came. I could even leave Mom a note telling her she didn't have to get up with me, I'd reset the clock for her.

Glad Mom wasn't home, I finished eating, cleaned up her mess, and made her bed. I got her alarm clock and set it for the time she'd get off work.

I'd started drawing when I remembered the water-colors in the store at school. I got the change I'd been hiding and counted it out. If I kept some of the two dollars Mom'd given me that morning, I'd have just enough to buy the cheapest box.

I took the rest of her change from school downstairs and put it on the note I'd left her. Then I went back upstairs to draw.

The next morning, I got Mom's alarm turned off before she woke up. Praying she wouldn't hear me, I checked the change I'd wrapped up in a piece of paper and hidden in my sweater pocket. When I was dressed and had my books, I tried her door.

I'd worried for nothing. The smell of beer in her room was stronger than ever. I slipped past her and downstairs. After I'd cleaned up her mess, I ate and hurriedly packed a lunch. Then I set her clock to wake her in time to get to work, took it back upstairs and put it on the table by Mom's bed.

I hate you. I'll never like you.
When Daddy comes back, I'll be free of you.

Up at the road, there was a flat rock beside our mailbox that was perfect for waiting. I got the small drawing pad out of my notebook and started drawing. When the bus finally came, I asked the driver the time.

The seat behind him was empty. I dropped into it and piled my books up beside me. When the bus stopped near the store and kids had gotten on, I looked up in the mirror and watched them go to the back. One of them sat down across the aisle from Clyde, said something that made Clyde laugh. I looked away out the window.

I'll never be able to do that.

The bus got to school early. I found my locker, figured out the combination. When I got to French, the boy who'd pulled my hair at lunch was already there talking to some others. I looked at the floor, found my place at the corner of the tables, and opened my book.

After Mrs. Lively came in, I started writing down what she said again. This time I tried to be sure I'd be able to read it when I got home. But it was hard. I kept seeing the edge of my drawing pad in my notebook, kept wanting to draw instead of listen.

At lunchtime, I went to the school store to buy the cheapest box of watercolors. Just as I was paying for them, a teacher came up.

"Did I miss you?" she asked. "I don't remember you from my watercolor class."

"I'm not in it," I said, trying to count the change faster.

"No? I'm Miss Joyce, the art teacher. Do you like to paint?"

The boy behind the counter nodded and swept the change off into his hand.

"No," I told her, feeling panicky. "These aren't for me." I didn't wait for her to think of more questions. I grabbed the paints and nearly ran to the cafeteria.

The corner tables by the windows were empty again. I sat down with my back to the room, took the lid off the box of paints, shut out the noise around me. Wishing I had water to try the paints, I hurried through lunch so I could draw.

The rest of the day, whenever I started getting scared, I made myself think about Mr. Beasley's promise to play. I listened to the teachers. I found it was like town. If I didn't look at people and stayed away from them, they'd mostly leave me be.

When I got back to the ugly, little house, I had only a couple of papers to take to Mr. Beasley. He'd said good ones. They weren't.

Half scared, I got one of my drawing pads out of its hiding place and tore out some wildflower drawings I'd done in the woods. I grabbed the school papers and hurried toward the pond.

Mr. Beasley was already there with his guitar. When he saw me, he put it aside and held out his hand. I handed my papers over with the schoolwork on top.

He pointed to the red 80 on the spelling pretest on top of the pile. "What's this mean?"

"It's just a practice test. The real one is Friday." I explained the different ways the teachers had said they'd grade.

Mr. Beasley listened carefully, nodding his head from time to time. Then he looked at my algebra paper and shook his head, sadly.

"Lord, what a mess," he said, banging his finger on each of the places where I'd erased and redone the problems. "You've got to do schoolwork nice. No teacher wants to see a mess like this!"

"I hate it!" I grabbed the paper out of his hands and wadded it up, ready to cry.

"That's the truth," he said. "Just one look and I sure knowed that. Where'd you get this, child?" His voice sounded strange.

I saw he was looking at one of my drawings. When he looked up at me, he wasn't smiling.

"I drew it," I said, mad, wondering if he'd hate it, too.

Mr. Beasley looked back down at the drawing and shook his head. "Seein' this here, I feel like I do lookin' on this ol' pond," he said, softly. "Peaceful inside, like somebody gentle's been near me." He looked up at me and smiled.

A strange feeling welled up inside me. *He likes it.*

"How'd you learn drawin' like this?"

"My daddy taught me," I said, suddenly feeling good because his daddy taught him what he liked best, too.

"What's your daddy's name, child?"

"Caldwell Burden." I looked away.

"I knows your father. He drawed me and my daddy one time while we was playin'. Where's your daddy, child? Didn't you tell me you ain't livin' with him no more?"

"He went away . . . the court . . . made me live with my mom."

"What's your name, child?" he asked.

"Claire."

"Claire," he said. "I figured it was goin' to be." His voice sounded strange again. Embarrassed, scared I'd told him too much, I started to get up to go.

He held my drawing out. When I reached for it, he moved it away.

"First time you sat down to try it, you drawed this good?" he asked gently.

"No."

"If you works on it, them school papers'll look every bit as good as this here."

"I don't care!" I grabbed the drawing away. "I hate school and it hates me. You're mean to say it's going to be different!" I saw his face and burst into tears. "I'm sorry!" I cried. "You're not mean! I'm just no good at school!"

"Hush, child. Don't go takin' on so. Sit yourself down here on the wall."

I sat down and struggled to stop crying. "It doesn't matter! I'm sorry! I . . ."

"Hush," he said. "It sounds to me like you're missin' your daddy."

I nodded.

"Your momma's got to go workin' and you don't know nobody here?"

I nodded again.

"I don't think you've put much thinkin' into bein' good in school," he said. "So I don't think you've got a way of knowin' yet if you can do good at it. When I was little, I was always thinkin' about growin' up and playin' good like my daddy. But I had to keep after it a long time to find out if I was going to play good like him."

His eyes are gentle.

"You are good at it," I said. "Your playing's beautiful."

He smiled. "That's 'cause I worked on bein' good." He picked up his twelve-string. "I been playing and playin'." He fingered the Bach melody. "I been puttin' all my time on this every day, till I almost got it like the sounds I'm hearin' in my head. Most of my fun's knowin' I can play good." He pointed at my drawing with his guitar. "What you drawin' all the time for?"

"I have to," I said.

"Yes. 'Cause you like it. 'Cause you got to be good at it, too."

I nodded. "But I'm never going to like school."

He laughed. "Maybe not, but that don't change the way you'd feel doin' good in school. You like every drawin' you make?"

I shook my head.

"All right then," he said. "Now you listen on this." After a few songs, he laid his guitar across his lap and stared at me. "I can't stay down here no longer, child. I've got to get on home. Best thing for you, too."

"Please come back tomorrow. I'll try to do better on my papers."

"I can't come down here tomorrow. I got to go workin' and get myself some money."

"Oh," I said, looking away.

"I'm goin' to be comin' down here again. You see this here ol' wall? You got bad troubles, child, you take one of the rocks off the top. Put it up behind this ol' white pine I'm leaning on. Unless I see one's gone, I got to go workin' till next week."

I nodded, feeling miserable. He looked as if he needed money. His clothes were worn and old, like him.

"You come on down here and see me next Wednesday," he said. "You bring me some good papers, I'm goin' to bring you some good songs."

"All right," I promised, smiling, too. "Good papers."

I was almost back to the house from the pond when I saw the squirrels were in the yard again. I stopped at the edge of the woods to watch them playing in the last of the afternoon sunshine.

One sat up on his hind legs and froze, looking at something. Suddenly, I saw all the things I'd gotten wrong trying to draw the squirrels before.

I hadn't made the top part of their hind legs big enough. Their front paws were tiny compared to the way I'd drawn them. I still wasn't sure how to draw the long fur on their bushy tails. I hadn't been able to make the hair coming straight toward me look right.

The sun's warmth felt good. I stood there enjoying it and watching the squirrels. I felt free, alive, and almost happy. I looked past the squirrels at the ugly, little house.

When the snow comes, I'll be stuck in there.

"I hate it!" I screamed.

The squirrels scattered to the trees. Looking at the empty yard and the house, I felt cold and miserable. I went up to my room and opened my algebra notebook. I'd promised Mr. Beasley good work, but I didn't want to do it. I wanted to try drawing the squirrels. Maybe if I did, I'd feel good again.

I wondered where they'd go when it got cold and snowed. I wondered what I'd do. I couldn't go outside and draw then.

An hour later, I'd finished the squirrel. I'd just made dots where the long hair on the tail faced me. It worked. He almost seemed alive. I'd caught him on my paper. Now even when it snowed, I'd have him to keep me company.

I tore the drawing out and held it up against the wall. I wished I had a drawing of Mr. Beasley to put up there, too. He'd said Daddy'd drawn him. He'd known I missed Daddy. He'd be my friend if I did my work. Maybe Mr. Beasley would let me draw him. But even if he did I couldn't put either drawing up.

I sat back down. I only saw Mom on weekends now, but her messes were always waiting for me. When I got up, her mess from last night was there. I'd clean it up. Now her breakfast mess was down there waiting for me.

At least I'll be able to tell if she drinks beer for breakfast before she goes to work. If she does, I'll really be in trouble. She'll get fired. The sheriff will find out that she isn't taking care of me. We'll have to go to Grandma's.

I folded the squirrel drawing in half and stuck it in the back of my algebra book. Mom wouldn't look there. At school, on the bus, even at home, I could look at it and remember the squirrels in the sun. And think of Daddy.

I flipped to the front of the algebra book. Even if I had a picture of Mr. Beasley, I couldn't take it to school. Someone might see it. They wouldn't want me to be friends with him just because he's an old black man. He'd have to be a secret like drawing, or I'd lose him, too.

Angry, hating people, I started working the algebra problems.

For the rest of the week school did get better. Listening to the teachers and doing my work made the day pass more quickly. But it wasn't completely the way Mr. Beasley said. I was still scared of kids. But most of them seemed to forget I was there. Most of them left me alone.

When the teachers weren't talking and I could hide my sketch pad, I drew: at lunchtime, in the library during study hall. Everywhere except biology class.

Best of all I didn't see Mom. She was still in bed when I left in the mornings. I was asleep when she came home. But on Friday night something woke me. I heard a crash downstairs. I rolled over to try to go back to sleep.

"Claire!" she bawled.

I stayed still, hoping she would think I was asleep.

"Claire!" She started banging on the kitchen wall.

I got up so she wouldn't come trap me in my room.

Downstairs, Mom was sitting at the table with a beer. There were two boxes on the table with good smells coming from them.

"You had supper?" she asked. She was really drunk.

I shook my head. She hadn't bought any food since the Sunday before and I was starving.

"Then celebrate!" She laughed and clapped her hands together like a little kid. "The boss got mad at June and fired her! Now I got her place! Means I got to work Saturdays now 'stead of Mondays, but I'm goin' to make money! Piles of it!" She laughed again and patted at her apron pocket until it jingled. Then she started slapping change onto the table until coins were rolling everywhere.

"Eat your supper!" she yelled, laughing. "You want some beer? I got plenty." She laughed again.

I shook my head and dug into the boxes. They were jammed with food. Fried chicken, mashed potatoes, salad, coleslaw, French fries. I got a plate and filled it.

Mom sat watching me eat.

"Would you like some, too?" I asked, wanting her to stop watching me.

She shook her head and looked away. "I want another beer," she said. There was a brown bag at her feet. She reached down and after groping in it came

up with another full can. She had trouble opening it. I
was eating as fast as I could.

She looked up and caught me watching her. She
looked angry, but then seemed to remember something and laughed.

"I got a good joke for you. The boss always lets the
cook take home the scraps, 'cause he keeps pigs. Well,
I done you proud." She was laughing so hard she had
to set her beer down. "I knowed you was hungry, so I
told the boss I had a pig at home, too." She laughed
and laughed till tears were running down her face.

I couldn't stay at the table. I got up and went back
upstairs, to bed.

*I hate her so much. I know hating's bad, but it does
me good to hate her. Sometimes, I don't think I'll ever
live long enough to hate her and Grandma and the
rest of them enough for taking me away from Daddy.*

The next morning after Mom had gone to work, the
sight of my plate still just sitting on the table made
me mad all over again. Mom had left the boxes of
food out on the table all night. They were stinking. I
was so mad at her and myself for not putting the food
away, I was shaking.

I scraped the mess off my plate and carried the
boxes out to the trash pile and threw them on top.
Back inside I found there wasn't any other food in the
house. The refrigerator was empty except for Mom's
beer.

Her change was still all over the table and floor.
There were so many coins I wondered if she knew
how much she'd had. I decided she couldn't possibly
remember. I picked some of it up and went up the
road to the store.

The same woman was working there. She frowned
at me but not as much. I was glad I'd taken time to
comb my hair and wash my face. She still didn't ask

me any questions. I made sure no one was coming in
before I went out the door.

Sunday, Mom never got up, but there was a box of
leftovers in the refrigerator. I stuffed myself, hating
her.

When I got up Monday, the smell of beer in Mom's
room was awful. I gathered up my things and crept
downstairs, glad she didn't have to go to work.

The kitchen was a mess again. I cleaned it up, made
my lunch, ran. So long as she was there, I was glad I
had to go to school.

Later that morning, in biology, I found a microscope on each desk and two packages of colored pencils. Startled, I turned back to Mrs. Carter.

Just then, Clyde came in carrying a box which he
took to her. She opened it, smiled, and asked him to
pass out what he'd brought. As he turned toward the
class, I went to my table.

Mrs. Carter said we were going to be studying botany. Clyde's mother had a greenhouse and had sent
flowers and leaves for us to study. After he'd passed
our table, I looked up and saw several strange green
leaves and two beautiful flowers. They were the same
purplish-blue color as the mountains. They reminded
me of the flower drawings Grandmother Burden had
had that her sister Claire had done. I reached out and
touched one of them.

Mrs. Carter started calling roll. I made myself concentrate on her. When she finished, she said, we'd practice first: using the microscopes, observing, and drawing.

I froze. I'd never thought about drawing being part
of a class's work.

*I can't draw in here! He'll see! No one can know!
Mom will . . .*

Clyde came back to the table. I looked up at him,
startled. He smiled. I looked away, saw the microscope.

I'll never be able to share it . . . or draw . . . with him here!

Mrs. Carter was putting up a large chart. She began explaining how to use the microscope. I frantically tried to listen. She was saying something about this being a stage microscope—which just enlarged the surface.

"Terrific!" Clyde whispered.

Later, she went on, we'd use the other kind which would allow us to look through the specimen. As she pointed to parts of the microscope on the chart, I began to feel panicky.

Clyde pushed the microscope on the table toward me.

"I already know how to use it," he whispered.

I bent over it trying to listen to Mrs. Carter, trying to get the panic out of my head, trying to do what she was telling us.

"You forgot the things," he said.

He held out one of the leaves. I backed off, scared he'd touch me. He put the leaf on the platform and took his hand away. I stayed still, waiting to see if he was finished.

"Go ahead," he said.

I looked back through it. There was only a green blur. I looked up at the chart, then back down at the microscope. The knobs were different from the ones on the chart.

"This one," he said, reaching out again.

I jerked my hand out of the way. He jumped. The girls in back of us giggled. I felt myself turn red.

"You use this to adjust it," he said, quietly, ignoring them and turning the knob. "Down makes it closer, up farther away. It just takes practice."

He moved away. I stayed still.

"Go ahead. I'll use it when you're through."

Feeling stupid, I leaned over it, turned the knob,

and caught my breath. The leaf's surface was suddenly there—enormous and beautiful. The thread down the center was a giant cord. I turned the leaf over and looked at the underside. It was incredible—completely different from the top—covered with hundreds of tiny holes. I reached out for the pencils.

"She said do the top," Clyde said. "The bottom's too hard."

Frustrated, I turned the leaf over and pushed the microscope back toward him.

"Aren't you going to draw it?" he asked.

I couldn't answer. I opened my notebook and got out two pieces of paper hoping to draw it while he was busy with his own. I put one paper partially over the other, slid them as close to the edge of the desk as I could and started sketching what I'd seen.

"Gee . . ." he began, looking over my shoulder.

I pulled the top paper down over the other and just sat frozen with my back to him. He moved away. I finished my drawing, covered it up, and stared at the floor, waiting.

"Next," he said, startling me so I jumped and looked up.

"Your turn." He pushed the microscope toward me. He looked away and opened his book.

He'd just left his drawing lying there. He couldn't draw. It was awkward and ugly and all out of proportion. I felt confused. Usually kids laughed when I did stupid things. He'd just looked puzzled and moved out of the way.

I looked back through the microscope. The next leaf looked almost the same until I saw it enlarged. I turned it over quickly to see the bottom. That was different, too. I moved it around trying to memorize it so I could draw it when I got home.

I felt strange suddenly and looked up. Clyde was watching me again. I flipped the leaf back over quickly and turned away to try drawing it. But I hadn't looked at the top enough. I reached out for the microscope.

Clyde was using it. I jerked my hand back to keep from touching him, turned away, wanting to die, knowing he'd laugh at me.

The microscope slid back in front of me.

"Finish the rest, I'll use it when you're through," he said.

I felt idiotic, but nodded. When I'd drawn the leaf and flower, I pushed all of them toward him. Mrs. Carter was helping someone. I took my paper up to her vacant desk and left it face down so no one would see it. When I started back, Clyde looked down at his drawing. I sat as far from him as I could and opened my book.

A few minutes later, Mrs. Carter came around collecting the drawings. I looked up, startled, tried to find words.

"She put hers on your desk," Clyde said.

"Okay," Mrs. Carter said, smiling. "That's fine."

I looked back down at my book. It wasn't fine. I felt like an idiot. He had to be sure I was one.

That afternoon in algebra class, Mr. Davis went up and down the rows checking our homework. When he stopped at my desk and began checking mine, he started smiling. I'd gotten all but two of the problems right. He explained the first. When I got it, I asked if the other was done the same way.

"Not quite," he said. Instead of showing me, he reached out and tapped Clyde on the shoulder. "Clyde? Will you help Claire? Clyde's the best we've got in math," he told me. "Maybe he'll help you while I check some others."

"Sure," Clyde said, turning around.

He turned my paper around, too, and looked down at it as Mr. Davis walked away. I stared at him, petrified. I hadn't imagined it. He really was beautiful. His eyelashes were incredibly long and black. He looked up and I looked straight into his green eyes. He looked back down.

"Which one?" he asked. "Oh, yeah. He marked it. The tenth. That was a bear. See, here's how you do it."

He got his paper and put it over mine. Somehow, I looked at it and was surprised. It wasn't like his biology drawing at all. It was so neat it nearly looked like a page out of the book. He picked up my book, moved the paper over beside mine, and began explaining the problem, softly, clearly, the way Mr. Davis had. I pulled myself into listening, into starting to correct mine the way he said.

Clyde started to put my book back on my desk. I jerked my hand out of the way, hit the book. The squirrel drawing slipped out of the book and off the desk. I grabbed at it as it fell, but Clyde caught the drawing and unfolded the paper as he held it out to me.

"Gee, that's great," he said, smiling. "Where'd you get it?"

My insides flipped. Then in my head I heard Mom yelling, "No drawing!" I grabbed it out of his hand.

For an instant, he looked startled. Then, he turned away. I sat staring down at his paper ready to scream.

I've done it again! I've been a freak again!

Ready to cry, I picked up his paper and held it over his shoulder. He took it without saying anything.

Mr. Davis was coming back up the aisle. My English book was in my lap. I stuck the squirrel drawing in the back of it and made myself finish fixing problem ten.

"All straightened out?" he asked, pausing at my desk.

I nodded, lying. I didn't dare look up. I knew he must still be smiling. I knew if I saw him, I'd cry.

It seemed at least a hundred years before class was

finally over. When the bell rang, I grabbed my books and fled. On the bus, I piled the books up between myself and the aisle so no one could sit down. I opened a book, turned my back slightly to the aisle, pretended to read.

I heard Jimmy getting on the bus yelling at someone and froze. He'd been in algebra. I'd die if he teased me.

"Let's sit in the back, okay?" Clyde's voice asked.

"Sure," Jimmy said, heading toward it. "The girls is back there!"

All the way home I listened to the kids talking and laughing.

I was scared when I got down the road and saw Mom's car. Then I remembered she had Mondays off and knew I'd hate Mondays.

The kitchen was an incredible mess. From the looks of it, she been drinking beer all day. The skillet was still on the stove and smelled burned. I went closer and saw she'd tried to fry leftover mashed potatoes. The whole inside of the pan was a charred, lumpy mess.

I sighed and took my books upstairs. Mom was in her bed asleep. More beer cans were on the table beside her bed and on the floor.

I put my books in my room and looked around trying to tell if she'd been in my things. They looked untouched. I sat down on my bed and wondered if Mom'd always been like this. Grandma had said Daddy started Mom drinking. Only I couldn't remember Daddy drinking before his paintings started going wrong a couple of years ago.

Grandma wasn't surprised Mom was drunk. She looked as if she knew she would be.

I shuddered and looked around the room.

I hate it here. I can't even draw with her here.

I changed into jeans and started back downstairs.

As I tried to slip through Mom's room, she half sat up. She looked awful.

"You didn't clean the bathroom yesterday," she said. "Do it. And fix me some supper. I'm hungry."

"All right!" I hurried downstairs hoping she'd stay in bed. Hating her, I cleaned the bathroom first in case she got up later. Then I cleaned out the pans and the sink. When I'd finished those and went to clear the mess off the table, I saw a quarter sitting by her coffee cup.

She left me a tip! Just like I was her waitress!

I picked up the cup and started to smash it on the table. I made myself put it down, carefully, and go outside. It was the only cup left. If I broke it, she'd know. She'd be after me about it.

I started running toward the pond, stopped.

Mr. Beasley isn't there. He said Wednesday.

I can't tell him anyway.

I turned back to the house.

I can't even go draw. My things are upstairs. If I go after them . . .

I looked down at my arms and saw the round white scars.

I don't want any more scars. I can't do anything if she's here . . . except wait on her. I hate her! I started running toward the river.

Once I'd found the flat rock, I went out on it. The charcoal drawing I'd made after the last time I'd been home was still there. I started bawling, wanting Daddy, wanting to go home.

When I'd quit caring and couldn't cry anymore, I just lay still, listening to the river. I heard a strange sound behind me and looked around. Terrified, I sat up and jerked my legs up close against me. A huge dog was on the sandbar at the end of the rock. He almost looked like a fox terrier, but was too big and gray and shaggy. I'd never seen a dog anything like him.

"No!" I whispered. "No!"

The dog lay down and put his head between his paws. He wagged his long, thin tail, and made the sound I'd heard before—a funny, moaning sound. It wasn't anything like a growl. It sounded like a moo. I saw he had a collar on. He was someone's pet. He was just a giant, ugly, friendly dog. I laughed with relief.

He wagged his tail.

"I'm scared of big dogs," I told him, smiling.

His tail beat harder against the ground. He raised his head a little, puffed out his cheeks and mooed again—longer and funnier. The sound went up and down as if he was trying to talk or sing.

"You want to be friends?" I asked.

He wagged his tail and crawled closer to the rock on his belly. His gray, shaggy coat looked soft. I put out my hand. I was still a little afraid of him, but I needed to touch his strange coat.

I held my breath as he came up on the rock. He was much bigger than me. His head was enormous. He sniffed my fingers and lay back down with his head between his paws. I leaned over to touch him. His fur felt soft, but wiry, too. I wondered if I could draw that.

"You're a mess," I said. His long tail, legs and belly were covered with burrs and beggar-lice from running through the bottomland.

He wagged his tail and nudged my hand with his nose. I laughed and put my arm over his back to hug him. He licked my arm.

"Don't," I said. "That tickles." I started picking the burrs off his coat. "You do belong to someone. Don't they love you and take care of you?"

He raised his head and looked over his shoulder at the trees on the bank. I looked, too, and froze with my hand in midair. Clyde was leaning against one of the trees, watching us, looking as if he'd been there a while.

"What are you doing here?" burst out of me.

He looked embarrassed and held up a book. "You're sitting on my rock with my dog."

"Oh," I said. I looked down at his dog. He'd put his giant head down on my knee. "I'm sorry. Call him. I'll go."

"You don't have to go. Most people are scared of him."

"Please call him. I am, too."

He laughed. "Not very. Most people scream or at least throw rocks at him the first time they see him."

"At him? That's awful." I put my hand back on the dog's head. He looked up at me, wagged his tail, and sighed. "Why? He's a nice dog."

"Because he's so big and different. They're scared of him. They don't wait . . ." He stopped talking.

"You were watching me."

"Jake heard you. I followed him to see what he was after. We were coming here anyway."

"You didn't have to stay!"

"I was scared you were hurt . . . needed help . . . I didn't know what to do. He won't come away if something's hurt!"

I looked away feeling sick inside.

Jake was just feeling sorry for me.

"Do you come down here much?" Clyde asked.

"Never," I lied, rubbing out my drawing.

"It's a nice place. See over there—the trees that hang over the water? Sometimes the air under them is green."

I nodded, surprised he'd seen it, too.

"You've seen it?"

"I won't come anymore. I didn't know it was your rock."

"It isn't my rock, silly. It's on your place."

I didn't answer. I looked back down at Jake and nervously started picking burrs out of his coat.

"That's easier with a comb. I do take care of him."

I felt myself blush and jerked my hand away from Jake. "Please call him. I have to go home."

"Don't go. Jake'll get mad at me."

I didn't answer. I felt stupid and awkward and wanted to get away from him. I'd been weird in class. He'd seen me crying. Now he was going to tease me for talking to his dog.

"Did you do your algebra yet?" he asked.

I shook my head.

"I didn't either, but I looked at it in class. It's tough. Want to? At your house?"

He whistled. Jake left me and went to him.

"Come on," Clyde said. "I'll come help you with it."

"No!" I scrambled up off the rock, terrified he'd see Mom.

He stopped and turned back. "Is something wrong?"

"No! My mom isn't home! She'd get mad!" I started up the bank well away from him.

"Oh," he said. "Then you don't live by yourself?"

I stopped cold and nearly fell. "What did you say?"

"You don't live by yourself?"

"No! Why? Did someone say . . ." I asked turning back, scared. In court the sheriff had insisted I might as well have been living by myself.

"No," Clyde said, looking embarrassed. "It just popped into my head. It was a dumb thing to say." He reached down and started scratching behind Jake's ears as he looked at me. Clyde didn't look mean. He looked nice.

"What's Jake?" I asked, thinking maybe I could find a picture of a dog like him and copy it.

"An Irish wolfhound," Clyde said, leaning down to hug Jake. Jake wagged his tail and licked Clyde's face. I turned away feeling awful.

I'll never have a dog with Mom around.

"Claire?" Clyde asked.

I looked back at him. He looked down at Jake.

"I could come over later. When your Mom gets home. To do your algebra."

I felt confused. It had been impossible to ignore him at school. He was so tall, I seemed to see him every time I looked up. Girls were always crowded around him, looking up at him, talking to him. In almost every class a girl named Margie was talking to him every chance she got. He usually listened to her. Why was he talking to me?

He feels sorry for me.

Besides, Mom is home.

I realized he was waiting to see what I'd say. I turned away.

"No, She'll be tired. She works."

"I could call you. To see if you got the answers."

"No!" I said, looking back at him in surprise.

"Oh."

I've hurt his feelings.

I felt funny inside. Beside Jake he didn't look as tall as he did at school.

"We don't have a phone," I said. I scrambled up the bank and ran.

Mom was still asleep when I got back to the house. I stood in the quiet kitchen wishing I lived alone the way Clyde said.

I'd have a dog if I did. A dog like Jake. I'd never go to school. I'd stay home and draw and go see Mr. Beasley and listen to him play. Jake and I would . . . till Daddy came back.

I saw the quarter lying by the coffee cup. *If I take it maybe Mom'll leave me more. I can save it to buy watercolor paper.*

She'll be gone the rest of the week. Except for her messes, I can pretend she doesn't live here. Just me . . . and Jake.

I took the quarter and crept upstairs to hide it with my stuff. There were more beer cans on the table by Mom's bed.

I closed my door behind me, spread out my books. I was tired when I got to the algebra. I just pushed the book aside. I could do it at lunch tomorrow or during study hall.

I crawled in bed. When I shut my eyes, I saw Clyde staring at me looking hurt. He'd tried to be nice.

I almost asked him if Jake was a freak.

Jake's an Irish wolfhound.

I'm the freak.

I pulled my pillow over my head so Mom wouldn't hear me crying.

Chapter Ten

"Claire! Claire! Where's my clock!" Mom ripped the covers off me. "You didn't set it! I'm goin' to be late! I'm goin' to get fired!" She hit at me, yanked.

I struggled to get away from her, fell out of bed and banged my elbow.

"Get up! Get up!" she wailed. "I can't find my keys! You got to help me! The boss'll fire me! I'll have to go back to Momma's!" She collapsed on my bed, wailing, "I'll kill you if I have to go back to Momma's!"

Terrified, I struggled up off the floor, saw her clock on my table where I'd forgotten it. I grabbed it, tried to show it to her.

"You've got time! You won't be late!"

"Couldn't find it . . . didn't know . . ." she babbled. "Can't find my keys. I got to get to work, Claire! Find the keys! Find 'em for me!"

I ran downstairs, found her purse, dug through it. I'd turned to go hunt upstairs when an impulse made me run outside to her car instead.

The keys were still in the ignition. Shaking, I took them out, went back inside.

She was still upstairs on my bed, wailing. Numb, hating her, I held out the keys. She took them and shut up.

I stood rubbing my elbow, wanting her off my bed, out of my room. "I have to get ready for school."

"It don't matter if you don't go, but I got to," she said. "You stay home if you want."

Panic welled back up inside me. It was time for my bus. If I missed it . . . "I can't stay home!" I yelled, running to my closet.

"S'all right," Mom said. "You want to go so much, I'll take you. I got time now. There ain't no use in me goin' early. The boss'd just put me to work. He's always keepin' me late cleanin' up. He knows I got to stay there." She got up and stumbled toward the door. "I need me some coffee anyway."

Scared she'd change her mind, and the bus would be gone, I dressed as fast as I could. By the time I got downstairs she was angry again that I'd forgotten to set her clock.

I couldn't eat. I just got my books and started out to the car to wait for her.

She followed me out, complaining nobody cared about her, never did anything for her. I made myself be quiet, look out the car window, tried to shut her out, but I couldn't. The stale smell of beer and cigarettes were too thick in the car. The long sleeves of my wool dress itched, reminding me of the scars on Mom's arms. I had forgotten her clock, almost gotten her fired, almost gotten us sent to Grandma's.

She let me out at school and left. The buses were already there. I got to French as Mrs. Lively was calling roll.

When I got to English, second period, the room was nearly empty. Clyde was sitting at his desk, reading. As I put my books down on my desk, he turned around and smiled at me.

For a moment, I looked down into his green eyes, wishing he'd like me. Then I remembered the way I'd hurt his feelings, run from him. I looked away and sat down, confused, wondering why he was smiling.

"Are you a ghost?" he asked.

I looked up, startled. He'd crossed his arms on top of my books and was leaning on them staring at me. I looked away again, shocked by how tall he was even sitting down, and scared by how close.

"You can't be," he said. "When you ran into me at the store, you were real."

He'd looked scared. As scared as Mr. Beasley had.
They both thought I was a ghost.

"Besides, Jake didn't growl at you. Dogs always growl at ghosts."

He's laughing at me. He's mad, like that boy in line . . . the one I told not to touch me.

"Claire?"

I looked back up, wanting him to move, hating him for laughing at me. He wasn't even smiling. He was still just staring at me.

My elbow hurt. I rubbed at it and looked down at my desk. He moved, held a paper over my books so I had to look at it. I saw it was his algebra homework, shook my head, feeling weird inside.

He's feeling sorry for me.

I closed my eyes so I couldn't see the paper. Kids had never felt sorry for me. It was grownups who'd found out I wasn't in school, poked around, and caused all the trouble. People feeling sorry for me was why I was stuck with Mom instead of still with Daddy.

If that's what you get, I don't want anyone feeling sorry for me ever again. It makes everything awful.

I heard Jimmy laughing, looked up at the door. He was out in the hall. Scared, I looked back at Clyde. He was still staring at me.

If he tells Jimmy he saw me crying, talking to his dog, he'll never stop teasing me!

Clyde turned abruptly away. Even more confused, I looked down at my desk. His algebra paper was still there. I started to give it back, saw Jimmy'd come in with Mrs. Morgan, the teacher.

I couldn't return it with them there. I stuck it in my English book.

When class was over, I still couldn't make myself try to give him the paper. Instead, I ran as soon as the bell rang.

Later, after gym, I'd already sat down in biology

before I saw Clyde was just finishing passing out
more flowers. I remembered his algebra paper,
started to get up to go get it, but Mrs. Carter began calling roll.

Clyde sat down, leaned toward me.

I leaned away. "I forgot your paper," I said, feeling
stupid.

"It okay. You can copy it at lunch."

I shook my head, realized I was starving. I'd been
too miserable and tired to eat the night before. With
Mom yelling, I hadn't had time to fix my lunch.

"You want the microscope first?"

I shook my head, opened my book and stared at it,
wanting to go home. My elbow hurt worse from the
exercises in gym. I closed my eyes, seemed to hear
Mom yelling we'd have to go back to Grandma's.

I struggled to see the studio at home, tried to remember sitting for Daddy. Finally, I saw Daddy's
face, began to feel safe again, smiled.

Something fell against my hand. Startled, I opened
my eyes, saw a purplish-blue flower in my lap. I wondered where I was, where it came from, looked up,
saw Clyde leaning on the table staring at me.

His eyes are gentle . . .

I looked away, startled, and realized he must have
dropped the flower onto my hand.

"Help me do this?" he asked.

I saw the microscope, shook my head, carefully put
the flower back on the table.

He asked if I lived alone. I wish I did. I . . .

"You can have the microscope," he said.

I nodded without looking at him and moved the microscope over as far away from him as I could. I tried
to concentrate on keeping my drawing covered instead of being aware he was watching me.

When Mrs. Carter told us to clean up, he stood up
to help her.

"Claire, wait a minute," he said, turning back.

I shook my head, hurried away.

In the hall, I remembered I didn't have lunch or money. Hungry, I got my books and went to the library to finish my homework. I sat down at one of the tables in the back and opened my algebra book. When I started trying to do the problems, I found out they were as hard as Clyde'd said. I took his paper out of my English book and looked at it.

Just looking at it, I saw the trick to doing them. I put his paper back in my English book, started the first problem again—messily, hoping it would look as if I'd figured it out myself.

I was halfway through the problems when I realized someone was standing behind me. I looked up, scared.

"It's okay," Clyde said, sitting down next to me.

I wondered why he was there and felt stupid again. He wanted his paper back. I pulled it out of my English book and shoved it over to him.

"It isn't a test. Why don't you copy them?"

"Stop feeling sorry for me?" I said, angrily.

He looked shocked. "You think I feel sorry for you?"

I looked away, embarrassed.

"I don't feel sorry for you. Where'd you get a stupid idea like that?"

I shook my head wishing I'd kept quiet.

"Should I?"

"No!"

"Because you were crying? People cry. You were all right, weren't you?"

"Yes," I snapped, knowing I wasn't and feeling cornered.

"I was just being friendly. I thought if I helped you with algebra you'd help me with biology."

I started pulling together my books.

"Never mind, I'll go," he said, getting up.

When I got to history class, Clyde was sitting sideways in his seat talking to Margie, the blond girl
across the aisle. I looked at the floor, sat down,
opened my book.

Margie kept talking about some movie she'd been
to. She was smiling at Clyde. He was smiling at her.
*She's pretty. She isn't a freak. With girls like her
around, he'll never like me.*

I looked down, hating her, wishing I'd never seen
Clyde. I wished I was still in Galway Fields, at Galway Hall, in the studio, and no one had ever felt sorry
for me and made me leave Daddy.

I kept hearing Margie's voice. When she stopped
talking, I looked up expecting to see Mr. Allen had
come in. Instead, I saw Clyde was still sitting sideways, staring at me.

I looked back down at my book and closed my eyes
so I couldn't see his arm across the top of my desk.

*I've got to stop being stupid. He'll start asking ques-
tions, he'll say something to the teachers. I'll get in
trouble, have to . . .*

A crash beside me made me jump, look up.

"Sorry, dropped my book," Clyde said, leaning over
to pick it up off the floor.

I looked around, startled, saw Mr. Allen at the front
of the room. Clyde had turned away. I looked at his
back wondering how he'd dropped his book, if he'd
been giving it to Margie.

Later, when I got to algebra, I sat down and looked
out the window. There were white pines on the hill in
the distance.

*Tomorrow's Wednesday. Mr. Beasley said he'd be at
the pond.*

I looked down at my book and tried to hear his music. I couldn't. I was too hungry. I closed my eyes.
*When school's out, I'll go eat, do my homework and
draw. Tomorrow, I can go listen to him play. Mom
won't be home. I can pretend I live alone.*

I heard movement, looked up. Mr. Davis, the algebra teacher, had come in. He must have already
checked roll. People were going up to the board to do
the homework problems.

When he called my name, I was ready to die. If I
got the problem wrong, I'd have to explain it, figure it
out in front of the class.

"Problem five?" he asked.

I made myself go to the board. As I started working, I was glad I'd seen Clyde's paper. I wouldn't have
to talk.

I finished putting it up and started to turn away
from the board. I saw the sea of faces, jerked back
around, wishing class was over and I was not starving.

When Mr. Davis said my answer was right and sent
me back to my desk, Clyde didn't look up. I wondered
if he knew I'd looked at his paper.

Chapter Eleven

The next afternoon, I took my drawing things along with my papers when I went down to the pond. I could hear Mr. Beasley playing before I got there. I stopped out of sight and listened to the rich, full music.

He is my friend . . .

He likes me . . .

He doesn't feel sorry for me or scare me or tease me.

I went on through the woods to see him. I smelled something good. A newspaper parcel was sitting on the wall beside him. When he saw me, he smiled.

I smiled back.

"You been lookin' peaked," he said. "So I got us somethin' to eat. You hungry?"

I looked down at the ground, suddenly feeling sick inside. I shook my head.

He's just going to feel sorry for me, too.

"I didn't have no time to eat if I was comin' down here. So I just fixed it up and brought it. I didn't want to be eatin' my own unless I had some for you, too."

"You go ahead," I said, trying not to smell it anymore. "I had something at home."

"You ain't got room for more?"

I shook my head again. "Don't feel sorry for me."

He picked up the newspaper parcel and untied the string. "I didn't know bringin' somethin' was feelin' sorry. Most of the school kids I know got a powerful hunger on them when they come home from school. Somethin' hot'd be right good."

"There's food in the house even if Mom isn't." I looked out at the pond, began wishing I hadn't come.

"What you got in there?" he asked. "That don't look like school papers in that box."

I looked down at my box of chalk and back at him. He set his newspaper parcel aside.

He wasn't hungry . . . he's just feeling sorry for me . . .

"It's my chalk," I told him. "I was going to see if you'd let me draw you."

He nodded.

He doesn't really want to see my schoolwork . . . he only wants to sit there and play.

I looked at his huge, old hands folded in his lap. I knew I should just go home and not bother him, but his fingers were so crooked and his knuckles so big. I needed to see if I could catch them on paper. Somehow I had to show his hands, moving easily, making his music beautiful.

He picked up his guitar and looked down at the mother-of-pearl inlay glistening around the opening and started playing.

I sat on the end of the old wall and watched him, trying to see him right. The beautiful guitar was part of him. His worn tuxedo, too.

I looked up, saw how the huge white pine he was leaning against seemed to frame him. I got out my chalk, put it in rows, began drawing. First his arms framing his guitar, then the tree framing both. I put in the curve of the tree high above, echoed it in his arms cradling the curve of his guitar. Even the toes of his heavy old work shoes echoed the music's patterning, repeating, circling. Even his white kinky hair and the frayed lapels of his tuxedo.

When I'd done all I knew how, and was frowning at it, trying to see if I'd got him right, he stopped playing. I looked up to see if he was going to leave.

"You finished?" he asked.

I nodded, wishing I could try drawing him again from another angle.

"Goin' to let me see it?"

I took the drawing to him and held it out.

"That's me?" he asked, laughing. "That's an ol' man you got sittin' under this white pine!"

I looked down at the picture, at the kinky white hair, the deeply wrinkled face, the deep-set eyes looking away toward the purplish-blue mountains.

"You don't like it."

"I like it fine. I'm just gettin' old." He reached out and almost touched his fingers to the drawing. "My knuckles hurt just lookin' on 'em, same as they do when it gets cold around here. You got yourself a gift, child. You showed me just what you been seein'—an ol' man playin'. What else you got in there?"

I gave him the drawing pad and watched him turn its pages. He looked sad. He stopped at some late summer flowers I'd drawn and looked at them a long time, shaking his head.

"This here's like lookin' on somethin' I 'member from a long time ago," he said. "Just lookin' on it makes me feel peaceful inside."

He's trying to be nice . . . I'm just making him think about his friend that died.

I turned away. He didn't look peaceful. His face had the same pinched, worried look the neighbor at home had had when she'd come ringing the doorbell every day. I'd quit answering it, but it didn't do any good. She'd just kept on prying, making trouble.

I began to feel scared, looked back at Mr. Beasley.

"You got some school papers, too?" he asked, smiling.

"It's all right," I told him. "I've got a lot of homework. I'd better go."

"I'm goin' to come down here Wednesday, next."

I took back my drawing pad and gathered up my chalk. "Thank you for letting me draw you."

He nodded and looked down at his guitar, picked it up again, and began playing a children's song. For a moment, I hesitated, watching his hands dance over the strings, so quickly, despite his huge old knuckles. Then I turned and ran . . .

He just feels sorry for me.

He just thinks I'm a little kid . . .

He didn't like my drawings. They just made him think about the ghost. I wish I was a ghost, would disappear.

Chapter Twelve

Saturday morning, I was awake and scared when Mom came banging into my room.

"I told you last night!" she said, frantically. "We got to get goin'. I got to get you to Momma's if I'm goin' to get to work on time!"

I sat up. "Please don't go back there! You said you didn't want to! Please . . . when she was here . . . she brought a cake. I threw it at her. Please don't go! Don't make me go!"

Mom looked startled. "You threw it at Momma!"

I nodded, got ready in case Mom tried to hit me. "It was after . . . she . . ."

"After!" Mom looked funny, looked away.

"Please," I begged.

"I got to, Claire. I got to! She's been callin' me all week at work, naggin' me. If I don't go, she'll be after me about it. The boss'll fire me for bein' on the phone. She ain't got nobody to help her can, Claire. She'll give us some of the food if we do. I told you. We're just goin' to stay the night. We'll come home Sunday. I got to. I can't stay there!" She looked ready to cry, seemed to remember. "You got to get up!" she screamed. "I'll get fired if I'm late! Then we'd have to stay there!"

She ran back out of the room. Sick inside, I gathered up my clothes, got dressed, and went downstairs. Mom was just sitting at the table. She looked up at me with the same terror I'd seen when Grandma ran at her.

"Don't fight with Momma, Claire," she begged.

"Just do what she says and stay out of her way. After I been workin' all day and come to help her . . . don't make her mad."

"Don't go!"

"I got to help her so she'll leave me be! If I got to, you got to, too. Soon as it's done, we're comin' home."

Going in to town, I clutched the back of the front seat till my hands hurt. Mom drove too fast. I tried to look out the window at the mountains, tried to keep from being scared Mom would just leave me at Grandma Simmons'. I couldn't believe she'd come help her after the way she'd been beaten.

Too soon, Mom was stopping in front of Grandma's house. She didn't turn off the motor. She just waited for me to get out. Then she hollered, "Tell Momma I'll be here as soon as I can," and drove off.

I just stood there on the curb watching the car drive away. Then I heard banging and turned to look at the house. Grandma was banging on the window. When she saw I'd seen her, she disappeared. I wanted to run, remembered I had no place to go.

I don't even know where Mom works!

Grandma could call the sheriff, turn Mom in. The beer cans were still on the table at home. I'd been to upset, Mom'd been in too big a hurry, for me to clean them up. It was too far for me to get out there to do it.

The front door opened. I saw Grandma coming down the front steps toward me, smiling.

"There's my grandbaby! I been waitin' for you since six o'clock! Come see what I made you!" She reached out to hug me.

Her smile was a grimace on her mean-eyed face. I backed away, held the sack Mom'd put our night clothes in out in front of me.

Her smile wavered, returned. "Come on into the house. I knowed your momma wouldn't get up in time to feed you. I got you a good breakfast."

"Mom fed us," I lied.

"You can have some more. Poor child, you're lookin' like nobody ever feeds you." She took the sack out of my hands and started toward the house.

Terrified, I followed her into the house, down the ugly hall to the kitchen. She turned on me with her horrible smile. "I made you some good fried pies."

I made myself stare at her. "I'm not hungry."

She looked uncertain. I remembered her screaming at Mom about Grandmother Burden's money.

She wants me to like it here, to want to stay here instead of with Mom.

If I'm careful, she won't hurt me.

I tried to remember the way Daddy stared at people when they bothered him. I tilted my head back a little, frowned slightly, stared at her with narrowed eyes. "Mom said I was to help. What do you want me to do?"

Grandma looked away. "She's turned you against me! Turned my only grandchild against me! After I went and give in to her beggin' for food!"

"She brought me to help," I said, knowing she was lying. "You'll have to show me what to do."

"We got to pick the stuff first." She yanked open the back door.

I followed her outside, took the bucket she thrust at me, went down the porch steps after her to the garden.

I couldn't remember ever being in that part of Galway Fields before. Daddy'd called it "Pig Creek." The houses weren't much larger or better than the tenant house Mom and I lived in, but the garden surprised me. Grandma's lot was a block deep. I couldn't see a street behind it, just rows of corn at the back behind other plants. I followed Grandma to the corn and watched while she showed me how to tell which was ripe, how to pull off the ears.

I was grateful when she went back inside and left

me there. After the musty, old smell in the house, the garden smelled good.

"Smells poor," Daddy'd said once about a smell like that. I tried to remember where we'd been, couldn't.

I wrinkled my nose at the fresh smell as I pulled off the ears of corn. I turned back a few of the shucks, to see how yellow the brown silk was where it had been hidden from the sun. The dirt between the rows was soft. I dug my bare toes into it, tried to just pick corn and not think.

By lunchtime I'd taken the bucket up to the porch and emptied it into a washtub many times. Grandma brought out a plate of sandwiches and a pitcher of lemonade. I wanted to eat slowly and just look at the garden, but Grandma stood right over me, gobbling her own food and yelling about Mom. I tried not to listen to her, tried to close out the sound.

"Damn fool, takin' you out there and leavin' you by yourself! Goin' to have nothin' but trouble just like I had with her! You need somebody to care for you."

I choked my sandwich down, hoping she'd go back inside and let me go back to picking corn. Instead, when I finished, she had me shuck the ears I'd already picked. For a while she was busy in the kitchen. Then she came back outside, and showed me how to clean the silks off the ears with a brush in a washtub of water.

I hoped we'd stop then, but we went back to the garden and started going down rows of green beans filling buckets until my arms ached.

Finally, she went inside to start fixing dinner. She left me on the porch stringing the beans and breaking them to can.

As the shadows got longer on the porch, I often heard Grandma go out of the kitchen to the front of the house. She came to the back door.

"What time did your momma say she was coming?"

"She has to work until seven on Saturday. She said tell you she'd be here as soon as she could."

"She's late!"

"She has to clean up before she can leave."

"She's late!" Grandma smiled. "You come in here and set the table. Your momma wants any dinner, she better get crackin'. Bring them beans in here!"

Scared Mom wouldn't come, I looked down at my thumbnail. It was thick from breaking away the strings. My hands were stained. I took the beans inside.

I'd hardly started setting the table when Mom hurried in. I was so glad to see her, I almost ran to her, but Grandma was in the way.

"I hurried, Momma, I hurried," Mom cried. "Half of town come in there! I been workin' hard all day!"

"Half of town! Half of town! And you standin' runnin' your mouth while I been workin' my fingers to the bone. Fixin' to feed you when you can't take care of yourself."

I kept small.

"Grew up a fool! Married a fool," Grandma hollered, slapping Mom.

"I hurried, Momma. I hurried!" Mom cried out, covering her face with her hands.

"Fool! Fool!" Grandma yelled to two more slaps. "Think I don't know how no-count you are! Get out there and finish stringin' them beans while I finish gettin' supper. Claire's got more sense than you!"

Mom ran out on the porch. I stayed still, scared Grandma would turn on me.

Instead, she smiled. "You go ahead settin' the table. Don't you be no fool like your momma! Lot it got you!" she yelled out the door. "No-count fool!"

When dinner was on the table, we took our places. Mom didn't look up. I tried not to look at her, because I knew she'd been crying. Grandma grabbed my plate away from me and began piling food on it. I was starving, but I knew I'd never be able to eat it all. I reached out for it, but she held it away and slopped gravy all over everything on it.

"Skin and bones!" she yelled. "Why your fool momma moved out of here I'll never know! You look like a scarecrow!" She slammed the plate down in front of me so hard, I was sure it would break.

The food looked awful with gravy all over it.

"You eat that up and your grandma'll give you some more," she crooned, leaning toward me, smiling.

I looked away shocked and scared I'd throw up. I wanted to scream how much I hated her, but knew I couldn't. I took a deep breath and tried to eat.

"I made you two kinds of pies. You eat all your supper and I'll give you some."

I just stared at the gravy-covered mountain.

"Eat! Eat!" she squawked.

Grandma finished first and went back to the stove to get the jars ready for the vegetables. Mom finished and went to help her. I quickly scraped the rest of the mountain off my plate into the trash. Grandma put a pan of hot soapy water on the kitchen table and told me to wash the dishes. Then she put Mom to work cutting the corn off the ears into a huge pan.

For a few minutes there was silence. The kitchen began to fill with steam. Tired, I leaned over the hot soapy water resting my hands, wishing they'd stop hurting.

Mom got up to take the pan of corn to the stove . . . I heard a clunk, looked up to see Mom'd bumped the pan on the edge of the stove and spilled some of the corn. Everything seemed to explode.

"You don't know no more than a nigger!" Grandma screamed, raising the huge metal spoon. Mom flung her arms up over her face, cried: "No, Momma!" as Grandma beat at her with the spoon.

I saw the scars on Mom's arms . . . seemed to hear Mr. Beasley. "You got to think on yourself, child."

"No!" I screamed. "No! You stop it!" I ran across the kitchen, grabbed the spoon out of Grandma's hands, threw it at the back door.

For a moment everything was frozen into shocked silence. I saw Mom's pocketbook sitting on a chiar and Grandma's hand rising.

"Run," I screamed, grabbing Mom's arm. "Run." I grabbed her pocketbook, dragged her toward the door, shoved her out in front of me, yanked the door shut.

"Run! Run!" I screamed, still pushing her.

"We left the food! We left the food!"

"No! No! We don't want her food! Wc don't want anything from her."

I dragged Mom after me around the house to the car, yanked open the door, jumped into the front seat.

"Claire!" Grandma screamed from the front door.

Mom froze. I grabbed her arm, yanked her into the car.

"Hurry! Hurry!" I wailed.

We pulled away as Grandma ran out to the curb.

"She'll kill me! She'll kill me!" Mom wailed.

"No!" I sobbed. "No! We got away. She can't hurt you now! You're safe!"

"Safe?" Mom cried.

"Safe!"

"We ain't got no food!"

"Stop at the store!"

The grocery in town was still open. Mom got out of the car, ran to the store. Numb, I huddled up in the front seat waiting.

When she came back with a cart, she looked bent, tired. I got out to help her put the bags in the car.

Mom looked down, saw she still had on her apron, began to laugh.

"We don't need Momma!"

I couldn't laugh. I just put the bag of six-packs of beer in the car, got in, waited to go home.

Chapter Thirteen

Monday morning when the bus came, I looked up surprised that I hadn't heard it coming. I picked up my books and the lunch I'd packed with some of the food Mom'd bought Saturday night. I sat down in an empty seat near the front and piled my things up beside me. As the bus began to move again, I leaned my head against the window, closed my eyes.

Saturday night at the store, Mom'd laughed, but she'd been drunk all day Sunday, was home drunk now.

At least she doesn't have to go to work today.

At least she left me alone.

I'd been so tired, I'd slept most of Sunday. I'd dreamed about going to art shows with Daddy the way I had when I was little. After all day in the sun waiting to see if people would buy his paintings, I'd usually gone to sleep in the car on the way home.

I smiled remembering how happy he'd been whenever he'd come back to his booth and found out someone had bought one of his paintings from me.

The bus lurched. I looked up and was surprised we were already at school. I was safe now. People would leave me alone. I could think about Daddy and draw.

I got to biology early. Clyde was there passing out the flowers and leaves. He'd already been by our table so I went in and sat down. He didn't say anything. When he'd finished, he left the room.

I looked up at the board. Mrs. Carter had put up the day's instructions. The flowers on our table were the same purplish-blue as the one Clyde'd dropped in my lap. I wondered what kind they were.

The instructions said we'd take them apart in class and draw them. Remembering the drawings Grandmother's sister Claire had done, I opened the colored pencils, lined them up, drew the flower. Then I started taking it apart and following Mrs. Carter's instructions.

People came in before I was finished. I tried to ignore them and Clyde beside me. Once I finished, I pushed the microscope toward him. Then I put my elbows on the table and leaned forward staring at my drawings.

"Hey."

I jumped. Clyde had tugged at my hair.

"You wouldn't answer," he said, looking embarrassed. "Where were you?"

I looked away.

"Help!" he said, and grinned when I looked back at him. "I asked if you'd help me. You know how to do this mess." He nodded toward my drawings.

I was surprised I hadn't covered them up. I turned them over.

"Thanks a lot!" He bent back over to look through the microscope, started drawing again. He didn't know anything about proportions.

His algebra paper kept me out of trouble. I didn't have to talk in class.

"Use the pin," I said. "Put it under the microscope so you can see how big things are next to it. Then do the same thing with the pencil on your paper. It'll show you the proportional sizes of the different parts. The rest is all right. The proportions are what's wrong."

He was just staring at me, looking shocked again. Feeling stupid, I turned my back to him and opened my book.

"It works," he whispered a moment later.

I didn't answer. I was trying to get Daddy's face back in my mind.

"Thanks," he said.

I could see Daddy now. I closed my eyes.

My chair lurched and I looked up, startled.

"Sorry," Clyde was saying to Mrs. Carter, "clumsy again."

Mrs. Carter was standing in front of our table looking at my drawings and classwork. She looked up from them at me.

"Claire, these are beautiful!" she said, smiling.

I nodded and reached out for them.

"Have you had any training?" she asked, not giving them to me.

I shook my head.

"We've an excellent art teacher here, Miss Joyce. I showed her one of your drawings last week. She said you aren't in any of her classes."

"No," I said, looking down at my book. "I already have all my classes."

"Do you have study hall?"

I didn't answer. I was too afraid she'd find out if I lied.

"Yeah, she's in mine," Clyde said.

I looked up at his smile, angry inside.

"You could take art then," Mrs. Carter continued. "Miss Joyce said she's usually in the art room at lunch. If you'd like a class you should go see her."

"No, I don't like to draw," I said. "I hate it!"

"Oh?" Mrs. Carter looked surprised. "You've finished your classwork?"

I nodded, holding my breath, hoping she'd go away.

If she keeps asking I'll get in trouble! I felt funny inside. Mom wouldn't mind that kind of trouble.

If they send home a note I refused to draw, Mom'd be happy.

Mrs. Carter looked at my drawing again, then put it back on the desk. She kept my classwork and returned to the front of the room.

Relieved that she'd stopped talking about it, I

pulled the flower drawing off the desk and started to wad it up.

Clyde snatched it out of my hand and held it away. "Give it back!"

"No. You're not going to tear it up." He stared at me with green eyes. "You don't hate drawing. Every time I see you at lunch that's what you're doing. It's all you do in study hall."

I shook my head, turned away, afraid Mrs. Carter would hear him and come back.

"Yes. You're either drawing or asleep!" he hissed. "Mrs. Carter's right. Go see the art teacher."

"Leave me alone," I begged.

"No!" he said.

I stared out the window in a panic. *If he tells her I'm always drawing! If she writes Mom a note!* I closed my eyes, remembered he'd thought I was always asleep, reopened them.

I have to hear the bell. I have to get away before she comes back to our desk.

Mrs. Carter told us to clean up. I looked up, terrified, expecting to see Clyde had gone to help her, was telling on me.

He hadn't. He was sitting there watching me. I turned away.

"God, you're shy!" he said.

The bell rang. I grabbed my books, ran out of class. I hurried to my locker, got my lunch, dropped my books inside, tried to close the door. A hand held it open.

"Get your drawings," Clyde said, towering over me. "The art teacher'll want to see them."

I backed away from him, not looking at him, wanting my locker closed, but too scared to try to close it.

"Look," he said. "You helped me in bio. If you're too shy to go by yourself, I'll go with you . . ."

I turned away and ran into the mobs of kids trying

not to bump into people. Behind me I heard a locker slam, Clyde yelling, "Claire!"

I ran into the girls' bathroom, past several girls at the mirror who laughed, into a cubicle and locked it.

When they'd left and the bathroom was empty, I came back out. There was a sofa in there. I sat down on it, made myself eat my lunch to try to stop shaking.

I was almost safe with Mom! She didn't leave me at Grandma's! She got food! She left me alone! But people won't leave me be! Won't stop feeling sorry for me!

I fought to keep from crying.

Later, when I heard someone coming in through the double doors, I went to the sink and washed my face. The girls were busy talking. I slipped past them to the door.

A few people were in the hall, but not Clyde. I got my history book, made sure he wasn't in class yet. At my desk, I stared down at my book, numbly trying to read it.

Clyde came in, sat down in front of me, sideways in his desk. Hating him, I didn't move or look away from my book.

He put my flower drawing down on top of my book.

"Okay. So you don't want an art class. I'm sorry."

I reached out to put it away where no one could see it.

"Dammit! Don't tear it up!"

I looked up, startled.

He turned red, looked away. "I meant you don't have to now . . . if you don't want anyone to know you draw it's your problem. But don't tear it up . . . it's beautiful."

He turned abruptly away.

Confused, I looked back down at the drawing.

He sounded as if he cared.

He's just feeling sorry for me. I've got to be careful. If he knows I draw all the time other people must, too. Mom can't find out!

I put the drawing in my notebook, closed my eyes, remembered he'd said I was always asleep, opened them.

Mr. Beasley said think!

He doesn't feel sorry for me. Maybe he did just bring his lunch the other day. Maybe he didn't eat because he knew I was hungry and lying. He played the Bach for me. He let me draw him. He said he liked it.

I felt funny inside remembering how sad Mr. Beasley'd looked when he'd seen the wildflowers I'd drawn.

They must have reminded him of the ghost. He said she was good to him . . . and I look just like her . . . I'll try to be good to him, too . . .

Wishing I was at the pond, I looked out the window at the distant white pines. Mr. Allen had come in the room, started talking. I opened my notebook.

If I get good grades, they'll have to leave me alone!

Chapter Fourteen

The next day, I made myself listen in school, do my work, not close my eyes, not draw. As soon as I finished eating my lunch, I went to the library. I found books with photos, looked through them trying to fix the things I liked in my head so I could draw them later.

When Wednesday came again and I got home from school, I gathered up my papers and took them down to the pond. I was afraid Mr. Beasley wouldn't come anymore, but he was already there playing. I ran toward him.

He nodded at me, smiling, and finished the song.

"You got some good papers?"

I nodded, happy he'd asked for them, and held them out. He began looking through them.

"I ain't lookin' for hundreds on 'em. It takes time to learn how to get those. What's this here?" He held the paper out.

"French," I said, seeing a dictation test.

He laughed. "I was hopin' it was somethin', 'cause it sure don't look like nothin' to me. Read me what it says."

I struggled through the paragraph, trying to say the words right. Then I started it a second time.

"Chantez-la bas," Mr. Beasley said.

I looked up surprised. He laughed, looking pleased with himself.

"Means 'blues sung low.' That's creole talk! Same as I was hearin' ever' time I went down to New Orleans.

You sure got to work on readin' it. You had to twice, 'fore you knowed what it was."

He looked through more papers. "Look here!" He held out an algebra paper. "There ain't no scratchin's on this here and you got yourself a good mark, too."

It was the paper Mr. Davis had corrected and Clyde had helped me with.

"This here ain't your writin'?"

"The teacher helped me."

"That's good. They're goin' to be glad to help you. All you got to do is know you're tryin'. Other folks, too. If they're nice, they're goin' to help you. You been makin' yourself some friends at school?"

When I didn't answer, he looked up smiling.

"Yes," I lied, not wanting him to feel sorry for me. "Some girls . . . that live near town. We don't have a phone. I don't have a way . . . to go see them."

He nodded and handed the papers back with a smile that would have made me feel good if I hadn't lied.

"You been workin' hard. I'm glad to see it. I told you you got a good head on your shoulders. All you got to do is give yourself a chance! Then we're going to see some good stuff! Didn't you bring me some drawin's?"

My heart seemed to jump at the disappointment in his voice. Then I felt confused, remembering the ghost, that I'd just lied to him, hadn't been good to him.

"I didn't have time . . . I didn't think . . . you'd want to see them."

"Sure I do. They're like comin' down here. I feel good just seein' 'em. It makes me happy, same as my playin' makes me happy." He picked up his guitar, smiled. "What you want me to play for you?"

Not the Bach. I didn't want to remind him of the ghost. "It's a Long Old Road," I said, remembering one of the other songs I'd heard him sing.

"That's blues, child. You want to hear blues when you've done so good?"

"Yes. It says 'but I'm goin' to find the end.' That doesn't sound like blues."

He smiled and sounded the opening chords. "It don't to me neither, child."

While he was singing, I wished I could stay there listening to him forever. *He wants to see my drawings. He is my friend.*

He soon started another song. It was something beautiful I'd never heard before, about a baby crying. Listening to it, I cried, too, but somehow the words and music made me stop hurting inside. When he'd finished and looked up, he was surprised.

"What you cryin' for?"

I tried to smile.

"Sometimes you worry me! What you got eatin' at you?"

I looked away, scared, not wanting him to feel sorry for me. "It was the song. It was so sad, I couldn't help it. But it's beautiful, too. That part made the sad go away." I smiled then, and he smiled back. "Thanks for playing it for me."

"I like to," he said. "Now you're lookin' almost like I give you some kind of present. Somebody likin' what I do makes me happy."

He set his guitar aside. "I got to get myself on home. I been pickin' apples, today. They're some old trees just off the road goin' down to your place. I already got myself all I need. I'm goin' to keep 'em cool so they'll last me the winter. You want some for your momma and yourself you best be doin' some pickin'. The critters are after 'em, too. There ain't no sense in leavin' 'em to fall on the ground and rot."

He stood up and looked out over the pond. "Lord, it's goin' to be one cold winter."

"How can you tell?"

He laughed. "My bones've been tellin' me. You got

to get old 'fore that's goin' to happen! Unless you're old you got to look on the signs. The apples're ready 'fore they 'sposed to be. All the trees are settin' new leaves. They got more acorns on 'em than I seen in a long time. Even the squirrels' tails are fat to help keep 'em warm. Yes, it's goin' to be a hard winter. You look to yourself, child. I'll come down here to see you Wednesday."

On my way home, I cut over to the road to find the apple trees. There were four with several kinds of apples. I picked a ripe one and started eating it. It wasn't pretty, but it was good inside.

I felt funny remembering the song that made me cry. Mr. Beasley'd said when I liked something he did and thought it was beautiful, he felt happy. I'd felt good when he'd said that.

Clyde's face when he'd seen the squirrel drawing popped into my head. I seemed to hear his voice telling me not to tear up the flower drawing, it was beautiful. I threw the apple away.

I just jerked the squirrel drawing out of his hand. He was nice and I was just mean.

The next day when I went into afternoon study hall, Clyde was already at his desk reading a book. He was sitting slumped to one side so he could put his feet out across the aisle. I just stood there looking at him. He muttered, "Sorry," moved his feet.

I sat down, embarrassed, realizing he must have thought someone was waiting to get by. I put my elbows on my desk, rested my forehead on my hands and closed my eyes as he turned around.

He was nice, like Mr. Beasley. He helped me when Mr. Davis had asked him to . . . and didn't make fun of me. He tried to get me to go see the art teacher, even offered to go with me. Then he left me be about it, and gave back my drawing. He'd even said he'd help me with algebra if I'd help him with the biology drawings. I had. But I hadn't been nice to him, ever.

I opened my eyes, saw he'd turned away, felt bad inside.

It's easy to be nice to Mr. Beasley. All I have to do is like his music. I don't have to talk.

I wished I knew how to be nice to other people, too. I looked back down at my books. But even if I knew how, I couldn't be friends with Clyde, couldn't let him come help me with my algebra. The first day I'd been with Mom, before she left for work, she'd said she'd kill me if I ever let any boys come to the house. She'd gone on and on about what they'd do to me until I was angry and frightened.

I felt funny. The boys she'd been yelling about didn't sound like Clyde.

I looked back up, saw the study hall teacher was taking roll. I went to the library and looked through books of photos again.

Clyde didn't come into algebra until Mr. Davis did. As Mr. Davis started calling roll, Clyde sat down sideways in his desk. Wishing he'd turn away, I opened my notebook to my homework. When Mr. Davis said pass it to the front, Clyde put out his hand.

I gave him mine, hoping he'd turn away. He didn't. He put it down on my desk and sat looking it over.

"You've blown most of them," he whispered. "I got a B in bio. Mrs. Carter said so after class. You'll get an F on this."

I looked up, startled, then away from his green eyes watching me.

"You mind getting an F?" he said.

I shook my head. The girl behind me held the other papers over my shoulder. I passed them to him.

"You do so mind," he said. He took the papers and turned away.

I sat staring at his back, angry, hating him. I'd already had to quit drawing, quit thinking about Daddy at school because of him. Now he was going to make trouble about my grades, too.

The next day at lunchtime, I went to one of the empty tables in the far corner of the cafeteria. I sat down with my back to the room the way I always did. I'd nearly finished my sandwich when Clyde put a tray, his algebra book and notebook on the table, and sat down next to me.

"Stop looking like I'll bite you. Jake didn't. I won't either."

I felt myself turn red, looked away.

"Move your stuff," Clyde said. "We're doing your algebra."

"No," I said.

"Yep. You helped me in bio. It's my turn." He pushed my lunch aside, tore paper out of his notebook, put the open algebra book beside it, held out a pencil.

"Hi," someone said.

I looked up. Margie was standing behind me with her lunch tray.

"Hi," Clyde said. "So then what happened?"

I looked to see if he was asking her, looking at her. He wasn't. He smiled. I looked away confused, heard her walk away.

"I already did the homework. I looked at yours the other time," I said.

"I thought so. So show me today's."

I shook my head. I hadn't been able to figure it out. My paper was a mess.

"Did you ever see a dog as big as Jake before?"

"No," I said, surprised, looking up.

He looked away. "Sometimes people are scared of me because I'm so much bigger than they are."

"Oh," I said, feeling funny, looking away, too. "She wasn't scared of you."

"Just do your algebra," he said, dropping the pencil on the blank paper in front of me. "You have to try to figure them out first or you won't learn anything."

He turned away and began eating his lunch. Not knowing what else to do, I started doing the problems. When I got stuck, I sat there feeling stupid until Clyde explained it. He finished his lunch, pushed his things aside, and leaned on the table watching me.

"Please don't look at me," I said.

He sat back up. "Don't look! Don't touch! Don't talk!"

Feeling stupid and confused, I put down the pencil and reached for my books.

He put his hand on top of them. "Stop it . . . just do your algebra, ghost!"

"I'm not a ghost!" I said, angrily.

"Right. But I sure thought you were. You know everybody says the mill's haunted? Because my great-grandmother died in it. She had long black hair, too, was young, beautiful." He laughed. "When you popped out of there you scared me half to death. I was sure I was seeing her ghost—till you ran. Ghosts don't run."

"How do you know?" I asked, stupidly.

Clyde laughed. "They're supposed to scare people, silly, not be scared of them."

"I'd run," I said, wanting to, knowing it was people that scared me, not ghosts.

"Yeah," he agreed. "Even if you were a ghost. You wouldn't like scaring people?"

"No!"

He was laughing. I looked away, feeling miserable. I was just being a freak again. This time he was laughing at me, too.

I reached out for my books. He moved them away.

"Look. If you don't hurry up, you won't finish. You'll be stuck with me in study hall, too."

I tried to see the next problem, tried to start doing it. "You don't have to help me."

"I don't mind," he said, softly. "It's fun." He reached out to touch my arm.

I jerked away, felt myself turn red, couldn't look at him.

He didn't say anything.

I stood up, wanting my books, wanting to run. He stood up, too. He was too tall. I turned away ready to cry.

"You didn't finish your lunch," he said.

"I'm not hungry!"

"Christ! Just eat your lunch!"

And he was gone.

During study hall, I went to the library, found a book of medieval buildings, leafed through it, pushed it aside. The photos were terrible. Besides, when I'd tried to draw the things I remembered the night before, I'd just made a mess.

That's all I know how to do.

Clyde plopped down across the table from me.

"I thought you told Mr. Allen you didn't like history?"

I looked up, startled. He wasn't staring at me.

"The first day . . ." he said. "You said you hated it."

I shook my head. "He said local history. I do hate that."

"You like medieval history?"

"No," I said, confused.

"Why've you got a book on it then?" he asked, pulling it toward him.

"It's just buildings. I was just looking at it."

"So?" He looked at the title, read, *"Medieval and Renaissance Architecture,"* opened it. "Wow, these are lousy photos."

I nodded.

"You quit drawing here. Was it me bugging you?"

I looked away, scared, shook my head. "I wasn't drawing. I hate drawing."

"You're a lousy liar," he said. He flipped the book open to the front. "You didn't check it out yet. You were going to take it home? You like drawing buildings?"

"No!"

"That's too bad," he said. "If you did you could go draw the mill this afternoon. It's neat. Come on, it's Friday. I'll even bring Jake. You liked Jake."

"No," I said.

"You're going to see someone else?"

"No!" I was suddenly scared he knew about Mr. Beasley. "No! My mom would get mad. I don't know anyone out there."

"I didn't think so," he said, getting up. "You'll get a B on algebra today anyway."

I looked up but he was walking away. I seemed to hear Mr. Beasley saying nice people would help me . . . if I let them.

At home that afternoon, Mom's mess was waiting. When I saw it, I started toward the door to go to the mill, but stopped. It would be the same as bringing someone home. She'd be angry. Kill me.

But she doesn't know about my drawing. Doesn't know about Mr. Beasley.

I stopped again. Mr. Beasley wasn't in school. He wasn't always asking questions. He was my friend. He didn't feel sorry for me.

I remembered the apples he'd told me about. I got the dishpan and ran up the road to the trees.

Picking the apples in the sunshine, smelling the faint apple smell when I broke the stems, I began to calm down. When I went back to the house, I set the dishpan of apples on the kitchen chair.

I wanted to go upstairs and draw, but I made myself clean up Mom's mess instead. Then I went up-stairs and tried to do my algebra.

I woke up in the middle of the night with the light shining in my face. Mom was frantically calling my name. I could smell beer. I was terrified until I heard fear in her voice.

"Claire! Claire! You still here?"

"What? What's wrong?" I asked, propping myself up on one elbow, and suddenly not as scared.

"Was Momma here? Was she?"

"No!"

"Where did these come from?"

By squinting, I saw she was holding a couple of the apples.

"They're off some trees up the road. I found them this afternoon." I flopped back down feeling relieved.

Mom plopped down on my bed and started crying.

"Thought Momma was after me! Thought she'd come and got you! She's still callin' me at work. Said she was comin' after you! Said I'm not fit!"

I was awake now and scared.

"She isn't fit!"

"She says I'm no good, Claire! I don't want you to go! You don't want to go to her, do you?"

"No! I hate her!"

Mom flopped over on my knees and began sobbing that horrible animal sound. "You're a good girl! You ain't mean to me like Momma is! Momma's always hurtin' me! You made her stop!"

I sat up, unable to stand the sound. "She won't hurt you anymore! Just stay away from her! She won't hurt you!"

"No more?" Mom sobbed.

"No more!"

Her sobs began to ease. My knees ached from her weight, but I stayed still afraid she'd start making that sound again if I moved. I couldn't bear that sound.

I hate her so much, but that sound makes the hate hurt me inside.

When she'd stopped sobbing and was quiet, I whispered, "Go to bed. It'll be better tomorrow."

"Got to be," she gasped. "Nothin' can't be no worse." She hauled herself off my knees and stumbled into her room.

Chapter Fifteen

Saturday morning I woke up to the smell of bacon and apples frying. For a moment I thought I was home with Daddy. Sometimes he fixed that for breakfast.

I started feeling happy and good inside until I opened my eyes and saw the drab, unpainted ceiling of the tenant house. Then, I was sure I'd been dreaming, but the smell was still there. I got up and went to the door.

When I opened it, the smell was much stronger. Mom wasn't in her bed. It was still made up. There weren't any beer cans on the table by it either. I remembered Mom saying Grandma had said she was coming to get me. Terrified, I crept back across my room to the window.

Mom's was the only car in the yard. Puzzled, I got dressed and went downstairs.

Mom was standing by the stove. When she heard me, she turned and waved the spatula at me.

"Smells good, don't it? I went up to the store and got us some fixin's so we'd have a good breakfast. Good thing it's Saturday and you don't have school. I almost woke you early till I seen you looked awful tired."

"It smells good," I said. I felt strange knowing she'd looked at me in my sleep.

"Was there a lotta apples?" she asked.

"Yes, there're four trees."

"Why don't you start in pickin' us some this mornin'? They'd keep all winter on the back porch. I ought to make sauce and can it if there's a lot."

"Why?" I asked, feeling scared. After Grandma's I

didn't want any part of canning. I didn't want to pick apples all day either. "You already said they'd keep."

"Yes, but Momma always . . ."

"You don't have to can them. Besides, when would you? You're working all day. You're not home like she is," I pleaded.

Mom smiled. "Yeah, that's right. I'm not home to do it. I work hard all day."

I began to be scared she'd tell me to do it.

I won't get to go draw outside! I'll be stuck in here!

"'Sides," she said. "They'll keep fine on the porch."

I waited awkwardly while she finished fixing breakfast. The table was already set restaurant style. She'd poured me a glass of milk.

I waited till she sat down before I did, waited till she started eating.

"These eggs need some pepper," she said. "You know, if we had the fixin's I could make us a pie tomorrow."

She rummaged in her purse for a pencil and looked around for some paper. Her napkin was the only thing. She started making a list on that.

"We need some brown sugar and flour. We ain't even got a pie tin! And raisins. You got to have them in a pie. I wish there was some walnut trees here 'bouts. There ought to be."

"I'll look," I said carefully. I felt strange watching her. She wasn't acting like the mom I knew at all. She was almost like someone nice.

"You be careful in them woods. There's snakes. You don't know what you're liable to run up against. I seen a lotta niggers at the store."

Anger welled up inside me. I tried to choke it down. I was far more scared of Mom than Mr. Beasley. *He'd never hurt me!*

"I'm glad you found them apples. I'll get us some pork at the grocery in town, too, on my way home. We'll have us a good supper, tomorrow."

I stayed quiet. She'd already been to the store that morning. She'd never go back again. She hadn't been back except for beer since we'd been at Grandma's to can. All week the only food we'd had had been leftovers from the restaurant.

"I got to hurry. I'll see what else we need when I get to the store."

She tucked the list into her purse. Then, she smiled at me. I felt mixed up inside, and wondered if I was dreaming. She'd never looked at me like that before. Still hating her, I tried to smile back, but I suddenly was scared I was dreaming, would wake up, and she'd be changed back into the mom I knew.

"I got to run," she said again, getting up. "You ain't got to pick many today. You leave yourself some time for playin'."

Even after I'd heard her car go up the road, I sat there still and shocked. Then, I shook myself awake. I took the dishpan out to the old shed in the yard. There were some crates in the back. I hauled several outside and got the broom to brush the cobwebs and dirt off them.

There was room for four crates in a corner of the small enclosed back porch. I fitted them into it. Then I took the dishpan up the road to the trees.

It was almost noon before one of the crates was full. My arms were ready to fall off from carrying the dishpan back and forth. I left it on top of the apples and went upstairs to get my drawing things. When I'd first gotten up to the trees to pick, I'd decided I'd come back and draw them when the crate was full. Now I was sick of apples.

I started toward Mr. Beasley's pond, stopped. I'd already drawn it once without him there. It had been too lonely.

I ran down the hill to the river, wondering what I'd find to draw. I'd already drawn the long rock where Jake'd found me.

I slowed up, remembering Clyde saying I should go draw the mill the day before. He'd said he'd take Jake. I wondered if they'd gone. Suddenly wishing I had, I turned toward the mill.

Clyde was the first person my age I'd ever liked who talked to me, who almost acted as if he liked me. When I'd first seen him, he was so good-looking, I'd never wondered what he was like. I just wanted someone that looked like that to like me.

I felt funny inside. All the boys I'd seen before who were that good-looking were awful. I didn't really know what they were like, just how mean some of them had been to me at school. But Clyde wasn't mean. Mr. Beasley said nice people would help me. He had.

I slowed up, remembering Mom, looked down at my sketch pad and chalk. Mom'd been wrong about Mr. Beasley. She had to be wrong about Clyde, too. *He won't be there anyway!*

When I reached the woods just before the mill, I got scared he might be there. I'd lied about drawing and I had my things. I turned around to go home.

Clyde was standing a few yards in front of me with Jake beside him. I stuck my sketch pad and chalk behind me.

Jake came wagging over to me, mooing, and leaned up against me. He was so heavy, he almost pushed me over. When he looked up with his cheeks puffed out, mooing, and his tail going, I had to pat him. I almost kneeled to hug him, but I remembered Clyde and looked up scared.

His smile vanished. "Don't run!" he said.

Jake pushed his nose into my hand. I looked back down, wanting to run, wanting to stay.

"You're here now," Clyde said. "Don't go yet."

"I didn't think—" I shut up.

"We'd be here? I knew you wouldn't come yesterday. You're glad to see Jake anyway."

I turned away, embarrassed. I'd almost said I was glad to see him, too.

"You were going to draw the mill?"

I nodded. *He's not mad I lied to him about drawing.*

Then I remembered Mom and Mrs. Carter and shook my head.

"We'll go home, leave you be," he said. "I have to get my stuff—it's at the mill."

I heard him start toward me. I walked ahead through the woods to the clearing. Jake bounded ahead of me, stopped at the edge of the woods. I stopped, too. Not far from him, a huge, dark red-brown horse was tied to one of the trees. It was wearing a bridle but no saddle.

"Do you like him?" Clyde asked, suddenly beside me.

The horse turned at his voice and tried to come to him. He had a small white star high on his forehead.

"He's beautiful," I whispered. Jake pushed his nose into my hand. "You, too," I said, nervously, patting Jake.

"Yeah," Clyde said. "Want to give him some sugar? I brought some."

I shook my head but followed him over to the horse. He took some sugar cubes out of his shirt pocket and held one out on his palm. When the horse carefully nibbled it off, I laughed.

"Try it. He won't bite you," Clyde said, smiling.

I hesitated. I'd never been this near a horse before.

"Just keep your fingers out of the way like this," he said, feeding the horse another.

When he turned back toward me, I put out my hand. Clyde dropped the sugar cube into my palm. Hesitantly, I stretched my hand out to the horse. His soft, velvety nose wetly nuzzled my palm.

"That feels funny," I said, backing away and wiping

my hand on my jeans. Jake stayed right beside me, pressing against me.

"Yeah," Clyde said. "He didn't bite you either."

I turned away, embarrassed again.

"Claire? Want to ride him?"

I started away. "I don't know how."

"I'll teach you. He's an easy horse. His name's Adair."

"Adair?" I asked, scared.

Mr. Beasley's ghost was named Adair.

Clyde was stroking the horse's neck and smiling at him.

"Yeah, but not like 'Can you take a dare.' Adair's the name of our farm . . . was my mother's name." He started untying the horse's lead from the tree.

"Oh," I said.

Then his great-grandmother was Mr. Beasley's ghost.

"He wouldn't throw you. I've had him since I was littler than you."

Mr. Beasley said she'd died when he was small.

"When was that?" I asked, upset, wanting to run.

"At least a hundred years ago," Clyde said, laughing. "You won't fall off."

"He's huge. I'm scared of him. You ride him."

There was a large flat rock in front of the mill. I went over to it and sat down. Jake came too and jumped up beside me. I put my arms around him, put my face against his soft, wiry coat.

Clyde picked a knapsack up from beside the tree where Adair had been tied. He led the horse over to the rock, put the knapsack down next to my chalk and sat down at the far edge.

"I wouldn't let you get hurt," he said. "I'd get in trouble if you did. I've been riding since I was three."

"I'm scared of him," I said.

"You'll stop being scared, just like with Jake. I'll ride with you, let you off if you're still scared."

"I just wanted to draw the mill," I said, letting go of Jake.

"I'll show you something better, something medieval."

"There isn't anything medieval in this country. It wasn't even discovered then."

He laughed. "You'd have to go see. I won't tell you anything else."

"I can't go home with you. My mom would get mad."

"It isn't there. No one would see us. I'd let you draw it, bring you back. You can't get there without Adair or I'd tell you where it is."

"Medieval?" I asked.

"I promise."

"You'd let me back off . . . if I was . . ."

"Yes. I told you I would."

When I didn't say anything else, he reached out for my chalk and drawing pad. I watched him open his knapsack, start to put my things inside.

"What's that?"

"My lunch and a book . . . if you didn't come." He closed the knapsack, put it on. Then he stood up and looped the reins over his arm.

"Stand, Adair," he said.

The horse posed still as a statue. Clyde moved to his side just in front of me and leaned over to make a stirrup with his hands. When he told me to, I put my hand on his shoulder, used his hands as a stirrup and suddenly found myself up on the horse's broad back. I put my palms down over the base of his neck. His beautiful dark red-brown hide was sleek and satiny. I could hold on with my knees. There were the reins, too.

"Well?" Clyde asked.

"Get on," I said, embarrassed at the fuss I'd made.

He laughed. "Just sit still. I have to move him so I can."

I froze as the horse stepped sideways, closer to the rock. Clyde got up on the rock, then was on the horse's back, too, putting his arms around me to hold the reins with both hands.

"See, you can't fall off. You were ready to have a heart attack for nothing!"

I looked down, hoping he couldn't see me blushing. I'd been so scared of the horse and trying to figure out what could be medieval, I'd never thought about him touching me.

"You can sit in back of me and hold on if you'd feel safer," he said, "but you wouldn't be. You want off?"

"No," I whispered. I couldn't say anything else without his knowing it was being up against him that I didn't want.

"You'll get used to it," he said, moving the reins so Adair began walking. "It's fun."

I didn't answer. We were going toward another woods on the far side of the clearing. There was a fence along the edge and an old road.

"Where does that go?" I asked, beginning to feel scared again.

"You'll see."

I already could see. The old road went down into the river. I tried to fight down my panic and just pay attention to the gently rocking motion the horse made as he walked.

When we got to the road and turned toward the river, I saw it had widened out again. The road came out on the opposite bank. Jake was waiting on our side. As we came closer, he ran across the river. The water didn't even come up near his belly. He ran up the opposite bank and bounded about impatiently on the other side.

"Okay?" Clyde asked, tightening his arms around me.

"Don't!" I said before I could stop myself.

"Are you scared of me or the horse?"

"Let's go. Jake's waiting."

It wasn't scary crossing the river. Despite the slosh-ing sounds, Adair still walked evenly. I tried to relax. As we started up the gentle slope out of the river, Jake took off, running in long, fabulous strides. I caught my breath as he streaked away from us.

"Tell me if you get scared," Clyde said, loosening Adair's reins.

As Adair ran after Jake, I was scared again until I saw Clyde's arms kept me from sliding around.

We came to the bend in the river above the mill. The cleared bottomland stretched off in the distance. Jake had already left us far behind. Adair went faster. His sleek hide rippled under my hands and the wind blew my hair. I felt suddenly, wildly happy.

When Clyde slowed Adair and pressed the reins against my hands, I was surprised and confused.

"I wasn't scared," I said.

"Your hair's blowing in my face. I can't see where we're going. Hold these."

I took the reins as Adair came to a halt. Clyde slid back away from me.

"What are you doing?" I asked, scared he'd get off and leave me on Adair by myself.

"Getting a string," he said. "Sit still."

"Oh," I said, feeling stupid again.

"Here," he said as he touched my hair.

I made myself stay still and not say the "Don't" that almost got out of me as he gathered up my hair and began tying the string around it.

"I never did this before," he said. "I'm not pulling?"

"No," I said, feeling awkward.

He finished tying the string, but still touched my hair. I felt strange inside.

"Claire?" he said.

"Let's go," I said.

He hesitated, then reached back around me to take the reins. I felt strange. He was holding his arms awkwardly so they weren't against mine.

Jake was running back toward us.

"Let's go!" I said, again.

Clyde slapped the reins and Adair started off. Jake whirled and streaked away from us. As Clyde began to relax, I stopped feeling awkward. The wild, free feeling flooded back up inside me.

We followed the bottomland until we came to woods and a fence where Jake was stretched out, waiting. Clyde turned Adair toward the fence along the upper edge of the field. We followed the fence until we came to a gate.

Clyde put the reins in my hands again, told Adair to stand, and slid off his back. Jake didn't wait for him to open the gate. He ran to the fence and soared over it. Then he loped back up on the other side, wagging his tail and looking pleased with himself.

"Gee, he flies, too," I said, looking down at Clyde and laughing.

He turned away to open the gate, led Adair through, latched it, and used it to climb back on. He hugged me as he took the reins.

"I was scared you wouldn't like it," he said.

"I do," I said, feeling nervous. "Let's go."

Jake ran along beside us but not close to Adair's hooves. We followed an old track past several small fields until we came to an old farm and the strangest barn I'd ever seen.

It was mostly roof—pitched high above low stone side walls. The end wall had three narrow openings arranged in a triangle near the high peak. Something about the barn looked familiar, but I knew I'd never seen anything quite like it.

"Do you know what it looks like?" Clyde asked. "Dad says whoever built it was homesick."

I shook my head. I knew what homesick was like. "It looks medieval," I whispered.

"Yeah, but what that's medieval? I'll give you a hint. Dad says the style is Saxon. It's the oldest thing anywhere around here."

"What's it like inside?"

"Go see," he said. He gave me the reins and slid off Adair's back. Then he reached up to take the reins, put them over his arm, and put both hands up to me.

"Slide off," he said. "I'll catch you."

"I'll land on you," I said, looking down at his out-stretched arms."

"And break me," he said, laughing. "Come on, I'll get out of the way."

I took his hands and slid off. He stepped back so I landed standing up between him and Adair. He didn't let go of my hands. He stood smiling down at me.

"Don't!" I said, pulling my hands away and turning and bumping into Adair.

Adair snorted. Clyde pushed him sideways. I turned away, embarrassed again, wanting to run.

"It's me you're scared of," he said.

I couldn't answer.

"Go see the barn," he said, leading Adair away.

Jake came running up to me and shoved his nose into my hand.

"Come on, Jake," I said, feeling confused and patting him. I ran toward the barn.

Inside, I stood looking up at the huge network of beams that held up the roof. Enormous pegs, bigger around than my arm, held the beams together. I couldn't remember ever seeing one tree as big around as high up as most of the beams.

I wished Daddy could see the barn. He'd have to draw it. We'd always been late getting places because he'd seen something and had to stop and draw it. Sometimes it was just a flower growing beside the road. Often all he had with him was an envelope and pencil. He'd sketch it with those and paint it later at home.

Suddenly, I could almost hear his voice the few times I'd found something special to show him.

"What's this?" he'd said, looking at it, smiling. "What beautiful thing have we here?" Then he'd draw it. I wanted him to come back so I could show him the barn.

"Hey," Clyde said. "Are you there?"

I jumped. He'd come inside and was standing near the door.

"It's beautiful!" I stretched my arms up at the roof high above me.

"What's it like?"

I looked around. None of the buildings in the book had beams like these inside. I looked at the way the timbers joined the low side walls. Some of them seemed to be curved, but it was just the way they'd been worked and put together. Something about that was familiar. I looked up at one of the high end walls. Sunlight was streaming in through the three windows. There were three pools of light on the dirt floor where the streams ended.

"It's a cathedral!" I whispered.

"Yeah! A cathedral barn! See the sides. If they hadn't closed them off to make stalls, they'd be the aisles."

I nodded and looked back at the timber framework.

"Where'd they find trees this big?"

"Dad says they were all over when the Europeans first came. They used them up. All the woods around here grew since then. How'd you figure it out?"

"The windows."

"Yeah. I like the way the light comes in through them." Suddenly he was standing on one of the pools of light. "I like it in here. It makes me feel small," he said.

I went and stood in another of the pools and squinted up at the windows high above me.

"Can you draw light like this?" he asked, turning toward me.

"No, I don't know how. I wish I could. It must take paints. I don't know how to use them." I stepped out of the light, remembering Mom.

I couldn't use them if I had them. She'd smell them.

"Will you draw it, Claire?" he asked, sounding awkward.

"Outside," I said, turning away.

When I'd found the best view of the barn, he brought his knapsack over, put it down beside me, and sat down cross-legged a little way away.

"How do you want me to draw it?" I asked.

"What do you mean?"

"I can draw it in charcoal or chalk."

"Both."

"You'd get tired of waiting," I said, feeling awkward.

"I won't. I've got a book anyway."

I opened the knapsack and took out my stuff. Nervously, I started blocking out the building in charcoal.

"You'd care if I watched?" he asked.

I made myself shake my head. He stretched out near me and propped his head up with one hand so he could see the sketch pad. I felt awkward again, but he kept on talking, asked, "Where'd you learn to draw?"

"My father taught me."

"That was fun?"

I nodded, remembering.

"How old were you then?"

"Five."

"That's when I got Adair," he said.

I stopped to look at him. "What were you like?" I asked.

"When I was five?" He grinned. "Littler than other people. A kid. Mom has lots of awful pictures. I'll bring one to school if you will."

I looked back at my drawing. "I don't have any. We never had a camera. Daddy used to paint me, but I don't have any of them."

"So you're not a ghost. You're out of a painting in a museum."

I looked at him, startled. He looked away.

"Was it fun? Being painted?"

"No," I said, looking back at my drawing and starting on it again. "You have to sit still forever."

"Was your hair long when you were five?"

I nodded.

"Don't let anybody cut it. Not ever."

I didn't look at him. He didn't say anything else. I kept working on the barn. I liked the sound of the charcoal on the paper. The way it sometimes squeaked. The way it sometimes crumbled off, unless it made a mess. Best of all I liked the way the barn seemed to grow out of the paper.

When I finished it, I held it out. It was good. I looked around to see if Clyde was still looking at it.

He'd gone to sleep. He was almost smiling. I liked the way he looked. It made me feel warm and good inside. I turned over to the next page in the sketch pad, got out my chalk, lined it up, started drawing him.

I was nervous he'd wake up, so I just roughed out his shoulders and concentrated on his face. I wished his eyes were open so I could find out what color green they were with my chalk.

When I finished, he was still asleep. I sat looking at him. Without thinking, I reached out to touch his face. It was warm. I pulled my hand away—backed away.

Then he was staring at me with green eyes.

"Claire?"

"What?" I asked, breathlessly, making myself stare back at him.

"What were you doing?"

"Drawing you." I turned away and saw his knapsack. "I'm starving. Did you say you had some food?"

"What else did you do?"

"Nothing. I stayed here."

I froze as I heard him moving toward me. He sat down next to me and reached for the knapsack. He dumped it out in front of us. There was a pile of sandwiches, a thermos, cups, a book, and a lunch bag full of something.

"Can I see what you drew?" he asked, yawning. "Did you finish the barn?"

I handed him the pad. When he opened it, I turned to see his face.

He likes it.

"You're on the next page," I said.

He flipped it over, and looked shocked. "Did I look like that?"

Feeling miserable, I leaned over to look at it. "You did. You don't like it?"

"It makes me feel mixed up," he said, sounding strange.

"I'm sorry," I said.

He closed the sketch pad and put it aside. "Don't ever show that to anyone!"

"I wouldn't!" I said, turning away.

"Claire! Did you know what I was dreaming?"

"No! How could I! Why are you so mad? I just drew you."

"I'm not mad. I'm sleepy and can't think."

"You didn't look awful! You looked nice. I'm sorry!"

"Nice?" he said.

"Yes! What's wrong with it?"

He turned away. "Nothing. Let's eat lunch. When I wake up, I'll stop being stupid."

He picked up two of the sandwiches and looked at them. "You want peanut butter?"

"Yes," I said, still feeling miserable.

"With lettuce? Or there's ham."

"Lettuce?"

"Yeah, it's good. Try it."

"May I have ham instead?" I asked.

He laughed and leaned toward me. "You can have anything you want," he said.

I turned away, startled.

"Lunchtime," he said, moving away from me.

I was starving and ate two sandwiches. When Jake turned up, I gave him part of the second. Clyde ate the other five sandwiches and drank most of the milk. Then, he started on the cookies in the lunch bag.

"Do you always eat that much?" I asked.

"Don't laugh. My mom thinks it's hilarious and I hate it. She's always embarrassing me by telling everybody how much I eat."

"Does she know it embarrasses you?"

"Yeah, but she can't help it," he said, laughing.

"I thought you didn't think it was funny," I said, confused.

"It isn't, she is."

"Because she embarrasses you?"

"No, silly. Because she makes the fuss."

"Oh," I said. I wondered what it was like to feel the way he seemed to be.

His mom loves him.

"You've got charcoal on your face," he said, leaning toward me. "Big splotches from pushing your hair back."

I backed away and put my hand up to rub at the splotches.

"I always get them."

"But you don't know you're doing it," he said. "I saw you didn't when you were drawing."

I nodded.

"They were there at the store. When you ran into me. I thought it was bruises. You looked like somebody had hurt you. But you didn't look scared. Not till Jimmy yelled. Then you looked terrified and ran."

"I looked awful," I said, embarrassed.

"Has someone hurt you?"

"No! It was charcoal."

"That's not what I meant," he said, sounding awkward. "You stood there touching me till Jimmy yelled."

I looked away.

"What happened to you?" he asked. "Ever since then, at school, you make sure nobody ever touches you. If I touch you, you jump like I've hit you. Claire, what happened?"

"Nothing," I said, turning away, wishing he'd stop talking. "I just hate people touching me!"

"But you were touching me at the store!"

"It was the color of your eyes," I said. "I didn't think about you being people till he yelled."

"People? Jimmy made me a person?"

"Your eyes aren't people."

"Claire!" he said, taking my arm.

"Stop it!" I said, yanking away. "I said I liked you! Leave me be!"

"You said you liked me?" he asked, startled. "When did you say that?"

"I want to go home!"

"Claire!" He dumped the sketch pad and chalk into my lap. "You said you'd draw the barn! In chalk!"

"Not if you talk!"

"I'll shut up!" He moved back away from me. I picked up the sketch pad, opened it in the middle and stared down at it.

"Claire?" he asked from somewhere behind me. "Why aren't my eyes people? Why do you act like you've never been around people? Why are you like a ghost? Why won't you let people see what you draw?"

"I'm not a ghost! I have been around people! I hate people! They're always picking on me! It's mean!"

"Draw the barn. I'll leave you be. I won't pick on you."

I made myself put the chalk in its rows, start drawing, keep drawing.

"Claire? Is it picking on you if I like you?"

I shook my head, tried to keep drawing.

"I don't want anyone being mean to you."

"You're not mean."

"Can I see the barn? In chalk? When you finish?"

I nodded.

"Okay. I'll read my book."

It was late afternoon before I finished the barn in chalk. It was better than the one I'd done in charcoal. I'd done the trees near the barn, too, and Adair standing under them.

I looked around. Clyde was stretched out reading. He looked up at me and smiled. I held out the drawing. Watching him look at it, I knew it was good.

When he looked up at me, the same way he'd looked at it, I smiled, too.

He likes me, the way Mr. Beasley does, because I can draw.

"It's beautiful," he said. "I wish I could show it to everybody and yell, 'Look what Claire did!' "

"No!" I turned away.

"I wouldn't. I just wish I could."

I put the drawing down between us. He leaned over it.

"Look at Adair! I'd've known it was him by the way he's standing. He always looks like that when he's asleep." He looked back at me, smiling, green-eyed.

I started to tell him he looked the way he had when I drew him but I was scared to. He'd gotten mad at me before. I turned away and began putting my chalk back in the box.

"Yeah," he said. "It's time to go home."

When we got back across the river and he'd gotten off Adair, he put up his hands. I took them and slid off. He moved out of the way again so I landed standing up between him and Adair. He let go of my hands, took off his knapsack to give me my chalk and sketch pad. He was smiling.

"You're not people," I said, and ran.

I didn't stop running till I was home. The house smelled of apples. I went back outside and ran up to the apple trees. I broke off part of some branches with leaves on them and ran back to the house. I took them upstairs and spread them out on the table.

The last of the afternoon sunshine fell on them—touching them with gold. I got my chalk and paper and sat down to draw.

Chapter Sixteen

Sunday morning when I woke up, I could hear Mom downstairs. I stayed in bed listening to her. She didn't sound drunk. She sounded sober. I wondered if she'd really gone to the store. She'd probably just forgotten.

I sat up and looked at the apples still sitting on my table. It didn't matter if she'd forgotten. I had Clyde and Mr. Beasley for friends. She couldn't hurt me anymore.

I flopped back down feeling happy—remembering the way it felt going fast on Adair, remembering how I'd felt when Clyde said he liked me.

After a while, I smelled apples and bacon again. When Mom called me, I wanted to stay in bed and not see her. But I didn't want her coming upstairs after me. It would spoil the way I felt.

I got up, hid the apples and called down that I was coming.

Downstairs, I found she really was sober. We ate without talking. She was so quiet, I was scared to look at her.

After breakfast, helping her clear the table, I saw the refrigerator was full of store food. I was still staring at it when Mom said she'd do the dishes. She gave me an old cardboard box and told me to go start picking apples.

When I got back with the first box full, the washer was going. As I went back up the road to the trees, I wondered again if I was dreaming. Everything was too different.

Later on, in the afternoon, Mom came up to the trees to help me. For a long time we just picked in silence. Then, looking down from the high place I'd climbed to, I saw she was looking up at me. She smiled. I smiled back.

"Funny, you findin' these," she said. "Your father was always findin' things and bringin' 'em to show me. Fixin' breakfast got me to thinkin' on him. He used to like to cook apples and bacon for breakfast. He ever fix 'em for you?"

She was still smiling. I nodded, uncertainly.

She looked away at the mountains in the distance. "Wonder where he is now. He could be a lot of fun when he had a mind to." She shook her head and laughed. "He liked to have fun. We never ended up where we started out goin'. He was always seein' somethin' and havin' to stop to look at it, draw it, show it to me." She looked back up at me. "He used to do that with you?"

I nodded again because she was still smiling.

"He always said there was somethin' beautiful everywhere if you knew how to look."

I smiled back and nodded. Still smiling, she looked away at the mountains again. "He said I was beautiful. He said I was just a flower growin' beside the road. He used to draw me, all the time. I was happy." She laughed, harshly. "Momma was even happy. She thought she was gonna get rich makin' him marry me when I was goin' to have you. Momma's been the fool some ways, too. Mrs. Burden seen to it she got nothin'. Seen to it Momma never put her foot in her house."

I felt sick inside. Ever since I'd found out she was my mother, I'd wondered why Daddy'd married her. Everywhere we went, women had always clustered around him and smiled at him the same way the girls at school did around Clyde. I'd always wondered why he'd married Mom instead of some woman like him. Now I wished I didn't know.

I got scared that Mom might know what I was

thinking. I looked back down to see. She wasn't paying any attention to me. She was still smiling at the mountains.

"I guess he drew you, too. I guess you know what it was like. Never lettin' you move till he was through." She looked back up at me, her smile gone. "Guess you know when he was through drawin' somethin' he was through with it! He sure was through with me!"

I looked away, remembering when he'd said I was ugly. He'd quit drawing me, too. *Mom isn't ugly. I wonder if he told her she was, too.*

Mom looked back up at me and smiled. "I'm tired. We don't have to pick 'em all today. I can pick some more while you're at school tomorrow. Come on down. You're lookin' tired, too. Today's been right nice. I hope that pork roast is good. I been thinkin' on it all day. You hungry? I'm starved."

I started to climb down. "Yes, I'm starved, too."

"You want to go to a show after supper?" she asked. "I ain't been to one in ages."

I was glad she'd picked up the box and turned away. I was scared to answer. I hadn't been to a movie for a long time, either, but she might drink beer with dinner and get mean again. I didn't want to say no. I wanted her to keep on being different.

"Maybe," I said. "I'm really tired."

She didn't drink beer with dinner or talk much. It was the first real dinner we'd ever had. Cleaning up afterward, I told her it was good. She smiled at me the way she had up at the trees.

"Come on to the show," she said. "We'll have us some fun."

She didn't talk going to town, but she didn't pick at me either, except when I forgot and asked if we were going to the first movie we passed.

"What'd'ya want to see a dumb thing like that for?" she asked. "I want to see somethin' good."

"You choose," I said quickly.

The movie she picked was awful. It was a stupid, brutal thing about cowboys and Indians. Mom cried when the hero got killed. Even harder than the stupid woman in the movie cried. I didn't cry. He'd been a mean drunk and had hit her. Watching it, I'd felt sick and scared. I was glad when he got killed.

When we came out Mom said, "Wasn't it wonderful!"

I kept quiet. I was scared to say it was awful. She wasn't paying any attention to me, anyway. She was smiling to herself.

I felt funny inside. The hero in the movie was the way she'd said boys would be. She was wrong. Clyde wasn't anything like that.

I looked over at Mom. She smiled at me again. I tried to smile back, glad we'd gotten to the car.

Going home, I stared out the window at the darkness, feeling confused. Maybe she was going to quit drinking. She was so different when she wasn't. I wished she would. I didn't feel scared of her when she was the way she'd been all day.

But I began to feel scared. If she quit, I'd have to be careful. From the things she'd said, it would never be all right with her for me to like Clyde or Mr. Beasley. Even though she was wrong about them, she'd be angry if she knew I'd gone to the pond or the Saxon barn.

The next morning, Mom had breakfast waiting when I came down ready to go to school.

"It must be lonesome out here by yourself all the time," she said. "I never thought about it."

I didn't know what to say. If she didn't have anything to do she might start cleaning my room and find my drawings.

"Maybe I'll go to town today. I ain't been just lookin' in the stores in a long time."

I grabbed at the idea. "That sounds nice. There's a new movie playing, too."

"Yeah. I could do that," she said, sounding tired. "I oughta pick some more apples."

"It's supposed to be your day off. You let me have Saturday off. You should get a day, too."

"I oughta. I work hard. You best go. It's late."

I grabbed my books and ran, happy to be getting away from her. As soon as I got on the bus and took the first empty seat, I opened a book and stared down at it. I stared at it trying to see Daddy, trying to shut Mom out of my mind, trying not to worry whether she'd go in my room or start drinking again.

When I got to English, second period, Clyde was already there. When I sat down, he turned around, put his arms on my desk, smiled at me.

"Hi," he said.

I remembered Saturday and the way I'd run from him. I looked up and saw the room was still empty.

"No people," he said.

I nodded, stared at his hands. They were huge. His sleeves didn't come all the way down over his wrists. I looked up at how much taller he was than me and saw his green eyes watching me. Mom was wrong. He wasn't the way she said.

"Claire? You want me to be a ghost, too?"

"Don't tease me," I begged.

"I'm not. You talked to me Saturday. You look like you won't here."

"I'll talk to you," I said, feeling my face turn pink.

"Okay. What did you do yesterday?"

"Mom and I picked apples, cleaned house, and went to the movies." I looked up, saw he looked surprised.

"That doesn't sound like a ghost."

"I'm not!"

"No. You don't have chalk on your face today, either." He reached up toward my face. I didn't move. I stayed still, felt surprised that the tips of his fingers were warm, then sorry, as he touched my hair beside my face and took his hand away.

"No. You're not a ghost."

I shook my head, looking down at the desk.

"So we'll do your algebra at lunch?"

"If you . . . want to."

"I do. But you want to draw? In study hall?"

I looked up scared, wished I hadn't, shook my head.

"Why," he asked.

I looked back down at the desk. "I'll go draw the mill . . . Jake."

"I can't. My mom's picking me up after school to go to the dentist. Why are you scared? About drawing here?"

"I'm not scared! I hate it here!" I turned sideways in my desk away from him.

"Don't run," he said, putting out his hand but not touching me. "You said you'd talk to me, here."

I took a deep breath. "Tell me what you did— yesterday."

At the end of algebra that afternoon, Clyde was talking to Mr. Davis when the bell rang. I didn't wait for him. He said he wouldn't be on the bus. I got my things and left.

Just outside, a station wagon was sitting at the curb. *Adair Farm* was painted on the door. It had to be Clyde's mom inside. She had short black curly hair, too. She was looking the other way so I slowed up.

She wasn't dressed anything like Mom. She could have been one of the neighbors in town.

I got scared Clyde would come out, see me watching her. I ran to the bus.

Back at the dirt road down to the house, I watched the bus go out of sight, then looked in the mailbox. The mail was still there. I hoped that meant Mom had

gone to town early instead of staying home. I didn't
want her home. I was too happy to want to see her.
Clyde had stayed where I was all day, seemed not to
see anyone except me.

Once I got close enough to the house to see her car
was gone, I started running.

The kitchen was clean. Two apple pies were sitting
on the table. I felt strange seeing them instead of her
mess. I reached out to touch one. It was still slightly
warm. I cut a piece and took it upstairs with me.

I got my things out to try to draw Clyde, but made
myself put them back. There was a history test tomorrow. He'd told me to study for it. I spread out my
notes.

Mom hadn't come home by dinner time. I tried not
to think about her. I made a pork sandwich and went
back upstairs to my history notes.

At ten, I finally gave up. I was so tired, I couldn't
see anymore. Mom hadn't come home. I knew she
must be drinking again. I climbed in bed and tried
not to care. When I closed my eyes, I saw Clyde, remembered how warm his fingers were touching my
face.

Something woke me up in the middle of the night. I
stayed still wondering what I was hearing. Mom's car
was running outside. I went to the window and
peered out. The car lights were still on. She'd run into
one of the trees in the yard.

Terrified, I ran downstairs and outside. If she was
hurt, I'd have to go to Grandma's.

When I got to the car, she was just sitting there
laughing. Angrily, I yanked the door open. The smell
of beer overwhelmed me. She was so drunk she
flopped over sideways on the seat. I wanted to hit
her.

"Jumped out in front of me," she giggled. "Right
into the middle of the road."

I ran back around the car to see what she'd done. The fender had hit the tree. It was mashed down onto the tire.

"Mom," I screamed. "Back the car up!"

"Feel sick," she cried.

She tried to get out of the car and fell. I ran back around to her. She was lying there on the ground, laughing. "My legs don't work," she said, giggling.

"Mom!"

She flung her arms up to protect her face. When I didn't hit her, when I just stood there shocked at myself, she started wailing.

"I tried not to! I did! I couldn't stand it no more! My head was hurtin' somethin' awful. I was goin' to die if I didn't get somethin'. You don't know, Claire. You just don't know! I wanna go to bed," she wailed, sobbing.

I hated her so much, I wanted to run and never come back. Shame welled up inside me, choking me.

She thought I was going to hit her! I wanted to! I wanted to hit her and hit her . . . so she can't ever be drunk or hurt me again!

"I wanna go to bed," she moaned, trying to get up. "I didn't go to no bar to drink it! I was drinkin' it in the car comin' home!"

I can't go back to Grandma's!

I helped her up and half carried her upstairs to bed. When I'd almost gotten her into it, she grabbed me and crushed me against her.

"You're a good girl," she blubbered. "You don't hurt me never!"

I yanked away, ashamed and sick with revulsion toward her.

"I'm just no good," she sobbed, "no good at all."

I ran downstairs and outside to get away from her. The car was still sitting against the tree with the lights on, the engine running, the door open. I went around and got in.

I thought I could remember where reverse was. I remembered to push the clutch pedal in first. Then I put it in gear and took my foot off the pedal.

The car jumped back from the tree and stalled. I got out to see if it had moved enough. It had. The tire still wasn't flat.

I took the keys out of the switch and turned off the lights. Then I picked up the empty bag from Mom's beer and carried it and her purse inside. The house was quiet. I sat down at the kitchen table still shaking.

Somehow I had to get Mom to work tomorrow. But the car had to be fixed. I looked in Mom's purse to see if she had any money. There was less than two dollars.

Nobody'll fix it for that.

Sick and scared, I went back outside. By sliding my hand up over the tire, I could feel the fender was only pressing into it a little. It was too dark and I was still shaking too much to see if I could fix it then.

At least she was going slow enough not to be hurt.

For a moment I wished she'd been killed.

That would put me at Grandma's faster than anything!

I remembered the sounds of Grandma hitting her. I ran back inside.

Upstairs, in my room, I reset the alarm. Then, I climbed in bed, hoping Mom was too drunk for my crying to wake her.

Chapter Seventeen

When the alarm went off at five, I was scared and couldn't figure out why it was blaring. Then I remembered the car. I wanted to go back to sleep and never wake up, but I made myself get out of bed.

Instead of trying to wake Mom first, I went downstairs to start a pot of coffee. I left it perking and went outside to look at the tire. It was still too dark to see.

I went back in and moved the living room lamp to the window. Outside again, I found it gave just enough light. The tire still wasn't flat but the fender was pressing against it. Even if I gave Mom the money I had hidden upstairs, she wouldn't be able to drive to the gas station at the store.

I went back inside and poured a cup of coffee. Then I took a deep breath and carried it upstairs. I was scared Mom would be mean again.

I put the coffee down on the table by her bed. Then I prodded her until she began to wake up.

When I first told her she'd had a wreck, she said she hadn't. She told me to go away. I kept at her.

"Go 'way," she said, hitting out at me.

I started screaming. "You've got to get up or you can't get to work! You've got to! We'll be back at Grandma's if you don't!"

"Momma?" she asked sitting up, looking terrified. "Where's Momma?"

"Mom, listen to me!" I repeated it all.

"I dunno how!" she wailed and started crying.

"I'll help. We can fix it," I pleaded. "We've got to."

I couldn't stand staying near her. I started down-stairs.

"Claire! Claire!" she cried, trying to get out of bed. "Wait, Claire! Don't leave me! I'm gettin' up!"

She looked horrible. I was scared to go back over to her.

"I brought you some coffee. It's there on the table."

She reached out for it. She was shaking so it slopped all over her, but she got the cup to her mouth and started drinking.

I told her I'd get breakfast and went downstairs.

She stumbled down after me and sat down. I poured her more coffee. When the oatmeal was ready, I put it in a bowl, put sugar and milk on it, and set it in front of her. She just shook her head and pushed it away. I pushed it back to her.

"Eat it!" I said.

She picked up the spoon and started eating.

"Do you have any money?" I asked.

She shook her head. "I spent the rest yesterday, 'cept a couple of dollars. What we goin' to do?"

"We'll have to fix it so you can go to work," I said. "You can't get fired."

I took the keys out to the car. There was a jack and lug wrench in the trunk but no other tools. I carried them around to the bent fender. If we tried to pry it out we might pop the tire. It was old and worn. I went back to check the spare. It seemed to have enough air in it, but I couldn't tell. Mom came out-side.

Before she could start crying again, I told her what we were going to do. She nodded dumbly and came to help. I put the long metal bar of the jack up under the fender and moved it until it was wedged behind the bent place. Then we put our weight on it to push it out. The fender gave a little.

I decided to try using the lug wrench too. Mom started putting her weight on the long bar while I was still getting the wrench in place. The fender bent free of the tire. Mom fell forward. The long bar shot out from under the fender and dug into my left hand. I screamed in agony. Mom screamed, too.

Then, suddenly, Mom stopped screaming. She grabbed me and half carried me back to the house. She dropped me into the chair by the table and grabbed a towel. She tied it around my upper arm so tightly I could feel it hurt over the pain in my hand. She grabbed the empty dish pan and pushed my hand into it. Then she got ice and dumped it over my hand.

"Hold still!" she said shouting. "Try to hold still!"

My hand hurt too much for me to look at it. I heard Mom run in the bathroom, then back past me upstairs. All the time she kept crying, "I didn't mean to! I didn't mean to!"

Then she was back beside me with rubbing alcohol and an old sheet. She sat down and stared at me, her eyes wide with terror.

"We ain't even got any bandages. I gotta use this. I gotta clean the place first. It's goin' to hurt. You want some beer? It won't hurt you so bad."

I shook my head, trying to keep from screaming on top of my crying. She probed at my hand.

"Thank God!" she said. "Thank God! It's just caught the skin. It ain't broke. It just hurts awful. You got to stay home, baby, and keep ice on it. It won't hurt you so bad."

"No! No!" I screamed, trying to push her away. "I can't stay home. They'll find out! They'll come poking! They'll make me go to Grandma's! I can't stay home! I can't go to Grandma's. I can't. She'll hurt me. They'll feel sorry for me and she'll hurt me. I . . ."

Mom put her arms around me and pulled me against her. "Poor baby. Life treats you bad."

"I can't go to Grandma's!"

"Nobody's goin' to make you! I'm not goin' to let 'em! I'm goin' to take care of you. Nobody'll make you go!" She patted my back. Held me close to her. "I'm goin' to see they don't."

"They will! They will!"

"No. You're goin' to stay here with me."

"I have to go to school."

She let go of me. I heard ripping sounds as she tore up the sheet. Then she was fooling with my hand again, gently, carefully, trying hard not to hurt me.

"There," she finally said. "It don't look too pretty, but it'll stay clean and heal. It ain't goin' to bleed no more." She untied the towel from my arm. "I'm goin' to get you some aspirin and some breakfast. You oughta stay home. Ain't nobody goin' to care if you miss one day. I wish I could stay with you, but ain't got no time off comin'." She smiled and patted my arm gently. " 'Sides. You fixed the car so I could go. I got to now."

I nodded numbly. "I have to go to school."

I stayed still while she fixed my breakfast. As long as I didn't move, my hand didn't hurt as much.

"You ain't left-handed?" she asked when she set breakfast in front of me.

I shook my head.

"Leastways there's that. I didn't even know. I didn't mean to hurt you. You was helpin' me. You been good to me. I'm goin' to see nobody makes you go to Momma."

"I hate her!"

"Me, too, Claire. Me, too. I always hated her."

I couldn't say anything. I treid to eat breakfast.

"I'm goin' to quit drinkin', Claire. I got to. We got us a home here, now. Nobody's goin' to take it from us long as I'm workin' and seein' to you. You stay home till you're feelin' better."

"I have to go!"

"Come on then. I'll help you get dressed."

She didn't say anything else until we were back downstairs. She'd gotten my brush, the silver-backed one Grandmother Burden had given me, and started on my hair. I felt scared. She had to know where I'd gotten it. But she was still gentle. I felt strange inside. No one had brushed my hair for me since Grandmother had died seven years ago. I could remember her brushing it when I was small. She was gentle, the way Mom was being now.

"You set on goin'?"

I nodded and looked up. She was smiling at me the way she had been Sunday.

"I'll carry your stuff up to the road for you. I'm goin' to do better, Claire. You're goin' to see I am."

She folded some aspirin up in part of a napkin and tucked that and one of the dollars into my sweater pocket. Then, she gathered up my books.

I followed her up the road. We'd just gotten to the trees at the curve when I saw the bus in the distance. I thought of Clyde on it and looked at Mom. She was still in her old robe. She looked awful. Shame welled up inside me.

If Clyde sees her . . .

"No! Go home!" I grabbed my books away from her.

"Claire! You're goin' to hurt your hand!"

"No! No! Leave me be!" I ran away from her toward the bus, still yelling. I looked back. She was just standing there looking after me. I made myself shut up and run so the bus wouldn't sit there waiting.

I got to it in time. I saw Clyde was sitting in the second seat. The first was empty. I sat down in it, yanked my books over my hand so he wouldn't see the bandage. If he saw it he'd start asking questions. I felt sick inside wondering if he'd seen Mom, wondering what he'd say if he found out what had happened.

Clyde leaned forward and touched my hair.

"Leave me be." I moved my head.

He put his arms on the back of the seat behind me. "You've been crying. What happened to you?"

"Nothing! Leave me be!"

"Claire? You're scaring me. What happened to you?"

"Leave me be. Stop picking on me."

"I'm not picking on you."

"You are unless you leave me be!"

"I don't understand. Yesterday, you . . ."

"I don't like you. Leave me be."

He sat back in his seat. Didn't say anything else.

When we got to school, I got off the bus as soon as it stopped and started running. Mom's car was parked in front of the entrance. She was standing there in her uniform, looking at me. I ran toward her, ashamed, frantically wanting her away from there before Clyde saw her or the car.

"Go to work!"

"Not till we see the nurse and she sees I'm seein' to you. Nobody's goin' to send you to Momma."

"Please go to work!"

"Come on to the nurse." She took my books out of my hands and steered me to the door and inside. I wouldn't let myself look to see if Clyde was seeing her, seeing the car. I looked at the ground, ashamed, hating Mom.

Mom led me right into the nurse's office, took my arm, and held it out to her.

"Got herself hurt this morning. I didn't have no money to take her to a doctor. Thought you'd best see it, make sure it ain't broken."

The nurse nodded, took my hand.

"Looks like you did a neat job bandaging it."

"I didn't have nothin' else. The sheet was clean."

The nurse nodded again and started gently unwrapping it.

"How did you manage to do that?" she asked, her voice getting mean.

I looked at my hand. Mom wasn't saying anything.

"We had a flat tire. I was trying to help fix it. The

jack slipped off," I lied, scared. "Mom didn't think it was broken."

She nodded and tried moving my hand. Gently, then harder. "It doesn't seem to be. Why didn't you keep her home?"

I didn't give Mom time to talk. I was too scared. "She wanted you to see it. She can't stay home with me. She works . . . she doesn't have any time off coming. Her boss is awful. He'd fire her if she stayed home."

"They'll sure do that," the nurse said, nodding. "Makes it real tough." She patted my arm, and smiled at Mom. "It's good you brought her in. I can give her a tetanus shot to make sure there won't be any problem. I've got some gauze and tape you can take home, too. You did a good job of bandaging it up. You should see some of the things that come in here."

"Tried to," Mom said, smiling. "I wanted my baby to be all right."

I was petrified the nurse would give me the shot in my arm and see the scars from Mom's cigarettes. I kept myself from looking at the scars on Mom's bare arms.

She didn't. She gave me the shot in my rear, said I could stay there and lie down if my hand hurt too much. I was scared to. The bell still hadn't rung. I was scared Clyde was waiting, would ask Mom what happened.

He was outside the office. Without looking at his face, I hurried Mom past him down the hall, and outside.

"You've got to get to work," I said. "Please don't be late."

She looked as if she was going to cry.

"Don't! It's all right. You made it all right. The nurse said so. Don't be late!"

I heard the bell ring. Clyde would have to go to class. I was glad he wasn't in French.

"Please go!"

"Nobody ever took up for me," Mom said, trying to smile. "We got us a home. We're goin' to be fine."

I made myself smile back. "Grandma can't bother us."

"No more," Mom said. "You go back to the nurse if you're feelin' bad."

I nodded and watched her drive off.

She believed me. She didn't notice Clyde. She thought I was taking up for her. She doesn't know I'm ashamed of her, hate her, would lie, do anything, to keep him, anyone, from finding out, from sending me to Grandma's.

I went inside hating her, hating myself, too.

When the bell rang at the end of my first class, I waited and let everyone else go out first, hoping I wouldn't see Clyde. He was outside the door. I started to turn away but he took my arm and looked down at my hand. I jerked my arm away from him, turned away.

"What happened to you?"

"Leave me be. I don't want to talk to you." I made myself walk away to my locker, get my books, sit down in class. I was glad people were there, but sick inside.

I've been stupid. I can't be friends with him. He's just like everyone else, asks questions, feels sorry for me, makes trouble.

I didn't look up when he sat down. I didn't look at him all day. I didn't take anything home. My hand hurt too much. I just wanted to go home, go to bed, not hurt anymore.

When I got home and saw the ugly, little house and the pies still sitting on the table in the clean kitchen, I started crying. Mom had fixed them for me and I hated her. I'd lied to her. I didn't want to be with her. I hadn't taken up for her. I'd lied to keep away from Grandma. I put my head down on the table.

Someone banged on the front door. I sat up, startled. Terrified it was Grandma, I crept into the living room to see if I'd locked the door. I hadn't. I started toward it. I was almost to the door when it opened and Clyde was in the room looking angry.

I turned away and, crying harder, started back to the kitchen.

He'll just hate me!

"Claire, stop it," he said, taking my arm and pulling me back toward him.

"No! Leave me be!" I cried, trying to pull away.

"No! You stop running. Stop yanking! You'll hurt your hand."

"It doesn't matter," I wailed, pushing at him and then crying out when I hurt my hand.

"Dammit! Stop being an idiot!" He sat down on the sofa, pulled me onto his lap, held me so I couldn't push at him. "Stop it!"

"Let me go!"

"No! You're hurt! You're acting like an idiot . . . hurting yourself worse! I won't let go till you stop and tell me what happened. If you don't, I'll go ask the nurse!"

I almost quit crying, terrified.

"What happened? Why were you running from your mom?"

I lied to the nurse. She believed me. I have to make him believe me, too.

"How did you get hurt?"

"I cut my hand."

"Why were you running from her?"

"She wanted me to go to the doctor!"

"What's wrong with that?"

"She made me go to the nurse!"

"Yes. Why didn't she bring you home? It's been hurting you like crazy all day!"

I couldn't answer. Shame welled up inside me.

"Well?" he asked, angrily, almost shaking me.

I felt myself turn red. "We don't have any money," I whispered. "Please go. Let me go."

"So? Why didn't she bring you home?"

"She can't stay with me! She'd get fired! Please go!" I tried to push him away. He wouldn't let go.

"Claire! You idiot! You're ashamed of it! You wouldn't go to the nurse because you're ashamed you don't have any money. You ran from me, too. I know where you live. I've lived on the next farm all my life. You wouldn't be living here if you had any money!"

"Please go!"

"No! I'm not a snob, you idiot! But you've hurt my feelings. You were sure I wouldn't like you. You ran away from me instead of letting me try to help."

"You'd feel sorry for me!" I wailed. "Every time I have anything, people feel sorry for me and take it away!"

"Claire!"

"They do They did already! I had my daddy and my home and I was happy. Then people felt sorry for me and made me go to Mom. If they find out we don't have enough money they'll take me from her, too!"

"Claire?"

"I can draw! I have Mom. I don't have anyone else! I want to stay here! People don't care if I'm happy! They just care if I'm where they make me go. They don't care about me at all!"

I hit him trying to make him let me go.

"Stop it! She's not all you've got!"

I shut up, shuddered, scared he knew about Grandma.

"Stop it. You've got me. Please stop crying like that! Please! No wonder you're scared of people! I don't want you to be! I want you safe and not scared and drawing and . . ."

"I was . . ." I sobbed.

"Stop crying. Doesn't your mom have any family to help her?"

"No! Mom tries to take care of me! It's hard for her!"

"It's hard for you, too," he said, tightening his arms around me. "Don't be ashamed of her."

I just cried harder.

"Stop it. I'm not picking on you, Claire. Stop running from me. I was trying to find out if you were okay." He let go of me enough to press my head gently against his chest and put his head down on top of mine. His sweater was soft against my face.

Grandmother was bigger than me. When I was little, she held me against her, too.

Mom did, too, when I was hurt.

I shuddered and tried to stop crying.

"Don't cry. I'm not hurting you?"

"No," I whispered. Suddenly, I felt totally, completely safe. I put my arm around his neck and pressed my face against his shoulder. He held me close to him until I quit crying.

"I better go," he said. "I called Mom from school and told her I was going to Jimmy's. If I don't get home, she'll call him."

"I don't want you to go."

"I have to."

I sat up away from him and slid off his lap feeling confused. He sounded as if his mother wouldn't want him there.

"Claire?" He leaned over, touched my hair. "Don't run away from me tomorrow. Don't be ashamed."

I tried to nod.

"My mom would help you. Daniel . . ."

"No!" I screamed, remembering how much his mom looked like the neighbors. "No! Don't tell anybody! They'll feel sorry for me!"

"Stop it!" he said, putting his arms back around me. "Stop. Don't be scared! I won't tell . . . anybody!"

"Don't. Don't. I have to stay here."

"You will," he said. "Your mom'll be home soon?"

I nodded, lying numbly.

"I have to go."

I stayed still a long time after he left.

He doesn't want his mom to know he was here. That's why he got mad when I drew him at the barn. . . . Didn't want anyone to see it. She wouldn't want him to like me.

I seemed to hear the kids who'd told me Mom was my mother, yelling . . . taunting.

But he likes me anyway . . .

He hasn't seen her drunk . . .

Somehow, somehow, I have to keep Mom from drinking.

I woke up in the middle of the night to the sound of her crying. It was that horrible, animal sound.

I pulled my pillow over my head and concentrated and concentrated until all I could see or hear was Clyde's green eyes.

Chapter Eighteen

Waiting for the bus the next morning, I began feeling awkward and scared. I'd sat on Clyde's lap and bawled, told him too much. If he'd gone home and told his mom . . .

But he wouldn't. He'd lied about where he was. He said he wouldn't tell.

I made myself get on the bus, sit down in the first seat, not turn away as he leaned forward in the seat behind me.

"You look like your hand still hurts."

He just feels sorry for me . . .

I shook my head.

"It does. I'll carry your stuff at school. You aren't stuck with a test first period?"

I shook my head, remembering the history quiz the day before. Taking it had been awful, I'd probably done terribly.

"I'll help you do your homework at lunch."

He's nice. He isn't people.

When we got to school, Clyde stopped at my locker, reached out and started working the combination.

"How can you do that?" I asked, startled.

"I memorized it yesterday, watching you."

I looked up at him and was surprised again at how tall he was. I remembered the way he'd sounded in the Saxon barn when he'd said it made him feel small.

"You don't like being tall," I said.

"I can't do much about it," he said, smiling and leaning toward me.

I turned away feeling awkward, but made myself not run.

"I get tired of bumping my head. And the dumb jokes! The stupid dentist says the same thing . . . every time. That he's scared to hurt me because I'm so much bigger than he is."

Tall's why he isn't people . . . why he knew people don't like Jake . . . because he's different.

I looked back up at him. He looked worried. I turned away.

"I better go to class. I'll be late."

"Claire?"

"I'll be late!"

As I came in the room, Mrs. Lively looked up and smiled. I nodded and sat down, wishing I'd done my homework. If she called on me, I'd have to lie to her, too. I'd lied to Clyde and the nurse about my hand. They'd believed me, but I hadn't remembered to tell them the same thing.

I opened my book, tried to concentrate.

Lying's how I got in trouble before . . . when I wasn't in school. I told the neighbor I'd been sick . . . but she'd seen me going to the store. I told her Daddy was sick . . . but she'd seen him, too. Seen that he'd been drinking.

I looked back at Mrs. Lively. She'd started the person the farthest away from me reading. She always went in a line. She saw me looking at her and smiled. I looked back at my book.

I hate lying . . . it makes me feel bad . . . I hate feeling wrong when I'm trying to do what's right.

I felt sick inside. I wasn't trying to do right. I'd made Clyde lie, too. He'd lied to his mom so she wouldn't know he'd come to my house. The last time someone came to my house, I was in third grade. There'd been a new girl at school. She'd asked me over to her house. I'd said no, knowing I had to go home. But I'd asked her to come home with me.

I felt myself turn red, remembering. Daddy hadn't

even said "Hello" to her. He'd just looked at her and asked where she lived. Then he'd just looked at me.

I never asked anyone else. No one else ever asked me.

If Clyde knows what the tenant house is like, his mom will know, too. She won't want him to be friends with me.

I made myself listen to Mrs. Lively in case she called on me.

When class let out, Clyde was waiting. I couldn't look at him. I let him take my books, went to English with him.

"You feel lousy," he said. "Claire, if your mom can't come get you, my mom would take you home."

"No!"

"You should be home."

"No! Just . . ." I pulled my books toward me.

"You promised you wouldn't run," he said, holding on to them. "We'll go see the nurse, maybe she'll . . ." He stood up.

"No!" I put my head down on my desk.

"Claire?" He sat back down, put his hand on my shoulder.

"Leave me be. I can't be friends with you. If . . . your mom took me home, my mom would be mad. She'd be mad you came to the house . . . She . . ."

He took his hand away. "She was mad at you? You already felt awful, and I just . . . made it worse . . . I'm sorry . . . I . . ."

My desk lurched. I looked up, confused. He'd turned away. His neck was red.

When class was over, he got up and left. I sat staring after him.

In study hall, doing my homework in the library, I looked up, saw him sitting across the room, turning his head away.

He thinks Mom knows he was there . . . was mad at me because of it?

When I got home, I went upstairs and got out my sketch pad. I carried it over to the table and opened it to the drawing I'd done of Clyde. I touched his chalk face. It was cold.

The string he'd put in my hair when we'd ridden Adair was still on my table. I tore the drawing out of the pad, carefully, and rolled it up. Then I managed to get the string around it. I put it under the bottom drawer of my dresser in the hollow space behind the baseboard.

It was Wednesday. I could hear Mr. Beasley playing before I got to the pond. I was just going to listen to him, not let him see me, come home. But the rich, beautiful sound made me start running toward him.

When he saw me coming, Mr. Beasley smiled and nodded his head. He looked happy to see me. I wanted to hug him.

Then he saw the bandage on my hand and quit playing. "What'd you do to yourself, child?"

I couldn't lie anymore. It just started pouring out of me. Mom's drinking, her running into the tree, her not wanting me to draw because it made her think of Daddy, my lying to the nurse. I couldn't tell him about Mom hurting me. He looked so upset and worried already, I was too ashamed and scared. But I told him how Grandma Simmons made Mom marry Daddy to try to get Grandmother Burden's money.

"I knowed somethin' bad was goin' on! I knowed it sure as I'm sittin' here! Your momma get mean when she's drinkin'?"

I shook my head, scared he'd know I was lying. "Mom says she isn't going to drink anymore."

He just looked at me a while. "You puttin' big stock in that?" he finally asked.

"She has to stop!" I said desperately. "If she doesn't, she'll get fired. We'd have to go back to Grandma's! Grandma hates her, hates me! Mom has to stop drinking!" I shuddered.

He peered at me, but I made myself stay quiet.

"I'm bound to tell you she's goin' to drink," he said sadly. "She's just goin' to. There ain't nothin' you can do to change it."

"But she doesn't want to! She said she doesn't!"

"That don't mean nothin'," he said. "When the drinkin' gets hold of people t'ain't easy to quit. It takes somebody strong carin' a powerful lot about somethin'. Your momma don't sound strong. It sounds to me like all your momma cares about is keepin' away from her momma. Ain't that the truth?"

"You're wrong! You've got to be!"

"I hope to be, child. I hope to be. But I can't go lyin' to you. You've got to be ready when it gets her again. When she gives in to it, she's goin' to feel 'shamed. You start in on her about it, you don't know what she's liable to do. But you sure got to get her so she's drinkin' at home 'stead of drivin' or gettin' herself fired. I got to figure something out. You know where your daddy's gone to?"

I shook my head, sick inside with shame.

"Ain't you got no more kin 'sides your grandma? Ain't your daddy got no friends to take you?"

I shook my head again, unable to look at him, wishing he'd stop asking questions. *Nobody wants me but Mom and Grandma.*

"Bad! Bad! Ol' Beasley's got to think. Where's your drawin's, child? Ain't you brought some for me to see?"

My heart seemed to stop.

He likes me. He's not just poking, feeling sorry for me.

I turned back toward him, saw him, old and black. *They'd never let me stay with him!* I looked away, angry.

"No! If she's going to be drunk, I don't want to draw!" I was ready to cry again.

"You hush that talk!" he said. "I ain't listenin' to it.

If she don't want you drawin', the only thing we can say for her drinkin' is you got time to draw while she's at it. Don't you go givin' me none of this quittin' drawin' talk! I'm goin' to get powerful mad. Your drawin's like my playin'. I play 'cause I feel like playin'! 'Cause I need to!"

"I don't feel like drawing anymore! Everything I do is wrong!"

"Your drawin' ain't wrong, child. When somethin' gets me down, I come down here and play. It eases my mind. I know my playin's good. Playin's what tells me I'm good. You do your drawin' like I tell you. You're soon goin' to see. Drawin's goin' to make you feel good again, 'cause it's good. Seein' me like it makes you feel good."

"I don't have any more paper," I lied, to make him stop. I'd never feel good again.

"Then I'm goin' to get you some," he said.

I looked up, saw his old worn clothes, shook my head. He was looking out over the pond, frowning.

"The law says you got some family, you got to stay with 'em unless somebody shows 'em it ain't no fit place. They ain't goin' to listen to me talkin'. From what you've told me, they ain't goin' to listen to you neither. And they sure ain't goin' to listen to your momma!"

"Then I wish I'd just die!"

"Hush that! You stop worryin' yourself so much! I ain't said there ain't nothin' we can do. I already told you I'm goin' to figure somethin' out. You let ol' Beasley do your worryin'. Now you listen good. If your momma comes home drinkin' you got to promise me you ain't goin' to carry on at her! Not when she's been drinkin'. You stay in the bed and play you're sleepin'. You've got to wait until she's off it again. Then you got to tell her she's got to drink it at home where she can't hurt herself. You got to make her believe that's the only way she's goin' to stay away from her momma. You got to swear it to me."

"That's not helping her!"

"It ain't your momma we're worryin' on, child. There ain't nothing' we can do for her, unless she does it herself. The thing we're goin' to worry on is you. You go gettin' your momma scared when she's drinkin' she's liable to hurt you!"

I felt cold inside. I already knew she could hurt me when she was drinking.

"You goin' to swear to it?"

"I promise," I said.

"On your soul?" he asked, staring at me so hard I couldn't look away.

"Yes. On my soul."

He smiled and nodded. "Now you let me do the worryin'." He picked up his guitar. "What kinda playin' you want to hear?" he asked, still smiling.

"It's a Long Old Road," I said.

"Yes, but ol' Beasley's goin' to find the way!"

I closed my eyes and shut out everything except his music.

When he quit playing, I saw he was staring at me.

"I saw your daddy once . . . out walkin' the roads a long ways from here. It musta been a long time before you were born."

He wasn't smiling. I looked away.

"Your daddy loves drawin' same as you. He knows it's good. He taught it to you."

I nodded.

"The time I seen him he wasn't travelin' high. I'm too old for travelin' myself, but the folks I know still goin' at it, they're as like as any to run across him. I'm goin' to town Saturday. I'm goin' to ask if they seen him along the way. I'm goin' to tell 'em when they go, they got to look out for him, tell him he's got to come home."

"Do you think you'll find him?"

"I don't know unless I try. I'm goin' to try. I've got to get on home now. I'm goin' to get you some more paper. You 'member what I told you about your momma."

I nodded, looked away.

" 'Member what I told you about this ol' wall? You got yourself troubles, child, you move one of the rocks."

I nodded.

"You look to yourself, child. You let your friends help you."

Chapter Nineteen

Thursday morning, when I got up and started down-stairs through Mom's room, she got up, too. I heard her coming down behind me, so I went on through the kitchen out to the bathroom. She came to the door and asked if I could manage by myself. I told her I could.

Mr. Beasley said not to worry about her.

When I couldn't stay in the bathroom any longer, I went back in the kitchen.

"Sit down," Mom said, smiling. "Breakfast is almost ready."

I sat down. Mom set the table quickly, put my plate in front of me.

"Aren't you going to eat, too?" I asked when she just stood over me."

"Goin' to after a while."

"Aren't you hungry?"

"Not much." But she got a plate and sat down, too.

"It's good," I said.

She didn't answer. I was scared to look at her, but I was hungry and ate.

When she cleared the table, I saw she'd hardly touched hers. She followed me upstairs to help me get dressed.

She was hurried about it, but careful not to hit my hand.

"Don't you get hot wearin' long sleeves all the time?" She was gently working the fitted sleeve of my dress over the bandage.

"No." I looked at the ugly scars on her arms. It was strange to me that she didn't seem to be aware of them. The only time she'd worn a sweater to work to cover them was that once after Grandma'd come with the cake. I wondered if people ever asked Mom what happened to her arms. What she told them, if they did.

"There," Mom said, finishing buttoning my dress up the back. "You goin' to be able to get that off when it's bedtime?"

I nodded.

There aren't any scars on her face . . .

I was mixed up inside, still seeing Mom put her arms up to shield her face when she'd thought I was going to attack her the way Grandma would have.

"We can brush your hair downstairs." Mom picked up my brush and brought it along. After she'd been brushing a while, she said, "You need a new brush. The bristles is worn out on this one."

I couldn't answer. My brush was the only thing I had that Grandmother Burden had given me.

Mom kept brushing my hair, gently and carefully, the way Grandmother used to.

"You got hair like Mrs. Burden," she said. "She always hated me. But she hated Momma more. Never let Momma in her house. Never called me to the phone to talk to her. I didn't mind that. Them three years was the longest I was ever free of Momma. Since then, I been moving out on Momma every time I got myself a job. But she never lets me be. She's always been callin' me at work, makin' trouble, till I'd get put off and have to go back to her. I never have stayed no place long enough to get me some money to leave town. Mrs. Burden give me some, but Momma got it from me. Mrs. Burden hated me, but she wasn't mean like Momma. Was she good to you?"

I nodded, too scared to answer.

"She wasn't so bad to me. She never was 'shamed of me in front of people the way your father was. Told

me I shamed him! Never told me why. Just said it.
Then wouldn't speak to me or look at me till he run
out of stuff to draw. Then I could sit there and he'd
draw me. Sit there all day, till he got tired!"

She sighed. "I didn't have nothin' else to do. Mrs.
Burden never let me touch nothin' or do nothin' . . .
never even let me touch you. Took care of you herself.
Even named you herself . . . after that sister Claire
of hers she got hangin' in her room. You seen that picture?"

I nodded, terrified.

"Mrs. Burden told me she'd learn you to be like
her—you look like her. When I seen you in court I
thought I was seein' her come to life. Didn't want no
part of her to take care of! Mrs. Burden learned you to
hate me, too. Learned you to look right through me on
the street like you didn't even know I was your
momma. I seen you, lots of times—with her, with your
father after she died. Even by yourself that time I was
workin' in the kitchen at your school."

I was too terrified to move. I hadn't known she was
my mom till then. Till the kids told me and made fun
of me. I'd come face to face with her after they'd told
me. She'd stood looking at me. I'd turned, walked
away, not looked at her, ashamed.

"You took up for me with Momma," she said. "Nobody ever done '' !! I couldn't stay with your father.
It was awful, but goin' back to Momma was worse. I
used to wonder if Mrs. Burden was good to you. She
never let me try to." She patted at my hair. "You best
go. You're goin' to miss your bus if your don't."

I didn't look at her. Her voice was too strange. I
started for the door.

"Wait! You're leavin' your lunch."

She ran upstairs before I turned around. She was
crying that horrible sound. I grabbed my lunch and
ran.

But the sound stayed in my head. Mr. Beasley'd said not to worry over Mom. But he didn't know what Daddy was like when he was angry . . . not speaking . . . not even looking at you. He'd never had Grandma Simmons after him, either.

I felt sick inside. If Mr. Beasley found Daddy and I went home to Galway Hall, Mom would go back to Grandma's. Mr. Beasley'd said she'd drink no matter what . . . that all she cared about was staying away from Grandma. But she'd asked if Grandmother Burden was good to me, said she'd wanted to be, too.

And I'd hated her. I'd been ashamed of her. All I wanted was to keep away from Grandma. But Mom thought I'd taken up for her. She said we had a home, now. She said she'd take care of me.

Nobody ever took care of her!

Maybe Mr. Beasley's wrong. Maybe she'll quit drinking.

I saw the bus was coming. I ran toward it.

Chapter Twenty

When I got to school, I opened my locker and just stood looking into it. My hand had quit hurting, unless I tried to use it. But there wasn't any way I could hold an armload of books without using both hands. I picked up my notebook and French book.

"Claire?"

I made myself turn away, tried not to see Clyde.

"Your mom said I can't even talk to you?"

I tried to nod, couldn't.

"I don't want her mad at you. I wouldn't do anything to make her mad. You won't let anybody else help you."

Mr. Beasley said, "Let your friends help you." But I can't be friends with Clyde.

I saw the mobs of kids in the hall, all laughing and talking to each other.

"Your mom was mean to you?"

I shook my head.

No. She wasn't mean to me. Everyone, always, was mean to her. I was, too.

"You'll be late to class." He touched my arm.

I looked up, startled. Clyde looked the way he had when I'd grabbed the squirrel drawing out of his hand, the same way when I'd yanked my hands out of his and turned away into Adair. I remembered Adair's snorting, how quickly Clyde'd pushed him away from me. How he'd said, "I wouldn't let you get hurt."

We were laughing together.

"Claire?"

"No! It's me that's mean!" I said, running.

In class, I stared at my book, made myself listen,

not close my eyes so I wouldn't hear Mom crying that horrible sound. When the bell rang, I wanted to stay there, still hear Mrs. Lively's gentle voice. I made myself get up, go out in the hall, through the mobs of laughing kids to my locker. I put my French book in, took my English book, went through the kids to class, sat down.

"You're not mean," Clyde said, sitting down sideways in front of me, puting his arm across the top of my desk.

I saw the sleeve of the same gray sweater he'd had on when I'd been crying.

He held me till I stopped.

"Claire? You're not."

I closed my eyes, tried to shut him out.

"You're mad at me? You think I'm picking on you?"

I shook my head, remembering how safe I'd felt on his lap.

"You're making me feel awful. You said you liked me."

I looked up, saw green eyes.

I do . . . I . . .

"Claire, are you okay?"

I looked back down at my English book, saw the folded paper in the back, pulled it out, pushed it across the desk at him.

"Claire?" He picked it up.

I looked down at my hands in my lap, scared.

"Don't show it to anybody," I begged.

"You're giving me this!"

I nodded, closed my eyes, tried to remember his face the first time he'd seen the squirrel drawing.

"Claire!" Warm fingers touched my face, jerked away.

I looked up, saw him turning away, people in the room, Mrs. Morgan coming in. I looked back at Clyde, reached out, almost touched his sweater.

He's not mean. He's not like everyone else. He likes my drawing.

When the bell rang, Clyde stood up, picked up my books, leaned toward me, smiling.

"You can't go to gym. Where do you go instead?"

"The library."

"Okay. You won't do your algebra, Claire? You'll . . ."

I nodded, stood up, too.

"You want your other books?"

"No."

"Okay. You'll wait? After class?"

Later, in biology, I looked up from my drawing, saw him leaning on the desk, watching me, smiling.

"You smile when you're drawing, but there's no chalk on your face."

I put my hand up to my face, looked away, seemed to hear Mr. Beasley saying, "Didn't you bring me any drawin's?"

I told him I didn't have any more paper! He said he'd buy me some. He said he had to go working to get money! I could see him old and bent, wearing worn clothes.

"Claire?"

I looked up into scared green eyes, away, saw the microscope.

"Are you okay?"

No!

I nodded. Pushed the microscope toward him, said, "Here. You won't finish," made myself draw.

At lunchtime, Clyde pushed my algebra book aside, smiled.

"You didn't need much help." He was leaning on my closed notebook and running his finger along the back of the sketch pad inside. He looked down to see what he was doing, pushed my notebook toward me.

"Why can't you draw here? It's almost the only time you smile."

"It isn't," I said, looking away.

"It is. Claire? I didn't ask her, yet, but my mom'd write yours a note or call her at work. She'd make it okay for you to come over."

"I can't."

"Okay. But you'd like the greenhouse. Mrs. Carter said we were through with botany except for the test."

"I can't." I reached for my notebook.

"No running," he said, taking it back from me. "I'll leave you be. But you'd like it. Sometimes the air's green—the way it is down at the river. It's warm and green."

"I can't."

"Okay! You can't! My grandfather built trellises all over the inside of the roof. The vines on them make it green. They're covered with flowers."

"Like the ones you brought?" I asked.

He smiled. "The ones the color of your eyes? Yeah. Mom says they're clematis *jackmanii*. Why can't you go if Mom's there? You'd like it."

She's not tall. She's not like you. She's like neighbors. She'll make trouble.

I turned away.

"All right!" he said. "All right! I'm sorry! I hate the greenhouse anyway!"

I looked up, shocked.

He looked away. "I just thought . . . when you gave me the squirrel . . . It was fun going to the barn? Riding Adair?"

I nodded, miserable.

"Claire?"

"I'll draw here."

"You hate that," he said.

I shook my head. Maybe Mr. Beasley was right. Maybe I would feel better if I started drawing again. I would if Clyde liked what I drew.

"There's nothing to draw here."

I looked up, saw green eyes. I smiled, feeling funny inside, pulled my notebook and the sketch pad toward me.

"Yes, there is," I said, opening the notebook. "See."

After school, when I got home, I got out my sketch pads and happily leafed through them, looking at the things I'd drawn in the woods. When I got to the drawing of Mr. Beasley and saw him old, I felt sick again.

He'll get me paper Saturday. I've got paper.

Ashamed, I opened the new pad I'd just started when I'd drawn the Saxon barn.

If I leave this for him he'll know I have enough paper.

I tore the drawing out and took it down to the pond, wishing Mr. Beasley would be there.

He wasn't. I looked around wondering how to leave the picture so it wouldn't blow away. The old rock wall was higher than the paper was wide. There was enough sky at the top to fold it over and let it hang down. It might not get torn up like that.

I looked around for something to hold it in place and saw the rock Mr. Beasley'd loosened in the wall.

He said move it if I'm in trouble. I've made trouble for him.

I pulled the rock out and used it to pin the picture in place.

Now he'll know I lied.

Maybe he won't be mad. Clyde wasn't anymore when I gave him the squirrel.

I looked at the pond. It was lonely without Mr. Beasley. I wished I had my chalk so I could try to draw it, lonely, now. I started to go home and bring it back, but Clyde said do my homework.

I wondered what it was like inside the greenhouse. Clematis *jackmanii,* he'd said. I wondered if there was a name for the color of his eyes, wished I could see them.

Friday afternoon, during study hall, Clyde and I went to the library. We sat in the back where the books were that nobody used. Clyde said if we were quiet and looked busy the librarian would leave us alone.

Clyde slumped down in his chair so his knees would go under the table and opened his book. "You ever read?"

"Sometimes."

His sweater was dark gray. It was trying to rain so that end of the library was gray, too. I wondered if he'd get mad again if I drew him.

"Did you read this?" He started to lean over to show me the book.

"Don't move!"

"What?"

I looked away. "You'd get mad again if I drew you."

"No. Claire?"

I was moving my things to the end of the table. I looked back, saw he was watching me.

"Look at the book . . . like you were," I asked, nervously.

He looked back down at it, grinning. "You're going to draw me? Here?"

"Don't laugh."

"I feel dumb." He quit laughing and looked at the book.

"Slide down more in the chair . . . stop. Don't move now."

I opened the sketch pad, started drawing fast, not believing he'd just done what I asked. I did his face slowly to get it right. For the rest, I just caught the pattern I'd set. I was nearly finished when I saw he was looking at the librarian's desk across the room.

"Please don't move. I'm almost finished."

"Look at the desk."

"No."

"Look!"

I saw Miss Joyce was at the desk, looked back at him. He'd moved, put down his book and was staring at me. I closed the sketch pad. I'd never get him back the way he was.

He got up. Scared, I looked at the librarian's desk again. Miss Joyce was gone.

Clyde came to my end of the table and sat down in the last chair on the side facing me.

"You knew who she was."

"I don't need a teacher. I know how to draw." I opened the sketch pad back up. "I do! See! Everything's in patterns that make you look here." I touched his chalk face. "The book's parallel to the back of your head. The way your arm's bent echoes the top of your head. Your chin's a smaller echo. All of it makes a circle. It carries your eyes around the picture to see the book and then you. I made you move so it was like that. I know how to draw! I don't need a teacher!"

"You didn't know how to draw the light in the barn. You said you didn't. You said you didn't know how to paint either—and this is all gray and black. You even made the book black. It's red."

"It isn't all gray. Your eyes aren't! The gray in the rest makes it better. I made the book black to fix the circle—so your face would be the most important part. If the book was red you'd look at that instead of your face. Red would make the book important. It isn't. Just you liking it is! There's light! The book's reflecting it on your face just the way it was from the window." I closed the sketch pad and turned away ready to cry. "You said you wouldn't get mad!"

"I'm not mad, idiot!" He held my arm so I couldn't get up.

"You're always after me!"

"Yeah."

He said it so quietly, I looked up. He didn't look mad. He was smiling. I looked away, confused, wishing I hadn't tried to draw him again.

"You hate this one, too."

"No, silly." He let go of my arm and pulled the sketch pad away.

"Clyde!"

I clapped my hand over my mouth and looked up at the desk. The librarian was busy and hadn't heard me. Clyde had only taken the sketch pad to open it back up.

"Why are you so scared?" he asked.

"I'm not."

"Maybe." He put one elbow on the table, leaned his head on his hand, looked from me to the drawing and back again, smiling.

"It's terrific. I'd be an idiot to hate it."

I smiled, happy he'd quit fussing at me.

"There's chalk on your face," he said, reaching out to rub it off my cheek.

I pressed my face against the warmth of his hand. He laughed softly. Feeling awkward, suddenly, I looked down but kept my face against his hand. He slid his hand down over my hair, pulled some of it toward him. As I looked back up, I saw him close his eyes, put my hair against his face, turn his face against it.

I remembered how warm and safe I'd felt in his arms. The way I had when I was small and got hurt and Grandmother Burden held me. I smiled and looked back up into half-closed green eyes leaning toward me.

The bell rang. Clyde jumped and looked around with a startled expression as if he didn't know where he was. He let go of my hair, shoved the sketch pad toward me.

"I don't want to just see you here!"

I looked away, startled by the harshness in his voice.

"It's okay. Just . . ." He got up, touched my arm. "Come on, Claire."

I got up, too, confused. He'd turned away toward his book at the other end of the table. I pushed the chalk off the table into the box.

"You're mad at me."

"You're crazy," he said, turning back, taking my books and the chalk. "Just come on."

Walking down the road that afternoon, I wished school had lasted longer. I wished I could stay there with Clyde instead of going home. I was almost to the house when I saw someone sitting on the porch steps. I froze, scared it was Grandma. Then I saw no car was there, saw it was Mr. Beasley. He raised his hand, waved. I felt cold inside.

What if Grandma'd come and found him! She's worse than Mom about black people. She'd try to use him to get me from Mom. She'd make trouble for him!

I made myself go toward him. I saw he was smiling and tried to smile, too. I was almost to the porch before I saw the big, flat package. It was wrapped in white butcher's paper and tied with red string. Blumenthal's, the art supplies store in town, always did their packages up like that when I'd gone there for Daddy. I still felt scared and ashamed, too, but my eyes got wide.

Mr. Beasley laughed. "You already know what it is! There's no foolin' you! Open it, child! I know it's right!"

I looked away. "But I lied to you! I do have paper!"

"Not like this you don't! It's all right, child. I knowed you was upset. I got you stuff just to be sure you had plenty. You got to draw, child. You ain't goin' to be a fool and quit?"

"No," I said, hearing Grandma call Mom fool.

No. I won't be like Mom ever!

"That's what I want to hear. I want you mad at any fool that wants you to quit! Just look at what I got you!"

I tore off the paper and string. Inside were two huge pads of paper, one for chalk, one for watercolors. Underneath them were two of the thick, beautiful paper boards Daddy had used for watercolors. I hugged all of it against me, started laughing and crying, too.

"You're a picture!" Mr. Beasley said. "I never seen nobody laughin' and cryin', too! I knowed it was right! I waited around outside the store till I seen somebody lookin' at the paper like they'd know what kind you'd want. Then I went inside and asked her to help me. I told her I got me a grandchild needs it for a present! She was a nice lady. She talked to me about paper and drawin' for a long time. Said I ought to wait on gettin' this here." He reached out and tapped the thick paper boards. "But I told her my grandchild draws so good it's got to be special! I couldn't get you no more than two. They must think that stuff is gold, the way they keep it locked up in them little drawers. You know the ones I'm talkin' about?"

I nodded, remembering, as he held up two fingers to show their depth.

"I'll get you some more when I can."

I quit smiling. "You don't need to. This is wonderful." I tried to smile again, scared I'd hurt his feelings. "It's the nicest present I've ever gotten."

"It's the best one I give," he said, smiling. "You were happy enough to split."

He narrowed his eyes and stared at me. "The lady tellin' me about the paper, she's a teacher down to your school. Her name is Miss Joyce. I carried her stuff out to her car for her. She told me where she lives in town. Said if my grandchild wants to come by her house Saturday mornin's, she's goin' to be glad to help him draw. Said she don't need no money for it, he's got to be good if I have to buy paper for him like this here. You listenin' to me?"

I nodded, too scared to look at him.

He laughed. "You ain't got to worry! I ain't sendin' you to her Saturday for my grandchild! Joyces been livin' in Galway Fields a long time. You know her from town?"

I shook my head.

"The man in the store says she's been teachin' a long time. Says she's always buyin' stuff for her students, helpin' them. It's long past time somebody knowin' more than you was helpin' you. I learned my playin' from somebody knowin' more'n me. That's why I play so good. You draw good, child, and you're learnin' more every time I see you, but that don't mean you know it all."

"I can't," I begged. "Mom would . . ."

"You hush your mouth and listen. I ain't no fool that's goin' to cause you grief with her. You got some extra time in school?"

"But Mom . . ."

"Ain't goin' to know about it unless you tell her!"

"But . . ."

"But! But! But! Lord, we got some goats in the woods today! You be thinkin' about it. You got some friends at shcool. You get them to help you figure it out so the school ain't goin' to tell your momma."

I looked up, scared, remembered the lie I'd told him about the girls near town.

"You just think I'm the ghost," I said, sick inside but wanting him to stop talking about Miss Joyce.

"Naw, ghosts ain't nothin' but a bunch of nonsense. I don't take no stock in ghosts." His voice trailed off. I looked up and saw he was smiling, but looked sad, too.

"There's some around here that sure believes in 'em," he said, shaking his head. "Seein' you, I almost thought I was seein' one myself."

"The ghost in the mill?"

"There ain't no ghost down there! There wasn't nothin' mean enough in that woman to go hauntin' nobody, though God knows she had cause. I musta been nine years old the time she died. All the land here 'bouts was her husband's, then. My family'd been slaves on it a long time before me. They just stayed on it, workin'. My momma was workin' in the kitchen. She used to take me along to help her." He smiled to himself. "I wasn't much help to her after young Mrs. Adair married into the family and come to live there. I was always gettin' in trouble with old lady Adair, for sneakin' out in the front hall to listen on young Mrs. Adair playin' her piano. The last time she caught me, old Mrs. Adair said if I was always hangin' around, I could just as well be some use. She put me to work carryin' young Mrs. Adair's stuff around for her.

"I used to carry her drawin' stuff all over—down to the river, to the woods, out into the fields. She was always findin' wildflowers and drawin' 'em, same as you. Till her child was born. After that she had to work like the rest of 'em. Never got no more paper, no more paints. Her husband was the meanest man I ever seen, the way he treated her."

He shook his head. "My momma said she sewed, too. Said she come there with a bride's quilt all covered with 'broidery—flowers like my momma'd never seen, all over the top of it. I never seen her sewin' no flowers, just makin' clothes for her baby."

"You liked her," I told his smile, feeling warm and good inside.

He nodded. "She was good to me. She taught me readin' and writin'. She told me to keep after book learnin' so I could be what I wanted for myself. When I got too big to be followin' after her, she got Mr. Adair to put me to work in the barns 'stead of the fields. She was always kind and gentle. She told me if

I be kind, folks was goin' to be kind to me, too." He
looked away, out of the yard toward the river. "I can't
say they ever was to her, but I listened to her. I
learned to gentle the horses better'n anybody they
got. When her son growed up and sold off most of the
land, the new people was glad to have me workin'. I
been good enough to have myself time left over, for
playin' like I wanted, doin' what I wanted. Young
Mrs. Adair seen to it I got to be happy."

He looked back at me and smiled. "I was sure
happy watchin' her drawin'. I forgot how happy till I
seen you drawin', too."

I looked away.

I just remind him of her. He just wants to remember her.

"Watchin' you likin' my playin' and lookin' happy,
set me on thinkin' about bein' small and listenin' on
her playin' her piano. I wanted to do the same for you
as she done for me."

I felt surprised, remembered the way he'd smiled
when I'd said his music was beautiful.

He was still smiling at me. I felt strange inside.

"What you goin' to draw on that paper I got you?"

*When my drawings make him happy, I'm like the
ghost, too.*

"Something you'll like," I said.

He pushed himself up off the porch steps. "I'll be
waitin' to see it. I best get myself on home, now. You
be thinkin' on lettin' Miss Joyce help you, child. I'm
goin' to be thinkin' on it myself."

When he'd gone, I sat down on the steps where he'd
been. I closed my eyes so the good, warm feeling I
had inside wouldn't go away.

*With Grandmother I felt good inside, the way I do
now.*

I could almost see her cutting daffodils in her garden. I'd run out of the studio, angry and crying at
Daddy because he wouldn't look at what I'd been

trying to draw. Grandmother'd put down the daffodils, gather me up in her arms.

"Your daddy needs to draw," she'd said. "There's no sense in our worrying him while he is."

"But I want to draw, too!"

"You'll be able to!" She'd kissed me, smiled at me. "Didn't I name you for my sister Claire? Let's go upstairs and see her." She'd given me the flowers to carry.

When I was settled on Grandmother's lap in the rocker by her bed, she'd nodded her head at the portrait hanging above it.

"I named you Claire for her so you could be just like her, kind, gentle, loving, beautiful, and good. You already look like her. You have her eyes and her hair."

I'd looked up at the portrait, at the beautiful dark-haired young woman who seemed to be smiling at me.

"That's not me," I told Grandmother.

"No, but you'll be just like her. You'll draw just as well as she did. Promise me you'll try to be as good and gentle and kind as she was. Help your daddy so he can draw. Don't ever let anyone who doesn't understand bother him or keep him from drawing."

"I won't," I promised, leaning against her, feeling good and warm as her arms tightened around me. "I'll be just like her. Just like you."

Grandmother must have known she was dying. It wasn't long after that when I got up one morning and Daddy said he'd taken her to the hospital and she had died. I just went to bed one night and she covered me up and kissed me, and I never saw her again.

Daddy said I could have her room if I stopped crying.

I looked at the ugly, empty yard.

I tried to be like you and your sister Claire! I tried to take care of Daddy the way you did so he could draw. All those years since you died when I was seven, I tried to keep people from bothering him.

Why didn't you leave the house and money to him instead of me! So he could stay there and draw when they made me leave! Now he's just gone, too. Just like you were when I was seven!

I tried to take care of him! They wouldn't let me anymore!

I looked around, desperately, wanting to get the good feelings back. The beautiful paper Mr. Beasley'd brought me was sitting on the steps beside me.

I couldn't do what Grandmother wanted. Maybe I can do what Mr. Beasley wants.

He wants me to be like the ghost. I'll try to be as good, gentle and kind as she was.

I picked up the paper, ran inside.

Chapter Twenty-One

Mom didn't get me up Saturday morning. She'd already gone when I woke up. Looking at the ugly, clean kitchen, I couldn't keep from remembering the way she'd sounded talking about Grandmother Burden and Daddy. And crying. Most of the time when she cried like that she came home drunk. She hadn't been, but I'd heard her crying again during the night.

I remembered what Mr. Beasley said I had to do when she started drinking again and shuddered. The idea of telling her to bring her beer home to drink scared me.

I don't want her to drink.

Mr. Beasley said the ghost was kind. I want to be like her.

Grandmother Burden said her sister Claire was kind, and good and gentle. She said I should be like her.

Telling Mom to drink at home when she's said she wants to stop won't be kind.

I went back upstairs and got out the drawing paper Mr. Beasley'd given me. But sitting at the ugly, old table in my room made me think about Mom.

I wish I was with Clyde. I don't think about Mom then.

I closed my eyes wishing we could ride Adair again . . . to the barn. I could try to learn to draw the light. But I couldn't get across the river without Clyde.

I looked out the window, scared.

Mr. Beasley must know the barn's across the river.

He'll know I can't get across by myself. If he figures out I know Clyde! If he tells him about Mom!

I ran outside, through the woods to the pond. My drawing was gone. The rock was back in its place. I ran back home, scared Mr. Beasley'd come along and ask me.

Back upstairs, safe in my room, I stared at the paper he'd given me.

I hate lying! I hate it. It just makes a mess.

I can't stay here! I hate it here! If he comes back asking! If Grandma comes!

I grabbed my chalk and the new paper and ran back outside.

I'll go down to the mill. Mr. Beasley wouldn't go there. Clyde might be there.

In the empty clearing at the mill, I saw the stone platform and the rock we'd used to get on Adair. I knew those were things I wanted to draw. I sat down and dumped out my chalk. I soon had the mill's outline laid out on the beautiful paper.

The picture grew.

Mr. Beasley's right. I feel better, drawing. I love the sound the chalk makes. The way the oil in it makes it easy to blend the lines, give the drawing the softness the old logs and stones seem to have.

The mill was lovely with the river bright behind it. I wished I'd brought my watercolors so I could try to catch the river's glimmer. But I might make a mess of it. I'd never used watercolors, though Daddy often had. I wished I had black ink, too, for the edges of the slates on the roof.

I stopped drawing and stared at the mill. Mr. Beasley hadn't said how the ghost died in it. I felt cold inside. Daddy'd stopped once to draw a mill. He'd said most of them had burned, that flour or ground corn dust in the air was explosive, a spark from the stones would set the air on fire.

I shuddered.

Mr. Beasley loved her. I hope it wasn't fire!

I looked at my drawing. From outside, the mill didn't look as if it had burned. I was glad I hadn't looked at the walls when I'd been inside.

I made myself draw. The light was changing. I'd have to hurry before everything I saw changed, too.

I didn't draw the river. I couldn't figure out how to with just chalk. I put trees behind the mill instead.

Going home through the woods, I found the small white flowers, growing out of dead wood, that I'd seen the day Mom burned Daddy's drawings. I wondered if they were one of the kinds of wildflowers the ghost had loved and drawn.

I can't show the mill to Mr. Beasley. She died there. I'll come back and draw these for him.

I leaned down to touch the flowers.

If he asks how I drew the barn, I'll tell him I waded across at the ford. But I can show Clyde the mill. He'll like it. I know he will!

Sometime late that night Mom came home drunk. When I heard her crashing around downstairs, I wanted to run down there and hit her and hit her until she could never be drunk again. Then I remembered what Mr. Beasley'd said. I stayed in bed.

There was a loud crash from the kitchen. I heard Mom coming upstairs and froze. She turned on the light in her room and came toward my door. I lay with my face in my pillow, terrified, afraid even to breathe.

"Shhhh," she was saying.

The door creaked open. I didn't move. She sighed and started closing it.

"Still sleepin'," she muttered. "Still sleepin'. She catches me, she's goin' to hate me, too, just like ever'body else. Ever'body hates me! Even Claire's goin' to!" She sobbed as the door closed.

Over the pounding of my heart, I could hear her

stumbling back downstairs, sobbing. There were more noises from the kitchen. I lay still listening to them for a long time. I kept trying to keep Clyde's face in my head, but it wouldn't stay. Mom's crying made my anger at her jumbled up and horrible.

Sunday morning, the house was quiet when I woke up. I stayed in bed listening for a while. Then I got up and dressed as quietly as I could. I crept to the door and opened it slowly and carefully.

Mom was in bed asleep. There weren't any cans on the table by her bed, but the smell of beer was awful. I crept past her and downstairs. The kitchen was sloppy but clean. I couldn't find any empty cans.

I went outside and looked at the car. It was the same. She'd gotten home without hitting anything.

I opened the car door, gathered up the empty cans, and hid them in the trash pile. Then, I rolled down the car windows so the smell of beer would be gone if Grandma came.

I went back inside, got the dishpan, and went up to the apple trees.

As I picked, I tried to remember the things Mr. Beasley had said to tell her to make her bring her beer home. Instead the things she'd said at my door kept popping into my head.

"I don't want to care about her!" I screamed, throwing the half-filled pan away from me. I watched the apples go bouncing and rolling away.

That's a lie. I want her to care about me. To care enough to stop drinking. I want Mr. Beasley to be wrong. I can't stand being with her or caring about her unless she quits drinking and I never have to hear her crying again!

I took the empty pan back to the house. It was after eleven but still quiet. I wondered what time Mom'd come home.

I made some coffee and took a cup upstairs. As I put it on the table I saw something under her bed. It was a grocery bag. I knew it had to be more empty beer cans.

I crept away to the foot of the bed and looked at her.

She isn't beautiful, now.

I started back downstairs, then glanced back over at her. She was staring at me, looking scared. I tried to make myself smile.

"I brought you some coffee," I said. "There's more downstairs, but you don't need to get up yet."

"Got to do the wash."

"I'll start it. I should have done it yesterday."

I went on downstairs.

She's trying to hide it. She's scared I'll find out. Maybe I can pretend I don't know. But she'll have another wreck. I'll be at Grandma's if she does. I'd never see Clyde or Mr. Beasley again!

If I wanted to be near them, I'd have to do what Mr. Beasley said. He'd said I had to make her scared. She'd looked scared.

I made myself get busy. When the wash was started and I'd cleaned the bathroom, I went back in the kitchen.

Mom was sitting at the table with a cup of coffee. She was leaning over it looking miserable.

"Mom?"

When she looked up at me, I was terrified. I didn't go any closer. I made myself start talking.

"I don't want you to go back to Grandma's! She treats you awful! I don't want to go back there either, Mom! I want to stay here. But I'm scared you'll have another wreck. If you do, we'll be back at Grandma's! I don't want that! She hurts you! I'm scared she'd hurt me!"

Mom turned away.

"Do you want to go back there? Do you?" I screamed.

She shook her head, dumbly.

"Then bring it home to drink! Please! I wish you didn't want to drink, but if you have to, bring it home . . . so you won't get hurt!"

"I don't wann. . . ." She started wailing that horrible sound. "I tried to stop, Claire. I tried to!"

I was still terrified, but I remembered the ghost was gentle and kind and made myself go put my hand on her shoulder.

"I know you tried. Just bring it home. I don't want to go back to Grandma's. I don't want you to go back. She hurts you. She's mean."

Mom buried her face against me and sobbed. I was about to throw up. I made myself stay still and pat at her back the way she'd done when I was hurt.

"Claire! Claire!" she blubbered. "She keeps on callin' me at work. She keeps yellin' I ruined her chances. She says I got to come home, got to bring you to her, got to do for her, same as she's always done for me."

"No! She hasn't done anything for you!"

"She gets in my head! Yellin' at me! Hittin' at me! I can't get her out! I tried to stop drinkin'! I tried to!"

"Don't talk. Don't cry. I know you tried. Just bring it home."

"You'll hate me!" she wailed. "Ever'body hates me!"

"No," I said, knowing I would. "No."

When she was finally quiet, I backed away.

"I'm going to pick the apples," I said.

She nodded dumbly. She looked as if I'd beaten her. I felt sick inside. It had almost been nice before. It was nice having someone fix my breakfast and care whether I was there or not. I couldn't bear seeing her looking as if I'd beaten her, too.

"Mom. You want to go to a movie tonight?"

"Yes," she said, starting to cry again. "Yes. I'll bring it home. We can't go back to Momma's no more."

I ran outside, away from the sound. I'd done what Mr. Beasley'd said. I made myself pick apples.

When I finally went back to the house, Mom was busy scrubbing the kitchen floor.

"Your breakfast is ready. You didn't eat yet, did you?"

"No, I was waiting for you," I lied, wondering how I'd eat.

Going to the movies that evening, Mom almost seemed happy. I didn't say anything when we went to another Western. I just closed my eyes. The hero was dumb. He wasn't like Clyde at all. He wasn't nice. He wasn't even tall.

"Wasn't it wonderful?" Mom asked when we came out.

I looked down at the ice cream cone she'd gotten me.

I'll see Clyde tomorrow. I'll take him the drawing of the mill. He'll like it. He'll be my friend.

"Yes," I told Mom, beginning to feel safe again. "Did you like this one better than the other one?"

All the way home, Mom talked about the movie, the parts she liked best, wanted to see again. Tired, half asleep, not listening to her, I smiled back when she smiled, watched the lights of occasional oncoming cars light up her face.

Mom's beautiful.

I wondered what Daddy'd done with the paintings he'd made of her. I'd never seen any signs of them cleaning the house. I wondered if he'd sold them.

Clyde said I was out of a painting in a museum.

I felt funny remembering how tired I got sitting for Daddy.

I'm not like Mom. I won't be. I'll be like the ghost.

I looked away out the window. We were almost home. I closed my eyes, wished I was already in bed.

"No!" Mom yelled, slamming on the brakes, throwing me against the dashboard.

I landed against my hand, cried out.

"Claire? You okay, baby?" Mom'd turned toward me, reached out.

"What's wrong?" I cried.

"Look there," Mom said, sounding terrified. "Always ruinin' ever'thin'!"

Grandma's car was sitting in the yard. The lights were on in the house.

"You threw out the beer cans?" I asked.

"Yes," Mom said. "There ain't no more left in the 'frigerator for her to find neither. What're we goin' to do, Claire? What're we goin' to do?"

"We can go back to town, come back later."

"She'd just wait!" Mom started to cry.

"No! You're bigger than she is. You don't have to let her hurt you!"

Mom turned to look at me.

"You don't! She's got no right to!"

Mom looked back at the house. "She's seen us!

Grandma had come outside, was coming toward the car.

"Get out of the car," I said. "We'll tell her we don't want her here. Tell her she's got no right to go in our house like that!"

"But . . ."

"Now!" I said. "Before she gets here! I'll help you. She can't hurt both of us!"

Mom pushed open the door. I slid out of the car behind her.

"Where you been, fool?" Grandma yelled, as she got to the front of the car. "I been waitin' here for hours!"

"We been to the movies," Mom said, moving behind me.

"Takin' that child with you while you play the fool! I come to get her. You're drunk as a pig!" Grandma yelled, coming around the car toward us.

"She's not!" I screamed, scared, hating Mom for just standing there behind me. "You stay away from her!"

"You shut up!" Grandma yelled. "I've heard enough

of your mouth. Go get in the car! I'm takin' you to town!" She hit out at me.

"No!" Mom screamed, yanking me out of the way. "You leave my baby alone! You get out of here! Always meddlin'! We don't need you! We don't want nothin' from you!"

Grandma drew back her arm. Mom slapped her, screamed, "Get out of here! We don't need you meddlin'. We got us a home!"

Grandma backed away from her.

"Get out of here!" Mom screamed, advancing on her. "Get out of here!"

I grabbed Mom's arm. She stopped beside me.

"Hittin' your momma!" Grandma yelled. "I ought to kill you!"

"You come tryin' to take my baby again, I'll kill you!" Mom screamed. "We got us a home! We don't want you meddlin' no more!"

"Mom!"

Mom put her arm around me. We stood there watching Grandma go get in her car, start it, drive up the road.

"She's gone," Mom said, staring at the empty road. "She's gone, Claire!"

"Yes! I told you! I . . ."

Mom took her arm away. "She's goin' to kill me. I hit my momma. She's goin' to kill me!" She turned from me toward the house.

"No, Mom!"

She started inside. I followed her. In the kitchen, she looked at me, stunned, shocked. She looked around the clean, ugly little room.

"I got me a home," she said, "and now Momma's goin' to kill me."

"No! She'll leave you be, now. She was scared of you!"

"No!" Mom started crying. "Momma ain't scared of nothin'."

"Get a phone," I said, desperately. "If she comes back, we can call the sheriff. He'd make her leave you be."

"No! I don't want no phone. Momma'd always be callin' me, worryin' me all the time, like she does at work. I'd never get no peace."

I turned away, sick inside. "You stood up to her. She'll leave you be."

"You stood up to her, too, and she was goin' to hit you. It don't do no good, baby. Once Momma makes up her mind to get somethin' she won't leave off. Leastways she won't be back tonight. She knows I ain't got no beer, knows the store's closed."

"Mom . . ." I tried to put my hand on her shoulder but she pushed it away.

"Go to bed, baby. I'm so tired."

Chapter Twenty-Two

Monday, when Clyde and I had finished eating lunch, I pulled my notebook toward me, opened it, and unfolded the mill drawing. He leaned over against me to see what it was.

"Hey, that's beautiful! When did you do it?"

"Saturday."

"I wish I'd been there. That's crazy, the way you did the logs. What happened to the river?"

I'd just been leaning against his shoulder, not thinking, feeling warm and safe.

"Huh?" He moved away and looked down at me.

"What?" I asked uncomfortably, looking away.

"Why didn't you do the river?"

"I was tired when I got to it. I didn't want to. I just put trees instead."

"We'll go back this afternoon so you can finish it."

"It is finished."

"Claire? Look at me."

"What?" I asked, not looking.

"You didn't know how to do the water, right?"

"It's all right if you don't like it," I said, reaching out for the drawing. He yanked it away.

"No. You're not tearing it up. I do like it, idiot. I told you it was beautiful. But you're lying. You don't know how to do the water, just like you didn't know how to do the light in the barn."

"I do," I said, desperately.

"Okay. I'll go get your chalk out of your locker and you can show me."

"No. I don't want to."

"Because you don't know how. Miss Joyce would show you."

"No."

"That's dumb! You love to draw. You said you wished you knew how to paint. It's stupid not to let her teach you."

"I can't."

"You have to. Mrs. Carter said Miss Joyce is usually in her room at lunch." He refolded the drawing and closed my notebook. "Come on. We'll get your sketch pad out of your locker. I'll go with you." He held out my notebook.

"No," I said, pushing it away.

He set it back on the table and got up. "Okay then. If you're stupid and won't let anyone help you . . ."

"I let you help me . . . with algebra."

"Dammit, you don't even like algebra! You let me help you because I wanted to!" He towered over me, angry. I looked away.

"No, I wanted you to."

"You hate algebra. When are you going to let someone help you with something you like!"

"You let me draw you."

"Not anymore. Go see her now or forget it!"

I looked up. He wasn't smiling. He was huge. He looked mad. I looked back down at the bandage on my hand, ready to cry, wanting him back like he was.

"That wouldn't be helping me."

"Sometimes you're just plain crazy! Okay! Be stubborn! Just forget it!"

He started away.

"Clyde!"

He didn't look back. He went to the stairs, up them, out through the double doors, was gone. Margie followed him up the steps.

I looked down at my notebook. Margie was in history class, study hall, English.

She's not crazy.

He won't like me anymore!

Even if I tell him why I can't, he won't!

I wished it was Wednesday, wished I could get home, go find Mr. Beasley.

But he's after me about Miss Joyce, too. He'd be mad at me, too.

I closed my eyes, tried to see Grandmother Burden, tried to see my house, tried to see Daddy.

Mr. Beasley said he'd try to find Daddy.

I opened my eyes.

I don't want Daddy! I want Mr. Beasley and Clyde!

Upstairs, I stood outside the closed door of the art room and hoped Miss Joyce wouldn't be there. I raised my hand to knock, but couldn't. I tried the knob. It turned so I pushed on it. The door swung open and banged.

Miss Joyce was sitting at her desk, reading. She looked up, startled. I was trapped.

"Hi," she said, smiling. "Can I help you with something?"

Scared and ready to run, I made myself nod.

"Why don't you come in so we can talk about it?"

I made myself walk toward her as she got up.

"You're . . . ?"

"Claire Burden."

She nodded. "And?"

"I don't know how to draw water and sunlight. I have to find out . . . how . . . Mrs. Carter said . . ." I looked down unable to go on and wishing I'd die. She was just staring at me.

"You're the girl with the flowers . . . who was drawing them in her class?"

I looked back up, surprised. She was still smiling. It was a nice smile like Mr. Beasley's.

Her eyes are gentle.

"See . . . I . . ." I made myself open my notebook, take out and unfold the mill drawing. "I didn't know how to do the water! It's all wrong!"

She took the drawing and put it down on her desk, leaned over it, moved back to see it better.

"No, it isn't all wrong. But you're right. It needs the water. The trees were farther back . . . about there, weren't they?"

I looked to see where she was pointing, felt surprised and nodded.

"The rest of it's very good. I like the angle you picked. Most people would have done it straight on . . . made the mill front a flat box. This is much nicer. It shows me more about it. The composition's excellent. Someone's already worked with you a lot?"

"My father."

She smiled. "That must have been fun. You've got talent."

I felt funny inside.

The last time I showed Daddy something, he said I didn't have any talent. He said it was terrible and I was no artist at all.

"Isn't he still helping you?"

I shook my head.

She looked back down at my drawing. "This is lovely, but it's lonely, too. Looking at it, I think you were missing someone very much."

I nodded. It hadn't been Daddy. "How can you see that?"

"The mill's abandoned. There's so much gray and black. You do know how to do sunshine. There's some near the woods."

"I meant the kind that seems to be touching something."

She nodded, smiling. "You love to draw, don't you?"

"Yes," I said, not as scared anymore.

"I do, too. It would be fun helping you. All your classes are filled?"

"Except study hall."

"None of the others are electives you could change?"

"No." I knew I'd have to get Mom's permission to change a regular class. Now, I was scared again. "I could come at lunch."

"You need to eat lunch. When's your study hall?" She reached for a note pad on her desk.

"Sixth period."

"Good! That's my free period. I can concentrate on you instead of a class. It's too bad you can't take it for credit now."

I made myself watch her write the note.

"I've already made plans for the sixth period today," she continued, "but give this to your study hall teacher and come on up, tomorrow. We'll start with water or that kind of light you like. I'm sure there're lots of other things, too."

"Can you mix mediums? I mean, could I have done the water in watercolors, and the rest in chalk and ink? Would it work on this kind of paper?"

"We'll find out tomorrow," she said, smiling. She picked the drawing up and looked at the back of the paper. I felt scared inside, wondering if she remembered Mr. Beasley.

"This is nice paper. It would work. If you've got more, you can try it yourself tonight. You'll bring me what you do? So I can show you where it went wrong if you run into trouble?"

I nodded. She was still smiling. She'd said it would be fun.

Daddy almost never smiled. It was never fun with him.

Miss Joyce went to the door with me. "We have plenty of supplies here. You don't need to bring your own things unless you'd like to."

"Thanks," I said, suddenly feeling good inside.

"Sure. I'll see you tomorrow."

I almost ran downstairs to look for Clyde. The bell

rang. He wasn't anywhere in the hall. I went to history. He wasn't in the room. Nobody was.

I sat down, suddenly tired and not feeling good anymore. I leaned over my desk, put my elbows on it, and my hands on both sides of my face so no one would see.

"Hey." The desk in front of mine bumped mine as he sat down. I moved my hands, made fists on my forehead, so he couldn't see I was crying.

"Stop it," he said, touching my hair. "Stop it. Stop it."

"You just walked off!"

"I had to. I was waiting up there. It wasn't awful. She was nice. You liked her so much you didn't even see me."

"You came up there?"

"Yes."

"You didn't think I'd go."

"No, I was scared you didn't like me enough to go."

"It was mean to make me."

"It wasn't. She's nice and you liked her. Stop crying, Claire." He gently tugged at my hair. "You're going to cry till we get to your house?"

I looked up, startled. "It's Monday! Mom's home!"

He looked away. "I'm sorry. I forgot. It made you quit crying, anyway."

I looked back down.

"Claire?" He tugged at my hair again. He'd put a strand of it across his face. "You like my mustache?" he asked, making a face.

"You look silly," I said, laughing at him, and wiping at my eyes.

"I feel silly. You like me anyway?"

I nodded.

"You wish . . . it wasn't Monday?" He looked down and began tracing the lines of tape on the bandage on my hand.

"Yes, I wish it wasn't Monday."

Chapter Twenty-Three

I didn't want to go home after school. I'd left Mom in bed sleeping that morning. I was scared she'd decided to drink all day. I didn't want to find her like that.

Instead, she was stretched out on the sofa, reading. She looked up, surprised, when I came in.

"Gawd, is it that late? I went upstairs to clean your room, but I saw this. I thought I'd try it. The day just went."

She held the book up for me to see. It was one of my dog books. I hoped I didn't look scared.

"Do you like it?" I made myself ask.

"No, it's real stupid. It's about a dog." She looked back down at it. She was less than halfway through.

"Want me to clean my room?"

"No. I didn't see nothin' that needed doin'. You keep it real nice. It's awful plain, though."

She looked at the pile of books I was still holding. "You gotta lot of work to do?"

I nodded, hoping she'd send me upstairs to do it.

"Dunno why you wanted to take all that college stuff. There ain't no way you can go. Can't see no-body wantin' to, no way." She got up and put the book on the sofa. "Won't take me long to fix supper. Ain't you got nothin' better'n this to read?"

I shook my head. The dog stories were the closest thing I had to her movies.

Mom went in the kitchen. I took my books upstairs and closed the door behind me. The dog book had been in the middle of the top shelf of the little book-case.

Listening carefully for her, I took four books off the

bottom shelf and got my chalk out from behind them. I put the books back in and looked around the room. Then I went over to the dresser and slowly slid the bottom drawer all the way out.

The picture I'd done of Clyde at the Saxon barn was still under it. I touched it, wanted to look at it, wished Mom was at work.

She might come upstairs.

I was too scared to take out the picture. I put my chalk in beside it and carefully slid the drawer back in. Then I sat down on my bed and tried to stop shaking.

I hate Mondays. If she's sober and doesn't have anything to do, she'll be poking into everything!

I fought to keep from crying. She'd see if I did. She'd ask why. I made myself go downstairs and help her get dinner.

All through dinner Mom talked about the dog book.

"Can we get a dog?" I asked, thinking about Jake, wishing I could touch his coat, hear him moo.

"For what?" Mom said. "They're filthy creatures. They track up the house and eat. They don't do nothin'. I can't even feed you right. What'd I want with a dog to feed, too?"

I nodded, sorry I'd asked.

"My daddy used to have one. Momma made him keep it out in the shed. He used to take up for it when Momma was after it. He never took up for me! I don't want no dog! I was glad when Momma got rid of it."

I don't want a dog. As long as I have to be with her, I don't want a dog.

After dinner Mom went back to reading. I went upstairs to do my homework. When I was through, I stayed up there. I was too scared to get out my chalk and watercolors and try them the way Miss Joyce had suggested. Mom'd hear me getting water. She might come see what I was doing.

I wish she worked every day.

I kept reading my history over again.

Finally, I drew Clyde in pencil in the back of my notebook. I left my history book open. If Mom came upstairs, I could pretend I was still studying. As I drew him, I tried to remember how I'd felt on his lap.

When I got up to the art room Tuesday afternoon, some of the kids from the last class were still there talking to Miss Joyce. I felt scared again, suddenly, and stayed at the door afraid to go in.

The room was huge. It wasn't as pretty as the studio at Galway Hall, but it had north windows, too. It also had skylights, with shades on them. All of one side wall was cabinets. Some were open. I could see all kinds of art materials inside, including a whole rack of narrow drawers for paper boards.

There were tables at that end of the room. At the other, a closet door was open. I could see a kiln inside. I wondered how clay felt under your fingers, if you could catch things in it the same way as with chalk on paper.

Most of the room was full of easels. There were several model stands, one low, wide one, one to lean on, another to sit on.

Several of the students were coming out laughing and talking. I backed up out of their way. Miss Joyce was coming to the door, too. She was still talking to a girl older than me. When she saw me, she smiled. I tried to smile back.

"Hi, Claire. Jeannie, this is Claire. She's going to be coming up during study hall."

Jeannie nodded at me. "During your free period? I'm green!"

Miss Joyce laughed. "I'll see you tomorrow. Try that tonight, will you?"

"If I get time. Tony's coming over. 'Bye!" She hurried off down the hall. I watched her go, looked back at Miss Joyce. She was still watching Jeannie, frowning. She looked back at me and smiled.

"Jeannie's one of my best students. I've been trying to talk her into going to college, but she's not interested. Are you?"

I nodded. "I want to go to college."

"Good. But that's a way off yet, isn't it? Which would you like to do first? Water or sunlight?"

"Water. I don't know how to use watercolors, either."

"You do have some though?" She was smiling.

"They weren't for a friend. That day . . . at the school store. I'm sorry, I . . ."

"It just took time to get up your courage?"

"Yes."

"We'll work on that, too," she said. She looked concerned, reached out for my bandaged hand. "What happened?"

I jerked my hand away. "It's just a cut! It's all right . . ." I felt myself turning red. "My mom just put on too big a bandage . . . to keep it clean."

She smiled and nodded. "Moms'll do that. Now, let's see about water, okay?"

"All right," I agreed, relieved she'd believed me.

We started working. She didn't just tell me what to do and go off to her own work the way Daddy had. She set up an easel beside mine. She showed me how to do something. Then she stayed there, watching, and stopped me whenever I started to make a mistake, and showed me again.

Daddy'd just told me what to do and gone off. He wouldn't look at anything until I was through. Then he fussed at all the things I'd done wrong.

"That's good. You catch on quickly!"

I smiled back at Miss Joyce. At home, when I'd finally gotten something, Daddy'd just nodded at it and told me what to do next.

I was surprised and upset when the bell rang. I looked up at the clock. It seemed as if ten minutes had gone by, not fifty.

"We accomplished a lot today," Miss Joyce said. "In a class we wouldn't have gotten past the first step. It's much more fun when no one has to wait. Do you think you'll remember how to practice some of the things we've done when you get home?"

"Yes. It was fun," I said, looking away, feeling shy of her.

"It was, wasn't it? I lost track of the time. I'll clean up today so you won't be late for your next class. To-morrow, we'll have to watch the time."

"All right," I said, not wanting to leave the beautiful room.

"Don't forget to bring me anything you try. I'd like to see it!"

"I won't forget."

Clyde was coming up the stairs to meet me. He laughed when he saw me. "You really hated it!"

"Don't," I said, embarrassed.

"It was fun?"

"Yes! The room's beautiful! It's almost like the studio at home. It isn't as pretty, but it's . . ." I stopped because he looked funny.

"At home? You don't have a studio at home."

I looked away. "In town . . . at my grandmother's . . . where I used to live . . . before I came out here."

"You were happy there?"

I nodded, feeling strange inside. I wasn't sure I had been happy there anymore, but I'd always thought I was.

"You wish you were back there, Claire?" He sounded awkward, suddenly, and started downstairs.

"No, not if I wouldn't see you. What did you do in study hall?"

"I read my book and missed you."

I stopped and looked up at him.

"It's okay. Just don't go at lunchtime, too. I'd never see you." He tugged at my arm, kept on downstairs.

"It isn't Monday."

"It may as well be," he said, disgustedly. "Mom's picking me up after school to go to town."

"For what?" I asked, stopping again.

"You didn't notice?" He stuck his arm out and I saw his shirt sleeve and sweater didn't even come up to his watch. "I'm growing!"

"I like you tall." I reached out to touch his gray sweater, wishing it hadn't gotten too small.

"You better. You have enough chalk and stuff? You want me to get you some?"

I shook my head, felt myself turn red.

"You're not just saying that?"

"No, Miss Joyce said she'd give me what I needed."

"Come on, we'll be late to class."

"I don't care," I said, but I followed him on downstairs.

When I got up the next morning, Mom was still in bed. The cans were gone but I could smell the beer. I reset the alarm clock and put it by her bed. She didn't stir. There was another grocery bag under her bed.

I got my things and went downstairs. She'd left a note on the table and a dollar. I wished it was a hundred dollars so I could run away and never come back, never worry about Grandma or her again.

I picked up the note. *I brung it home,* it said.

I shredded it and shredded it until the pieces were too small for me to tear anymore. Then I gathered them up, took them out to the bathroom and flushed them down the toilet.

When I turned away, I saw a bright red plastic hairbrush beside the sink. My old silver-backed brush that Grandmother had given me was gone. I nearly ran upstairs after Mom to find out what she'd done with it. Instead, I frantically searched through the trash in the bathroom and the kitchen.

I found it on the garbage heap out back. I cleaned it off and hid it in the shed under a crate in the corner. Then, I went back inside.

Brushing my hair, I knew I'd hate her every time I used the plastic brush. I threw it across the room against the wall.

She did it for me. She got it for me because she thought it was pretty.

She threw my old brush away because it reminds her of Grandmother. She doesn't want me to be like her. I don't want to be like Mom!

Will she throw me away, too, if I'm not?

I picked up the brush and put it on the counter. Back in the kitchen I gathered up my books and the dollar. I didn't want any breakfast. I hadn't fixed my lunch. I would just buy it.

I ran up the road to wait for the bus. When it pulled up, when I saw Clyde smiling, I stopped being scared.

He got up so I could sit by the window, and he could put his feet out in the aisle. He kept smiling as if he had a secret. Once the bus was moving again, he took my bandaged hand.

"When's that coming off anyway?"

"Pretty soon."

"Is it going to be scarred?" He traced the tape around my hand.

"Some. That tickles." I tried to pull my hand away but he wouldn't let go.

"I got you something in town."

"Why? I mean . . ."

"I wanted to. I'll give it to you at lunch. What's wrong?"

"Nothing. It's just . . . Mom got me something and now you have, too. It isn't my birthday."

"That's okay. What'd your mom get?"

"A brush," I said, wishing I could tell him about it.

"To paint with?"

"No, for my hair."

He laughed. "A hairbrush isn't a present."

"She thought it was. It doesn't matter. What did you get me?"

"If you stop asking questions, you'll see at lunch."

At lunch, I sat looking at the silver chain Clyde'd taken out of his pocket and handed to me. There was a flat disk at the end with my name on it.

"You don't like it," he said.

"I do!" I said, struggling to keep from crying. "It's beautiful! I want it! But Mom . . ."

"Damn! I'm an idiot! I didn't think about that. I was waiting for Mom and saw it. I got it because it was pretty and I wanted it for you. I forgot about her. You want me to take it back?"

"You can't. My name's on it." I looked up and saw he looked miserable. The chain was long enough to slip over my head. I put it on.

"But . . ."

"I'll hide it. She won't see it."

He still looked worried. "I don't want her mad at you."

I looked away remembering he'd thought Mom'd found out he'd come to the house and been mad at me.

"She won't be. It's beautiful." I touched the chain, the disk with my name. "I'll wear it inside my shirt. Nobody'll know I have it."

"But me," he said. "I'll know."

I nodded, feeling warm and good inside.

That afternoon, looking for drawings to take to Mr. Beasley, I found the apples I'd drawn after Clyde and I'd been to the Saxon barn. I felt happy again, seeing them. I put that drawing on top of my papers and went to the pond.

Mr. Beasley was already there, playing in the afternoon sunshine. He stopped and put his hand out for my papers. His smile got bigger looking at the drawing.

"You were happy doin' this here. I can feel it just lookin' on it, same as I feel the sunlight fallin' on me. You fulla sunshine, child. You just got to keep it safe way down inside yourself where your momma can't get it. She been drinkin' much?"

I looked down, ashamed for thinking he'd been wrong, and nodded. "I did what you said. She said she'd drink it at home. She did."

"How much is she drinkin'? Enough to get her fired?"

I shook my head, wishing I could ask him how to get Grandma to leave us alone.

"You keep yourself safe from her, child. You been workin' hard in school. Most of these papers're lookin' right good."

He put the apple drawing back on top. "I like that the best. I was likin' the barn you left me best till I seen this here. I put the barn up on the wall at home. That ol' barn's so old, time's just forgot it and left it standin'. Lookin' on it, I 'most feel like time's goin' to forget me, too. Seein' this here makes me happy like you musta been drawin' it." He frowned.

"I went to see Miss Joyce," I said, quickly, scared he was going to ask how I got across the river. "I went Monday."

"Yeah?" His face lit up, and he laughed with pleasure. "You did! Is she goin' to teach you?"

"Yes!"

I told him about it. How nice Miss Joyce was. How good she was showing me. How much I liked the room and wished I could be there more. When I'd run out of things to say, we just sat looking at the sunlight on the pond.

"She'll teach me to draw light like that, and water," I said.

"I'd like to see that. Sunshine just like you. What you want me to play for you?"

"Play me the one about the baby crying and the ghost's song," I asked, remembering the mill drawing and wishing I could show it to him, too.

Mr. Beasley laughed. "She wasn't no ghost. She was flesh and blood same as you. Are you goin' to cry if I play the other one for you?"

"Only because I'm happy," I said.

"S'all right then if you do. I don't mind that kind of cryin'."

I could hear the song in my dreams that night.

Chapter Twenty-Four

Friday afternoon, I ran upstairs to the art room, happy. All week I'd had fun with Miss Joyce. I could almost paint the water in Mr. Beasley's pond now. Today we'd start sunlight on water.

As I got to the door, the last kids were leaving. Miss Joyce was there with Jeannie, the girl she'd been talking to the first time I'd come during study hall.

Miss Joyce tried to smile, but looked upset. "Excuse us a minute, Claire, would you? I need to talk to Jeannie."

When I nodded, she closed the door and went back inside. I waited forever, not hearing anything, afraid she'd forgotten me. At last the door burst open. Jeannie ran out, crying. I looked after her, wondering what was wrong.

"Come in, Claire."

Miss Joyce looked mad. She usually left the door open. This time she closed it behind us.

"I could come back Monday," I said, scared.

"No. I need to do some drawing."

"Something's wrong?" I asked.

"Plenty. Jeannie's pregnant. She was going to quit school and get married. Idiot!" she said, angrily. "She could do so much, Claire! She has talent! She loves drawing! Now she'll just quit . . . have half-a-dozen kids and won't even be happy married to that immature . . ." She stopped. "I'm sorry. I'm terribly angry."

"You don't like boys?"

She looked surprised. "Boys are fine! It's being stupid that isn't! It's having talent and just throwing it away that I don't like! What do you do Saturdays?"

Her blue eyes were like Mr. Beasley's. I couldn't look away from them.

"I help Mom at home."

She nodded. "You live near town?"

"No."

"Would she bring you in? A friend of mine and I have been teaching together on Saturdays. He knows much more than I do. I'd like him to work with you."

"We don't have any money for a teacher."

"He wouldn't charge you. I took your mill drawing to him. He was very impressed. He's a professor at the university, Claire."

She smiled.

I looked away from the blue eyes. "Mom works Saturdays."

"She could bring you in when she goes to work."

"I'd have to talk to her," I said, wanting to run.

"I'll be glad to. I tried to call last night, but you aren't in the book."

"We don't have a phone."

"I could reach her at work?"

"She's a waitress. Her boss gets mad if people call her at work."

"Then I'll write her a note." She went to her desk.

I stayed still, terrified, wondering how I'd get out of it.

She came back smiling. "I won't expect you tomorrow, okay? You may read the note if you like."

"Mom's tired Saturdays."

"Probably so. Being a waitress is hard work. It's good that you help her at home." She looked tired, suddenly. "Jeannie'll end up doing something like that. Without finishing school, she'll never be able to get a good job when she needs one. I put my phone number on the note and asked your mother to call me."

I tried to nod, sick inside.

The period was too far gone for painting. I stood up.

"I'm sure I can convince your mother. Now, I'd better go see if Jeannie got to class all right," Miss Joyce said, sighing. "She's going to have enough trouble as it is. I mustn't make it worse for her."

She went downstairs with me. Without thinking, I went in the library. Clyde was sitting by himself at our table, reading. I went back outside quickly, before he could see me, and down the hall to the girl's bathroom.

I read Miss Joyce's note. The things she said about me were wonderful. I wished I could keep it, could show it to Clyde and Mr. Beasley. I tore it up carefully and flushed the pieces down the toilet.

It was cold when I got up Saturday morning. Mom had already gone to work, but she'd built a fire in the stove in the living room. It was warm in there. In the kitchen, I looked in the refrigerator to see if she'd gotten milk.

There was just beer.

I went back in the living room and sat down. I stared at the stove wondering what I'd do Monday. I couldn't go back to Miss Joyce. I wondered if she'd get Mom's number at work from the office and call her. I wondered what Mr. Beasley would tell me to do.

I saw I'd picked at the bandage until it had come off my hand. The place was as red and ugly as some of the scars on Mom's arms.

I heard someone come up on the porch. Terrified it was Grandma, I crept to the window, peeked out. It was Clyde. I ran to the door and opened it. He'd just raised his hand to knock. He looked startled.

I flung my arms around him. "I'm so glad to see you!"

"Claire?" He put his arms around me.

I pressed my face against his sweater, remembered how safe I'd felt.

His arms tightened around me.

"It's freezing. Come inside," I said.

He let go of me. I took his hand, pulled. He came inside, closed the door. When he sat down on the sofa, I laughed, happy he was there. I sat down next to him, pulled the chain he'd given me out from under my sweater, and leaned against him. He smiled at me with green eyes. I reached up and touched his face. He put his arm around me, leaned down, and kissed me. I leaned against him, happy.

"It isn't green, but it's warm," I said.

"What? You're being silly." He put his other arm around me.

"No. It isn't green like the greenhouse, here."

"Oh," he said.

"It's ugly. But it doesn't matter. You're here. Your eyes are green." I kissed him, put my head against his chest, stared at the stove. There was a crack where the door didn't close properly. I could see flames inside.

"What happened to the ghost?" I asked, scared, watching the flames. "How did she die?"

"She hanged herself."

No! Not Mr. Beasley's friend!

"It was the ghost's greenhouse? That's why you wanted me to see it?"

"No, silly. It wasn't her greenhouse. Her son, my granddad, built it. It's pretty. You'd like it."

"But you said you hated it!"

"That doesn't matter. I wouldn't anyway if you were there."

"It does matter!" I said, thinking about Mom's hating drawing. "Why do you hate it?"

"I don't really. It just used to make me mad. Granddad used to spend all his time out there. He never wanted to do anything else. He didn't care about anything else. When Mom was little, he sold off most of the farm. He expected Grandma to take care of Mom with the money from that and just leave him alone to do what he wanted in his glass cage!"

Scared, I pressed my face into his sweater.

"The only time he knew Mom was alive was when she helped him in the greenhouse."

"Your mom hated him, too?"

"No, she felt sorry for him. He was just a pathetic old man." He tightened his arms around me. "Mom's not like him. But your mom is. I hate her! I wish she'd take care of you."

I jerked away from him. "She does take care of me!"

"She doesn't. You can't have any friends. You even have to hide that." He reached out to touch the chain he'd given me. "There's something weird about her."

"There isn't!"

"There is! You can't go to my house. . . . Why were you so scared of Miss Joyce?"

"I hate her! I wish I'd never gone! She's just like you! Always after me! Always asking questions . . . trying to make me—!" I shut up, scared.

"What?" Clyde demanded, taking my arm. "What is she after you to do?"

I pushed him away. "Be mean to Mom!"

"Mean to her? How?"

I jumped up and ran outside, away from him and the fire.

"Claire!" He ran after me, caught me. "Tell me! What would be mean to her?"

"Drawing!" I yelled, trying to yank away from him. He let go.

"Drawing! Claire, you idiot, your drawing's not mean . . ."

"It is. Mom hates drawing! She ought to hate it! You're just like Daddy! Miss Joyce is, too. All you care about is me drawing! You don't care about me!"

"Claire? I do!"

"You don't. Daddy was mean to Mom! He never cared about her! He was the one like your granddad, not Mom! She ought to hate him and drawing, too! Just leave us be!" I screamed. I turned to run back inside.

"Claire!" He tried to grab my arm, accidentally caught the chain. I yanked away so hard, the chain broke. He stood staring at me, shocked.

"I hate you!" I ran inside and slammed and locked the door.

"Claire!" he yelled, pounding on it. "Stop it! Open the door!"

I ran upstairs and slammed my door, too.

After a while the banging stopped. I just sat on my bed, confused, rubbing my neck, not knowing why I'd acted the way I had.

It's Mom I hate, not him. He's right. I can't have any friends unless I hide them from her. I can't even have my old brush or the chain. I can't draw or do anything I want unless I lie and trick people. I always have to be scared Mom'll find out, or Clyde, or Mr. Beasley, and Grandma'll come after me.

I was freezing. I went back downstairs, out on the porch. He was gone. The chain was gone. I went back inside, curled up on the sofa and stared at the flames until I couldn't see them anymore.

Mom woke me up when she came home. She had a grocery bag that looked as if it was beer, but smelled good.

"You was waitin' up for me?" she asked, smiling.

I tried to nod.

I have to be like the ghost. Mr. Beasley said so. I have to be good, kind, and gentle.

"Come on in the kitchen," Mom said. "Joe fixed me some supper, 'cause the boss went home early. Joe had to go too, so I brung it home."

I followed her in there, starving.

"Joe's a good cook. I wish he was the boss." She sat down, pulled off her shoes.

"You look tired," I said, feeling tired.

"I am. Half of town must of come in there tonight. I'm glad I don't have to work tomorrow. The boss misses part of a day, he thinks he has to yell twice as much to make up for it."

"He must be awful."

"He is. I'm goin' to eat myself some supper, have myself a bath and get to bed." She looked around the ugly kitchen. "I been wishin' we could get us a TV."

"They cost too much," I said without thinking.

"Yes." She looked miserable. "Everything costs too much."

"I don't mind not having one. If you wanted one maybe we could find a used one. They'd have to be cheaper."

"Still too much."

"We could save for one."

"I guess." She smiled at me. "I could put some of my tips aside."

"Do you have a little box? An old jewelry box or something?"

"I'll go see."

She came back downstairs a little bit later with a small, cardboard box about three inches square. I felt sick inside remembering the way I'd screamed at Clyde, thrown the chain at him.

"Here," I said, taking it. I got a knife and made a slit in the top. Then I got the leftover tape from bandaging my hand and taped the box shut. With a pencil, I wrote *Mom's TV* around the slit in big letters.

He'll hate me, now.

I started drawing flowers on the sides of the box.

Mom slapped me so hard I dropped the box and pencil. I stared at her terrified, dazed, and dizzy. Her face had gone white.

"Oh, God!" she screamed. "I didn't mean to, Claire. Forgive me!" She burst into tears. "Forgive me!" she wailed. "Ever'thin's been so good, Claire. Don't make it bad!"

I stayed still, frozen and scared.

"Don't ever do that, Claire. Don't ever draw! You got to promise me you won't! Never!" She groped in her purse until she found her cigarettes and lit one. Her hands were shaking.

"I was just trying to make it pretty," I begged. "I was making it for you."

"That don't make it pretty! All them flower drawin's all over the house that Mrs. Burden's sister made! You sittin' there lookin' like that paintin' of her!" She drew in her breath, shuddered. "You was makin' me somethin'. But you can't draw! There ain't nothin' pretty about it. You best go to bed. I'm tired, Claire. Momma's been after me again, threatenin' to come get you, yellin' I'm not fit. Don't you go gettin' on me too. You got to promise me you won't draw."

I tried not to stare at her trembling cigarette. "I won't," I told the cigarette. "I promise I won't."

"Go to bed, baby. You got to be tired. I'm tired. I'm so tired."

I lay upstairs, scared, listening for a long time, wondering if she was drinking. The house was quiet.

The ghost killed herself! Mr. Beasley's ghost. Clyde's great-grandmother . . . she hanged herself in the mill.

When I got up the next morning, her bed was empty. I went downstairs. She was passed out on the sofa. I went back in the kitchen and sat down at the table. The little box was still sitting there. She'd put tape around the sides, sloppily, where I'd started to draw. On top she'd put my name over hers so it said *Claire and Mom's TV.*

If Grandma comes today . . .

I picked the box up to crush it and heard something

clink. I looked through the slit and saw coins inside. I put it back on the table and pushed it away from me.

I don't know how to be good, kind, and gentle with Mom.

When Mom woke up, I cleaned the house. She started drinking beer again before dinner time, and went back to sleep on the sofa.

I went outside and sat on the porch steps. It was cold. For a moment, when Clyde kissed me, I'd been warm.

He'd hate me now. I put my hands in my pockets and bumped the dimes I'd picked up cleaning the floor.

I could go call Miss Joyce. I could tell her Mom had to work nights now and sleep days. I'd tell her I didn't have any place to stay until Mom got off from work. I'd say she hoped to get it changed at the first of the year. Maybe Mr. Beasley could find Daddy by then. Maybe Clyde wouldn't be mad . . .

I started running to the store. Inside the phone booth, I found Miss Joyce's number, put in a dime, started to dial.

I put the phone back on the hook and heard my dime clink down into the coin return. She'd been too mad about Jeannie. She'd been too sure I had to go to the teacher on Saturdays. I hadn't figured out what to tell her if she asked who stayed with me at night.

She'd feel sorry for me.

I turned away from the phone.

It was almost dark and beginning to rain. I was freezing. I started running toward home.

I hadn't gotten far before a car came along behind me. It slowed down and then drew up alongside of me. I got scared it was Miss Joyce and turned toward it.

It was a large station wagon. For an instant, I thought it was Clyde leaning over to roll down the window on my side. Then I saw it was his mother, much smaller than him but with almost the same face and green eyes.

"Are you all right?" she asked.

"Yes, thank you. I was running because it's getting late."

She smiled. "And very cold. Open the door, dear. I'll give you a ride home."

She's like the neighbors in town. Feeling sorry, making trouble.

"No, thank you," I said, backing away from the car.

She pushed the door open. "It's all right. I'm Sylvia Bowman. You must know my son, Clyde, from school."

I shook my head. "I just moved here. I don't know many people."

"You live in the tenant house?"

I nodded. "I'm almost home."

"Get in. I'll take you. It's safer." She was smiling, but she wasn't going to let me walk home. I got in the car.

"You're . . . ?"

"Claire Burden. Thanks for the ride. You can let me out at our mailbox."

"It's too wet and cold and no trouble to take you home. Aren't you out rather late?"

"We don't have a phone. I had to go call my aunt. I forgot my coat. My mom will be mad."

She nodded. "Why haven't I seen you before? Most of the kids along the road have been over some time or another."

"I'm not home very much," I lied.

I didn't dare look at her. We'd pulled into the yard of the ugly, little house. Mom's heap was just sitting there.

"Thanks for the ride," I said, trying to get out quickly.

"It was nothing. I'll tell Clyde I saw you. Why don't

you come over next Saturday? We're the next farm. I'll ask some of the other kids, too."

"Thanks, but I can't. My mother and I usually visit relatives."

"Perhaps another time."

I nodded, got out quickly, and ran toward the house.

Inside, I listened to her car going away up the road. Mom was still drunk and asleep. I was frozen. The fire had gone out in the stove.

I didn't get up to go to school the next morning. I just stayed in bed. When I did go downstairs, Mom was sitting at the kitchen table drinking a beer.

"Ain't it Monday?" she asked.

"Yes."

"Tired of school?"

I nodded.

"I used to get tired of it, too. Always some damn teacher after you. Gimme 'nother beer, Claire."

I handed her one from the refrigerator and tried to eat breakfast. There still wasn't any milk. I went back upstairs and crawled into bed.

Late in the afternoon, near time for the bus, I slipped out of the house and walked up the road to the woods. I waited, watched the bus go by without anyone seeing me. I didn't see Clyde. I wished I had.

I wished he hadn't made me go to Miss Joyce.

Mom's right. Boys just make you do what they want.

Going home, I stopped at the apple trees. There were some holly bushes near them. The frost had made the berries turn red.

I broke off several branches to take home. When Mom went to work tomorrow, I could draw them. I wondered how long it would be before the school would try to find out why I wasn't coming anymore.

Mom was still asleep on the sofa when I came in. I

took the holly in the kitchen and saw an empty clean glass I'd left on the table. I got a knife out and cut the holly off short. I tried to arrange it so it looked pretty. I felt tears start to well up.

"Claire? You home?"

"Yes. I'm in the kitchen."

I heard her get up and come into the room. She went to the refrigerator, got a beer out and opened it.

"What're you doin'?"

"Fixing this," I said, turning around to show her.

She glared at me, drunkenly. "Ugly stuff. What d'you want it for?"

"I'm sorry. I'll throw it out."

"Jus' like Momma!" she screamed, slapping me. "You told me to come home and drink. What're you cryin' for?"

I ran out the door away from her. I dropped the glass and threw the knife as far as I could. I didn't stop till I got near the pond.

Mr. Beasley was sitting on the wall, by himself, looking at the pond.

Poor Mr. Beasley. He loved the ghost. She cared about him. She killed herself.

I went over and sat down beside him.

"What happened to your face?" he asked.

I put my hand up and felt it was swollen. I'd been so glad to see him, I'd forgotten about it. I couldn't answer. I was so ashamed.

"Was she drinkin'?"

"No," I lied, shaking my head, wanting to die, wishing I hadn't come troubling him.

"Has she hit you before?"

"No! Never before. She was tired and worried about money. I dropped some dishes."

He looked angrier. I was scared he knew I was lying.

"It was my fault. I didn't get up early enough to do them before I went to school. I was in a hurry. Made a mess. I didn't come to move the rock. I just wanted to see the pond."

He nodded. "You're a good child. Don't you go worryin'. Things'll get better for you."

I looked away. One of the neighbors had said something like that, before she'd made trouble. I was lying to everyone again, trying to trick them. I hadn't told Mr. Beasley about Grandma beating Mom. Would he be angry for Mom if he knew? Would he think I'd just wanted him to feel sorry for me?

"It's all right," I said. "It was my fault."

He nodded and smiled. "I'm goin' to be here Wednesday. Same as always. You be sure and come down here to see me. I been 'membering another one of Mrs. Adair's songs. I want to play it for you."

"I'll be here," I said, still lying.

"You best be gettin' back where it's warm, now."

He hauled himself up off the wall.

I didn't wait till he was out of sight before I started running home.

I'm not like the ghost! I'm not good and kind. I just make trouble. Make people feel bad. I'm treating Mom the way Daddy did.

I heard Mom crying, calling me. I ran toward the sound, terrified Grandma had come, was beating her.

When she saw me, Mom flung out her arms. "I was scared you'd gone!" she wailed. "Scared you'd left me! Baby, don't make trouble! Try to be good. You got to. We got us a home here. Don't go bein' mean to me!"

I ran into her arms. She hugged me, held me close against her.

"You all I got, Claire! You all I got! I ain't got nobody else."

I started crying, too. She was drunk and awful but she needed me.

"I'm sorry," I sobbed. "I'm sorry. I'll be good, Mom! I will!"

Chapter Twenty-Five

I woke up the next morning before the alarm went off. I'd been having the same nightmare over and over. I kept dreaming I'd fallen into the river by the mill and was drowning. There were people on the bank, but I didn't know any of them. They didn't seem to see me. They just kept talking and laughing. They never looked at me.

I didn't want to sleep anymore. I was scared I'd have the dream again. I didn't want to see Mom either. I reset the alarm so it wouldn't go off until time for her to get up and go to work.

She'd made me promise I'd go to school. She said I'd have to or they'd send me to Grandma's. She'd said if I went, she'd have to go, too.

I got dressed and started downstairs.

When I stopped to put the alarm on the table by Mom's bed, I saw she looked peaceful. She'd said she loved me. She'd cried and cried last night. I stayed still, staring at her, wishing Grandma could have loved her or Daddy or someone. Then maybe she wouldn't hate drawing so much.

I went up the road to wait for the bus long before time. When it finally came and I got on, Clyde rose up from the second seat and blocked the aisle so I couldn't go by.

"Sit down!" he said, angrily, towering over me.

I sat down and tried to put my books on the seat so he couldn't sit next to me. He yanked them out of my hands, sat down, and turned toward me. Scared, I turned away to the window. When he didn't say anything, I looked to see if he was still there.

"I'm mad at you. I've been mad at you all week-end."

I looked back out of the window, sick inside.

"You've just been acting completely crazy. Having fits at me, running down the road, lying to my mom! You told me you didn't have any relatives! I came over last night and nobody was there. The house was empty—the doors were wide open—the lights were on. Where were you? Where was your mom?"

"We went for a walk," I whispered.

"And left the house like that! Why were you running down the road? My mom had a fit. You shouldn't be out by yourself like that! You're going to see my mom this afternoon."

"No! You promised me."

"I was wrong. You could get hurt. Claire, you don't know anything. It's like you've never been around people at all."

I looked back out the window. We were going down the road to school. I could get away from him, there.

"Leave me alone," I begged.

"I won't!"

The bus stopped I tried to take my books from him. "Just leave me be! You're always . . ."

"What's he always?"

I looked up. Jimmy had stopped on the other side of Clyde and was looking down at me, smiling. Clyde looked up at him, too, and then back at me. He still looked mad.

If he gets mad enough, he won't care anymore. He won't keep after me about his mom. He won't find out.

I smiled at Jimmy. He looked surprised. Then, he half closed his eyes and stared at me. I half closed mine and stared back at him trying to look the way he did. He laughed.

"Go on," said a girl behind him. "You're blockin' the way." She pushed at him and stared angrily at me. I opened my eyes wide and stared back at her. Jimmy laughed and went on off the bus. I looked at Clyde. He was mad. Madder than I'd ever seen him. I'd succeeded.

I felt sick. I looked away, waiting for him to get off the bus.

He didn't move. He waited until everyone else had gotten off.

"Let's go," I said, terrified. "I'll be late."

"I don't care," he said. He stood up and I got up, too. I pushed past him and ran off the bus. He caught up with me and yanked at my arm to stop me.

"Claire! Don't fool with him. I mean it!"

I tried to pull away. "I like him," I said. "I hate you."

"You don't. You don't know what you're doing. He isn't like me."

"I hate you."

"You don't know anything and your mother's a fool!"

"Shut up!"

"No! You don't know anything! He'll find out you're home by yourself and don't know anything. He'll come for you. You should hear the things he says about Arlene. He doesn't care about her! Just what he gets from her! He wouldn't care anything about you either!"

I started away from him. He grabbed my arm again.

"If he comes down to your house, don't let him in. He'd hurt you, Claire! You can't just open the door like you did Saturday. You can't just go running down the road by yourself at night!"

I tried to pull away, beginning to understand what he meant.

"Are you listening to me?"

"Yes, stop it! " I begged, embarrassed.

"I can't till I know you understand. You've scared me."

His voice made me look up at him.

"I love you. I don't want anybody to hurt you. He would. Other guys would have, if they'd been at the barn."

I turned away again, shocked.

I don't want him to hate me!

"Come on," he said, gently. "Let's go to class."

All through French, I kept remembering the things Mom had screamed the first horrible day at the tenant house—about boys and what they'd do to me. I tried to shut it out of my mind. I remembered the way Jimmy'd looked at me and felt embarrassed. Then I realized Clyde had looked at me like that. I remembered how upset he'd been when he'd seen the picture I'd drawn of him asleep at the barn. He'd wanted to know if I could tell what he'd been dreaming. Then he'd quit talking about it, just told me not to show it to anyone.

He's been looking at me like that almost all the time, lately.

I looked up, scared the class was looking at me. Mrs. Lively was writing on the board. Everyone else was copying it. I opened my notebook quickly and started trying to copy it, too.

When everyone had finished, she had us read aloud. She called on me first. I tried to hurry through it, but she kept making me stop and go back. At last, it was someone else's turn.

I looked down at my book wondering how I could face Clyde. He was right. I hadn't known anything. But I liked it when he looked at me like that, and I liked being near him, and now he was mad at me.

I felt lonely, suddenly. Mr. Beasley was already angry. He was feeling sorry for me. He and Clyde were both mad at Mom. I shuddered, thinking of Grandma. They didn't know about her.

I jumped when the bell rang. One of the boys in the class was still reading. I was glad the teacher let him keep on. I hoped Clyde wouldn't be waiting for me. I wasn't ready to see him even if he still wanted to see me. I was still too confused and scared he'd be angry.

Until Miss Joyce got mad at Jeannie everything was all right. Now everything's awful.

Mrs. Lively stopped the boy that was reading and said he could finish tomorrow. I was the last one out of class. Clyde was still waiting. I couldn't look at him.

"Parlez-vous français?" he asked.

I looked up, surprised.

"I don't know anything else but that," he said, not looking at me. "In French and drawing you know it all."

I looked back down, ready to cry.

He still wants me to like him.

"Don't," he said. "I'm sorry, Claire. I just . . . was worried about you."

In English, I couldn't listen to Mrs. Morgan. I kept looking at Clyde instead. The way his hair curled, the way he sat slumped to one side so he could put his legs out by the desk in front of him.

After class when I'd already put my books in my locker and he was putting his away, I couldn't help staring at him. When he started to turn toward me, I looked away. He closed the door and took my hand.

"What are you going to do in gym?" he asked.

"Something stupid," I said. His hand was warm. I could feel calluses on his palm. He began to walk away toward the gym but I didn't move. Holding his hand, I almost felt safe again. I remembered how warm, how safe I'd felt on his lap, in his arms.

"Come on," he said, tugging, looking puzzled.

At lunch he kept trying to talk but I couldn't think of anything to say. When we'd come into the cafeteria, I'd seen Jeannie and Tony. They were sitting at the end of a table by themselves so close together their faces were nearly touching. I couldn't see Jeannie's face, but I'd seen Tony's.

"Eat your lunch," Clyde said, leaning toward me.

I looked up. He reached out and touched my face where chalk usually was. His eyes were half closed the way Tony's had been. Clyde took his hand away and turned back to his lunch. I sat still. My face was still tingling where he'd touched me. I wished he still was.

Jeannie and Tony have to get married.

I realized Clyde was looking at me.

"You're still upset," he said, leaning toward me again.

I nodded, wished he'd touch my face again.

"I'm sorry. Don't cry."

I was only half listening.

Mom had to get married. She said Grandma made Daddy marry her. Mom said she was fifteen.

"Hey," Clyde said, touching my arm. "Where are you?"

I looked up at him. He was smiling at me.

He's fifteen. He isn't like Daddy. Or Mom. Or Grandma. He isn't like Mom said boys would be. He wants me to draw, be safe.

"I scared you?"

"Yes."

I looked back down at my lunch. I still hadn't eaten any of it.

"Jimmy won't bother you. I'll see he doesn't. But I want you to go see my mom. It isn't fair . . ."

I shook my head.

She'd hate me the same way Grandmother Burden hated Mom.

"She's nice, Claire. She'd love you. She's going to be asking me about you. I don't want to lie to her. I want you safe! I'm scared that you're not!"

"She'd like me?"

"Yeah, Dad too. They don't care where you live. They'd want you to be safe. I want you safe, too."

I looked up. He was still leaning toward me, smiling.

He isn't always after me to be different from me, just to be safe. He says he loves me.

"Claire, come home with me this afternoon, talk to my mom. I have to be sure someone's taking care of you."

Mom says she loves me, too, but she doesn't. She doesn't want me to draw. She doesn't care if I'm safe.

"It's getting late," I said. "We'd better go to class."

At my locker, I watched him working the combination.

He'd hate quitting school.

He looked down at me. "What?" he asked.

I felt scared and looked around. A group of girls was watching us. I looked away. He'd seen them, too. He looked back down at me.

Daddy hated Mom. Clyde might hate me.

"So people know I like you," he said.

"I wish you were invisible. I wish we both were—or ghosts."

"Claire?"

"They're always looking at you."

"So, I'm good-looking, silly, and the tallest thing here."

"I wish you weren't! I wish you were just nice the way you are without that." I turned away and went to class.

If I run away, if Mr. Beasley finds Daddy, there'd be plenty of people to like Clyde. Nobody else liked me ever.

Clyde put my books on my desk and sat down.

"You mean you just like me? It doesn't make any difference what I look like?"

I nodded.

"You love me Claire?" he asked.

I nodded again.

After class, I realized it was time to go to the art room. I reached in my locker for my books instead.

"You don't need those."

"I haven't done my homework."

"You have to draw, Claire. I'm not letting your mom make you quit!"

"I'm not quitting. Miss Joyce said it was all right not to come if I had homework."

"Claire."

"I'll go tomorrow."

We went to study hall. After the teacher called the roll, we went to the library. I didn't look up at Clyde or say anything.

"You've been shy of me all day," he said.

I looked up, felt small and scared. "Were you ever shy?"

"Some. I'd have done anything to get you to like me."

"Please don't stop liking me."

"Silly, I couldn't stop liking you."

"Do you promise?" I asked, looking away.

He laughed. "I promise I won't quit liking you no matter what. Why are you being spooky?"

"I'm not."

The ghost was kind and good. I'm not. I can't be like her.

"You're acting strange. You're going home with me after school."

"No. I can't . . . I promised Miss Joyce I'd practice painting water."

"You can do that tomorrow. Come see my mom instead."

"No. I promised her . . . I'd go paint the river."

"Claire?"

"I did! I can't talk anymore! I have to do my homework! I'll get in trouble if I don't!" I opened my algebra book, started trying to do the problems.

"Claire."

"I mean it! If you want to talk about it come talk to me while I paint the river."

He didn't say anything. I didn't look up. I tried to make myself figure out the first problem.

"Help me with this?" I asked.

He leaned over against my shoulder, looked down at my book.

"Okay, I'll come down to the rock, the one where Jake found you. But only if you'll go home with me after to see Mom."

"I will," I said, "I promise."

When I got home, the ugly, little house was clean, cold, and empty. I started to go down to the rock to wait for Clyde, but I was scared he'd get his mom to come, too. I went upstairs, got Mr. Beasley's paper and my watercolors. Then I ran down the hill to hide where I could see if Clyde was by himself.

When I'd seen he was, I followed him down to the rock. He was already sitting on it, waiting for me, smiling. I took a deep breath to try to stop being scared.

"You didn't bring Jake."

"No, Mom wasn't home. She'd said she would be. Come paint. If I'm not there when she gets back, she'll be worried."

"No." I felt scared. "I can't paint yet."

"Okay." He got up and came toward me, took the paints and paper. "Then we'll just walk. Did you ever follow the river upstream?"

"A little." I started off up the sandbar away from him. I'd pretend it was just us—that we were ghosts—that we'd never have to go home, that he'd never find out about Mom, or that I'd tricked him.

"Have you seen the rocks? Will you paint the river from there?"

"If you want me to," I said, not wanting to think anymore.

"Wait for me. You'd remember if you'd seen them. They're huge."

"I haven't seen them."

"What's with you?" Clyde asked. "You're a million miles away."

"I'm not."

We'd come to the end of the sandbar and the mouth of a creek. I looked up it, wondering if it led to Mr. Beasley's pond. I remembered how angry he'd looked when he asked if Mom had hit me.

"I wish there weren't any other people!"

"Claire!"

"I do! Just us!"

He'd crossed the creek on stones. I followed him across and tried to scramble up the bank. He put my paper under his other arm, took my hand and pulled me up.

"Just us?"

"Yes. Just us. Nobody else, ever!"

I yanked at his hand and started running. He ran past me and pulled me along after him through the pine woods. He started laughing. I ran wildly after him in and out of shadows and sunlight until I was out of breath.

"Stop!" I gasped, pulling at his hand.

He dropped the paper and paints, stopped suddenly and turned. I ran straight into him. As his arms went around me, I buried my face against his chest, gasping for breath. He was still laughing, and tightened his arms around me. He put his face down against the top of my head.

I stayed still listening to his heart pounding, not wanting to ever move again.

"Come on. I'll show you the rocks," he said, letting go of me, kneeling to pick up the paper and paint.

It wasn't much farther. Looking up at the gigantic bluff, I knew the river must have cut through a mountain. Clyde started up the rocks, pulling me after him. They were easy to climb. There were several levels where wide, flat places had been left.

Almost at the top, he followed one of the ledges around an outcropping to a much wider, flat shelf. The view was up the river for what seemed like miles. The deep purplish-blue mountains were hazy in the distance.

"It's beautiful," I whispered.

"I like it here." He put my things down, sat at the back of the ledge, leaned up against the rocks rising up behind him.

"Sit," he said.

I sat down near him.

"Jake and I used to come up here fishing," he said, looking at the mountains.

"From up here?"

"I had a book," he said, grinning. "It's crazy up here. It makes me feel small."

I shuddered. "Me, too. I hate it! I hate being little and pushed around and never safe."

"Claire, you will be."

"I'm not. I want to feel safe. I did when my hand was hurt, and I was crying, and you held me."

He looked away. "You weren't very safe. You were hurt and scared and everything was a mess."

He was looking awkward.

"No, I felt safe."

"Claire, why do you keep saying it? Why are you scared?"

"My mom'll be mad if I go see your mom. Everyone's just making trouble. They'll send me off somewhere where no one cares about me. I'll never see you! I'll never be safe!"

"You will be." He reached out and touched my hair. "My mom won't embarrass your mom or cause trouble because she doesn't have enough money. She'll help you."

I took his hand and pressed my face against it. "Please, hold me. Let me feel safe like I did."

"Idiot, I can't keep you safe like that!" He pulled me onto his lap and put his arms around me.

"You are," I said, burying my face between his neck and shoulder.

"You're cold," he said, tightening his arms around me. "Why didn't you wear a coat?"

"I'm not cold anymore."

"You're . . ."

"Please. Don't talk. Just let me pretend we're invisible, I don't ever have to go home. Just let me feel safe because you love me."

"Feel safe. I love you. We're invisible. There isn't anyone else anywhere. Just us."

"I love you." I put my arms around his neck and pulled his face toward mine to kiss him. Then I just looked into his green eyes.

"You like me anyway?" I asked.

He laughed and tightened his arms around me. "Idiot!" he said.

"You won't like anyone else?" I asked, leaning toward him.

"No," he said. He kissed me until I was scared and turned my face away from his. Then I remembered what I had to get him to do and pulled his face back toward mine.

"Claire?" He pushed me away and stared down at me. "You're scared."

"I'm not!" I put my arms around him, pressed my face against his sweater and listened to his heart pounding. "Not of you! I'm not!" I reached up to touch his face and hair. "Your hair's soft. I never touched it before." I gathered up my hair, put it against his face, pulled his face toward mine.

He pushed me away and stared at me, looking scared and confused.

"What are you doing?"

"Nothing," I said, looking down, away from his eyes. "I just want to be near you, touch you."

He put his arms back toward me.

"I'm not scared! I won't be. I want to stay here and never go home. I love you! I want you to love me!" I tried to put my arms back around his neck.

"Stop it, Claire."

"No! If you love me . . ."

"Stop it! You don't know what you're doing."

"I do know. You said you wanted what I wanted. I want . . ."

"No!" he said, dumping me off his lap. "I shouldn't have brought you down here. You've been crazy all day. What's happened to you?"

"I'm not crazy! You don't love me!"

"I do." He got up and yanked me up to my feet, too. "And you're going home before I listen to you."

"I don't want to go home!"

"Neither do I." He started down the rocks pulling me after him.

"Then don't!" I wailed, sitting down, forcing him to stop and turn back toward me. "I won't see you anymore if you do! Everyone'll feel sorry for me. They'll take everything away from me again. Stay here!"

"Claire, they won't!"

"They will! I want to be with you! I'm safe with you. Please! They'd have to let us get married! I want to be with you!"

He let go of my hand. "You fool! Not like that you don't! You think you've got a mess now! You're crazy! You don't have any idea—how kids get treated!"

"Your parents are like that?"

"Stop it!" he yelled.

I started crying. "You don't want me either. Nobody does. You said your mom and dad would love me!"

"They would! Dammit! You've been asking me all day! Claire! They'd be so mad at me. I'd hate myself! I can't take care of you! I'm a kid! I don't want you to quit school! Quit drawing!"

"You said you loved me. You could help me and you won't."

"That wouldn't help you! Get up!"

He was so angry, I got up.

"Come on," he said, turning away.

I followed him, confused and embarrassed. He didn't say anything or even look at me until we got to the yard of the ugly, little house. Then, he pulled me back against him.

"I hate your mom! Why can't she take care of you? Why can't everything be okay?"

"Don't leave me here!"

"I have to! Mom's not home! I'm not taking you there!"

"I don't want your mom. I want you," I said, crying again.

"You can't trust me," he said, pushing me away.

"You just don't want me!"

"I do!" he yelled, running away from me. "You don't know anything!"

I stood there, crying, watching him go.

Mom had screamed I couldn't trust boys, they were bad. He said Jimmy was. Arlene, too. He said I don't know anything.

But I do. I trusted him. He isn't bad.

I turned to go in the house.

I'm the one that's bad. He called me a fool.

I'm like Mom.

And he doesn't want me. He doesn't even want me to see his mom anymore.

I went inside. The house was cold and empty.

He hates Jimmy. He hates Mom. He hates me.

I looked at the ugly front room, hating it, hating Mom, hating myself. I was freezing. I built a fire in the stove.

Mr. Beasley said draw.

I got my things and carried them down to the stove.

I couldn't draw. *Mr. Beasley said be good and kind like the ghost. Grandmother Burden always said that, too. "Be kind and good and gentle as my sister Claire."*

I pushed the chalk and paper off on the floor.

I'm not good or kind or gentle.

I'm like Mom.

I curled up on the sofa and cried.

Not long after dark, I heard a car. It sounded like Mom's. Frantically, I tried to gather up my drawing things. I swept them into my skirt and ran upstairs. I yanked the covers back on my bed, dumped the things, covered them up. I got back downstairs just as Mom came in the house. She was drunk, horribly drunk.

"Liar!" she screamed. "Liar! All this time I been killin' myself for you. You went and told people I ain't fit!"

"No, Mom!"

"You did! The sheriff came to work with papers! Says I got to go back to court! Show 'em I'm fit!"

"No, Mom! Grandma must have called him!"

"He said it was you telling. You got me fired!" Mom screamed, coming toward me.

I backed away into the kitchen. She followed me.

"I can't go back to Momma no more! You made me hit her! She'll kill me if I go back to her!"

"No! Don't go back to her! Don't let her trick you!"

"I'm not! But you're goin'! I called her and told her I'm bringin' you so she'll leave me be! You get upstairs and get your stuff! I'm takin' you to her!"

Mom doesn't even want me anymore.

"No, please no!" I begged. "I didn't tell on you!"

Mom lurched toward me, nearly fell. I froze as she looked down to see what she'd stepped on.

I dropped some chalk!

I fled upstairs.

"You been drawin'!" she screamed, stumbling, crashing upstairs after me.

Frantically, I tried to move my dresser over in front of my door.

"I told you! I told you never to draw! I ought to kill you! All this time I thought you cared 'bout me! I kept you from Momma! I hit her for you! You never cared nothin' for me! You're no good! You hate me just like ever'body!"

I grabbed the door, held it closed as she crashed against the other side.

"No good!" she screamed, pounding on it. "No good! Hurtin' me! Trickin' me! Just like Momma!"

I'm no good. I'm worse than Mom. I'm like Grandma. Mr. Beasley and Miss Joyce'll find out.

Clyde already knows.

I can't go to Grandma, be like her.

I opened the door.

Chapter Twenty-Six

Freezing . . . hurting all over. Someone screaming
. . . a light on somewhere else. I tried to see . . .

The light's on in Mom's room. . . . Someone's hit-
ting something on the floor . . . yelling . . .

"Killed her . . . teach you . . . ruined my chances!
Now I'll never get that money!"

Mom . . . that's Mom! Grandma's hurting Mom!

I tried to get up . . . saw small pieces of something
white all around me . . .

I heard someone near me crying . . . then trying to
move me . . . hurting me . . . I screamed, tried to
push them away . . .

Quiet . . . hurting . . . hard under me . . . blankets
over me. I tried to move . . . it hurt too much. I tried
to see . . .

No one's there . . . it's white all around me.

Mr. Beasley's paper's snow . . .

I started crying, tried to get up.

Sounds . . . someone's touching my face . . . some-
thing wet's falling.

"Mom! Mom! Leave her be! This is Claire!"

"Oh, no! Oh, son!"

Gentle hands touching me . . .

Clyde came back.

"She's alive, son . . . go wait for the ambulance . . ."

Black curly hair.

"Help's coming . . . you'll be safe now."

Not Clyde. I tried to turn away.

"Try to stay still."

Another blanket's over me.

"I'll try to help your mother."

"Mom!" I tried to get up . . .

Siren . . . closer . . . stopped. Noise . . . Clyde's yelling . . . Men's voices closer.

"This one was conscious? Will you take that boy outside!"

Clyde's yelling going away.

Someone touching me, hurting me. Someone moved on the other side of me.

"Why can't the crazies stick to the furniture?"

"Looks like this one started on the people and kept goin'."

"You ever seen a mess like this? Paper, stuff, all over?"

"No. Careful, now. She's conscious. You goin' to be okay, girl. You just hang on. We got to take you to the hospital now."

Moving me onto something . . . hurts . . . hurts . . . Clyde's voice. I tried to see . . . white ambulance . . . *Someone's already in it . . . face is awful . . . horrible.*

Mom. It's Mom.

Someone touched me. I screamed, tried to push them away.

"It's okay now, girl. You're safe. We'll be at the hospital in no time."

I heard someone crying and opened my eyes. I didn't hurt anymore. I felt strange and unreal, but I didn't hurt. I looked around the white ceiling, wondered if it was me crying. I didn't think so.

Mom!

I tried to move, tried to see who was crying.

A man in white was standing at the end of my bed. He had on a white cap.

"Doctor?" I whispered.

"No, I'm an orderly. You're in the recovery room waking up from the anesthetic."

"Who's crying?" I tried to move, to see, but my body wouldn't.

"Another patient."

"Someone's hurting Mom! Make them stop!"

"It isn't your mom. Can you feel this?" He seemed to be wiggling my foot. I could see he was, but couldn't feel it.

"No! Help my mom!"

"They're helping her. See if you can raise your knees. I can't take you upstairs till you do."

"I can't! Make them stop hurting Mom!"

"Nurse!"

Someone came to the head of the bed.

"Make them stop hurting my mom!"

The nurse leaned over me. "Can you raise your knees?"

Before I could answer, I saw he'd pushed my feet so my knees went up.

"Okay, I'll send another orderly in to help you. Let them know she's coming upstairs."

As she left, the man came up to the side of the bed, began rolling it.

"I'll take you upstairs now. It's quiet there. You'll be okay."

"Mom!"

"She'll be okay, too."

Someone asked something.

"No," he said, angrily. "Beat up . . . somebody . . ."

I woke up in another white room. I still felt unreal, but when I tried to move, I could. Mr. Beasley was sitting in a chair by the bed. I started crying and tried

to put my hand out to him. It wouldn't move, something was holding it down.

Mr. Beasley put his huge, rough hand gently over
mine.

"There ain't nobody goin' to hurt you no more. You
all bruised up and your arm's broke, too, but they already got it fixed up. You goin' to be fine, child. You
goin' to be fine." He sounded angry, but tears were
running down his face.

"Mom?" I whispered.

"Here in the hospital, too. Who hurt your momma,
child? You know? They're goin' to be comin' to ask
you. 'Bout that and her hurtin' you, too."

"Grandma," I whispered. "Grandma hurt her."

"Lord, child! Lord! I wish you'd told me how bad
they was, told Clyde, told anybody, so's we'd . . .
thank God, your momma didn't hurt you no worse.
You're goin' to be fine and you ain't got to be scared
no more. Clyde already told the sheriff how scared
you was of your momma. Told him it had to be her
hurtin' you, 'cause she hated your drawin' so much.
She's goin' to jail!"

"Grandma?"

"No, child, not like your momma's goin' to! But
don't you go worryin'! They ain't goin' to let your
grandma have you! The Bowmans'll see to it. I'm goin'
to get you more paper, more chalk. Once your arm
heals, you goin' to be able to draw all you want. Any
time you want."

He was crying. I tried to take his hand, wished I
could make him stop.

"You sleep, child," he said, patting my hand. "Close
your eyes, and sleep. Nobody's goin' to hurt you no
more. I got to go. I got me a ride waitin', but I'm
comin' back to see you. Mrs. Bowman's goin' to come
to see you, too. They won't let Clyde come. He ain't
sixteen."

After Mr. Beasley left, I looked at the high white

ceiling wishing Mom'd killed me. I could still hear
her, when she'd finally stopped hitting me, crying and
trying to hold me, but screaming at me: "I hurt my
baby! You made me hurt my baby! Why'd you draw!
Why'd you make me hurt my baby!"

Someone gently touched my face and I opened my
eyes. I saw green eyes and black curly hair. For a moment, I thought it was Clyde. Then, I saw the face
was too small, the hair too long. His mother smiled.
Her hand stayed gently against my face.

"Yes, she's awake," she said, without looking away.
"How do you feel, dear?"

"I hurt." My face felt huge and ached terribly. Her
cool hand felt good against it.

"We've got some medicine to help that, and supper,"
another voice said.

Mrs. Bowman moved out of the nurse's way. I tried
to see if Mr. Beasley was still there but couldn't. Mrs.
Bowman went around to the other side of the bed.
She stayed near as the nurse hovered over me, taking
my pulse and blood pressure, giving me a shot, and
taking my temperature.

"Are you hungry?" the nurse asked.

"No."

"Mrs. Bowman'll tell us if you're hungry later. The
shot will ease the pain." She helped me drink some
water.

When she moved away, I turned to look at the chair.
Mrs. Bowman was in it, now.

"He went home?"

"Daniel? Yes, I sent him home this afternoon. He
was worn out. I'll stay with you now. Miss Joyce was
here and brought you some flowers. Would you like to
see them?"

She didn't wait to see what I'd say. She got up and
started across the room.

"Yes?"

I saw a woman had come in the room. She stared at me.

"What happened to that girl? How'd she get her face messed up . . ."

"Go along," Mrs. Bowman said, taking her arm and turning her toward the door. "She's been hurt! Don't upset her!"

The woman was still staring at me over her shoulder, looking sick. "I was just looking for my mother! The nurse said her room was down here."

I started crying. Mrs. Bowman came back and put her arms around me.

"Oh, Claire! How awful for you. Your face is all bruised, all swollen. It must hurt horribly. But it isn't cut, your nose isn't broken. You'll look just the way you did! You'll be just as beautiful!"

Mom! Mom always put her arms up so Grandma couldn't hurt her face, couldn't make ugly scars on it like her arms.

"No!" I pushed her away, screaming.

Mom won't be just as beautiful! Now her face'll be like her arms!

"The medicine will help you sleep. You'll feel better tomorrow, dear."

Mrs. Bowman gently pulled the covers up close around me.

"Sleep tight, dear," she said, bending over to kiss my forehead. "I'll come back and see you in the morning."

Grandmother Burden always said that, always pulled the covers up like that when she kissed me goodnight.

The cool, gentle hand touched my face, stayed there.

"Sleep tight."

Still sobbing, I tried to turn away, couldn't.

Nobody ever cared about Mom. Nobody was ever gentle to her. Nobody ever kissed her goodnight. . . . She thought she finally had a home . . . she thought

*somebody cared about her the way Grandmother Bur-
den cared about me . . . and I didn't . . . all she ever
had was being beautiful . . . and I ruined it. I wasn't
good or kind or gentle like the ghost. I was like Grandma and ruined it for Mom.*

Chapter Twenty-Seven

The next morning after breakfast, Mrs. Bowman came back with two policemen. One of them had a camera. He started taking pictures of me.

I can't be like Grandma. I have to help Mom.

Mrs. Bowman sat down on the side of the bed, put her hand over mine.

"I'm sorry, Claire, but they have to ask you some questions."

"It's all right," I said, so scared they wouldn't believe me that I started crying, "I want them to. Grandma hurt me! She hurt Mom, too. She was always hurting Mom. Mom's arms are all scarred up from Grandma hurting her!"

"Your grandma! An old woman?" one of the policemen asked.

"She's not an old woman!"

"Claire, why would she hurt you?" Mrs. Bowman asked.

"My Grandmother Burden's money. She was trying to get me away from Mom. I was scared of her. She kept coming out to the house after me. This time Mom wasn't there. When I wouldn't go with her, she hurt me. Mom came home drunk, and tried to stop her. She hurt Mom. I should have gone with her!"

Mrs. Bowman put her arms around me. "No! If she'd been after you, your mom should have gone to the police, gotten help."

"No! They'd have found out Mom was drunk. They'd have sent me to Grandma. Mom didn't hurt me! She tried to take care of me! Don't let Grandma hurt her anymore!"

"Then who made that mess? The boy said you told him your mother hated your drawing!"

"Grandma . . . so people would think Mom hurt me . . . and would make me come live with her . . . only Mom came home drunk . . . thought Grandma'd killed me. Tried to hit her. I couldn't stop Grandma. Please! She'd do anything to get Grandmother's money! Anything!"

"Claire, Claire!" Mrs. Bowman held me close against her. "That's enough," she told the policemen.

I tried to push her away. "She said nobody'd believe me! She hurt Mom before . . . last summer. I was going to tell then . . . but she said nobody'd believe me! They'd just see Mom was drunk and . . ."

The nurse gave me a shot. Mrs. Bowman held me against her.

"It's all right, Claire. It's all right. It's over now. She won't hurt you or your mother anymore. Just cry. You're safe. You'll feel better."

When I woke up again, Mrs. Bowman was sitting in the chair by the bed, reading. I looked away, saw red roses in a vase on the table on the other side of the bed. The vase was cut glass. The sun was shining on it, making rainbows. I lay still, looking at it.

Mr. Beasley's guitar makes rainbows. It catches sunshine like that.

I tried to remember the way the hair on my arms and neck tingled when he played, how the air around me seemed to come alive.

It's when he plays that his guitar is really beautiful.

I remembered Mom's face and looked away from the rainbows.

Mrs. Bowman smiled. "Good, you're awake. You must be starving."

"Grandma?"

She sat on the side of the bed, took my hand.

"They'll be arresting her. Your grandmother Burden's lawyers say she's been harassing them for some time about the will. The sheriff said she called him that afternoon saying you'd told her your mother was always drunk and not feeding you or taking care of you. Your grandma'd bothered him about your mother too many times before. Instead of believing her and coming after you, he just took your mother a notice at work that she'd have to see a social worker with you."

Her cool hand gently touched my face.

"Clyde said you told him every time people felt sorry for you they took away something you had."

I tried to nod.

"It must have seemed that way . . . when they took you away from your father. They were trying to help. They just didn't find out enough, make sure you had been helped. You were trying to be safe. You were too scared to trust anyone."

"Please tell Mom she doesn't have to be scared anymore."

"She'll know. The doctors say you'll be able to leave the hospital soon. I'm going to take you home with me. When you're able to go back to school, you can stay with Miss Joyce. Daniel asked her to help. She says he made you come take a class with her. I'm glad. She likes you very much. She'll be able to take good care of you."

Miss Joyce wants me to come live with her, have fun drawing? I wish I could.

"I lied to everyone. I tried to trick everyone."

She held me gently against her. "It's all right. Everyone understands. Daniel came back while you were asleep. He brought you something. He says it's just for you." She let go of me and got a box off the table beside her chair, lifted the lid.

It was a huge box of chalk, every color laid out in a rainbow.

I turned away, crying.

I'm not like the ghost. She was good and gentle and kind.

Mrs. Bowman pulled the covers over me, began gently rubbing my back. "Crying's good. It'll make you feel better."

I'll never feel better. I ruined it for Mom.

"Daniel's a special old man," she said. "My father told me he taught him to read and write, was always after him to stay in school, learn, do more with himself. I'm glad Daniel's your friend, Claire. Clyde thought Daniel knew you were scared, was helping you."

I closed my eyes, sick inside. *All that time, Mr. Beasley knew Clyde. They knew I was lying when I told both of them I didn't know anyone out there. But they still tried to help me . . . were still my friends. Mrs. Bowman says she's glad Mr. Beasley did . . . says she wants to help me, too.*

Clyde must not have told them about the rocks, must not have told them I was no good. Wasn't gentle and kind like the ghost . . .

Chapter Twenty-Eight

Several more days went by. Doctors and nurses were always in and out of my room. They brought in equipment and food. They took me to other rooms to run tests.

Mrs. Bowman came to see me often. When she was there I remembered being small and safe with Grandmother Burden. When she did things for me, I didn't hurt as much. I was just glad to be safe and not scared of Grandma anymore.

Mr. Beasley came to see me several times. He brought me drawing paper . . . said it was no fun playing without me there to listen. Miss Joyce came too, talking about school and drawing. I tried to listen.

One morning, Mrs. Bowman came back in the room smiling. The doctors had just been there. She'd gone outside with them to talk.

"You can go home with me today," she said. "All the tests say you're going to be fine. The cast will be in your way a while yet, and you'll still hurt some, but you'll soon look exactly as you did." She hugged me, gently. "I've already called Tom. He'll be along soon to take us home."

Clyde's dad didn't look like Clyde at all. He wasn't nearly as tall, his eyes weren't green, but he was nice like him.

Downstairs, we stopped just inside the glass doors to wait while Mr. Bowman went to get the car. I was surprised there was no snow outside. I was sure I remembered snow around me after Grandma'd gone.

It was Mr. Beasley's paper. Mom made his paper snow.

A woman was coming up the walk. As she got to the door, she began to stare at me. She looked as if she was going to be sick. Mrs. Bowman turned the wheelchair away so I couldn't see her.

"What . . ." I heard the woman start asking as she came inside.

"Go along, please," Mrs. Bowman said, firmly, putting her hand on my shoulder. The station wagon pulled up then. Mr. Bowman got out to put me inside.

"I don't want anyone to see me!"

"People!" Mrs. Bowman said.

"We'll be home soon," Mr. Bowman said, picking me up. "No one there'll make you feel badly!"

In the car, Mrs. Bowman put her arm around me and pulled me gently toward her so my face rested against her.

"That doesn't hurt?" she asked, softly.

"No," I whispered. She was warm.

She and Mrs. Bowman are people, but they're helping me.

Going down the road to their house, I looked out and saw the greenhouse at one end of it.

Clyde will be there. He got his mom to come get me out of the snow.

But he knows I'm no good.

The car stopped in front of the house.

Mr. Bowman carried me inside to a pretty room with a four-poster bed. After he put me down, he pulled the covers up around me.

"I've got to go back to work," he said. "But Sylvia'll see you've got company."

He kissed Mrs. Bowman and went out. I looked away, feeling strange inside.

I've never seen anyone kiss someone except in Mom's movies.

"My room's next door," Mrs. Bowman said. "The

bathroom's in here." She opened the door and left it ajar. Then she went to the windows and opened the curtains. "There's a nice view when you want to get up."

She came back and sat on the edge of the bed, smiled and nodded at a vase of flowers sitting on the bedside table.

"I see someone's been getting things ready for you. There's wood in the fireplace, too. Would you like me to light it?"

I nodded, suddenly feeling shy of her and scared in the new place.

She went to the fireplace, put a match to the kindling, and came back.

"Clyde wants to see you. Do you feel like seeing him?"

No. He knows I'm no good.

I shook my head.

"You'll be just as beautiful, Claire. You'll look exactly the same."

I turned away.

It won't be the same with him.

Beautiful's no good. It's nothing if you're ugly inside.

Mrs. Bowman touched my shoulder. "It will just take time, dear. I wish so much I could help you feel better. Wait, I've got something special. I'll get it."

She went out of the room. I waited, wondering what she meant, scared she'd gone after Clyde. When I heard her coming back, I turned to see what she had. She came in smiling, unfolding a quilt.

At first, I just gasped at the hundreds of brilliant, beautiful, multicolored embroidered flowers crowding and filling the quilt's surface. As she tossed it out over me, I wondered how anything could be so beautiful.

"It even has your name on it," Mrs. Bowman said, smiling and holding the edge up for me to see, "at least part of it."

I stared at the edge, saw *Claire Beauchamps, Long River, 1898*. The tiny, embroidered signature was exactly the same as I'd seen at Galway Hall so many times.

"No!" I screamed, pushing the quilt from me. "No! I can't be like her!"

I turned away, screaming, wanting to die, wishing Mom had killed me. "She was my grandmother's sister! Grandmother named me for her! Said I had to be like her! Mom hated me for looking like her!"

"Son! Son!" Mrs. Bowman was at the door, gone.

"No! No!" I begged.

When I heard her coming back, I sat up, ashamed.

It was Clyde. When he saw me, he started crying. I turned away, curled up in a ball, crying, wanting to die. He pulled the covers back up over me, lay down behind me, pulled me against him.

"Oh, Claire, I was so scared she'd killed you!"

I tried to pull away.

"No! I won't let you go. I left you there when you begged me not to. Don't hate me, Claire! Don't. I didn't know she'd hurt you! I was scared to come back, scared she'd be home and get mad at you! Mom didn't get home till late. She said you'd be all right. Said she'd go see your mom the next Sunday. When you didn't come to the bus, I was scared you'd run away, scared you wouldn't let us help you. I got off, went down to the house. Claire! You asked me to help you, and I just left you there, came back too late! It was my fault!"

"No!"

"It was! You wanted to be with me. You felt safe with me." He tightened his arms around me. "I didn't want to take you home, but you trusted me. I had to try to help you. I couldn't, not the way you wanted! I was scared you wouldn't love me anymore if I did. But I didn't help. You just got hurt." He started crying again.

"Don't," I said. "Don't. You didn't know she'd hurt me. You never hurt me."

He pressed his face into my hair. I could feel his breath warm on my neck.

"You don't hate me, Claire?"

"No, I love you. I . . ."

The door banged open and he jumped away from me. I sat up, scared.

"Damn you, Jake!" Clyde yelled.

Jake cowed, lay down, put his head between his paws and moaned.

"I'm sorry," Clyde said, putting his hand out to him. "Mom'll be back with Daniel soon, anyway."

I turned away, embarrassed and confused. Clyde pulled the covers back up around me and patted the bed. Jake jumped up on it, mooed, and lay close against my back.

"Replaced by a damn dog," Clyde said.

"I . . ."

"It's okay, Claire. Mom won't get mad at him. She would at me." He touched my hair, sat down on the edge of the bed on the other side of Jake. "Claire? I'm so glad you're safe and here. Please let Mom and Miss Joyce take care of you. You mind being here?"

"I shouldn't be. I tried to be like the ghost! I couldn't!" I started crying.

"Like the ghost! Claire?" Clyde leaned across Jake. "What are you talking about! Nobody wants you like her!"

"My grandmother Burden did! The ghost—your ghost, Mr. Beasley's ghost—was her sister!"

"But she killed herself! Claire? She didn't want you to be like that!"

"No. The ghost was good and kind and gentle. Mr. Beasley said so. Grandmother did, too. She said I had to be like her. I tried to!"

"No, Claire! She was so miserable! Her life was awful! But Daniel doesn't know. He was just a little kid!"

"But . . ."

"No but! I've got her diary so I know! I found it, messing around in the attic last summer. That's why her quilt scared you? You thought she was perfect? And you had to be?"

I was too mixed up to answer.

"No. Mom got the quilt out because it was pretty. Nobody here wants you miserable like her. We love you too much." He touched my hair. "I'll give you her diary. You'll see. You won't want to be like her anymore."

I lay still, confused, glad his hand gently stroked my hair, glad Jake's warmth was near me.

"Claire? Feel safe. Please don't mind being here."

"I feel safe," I whispered.

I heard voices, footsteps on the stairs. Clyde got up and went to the door.

"She's okay," he said. "Jake and I took care of her."

Later that evening, after dinner, I was half asleep, still half hearing Mr. Beasley's music in my head. Before he'd gone, he'd asked if I wanted anything out of the tenant house. I'd asked him to get the silver-backed brush Grandmother'd given me out of the shed where I'd hidden it from Mom. He'd promised he would.

Someone knocked at the door, opened it.

"You awake?" Clyde asked, softly.

I tried to nod. He pushed the door open, went over to the window, and opened the curtains.

"It's snowing, Claire! I love snow. It's neat!" He came toward me, smiling.

"Mom said I could come see you . . . if I read to you." He leaned down to me. "Mothers! She acts like . . ."

"Don't look at me," I said, seeing him stop smiling and look hurt instead. I put my hand up to try to cover my face.

"It makes me hurt. Your face hurts? Your arm still hurts?" He touched my fingers where they stuck out of the cast.

"No."

"Don't lie to make me feel better! Look." He pressed something against my fingers.

I looked down, saw a small, old, leather book. Its cover had been cut into a paisley design, and colored inks had been rubbed into it.

"That's beautiful," I said, running my fingertips over the design.

"Yeah," he said, smiling. "You still touch things. It's her diary." He pulled it away, opened it. "You get me reading it so Mom won't come chasing me off."

He went around the bed and sat down in the chair beside it. "She was your grandmother's sister?"

I turned toward him, nodded.

"You knew she'd married my great-grandfather? Lived here?"

I looked around the room, startled. "No! Grandmother never told me where she went or what happened to her—just that she'd died when Grandmother was little."

"That's weird. I never showed this to Daniel—it would just make him feel bad. But I asked him about her when I found it. What she looked like and a bunch of other stuff. It wasn't even a week later when you popped out of the mill at me." He laughed. "God, you scared me! And him, too, at the store. I really thought you were her! After me! Now, it's dumb . . . but it's almost like she wanted me to find her diary, be at the mill when you were, love you. Claire, you know where Long River is?"

I felt funny inside. "It's a farm on the other side of Galway Fields. Grandmother's family lived there when she was little. She took me there once."

Clyde nodded, held the book out. I saw *Long River, eighteenth day June, 1898* in the same small, neat handwriting I had seen on her drawings at home and just that day embroidered on the quilt. Clyde pulled the book away, started reading:

> —*Dear Little Leather Book. It's late at night and all the house is sleeping. Momma said I was to sleep, too, but I can't. You'll soon know I always have a candle stub hid for when I have to draw.*
> —*Yesterday, Poppa took Momma, little sister Evelyn—*

Clyde looked up. "Is that your Grandmother Burden's name?"

I nodded, feeling still stranger inside as he looked back down and went on reading:

> —*and me to Galway Fields. Momma got me a length of purplish-blue silk, the color of my eyes—*

Clyde looked up and grinned. "That's right anyway. Her eyes are the same color as yours."

"I look just like her," I said. "Grandmother had a painting of her in a dress that color."

He looked surprised. "They kept it? The paintings?"

"Yes. Does the diary say who painted it? Was it one of the Burdens?"

"No," he said, looking back down at the yellowed page, "but she knew them. Just listen."

> —*the color of my eyes for making me a gown for the Burdens' summer ball. Poppa says Mr. Adair will be there. I wish Poppa was not so set on him. He doesn't look gentle like Poppa, though he's as old. His eyes are cruel when he smiles.*
> —*I try to tell Momma. All she'll say is times are hard. I have to marry Mr. Adair if he'll have me, so he'll help Poppa keep Long River.*

*—Momma got me more 'broidery thread in town.
It's been a year gone since she got me the stuff to
make a bride's quilt. Poppa's been saying I must
not want to marry, I've been at it so long. I hope
it takes forever. I've been covering the whole
quilt top in flowers the same as the Burdens have
in their glass room at Galway Hall—*

"That's my house! Grandmother's house! But it
doesn't have a greenhouse."
"Does it have a room like this?"

—It's all glass doors down one side.

Clyde looked up and I nodded.
"That's the studio."
He smiled, read:

*—It's full of strange plants. I been copying their
flowers onto my quilt.
—Once we picked our stuff, Poppa took us to the
Burdens'. Mrs. Burden give me a new book of
music for playing on my harpsichord. After I
played for her, she and Momma got talking. They
give little Evelyn and me leave to go to the glass
room so I could draw more flowers.*

"She is like me," I said. "I . . ."
"She's not!" Clyde didn't look up.

*—While I was there, the tallest man I ever seen
come in from the garden with Clement Burden.
Little Evelyn was scared to see him and hid behind me. Clement told me the stranger's name
was Clyde Joyce. He made me show him my
drawings, since he draws, too. Clement went on
in the house leaving Mr. Joyce with Evelyn and
me. He hardly stayed, but he had you in his*

*pocket, Book, and give you to me for drawing
flowers. He said my drawings was beautiful, but
not so much as me.*
*—I didn't show you to Momma, Book. I was
scared she'd make me give you back, Mr. Joyce
being a stranger. He didn't seem one to me. His
hair's so black and curly, but it's nothing to his
eyes. They was a green I never seen in nature.
Oh, Book, why can't he be Mr. Adair? Your loving friend, Claire Beauchamps.*

Clyde's green eyes stared at me, eyes like Clyde
Joyce's in the diary.

*—Sixteenth day July, 1898. Yesterday the Burdens
had their ball in the glass room. The plants was
back against the walls, filling the air with scents.
Men come from the university to play music.
Huge candelabra was lining the walls, all silver,
making the very air magic.*
*—Mr. Joyce was at the ball. He hardly knowed I
was. Just once all evening, when Mr. Adair finally left me to see to his mother, he come up to
me, bowed low before me, asked me to dance.*
*—For a while, I looked up into his green eyes. He
held my hand, touched my waist, whirled me
about. There was no floor beneath my feet. All I
could see was his eyes and handsome face. Then,
when the music stopped, he give me back to Mr.
Adair. I hate Mr. Adair. He smiles with his mouth
but his eyes are cruel. They never smile like Mr.
Joyce's.*

Clyde's voice sounded strange. I kept quiet, watching him.

*—Eighteenth day July, 1898. Momma says Pop-
pa's hired somebody to paint me in my ball*

*gown. I crossed my fingers quick wishing, but
that could never be.
—Twenty-second day July. The painter's Mr.
Joyce. I was so shamed. I'd been out in the woods
all morning finding and drawing Indian pipes.
Little Evelyn and me come back a mess and
laughing. We run in to show Poppa what we'd
done. And there he was. I felt so shamed. Poppa
looked shamed, too. I couldn't look at Mr. Joyce.
Poppa sent me to wash and dress like I was six.*

Clyde looked up, grinning. I looked away embarrassed, remembering how dirty I'd been when I'd run
into him at the store.

"You weren't a ghost," he said. "You were warm and
touching me. I knew you weren't her."

"Mr. Beasley fussed at me."

Clyde laughed. "For being a mess?"

I nodded, ashamed.

"He fussed at me, too, for scaring you," he said,
gently squeezing my hand.

"You didn't scare me." I looked up, saw him smile.
"You weren't like any of them."

"I hope not," he said, looking back down at the book
in his lap.

*—Mr. Joyce told me to look out the window at the
river while he was painting me. Poppa stayed
there watching him. I stood there all afternoon
while they talked horses. I love the smell of the
paints. I wish Poppa hadn't been there.
—Twenty-third day July. Mr. Adair come calling
today. He hardly talked to me. I didn't mind. I
wish he had not walked with me in Momma's garden either, had not told me Poppa's give him
leave to marry me. He can't even read. When he
touches me, I want to run away. He stayed
watching Mr. Joyce painting me. I was glad when*

he went home to his mother. Mr. Joyce never talks to me. I wonder if he even sees me. I dare not try to draw his face. He's gone home.
—Twenty-ninth day July. Today while I was standing, Mr. Joyce come over to me and turned my face toward him. He told me to look at him and smile the way I do at Evelyn. His hand was warm. I smiled at him. His family's the same as us and worse. His father's gone. It's just him and his mother. He's going north to paint.

Clyde looked up. "He must've come back—if he's related to Miss Joyce."

I looked away, confused. Clyde turned a page in the diary, kept his other hand on mine.

—He's almost finished painting me. He let me see the picture. I never knowed I looked like that. He said he'd be finished tomorrow and going home. He said he can't come back here, asked me to go meet him Monday by River Bridge. I mustn't go meet him. Momma'd kill me if she knew what I was dreaming.

I tried to pull my hand away. Clyde held onto it.

—First day August. He's gone. I begged and begged him not to. He said he had to. He's got nothing but his paints, and I've got Mr. Adair. I shouldn't have gone to meet him! I had to, but he doesn't care!

"You weren't like that!" I said. "You weren't."
"And you're not like her!"

—Eleventh day October. Mr. Adair was here again today. I must marry someone. Mr. Adair says he'll pay Poppa's debts if I do. I am with

*child. There's no hope for me now. Last time I
was to town, Mr. Joyce had gone.*

"No!" I said.
"Yes," Clyde said.
"That's why you made me go home!"
Green eyes stared at me. "No! I loved you! He
didn't love her. He just used her!"
"Poor ghost!"
Clyde looked surprised, looked back down.

*—March 1899. I am so tired. They don't even
care what day it is here, except Sunday. I never
know anymore or care, myself. Now Mr. Adair
hopes for a son. At least he leaves me to my
drawing and harpsichord and tells his mother she
must, too. There are no books here save the Bible
and this. No one here can read or write or be
kind except Daniel. I don't even know what day
old Mrs. Adair brought him to me. She yanked
him into the parlour by the ear saying he was no
good in the kitchen so he could wait after me.
Poor little black child. He can't be more than
seven. He sat where she throwed him as if I
would hit him, too. When I started playing again
and looked to see what he was doing, he was
smiling. I haven't seen anyone smile for pleasure
for so long. He's a clever child. I'm teaching him
to read and write. He knows no one must ever
know I am. He carries my things about.
—May, 1899. Last week I had a son, born too
short a time since I was married. Mother'd come
to visit and stayed to help me. When she saw his
curly black hair and green eyes, how fat and
healthy my baby was, she said I was disgraced,
had disgraced her and Father, too. I named him
Charles for father, but he doesn't care.
—Summer, 1901. Everyone here hates me save my*

*child and Daniel. Now Mr. Adair says Daniel's
too old to help me anymore. He's taken him away
from me. I begged him till he promised to let
Daniel work in the barns with the horses, but I
won't see him anymore. It's two years gone since
I seen Mother or Father or Evelyn. Mr. Adair
gave back Father's debt. Long River's sold. I
don't know where they've gone. I wonder that
Mr. Adair keeps me or my child, he hates me so
much. I've never been back to Galway Fields.
When I've finished working in the mill, I'm tired
enough to die.*

*—October 1901. I found a place in the attic to
hide you, Book. Maybe someday my son will find
you and know I loved him, if he can read. There
is a way I can be sure he has a home. When I'm
not there for her to hate, old Mrs. Adair loves
him. I saw Daniel at the barns, begged him to
look after Charles when he could, tell him I asked
him to name a child like himself Clyde.*

*—Forgive me, God. Coming home from the mill I
saw Indian pipes growing up out of a dead tree in
the woods. I remembered finding them and
drawing them with Evelyn so long ago. I don't
know how seeds can fall on dead wood, grow out
of decay, and somehow bloom.*

Clyde put down the book, put his arms around me.
"Don't cry."

"I have to. Poor ghost! Nobody loved her! They just
treated her like Mom! Mom had to marry Daddy, because of me! Daddy and Grandmother just hated her.
Just like the Adairs hated the ghost." I put my arm
around him, cried against him.

"You're not like her. You don't want to be?"

"You wouldn't let me be. You loved me so I
wouldn't be like her."

"No, silly. I love you because you aren't!"

"It doesn't matter. Just so you love me."

"It does matter! I love you! I don't want you miserable like her." He held me close against him. When I stopped crying, I just listened to his heart beating, felt safe, then pushed at him.

"Your mom. She'd get mad at you."

"Let her get mad."

"No. She wouldn't let you come see me."

He let go, moved to the chair. Got up again, held out the silver chain he'd given me.

"I got it fixed," he said, as I took it, raised it up to put it over my head.

"I love you," I said.

He turned away, started out of the room, stopped at the door, but didn't look at me.

"I didn't want to take you home."

"When was that?" his mother asked from down the hall.

"It's the last line of the story," Clyde said, turning to pull the door closed behind him. "Claire's almost asleep, leave her be."

I watched the door close, looked down at the disk on the chain, saw it said *Clyde*. Surprised, I turned it over, saw *Claire* on the other side. I started to look at the door, saw the other Claire's diary lying on the bed. I pushed it under the covers, turned away from it, watched the clean cold snow lightly wash against the window panes.

Chapter Twenty-Nine

The next afternoon, I got tired of being in bed. I'd spent the morning looking at Claire Beauchamps's quilt, tracing the flowers into my memory. I didn't want to reread her diary.

Mrs. Bowman said I could get up and get dressed. Following her downstairs, I tried to realize the ghost lived in this house, walked down these steps, stood in the front hall. But looking in the living room, I couldn't imagine her there with Mr. Beasley. The fieldstone fireplace was old, but the furniture was modern. There wasn't any harpsichord. I turned away and asked Mrs. Bowman if I could see the greenhouse.

Just inside the door, I stopped to feel the warm moist air, tried to take in the many colors, a dozen smells; damp earth, blooms I couldn't identify, the acrid smell of fertilizer.

There were several small blooming trees beside me. When I looked up, I saw the vine Clyde had told me about covering the trellises inside the roof. There weren't any more of the purplish-blue flowers he'd given me on it, but the air was almost green. Looking at the vine's streamers hanging from the trellises, I remembered the vine on the old dead tree in Grandmother's garden.

"Clyde said you'd like the greenhouse," Mrs. Bowman said.

"It's beautiful." I turned to look at the pots and pots of flowers. "Daffodils."

"Yes, they just opened yesterday." She touched the yellow flowers, bent down to smell them. "These don't have much fragrance, it's the later ones that do."

Suddenly, I needed to touch them, too, feel their texture, see if I could catch them on paper. I started to reach out, saw the cast on my right arm. I leaned down to smell them, touched them with my left hand, wondered if I could show the granular yellow pollen with chalk.

"I'd better go get dinner started," Mrs. Bowman said. "Clyde'll be home from school soon. You can stay out here if you'd rather."

"Yes," I said. "It's all right if I touch the flowers?"

"Of course. Pick some to take upstairs, too."

When she'd gone, I kept looking at the flowers, touching them, wishing I knew their names and could draw them.

Clyde's grandfather . . . the ghost's son, Charles Adair . . . locked himself away in here . . . looking for the ghost, his mother . . . trying to make this place like her?

Watching that other Claire drawing and playing, finding wildflowers with her, was fun for Grandmother and Mr. Beasley. She cared about them, her Evelyn and her friend Daniel. She needed them to care about her. They knew she did.

Most of these flowers are on the quilt. They're in the drawings that Grandmother showed me, smiled at, said her sister Claire had done.

Feeling lonely, I sat down on an empty bench and just looked.

Daddy locked himself away, too. In another glass room . . . Did he want to be there?

Grandmother wanted him there. She told me to keep him there.

When I nagged him to stop drinking and paint more, he said I was ugly. He ran away.

I heard the door, saw Clyde duck his head to come in. He came over and stood in front of me, tall, beautiful, blocking out the greenhouse.

"Sit," I said, trying to smile, glad to see him.

He sat down next to me. "Were you drawing?"

"No, I can't with this cast. Why'd you think I was?"

"You've got stuff on your face," he said, gently brushing at my cheek and showing me the pollen on his fingers. "It looks like chalk."

"I was looking at the flowers. They're beautiful. Do you think your granddad ever saw her diary?"

"I don't know. It wasn't with his stuff. Anyway, he had the quilt and Daniel probably told him she liked flowers. Only Daniel would never come in here . . . Quit thinking about them, Claire. Look at me."

I did and smiled so he'd quit frowning.

"Daddy was like your grandfather," I said. "Locked away. All he wanted to do was draw. He didn't care if anyone liked what he drew. He didn't care about Mom, or me. Poor Mom. She never had anybody that cared about her."

"What about you!"

"Grandmother Burden cared about me when I was little. She wouldn't let Mom take care of me."

"That was smart of her."

I looked away. "But Mom wanted to take care of me!"

"Yeah, by not wanting you to draw!"

"She couldn't help it. She couldn't be happy if I drew."

"She couldn't've been happy no matter what you did!"

"Don't get mad at me!"

"I'm not!" he said, mad. "I just don't believe what you told the police, that your grandma hurt you! You were too scared of your mom!"

"It was Grandma!"

"Claire, Mom says the court may send you back to your mom."

"No!"

"Yes!" He put his arm around me. "I'm sorry! I shouldn't've told you. Miss Joyce is coming out to talk about it. I should have . . . Claire!"

I'd pushed him away, gotten up. He grabbed at my arm.

"You can't go back to her!"

"I won't! I can't!"

"She did hurt you!" He stood up, towered over me, angry.

"No! It was Grandma! Leave me be!" I said, turning away. "I've got to talk to Miss Joyce. I'm going upstairs till she comes."

"No! Talk to Mom!"

The fear in his voice made me turn back toward him, reach out and touch him.

"I won't go back to Mom! I couldn't see you if I did!" I ran upstairs away from him.

When Miss Joyce got there, she came to my room.

"I'm so glad to see you," I told her. I started crying again.

She hugged me, sat down on the edge of the bed. "I thought you were up and around. What happened?"

"I am . . . I was. I need you to help me."

"If I can, of course I will."

I looked away from her smile. "Clyde says they may send me back to Mom. I can't go back to her! I can't let her go to jail, either."

Miss Joyce started to speak. I didn't let her.

"I'd hate myself if I did. I'd feel as if I was Grandma! I'd never be able to draw again if I let Mom be locked up in jail!"

"Claire!"

"Please help me. Mom won't want me back. With her face scarred, she'll hate me. Being beautiful was all Mom ever had. Grandma's taken that away from her, too."

I told Miss Joyce what it had been like for Mom with Grandma, with Daddy. How Grandmother Burden took me from Mom, and then gave Mom money to go away. How Grandma got that from her, too.

"Every time I ever saw Grandma, she said Mom had ruined her chances. It's not true. She ruined Mom's.

"Mom hated drawing, but I don't blame her. If I'd been her, I'd have hated it too! She hated my looking like Grandmother's sister, my being like Grandmother. But she tried to take care of me. She thought she had a chance with me! She thought we had a home. She'd never had one where someone cared about her!

"I didn't want to be with her! But I was so scared of Grandma, I made Mom think I cared about her, wanted a home with her. I promised her I'd never draw.

"When Grandma made trouble with the sheriff, Mom got upset, got fired. She came home knowing she'd have to go back to Grandma. Only she'd stood up to Grandma, because of me. She'd hit Grandma for trying to hit me! Grandma'd told her she'd kill her. Mom came home drunk and caught me drawing!"

"And battered you!"

"I let her! I thought I'd just made a mess with you, with Clyde, with Mr. Beasley. I'd ruined everything with Mom, too. I let her. I wanted her to kill me."

"Claire!"

"I did, but I don't want to die anymore. I won't stay with anyone else that doesn't care about me! But I can't let Mom go to jail! Daddy treated me the same way he treated her. With you, Clyde, with Mr. Beasely, I'd thought I had a chance, the same way Mom did with me. I can't draw unless she has one chance. I have to try to help her, or I'll just be like Daddy and Grandma. I can't draw if I'm like that!"

"Claire, how can you help her? You're a child. She's the parent. Some parents aren't worth helping! Aren't worth making yourself miserable over!"

"I have to try to help her."

"What could you do? She belongs in jail!"

"She's been in jail all her life with Grandma! I don't even know her name! I've never heard Grandma call her anything but 'Fool!' She always kept saying she'd wanted to go away somewhere else and have herself a life. She'd need money to do that."

"You want me to give her money?"

"No! I want you to sell Daddy's paintings for me. There're dozens of portraits of me in Grandmother Burden's house. People used to buy them, before he quit selling them. They're beautiful. But I don't want them. They'd just make me remember he didn't care about me, made me sit there all those years while he painted them.

"If you gave Mom the money from them, told her how I got it, so she could go away, have a home and a chance away from Grandma, maybe she'd know someone did care about her. She'd go anyway!"

"You sound awfully sure of that."

I nodded, remembering the way Mom couldn't look at me when she'd said she was going to take me to Grandma. "She'll go. She won't want me back. I thought you'd understand. I thought you'd help me."

"I understand you care more about her than she deserves."

"I never wanted to. I was always ashamed she was my mother."

"I don't see any way you could have been proud of her, except when she stood up to Mrs. Simmons for you."

"She took me to the movies. She bought me ice cream. She stood up to Grandma for me. Daddy never did any of that. He expected me to take care of him. When the school and neighbors meddled, he just drank more, ran away. Mom tried to take care of me, tried to keep me from Grandma."

Miss Joyce put her arm around me. "I guess you

feel she cared about you the best she could. That's why you have to try to help her?"

"Yes." I leaned against her, crying. "Being with her and caring about her wouldn't help her. She'd just hurt me again. There isn't any other way I can help her except try to help her get away from Grandma, be free, once. It's the only way I can tell her I did care about her, forgive her, not hate myself."

Miss Joyce nodded. "I'll sell the paintings for you. They've given me custody of you while she's still in the hospital, so I'll be able to. But, Claire, you must give me your word. If she won't take the money, won't abandon you, so I'll have permanent custody of you, you'll have to tell the truth, that she hurt you."

"I won't let them send me back to her."

Miss Joyce hugged me, let go.

"You'll have to stay here a while longer. My apartment's too small for both of us. Your grandmother's house will have to be cleaned."

"I can go home? To Galway Hall?"

"Yes, your Grandmother Burden's lawyers said that was best. Was it ever a home?"

"Yes, before Grandmother died. She loved me. I trusted Mr. Beasley, Clyde, and you, because you were like her. It was fun drawing with you. You'll make the studio the way it should be."

"I'll certainly try."

"Can I go tell Clyde? That I'll be with you! That I'm going home!"

"Yes, but, Claire . . ." She hesitated, frowning. "You're so young. There's so many things to do. I hope you're not getting serious about him."

"He's my friend! He helped me. He made me come see you!"

She looked surprised.

"Mr. Beasley told me to, but then I was too scared of Mom. Clyde knew I wanted to. He said he wouldn't be friends with me if I didn't do something I wanted to, didn't learn how to draw the things I didn't know how to!"

She nodded, still looking surprised.

"Don't tell him it was Mom who hurt me! He wouldn't understand! He'd want her in jail. Want us to do what was right!"

"I couldn't help you if I didn't think it was right. It's not a question of that, but of you caring about her and needing to help her."

"Clyde just hates her. He's scared I'll have to go back to her."

"Then you'd better go tell him that's not going to happen."

I ran downstairs looking for him. His mom and dad were in the kitchen, said he was outside. I went back into the hall, looked out the front door. He was just coming up the walk through the snow.

I closed the door behind me, ran down the porch steps toward him.

"I'm going home! With Miss Joyce! I'll be with her!"

I slipped, almost fell on the icy sidewalk.

"Claire! You just got out of the hospital!" He caught me, put his arms around me, pressed me against him. "You'll be with Miss Joyce? They won't let your mom have you back? You'll be safe?"

"Yes! I told you I would be!"

"You just ran away from me. You thought I . . ."

He held me away from him to look at me.

"What?" I asked, shivering.

"Claire, you idiot! It's snowing and you haven't even got a coat on! Come inside!"

"No! I'm too happy to go inside"

"You'll freeze out here!" He tried to turn me toward the house.

I reached down, scooped up a handful of snow. "You love snow?" I asked, putting it against his face. When he nodded, I laughed and dropped it down inside his collar. He yelled and let go of me to grab at it.

Giggling, I dashed away from him, picked up more snow, threw it at him, grabbed more.

"Stop it!" he said, coming toward me. "You'll fall down and get hurt!"

I looked up at him surprised again at how beautiful he was. "You'd never let me!"

"Please. You just got out of the hospital. It's freezing out here. You haven't got a coat."

"All right." I dropped the snow and put my arm around him before he could move. "I'll go inside if you promise me two things."

"What?" he asked, brushing the snow out of my hair.

"Get the picture I drew of you asleep at the Saxon barn out of the tenant house for me. It's underneath the bottom drawer of the dresser upstairs."

"Claire."

"It's mine and I want it! Anyway, I know why you didn't want me to show it to anybody. You thought I'd show it to Mr. Beasley and he'd know how much you liked me and get after you."

"He already has. You gave him the drawing of the barn with Adair asleep beside it, remember?"

I giggled, tightened my arm around him. He'd turned red, but I didn't stop. "That's why I want the drawing, silly! Every time I see it, I'll know how much you cared about me when you made me go home. Look at me. Will you get it for me?"

"Yes, I'll get it for you." He still looked embarrassed, but he put his arms around me, looked down at me. "There isn't any chalk on your face."

"But you like me anyway?" I asked, laughing.

"No, silly, I love you anyway, but your teeth are chattering. What else do I have to do to make you go inside?"

I laughed, feeling warm, safe, and happy. "Kiss me."

"Idiot!" He kissed me, held me against him. "That's not fair. Now I don't want to go inside, either."

"It's okay," I said. "Next time, I won't be an idiot. I'll wear a coat." I touched his face, kissed him.

He took my hand, turned to the house. We started up the walk.

"Claire? That's a promise?"

"Yeah."

Epilogue

Galway Hall
Saturday, April 12th

Dear Ghost,

Sometimes late at night, I still wake up scared
Mom or Grandma's come back, is in the room
with me. When I do, I reach up and touch the
carved headboard on Grandmother's four-poster
bed. Then I know I'm safe and home. I know if
I'm scared and call her, Miss Joyce will come in
and sit with me and talk till I'm not scared anymore.

When I first came back here, I missed Mrs.
Bowman. She's so gentle and loving. I wish I'd
had a mom like her. Miss Joyce isn't like her, but
she likes me, cares about me.

For months after we came here, I would get
back up most nights and go downstairs to the studio to draw. Miss Joyce would hear me and come
down. She understood I had a lot of catching up
to do. She said she didn't want me to have to do
it alone. But she doesn't get up anymore. I asked
her not to, told her I wasn't scared by myself. I'm
not. Besides, she's grouchy enough in the morning
without being up too late.

It's been weeks since I got up. Last time, I
didn't draw very long. It's more fun in the daytime, when there's light to see outside, when Miss
Joyce isn't sleepy. When she's teaching me or
looking at my drawings, she's warm and gentle
and fun. On Sundays when Mr. Beasley comes

and plays all the songs he loves and we draw, the studio's the way it should be.

I don't draw much anymore when Clyde's around. Miss Joyce won't let him come over very often, says I see him enough in school. There're too many other things I've never gotten to do before, that are fun with him, for me to draw when he comes over. He still has to see everything I draw. He still smiles at them and then me. He doesn't know much about art. He even smiles at the goofs I don't want to show him. I wish I thought Miss Joyce would understand if I told her he'd never let me be stupid like Jeannie. I couldn't be so stupid, anyway. It would hurt him, too.

Clyde didn't want me to come back here. He wanted me to get Miss Joyce to sell the house so we could live somewhere else. I made him come see how beautiful Galway Hall is, made him stand in the studio, see Grandmother's garden covered with snow outside the many-paned windows. Clyde said the studio was a glass cage. With my arm around him, I tried to get him to remember you were happy here once, ghost, drawing, waltzing with your green-eyed stranger. He'd said you'd want us together.

But I was almost scared no one could be happy here again. Even Daddy's painting of the vines covering the old dead tree in the yard wasn't the way I remembered it. He painted it in the rain! I asked Miss Joyce to sell it, too. I don't want the vine crying! I'm glad he ran away! I don't want to be like Grandmother, making someone try to be what they can't!

I don't think about Daddy or Mom much, anymore. After we'd been here a while, and Mom'd gotten out of the hospital and gone, Miss Joyce asked if I worried about her. I don't. Mr. Beasley was right. You can't help people unless they help themselves, too. It's strange how much alike Daddy and Mom were, trying to do what their mothers wanted, even when it was wrong for them. You were like that, too. I was, but I won't ever let anyone else make life a cage for me again. I wish you and Mom had been loved, too.

It's getting warmer now. The daffodils at Galway Hall are golden. I've caught them on paper. When summer comes, when the vines your Evelyn planted grow up again around the old dead tree, and streamers freely cascade down toward me from its dead limbs in a glistening, white waterfall, then, while the blooms are touched by the sun's last light . . . shimmering . . . and all the air is green below, I'll paint the tree: for you, Mr. Beasley, Miss Joyce, Clyde, and me. Because I know seeds can take root in dead wood, grow out of decay, and somehow bloom.

I'm not and don't want to be you, ghost. I'm free of the past, now, and tired of it.

I promised Miss Joyce I'd finish my homework for Monday before Clyde gets here to take me to the movies. This wouldn't all fit in your little leather book, ghost, but Clyde's going to hide it and your diary in the mill . . . so you'll know we found each other.

The glass cages are broken.

Clyde likes hot fudge sundaes as much as I do. There aren't any cowboys in his movies.

Goodbye,
Claire Burden

the Judy Blume Diary

The Place to Put Your Own Feelings

This diary is wonderfully different from most because it can be started on any day of any year. It's a <u>special place</u> to write about your own <u>special feelings</u>. Spiral-bound, THE JUDY BLUME DIARY features a letter from the author, quotations from her books, and 36 black-and-white photographs.

Like your thoughts, THE JUDY BLUME DIARY belongs to you. It's the place to put your own feelings, whenever and however you like.

YEARLING $6.95

S.E. HINTON

**knows how to write for
the young and the restless.**

Telephone _____

Ship to (if different from above)
Name _____
Address _____
City/State _____ Zip _____
Telephone _____

Credit Card Information
Credit Card # _____ ☐ Visa   ☐ Mastercard
Expiration Date (mm/yy) _____ ☐ AmEx   ☐ Discover

Qty.	Author	Title	Price	Total

Use this order

form, or call

1-888-INDIGO-1

Total for books _____
Shipping and handling:
  $5 first two books,
  $1 each additional book _____
Total S & H _____
Total amount enclosed _____
Mississippi residents add 7% sales tax

Visit www.gensers press.com for the latest releases and specials.

AGAINST THE WIND

GWYNNE FORSTER

Genesis Press, Inc.

Indigo Love Stories

An imprint of Genesis Press, Inc.
Publishing Company

Genesis Press, Inc.
P.O. Box 101
Columbus, MS 39703

ISBN: 1-58571-213-2
Manufactured in the United States of America

First Edition 1999
Second Edition 2006

Visit us at www.genesis-press.com or call at 1-888-Indigo-1

To my husband, who for nearly thirty years has always been there for me when I needed him; who supports and encourages me in all that I do; who is my solid rock; and who is my love.

CHAPTER ONE

Leslie Collins glanced at the rear view mirror of her ten-year-old Taurus and momentarily relaxed her foot on the accelerator. Her heart pounded in her chest, and she felt as if her blood had begun to flow backwards, curdling, it seemed, by the seconds, and perspiration matted the hair at her temples. If that brown Chevy wasn't trailing her, why has it stayed two cars behind her on three different highways since she'd left Westminster? She had been careful to cover her tracks, but she had learned that the man had the tentacles of an octopus, a sensory system capable of finding her no matter where she went.

She accelerated rapidly, putting several more cars between hers and the Taurus, drove without signaling into the parking lot of a huge mall, and found security beside an eighteen-wheel Mack truck. From there, she watched the brown Chevy continue down Route 295. She spun her car around and headed in the direction of the Chesapeake Bay Bridge, feeling as if she were a vagabond looking for a place to camp for the night. Preston, a small town bordering Talbot County, Maryland, seemed as good a place as any, and she took a room in The Talbot Women's Residence, a comfortable lodging near the town square. The next morning, she got such information as she could on job opportunities and headed for Saber Estates, just outside of Dexter, about twenty miles from Preston. If she could get the job and keep it for the next six months, she could save enough money to finish her master's degree. And she'd take any job, even if it meant shelling beans eight hours a day.

The expanse and obvious wealth of Saber Estates surprised Leslie. She stepped out of her ancient Ford, took a deep breath and looked around. Lush greenery, flowering fruit trees and yellow April flowers bordering a green-shuttered, white Georgian mansion greeted her eyes. Everything about the locale gave her a sense of peace and security. Her future, indeed her life, depended on finding a job in a safe environment, far away from Westminster. She had left her secure position as bank officer in a small, but prosperous, bank in Westminster, Maryland, and gone job hunting once more, but after two months, she was still looking. She'd been told at the women's residence that the owner of Saber Estates was a tough taskmaster who demanded impeccable behavior from his employees. Just what she needed: employment with safety. Protection. He had an opening, but if he turned her down, she'd have to move on.

Fifty feet away, Jordan Saber examined his strawberry crates and estimated how many he had to buy. The promise of a bumper crop of berries, the best in several years, buoyed his spirits. If central Maryland was spared its usual early spring hail storms, he'd turn a good profit. He spied Leslie just as he finished stacking the usable crates, closed the shed and started to the house.

What's this?' he said aloud, seeing Leslie, a slim, young African-American woman dressed in stone washed jeans and a snug-fitting sweater, stretching like a young cat. In late summer, some townspeople cam to the Estates asking for unsold or blemished fruits and vegetables as hand-outs, and he was glad to oblige them when he could. But the whole town knew that he didn't "hand-out" before mid-

July. He was on the verge of discouraging her when she ran up to him and stopped dead in her tracks, as though stunned.

Leslie clasped one hand over her stomach, because that was where her pounding heart has settled. Nothing that had happened to her in her twenty-eight years had prepared her for Jordan Saber. He loomed over her, his impatience reflected in hypnotic green eyes, but that made no impression on her. She had temporarily forgotten where she was and why she was there. She hadn't spent much time paying attention to men, and especially not to white ones; if she had, it wouldn't have helped. This was a man who turned heads.

"Well?"

She wondered if he realized that his looks had disconcerted her and if he was overly concerned with them. Surely women had left him with no doubt as to his attributes.

"Morning, Miss. What can I do for you?"

Remembering her unemployed status restored her presence of mind. "Good morning. Can you tell—?"

"What's the problem, Miss?" They spoke simultaneously. His long legs propelled him at a pace she couldn't match despite her five-foot-seven-inch height, so she raced ahead of him to get in her question. Whoever he was, he was formidable. The man wasn't unpleasant, but his obvious disinterest almost caused her to leave.

"Where can I find Jordan Saber?"

He stopped walking and gazed down at her. "I am Jordan Saber. What can I do for you?"

"I'm looking for a job, and I can do—"

"I'm afraid I don't need any workers," he interrupted. For a minute, he thought she'd wilt right there, but she straightened up and looked him squarely in the eye.

"Mister, I have to find a job. I heard that you needed clerical help. I can keep books, do accounting, computer programming, typing, any office work, but I'll do anything. I've looked everywhere, but everybody tells me they're laying off people."

He walked on, and she grabbed his right arm, surprising him. "I fired my bookkeeper for dishonesty, and I haven't decided to hire another one. The only workers I need are lettuce pickers."

"I can do that. Pick lettuce, I mean." He meant his facial expression to imply that the very idea was ludicrous. His lettuce pickers were hefty men, able to carry two to three bushels of lettuce at a time and, anyway, he wouldn't put a woman in that rough bunch of men.

She must have realized that he was going to say no again, for she raised her chin high and molded her hands to her slim hips in an obvious effort to communicate to him the extent of her determination. "Mr. Saber, I need a job badly, and I'm not afraid to work."

They reached the back porch, and he stopped, stuck his hands in the back pockets of his overalls, and gave her a long penetrating stare. No, he didn't doubt that she was desperate; he didn't doubt it one bit. She looked it. But she didn't beg, and she wasn't whining. So she had his respect. He opened the screen door and nodded for her to precede him.

"Come on in. We'll see."

She let out the breath she'd been holding as she waited for his answer and hesitated as though uncertain. He stared down at her. Bemused. She was obviously intelligent, but so skittish. "Come on in. We're wasting time," he told her. "I'll see what Julia can do for you."

"Julia?"

He could see that he made her ill at ease, so he smiled. But that brought a wide-eyed look of surprise. Damn. He couldn't be that daunting.

"Is Julia your wife?"

He realized then that she would rather not enter the house alone with him and wondered what had made her wary of a normal man. "Julia," he called, "could you please step her for a second?" Softening his tone, he asked her name.

"I'm Leslie Collins." He heard the pride and sensed again her determination. She was rather interesting look-ing, with long, thick, unstraightened hair and large, wide brown eyes, her face devoid of make-up. And she cloaked herself in an arresting dignity. He eyed her with approval; self-pride was a trait that he admired. He watched her from the corner of his eye. She'd be better than good looking if she took one-third as much trouble with herself as some of the glamour girls he knew.

"Julia, this is Leslie Collins. Could you please set a place at the table for her? We'll talk while we eat breakfast. Where's Cal? Hasn't he come in yet? Miss Collins, this is my housekeeper and friend, Julia Baker. Mrs. Baker and her husband live here with me." Leslie noticed that he asked questions without waiting for the answers.

Leslie saw in Julia Baker a handsome blonde who looked like anything but a housekeeper, a fifty-ish woman with a fine-looking, slim figure and the self-confidence of a modern matron in her own home. And she wasn't wearing an apron. If she replaced those jeans and sneakers with a cocktail dress and sandals, she could go dancing without doing anything else to herself.

She extended her hand. "How do you do, Mrs. Baker?" The woman's firm handshake and cordial demeanor comforted her like a warm fire after a trek through a blizzard.

"I'm glad to meet you, Leslie. Please call me Julia." She pointed to a short hallway. "There's a bathroom just around there, if you'd like to wash your hands."

Leslie had already eaten breakfast, but she suspected that this man would talk with her while he ate his breakfast, and not a minute after he'd finished it. She quickly washed her face and hands and joined Jordan, who had seated himself at the table. Then she watched in amazement as Julia stood facing him and began to say grace just as Jordan was about to put a hot muffin into his mouth. He left his hand, muffin and all, poised at his lips while Julia spoke the few words. When she finished, he popped the muffin into his mouth.

Julia looked at Leslie with an amused twinkle. "Without us women, men wouldn't be anywhere near civilized."

Jordan ignored her, and Leslie sensed then that, formidable through he seemed, Jordan Saber might be human. Still, she wasn't planning to test the theory. She already

knew that a man who behaved decently could have a very dark side.

"Come sit down, Julia. Miss Collins is looking for a job. She'd prefer office work, but she says she'll take any kind of job, and if occurs to me that you've been needing some help." He turned to Leslie. "I don't need a clerk. I've learned that it's best to manage my own affairs, and unless they get to be too much. I'll keep my own books. Another thing. I am not going to hire you to work in a field with twenty men. The work's too hard, and the hands can't be expected to change their manners just because you're out there."

Leslie braced herself and prepared to reason with him. "I wouldn't expect them to. They can do what they like; I just want the chance to earn a living."

He scowled at her. "Where'd you come from? Don't you know what laborers are like when there're no women around? That's my decision and it's final. Julia's been needing someone to help her prepare meals for the hands—the men who work for me. They live in a workers' dorm that I built out beyond the barns, but that's not your business. I don't want to think about the reaction of those men if you go in that dorm, so my advice to you is stay away from there. You need to be here by six-thirty. You get Saturday afternoons and Sundays off. If you work overtime, you get paid time-and-a-half for it. I'll pay you the same thing I pay the men." When she raised her eyebrows, he snapped, "Don't worry, you'll earn every penny of it—three fifteen a week, and meals to start. When most of the hands came here, they were down on their luck—homeless, socially and

financially bankrupt. I've insisted that they save, and they're proud of what they're accumulated. Do you have a bank account? If you don't, then please open one. One-half of your salary goes into your bank account every week and I keep the bankbook. You can check your balance every pay day." She gasped and opened her mouth to protest, but he didn't pause.

"I advise you not to go to Pepper's Tavern at any time. It's not a place for people with self-respect."

Leslie clenched her fists, trying to control her anger. When she spoke, it was with dripping sarcasm. "Anything else, sir?"

Jordan ignored the taunt. "Yeah. Outside of this house, no alcohol is allowed on the Estates, except two beers or a half bottle of wine per person with supper on Saturdays, and I furnish that. I can't abide drunks. Those are the same terms the men get. Take it or leave it." Before she could say a word, he was out the door and headed for the fields.

"Just a minute, you!" She yelled after him. Furious, she placed her hands on her hips and stared at an inscrutable Julia.

"Don't take it so hard, honey," Julia told her coolly, "that lion can be a lamb, believe me."

"If you say so," She fumed, still boiling with the impulse to tell him what he could do with his job. But she knew she had to hold her tongue; she couldn't afford to lose the job, and he offered her the security she needed at the time. But he irritated her.

"He can't keep my bankbook with half of my salary in it," she seethed.

"I'm sure you expected to make a lot less than that. Right? Jordan is an honest man. If you've got him for a friend, you can consider yourself fortunate indeed. Come on. I'll show you the house."

Leslie had already noticed the wide center hall that connected the front vestibule and the kitchen. Carpeted with a brown patterned Persian rug and decorated with landscape paintings and family portraits, it suggested a casualness that belied the facts. Like the living and dining rooms, with their large wood-burning, marble fireplaces, matching Royal Bokara carpets, rich butter-soft leather seating and silver appointments, the hallway bespoke good taste and the funds to support it.

"You can see he's not a compulsive buyer," Julia said. "He decides he needs something and then goes looking for it. If he doesn't find it, he doesn't buy. I'd say that's the key to his personality."

At Leslie's raised eyebrow, she added, "Oh, he's a complicated one, all right. This is Jordan's office," she explained of the room next to the dining room. "It used to be the breakfast room, but we never used it. We call it the den."

She crossed the hall and pointed to a door at the edge of the vestibule. "That's my and Cal's apartment. We have a living room, bedroom and bath. Jordan sleeps upstairs, and there're two more bedrooms and baths up there. When I get time, I'll show you the laundry rooms, recreation room and bath downstairs."

"This is a big house. Who cleans it?"

"We have someone come in and clean once a week. I take care of Jordan's bedroom and bath, but you and I can

collaborate on that. Now let's divide the chores. We have dinner at noon. All the dinner meal, including the food for the hands, is prepared here. Jack—he's the house master at the men's quarters—comes at noon for the men's dinner and brings the pots back clean. Jack roasts a ham or turkey or fries chicken for their supper. What can you cook?"

"Most things. I'm a pretty good cook." It wasn't Julia's business that, in exchange for room and board, she'd cooked for the family in whose home she stayed while an undergraduate at the University of Maryland. She added, "I prefer to bake."

Julia smiled as though to say, so far, so good. "Where do you live?"

"About forty-five minutes or an hour from here," Leslie answered, intentionally vague; the less Julia knew about her, the better. But she would learn that not even Jordan could get around Julia.

"Dexter isn't more than thirty minutes walking," Julia said of the nearest town.

"I don't live in Dexter." She said it grudgingly.

Julia put the scouring pad down and waited, but Leslie said nothing. "Planning to say where you do live, honey?" Her tone was cool and decidedly unfriendly.

"Preston. At the women's residence."

Julia dropped her jaw. "How on earth will you get here by six-thirty? Jordan won't tolerate tardiness. I don't mean to pry, Leslie, but we do need to know who to contact in an emergency."

"I'll be here. Just call Mable Haynes on Bush Street in Westminster, if anything should happen to me." Julia scru-

tinized her, and from the length of her potent silence, Leslie couldn't help wondering whether the angel of minutes earlier had started to sprout horns.

"We'd better get busy. Here're the day's baking requirements. Can you handle them?"

"Sure. Anything else? I intend to earn my salary."

She wanted to bite her tongue at the slip. Julia's stare was a reminder that household help got wages, not salary. She'd have to watch herself.

"You've done well this morning. Leslie," Julia told her just before noon. "Jordan will be pleased."

Julia took a compact from the right pocket of her jeans and ran a powder puff across her nose. "It's a woman's duty to look good all the time," she explained. "Easy as pie, too, in an air-conditioned house." She brushed her left eyebrow back into shape. "My Cal loves to look at me."

Leslie thought it best not to say any of the half-dozen things that came to mind, but she wondered whether she wanted anything or anybody that she had to work so hard to keep. Feeling that she might have found the niche she needed, Leslie stepped outside to enjoy the warm sunshine and familiarize herself with her surroundings. To her surprise and delight, an African-American man approached with a basket of eggs. She had wondered if she'd see any brothers at the Estates and smiled her greeting at the pleasure of it. But the man merely touched the brim of his hat with his right index finger, nodded with a slight smile and walked on past her. Well, well. The strong, silent type. Maybe. She picked a few jonquils for the table and went back into the house.

Jordan strode into the kitchen followed by Cal. "Leslie, this is Cal, my foreman and Julia's husband. Whenever I'm not here, he's in charge. Cal, this is Leslie Collins."

Cal shook hands with her, and she liked him at once

"What's for dinner, Julia? I'm starved," Jordan said, emphasizing it with a pat on his stomach.

Julia's smile was that of an indulgent mother. "That's normal for you. Leslie made biscuits and you other favorite, apple pie." She turned to Leslie. "Those are two things that Jordan loves."

The four sat down to dinner, as they called the noon meal, and it amused Leslie that Julia again imposed grace on Jordan.

"You'll get used to it," Cal told Leslie. "It's a ritual that they play out at every meal."

Jordan buttered a biscuit and bit into it. "Well, I'll be damned. Julia, your biscuit-making days are over around her," he joshed. In a more serious tone, he added, "These are delicious, Leslie. I've never had better." When she appeared embarrassed, he pinned her with a perceptive, green-eyed stare, seeing both her reservedness and her intelligent countenance and sensing that she was more than she appeared to be. He'd heard her yell at him as he'd walked away from her that morning after he'd hired her. She had guts.

He ate a normal-sized meal, pushed his place aside and took a healthy helping of pie. He tempered his desire for everything but good food. A glance brought Leslie into his field of vision. He summed her up. A black Madonna in a green-checkered apron. For some reason, he didn't want to

become curious about her but, with his experience, he could see that she was a pearl whose oyster hadn't been shucked. Only a foolish man would get inquisitive about that kind of woman.

"Who was the man who brought the eggs to you around noon today?' Leslie asked Julia as they cleaned up after dinner.

"That's Ossie Dixon, one of the hands and my favorite.' Her right eye closed briefly in a suggestive wink. "Interested?"

Leslie wished she hadn't mentioned him. "That didn't cross my mind, Julia. I'm not looking for a man, and especially not where I work."

Julia dried her hands and massaged them with lotion. "He has quite a story. He's been way up and way down, but he'll make it. He's a good man."

Leslie would have liked to know more, for she had begun to suspect that Saber Estates was a refuge of sorts. She wouldn't probe, though, lest Julia misunderstand her motive.

Bone weary, but happy, Leslie began the long trip home, hoping that her luck would hold and her old Ford wouldn't choose that day to declare its mortality. Breakdowns were becoming a common occurrence, and she could barely afford the cost of towing and service. It was the morning trip, leaving home before daybreak, that worried her. She knew that if he ever found her alone on that deserted road with a car that wouldn't run, she wouldn't survive. And she was tired of running. Oh, God, she was so tired of picking up and looking for another place. Preston was the

third town in which she'd lived during the past eighteen months. If she'd been guilty of any wrongdoing, any transgression against anyone, she wouldn't complain about taking her medicine. But she'd been the victim. All she'd done was insist that her civil rights not be violated, and in spite of the trouble it had caused her, she' do it again.

Leslie got to work half an hour early one morning of her third week at Saber Estates, and Jordan observed that she didn't seem happy to find him standing beside the big oval kitchen window.

"Good morning, Leslie. Julia tells me that you two are getting on very well." He stirred his instant coffee, not looking at her or the cup but into the distance, thinking about her inexplicably strange behavior, of her friendliness with Julia and Cal, but not with him.

"You're early this morning," he went on, making conversation.

Her voice came to him soft and refined, and he liked it. "Good morning, I didn't expect to see you in here."

He frowned at her seeming disinclination to talk with him. Did she dislike him, or just men in general? "Why not?"

Her answer was a careless shrug. She was deliberately irritating him, and he decided not to be nice. "I live here, and I own the place. So I go and come as I please." This time, she moved her shoulders in another, more elaborate shrug. "You took your time deciding whether to return my greeting," he went on. "Testy this morning, eh?"

He thought she'd been insolent, but he didn't say it. Instead, he baited her. "At first I thought the cat had your

tongue, but it looks like you've been out fencing with a pit bull."

Leslie had arrived in a light mood and had planed to get a cup of coffee and relax for half an hour before beginning work. She was cross with Jordan without cause—just because he was there, and she knew it was unreasonable. It wasn't his fault that he made her conjure up images that had no business in her mind. She didn't know his motive for being there, and experience had taught her that trusting a man could be a big mistake.

She sat down, pulled off her rain boots and asked him, "Do you respond to people who talk to you without giving you the courtesy of looking at you? Well, I don't. As far as I could tell, you were speaking to the window. And if I've done any fencing today, it's been right here in this kitchen." She looked him right in the eye when she said it, and he stared at her for what seemed like minutes. Heat burned her face, but she didn't back down and held his gaze as long as he held hers.

He yielded; if he hadn't, he'd probably have taught her a lesson that they would both have regretted, because he didn't back down for women or men. He let his gaze stray over her brown face and shook his head. A conundrum if he ever saw one. If she was wary of him, she certainly wasn't showing it right then. He suppressed a smile. Her intelligence, wit and temper were a combination that had always appealed to him in a woman.

"I've probably been called a lot of things behind my back, but I'll wager this is the first time I've ever been called a pit bull. And right to my face, too." Her face was ashamed

and he couldn't help enjoying her discomfort. He turned toward the stove to get hot water for another cup of instant.

She stood and tied her apron. "If you'll wait a few minutes, I'll get you a decent cup of coffee. That stuff's not fit to drink."

He looked around at her and grinned, deliberately aggravating her. Let her squirm. Pit bull! "Should be good enough for a pit bull," he chided. When she seemed alarmed at the turn of the conversation, he decided to let up. "Thanks, I'd appreciate some. I hate instant coffee." He smiled to put her at ease. "Why are you here so early, Leslie?"

"No traffic."

His eyebrows shot up. "Is there ever any?"

"For me, two cars equal traffic."

He didn't believe it and let his expression tell her so, but when she turned her back and headed for the pantry, he let it drop. All right, if she didn't want to be friendly, it was no skin off his back.

Leslie had refused Jordan any space in her mind since that morning in the kitchen when, for the second time, she'd been staggered by his uncommonly good looks. And he gave her plenty of assistance, ignoring her most of the time. Indeed, he barely spoke to her even at meals, except to tell her he enjoyed the food she cooked. And she was glad for his coolness. He was not a man easily ignored. But she didn't so much ignore him, as she refused to let herself see him as he really was——six feet five, with black hair, green eyes, physically trim and knock-out handsome. Her defense against him was to pretend that he wasn't there by

not speaking to him or looking at him unless she was compelled to do so. If she seemed rude, she couldn't help it.

Jordan was demanding and most times, not particularly friendly, except with Cal and Julia. And even though she sensed he was a gentleman, she told herself that she didn't really like him. Sometimes, when her emotions betrayed her and her response to him confused her, she let herself believe that she disliked him, though she couldn't pinpoint a reason.

On one of her homeward journeys, as her mind wandered, it occurred to Leslie that Jordan was something of an enigma. That morning she'd heard him speaking on the telephone and had been surprised at the level of his language. He'd sounded like a very polished, sophisticated man. "Not your typical farmer," she said aloud. She'd notice that he never came to the table without washing his face and hands. He was always cleanly shaven and, even though he worked beside his men, his hands were always clean, his nails well shaped and manicured. Since when did a working farmer have hands like Jordan's? She pondered. Strong, elegant, beautiful hands. She wondered what it would be like if he touched her, and she shuddered. Was she crazy? She wasn't going to waste thoughts on Jordan Saber or any other man. She shook her head as though to clear it of him, and laughed at herself. She already knew it would take more than a shake of her head to get Jordan Saber out of it.

The next morning, as she gathered flowers for the dinner table, she slipped on the dew dampened grass and fell into a patch of thorny rose bushes.

His deep voice startled her. "Taking an early siesta?"

"I'm stuck here."

She watched as his brow creased in bewilderment. "Stuck? What do you mean, stuck? Can't you get up?" He grinned at her, and she wished she'd been looking somewhere else. Her insides quivered, and the earth seemed to shift beneath her.

"I can get up, if I want to leave my clothes here," she told him, testily. "I'm caught in these thorns." She gestured toward the rose bush, and he hunkered down before her, still showing his white teeth in a roguish grin.

"Let's see what we have here. Hmm. At this rate, I won't get any biscuits for dinner." He peered down at her and must have assumed that she didn't want him too near her, for he said, "I'll be out of your way in a minute. Just hold still."

But he couldn't have guessed more incorrectly; she'd almost frozen, shocked by the thrill she got from his nearness.

He picked off a thorny bush that had hooked itself into her blouse. "What's the matter, Leslie, don't you trust me? A guy doesn't have to be a genius to do this."

Being so close to him unsettled her, and she didn't know whether she didn't trust herself to answer him or was numbed by the memory of another man who got too close to her. Jordan managed to pick the thorns from the back of her blouse, and she started to get up, but he stopped her with both hands on her shoulders.

"You want a head full of these things, too?" he asked her, nodding toward the branch that hung just above her.

"Hold on." Without another word, he put an arm around her shoulder and the other under her knees, tilted her slightly and slid her from under the rose bush. He stayed here, hunkered before her, looking at her as if attempting to assess her in some way. Then he stood, lifted her to her feet, picked the flowers up, and handed them to her, dusted off the back of his overalls and walked away.

Coming to her senses, she called after him, "Thanks."

He stopped, turned around and grinned at her. "You're welcome, provided you mean it. It was my pleasure."

She knew he could see her embarrassment from the distance that separated them. Feeling herself unsettled in strange ways, she walked slowly back to the house. Maybe she should leave Saber Estates before she had another experience like the one she'd had with Faron Walker; Jordan didn't seem the type, but she hadn't suspected that Faron was, either. And another thing. She hadn't liked Faron at all. But Jordan….

As she reached the back porch, she looked up into the censoring gaze of Ossie Dixon, who didn't return her greeting but sucked his teeth as though in disgust, held the screen door open for her, and went on his way. She didn't know what she'd done to earn his displeasure, and she didn't plan to spend a minute worrying about it.

That evening after work, when she turned the corner into Euclid Street, where the women's residence was located, immediately a brownish sedan headed straight in her direction, paused as if to allow the driver a good look at her, and then sped away. Inside her room, she locked her door and leaned against it. She couldn't be certain that it was he,

but who else? Surely not...Oh Lord, how had he found her? She hadn't left a trail, not a single clue as to where she was going. She calmed herself with the thought that it might not have been Faron.

She changed into a blue corduroy jump suit and went to the dining room for supper, looked around for company and joined Berle Cox, an administrative nurse at a nearby hospital.

Berle welcomed her with a wide grin. "Girl, you're a knockout in that shade of blue. How's the new job? You gonna stay there, or you just passing through?"

She liked Berle and welcomed her friendship, but the less people knew about her, the less of a chance Faron had of finding her. "I hope I'm fixed for the next six months or so. I have one more semester before I get my masters degree, and I'm hoping this job will put me over."

Berle peeled a radish and put both the peeling and the radish in her mouth. "Where'd you luck out?"

Leslie pretended diffidence. "Honey, if the word gets out, half of this residence will be trying to take my job. They're too hard to get. I'll tell when I'm ready to leave, and somebody else can get a break."

Berle nodded. "You've got it right, girl. Some of these women could take salmon from a grizzly. A job or a man; to myself." She was tempted to be friends with Berle, but her mind told her the less anyone knew about her, the safer she'd be. With friends, a person could get loose-tongued. Better not.

If Leslie though Jordan an enigma, he'd taken to referring to her mentally as "that riddle with Julia." You would

have thought he was a snake the way she acted around him. Her wariness of him was barely short of rudeness. And as friendly as Cal was, she seemed hardly more comfortable with him. He recalled her reluctance to enter the house with him when she'd come looking for work. What kind of experiences has she had with people—no, with men? That was it. She was wary of men. He walked on to the barn, puzzled and not liking it one bit. She gave him a strange feeling. He wasn't a ladies' man, and he had his ego under control. But damn. He wasn't used to having women look straight through him and not see him. He'd swear that Leslie even managed to look around him if he got too close. Any place, but not at him. And he probably wouldn't give a hoot, but the more he saw of her, the more she appealed to him. And her scent. From the first thing in the morning until she left in the afternoon, her delicate woman's scent could tantalize him. Sweet and clean as an early morning spring breeze. He whistled sharply. She worked for him, which meant she had no business being in his head.

He finished examining the tack and was walking to the garage to get his pickup when he noticed a strange man leaning against the garage door. It wasn't that the man was ill kempt and apparently down and out, though that was an apt description. Jordan didn't judge a man harshly for that. He'd seen too many such men scramble to their feet when given a chance. But he knew when a man was honorable, and this one wasn't.

He walked up to the man. "Do you want something?"

"You got a woman here named Collins?"

He didn't like anything about the man, and he'd wager that he wasn't a friend of Leslie's. "What do you want with her?"

"Don't know that it's any of your business."

Jordan tensed. The man had to be a stranger to the region; every man within miles was familiar with Saber Estates, and most of them recognized Jordan. He liked this less and less.

"Is that so? Are you a process server? Where's your ID?" He noted the shifty glances, the nervous foot shuffling.

"I'm not serving anything, and I don't see that it's your business."

Jordan moved closer, and the man backed away. "If it's not my business, get off of my property. If you put one foot back on my land, you're going to jail—after I give you a work-over that you'll never forget. And don't you doubt it." As the man hastened away, Jordan was certain that his intent had been criminal. He made a mental note to have a talk with Leslie, as it occurred to him, not for the first time, that he knew nothing about her. He corrected that. He knew that she was neither a farm laborer nor a household servant, and he'd only given her that job because he'd sensed her desperation. And all that polish. He meant to ask her where she had learned her domestic skills.

CHAPTER TWO

The Friday morning of her fourth week at Saber Estates, Leslie did the unpardonable: she rushed into the kitchen one hour late, ten minutes before Jordan came in for his breakfast. Julia had become increasingly anxious about Leslie's daily trips and, on this particular morning, feared that Leslie might have met with an accident or some other misfortune. She has sensed that Leslie lived right up to the edge of peril. But Leslie didn't extend herself, never volunteering personal information and resisting answering questions about herself, so she kept her distance. She still hadn't decided that she liked Leslie, though it was impossible not to respect her.

She could only stare in amazement when Leslie burst into the kitchen with her entire body soaking wet. Quickly collecting her wits, she dropped the breakfast preparations and rushed Leslie to the basement, hoping to get her dry and warm before Jordan returned for his breakfast. But fate wouldn't have it that way.

She knew her scheme to get Leslie ready for work before he got there was doomed when she heard him call, "Where is everybody?"

Impatience didn't begin to describe his mood right then. It didn't help that the rain had caused a flooding in his sweet potato beds and that he'd had to devise an emergency draining system while the rain poured down in torrents. He was hungry and damp, and there was no food and no one was cooking it.

"Julia, what's going on here?" He started to pace the floor but heard low voices in the basement and bounded down there two steps at a time.

Leslie was looping the belt of his white terry cloth robe around here, and when she looked up and saw him looming over her and wearing what he supposed was a ferocious scowl, she backed away.

"What are you doing in my clothes, and where is my breakfast? Where's Julia? Two women in that kitchen, and I still can't get a meal." Maybe his anger needed release, or maybe he relished the opportunity to get to her. He didn't know. But he began stalking her the way a jungle cat stalks its prey, reveling in the unholy joy it gave him. He knew he shocked her but, for her attitude toward him, she deserved it. She didn't seem overly perturbed, and that annoyed him. She glared at him, turned and strolled up the stairs. He didn't doubt that she'd have loved to swear at him, and he wished she had; he allowed a person as much room as he gave himself, and he'd gotten her thoroughly mad. But the lady had just raised her head and walked away.

Not to be outdone, he yelled after her. "What's the matter with you? The least you could do is explain yourself."

Still holding Leslie's wet clothing; Julia rushed into the recreation room where he stood with his hands in his back overall pockets and a scowl on his face.

"What's got into her? And what's she doing in my robe? What's going on her, Julia? Am I going to get any breakfast?" As furious as he was, he remembered to soften his voice. Jordan cared deeply for Julia, and he treated her like

the mother figure that she had been for him since child-hood.

"Will you simmer down? Leslie got soaking wet coming to work this morning. It was raining so hard that she could barely see in front of her and fell into the ditch. By the time she got here a few minutes ago, she was soaked, muddy and shivering. On top of that, you have to scream at her like a madman. Jordan, really, sometimes I just wonder why you like to make people think you're such an ogre."

"I told her to be here by six-thirty, and you're telling me she was an hour late." He continued pacing, but his voice had lost its sharpness.

"Didn't you hear anything that I said?"

"Yeah," he growled. "You said she fell in a ditch, got wet and... What did you say? What was she riding in, a truck? Somebody tell me what's going on around here?" Julia laid a soothing hand on his arm.

"Jordan, you have never showed any interest in Leslie, so I figured you didn't care that she gets here before six-thirty every morning by leaving home while it's still dark and driving a jalopy that finally gave out last night. She got here this morning by pedaling an old bicycle all the way from Preston. And you take your hat off in the house."

As though oblivious to Julia's command, he leaned against the edge of the pool table. "I ignore her because she's wary of me, and because she goes out of her way to avoid being alone with me. Julia, I have never closed my eyes to the suffering or misfortune of any of my employees. Why didn't you tell me about this?"

"The occasion didn't arise," she replied, not bothering to keep the testiness out her voice.

"Where does she live in Preston, and why couldn't she find a job closer to home than this?

"When are you going to learn to give a person one question at a time? She lives in the women's residence, and I'm sure that she'd exhausted every other lead when she came here asking you for a job. You know the unemployment rate in this country. Anybody who's got a job is keeping it."

"In the women's residence? Damn!" Apparently musing over what to do with that information, he remained silent for a time before he asked her, "Julia, may I please just have some breakfast?"

"Sure. I'll be up just as soon as I get these things into the washing machine." She found Leslie sitting at the kitchen table, still wearing Jordan's robe and apparently too drained even to consider starting the breakfast.

"Am I fired or not?"

"I'm sure that hasn't crossed Jordan's mind. Go in my bathroom and get a shower. There's some shampoo in the cabinet beneath the bowl, and you may use my hair dryer and brush. Keep the robe on until your things dry. I'll get the breakfast on the table. And don't you let Jordan upset you. He's all bark and no bite."

Leslie looked at Julia, an expression of surprise claiming her face. She smiled her thanks.

Leslie blow-dried her hair, brushed it around her shoulders and started toward the kitchen. When she saw Jordan sitting there, she stopped, uncertain of his mood. If he

started in on her again, she knew she'd give him as good as she got.

He looked up and smiled. "Come sit down, Leslie."

This man is as mercurial as a thermometer in rapidly shifting temperature, she reflected. Both of her eyebrows arched at the change in him. When she sat down, but didn't start to eat, he stopped eating.

"We're going to talk, but first eat your breakfast." She made no move to begin.

"What's the matter? Aren't you hungry?" he asked, his voice low and gentle. If he had deliberately attempted to seduce her with it, he'd have been less successful. She resisted the unintended seduction and eyed him evenly.

"Has Julia said grace yet?" His head came up sharply, and he stared at her for what seemed like heart-stopping minutes before a broad grin slowly transformed his face into the quintessence of male beauty. She sat mesmerized, enthralled by the dancing lights in his soft green eyes. She hadn't realized that she stared at him until he laughingly teased her with, "Did I get some egg on my face?'

She didn't move a facial muscle and quickly shifted the focus from her to him, though she had no idea where the question came from. "Do you have any children, Mr. Saber?" Now he could be shocked, she told herself with some satisfaction.

"No, I don't have any children, Leslie. I've never been married." He said it softly, as if to reassure her of his gentleness. "And while we're getting personal, call me Jordan. Everybody else on the Estates does. And don't call me `sir',

either. I'm not old enough to be your father." He frowned, as if trying to imagine why he'd added that.

Leslie had his attention. He was looking at her, wondering what was so pleasantly different, when Julia joined them for coffee and immediately supplied the answer.

"Why Leslie, I never dreamed that you have such beautiful hair."

"So that's what's different. Looks good. Why don't you wear it that way all of the time, Leslie?" Jordan queried.

"I can't when I'm working. It gets in the way.'

Julia cleared her throat to head off the bite of his tongue, but she needn't have bothered. He didn't exploit the vulnerable; indeed, since childhood, he had defended and protected them, female and male alike.

Aware that his deep voice could shock, he spoke softly. "Leslie, if you didn't look in the mirror when you brushed your hair, I suggest you do it now."

"Why?"

"Because you look damned nice, that's why." He growled. "And I like it. If you didn't have such a hassle getting here, maybe you could manage it every morning.

"Oh my," she muttered with studied impudence, "the lion has just replaced the lamb." At that, Julia snickered, was unable to control her amusement, and finally began to laugh hysterically. Caught up in the light heartedness, Leslie dropped her face into her hands to hide her amusement, as though uncertain as to how he'd tolerate being laughed at. But she soon threw her head back and laughed aloud. Jordan looked at her, spellbound. He'd never heard

her laugh before. It was music. Come to think of it, he had never seen her smile.

"My Lord," he said to himself, "she's damned lovely." And just as irreverent. He promised himself that he would find out who Leslie Collins really was.

Julia sobered and explained that she'd lent Leslie her new designer shampoo that was guaranteed to make hair wavy, bouncy, shiny, softer and whatever else you wanted. "Cal bought it for me, because I like to try new things. It sure is good for Leslie's hair."

Fully attuned to her now, he observed Leslie's embarrassment. "I didn't mean to make you uncomfortable."

"Oh, I don't mind. The blow-drying gets some of the kinkiness out of it, and it's straighter than I usually wear it, but it'll curl up again in a few hours."

Julia got up and took her place at the sink. "I've got to start the clothes drier. You sit here and finish your breakfast, Leslie. I'll bring your clothes up in a few minutes."

Leslie thanked Julia and sipped her coffee, but she didn't look at Jordan. If he hadn't already upset her that morning, he'd ask her why she got out of sorts whenever she found herself alone with him. Hell, that kind of behavior could give a man ideas.

He leaned back in his chair and strummed his fingers on the table, amused that her gaze shifted from one of his hands to the other one. "Why do you live at the women's residence, Leslie? Not many young people live there. Most of the residents must be twice...." he paused and looked closely at her, "...even three times your age. Can't you find

an apartment?" He didn't believe in tiptoeing around a matter that needed airing.

"Why are you settling for that?" he persisted, when she continued to eat and didn't respond.

"It's what I can afford."

"What about a room in a private home."

She shrugged, "I've had it with that. I'm doing the best I can, Mr. Saber."

She tipped up her chin, obviously intending to glare at him and force him to back off, but he let only gentleness and tenderness reflect in his eyes, and warmth spread throughout his body when she melted and half-smiled.

"My name's Jordan," he reminded her. "Are you leveling with me? I think it's reasonable for me to expect that much." He sharpened his tone a little, hoping to discourage the honeysweet, inviting expression on her face. And he told himself to get his reaction to her under control.

Leslie sighed in resignation. It was as she had feared. She hadn't wanted these people to involve themselves in her life. She'd had four weeks to observe the camaraderie among them. No, it was more than that; the Bakers cared deeply for Jordan and him for them. They were a family, and she realized that she wanted to belong, wanted to be a part of them. Julia treated Jordan more like a son than an employer. She regarded him carefully, wondering how much she could confide.

"I don't remember my mother, and I lost my father when I was ten. He was very good to me and I knew he loved me, but he was reserved and rarely showed affection. I missed him. Still do. My mother's best friend took me to

live with her, her husband and four daughters, and I grew up as one of her five girls. I lived with them until I went away to school and, even then, I spent the big holidays in their home. I'll always regard Mom and Pop Haynes' house as my home."

"Do you have to continue staying in Preston? Your car is ready for the junk heap, and I can't let you pedal so far twice a day and work, too."

"It's not so bad. No one bothers me at the women's residence, and my room is comfortable and quiet. So I'll manage."

He made a mildly profane comment. "There's a very nice apartment above the garage that was built for the chauffeur that my uncle never hired. Julia stayed there for a while when she first came to work here. It's very comfortable, and you may have it for as long as you want it." Observing her skepticism, or was it suspicion, he added, "I provide housing for all my other employees. There's no reason why you should be an exception. I'll drive you to Preston this morning to get your things, and you can move right in."

Nothing came without a price. Good as it sounded, she had to think about it. When she didn't respond, he prompted, his manner gentle. "Leslie, will you please say something?"

On the verge of telling him to stop handling her with kid gloves, she reflected that she was partly responsible for that. So, instead, she asked him, "Why are you doing this? You can find a cook anywhere."

"Leslie, I'm not known for patience, and I've got work to do. I have no ulterior motive in offering you that apartment. It's empty. Do you want it or not?" He made as if to leave the table, glanced at her and saw the unshed tears glistening in her eyes. What a woman! She refused to shed them.

"My God, woman, I didn't mean to upset you. I was trying to help." He realized that he was roaring. Probably frightening her. He ran his fingers through his hair in an uncharacteristic gesture of helplessness.

"Leslie, I'd so soon hurt myself as you. You're as vulnerable as a newborn baby." Without thinking, he took her hand. "Do you suppose I'm such a bastard that you have to be afraid of me?"

She looked at him, obviously disconcerted, and he gazed down at her in surprise. She wasn't only uncertain of him and of his motives, he realized. Whether she knew it or not, she was attracted to him. Damn, he thought. She's vulnerable in more ways than one. His own reaction told him that she was no less susceptible to him than he was to her. He shrugged if off; he wasn't about to harbor an attraction for one of his employees. Besides, he wasn't looking for a woman. He gazed at her inquiringly, waiting for her answer.

"No. Oh, no! You haven't hurt me," she said at last. "I don't know why I'm reacting this way. This is the first time I've even been near tears since...."

"Since what?" Jordan stiffened. He knew there was more than she'd told him. "What?" He stroked her shoul-

der, wanting to put her at ease, but she leaned away from him.

"Look, Mr. Sa..., I mean, Jordan. I don't want to talk about it. Thank you for letting me have the apartment, but I don't want you to go all the way to Preston just for me." And I don't want to be obligated to you or to anybody else, she might well have added.

Patience, man, Jordan lectured himself. "How do you plan to bring your things here? Think you can drag them piece by piece on that old bicycle?" He reached toward her in an effort to soften the bite of his words.

She drew back, immediately on the defensive. "Don't touch!" She didn't want to experience that frustrating heat that had seared her minutes earlier when she felt his hands on her.

"What?" Jordan scowled at her. "Don't what? Don't touch you? You'd better rid yourself of your fancy notions, woman. You're as safe with me as a saint in heaven." His anger was almost palpable, but Leslie stood her ground, giving him a very level look.

"I'm glad to know that." She wouldn't let him know how his words had cut her.

Jordan glared at her. "For goodness sake, Leslie, cut me some slack here. I was only trying to put you at ease. You may have had some unpleasant experiences with men, but you ought to have sense enough to realize that not all men are vultures. If you can't see that, maybe you'd better leave. Damned if I'm going to tiptoe around you."

"If you want me to leave, I'll go." Her pride wouldn't let her disclose how much that prospect disturbed her.

"I don't want you to leave," he growled, as if aware that she had boxed herself in. "I just want you to realize that I am not harassing you and that I never will. I put my arm around your shoulder protectively and you behaved as if that was perfectly natural. Five minutes later, I merely reached toward you, and you got your back up. Settle down, Leslie. If you want space, I'll give you plenty of it, with pleasure. Do you want to see the apartment or not?"

Leslie knew why she was always on the defensive. Because she wasn't independent, she considered herself to be vulnerable, and vulnerability attracted abuse. That was the law among animals, but people were not wild animals; they lived in civilized communities with laws and customs to protect each member. Yet, when she had needed that protection, it hadn't been there for her, and she'd been left to her own devices. Nearly five years after a humiliating, almost ruinous experience, she was still continuously looking over her shoulder and worried for her safety. If she had learned anything, it was that she should never relax her guard around men. She had vowed that she would never depend on them for anything and, so far, she had kept those vows. She looked at Jordan Saber, felt—even across the expanse of the big kitchen—his towering strength. She would take the chance, she decided, but she'd keep her eyes and ears open, and she'd be ready to leave at the merest suggestion of a problem between them.

Her silence annoyed Jordan, but he suspected that she had reason to hesitate before making such a move. "Let's get one thing straight," he told her, guessing the source of her reticence. "If a woman doesn't want me, I don't want her.

And I know when she does and when she doesn't." He knew she didn't find his last remark comforting, and he knew why.

"Go down and get your clothes from Julia and hurry back up here. I'll show you the apartment and, if you like it, we'll take it from there."

She wished Julia would go over there with them but, after mulling it over, she felt ashamed. I'm the problem, not him, she told herself. He was a generous man, and she would thank him, but she'd taught herself not to have to learn anything twice. Her face burned when she remembered how she'd reacted when he touched her. It had been an innocent gesture, but so had Faron's little friendly touches that got bolder and bolder. Yet, she knew that Jordan didn't need to impose himself on women. She walked downstairs, seeing in her mind's eye his elegant facial contours, long curling black lashes and moss-green eyes. He had to be the envy of men and the goal of countless women. That alone was enough to comfort her.

CHAPTER THREE

Jordan leaned against the doorjamb, enjoying Leslie's surprise as she examined the apartment—a large, light and airy living room, small bedroom with a picture window, porch and steps that led down to the garden, and a serviceable kitchen. It pleased him that he'd recently renovated the bathroom when he'd thought Ossie might like to stay there. The sunken tub, glass enclosed shower and pale green wall paper with assorted sea shells had given Ossie an excuse to refuse. "Too feminine," he'd said, though Jordan knew the truth: that Ossie hadn't wanted to live apart from the other workers. Leslie swung around to look at him, her face beaming with a happiness that made his heart skip a beat. But his enjoyment of her pleasure was short lived, for a frown quickly wiped out her glow.

"What is it?" she asked him.

His mind had been at work, but he didn't let a person look at him and know his thoughts. He allowed himself a lazy half-smile. While Leslie had been looking over the apartment, he had been thinking over some of the things she'd told him.

"Leslie, have you borrowed money from anybody?"

He knew she wanted to reveal as little as possible of herself, but he didn't intend to give her an alternative. Without seeming to pressure her, he'd get what he was after, no matter how relentless he had to be. He had a right to certain information about his employees, and he didn't pretend everything was fine when he could see that it wasn't. Where there was smoke, look for fire.

She took a deep breath and let it out. "I had to borrow money from a small finance company to finance a part of my education. The interest rate is very high, but at least I could get the loan without collateral. Repaying it has meant that I've had to put school on hold for a while."

"Probably a loan shark," he muttered under his breath.

School, huh? Probably the key to Leslie—or one of them, but he'd let that go for the present. He didn't mention another thing that was baffling him. She was here in this apartment alone with him, and she didn't appear to be anxious. That pleased him, but he had no intention of mentioning it to her. She also seemed to have forgotten their conflict of only minutes ago. Well, better that than an atmosphere of animosity, he mused.

Seeing the joy on her face, he urged, "All right, let's go." He looked down at her and realized that sometime since seven-thirty that morning when he'd bullied her, he'd developed a lot more compassion for her than was healthy. Damned if he could figure it out. "Come on, Leslie," he roared—that demeanor being safer— "let's get going."

Leslie headed back to the kitchen to tell Julia where she was going. Jordan might ignore the fact that her being away for a couple of hours in the morning would upset Julia's work schedule, but she didn't want to make an enemy of the woman. She stopped short as she reached the bottom of the stairs leading from the little apartment. Sometime in the course of the morning's events, Jordan has ceased to be a gruff, demanding boss who, in her mind, could, if he so decided, use his power and authority to wreck the lives of those beneath him. Somehow, his gentleness and compas-

sion had made a mark with her and, in her perception of
him, had replaced his toughness. Unless he had a multiple
personality, he was a good man. He had barked at her
because she'd broken his iron-clad rule and come to work
late, but as soon as he'd learned she had a problem, he'd
reached out to her, offering her compassion and assistance.
She skipped into the kitchen.

"Julia, Jordan's going to give me the apartment over the
garage, and he wants me to get my things from the women's
residence in Preston right now. I know this'll upset everything here."

Julia crammed leeks into the blender, put the lid on it
and turned to face Leslie. "That's the best thing I've heard
recently. It's a lovely apartment, and you won't have those
long trips every day. You go on. They'll get cornbread
instead of biscuits."

"Oh, no. If you measure out five pounds of flour and a
pound and a quarter of lard, I'll get them made before Jack
comes for the steam table."

"We'll see. Now run along and, for goodness sake, put
on some lipstick. A woman ought to rouge her lips. Hurry.
You know how far Jordan's patience goes when he's waiting
on somebody."

Jordan leaned against his big, silver gray Town Car waiting for Leslie. His pick-up would probably have been more
suitable for transporting her belongings, but he had wanted Leslie to know, somehow without being told, that she
deserved his courtesy, that she wasn't merely a servant. He
didn't welcome the intruding thought: if she wasn't a servant, what was she? She cooked, cleaned and did laundry,

and he paid her for it. Frowning, he wondered if he wasn't going overboard over nothing and if he'd regret it. She wasn't his responsibility, or at least, she hadn't been. And he didn't want a woman leaning on him. He was sick and tired of clinging vines. They could fall in love right on cue—as soon as they found a man able to take care of them in the style to which they aspired. He had no more use for them than he had for unfaithful bed-hoppers like Joan, his ex-fiancée. He liked and admired capable, intelligent women who could meet a man halfway. He wasn't normally gullible; far from it. Was he making a mistake with Leslie? It surprised, almost shocked him, that he felt so protective toward her. She was nothing like other women he'd known but, still, it bore watching. Lean on him? He laughed in self-derision. She certainly hadn't given any indication that she wanted to lean on him or anybody else.

Leslie skipped off the porch and down the steps, capturing Jordan's attention. He surmised that it was the first time he'd seen her express youthfulness or lightheartedness. The hell with being gullible. He wanted her to forget whatever it was that had clipped her wings, to smile and laugh. He wanted...

"Oh, Jordan," she whispered, as she caressed th automobile's sleek lines. "I didn't know you had one of these. It's beautiful and so elegant. But shouldn't you take the truck? My stuff is old, and I wouldn't like anything to soil your nice car."

"None of that," he tempered, gruffly, "I want the people at that place to see that you'll be with good folks." He opened the door on the passenger side and placed his hand

lightly on her elbow to assist her. She flinched slightly, and it didn't pass unnoticed. This flower closed its petals if you got too close.

The hell with it, he thought. I'm not going to ignore my upbringing just to suit her.

Leslie sat against the door of the car, as far away from Jordan as she could get, surreptitiously watching him as he drove. His hands with their long, tapered fingers fascinated her. Hands that might have sprung from an artist's palette. Elegant. Strong. And he sat behind the wheel as if it were he rather than the car that had the horsepower. Unaware that he knew she was watching him, she fastened her eyes on his profile but, caught with her thoughts unsheltered, she quickly looked away.

"Where did you learn to cook so well?" Jordan asked, reducing the sudden tension.

"After I finished high school, I had two summer jobs working in a restaurant. The first summer I was a waitress. The next, I worked as a short order cook."

He'd begun to understand that Leslie never volunteered information about anything, including and especially herself. If he wanted more, he had to ask for it. He digested that for a moment. "What did you do in the winters?"

"I went to the University of Maryland on an academic scholarship, but I stayed with a family and cooked the dinner and weekend meals in exchange for room and board." He smiled and didn't dare ask himself why he was so inordinately pleased with that reply. He'd been right. She was neither a house servant nor a laborer.

"Come on. Leslie. You're hard ground after a long drought. Hell, I need a pickax to get anything out of you. What were you studying? Did you get your degree? What did you do the other summers?" When he glanced at her, he had the pleasure of seeing her grin mischievously.

"I worked as a secretary in the summer following my sophomore year in college, but my boss was a boorish as..." She hesitated and, when he glanced at her, he saw something—fear, pain or a bad memory—flicker briefly in her eyes. He quickly interrupted her.

"You don't have to say it. I'm beginning to understand a lot of things. Go on."

Her voice was stronger now. Melodious. Prideful. She spoke eagerly. "Well, I've got my bachelor's degree, and I'm still studying." The sudden swerving of the car in from of them distracted his attention from their conversation, and averting a multi-car collision took all of his skill as a driver. At the residence, they collected her things, and Jordan packed them into the Town Car and headed back to the Estates.

"Over here, Ossie," Jordan called as he stepped out of the car and saw the man walking toward the house.

Leslie watched the man stroll casually over to them, his face displaying a warmth and receptiveness that she hadn't previously observed in him.

He walked directly up to Jordan, smiled, braced his elbow against the car and supported his head with his hand. "What can I do for you, Jordan?"

"Ossie, this is Miss Collins."

She noted the warmth in Jordan's equally casual manner, and it occurred to her that they seemed more like friends than employer and employee.

Jordan opened the car's trunk. "Give me a hand with her things. She'll be staying in the apartment that I offered you last winter."

"Hello, Ossie."

"How do you do?" he replied, though he barely spared her a glance.

She reached for her portable typewriter, but Jordan stopped her with a hand on her shoulder. "We'll take care of this. You go on up and show us where you want us to place things."

She was about to thank him, when she noticed the direction of Ossie's gaze. He stared at Jordan's hand on her shoulder, scowled, and she knew he'd drawn the wrong conclusion when he trained knowing eyes on her and let her see his disapproval, his distaste. She could almost measure the change in Ossie, from a tepid acknowledgment of her presence to outright dismissal. Like an unheralded chill at the sudden setting of an autumn sun. She glanced at Jordan although, as she'd expected, he hadn't noticed their wordless exchange. When a brother looked at an African-American woman, she knew what he saw. And Ossie Dixon left no doubt that he didn't like her and had no use for her.

After Ossie left them, Jordan helped Leslie rearrange the apartment and made notes of things she would need. He had begun to measure the filter in an air conditioner when she screamed. He looked up just as the step stool on which she was standing tilted to a dangerous angle and, with light-

ening speed, he made it to the closet just as she fell backward and into his arms. He stared at his right forearm, wrapped firmly across her chest and all but clasping her breasts, and at his left hand splayed across her belly. He settled her on her feet, and she turned to face him, her face wreathed in obvious amusement—no doubt at her folly—when her mouth moved to within an inch of his own. He knew the second she realized the position of his hands and how they felt, for she gasped as though shocked. For a moment, she stared at his lips. Then she shifted her glance to his eyes. That blatant, if innocent, invitation sent his blood pressure to a dangerous high, and he swallowed hard. But as if on automatic pilot, she gathered her wits and, with seeming reluctance, leaned away from him, obviously shaken. But not before he'd seen that she wanted more of him. Not before he realized that he wanted her and had wanted her for weeks. He let himself breathe and dropped his arms, releasing her.

So close. Her voluptuous, unpainted mouth had been so close. His if he'd wanted to take it. But he was fairly certain that she had no idea what had just happened between them and that, if she figured it out, she'd probably be gone before nightfall. No one could tell him that she wasn't repressing some deep-seated fear. He was sure of it. He had felt her tremors of excitement and seen her wet her trembling lips as, flushed with blatant desire, she stared at his mouth, but she'd nonetheless moved away from him. He had to defuse the situation and do it quickly, so he grinned, seeking leverage with humor.

"Leslie, you're going to have to stay off stools and ladders. I won't always be around to catch you."

He had to hand it to her. The woman was a thoroughbred. Even so, her sally surprised him. "Advice is cheap as well as useless: wise men don't need it and fools won't take it."

He cocked an eyebrow. "You're fast with the repartee, too, when you want to be, aren't you?" Or when she forgets her self-consciousness, he mentally corrected. She'd be delightful company, if she could lose that wariness. A thought jarred him. What had happened to his highfalutin scruples about not consorting with a woman who was his employee? Thinking that he'd best put some distance between them, he finished with the air conditioner and started for the door. Then he turned to reassure her that their relationship had not changed.

"If you need anything at all, Leslie, just let me know. You'll have your own telephone sometime tomorrow, and I intend to install an intercom here so you can reach Cal, Julia or me conveniently whenever you want to." With that he was gone.

Leslie looked around. Home. Her own place. She opened the door and stepped out on the porch. Blue clear sky, bright sunshine, green trees, flowers everywhere and God's great earth, lush and beautiful for as far as she could see. She loved everything her eyes beheld. And not a sound. Then, the quiet, almost spiritual in its all-enveloping splendor, yielded to the click-clack of Jordan's horse's hooves as he cantered in the direction of the brook, his presence in her world adding to her sense of peace and security. She

watched him astride that big horse, master of that powerful animal, and remembered the feel of his hand gentle on her shoulder, yet strong as he'd held her when she almost fell. Her gaze followed him until he was out of sight.

She had told him not to touch her. What else could she do to protect herself when what she really wanted was just the opposite, a want that didn't belong in her relationship with this man? It was unthinkable. But his hands. Frissons of heat had darted all through her when he'd held her those few minutes. She gripped her left hand with her right one and shook her head. She had to get him out of her mind. She didn't want to think such things about Jordan, because nothing could come of it. She wouldn't let anything come of it. Besides, he wouldn't get involved with his African-American cook, any more than she would consort with her white boss. Life was hard enough without that burden. Like pulling a bag of rocks up the side of a steep mountain while everybody stood back to watch you fall flat on your face. Not for her. She changed into jeans and T-shirt and went back to help Julia.

"All settled in? How do you like it?" Julia asked her.

As she washed her hands, Leslie observed Julia's pristine, sharply creased jeans. The woman could cook a meal and stay as spotless as an alter cloth. "I'm all set," she told Julia. "And it's...I adore it. I, uh...I think I have time to make the biscuits before Jack gets here."

"I'd say so."

"What is it?" Leslie asked Julia half an hour later when she caught the woman looking her inquiringly.

"You've been humming and singing ever since you started those biscuits. I'm glad you're happy, Leslie."

She let herself laugh aloud, and joy suffused her as she anticipated the pleasure of a quiet evening in her own place. She had intended to look at the clock beside the window, but instead, her glance caught a looking-glass that was framed in red and white check that matched the kitchen curtains. It leaned against a window pane as though part of the décor. For heaven's sake. And to think that in all these weeks, she hadn't noticed it. This had to be the only kitchen in the country with a mirror over the sink. She said as much as to Julia.

Julia's wink suggested that she might have even more interesting secrets. Patting her hair, she said, "I just put it there this morning. I got tired of scampering around there to our apartment every time I hear Cal coming in the door."

Leslie stared at her. "You mean…"

"Honey," Julia began in her best Southern drawl and as though patience was needed, "that man has never seen me looking anything but good. I get up first every morning and take care of business long before he opens his baby blues." She bent to open the oven. "It's working, so I don't see any point in changing."

Leslie shook her head in wonder. "Yeah. Like Yogi says, 'If you ain't broke, don't fix it.'"

Her first night in her apartment would have been Heaven, if somebody hadn't tossed pebbles at her bedroom window. Ossie or Faron? It could have been either. One disliked her and the other hated her. After checking the lock

on the front door, she closed and locked the windows, turned on the air conditioner and went back to bed. Maybe she should tell Jordan, but if she did, she'd invite more of his probing. The night sounds lulled her to sleep.

Leslie couldn't have been more surprised when she answered her telephone several nights later and heard the voice of Berle Cox, her acquaintance at the women's residence. "How'd you find me, Berle?'

"I was looking out of my window when Jordan Saber brought you here to pick up your things. The rest was easy."

A wave of apprehension swept through her. If Berle had reached her so easily, so could Faron. She wouldn't appeal to the woman; that, too, was dangerous. Instead, she said, "I sure hope you're tight-lipped, because I don't want everybody to know my business. How are you, Berle?"

She could imagine Berley pushing her glasses up on the bridge of her nose. More than once, she'd almost asked her when she didn't get a pair that stayed in place. "Me? Same as always. Nothing interesting ever happens to me. Now, if I got a job working for a hot number like Jordan Saber, I'd...."

Leslie didn't let her finish. "I work for him, and he pays me twice monthly, Berle. That's it. Period."

"I hope you're not complaining. At least you can look at him."

Leslie couldn't decide whether Berle was fishing for something to gossip about merely making conversation, so she made her reply as vague as possible. "Looking doesn't do a thing for me Berle."

A deep sigh reached her through the wires. "Six feet, five or so, jet black hair, moss green eyes and a smile to die for. Girl, when it comes to that man, just looking would do a lot for me."

Leslie hardly believed her. "You serious? You don't think he's off limits?"

She heard Berle suck her teeth. "Child, you Southern girls give me a pain. I'm from Minnesota. Up there, we don't get balled up in this color mess. If he looked my way, I'd grab him before you could say Berle."

Leslie sucked in her breath, as Berle's remark sent blood flying through her veins like a liquid comet. But she didn't give away her emotions. "Well, if that's what winds you up, I understand he goes to Abel's Feed and Grain every Monday morning."

She conceded that she sounded more clever than she felt. Seeing Berle with Jordan wouldn't make her sleep nights.

"Don't tempt me, girl." When Leslie didn't reply, she added, "Call me sometime, and don't worry. I won't tell anybody where you are."

Leslie stared at the phone long after she hung up. She hadn't dared ask what prompted that last remark, but she was grateful for the assurance.

She didn't work on Sundays. However, since moving to the Estates, she took all of her meals with Julia, Cal and Jordan, so she insisted on helping Julia with the weekend cooking. They ate late on Sunday mornings, and when Leslie walker into the kitchen at eight o'clock one Sunday, she got a surprise.

"Who are you?"

"I was about to ask you the same question," the big blond man replied, with a rakish grin. "Jordan usually goes for blondes, but looks like his taste has improved. I didn't know Jordan had gotten married."

"Neither did I," she replied, expertly sidestepping him as he walked around the table and extended his hand. She didn't like his easy familiarity, so she pretended not to see his hand, bounded up the stairs and knocked on Jordan's door. It hadn't occurred to her that her presence at Jordan's bedroom door would rob him of his composure, but when he opened it, he gaped at her, speechless. And she couldn't help staring at his wet black hair, washboard belly and the towel that clung precariously to his hips.

If ogling was bad manners, so be it, she couldn't hide her admiration and didn't try. Mom Haynes always said that when you see evidence of God's perfection, you should bow before it. She wouldn't go that far, but Lord…

To her embarrassment, her voice cracked when she spoke. "Jordan, did you know there's a man downstairs, tall and blond?"

He savored her freshness, the soft curls caressing her face, and her inviting floral scent, as fleeting as petals on the wind. As his gaze roamed over her, he felt the heat rush through his body, startling him. "What the hell?" he muttered to himself. He must be getting some kind of glandular dysfunction.

"That's Cal's younger brother. Wait while I get into something, and I'll go down with you." When it came to Turner, her apparent lack of ease around men was anything

but foolish. He wouldn't go any further than she let him, but he'd certainly test the water.

Turner met them at the kitchen door with his electric smile in place, but Jordan knew it wasn't meant for him. Turner had arrived the night before, after Leslie had gone to her apartment, his visit impromptu as usual.

"Where did you find her, Jordan? She's skittish as a young colt. Cute, though. Just needs to be broken in." He reached out if he meant to touch her, but Jordan restrained him. And not very gently.

"Turner, this is Leslie Collins. Keep your hands off her, and don't crown her."

"Last time I looked, she wasn't wearing a ring. Do you have his ring, Leslie?" She looked from one to the other. Jordan knew his face had the turbulence of a mid-summer thunderhead. But he made himself stay relaxed, as though unconcerned. After all, what was he getting so riled up about? He squelched the urge to laugh when she looked at Turner in a way that should have shriveled him.

"I figure you're getting this information for the Gallup Poll. Right? Otherwise, you wouldn't be so personal, would you?" A scowl settled on her face, and she added, "Are you sure you're Cal's brother?"

"You're not the first person to wonder about that. It could be the twenty-year age difference." They looked around and saw Cal leaning against the doorjamb. "Miss Collins is off limits to you, brother. You'd do well to take Jordan's advice."

Turner's half-mile smile was aimed to reassure them. "All right. All right. I was just testing the water. Why is

everybody so uptight? I never take anything that isn't given willingly."

Jordan had never been certain what he thought of Turner. He wasn't what he appeared to be. He had a ready grin, but he wasn't fun loving. He picked off women like buckshot picking off black-birds, yet he never had one woman for a steady companion. And he didn't come around his brother often. He looked steadily down at Turner from his advantage of three inches.

"Don't try me on this, Turner. I won't tolerate it even for one second." Still smoldering and not remembering that he'd promised himself he'd avoid touching Leslie, Jordan draped his arm around her shoulders and steered her to his den.

"Let Julia cook. You shouldn't be in there with him." He didn't question his proprietary manner and neither, apparently, did she.

To his amazement, she didn't move from his arm. He opened the door, expecting her to refuse to enter it with him, but she did, adding to his incredulity.

"Is he going to stay here?"

"He'll be gone in the morning. He isn't really brutish. He just loves to tease, but the problem is that he tends to take teasing too far. Unless you're receptive, that'll be the end of it. He knows me well, and he isn't foolish." She seemed at ease with him, so he took a chance. "Leslie, what makes you uneasy with men? Tell me. Let me help you. This isn't normal, Leslie."

Immediately, her demeanor changed. Within that second, she had become evasive. Uncomfortable. "I told you

some things, Jordan. Please. I don't want to go into it now. I'd better help Julia."

He'd give a lot to know what made her so evasive. He remembered that man he'd found loitering around the garage. "Leslie, I've been wanting to discuss something with you. A couple of weeks ago, a man came here asking about you, but he wouldn't state his business. I sent him away because he looked like a reprobate. I didn't like it. Would you know what he wanted? Since then, I've learned that he's been pestering the neighbors and he's given them a pretty good description of you. Of course, they're my friends, so they wouldn't tell him a thing." He observed her intently and couldn't miss the apprehension that clouded her eyes.

She shook her head. "I don't know what he wanted with me, Jordan."

"What about the finance company that you owe?"

She brightened. "Could be, though I'm not behind in my payments. Still..." Her voice trailed off. "I'll go help Julia."

He stood there staring at the open door. Not much shocked him, but that bad performance of hers had come close. She hadn't told him the truth, at least not all of it. He rested his hip against his desk. What was he supposed to do now? A few minutes earlier, he would have boxed Turner's ears to protect her. Still would. He grimaced. Taking on Turner wasn't something you did casually; he was as good as a man got. One thing was certain: he didn't know enough about Leslie. Maybe this was just the medicine he needed to straighten up his head and get her out of it. Leslie appeared to be principled. But hell, the woman was in trou-

ble and too scared to accept the help that was right there for her. He went back upstairs, got his jacket and headed for the garage. He didn't want to see Leslie right then; he'd get breakfast in town.

Leslie didn't question Jordan's right to an explanation of her behavior or as to why a man he described as disreputable-looking would inquire about her. If she were in his position, she'd probe too. She'd give anything if she could tell him all that she had stored inside herself, and especially if she could tell him about Faron Walker. She longed to open up to him with the truth, but more questions would follow, and she couldn't bear to relive the cross-examination, the suggestive——if not out-right——accusations, such as the ones' she'd faced in court. And she didn't want to be diminished in his eyes. Worse still, Faron had promised to kill her if he found out that she had told anyone that he was looking for her.

She had done nothing wrong, but even in her vindication, they'd draped the heavy curtain of suspicion over her. If Jordan didn't want her to stay, she would have to leave, and she would. She could stand up to almost anything but his scorn. She gazed through her bedroom window at the lush fields that reached as far as she could see and asked herself why it was so important that Jordan think well of her. She turned away from the window and switched on the radio, unwilling to pursue the thought, afraid of where it might lead.

Late in the afternoon several days later, Leslie and Julia sat on the back porch shelling June peas for supper. In Leslie's mind, Julia's perfectly manicured nails should have

been holding a porcelain teacup in a salon, not shelling peas on the back porch of a farm house. She looked at her own tapered and buffed, but unpolished, nails.

"Julia, you do the job of two people. How do you manage to look as if you've never worked in your whole life and wouldn't deign to consider it?"

Julia patted the blonde French twist at the nape of her neck. "I figure I don't have to look frumpy just because I chop onions. Besides, I never know when Cal will walk in here, and I intend to keep his head so full of me that there won't be room in to for any other woman."

"Yeah, but you could pull off those jeans and sneakers, slip on an evening gown and sandals and go straight to a gala."

"I wasn't born beautiful, Leslie. You were. All you have to do is wash your face and blow-dry your hair. Men love to be around attractive women, even if they're not interested in them. So I give 'em plenty to look at."

Leslie pondered raising a matter that had long bothered her. "What if a man you don't want gets interested?"

Julia's well-shaped eyebrows shot up. "You can't worry about that. It's natural. I get a bang when a man does a double take and looks at me a second time. Makes my blood race. That's what this man-woman thing is all about. Cal is my world, and when he gives me that look that says he's got loving on his mind, I get dizzy. You see me looking like this in the kitchen and you wonder why. It's because that man responds to me. When I want something from Cal, I let my hair down, put on something feminine that he likes, tell him how wonderful he is, and he'd give me the moon if he

could reach it. Try it. There isn't a man walking who would-
n't eat it up."

Leslie tucked several strands behind her left ear and
paused over her next words. She'd always thought it best to
be honest with a man. "But Julia, that's manipulative."

Julia shrugged. "Right. But from what you've seen of
Cal, you wouldn't suggest that he's too stupid to know what
I'm doing, would you?"

"Course, not. Which is why I don't get it."

Julia grinned, and the grin broadened into a wide smile,
as though she savored a rich memory. "He likes it. He
knows I'm strong-headed, but he'd rather I tease and pam-
per him than demand what I want like a bully squaring off
for a fight." She licked her lips. "He likes me soft and sweet,
and I give him all the sweet stuff he can handle."

"If that's what boils his water," Leslie said, and covered
her amusement when Julia patted her hair, looked at her
nails and grinned at some private thought.

Julia pointed an unshelled pea at Leslie. "You'd be right
gorgeous, a head turner, if you'd just let your hair hang
down and put on a little lipstick. You're kicking God's gift
square in the teeth. You have to be a real woman twenty-
four hours every day. No matter what."

Leslie figured she'd already turned one more male head
than had been good for her and besides, it suited Julia to
flaunt her femininity; she'd rather do what came naturally.
Hearing the crunch of heavy steps on the graveled walkway
leading to the back yard, they sat forward, alert. Cal and
Jordan had just left for Dexter, and they hadn't heard a car.
Anxiety tested her courage, and she could feel the tension

reverberating around Julia. A vision of Faron crowded all else from her mind. Suppose he had seen Cal and Jordan leave! The sight of Turner brought such relief that she welcomed him with more warmth than she felt. He explained that he was on his way back to Washington and thought he'd drop in.

"How've you been, Leslie? You're pretty jittery, aren't you? Well, worry not, honey, you're safe with me. Jordan's laid claim, and I'm not one to go after another man's woman."

Jordan's woman? He had to be out of his mind. She opened her mouth to deny it, but decided that it might be safer not to. "What do you do in Washington?" she asked him.

"I live and work there. I run a software design business. I've just decided to develop some programs for farmers, cattlemen and horse breeders, and I'm working my way through Maryland, Virginia and Kentucky to find out what people need and how to package it."

Her interest piqued, she warmed up to the conversation. "What kind of information would you need to write a program for a big operation like this one?"

In his element now, Turner took a pencil and some paper out of his briefcase and began to list items and draw diagrams. She pulled her chair closer to examine Turner's sketches, and was soon so engrossed that she drank the lemonade and ate the cookies without realizing when Julia has put them there.

Julia surveyed the cozy scene and contemplated the probable fallout, because Jordan had warned Turner not to

play loose with Leslie as he did with so many women. She loved Jordan, and she didn't want any antagonism between them. But she'd never before seen Leslie so enthralled in anything, so she decided to cook the supper and let Leslie enjoy herself. As she worked in the kitchen, a thought plagued her. Would Jordan have challenged Turner about any cook or other female employee, or just about Leslie? He hadn't trusted Turner with her. Jordan protected the vulnerable; that was as much a part of him as his hands, but he'd walked out of the kitchen with his arm around his African-American cook. She liked Leslie, and she could see that a man, any man, would want her. She didn't like what she was thinking, and she hoped they'd used some sense and stay away from each other.

She punched the intercom, called the men's quarters and asked Ossie to bring her a bunch of scallions. She enjoyed talking with Ossie, and knew he'd do most anything for her, so she couldn't understand why he soured from the time she'd spoken with him until he walked into the kitchen. He's opened the door with his usual smile, but had seemed to become angry when he saw Leslie and Turner huddled over Turner's sketches. She hoped Ossie wasn't sweet on Leslie.

Jordan found Leslie and Turner head to head and deep in a quiet, almost whispered discussion of the technicalities of computer program design. He observed them for a few minutes, then spun on his heels and walked away. Out in the barn, he saddled Casey Jones, his big bay stallion, and galloped out to the brook. He wanted his supper, but he needed to cool off, and he needed to think. If you men-

tioned a man to her, her knees got rubbery. She was uneasy
with men, and he knew it; at least that was what she had
led him to believe. She kept plenty of space between him
and her and, just four days ago, she had definitely not
wanted to be in the kitchen alone with Turner. Now she
was sitting head to head, shoulder to shoulder with him as
comfortable as a queen holding court. He remembered the
coolness with which she had misled him. Perhaps she was-
n't afraid of men. That could be a screen. May be she just
liked Turner; most women did. He didn't know what to
think. And what was Turner doing back there so soon? He
lived within seventy-five miles, but they hardly saw him
twice a year. Instead of cooling off, he got madder.

Julia stepped out to the porch. "Cal and Jordan are
back, Leslie, so supper will be served in a few minutes."
Surprised that so much time had passed, Leslie apologized
for not helping with the meal.

Julia waved her hand, dismissing it. "Don't mention it,
Leslie. Wasn't much to do."

"Where's Jordan?" Leslie asked, but Julia had stepped
back into the kitchen.

"Wherever he is, he's mad as hell." Turner folded his
paper and put it in his shirt pocket.

"Mad? About what?"

Turner responded with a brittle laugh. "He saw you out
here with me. Lady, that man wants you."

Even as she denied it vehemently, he narrowed his eyes.
"Leslie, Jordan is a civilized man. He uses his head before
he uses his fists, though God knows you don't want to be
the one standing there when he starts to swing. But if I had-

n't backed off last Sunday, he would have taken me on in a minute. Jordan and I were teenagers together when I spent my summers here with Cal and Julia, and I used to whip him as often as whipped me. But roughness isn't his style. He'd beat the brains out of anybody who bothered Julia, and that includes Cal, but fight over any other woman? I never thought so."

"What exactly are you saying? I'm his employee. The only thing he wants from me is a good day's work and a steady supply of buttermilk biscuits and apple tarts."

Turner's laugh carried a hard edge and no humor. "It's a good thing I'm smart enough not to believe you. If you don't want him, you'd better get out of his way. Excuse me, Leslie, but I've got to find him before he gets back here." He grinned at her. "Somehow, I think I'd be safer meeting a rattler."

In the stable, Jordan stood beside Casey Jones grooming him. He sensed Turner's presence without turning around and addressed him through clenched teeth. "To what do we owe the pleasure of your company this time, Turner? You don't usually need to see your family so frequently." Jordan knew his expression signaled his readiness for just about anything, and it didn't surprise him when Turner didn't reply with his usual sarcasm.

"Don't get your back up, Jordon. I came back here expressly to see you." At Jordan's look of disbelief, Turner laughed. He hoped his suspicions were correct; Leslie wasn't what he would have expected Jordan to choose, but he could do a lot worse. All the stupidity about inter-this and inter-that didn't make sense to him anyway. Women were

women and men were men, and a drunk was obnoxious no matter what color he was. Besides, a man went for the music that made him dance, and if that was the case, bully for both of them.

"You told me not to crowd her," he told Jordan. "Do you think I have to go on another man's turf in order to get to a woman?" He was careful not to give Jordan complete reassurance; a little jealousy would be good for him, because he wasn't used to it.

Jordan frowned and rubbed the back of his neck, a signal that he didn't care for the remark. And he confirmed that when he said, "You're way off. Talk what you know."

"Whatever you say," Turner told him. From where he stood, the denial was as weak as a puff of smoke battling a March wind. He might as well have agreed. "You know anybody around here who'd be curious about Leslie?"

"The guy looked a little weather-beaten, but when he started talking I got the impression that he had some education. I guess what I'm saying is that the man had probably seen better days.'

"He asked about Leslie?"

"Yeah. And you, too. Wanted to know whether she stays at your place and what her relationship was to you. Didn't seem very hostile, but he doesn't know any more now than he did before he asked. Jordan, I could swear he followed me from here. Otherwise, why did I see him in Frederick and again in Boonsboro, places where I stopped on my way to Hagerstown? I'm pretty sure I saw him in a bar in Frederick. He stared at me so that I got edgy and came pretty close to confronting him. But Boonsboro? He was fol-

lowing me all right, all the way to Hagerstown. That's where he finally approached me. You want to watch your back, Jordan, and keep Leslie in front of you where you can see her."

Turner's description of the man puzzled him. It could be the same one, but something didn't tally, and he couldn't quite put his finger on it.

"You staying over tonight?"

"Can't. I'm leaving after supper. I've got to be at my office early tomorrow morning. Why?"

"If you see him on the way out, stop somewhere and call me. You didn't mention this to anyone else, did you?"

They started toward the house, and Turner stopped and rubbed his jaw with his index finger, as though unsure of his next move. "Naturally, I didn't mention this to anybody, but maybe you should tell Cal."

"I will eventually. And thanks, I owe you one."

Leslie had finished work for the day and was preparing to go to her apartment when Julia placed a hand on her shoulder, detaining her. "Jordan wants you to stop by the den before you go to your place."

Julia had noticed the coolness between them at dinner and had sensed Jordan's displeasure with Leslie, though she was certain that Leslie's work was not at the root of it. She watched Leslie through half lowered lashes. Surely Jordan wasn't annoyed because he'd found her talking with Turner. Whatever the problem, it wasn't child's play, and it bore watching. She spoke to the younger woman.

"Don't be afraid of Jordan, Leslie. There's no reason to be. If you have a problem, let him help you with it. We're a family here, and you're one of us."

Leslie gaped at her nonplussed. "Thank you. I...well, thank you.

"You wanted to see me?" She stood her back against the closed door, her gaze fastened on the portrait of Jordan's parents that hung above the big mahogany desk where he sat, his shoulders lunched forward. She leaned against the wall and waited. He chose his words carefully. "As I recall, we have something to discuss. I want to know what that man wants with you." He almost prayed that she'd trust him. He felt something for her; more than he knew was healthy.

"I don't believe her, and permitted himself to show the anger that boiled up in him. "The perhaps you can explain why a man trailed Turner in three different towns, cornered him, and raised questions about you?'

She stood straight and looked him in the eye. "The person you should grill like a trial lawyer is the man who's looking for me. I don't control him."

Incensed at her refusal to trust him and her willingness to throw away circumstances the he knew she valued, he bounded around his desk and grabbed her by the shoulders. He wanted to shake her. "Don't be a fool, Leslie. Can't you see that I want to protect you? Or don't you care? If you leave here, where will you go? Back to that cell for the aged where you were living? He'd certainly find you there. Dammit, why can't you trust me?"

She looked up at him, and her gaze suddenly fastened on his mouth as she sucked in her breath, shocking him out of anger and into sensuality. His hands, hands that he normally controlled automatically, went of their own volition to either side of her head, drawing her to him. But just as he lowered his head, his mind regained control and he stopped and backed off. Displeased with himself for having most succumbed to an urge he'd had for weeks, one that surely spelled trouble, rage surged within him, and he didn't bother to snuff it out.

"What else have misled me about? That heart-rending tale about your childhood and how you got through college, how much truth was in it? And your wariness of men, of me. You're not scared right now, are you? Four days ago, you were so afraid of Turner that a thirty-foot long kitchen wasn't big enough for the two of you. But this afternoon, I find you practically sitting in his lap, as happily as you please. What did he offer you? A place to stay while you finish your degree? Did you try seducing him like you did me just now?" He knew he was being unfair, but so was she.

Her facial muscles twitched in anger, and she drew back her hand, but quickly got a grip on her temper and let it fall to her side. "How dare you!"

She' come near to striking him, and the fire in her eyes blazed with the brilliance of a belching volcano, fire that spelled passion, womanly passion. Her refusal to let him bend her ignited in him a powerful urge to have her and, even as he flamed in anger, desire rioted through him.

"Damn you!" he swore.

He pulled her to him, lowered his head and bruised her lips with his angry mouth. She pushed at his chest, but he held her until she became pliant and her fingers wound their way to his shoulders. But when he drew her closer to him, she backed away. Nobody had to tell him that because he'd moved in anger, her pride wouldn't let her succumb to what she felt, or probably even to admit it even to herself.

She proved him right when, in a voice as dull as warm buttermilk, she said, "I never expected that from you. I said I didn't know what he intends to do if he finds me. I still don't."

He stood rooted to the spot as she walked out of the room.

He'd been out of bounds. Way out. But she hadn't been straight with him when he'd wanted, needed some reassurance that his faith in her hadn't been misplaced. And he hadn't intended for her to enjoy that kiss, but she had. She'd melted those wide brown eyes so smoky you'd have though they were hazed over with fog. And her lips, so soft and yielding, sweet as new-born innocence. He's stopped because he'd had to. Another second and she would have him on the edge. He sat down to think and made up his mind. He'd find the man. And then what? Leslie was definitely fudging the truth when she'd disclaimed knowledge of any man's reason for wanting to find her.

He slammed his fist on the desk. She hadn't actually said that. She had avoided lying by saying she didn't know what he intended to do to her. That was something, but it wasn't good enough. And another thing. She hadn't divulged the name of the finance company the she owed.

Why hadn't she? He'd also like to know why she had seemed so much more at ease with him since Sunday, when she'd seen him almost naked. And she managed to conquer her guardedness around Turner, too. Something was rotten in Denmark. He put on a business suit, got into the Town Car, and drove to Preston. He would never permit himself to be ignorant about anything vital to himself and those close to him. And he was ignorant about Leslie.

She hadn't lied, though she'd skirted the truth; she knew why Faron Walker wanted to find her, but not what he aimed to do to her. Only he wanted revenge. She didn't want to meet Julia and her questions, so she started toward the side door but, with her hand on the knob, she drew back. It wouldn't surprise her if Faron Walker was loitering outside, and if he....She didn't let herself complete the thought. She walked rapidly down the hallway, out the kitchen door, and up the winding steps to her apartment. Sitting on her bed drinking tea, the door locked and curtains drawn, she let her mind wander back to that second, that single second, when Jordan Saber's lips caressed hers. Oh, he'd been angry, mad was more like it, and had done what conquerors do. He had displayed his power. Yet, he'd handled her with such gentleness. She didn't dream he'd ever kiss her or even that he might want to, and she didn't kid herself. He hadn't been motivated by affection, but by frustration. She'd pulled back, because she hadn't wanted him to know how much she enjoyed it.

She drained her cup, set it on the marble-top night table and grinned. She couldn't help it as laughter poured out of her. By now, he was probably swearing, furious with

himself, but he couldn't take it back. Never. That second belonged to her, and it would have to do for all time, because she definitely wasn't going that way.

She crawled into bed, turned out the light and immediately sat up. What seemed like a fist full of pebbles hit her bedroom window. The meanness had begun to occur with increasing frequency. She suspected Faron, but she couldn't get a court order on a hunch. She glanced at the intercom that Jordan had installed in her room, wondered if she should call him and decided against it. She'd had enough of his questions.

Jordan stretched out on his bed, locked his hands behind his head and contemplated his next move. He'd gone to the women's residence that evening to learn what he could about the mystery surrounding Leslie. He hadn't expected that the manager would be a shrew with an intense dislike for Leslie, or that she would indulge in groundless gossip and baseless accusations about Leslie. When she had informed him that she knew Jordan Saber well, and she was disappointed that he'd "take up with Leslie," the lie'd enabled him to put everything else she'd told him into proper perspective. The phone rang, and he glanced at his Rolex before lifting the receiver.

"I didn't see the driver," Turner informed him, "but an old brownish sedan was parked just a couple steps from your gate. I'd bet my boots that was the same car that parked right behind mine in Boonsboro. But the driver wasn't in the car, so he had to be prowling around. Watch it, Jordan."

"Thanks. I will." He hung up and sat there in the dark, nursing an eerie feeling. The man had known that he was away from the Estates and that Leslie was probably not well-protected. What if he attacked her in his absence? That was a complication that he didn't need. He slept fitfully.

Early the next morning, Jordan headed for the orchard where Cal was inspecting fruit trees. The unusually cool, long spring meant a late peach harvest, but it promised to be a heavy, healthy crop. As he walked down the long row, he removed his hat to let the early morning breeze flow through his hair as it brushed his face. He loved the Estates with the gently swaying trees, the green bush that cooled the air in mornings, the plants that responded to eagerly to thoughtful care and the brook that lulled him into peace-fulness, subtly, like a woman's sweet whispered entreaties, every time he neared it. When he'd had to choose between his career and saving the farm, there has been no contest.

The farm was his life, and he had willingly undertaken the back-breaking work and made the sacrifices to build it into the prize that was Saber Estates. He missed teaching full time, especially the graduate students, but he'd saved the farm, and that mattered more. If he got through this year, he'd be financially sound.

Cal was looking at the base of a tree that bore white peaches, one of Jordan's most prized varieties. Jordan never thought of the man as an employee; he was brother, friend, surrogate father and confidant. Cal had guided him through those awkward years when he was bursting into manhood. His uncle Riddick, from whom he'd inherited the nucleus of the Estates, had been a gentle, caring man,

but a washout as a surrogate parent. Jordan knew that his
system of values had come from Cal, who had taught him
perseverance, honor and the value of self-control. And
watching Cal with Julia had been his guide to the myster-
ies of man-woman relationships and the rewards of loving.
He broke his stride and paused beside Cal.

"Any insects?" he asked him.

"No, but the bark's peeling. I think it's just showing age.
And you shouldn't be. It's pretty early in the morning to be
so sluggish, Jordan."

Jordan shrugged. "Sometime my mind balks at the
workout I give it. Say, I've been meaning to let you in our
some rather depressing happenings around here." He told
him that Leslie was being harassed by one or two men, her
failure to explain it, his conversation with the manager of
the women's residence the previous evening and about
Turner's message.

As he usually did, Cal thought for a while before
answering. "Jordan, I've always admired Leslie's courage,
and what you've just told me hasn't changed my good opinion of her." He pulled a strip of diseased bark from the
peach three. "That woman at the residence is the reason
why whoever's looking for Leslie knows she's here. Did you
straighten her out?"

"Cal, when a person has a tongue as loose as that and
shows so little respect for the truth, you don't tell them anything."

"You're right. We'll have to trap him."

"Bet on it."

CHAPTER FOUR

Jordan headed back toward the stables to get Casey Jones, his bay stallion. He wanted to examine his experimental corn seedlings near the brook. "Great morning, isn't it" he said to Ossie, who sat on a workbench in a corner mending a saddle.

"Yeah. Too bad it won't stay like this all day. We could use some rain, too. The grass at the edge of the ravine is getting brown. Maybe we ought to turn on the sprinklers."

Jordan knocked his hat back with his thumb and forefinger and laughed, as he always did when Ossie referred to the irrigation system as sprinklers. "Not a bad idea. I'm taking Casey down to the corn patch. Be sure and mend that stirrup. Be back in about an hour."

"Sure thing. Oh, Jordan. Any reason why a Ford, maybe green, maybe brown, parks down there near the gate some nights? I've seen it there twice. Whoever's in it drives off just as I get to the gate. You know anything about this?"

Jordan paused in the act of straddling his horse. "Something's going on, Ossie, and I can't get a handle on it. If you see that car again, get the license number."

Ossie wiped his brow with his shirtsleeve, already damp from the rising humidity. "I thought maybe it was somebody visiting Leslie. I think he's kinda short, because I couldn't see much of a figure in the driver's seat. Oh, well..." He looked up at Jordan and shrugged. "Maybe it's nothing, but I'll keep an eye out."

Jordan took Casey on a slow gallop toward the brook. Ossie didn't know how close he'd probably come to the

truth. If the man hung around the Estates regularly, he'd have to lock the gate and give the men keys, and he hated making a fortress of his home. But he couldn't shake the notion that the mysterious stranger represented a threat to Leslie, and his persistence suggested that he sought vengeance. He took out his pocket recorder and gave himself a reminder to visit a private investigator.

Leslie opened the kitchen door and stopped. Ossie leaned against the counter sipping coffee as Julia laughed almost hysterically.

"You can put the guy's brains in half of a peanut," Ossie said. "It's not funny, Julia. Suppose you had to work with him every day. Cal says he can't tell the difference between up and down, and Zeke swears Rocket thinks a cocktail is the rear end of a rooster." He laughed. "Zeke blew my mind when he said that."

Julia wiped the moisture from her eyes. "Come on now, Ossie, you and Zeke and that husband of mine leave Rocket alone. You're stuck with him, anyway."

Ossie held out his cup, and Julia refilled it. "I know. Jordan's aware of the guy's limitations, but he says the man has to live. And who am I to talk? Jordan is a rare man; there's nothing I wouldn't do for him."

"I know that, Ossie, and so does Jordan."

Feeling as if she were eavesdropping, Leslie went to the broom closet and hung the brushes she carried, cleared her throat and smiled a greeting to Ossie? "Morning, Ossie. Who's the guy with all the brain?"

Ossie turned around to the sink, damped the remainder of his coffee in it and nodded toward Leslie. "Morning,

miss. I'll bring eggs in around nine-thirty," he told Julia, walked out and let the screen door slam.

Julia stared at Ossie's departing back. "Well, I'll be...What got into him?" Leslie didn't care for Julia's inquiring look and bristled when the woman asked, "You sure there's nothing between you and Ossie? He's such a fine man. I never knew him to act like that. You'd have thought he saw a UFO coming at him." She shook her head as though in wonder.

Leslie took a deep breath and let it out slowly. Her patience with Julia's thinking on the subject of Ossie and herself had just about worn out. "Why would you think there's anything between me and that man?" she asked Julia, not caring about the sharpness of her tone. "He hardly acknowledged my presence. As soon as he saw me, the fun went out of him. If you want to know why he acts as if I'm poison, ask him."

Leslie supposed that her reply had annoyed Julia, because she could see the woman deal with her temper. With admirable control, Julia stopped stirring soup and laid the spoon on a saucer. "I thought you'd have figured out by now that Ossie's well thought of around here. He's educated way past what he does out there. He was down on his luck before Jordan brought him here, and one of these days he's going to be right back where he was. I thought the two of you might get together."

Leslie bristled, but did her best not to show it. "Just because we're both African-American doesn't mean we have to be attracted to each other, Julia. In fact, Mr. Dixon dislikes me." She measured out the flour for the apple

turnovers she'd make for lunch. "And I'm not crazy about him, either."

Her head jerked up when she was certain she heard Julia murmur, "Too bad, 'cause it sure would be less of a problem."

"What did you say?"

Julia walked over to Leslie and faced her. "I only want what's best for you, Leslie, and I'm almost twice your age, so grant me a little experience with life. Many a person had drowned swimming against the tide."

"That isn't something I'm in a habit of doing." Leslie said, feigning ignorance of Julia's meaning.

"Well, I hope not. Believe me, Leslie, I sure hope not."

Half an hour before dinner, she ran over to her apartment, washed up, kicked off her jeans and put on a broomstick skirt and peasant blouse. Then she brushed out her hair, glanced at the lipstick Julia had given her, decided against it and ran down the steps that led from her apartment to the garden.

"What's all this?"

The sound of Jordan's voice brought her to a dead stop. He let out a long whistle, and she'd have given anything if she'd still been wearing her jeans.

He didn't let her off. "You're a sight for sore eyes, Leslie, and the sight gets better all the time."

He was going to make her walk back to the house along with him, and if they walked into the kitchen together, Julia wouldn't miss it and she'd probably have something to say about it.

He stood within two feet of her, and she couldn't see around him, though she tried. He smiled pleasantly enough, but his body sent her a different kind of message, one that held nothing as innocuous as a friendly smile. The smell of him tantalized her nostrils, and heat seemed to spring from him to her, a special kind of man's heat. And it had a strong energy that seemed to coil around her, roping her in, a slow taming of her senses like something being marinated in preparation for a feast.

He grinned in that way that made her heart bounce up and down in her chest. "After you. Aren't you going to give me some dinner?"

She moved around him with quick steps and started for the back porch. "Julia gives you your dinner."

He reached past her and opened the screen door, brushing her arm as he did so. "Yeah. But you're the one who gives me what I really like."

Stunned at the suggestiveness with which he'd imbued that innocent statement, she whirled around and faced him. "Right now, you stand pretty tall in my books, Jordan, so don't mess up."

His smile had almost blinding brilliance, the weapon of a man certain of his masculinity and of its effect on any female whom he cared to bless with it. "Not to worry, Leslie. I'll always take my cue from you."

She glared at him, and she hoped she did it convincingly, because he stood within inches of her, battering her senses. "What are you taking about?"

His finger touched her arm, urging her on to the porch. "Same thing you're talking about, Leslie. Exactly the same thing."

She whirled around and stared into the icy gaze of Ossie Dixon. She didn't doubt that the man was more certain than ever of something that did not exist and never would. As she walked on into the house, Dixon's friendly words to Jordan reached her ears.

"I've had the sprinklers on all morning, and the tack's in order. Think I can leave here right after dinner?"

As she looked back, she saw Jordan's arm on the man's shoulder and heard him say, "That's great, Ossie. Turn off the irrigation system and do what you have to do. See you in the morning."

Well, well. Ossie had made up his mind about her: if he saw what appeared to be familiarity between her and Jordan, it was her doing and she whom he despised, but Jordan remained unscathed. She got a pitcher of lemonade and put it in the middle of the dinner table.

"My, my. Don't we look pretty," Julia remarked.

"Yeah," Cal said. "The presence of pretty women looking pretty eases away a man's stress, cures what ails him and does him soul good."

Leslie grabbed the opportunity to turn Cal's attention to Julia. "In that case, you must stay happy."

She needn't have bothered, for he kissed his wife on the mouth, caressed her check and replied, "This woman knows what it's all about."

Leslie hadn't realized Jordan had joined them until he said, "You lovebirds hold off for another hour until we eat.

Then Leslie and I are going to give you all the space you need."

Cal winked in man-to-man agreement, but Leslie didn't miss Julia's wide-eyed amazement. Ordinarily, she would have asked Jordan for an explanation, but she decided to let Julia stew. She had planned to spend the afternoon working on her thesis, but...Well, she'd wait and see.

Jordan bounded down the stairs and into the kitchen just as Leslie opened the kitchen door on her way to her apartment for the afternoon.

"Hey, wait a minute," Jordan called after her. "I thought we were going to——"

"You didn't think any such thing," she interrupted, "because I didn't agree."

He put his hands in the pockets of his white slacks and let the look in his green eyes sear her. "But you didn't disagree, and that's tantamount to saying yes."

A green-eyed, black-haired man posed danger enough without wearing a red shirt, and she didn't doubt that he know it. She took a step back. "Jordan, I have to work with your other employees, and I'd rather not be the source of friction, animosity and gossip."

He grabbed her arm. "What on earth are you talking about?"

Well, she was the one likely to get the fallout. If he didn't know, she'd tell him. "I don't know about the rest of the people, who work her, but Julia doesn't want you with me, and Ossie doesn't want me with you. What's more, both of them have made that clear to me."

A frown creased Jordan's face. "Wait a minute. What are you saying?"

"I'm saying you must have heard about race relations in this country and especially in this region. I'm African-American and you're white. They don't approve of any familiarity between black me and white you. Get it?" She brushed past him and started up the steps to her apartment.

He raced after her. "What are your views on the matter?"

She looked up into his eyes, but the tenderness she saw there didn't seduce her into believing he offered her an uncomplicated relationship, and she'd had enough problems. "I've had a rocky life, Jordan, but I've always been able to carry my burdens and solve my problems. This problem will be here long after you and I have angel's wings. No, thank you,"

"Does that mean I can't drive you out to the Bay this afternoon? I have a wonderful boat over there that I won at a fair. I almost never sail it, because neither Julia, Cal nor Ossie likes being in the water, and I spend most of my time with them."

She slapped her hands to her sides. "You didn't hear a word I said."

He shrugged. "I heard you, but I just don't see color when I look at people. I don't care what their mother tongue is nor how well or poorly they speak English, and I don't judge people by their clothes. If I did, except for Cal, not one of these men who work for me and whose loyalty I'd bet my life on would be here. I think a lot of Julia and Ossie; they're family and best friends, but they don't tell me

what to do and don't meddle in my affairs. You use your sharp tongue with me. Give them a taste of it. You're going with me?"

"I uh—"

His fingers skimmed down her arm. "Come on," he coaxed. "It's Saturday afternoon, and you spend all of your time either in your apartment or working in the house." His grin shattered her defenses. "Besides, I thought you put this on because you wanted me to see you looking nice like this. You look —" He turned away and stared into the distance. "An afternoon together won't be the start of the World War III, Leslie. So what do you say?"

Without thinking, she covered his hand with her own. "Okay. Meet you at the garage in twenty minutes."

He rewarded her with a dazzling grin. "Make it ten."

Jordan waited beside the Town Car, his head buzzing with questions. Leslie had agreed to get on that boat with him. He wondered if she realized that they would be alone on the Chesapeake Bay inside that boat. Recently, she'd shown no sign of unease with him, and he welcomed the change, but why? He kicked the whitewall tire, though he did it gently. He was tired of guessing; the thing to do was ask her about it. And that talk about race relations bothered him. He hoped neither Julia nor Ossie made the mistake of mentioning that to him, because friendship didn't cover everything. If he wanted to brighten Leslie's day and she didn't mind, it was nobody else's business. He ignored the next questions that popped up in his mind: why was he doing it and had he forgotten what happened when she fell off that stool into his arms? He shrugged. He controlled his

emotions; they didn't control him. Then he laughed aloud at himself as he caught in his mind's eye as a vision of Leslie with her skirt billowing in the breeze while she picked roses the previous morning. He suspected he hadn't yet been tested.

He'd said ten minutes. She looked at her watch. Twelve. She dabbed perfume behind her ears, grabbed her shoulder bag, locked the door and tripped down the steps. She didn't know why he'd asked her to go with him, and maybe she should've said no, but he made it seem so natural. As if they were ordinary couple. But it wasn't natural, and they weren't the average man and woman going for an afternoon outing. A whole world separated them, though he didn't seem to think so. Or, if he did, it didn't matter. It wasn't just the color thing. The loan company owned half of what was in her bankbook, and that wasn't much, but Jordan had wealth, power and status. And he was a catch, too. She'd bet every penny she had that women flocked to him like bees swarming around honey.

A few paces away from the car, she stopped. His left foot rested against the edge of a front tire, and he leaned against the open door on the passenger's side staring into the distance, while the breeze frolicked through his black wavy hair. She swallowed in an attempt to get rid of the lump in her throat, but it stayed there. This man could mean more to her than was healthy. More than was wise. As if he knew he had the advantage, at least for the moment, he clasped her arm, almost caressing it, to assist her into the passenger's seat, and his hot energy jumped through her sheer cotton blouse and burned her all over.

Every minute he touched her, something like electricity shot through her. Exciting her. And warning her, too. Turner had said that, if she didn't want Jordan, she'd better get out of his way. A chuckle bubbled up in her throat, and she let it out. Maybe it was Jordan who should get out of her way.

"Let me in on the fun," Jordan said, backing the car out of the short driveway. "I like a good laugh too."

She felt free. Liberated. Faron Walker has stood up in court and yelled to her, "Wait'll I get out. I'll never let you rest." Not since the public defender had called to tell her that he was out of jail had she been a free person. Free to read in the library, sit in a park, browse in a museum, go to church or a concert, or stroll along the street like anybody else. She couldn't even work in a public place, and had been forced to leave her job as a bank officer when she'd spied him lolling against a car in front of the bank's door. She didn't mind wearing an apron, cooking, cleaning and finding excuses not to leave the Estate, but oh, it felt good to change the scenery, to put on a feminine dress and go out with a good looking man. Her mind and her spirits soared. She laughed aloud. Jordan's head snapped around. She knew she'd surprised him, but she wouldn't dare tell him how alive she felt.

"What's going on, Leslie?"

She leaned back, folded her arms and rubbed them fro shoulders to elbows. "It's such a beautiful day. That's all."

His raised eyebrow told her what he thought of that. He added, "Any special reason?"

In that air-conditioned car, her arms tingled as though attacked by prickly heat. She finessed his questions. "Blue skies everywhere. Jordan, why did you ask me to go boating with you? You can have your pick of company, women or men."

In a sober, thoughtful tone, he said, "I want to know who you are when you're not wearing an apron. You're an enigma, Leslie, and you interest me. I've always found intelligent, independent women intriguing, but you're also purposeful as well as charming." He half-laughed. "And I don't faze you one bit. I like you, and I want to get to know you."

Put off by his candid answer, she joshed, "I thought it was my peasant look today."

He took his glance from the highway long enough to look at her. "Is that what you call it? It's pretty and feminine, but it's got nothing to do with my asking you to come with me."

She didn't want them to get into a discussion of him and her. Better change the subject. "Where do you keep your boat?"

She sensed his pride as he leaned back in the driver's seat, rested his arm against the door and put the car into cruise control. "Over in St. Michael's. Another ten miles from here. She's a thirty-foot cabin cruiser."

She turned to him. "You mean you own a boat that big?"

He nodded and switched into the left lane in order to pass a slow moving RV. "Leslie, I don't make bills unless I can pay them off at the end of the month. If I'd had that much cash to spare, I'd have my thoroughbred farm. As it

is, I'm depending on my peach crop for that. We have unusually heavy yield this year, so I ought to be able to get my horses in the spring."

"You planning to race horses?"

"No indeed. I'm going to breed horses, and I've got some good fallow land I've been saving for that."

With her curiosity piqued, her mind sprang into action. "Why don't you sell the boat?"

He shook his head. "I wouldn't get a third of its value. Boats are like cars; the minute I took possession, it became a used vehicle."

She wanted him to talk to her, to tell her about his life and his work. "But I thought you were a farmer," she said to encourage him.

"I am, but one long drought can wipe out a farmer. I've diversified, but even with vegetables, fruit trees and pecan trees, I'm vulnerable. Besides, I love horses."

He pulled up to the dock, cut the motor and they got out. Crisp salty air stung her face, and to her dismay, the sun disappeared behind the clouds. She observed the vestiges of wealth: schooners, sailboats, yachts and cabin cruisers everywhere. Some with flags that told of their long voyages from Canada and Mexico.

He took her hand. "Come on over her, I want to pick up something."

They entered a small shop that smelled of roasting chickens, cheeses, barbecue, garlic and baking bread, and a matronly woman greeted Jordan with enthusiasm and not a little deference.

"Here you are, Mr. Saber," she said, blessing him with a smile and handing him a yellow basket and a bill. "Any time you need anything, you just call."

He paid with his credit card, and she couldn't help noticing that he folded a bill and pressed it into the woman's hand.

"God bless you, sir," she said and clasped her hands in a prayerful attitude. "Y'all have a safe trip, now."

He thanked her and, with the basket in one hand, he grasped Leslie's right hand with his other one and headed them toward the boat.

"It's gotten cloudy. We'd better hurry.'

He stepped on the deck with her seconds before a loud bark of thunder split the silence, closed the door behind them and led her below. She stared in awe at the walnut finished paneling soft leather seating, recessed lighting and parquet floors.

"Jordan, this is plain decadent. I had no idea…." She left the thought unfinished. No point in letting him know she'd never been on a boat before. "What's in there?" she asked, pointing to a brass-handled door.

"Captain's quarters," he replied and hastily followed the words with, "Let's put this stuff in the kitchen. I was hoping for a sunny afternoon."

So he had a bedroom in there and didn't want her to focus on it. Hmmm. He showed her the tiny kitchen, put the food and drinks in the refrigerator and led her back to what she supposed was the lounge.

"I don't hear any thunder. Want to go up on deck? If the weather's clear, I'll take her out. Okay?"

He stared up the steps, reached back and took her hand. And it felt so right, as if her whole body was in tune with his, as it had never been with anyone else's. The way a composer's music sounded better when he played it than when anybody else tried. The way poetry took on new meaning and added brilliance when read by the poet. The way she squeezed his fingers at the very moment he squeezed hers.

They stepped on deck, and he turned to her with a grin all over his face and the eagerness in his voice. If anyone had told her that he could express such child-like enthusiasm, she probably wouldn't have believed it. She looked out over the Bay. Water as far as she could see. Water the color of his eyes. If she didn't back up in a hurry, she'd fall through the cracks.

He took the boat over the gentle waves, exhilarated as always by the sense of freedom and adventure it gave him. Did she enjoy it as much as he? He hoped so. She stood near the boat's prow with the wind blowing her hair from her face and her skirt blowing like a colorful kit in a March wind. She had her face to the breeze, as though embracing it. But she was so quiet.

"Leslie, can you come over here for a minute?"

She came to him in quick, lithe movements. Youthful. He'd never thought of her age, but it occurred to him now that she always acted much older than her twenty-eight years.

He put an arm around her waist. "Are you happy? Do you enjoy this?"

"It's wonderful. Another world. A wonderful world. Thank you for bringing me."

He didn't want her thanks, only her joy. "This is my pleasure, Leslie. I've been on these waters a lot of times, but I'm enjoying it more today. Maybe it's because there's peacefulness about you and I haven't seen before. I'm going to anchor a few feet from here, and we can get something to eat. Okay?"

"I guess so. I'd forgotten about food. After all, we only had lunch three hours ago."

He dropped anchor, reached for her hand and started down the steps. "That salt water always gives me an appetite. You mean you're not hungry?"

She shrugged, "Truth is, I'm too excited to be hungry, but I'll eat if you do."

He put a white cloth on the table and opened the basket. When she started toward the kitchen to get plates and glasses, he stopped her. "This is my treat. You're my guest, so I do the work, what there is of it."

He set out the smoked salmon, shrimp and water cress sandwiches, lemonade and brownies and pulled out a chair for her. He had a shrimp sandwich half way into his mouth when she stopped him with a hand on his wrist.

"Aren't you saying grace?"

He took in the devilish twinkle in her wide brown eyes and didn't bother to control the laughter that roared out of him. When he could manage, he said, "Okay, you say it."

But she was staring at him as if seeing him for the first time, a seeing that was intimate and filled with longing. Quickly, he bowed his head and said the few words Julia had taught him when he was nine years old, because he had to diffuse the situation before he did the unthinkable. As

long as they were on that boat, he wouldn't dare touch her and let her think he'd brought her only for that reason.

Feeling barely short of holy, he put their dishes in the dishwasher and got them back on deck. "I'm calling Cal to tell him they can eat supper by themselves. The men are off this afternoon, so Cal can take Julia out to supper if that's what suits them."

He dialed Cal and Julia's private phone number. "I thought we'd stay out here till dusk, Cal, so Leslie can see the lights from the boats and the restaurants."

He could imagine Cal's slow smile crawling over his face. "I'm glad you called, Jordan. Julia's been throwing hints ever since you left. She said you wouldn't get off the boat any sooner than you had to. We'll see you in the morning."

`He watched the glow on Leslie's face as they stood on the deck at sunset. He might ruin what had been a pleasant interlude, but he had to know. He took her hand, walked over to a bench on the starboard side of the cruiser and sat with her.

"Leslie, I know I'm risking putting a damper on things, but I have to know." She tried to move her hand from his, but he sandwiched it between his two. "Leslie, when you came to the Estates, you were afraid to be alone with me. What happened to change that? I need to know."

He could feel her whole body relax and knew at once what she'd thought he would ask her. "I ...Ever since you made Turner stay away from me... He took you seriously, so I did too. And I guess I... well, the more I get to know you...You're...I trust you. That's all."

He welcomed that news, but he hoped she understood that there were different kinds and levels of trust. "Is that why you were so comfortable with him when he came back a few days later?" His breath stalled in his throat while he waited for her answer.

"I suppose. He said if he got out of line with me, you'd let him have it, and I believed him. Then I found we were both interested in developing computer programs for big businesses. He turned out to be nice."

He let go of his breath and got up. "Where's your pocketbook?"

She pointed to the shoulder bag that hung on her arm. "Right here."

"All right. I'll take this refuse out to the dock; then we'll go."

So she trusted him. But did she have enough confidence in him to let him kiss her senseless? Straighten your head out, man, he admonished himself. This is new ground, and you aren't sure you're ready to cultivate it.

On a Sunday evening in mid-July, Leslie, Cal and Julia were well into a game of cut-throat Pinochle, but Leslie couldn't keep her mind on it. Jordan had grilled her about a man who'd followed him from place to place for half a day in Dexter and, when she'd denied knowing the man, he'd lost his temper. She hadn't lied, because she didn't know a man such as he'd described. Certainly the man did not have Faron's physique and wasn't his facial type, but she hadn't seen him in almost five years.

"Cal, why does Jordan spend so much time in that den these days. Is he being anti-social?"

"No, Leslie. He's gotten way behind with his book-keeping since he started working on that corn yield research project with those people out in Wisconsin."

"What corn-yield research project?"

"I guess Jordan doesn't tell much. He's a specialist in plant development, particularly certain grains. He's got a large plot out there behind the potato field that he uses just for improving plant yield and quality."

Leslie laid an Ace on Cal's Queen. "He's a man of many talents.'

Julia tossed out a trump card and took the game. "He's got no more sides to him than I see you've got, and I have a feeling that you've got some I haven't seen yet."

"Probably have," Leslie replied, down playing the sig-nificance if Julia's remark.

She couldn't imagine why Jordan's bookkeeping required so much time. Well, bookkeeping and accounting were what she did best. When they finished the game, she made a fresh pot of coffee and put a hefty slice of her apple pie into the microwave oven to warm, and then hesitated, thinking that he might not appreciate either her concern or her suggestions. "Well, nothing ventured, nothing won," she told herself, putting the coffee and pie on a tray and heading for the den. She paused at the door, suddenly nerv-ous and uncertain, but she made herself knock in spite of his jitters.

"Yes." It was curt and unfriendly. But having gotten that far, she wasn't going to be scared off. She went in and closed the door behind her. His hand remained suspended over a wide sheet of paper. She pulled out the desk sleeve

and put the tray on it. He looked first at her and then at the tray. Leslie then watched in amazement while Jordan slowly transformed his fierce scowl into a shimmering smile of unadulterated pleasure. He looked up at her, grinned and warmed her all over.

"You spoil me," he said. "Thank you. Maybe this was just what I needed. I've been over this sheet and these receipts a dozen times, and they just don't tally."

"If you computerize this, twenty or thirty minutes a day is all the time you'll need to keep everything current."

"I know that. I had my business computerized, but my accountant not only programmed a hefty take for himself, he put a virus in the system when I caught him. You can't imagine the damage that caused. Not again!"

"Do you trust me enough to let me do it?"

The pie almost fell out of his mouth. He regarded her soberly, "Why don't you sit down? Are you telling me that you can set up a computerized bookkeeping system for me?"

"Not only that, but I'll teach you how to operate it." He raised one eyebrow, put his fork down and finished chewing his mouthful of pie.

"Are you serious?"

"Of course, I'm serious. I could do that before I ever got my bachelor's degree. Don't you remember that when I came here, I was looking for a job as an accountant? The degree I'm working for now is a master's in business administration. Get me a DOS system computer, and we're in business. I'll set it up in a few weeks in my spare time. It'll take you about an hour to learn the system, and I'll write

out the instructions clearly in case you ever forget. What could be simpler?"

"Tell me what you need, and I'll buy it tomorrow. But I can't let you do this at your wages. We'll have to discuss your pay."

"Jordan, please don't spoil this for me by talking about money."

A week later, Jordan walked into the den to find Leslie and Cal setting in the middle floor proofreading receipts and invoices against printouts.

"She's got this thing operating, Jordan. Everything's in there, everything you put out and everything you take in, even the men's bank balances, in case the books get lost. You name it; it's here. She's a gold mine, boss."

Jordan's expression revealed to her more than an appreciation for her skills as an employee. "Yeah. She's precious, all right."

Seeing his embarrassment, Leslie joshed, "Tomorrow you get your first lesson, if you have the time and want to, that is."

Understanding her perfectly, he said, "I'll make the time. You just say when."

Cal looked from one to the other wondering whether they knew what was happening.

Leslie and Jordan's awareness of each other was not lost on Julia. She saw that they did not look at each other when they spoke, and that Leslie made an even wider circle than usual around Jordan whenever she had to pass him. They didn't tease or joke with each other, although each of them

exchanged pleasantries with Cal and her. She decided that whatever it was, it was on its way to becoming a problem.

And it was a problem that troubled Leslie as well, for her mixed feelings about Jordan were beginning to wear on her. He thrilled her, and he made her apprehensive. He was wonderful, but he was off limits. Yet, in spite of the lectures and warnings she gave herself, he was seeping into her whole being day by day, glance by glance, and she hungered for information about him.

"How long have you known him?" she asked Julia as casually as she could manage one afternoon after dinner.

"Who, Jordan?" Julia guessed. "I've worked here for twenty-seven years. Came here when I was twenty-one and lived here since."

"But Jordan couldn't be more than..."

"Thirty-six. I came work for his uncle when Jordan was nine. His parents had died of food poisoning in the northwest, where they were both university professors. Seems they picked wild mushrooms and got some bad ones. Fortunately, the boys were away at boarding school and didn't eat any. Jordan's paternal uncle brought Jordan and his older brother to live with him here. In those days, the farm was only about five hundred acres. Jordan's brother was nineteen and didn't want any part of farm work, so he just took of and nobody ever hears from him. Jordan was raised by me and his uncle. Cal, too, later on."

Leslie wavered for a minute and decided to ask questions that had bothered her most about Jordan. "Julia, why do I have the feeling that Jordan isn't a farmer, although I

see him farming. Did I see the real Jordan in that gray silk suit yesterday when he went to Baltimore?"

"Honey, you've got good instinct. Jordan's uncle died six years ago, leaving a barely profitable farm of about five hundred acres. Jordan was a full professor of agricultural science at the university, still is for that matter. But since he's a tenured professor, he was able to switch to part-time teaching temporarily and take over the farm. He soon reduced his teaching to Monday nights and built the farm up to what it is today—two thousand acres with just about the largest and best quality output anywhere around here. What made you think that he was something other than a farmer?"

"At first, it was his vocabulary, his speech and his beautifully manicured hands. Especially his hands. I didn't think farmers had hands like that. After a week, I couldn't see a working farmer with his level of sophistication. Not even those ridiculous overalls that never fit could hide it."

Julia laughed. "I'll have to tease Jordan about that. Come think of it, I don't remember seeing a farm worker or a cook with your level of sophistication, either."

Leslie forced a laugh. "Really?"

"Hmmm," was Julia's reply, letting Leslie know she hadn't been fooled by the casual behavior and evasiveness.

"Where's Julia?"

Startled, Leslie swung her gaze from the scene past the kitchen window to Jordan relaxed indolently against the door jamb.

"Julia went to her room to write some letters."

A roguish grin spread over his face. "That's interesting. Cal decided to go write letters, too. That leaves just you and me. What'll we do? You want to write some letters, too?" He was laughing now. He couldn't help it. Leslie was getting madder at him by the second. He hadn't realized how much he would enjoy teasing her.

She hadn't seen this side of him, and he knew he had her nonplussed.

"Will you please go away and leave me alone?" she sputtered. "What's so funny?"

He straightened up slowly and sauntered toward her, and she took a step backward for every one he took forward.

"What's the matter with you, Jordan? I never saw you act like this."

He tried to stop grinning, but it wasn't easy; she looked `a pickle. He stopped right in front of her, almost close enough for his shirt to touch her blouse.

"Jordan?" She croaked it out, as if being that close to him tied her in knots. His grin got broader. Winking wickedly at her, he tweaked her nose. She backed away, landing against the wall. He didn't crowd her further, just stood there with his hands in the pockets of his slacks looking at her. He could see her getting a grip on her emotions.

"Jordan, why did you do that? What's come over you?"

He presented to her the picture of innocence. "Beats me. I guess the devil made me do it. You know what they say about idle hands. Well, I don't have anything to do right now, and you won't write letters."

She poked him in his rock-hard chest. "How old did you say you were?"

He couldn't restrain the laughter, because she was trying so hard to be annoyed. But she didn't fool him; her body language old him she wanted him near. She could pretend all she wanted to. "I didn't say, but I'm a man, if that's what you're after."

"Don't be ridiculous. I know you're a man."

"Do you?" he asked her, his voice soft and the grin gone, replaced by sober reflection. "How do you know I'm a man, Leslie?"

She opened her mouth to answer, but closed it as he moved closer.

"Don't tell me you figured that out from the couple of times you accidentally found yourself in my arms," he mocked, the teasing gone.

"What do you want, Jordan?"

This time, he was giving no quarter. "What do I want? If I told you, you'd be out of her as fast as lightning." He looked her in the eye, let her see his smoldering passion. "And don't push me, not even a little bit, because if you do, I'll tell you what I want, even if you don't want to hear it." And damn the consequences, he thought, but didn't add.

Fully a minute passed before he moved or made a sound. Then he tipped her chin up with one finger and stared into her soft brown eyes. Eyes that made him question his goals, his priorities and all of the reasons that he had ever given himself for remaining unattached. She caught her breath and ran her tongue around the rim of her lips. And still he stared.

Finally, clearly unable to stand it any longer, she whispered to him. "Don't. Don't toy with me. I'm no match for you."

He realized he'd gone too far. "You know you needn't be afraid of me, Leslie," he told her, his voice conveying gentleness and tenderness. "You may some day find that I'm the one who's no match for you."

What had begun as a tease had become serious, and he knew she wasn't ready for a serious discussion of what was happening between them. He stepped away, hoping to defuse the situation quickly.

"Is there any coffee in that urn?" he asked, disconcerting her. Her relief was picture clear. He asked her whether she knew how to ride.

"Ride what?"

"A horse, Leslie," he explained patiently, gruffly. "What else would you ride on a farm?"

He gazed down at her, wanted her badly, but his common sense told him the he had better bide his time.

"How would I know? I'm a city girl. Anyway, I don't ride."

"Everybody else on the Estates can ride a horse, so I'll teach you. You'll enjoy it. There's nothing as relaxing as cantering along on your favorite horse." He grinned. "Or galloping like hell, if that's your fancy."

He wanted to do something nice for her, to make her feel….cherished. He thought for a minute. "If you want to go into town for anything tomorrow afternoon, I'll take you. Just let me know." He left without waiting for her reply.

Leslie watched as he strode toward the stables. Long rhythmic strides punctuated his sexy gait. What made him so sure she didn't want to know what he wanted from her? She'd gotten tired of bantering and teasing. He charmed her like a sleek jungle animal that simultaneously menaces, entices and beckons. And she hadn't wanted him to leave her, but to stay there with her. Not strutting his male prowess, a handsome peacock with his plume spread wide and his cone at full height, but just being himself as he'd been on the boat. Sweet and tender. She'd have to pay more attention to Julia's ways with Cal, because there was a lot she didn't know.

She noticed him watching her all through supper that evening, and she wished he'd stop it. The butter intended for her biscuit slid instead to her jeans, and to her chagrin he saw it. That and the way her fingers shook when she reached for crab cake. She made herself look at his face, intending to censure him, but his smile sent butterflies swirling around in her stomach. She stared at her plate, because she could feel Julia's eyes on her.

"How about going for your first riding lesson around seven-thirty this evening, Leslie? It'll be cooler then, and the horses will enjoy the chance to stretch out."

She knew he'd spoken to put her at ease, so she agreed.

"All right. What'll I wear? Jeans? I don't have any boots."

"Wear sneakers. But put on a long sleeved shirt to ward off the mosquitoes."

She met him at the barn at seven that evening, after she'd given herself a good lecture and gotten rid of her jitters.

"Get on the horse' left side, put your left foot in the stirrup and extend your right leg over the horse's back. Okay?"

"Okay. I think."

He patted her shoulder. "Don't worry. It'll take a little time, but you'll get it." He led the horse from the stall and stopped in front of Leslie. "This is Serenity. She's sweet, gentle and loyal. Get acquainted with her. Like most females, she loves hugs and kisses, so...."

Leslie shuddered. "I'm supposed to hug this big animal? Maybe she just loves your hugs and kisses. I'm doggoned if I'll—"

His grin told her she was being had. "Sure. Most females would. Right?"

She did her best to glare at him. "How would I know?"

He moved closer, and his big hands positioned her to mount the horse. "You're a female. That's how you know. Remember what I said now. Left foot in stirrup."

She did as he said, swung her right leg over Serenity and, to her amazement, found herself sitting on a horse.

He took off his hat. "Lady, you're a quick study. Now, let your body sway with the horse's gait. Pull the rein gently."

She did, and he mounted Casey Jones and headed them toward the brook. Jordan saluted Ossie, who passed them on his way to the house, but Leslie pretended not to see him.

Julia smiled when Ossie walked into the kitchen. "Ossie, you're just in time to help me with this. There's a leak under here somewhere. Cal's gone into Dexter and Jordan's teaching Leslie how to ride. I'm so—"

Ossie sucked his teeth and interrupted her. "That's not all he's going to teach her."

Julia swung around and looked at Ossie. "You notice it, too, huh?"

"You'd have to be blind to miss it," he said, getting on his knees and crawling as far as he could under the sink. "And she'll wake up soon as he gives her something to play house with."

Julia wrung her hands. "You don't think Jordan would do that, do you?"

Ossie crawled out. "He's a man, and she's a good looking woman. He'll take whatever she gives him."

Julia shook her head. She hadn't expected Ossie to take sides against Leslie, but she'd learned that he had integrity and didn't mince words. She looked toward the sky and threw up her hands. "I just don't think she's right for him. I know she's smart and all that, but that'd be an unnecessary burden for him."

"You got it," Ossie agreed. "And he's not right for her, either. She's got some education; you can see that, but she could use some mother wit. Where does Cal keep his pliers?"

She found a pair and gave them to him. "You can't fault her work, nor her manners. Nothing," Julia said. "What about children? Jordan doesn't have any children."

Ossie's laugh was little more than a snarl. "That was my point in the first place. You know, I just couldn't believe it when she moved here. She could at least have given him a hard time. Don't misunderstand me, now. I think the world of Jordan, but he's a man."

"When that's a complication we don't need," she said.

She tried the spigot. "It's not leaking now. Thanks so much, Ossie. I don't know what we'd do without you around here."

She'd just combed out her hair and slipped into a long, red cotton shirt with a mid-thigh slit in time to rush to the front door and greet Cal. His whistle was music to her ears, and she kissed him until they were inside their apartment with the door locked. He held her at arm's length, and she loved it when he swallowed, licked his lips and let his eyes tell her what a delicacy she was. An hour later, feeling like a pile of sweet mush, she rolled over in his arms and kissed his neck.

"Jordan's out teaching Leslie how to ride.'

Cal pinched her bottom and stroked her arm. "It's a good thing. Everybody here should be able to ride."

She sat up. "You mean you haven't noticed what's going on with them? Ossie just said he has no use for Leslie, and if he doesn't leave Jordan alone, I won't."

"You're not serious."

"Why not? The last thing we need here is a disruptive influence. I trust Ossie's judgment in this."

Cal pulled her down in the bed. Then he sat up and glared down at her. "Jordan Saber is thirty-six years old, and I believe he said Leslie is twenty-eight. What they do is

their business, and neither you nor Ossie has one damned thing to do with it. I don't want to hear any more of this, and I don't want to see you treat Leslie any differently from the way you have been. If you want a commotion around here, you interfere with Jordan's private life. You're one person here who ought to know better; as much as he loves you, Julia, he won't stand for that.' He turned out the light. "Now go to sleep."

But she couldn't sleep. God forgive her, if she was wrong, but it just didn't seem right.

Leslie sat straighter on Serenity and looked over at the man who smiled as he rode beside her. "I never dreamed I'd like this so much. How'm I doing so far?"

"Great, but we won't stay out too long this time. Your muscles have to get used to this. You might want to loll around in a hot tub before you go to sleep."

She was a shower person, but he didn't need to know that. "Are you going to take me out again?" she asked, not caring if he detected the eagerness and excitement that she felt. When he nodded, she let a grin take possession of her face. "I can hardly wait."

They'd reached the stable, and he dismounted quickly and walked over to where she sat astride Serenity. He held up both hands, and her heart begun a wild race in her chest. Did she have the nerve to put her arms around his neck when he helped her down? She reached out to him, and he lifted her close to his body and let her slide down. With little more than air between them, he stared into her eyes, his own pools of fiery desire, until she sucked in her breath at his glittering promise. Shaken, she stepped away from him,

but he didn't have to tell her that if she had made one move, she'd still be in his arms. He'd as much as said, it's your call.

CHAPTER FIVE

Jordan stood on the porch darkened by the black sky. Midnight air, hot and damp, swirled around him, and he used the back of his hand to wipe the perspiration from his forehead. The perfumed odor of Julia's roses, blown on the summer wind, teased his nostrils, reminding him of woman. Fresh. Sweet. He'd come down to the kitchen for a glass of lemonade and, for reason he hadn't explained to himself, had stepped out on the porch and looked up at Leslie's apartment. It, too, stood dark and unwelcoming in the silent night. So near she was, and yet so far away. He was beginning to accept that he couldn't rest until she belonged to him. After that....She was in him. Way down deep where he lived dreamed and ached. And he couldn't deny it. Didn't want to. If only she'd relent and rid them of that barrier that prevented them from finding out what they could be to each other. He shook his head. Why was she so intractable?

He stared at the windows of her apartment for some minutes more before turning to go back into the kitchen. As he opened the door, he could have sworn that something crashed somewhere against a window. He stood on the porch, wishing he had a flashlight. Again. This time, he traced the sound to Leslie's window. He dashed back into the kitchen and turned on the lights above the steps that led to her apartment, but by the time he got back to the porch, he could hear the footsteps of a man running. Too late. It was time he did something about Leslie, and he'd begin by

putting one of his workers on night watch. He left the light on and went to bed.

The next afternoon, Saturday, Jordan joined Leslie, Julia and Cal in a game of bridge, but after a few hands, he tired of it. He couldn't get his mid off Leslie and whoever had thrown pebbles at her windows the previous night. It aggravated him. Then she smiled his way, and he felt his heart turn over. He savored the innocence reflected in her soft brown eyes, the natural pout of her full, luscious mouth. The make-up free, natural beauty of her butterscotch brown face. The fragile strands of black hair hanging all the way down to her full breast. He thought of her uninhibited warmth and how she blazed when he touched her. And he remembered the pebbles crashing against her window. She could be the opposite of the woman that her demeanor proclaimed. Still, he doubted it. Something in him wanted to shield her, care for her, protect her, and his instincts had never been far off the mark. He excused himself and went to the kitchen for a glass of water. He needed a resolution to his nagging passion. And soon. Maybe a change of scenery would be good for all of them, and it wouldn't hurt him to see Leslie in another environment, not just with him, but with their friends as well. And he wanted Julia especially to see Leslie out of her role as cook, away from that kitchen.

He stuck his hands in his pants pocks and sauntered back into the living room. "Look, I have an idea. Let's all go over to Baltimore for supper. I could taste some crab cakes and we'd give the ladies a break. How about it, Cal?" He looked at Leslie, who nodded her agreement.

Cal stood. "Sounds good to me." Putting an arm around his wife, who had her hair in elegant French braid, Cal told her, "I know you have to take off those shorts, Julia, but leave your hair up."

"And you leave yours down," Jordan commanded Leslie, without thinking. He saw the knowing looks that passed between Julia and Cal, but ignored them, and said to Leslie. "I wish you'd wear that pretty red sun dress. I liked it a lot."

He noticed that she glanced at Julia. "I'd love to wear it, but I have to iron it."

"We can wait," he said, letting all of them know that the only opinions he cared about were Leslie's and his own. When they got back to the Estates, he walked with Leslie to her door, opened it, kissed her cheek and, in a playful attitude, shoved her into her apartment. He didn't know when he'd had so much fun. Julia had flirted with every Joe she saw, while Cal regarded it with amused indulgence, and Leslie frankly censured Julia's frivolous behavior.

The next morning, Jordan gave them another surprise. "I'm leaving this afternoon for the University of Wisconsin," he told them, "and I'll be gone most of the week. You won't need me," he said to Cal, "but I'll leave my number just in case you do. And I want you to turn the flood lights on at night and put Sanchez on night watch. The weather forecast doesn't look to good, but I hope we don't get any storm damage."

They weren't lucky. Jordan left on Sunday afternoon, as planned, but by nightfall, the sky had blackened, and the wind threatened. Cal had the men tape every window,

board up the barn doors and windows, secure the stables and tie the low-lying limbs on as many trees as possible. He bolstered the windows and door of Leslie's apartment as well as he could and had her spend the night in on of the guest rooms. Then he called Jordan.

"The storm's pretty close to us, Jordan, but there's nothing you can do that we haven't already seen to. Stay out there and finish your business."

"Thanks, Cal." He seemed to weigh both his words and the tone of his voice. "How's Leslie?"

"Don't worry, Jordan, I'll look after her. She's fine, except she's a little upset about what the storm might do to your peach trees." He spoke in lowered tones. "We all are, son."

"Yeah. Well, keep her there with you and Julia." Cal hung up, certain that Jordan was more concerned about Leslie than about his peach crop. By midnight, he knew that they were in for a lot of damage. The storm roared in as violently as any he had witnessed.

"Go on to sleep," Cal told Leslie. "Tomorrow, we'll salvage what we can, but I don't expect that'll be much."

At five-thirty the next morning, he found Leslie peering out the kitchen window at the tree limbs, uprooted saplings and the rubble that was strewn everywhere.

"I guess he won't be able to start his horse farm," she said. "He was counting on the money from the peaches. What do you think he'll do now, Cal?"

Cal regarded her carefully. He didn't think she was this concerned because her boss would have to wait another year for his dream, but all he said was, "If we'd had anoth-

er week, we would have made it. It's bad, but you can bet he won't let it bury him. The trees aren't in such bad shape, Leslie. I was out there. But more than half the peaches are on the ground. Some are ripe, some hard. Well, you know."

Leslie swung away from the window and grabbed Cal's arm. "You mean to say that some of the peaches on the ground are already ripe? How many?"

"Well, most of the ones that fell are ripe. Some are bruised, and a few are green but sound. What are you thinking?" he asked her, as Julia walked in, clearly distraught.

Before Leslie could reply, Julia cut in. "It doesn't make a difference how he gets money form the peaches, so long as he gets it, right?" She began putting on her rubbers. "We're going to make preserves, Leslie."

Leslie didn't hesitate. "Sounds good to me. Let's get busy."

To Leslie's astonishment, Julia put on an apron. "Cal, could you ask the men to get some of those bushel baskets you use for string beans and start gathering peaches. They have to be graded for ripeness and damage. Then we have to go to Hagerstown and get some supplies."

Perplexed both by her message and her apron, Cal turned to his wife. "What at you going to do with hundreds of gallons of peach preserves?"

"Bottle, label and sell them under Jordan's logo," Leslie put in.

Cal looked hard at her. "I didn't know that Jordan had a logo." He knew his wife was an optimist, but this whole scheme was an enormous gamble. That fact didn't perturb

Julia, who repaired her lipstick and smiled broadly at Leslie's eagerness to do anything necessary to keep Jordan's dream alive. Cal knew Leslie had passed Julia's test: she'd go all the way to the wall for Jordan and, for that, Julia would forever lover her. She needn't worry any more about Julia not wanting her with Jordan. He'd bet anything on that.

"Then the three of us will have to design a logo," Leslie informed them airily, "though I can't even draw a straight line."

"But that won't stop you," Cal said to himself.

Leslie rolled up her shirt sleeves and began searching for stock pot. "Come on. Shape up," she ordered. "We've got a lot to do."

"Sure thing." Cal regarded Leslie with new insight and added, "Jordan's a lucky man to have the love of a woman like you."

"What?" Leslie spun around, startled. She couldn't have heard him correctly.

Cal shook his head and smiled his slow, patient smile. "Don't you know that you love Jordan? Well, if you don't, let me be the first to tell you do. I'll get the men started, and we'll head for Hagerstown as soon as we can get us some coffee and a biscuit. I'm glad you're here, Leslie, and I hope you stay." She stared at him. Staying hadn't been in her plans. Neither had loving Jordan.

By mid-afternoon, they had everything they needed, including every available one-pint barrel-shaped glass jar in Hagerstown and Dexter. All eleven of the men willingly worked until well beyond nightfall to help them. Even

Rocket, whom they all regarded as being mentally in the clouds, skinned more than a dozen baskets of peaches.

Julia looked at the peaches that remained to be graded and preserved, and her shoulders sagged. "Maybe we'd better call it a night and finish tomorrow."

Knowing that she wouldn't rest until they'd done everything they could, Leslie shook her head. "No way. We finish tonight."

Julia stared at her. "I believe you'd work at it all night, wouldn't you?"

She didn't care what Julia thought. She nodded. "If that's what it takes. In another day, half of this fruit will be unsalvageable. We can sleep when we finish."

"That's my girl," Ossie put in. "Wear yo sef out of de man. Doormats are rare these days."

What Ossie thought didn't faze her. "If nastiness is what turns you on, Mr. Dixon, you ought to be fired up all the time."

But she saw that Cal did care. His head snapped up, and he laid his knife on the table. "Exactly what do you meant by that crack, Ossie?"

"Don't worry," Ossie replied. "She understands me perfectly.'

"So do I," Cal said, getting up and walking over to Ossie. "We need to have a talk, man."

Ossie stood. "What about?"

Cal nodded toward the back door. "We'd better step out side."

Ossie dusted off his jeans and followed Cal out on the back steps, and she wondered how Ossie could be so mean about something that wasn't his business.

"All right. What's the problem?" Ossie asked Cal.

Cal knew why Ossie had unloaded on Leslie and, as long as he was in charge, he wouldn't stand for it anymore than he'd tolerate Julia's sniping about Jordan and Leslie.

"The problem," Cal said in measured tones, "is that you've been making these digs at Leslie ever since we started working on these peaches. That last crack was beneath you, and she doesn't deserve it. I want you to apologize to her, and don't do it any more."

It didn't surprise him much when Ossie raised an eyebrow and said, "Sorry, Cal. I don't eat my words."

Cal laid his head to one side, looked at the man and knew he wouldn't budge. "In that case, you may discuss it with Jordan, but don't do it again while I'm in charge here. Come on, let's go back in there. We've still got work to do."

Ossie put his hands in the back pockets of his jeans and gave Cal a long look. "Because she refuses to quit until it's finished?"

Cal raised himself to his full six feet, two inches, and the stood toe to toe and head to head. "Damn straight. Let's get to work."

By Thursday morning, Leslie relaxed, tired but happy. They'd saved every peach. The ripe, damaged ones went into preserves. The green peaches had been dried and placed in the sun to ripen, and the ripe, unblemished peaches were already on the way to the markets. When the three of them sat down to supper Friday night they smiled

at each other but were almost too tired to eat. And for the first time since she'd come to the Estates, Leslie had a feeling of oneness with them.

"Thank God, Jordan will be here tomorrow," Cal proclaimed. "I never told him what we were doing when I called him from Hagerstown. He'll see when he gets here."

Leslie sat up most of the night pondering the market potential of the logo designs. With the help of pictures in some country and gardener's magazines, the three of them had developed several ideas from which Jordan could choose. When she finally got into bed, she hugged herself. "I think I'll die if I can't see him, touch him tomorrow. I think I'll just go crazy."

This time, she wouldn't be reticent—and she wouldn't worry about what people would think. Julia had her Cal, didn't she? And if Ossie wanted to be full of attitude, that was his problem.

At about two-thirty Saturday afternoon, she heard the motor of the Town Car—Jordan had garaged it at the airport— and ran as fast as she could from the kitchen to her apartment. She quickly took her hair down and brushed it out, put on some lipstick and a dab of perfume. Then she slipped into the red sun dress and her white sandals.

"I can't let him see me in jeans and these old sneakers," she told herself. In a minute, she would see him. Oh, she couldn't face him. She smoothed her hair and looked at herself again. Her blood raced, and anxiety knotted her belly as she anticipated the feel of his mouth on hers. He wouldn't get away this time. If she had to make the first move, she'd do it. Even with her limited experience, she

knew when a man wanted her, and Jordan Saber was on fire for her. She calmed herself, reminded herself who she was and what she wanted from life, but her treacherous mind conjured up a picture of his mouth at her breast, and shudders shook her.

Knock! Knock! When she doesn't answer immediately, he called, "Leslie, open up and let me in." It would be the first time he'd been to her apartment since the day she moved in. She went trembling on liquid legs to the door, hoping she wouldn't betray herself.

"Hi." She said it softly, almost breathlessly. The cook, housemaid and accountant were gone. It was the woman standing there.

"Hi. Aren't you going to let me come in?" He noticed how nice she looked in the middle of the day in that red dress and her hair around her shoulders, and he hoped it was for him. He had almost killed himself exceeding the speed limit all the way from Baltimore to get back to her. And then, to discover what they had done for him! When Cal showed him, speechless, he had said nothing. He'd simply turned around and gotten to her as fast as he could.

"Y...yes, sh..sure. C...come in." He stopped right in front of her.

"Did you miss me?"

She wanted to hurl herself into his arms, but she stood there, her composure shot. "Yes. I mean, no! I mean, was I supposed to?"

He stepped closer and gently lifted her chin. "Did you miss me, Leslie?" His voice had a huskiness she hadn't heard before.

"Jordan. I...Jordan... Oh, Jordan!" He took off his hat, threw it across the room and gathered her into his arms. Then he gently touched her lips with his, as though waiting to see if she would reject him, but she just moved into him, locked herself to him. He's hungry, she thought. Hungry. Starved like me. He pulled her closer and moved his mouth over hers, increasing the pressure, deepening the kiss. She didn't back off. The more he wanted, the more she gave, and the more she wanted to give.

She trembled in the grip of her true awareness of herself as a woman. None of her dreams of him measured up to the feeling of his mouth, gentle, but urgent and hungry on hers, of his hard body pressing against hers, of his arms caressing her. She felt him in every molecule of her body. She tried to get closer, seeking to satiate something that she couldn't name, couldn't identify. She squeezed him to her until her arms ached. And still she tugged him closer. Lord, he felt so good. So good! She reeled under the onslaught of her passion. Groaning in the sweet delirium of new-found ecstasy, she held his head in her arms to increase the pressure of his mouth on hers and nearly blacked out when his hand went to her buttocks to settle her between his thighs.

Jordan ran his tongue around her lips and soon realized that she didn't know how to respond. "Sweetheart, open your mouth for me. I want to kiss you." She parted her lips, and he gave her his tongue, intending to explore every centimeter of her sweet mouth. But she pulled it in as far as she could get it, and sucked on it as if it were the sweetest thing she'd ever tasted, the essence of life itself. Her moans, strung out with desire, with longing fed over months of

daily torture. At last she was in his arms, her breast pressed against him, her arms tight around him, and her warmth heating him to boiling point.

He teetered toward problems with his control, but he reeled himself in. She fitted him perfectly. He'd known that she would. And the best fit was yet to come. Trying to control the heat settling in his loins and wanting to keep full arousal at bay, he started to turn sideways, still holding her. But she wouldn't give him a centimeter, just moved into him again. The hell with it, he thought, I want this. I need it. And she's mine! He put his hands in her hair, held her head still and made love to her with his tongue, his mouth, until she moaned aloud.

"Sweet, so sweet," he whispered, kissing her again and again.

When he brushed his fingers gently over her breast, she cried out, "Oh Jordan, Jordan, something's happening to me.'

"I'm what's happening to you," he wanted to say. But he didn't. He did step back a bit, giving her a little space. To his amazement and pleasure, however, she moved into him, as though bereft at the separation. It was too much. He lifted her into his arms, pressed her head to his shoulder and started toward her bedroom. Already nearly out of his mind with desire, he felt her kiss his neck sweetly and tenderly, and his arousal was swift and total. He wanted to take her right there in the middle of the floor. She caressed his face with gentle hands and stroked his hair. So tender, he thought, so trusting and loving.

So trusting! What on earth was he thinking about? She was an innocent, and she trusted him. He stopped at the overstuffed leather chair and sat down, resting her on his knees. He didn't dare hold him any closer but, to his horror, she slid up to his lap snuggling as closely as possible. Her immediate change of demeanor stunned him.

"I was trying to hide it from you," he told her. "That's why I sat you on my knee."

Minutes passed, and she didn't respond or look at him, and he knew something had gone wrong.

"Honey, I want more from you. I need more, but I know you're not ready for it."

He sense her withdrawal and decided to deal with it right then. "Please talk to me. I know your experience with men had been limited, and I know there's a reason, because you're young, beautiful, warm and loving. I told you I'd protect you as long as you're her, and I will. I'll even protect you from myself, if that's what you want. I won't touch you, Leslie, unless you want me to.

"I've wanted to hold you almost since the day you came here, but I gave you the space you seemed to need. When I was away, though, I missed you. You've become important to me."

He stopped speaking, because she was looking at him, concentrating on his every word. And judging him. Scrutinizing him. Making up her mind. He waited. What else could he do?"

"I can't stay here indefinitely, Jordan." At his gesture of dismay, she explained. "I've got another year of my master's degree. I'm not sure how to react to what you're saying to

me. I know I feel, but I've worked so hard and so long to get that ticket to independence that it has to be my first priority. And another thing. You have to give serious thought to the social consequences of an involvement with me before you get in any deeper."

He put both hands on her shoulders and set her away from him so that she could see his face. "Do you think I'm blind to what goes on in the world? My only concerns are for our feelings for each other. Your opinions and mine. I don't give two hoots about anybody else's judgment, attitude or reaction. Do you understand that?"

She gazed at him, as though searching for the truth in him. Then she lifted her face, and he had the feeling that she wanted to be picture clear to him. "I feel closer to you than I've ever felt to anyone, but I'm not sure you can rely on that; I'm different from other women, I—"

He didn't want to hear that. "What do you mean, you're different from other women?" It amazed him that his voice sounded so calm.

"There's a reason why I'm not comfortable with men. It's not my fault, and it's neither biological nor health related. You said you care for me, and I'm not sure that's wise."

She attempted to move away from him, off his lap. But he held her and rocked her gently, soothing her.

"And you still can't tell me about it?"

She shook her head. "I want to, and I've tried, but I... I can't deal with it." Her eyes pleaded with him. "I'll disappoint you."

"I'll be the judge of what pleases me," he said, his voice strangely gruff and deepening with passion. "When you

learn to trust me completely, all of your doubts will be history."

She tightened her grip on his shoulder as if she wanted to make sure she had his attention. With her nestled in his lap, what and who else did she think could be on his mind?

"Maybe," she said. "I don't know. But we'd better back off a little, Jordan, and let me find out if there's anything to this other than the rocks that fly around in my middle when I get near you."

He couldn't help laughing. She'd nailed it right on the head. He stroked her cheek. "At least you feel it too."

"I'm serious. If we get involved, we won't walk away from it unscathed. I know I won't. And we're not the only ones. Some of the relationships dear to you may go up in smoke because of us. I'm not sure I want to—"

He refused to give her a chance to say no. "All right," he cut in, "but will you at least let us spend time alone together so we can find out whether this thing between us is for real?"

Her silence lasted a little too long for his comfort, but she finally said, "Yes... Okay. So long as that doesn't interfere with my studies."

He didn't care how many degrees she planned to get. Hell, he'd help her. But now that he knew how deeply she cared for him, even if she didn't admit it; he was going to have her. It struck him as forcibly as a sculptor's chisel hits stone that he wanted her for himself alone. Permanently? He didn't know. But God help him, he was teetering toward it. She wasn't going anywhere. He'd never been a patient man, but he was going to learn forbearance if it

killed him. Somewhere back in his mind, he remembered that she had secrets, maybe dangerous ones, but he suspected it was too late to worry about that.

Leslie sat on the edge of her bed for an hour after he had kissed her fleetingly and left her. If she was dreaming, she didn't want to wake up. If she was awake, she didn't want to break the spell. She caressed her arms, her breasts, everywhere he had touched that she could reach. She laughed aloud, and then she cried. She had wanted to know what it would be like to have him hold her, caress her, kiss her. She just wanted to know. Now she knew, and for two cents, she'd fly. She fought the delirium. And the fear. What if she really was in love with him as Cal had said, and he decided she was just another puppet in the parade of women who wanted him?

She'd never thought that there would be an insurmountable obstacle to what she wanted most—her master's degree—because she was willing to do any kind of work, no matter how hard or unpleasant, to accomplish her goal. Jordan Saber was an obstacle, because he made her have dreams that had nothing to do with a master's degree in business administration. To let him get next to her, to love him as she knew she could, would end all of that. She wouldn't do it.

She tried to ignore the whispers of her conscience: You know what you're afraid of, and it isn't not getting your MBA, or being dependent on him. You're afraid to let him make love to you, to touch you, really touch you. Tell him. Tell him everything. Never! She vowed.

After supper that evening, Jordan sat in his den with Leslie, Julia and Cal and thought of his luck in having the three of them in his life. Three people who had done a Herculean job for him at a time when he needed it, and with no thought as to recompense. Because they cared about him.

He wasn't yet sure about Julia, but he didn't doubt that Cal had accepted Leslie as one of them. "How're we going to market these preserves, Leslie?" Cal wanted to know. "You're the expert in business administration." She pulled out the logo designs, and they agreed on one that Jordan decided would thereafter go on every carton and crate of produce that he shipped.

As they settled on a marketing strategy, price and schedule, it occurred to Jordan that Leslie was in her element, just as she'd been when she computerized his business. She didn't attempt to downplay her attributes as she so often did, and he could tell that, in her mind, she was one among equals. To him, that had never been in doubt.

"All right," Jordan said, "that's it. Can either of you think of anything we've overlooked?"

"Not a thing," they replied in unison. Leslie handed Jordan a sheaf of paper.

"What's this, hon...Leslie?" He had almost called her "honey" before quickly checking himself. If she noticed it, she didn't make it obvious.

"It's advertising copy. I thought it might be helpful to give this to local radio and television stations and newspapers. There's also a design for fliers."

If Julia and Cal hadn't been present, he would have done a thorough job of kissing her.

At the end of the week, he opened a bottle of vintage champagne and the four of them drank a toast. He was in a mellow mood. He'd come back home thinking that he was one year or further away from his dream. But they had salvaged the peach crop for him, in fact, gotten the ripe ones to the market early when he could command highest prices. This week, he had seen firsthand how smoothly Leslie and Julia managed the labeling, packaging and shipment of the preserves. The product was very professional and eye catching and five supermarket chains had agreed to take the preserves on the advice of their local branches. If he wanted to, he could market the preserves on a regular basis, and it was an idea that had plenty of merit. He and Leslie could make a great team.

"Got a minute, Jordan?" Cal asked.

They'd finished celebrating, and he wanted to stretch out and organize things in his mind, namely, what he'd sacrificed in Wisconsin in order to get back home quickly, the turn his business was about to take, and Leslie. He couldn't let her dangle in uncertainty, and he didn't intend to let her do that to him. He didn't want to spare Cal a minute, but he would.

"What's up, Cal?"

They walked back into the den, and Cal closed the door and ran his fingers through his thinning hair. "Ossie's taken a dislike to Leslie, and I thought he was rude to her. Fact is, I know he was. Real rude. I spoke to him about it, and he refused to apologize to her. She doesn't know this part,

though." He walked a few paces, looked down at his shoes and gritted his teeth. "He should apologize, Jordan. I told him I'd speak with you about this."

He remembered Leslie's having told him that Ossie didn't want the two of them together. "Did his comment involve me?" he asked Cal.

At Cal's widened eyes, he added, "I don't expect everyone to understand my feelings for Leslie, but I do expect everybody on my property to keep their negative opinions to themselves."

He reached for his hat and felt Cal's hand heavy on his arm, detaining him. "Where're you headed?"

"You don't have to ask that because you know. I've been through a lot with Ossie, and he's almost like a brother to me. But he's going to apologize this very day."

"Now wait, Jordan. Don't be hasty. You don't even know what he said."

Jordan put on his hat and started for the door. "He said enough to get a reprimand from you, and not many of the men who have worked here over the years can brag about that. I don't need to know more." He walked off, saddled Casey Jones and headed for the men's dormitory.

He tethered the stallion to a hitching post near the dormitory, as the men jokingly referred to the single-room-occupancy apartment building in which Jordan housed them. In the lounge, several men watched the Baltimore Orioles lose their third straight game, and a few feet away, four men concentrated on a game of rummy. His gaze fell on the recreation area in the back. Rocket sweated on an exercise machine, two of the older African-American

men—Zeke and Roland—enjoyed a game of billiards, while Sanchez and McGuiness, the youngest of his workers, played table tennis. It didn't surprise him that Ossie wasn't among them, because the man spent his leisure time shaping his future. The harmony among the men—black, white and Hispanic, educated and nearly illiterate, some with families but most without—always amazed him. He attributed it to the possibility that each recognized himself in all of the others. Failed men who'd been offered another chance and who'd grabbed at it and used it.

He walked over to Jack, the housemaster, who reclined in an overstuffed leather chair reading an issue of *Time* magazine and spoke into the public address system. "I want to thank all of you for what you did to salvage those peaches. I know you did it out of loyalty, but you'll all get bonuses in your next pay."

After the applause died out, he said to Jack, "Any idea where Ossie is?"

When Jack sat up straight and raised one eyebrow, Jordan knew that every man who worked for him was expecting Ossie to get a reprimand.

"He was down here for a couple of minutes to get a soda. I'll call him."

Jordan shook his head. "Thanks. I'll call him." He dialed Ossie's phone number. "This is Jordan. I'm downstairs. I want to speak with you."

"I didn't know you'd come back. I'll be right down."

It wouldn't be an easy exchange, because Ossie had once enjoyed the respect of corporate titans and everybody else who knew him. He was a proud man, and he didn't back

down readily. But he'd have to do just that, because he'd gone too far.

He didn't greet Ossie with his usual warmth. He couldn't. He walked with him into the dining room. "Cal told me you were rude to Leslie and that you refused to apologize." He saw Ossie's nostrils flare in anger. "Before you harden your position," he told him, "think about what I'm going to say."

Ossie shrugged. "I'm listening."

"You and I have been together through more difficulties that most blood brothers or fathers and sons, and we've built a relationship that has come to mean a lot to me."

Ossie rested against the back of a chair and crossed his ankles, "But."

"Yes. But. Didn't it occur that you were disrespecting a woman that I care about? Do you believer I'm using Leslie, and is that the kind of man you think I am?"

"Look, Jordan. I—"

Jordan raised his full height. "I haven't finished. I'm not going to bend on this, Ossie. If Julia forced me to choose between her and Leslie because of some ridiculous notion about what's good for me, as much as I think of Julia, she'd have to go. And that ought to tell you something. Nobody on Saber Estates is going to mistreat Leslie because of me and do it with impunity. I'm giving you a choice."

Ossie ran his hand over his short hair in what Jordan recognized as a gesture of frustration. "Every time I see the two of you together, my back gets up. She's got no business with you. She belongs with her own folks. I don't like it."

Impatience began to wear on him, and when he ground his teeth, he knew he had to control his rising anger. "Ossie, I don't give a damn if you don't like it, because it isn't any of your business. I want you to apologize to Leslie and to treat her with respect." To his surprise, his fist hit the table. "If I saw you with a woman, white or any other color, I wouldn't consider it my business, and I'd be courteous to her. And by damn, I demand the same of you. Anybody who doesn't like seeing me with Leslie can ignore it or leave."

Ossie stared at him. "You'd scuttle everything you've built up here?"

Jordan walked as far as the door, turned and said, "I am still a tenured professor at the University of Maryland, which means I've got a permanent job. Neither these two-thousand acres, nor anything nor anybody on them is worth my self-respect, and if I permitted you to behave toward Leslie as you did, I wouldn't be worthy of your respect or anybody else's."

Ossie took a deep breath and blew out a lot of air. "Who'd have thought it? See you."

"Before you sleep this night, Ossie."

He walked out, closed the door and jumped on his horse. He sat astride Casey Jones gazing at the summer sun—big, round and intimidating—as it prepared to sleep for the night. Putting an end to the day. Forcing him and everybody else to look toward the morrow.

He let his gaze wander over his lush fields, all that he'd driven himself to accomplish. Progress that had come sweat by drop of sweat, and acre by acre. And in it all, he saw her.

Somber. Laughing. Skipping. Teasing. Her face peeped out at him from every bush, tree and grove. He ran his hands over his eyes, and she was no longer there. He remembered that he'd chased her in his dream, and she'd laughed at him and refused to tell him her name. He was damned if he'd put up with the uncertainty. The torture of not knowing who shadowed her and why. He had to settle it. Now! She cared for him, and if he had to, he'd used that to advantage.

And Ossie. Sadness weighed on him as he contemplated losing Ossie, as good a worker and friend as a man could want. He shook his head, slapped Casey Jones on his rump and headed for the barn. If Ossie knew how much he cared for him, the man wouldn't find apologizing so difficult, but if he didn't do it, he'd tell him to go.

It was Ossie's love for Jordan that propelled him to the white Georgian mansion as darkness settled in. He had procrastinated until he could no longer justify his stubbornness. He knew he'd gone too far with Leslie and that he'd crossed the line of decency with his rude statement to her. He didn't know what had gotten into him, because he had always prided himself on behaving as a gentleman. Even when he'd been down and out—living on the streets of Baltimore—he had never approached a woman for a handout though he knew they were more likely to give; he hadn't wanted to embarrass them with his presence. He walked slowly, remembering the punishments he'd gotten as a child because he'd refused to apologize for something he'd done.

He stopped at the barn and leaned against the old tree where Jordan had kissed Leslie at high noon in the presence of anyone who cared to see it. And that wasn't the first time

he'd kissed her in public. When a man did that, he was making a statement. He walked on. If he was honest, he'd admit that Jordan wouldn't misuse Leslie or any other human being. Besides, the woman carried herself with as much dignity as anyone he knew or had known, and what she deserved from him was not rudeness, but respect.

He reached the back porch, stopped and jammed his hands in his pockets. "Don't beat yourself to death about it, Dixon," he admonished himself. "Do what's right."

Just what I need, he thought, following the voices down to the basement, a big audience. He stepped into the recreation room and, as he'd expected, got the undivided attention of Jordan, Cal, Leslie and Julia.

"Good evening, everybody," he said before looking directly at Leslie. "I have no right to speak to you as I did, and I won't do that again." He tipped his hat. "Good night, all." Then he turned on his heel, ran up the stairs and headed for the dormitory.

Halfway between the house and the barn, he stopped. He didn't know a thing about Leslie, he mused, but he did know that he was a God-fearing man, and it wasn't his place to judge her or anybody else. That was God's prerogative. One more thing for Confession the next Sunday. Any way you measured it; he'd been out of line. He could see why a woman would want Jordan and find him irresistible. Jordan said she meant something to him, and he suspected it went deeper than that. It would take a lot for him to embrace the idea of black women with white men, and he'd have to pray about his attitude. Yeah. He'd have to see what he could do to make amends.

Ossie's statement hadn't mollified Jordan, however, and he'd started up the stars after Ossie when Cal stopped him. "Let it be, Jordan. For Ossie, those few words were tantamount to your getting down on your knees and begging for forgiveness."

Jordan ran his fingers through his hair. "But—"

"Just let it go, son. The man humiliated himself."

Jordan slapped his fist into his left palm. "With that half-assed apology?"

"Yeah," Cal said. "I remember making you go without supper one night because you refused to say even that much. Let's close it."

"I...I'll leave it for now."

Cal slung an arm around Jordan's shoulder. "Good. Sleep on it."

Jordan went back down to the recreation room where Julia had begun teaching Leslie how to shoot pool.

"Julia, will you excuse us? I have to speak with Leslie."

Julia looked from one to the other and headed upstairs without commenting.

"You want to talk to me about Ossie?" Leslie asked him.

"No. That's between him and me." He looked at her for a long time. With that smile, she could bring a man down more easily that a chain saw could fell a tree. He shook his head, and then surprised himself when he walked up to her, grabbed both of her shoulders and stared down into her face. "You wanted us to back off and get to know each other, understand each other and develop a friendship. Friendship is based on trust. Now, I'm asking you for a few simple truths. Have you committed a crime?"

Seemingly unperturbed, she shook her head. "No, Jordan. I am not a criminal. What else?"

He had to ignore her unshed tears, though it hurt him to see them. "All right. You said you're not married. Are you engaged?"

At that, she bristled and tried to move away, but he held her. "If I were engaged, I would never have kissed you. I am not a cheat."

No. He hadn't thought she was. She stared into his eyes, and he had to fight the demands of his loins where her eyes took on that smokey haze that he knew signaled a woman's rising desire. The she wet her lips and, in spite of his intentions, he pulled her to him, bent his head and took her mouth. Shock reverberated through him when her body trembled and her lips parted. Her eagerness for his kiss scattered his senses, and he had to pull away lest she drag him into full arousal.

"Leslie, you care for me. I know it. Yet you don't trust me. You have to tell me now what you fear and why. I can't stand knowing you're in danger and being unable to protect you. Tell me you don't care for me, and I'll leave you alone." He nestled her to his body and waited.

After long minutes, she raised her head from his chest, stepped back and let him see her face. "Promise me you won't ask me any questions, that you won't grill me. I can't go through that again. Just accept what I tell you. Can you do that?"

What could he say? "I can try. At least for now. And I'll believe what you tell me."

She looked into his face, but he'd already seen that she was wringing her hands. He wanted to take her in his arms, but he didn't touch her.

"My boss tried to rape me and almost succeeded. I still have two of the bruises he gave me. I brought charges against him, and the trial lasted three weeks, during which time almost everybody who ever knew me was called to testify against me. His lawyer tried to prove that I was little more that a street woman, but he couldn't, although he grilled me all day for three consecutive days. My boss was a prominent man, but thanks to three women—former employees of his—who came to my aid, he served three years in jail. At the sentencing, he swore that when he got out, he wouldn't let me rest. I know he wants vengeance, but not what kind, and I can tell you he promised to kill me if I ever mentioned his name or brought any more charges against him."

Whatever he'd thought he'd hear, it wasn't anything like that. He folded her to him and stroked her back. "That explains everything, but I want you to try and forget that it ever happened. He didn't succeed, honey, and that's what matters."

He could barely decipher the words muffled against his chest. "Are you satisfied?"

"I'll be satisfied when I can get my hands on him." He hugged her to him. "Thank you for trusting me. You're safe now. Do you understand? You're not in any danger."

She nodded, but skepticism clouded her face. "He lost everything, including his family, because of it, and I guess he intends to make me suffer."

"But he won't succeed. Not if I have my way." He had
to do something to lighten her mood. "Want to see a movie
tonight?"

She shook her head. "I have to work on my thesis."

He ran his forefinger across her bottom lip. "You can do
that after the movie. Tell you what. I'll buy you a big bag of
popcorn."

She laughed, and he didn't want her to stop, didn't want
the dancing lights to fade from her eyes. "Kiss me. Leslie,
put your arms around me and kiss me."

"Right now?"

His eyebrows shot up. "Yeah. Now."

She reached up, kissed his cheek and got out of his arms
before he could stop her. He couldn't believe it.

"Go mend some fences, do your books or something.
I've got work to do."

She dashed up the stairs, and he watched her go. He'd
have to be careful, because that incident could have shack-
led her with a deep-seated fear of intimacy. But that would-
n't stop him. He'd had bigger challenges and overrode every
one of them. Still…

He shook his head. It wasn't good.

CHAPTER SIX

It had been a week since Jordan left for Kentucky, and Leslie an antique marble table in the foyer, the doorbell rang in short but insistent peals. She opened the door to find a woman and a very handsome small boy who reminded her of someone.

It appeared from the woman's tired, worn expression that she was about to ask for help. But to Leslie's amazement, she displayed cool professionalism. "Is this where Jordan Saber lives?"

"Yes, but Mr. Saber is away on business. May I help you?" Leslie noticed that the boy seemed nervous and apprehensive. She smiled and patted him on the shoulder, hoping to put him at ease.

"This boy claims to have an uncle with a background similar to Mr. Saber's," the woman said, "and the California courts have been looking for the boy's uncle for nearly eight months. His parents died in an automobile accident. We've had him in foster care, but he insists his father had a brother named Jordan. I'm his case worker. He's stubbornly maintained that he can't be adopted because he has an uncle somewhere, but he didn't know where that uncle was. He's a ward of the court until we find his uncle. If Mr. Saber doesn't want him, we'll find a foster home for him and take it from there. When will Mr. Saber be back?'

"In a couple of days. Come in, and I'll get someone who may be able to help you." She looked down at the young boy. "What's your name?"

"His name is Clifford, and I'm sorry, but we don't have time for a visit. I'll bring him back next week."

She took the boy's hand and turned to leave, but at his unspoken appeal to her, Leslie whirled around. "Julia, come here please." She told Julia the story.

As Julia studied Clifford, her face bloomed into a smile. "This is Jordan Saber's home. If this boy is his nephew, he belongs here. Son, what is your full name?"

He looked steadily at Julia, his gaze intense as though deciding whether to cast his lot with her. Apparently satisfied, he replied, "Clifford Saber, ma`am. Can I stay with my Unca Jordan for good? I want to stop moving."

Julia regarded him with admiration. "And what was your dad's name?"

The boy showed no emotion. "His name was Haskell Saber."

"Sure. You're a Saber all right. You're named after your grandfather, and you look just like your uncle Jordan did at your age. How old are you, Clifford?"

"Eight, Ma`am."

Julia turned to the social worker. "Madam, this is Clifford's home now. You may come back next week and talk to Jordan, but you can leave Clifford with me."

"I'm sorry, but I can't do that. Ask Mr. Saber to call me." She handed Julia her card.

"Do you think he'll call her?" Clifford asked Julia.

"You needn't worry about that, son. You're a Saber, and Jordan takes care of his own. My name's Julia, and this is Leslie. We'll see you Monday."

Clifford was interested in how he would be received. He looked at Leslie. "Is my Unca Jordan nice?"

She guarded her expression, lest she betray herself to Julia. "He's a wonderful man."

The social worker took Clifford's hand. "Come along. Something tells me you needn't worry any more. I think we've found your uncle and that you're going to be happy with him."

Clifford didn't want to leave. "I sure will be glad when Monday gets here. Bye."

Leslie's lectures to herself did nothing to abate the anxiety with which she awaited Jordan's return. She stared out of the windows, forgot to put baking powder in a batch of biscuits and, more than once, Julia had asked if she was having a problem with her hearing. She discarded the pretense of calm and accepted that she couldn't wait to see him, couldn't stop thinking about the kiss he'd given her. Seven days. When he'd first left, she'd bent dreamy-eyed over her thesis, her thoughts only of him. Then, she'd browbeat herself into finishing chapter six and outlining the remainder of her study. She couldn't sublimate any longer; she needed to hear his voice.

"Jordan! Where are you? What happened? I was on my way out of my mind when this phone rang. I didn't know whether to be worried that you might be in trouble or angry at you for not calling." She reveled in the sound of his velvet voice with its deep masculine resonance, not even attempting to conceal her joy.

I'm fine. But I barely get a minute to myself before midnight, and I wouldn't call you that late."

She sat up and turned on the light. "What about the horses? Did you get what you want?"

"You bet. These Kentucky horse breeders know how to do business. You okay?"

"Life's different when you're not here. Real different. It'll be good to have you back."

She could imagine the scowl of his face when he roared, "Woman, when are you going to say what you think and feel?"

She gripped the phone. She'd already said more than she should have, and she didn't think it wise to pour out her soul to him about what he meant to her, when she couldn't become involved with him. She pressed her left hand to her forehead. Oh, how she wanted to tell him how precious he was!

Instead, she said. "And you know what I'm thinking and feeling, do you?"

His long silence unnerved her. "If you don't feel any more than you're telling, I wasted my two bucks."

She laughed because she couldn't help it. A crazy happiness zinged through her. "It was a good investment. Believe me," she said. "Hurry back."

She could almost feel his frustration. "I will, and I hope you stand behind your words." he grumbled. "Getting a speck of encouragement from you is about as easy as pulling hens' teeth, and they don't have any. See you next week."

She blew him a kiss through the wire, hung up and was soon dreaming about him.

As if Jordan had been away for years, Leslie prepared a feast in honor of his return. About twelve-fifteen that Saturday afternoon, they heard the Town Car ease into the garage. Julia rushed out to meet Jordan as he closed the garage door, but Leslie stayed inside, while Julia told Jordan of the death of his brother and sister-in-law and of Clifford's arrival. After a few minutes, Leslie walked out of the kitchen and stopped on the steps a few feet from the garage.

Jordan walked quickly to where Leslie stood, composed and regal with her hands clasped in front of her, and stared down at her. The promise in her eyes sent his blood roaring through his body, and he knew his own eyes pledged her everything. All that he had ever wanted, needed to see in a woman's eyes shone in her slumberous gaze. He stepped closer, near enough to touch her. But instead, he only looked into her rapturous face, reading in it all that her unspoken words told him. When her face bloomed into a smile, warm, loving and inviting, his heart leaped into a spin. Then, for anyone who wanted to see it, he removed his hat and folded her in his arms.

She whispered, "Thank God, you're home safe." And he lowered his head and covered her lips with his own. Let them think what they liked; he didn't care, and he didn't intend to keep what he felt for her a secret.

He broke the kiss, though heaven knows he didn't want to, and looked at the social worker's card. "Come go to Easton with me. I'm going to check this out."

She'd never been to Easton, the county seat, and had no idea where it was. "Right now? What about dinner?"

He put the card back in his pocket, splayed his hand in the small of her back and started with her toward his car. "Easton's twenty-two miles from here. Dinner'll have to wait. Today's Saturday, but I'll call in some favors. Clifford sleeps here tonight."

He greeted Clifford, seeing in the boy a likeness to himself and to his own father. "I'm sorry about your folks, son," he said. "From now on, your home is here with me. You're all the kin I have and, as far as I know, I'm all you have." He put both arms around the little boy and hugged him. Clifford hugged him back so fiercely that Jordan knew the boy had been worried about the reception he'd get from his uncle. He held the child for a while, and then he scrutinized his face.

"I understand you want to be assured that from now on, you'll stay with me, that you're sick of moving around."

Clifford looked over at Leslie and smiled, as though recognizing an ally. "Yes sir, that's right. That's what I told the social worker. Am I staying?"

Jordan grinned, liking the boy's spunk. "Well, Clifford, I also have a few requests to make. If you can manage them, you and I will get on fine. Don't ever lie to me, Clifford. Always do what you know is right, always! I expect you to keep your word, and I'll keep my word to you. And you must obey me. I'm your blood uncle. But you must also obey the other adults in my home. Do you understand?"

"Yes, sir. I can do that."

An hour and forty-five minutes later, Jordan drove Leslie and his nephew to the front of his white Georgian home and let them out. "I'll be inside in a minute."

When he walked into the dining room, they'd already seated themselves at the table, along with Cal and Julia.

Jordan looked around the table and settled his eyes on Leslie. He tried to avoid looking at her too often during the meal, but ten days away from her and his eyes couldn't get enough. He knew he had to bank the fires raging within him, because her reserved manner told him that she wasn't ready for what he needed and what he needed to give her. Clifford seemed to have attached himself to Leslie, and he didn't blame the boy; she'd gotten to him too. No one spoke. Cal never uttered an unnecessary word, but Julia usually found something to say. Then he realized they all had focused their attention on him, wanting to know about his plans for Clifford and for the stud farm. He sipped his coffee and leaned back in his chair.

"Clifford, you and I are going to spend Monday together. We're going to enroll you in school and buy you whatever you need." Later, alone with Clifford in his office, he allayed the boy's fears.

"This is your home now. I want us to be like father and son. Whenever you need me, no matter what for, I'll always be here for you. Don't forget that."

Clifford rested his elbows on his uncle's knees, testing his right to do so, and looked up at him, already in love with the man. Jordan stroked the boy's thin shoulders gently, recalling the day nearly three decades earlier when his uncle had sat in the same room and said similar words to him. He hoped he'd do a better job of parenting than his uncle Riddick had done. But for Cal, he would have been rootless.

Clifford treated Jordan to his own brand of Saber charisma, giving him a brilliant smile before testing the water. "Unca Jordan, can Leslie go with us Monday?"

"Sure, if she wants to. What's the matter?" he asked when Clifford rubbed his stomach. "Did you eat too much?"

He took his own measure of the problem when Clifford dropped his head, not bothering to cover up his shame. "I guess so. I had most of a pan of cookies for desert. You're not angry, are you?"

"Why should I be angry? What you did wasn't smart, and now you know it. I don't think you'll do that again."

"No sir. Not as long as cats scratch, Unca Jordan. You can believe that."

Jordan raised his left eyebrow. Where had that come from? It wasn't anything his brother Haskel would have said.

After supper, Jordan got Cal's report on events during his absence, called Turner and learned that their mystery man had asked his department at the University for a character reference on him. Jordan didn't agree with Turner that they might have misjudged the nature of the man's interest in Leslie. The man that Jordan had confronted on the Estates and had seen later in Dexter was not an honest man, and he hadn't seemed the type to go to a university for any kind of information. Well, his judgment wasn't infallible. He told Turner about his plans for the stud farm and learned of Turner's ideas for computer programs that would simplify farm and animal husbandry management.

A frown clouded his face at Turner's boldness when he said, "What are you doing about Leslie? You've got first dibs, man, and you'd better make the most of it. That girl's a gem. But if you don't want her, tell me in plain words. I need to know."

He didn't want to discuss Leslie with Turner or anybody else, but the man had just admitted having an interest in her. "I thought I told you to back off from Leslie."

"You did, and I have. But Jordan, if you can see her, so can every other man. I thought you wanted her. Don't you?"

Jordan gave in. "Yes. But I've got to get the matter of this man cleared up. I've been clobbered once, and I'm not stupid enough to let it happen again."

"Why don't you just ask her who he is?" Good question, but he knew she was too frightened of the man to reveal his identity. Anyway, he considered his problems with Leslie to be his own business.

"Yeah. Well, if you learn anything else, give me a call. And thanks, man."

"Right. Give the folks my best." He hung up.

Night fell, and Jordan leaned his hip against the banister on the front porch. In the cool evening, trees swayed gently in the light breeze that brought with it the smell of chestnuts roasting over in the men's lodgings and a frosty reminder of the coming winter. He looked up at the stars and at the half-moon lying on its back. For ten nights, he'd tossed in his bed in a lonely, barely serviceable motel room, wanting her. He hadn't slept. Nothing, neither cold shower, counting sheep, deep breathing nor yoga postures had

tempered his desire for her. He hadn't even considered finding an old girl friend, because he'd known that it would be
useless. When he'd looked up and seen her standing there
on the steps waiting for him to make the first move, his
heartbeat had accelerated at an almost frightening pace,
and it had taken all of the control that he could muster not
to pull her into his arms and unleash his passion. He could
stop asking himself whether he loved her. For the first time
in his life, he truly cherished a woman, put her interest
above his own and wanted her exclusively.

After supper, he allowed Leslie to set the pace, let her
take the lead. And what had she done? She had gone to
him, kissed his left check and told him goodnight, as if
nothing else was to be expected. Julia had been speechless,
her expression confirming the incredibleness of the scene.
But she hadn't been as shocked as he. That Leslie had done
that in Julia's presence was out of character; that she had
done it all was nearly incomprehensible. Going to her right
then was out of the question. So was going to sleep. He'd
have to sweat it out.

And he was not alone. Leslie hadn't slept in her apartment since Jordan had left for Kentucky, and while she'd
lived in the house, she had begun to feel as if she were a part
of a family. Going back to that old arrangement, living
apart from Jordan, Julia and Cal, had brought her back to
reality. She wasn't one of them, and no matter what Jordan
felt for her, the future held nothing for them. She knew
she'd disappointed him, shocked him was probably more
like it, but she didn't want to be a victim, duped by her own
passion and her need for his love. And if she let herself

behave with him in the way that she wanted and which seemed so natural, she'd be lost. He wanted them to get to know each other as friends, and she'd agreed, but she had no intention of plunging into an affair with him.

She rolled over, twisting the top sheet around her body, symbolically binding herself when what she wanted most was freedom in his arms. He'd kissed her in front of half the people who worked for him, a public declaration that she was more to him than his cook. And to what end? She could imagine Ossie's disgust, and she heard again Julia's words of caution: Many a person had drowned swimming against the tide.

She tossed until the bedding confined her entire body, as one mummified for all time. Exasperated at herself, she got up. No matter what she told herself or how she rationalized, the big hole in her chest wouldn't go away. He roamed at will in her mind, saturated her thoughts and warmed her blood. She put on her robe and stepped out on the balcony in the crisp September night. Maybe if she got chilled, the heat that seared her body would go away. She heard footsteps and stepped quickly back into her apartment. Carefully, she pulled back the curtain and gasped as she saw Jordan place a booted foot on the bottom rail of the fence and look off into the distance. A glance at her clock told her it was three o'clock in the morning. Her body wanted to go to him, but her mind immobilized her. She couldn't take that step.

"I thought you wanted me to drive over to Westminster before we went back home, Leslie. We've got time," Jordan

said the following Monday morning on their drive with Clifford into Dexter. "What changed your mind?"

He figured something she had been so enthusiastic, and now didn't appear to want to go."

"Well, I don't want to go put you out. Besides, by the time you get Clifford's affairs straightened out, there won't be time."

Jordan reduced the speed, took his gaze from the highway and glanced at Leslie. "What had you wanted to do there?"

"I wanted Clifford to meet Mom Haynes and her two younger daughters. After all, the Hayneses are my family. All that I have, anyway."

Jordan stared at her. "Lady, you have the ability to madden me. Your family! Hell, your family is out at Saber Estates whether you like it or not. We'll go if we have time after we get Clifford enrolled and fitted out for school. All right?"

When he patted her hand and winked at her, warm contentment swirled around her, and she nodded her agreement, leaned back in the bucket seat and closed her eyes.

They discovered that registering Clifford wasn't so simple. He'd been in several different schools during the past year, thanks partly to the inability of school officials to find a suitable school for him, as he performed at a level beyond his age. In addition, his parents had lived in two different states in the months just prior to the accident that took their lives. Jordan suppressed what would have been a sharp whistle when he saw that the boy's report cards indicated a superior intellect.

"He'll have to go to school for gifted children, probably in Baltimore," the principal told them.

Both of Jordan's eyebrows shot up when he got his first indication of what it would be like to raise Clifford.

"I'll go anywhere, sir," Clifford told the principal, "if I can stay at the school long enough to make friends, and if I don't have to stay away from Leslie and my Unca Jordan. I'm not going to leave my Unca Jordan."

The three of them watched as his chin went up and his chest out, while he tilted his head defiantly to the side and gave the principal a very level stare.

Jordan nearly laughed. This eight-year-old kid was taking a man's measure. The principal viewed the matter with less approbation, however, and advised Jordan that, if Clifford went to public school, he would adjust more satisfactorily if he had a good tutor.

"We don't want to risk his losing interest in school because of boredom," the principal said.

"Fine. If you can recommend a qualified teacher, I'll hire him, or her." He looked at Leslie and grinned, daring her to accuse him of being a chauvinist.

The shopped for the things Clifford would need for school, and the thought returned to him repeatedly that the boy had known difficult times. And he wondered at Leslie's silence, her apparent withdrawal from them when, minutes earlier, her enthusiasm and gaiety has matched Clifford's, reminding him of the way he felt in warm sunshine on a winter day. He shook his head and pushed back his sadness. Every time he thought he'd gotten close to her, she did

something, knowingly or not, that told him how wrong he'd been.

He jammed his hands in his pockets and stared at Leslie, searching for gentleness, compassion and sweetness that drew him to her, nail to magnet. That could tie him in knots and make him long for her and want her when she was miles away from him.

The saleswoman handed Clifford his parcels, and the boy's grin of happiness enveloped them as he reached for Leslie's hand. She wrapped her fingers around Clifford's, and his heart jumped into a fast trot as he gazed upon her brilliant, answering smile, her somber mood of minutes earlier nowhere in evidence.

Jordan luxuriated in her sweetness as she openly adored him for the happiness he'd given Clifford. The look in her soft brown eyes sent pure joy zinging through him, and he walked over to her. But he didn't touch her. It was too dangerous. When he touched her again, he wanted them to be alone, in total privacy and with plenty of time for what was ahead of them.

They left the store with Clifford dancing between them, and he envisioned them as a couple with a child. Their child. He corralled his thoughts when, from the corner of his right eye, he saw a lone man, a familiar figure, watching them from the doorway of the post office across the street. He didn't want to draw Leslie's attention to the man, so he stared straight ahead. If the stranger had wondered as to her whereabouts, those doubts were now dispelled.

Leslie wished Jordan wouldn't create intimate scenes between them when they were in public places. Yet, his boldness enticed her. As if he couldn't stand there and not touch her, not have some physical contact with her, he had started toward her. Slowly. Purposeful. Graceful. A gazelle in slow motion. Her gaze had glued itself to him as the excitement of not knowing what he'd do took hold of her. He must have read her well, for his eyes had seemed ablaze with wildfire and determination with a recklessness that she hadn't seen in him before. He hadn't touched her, and she'd been glad. When Clifford had looked from Jordan to her and back to his uncle, she'd known she hadn't imagined their unspoken exchange. Jordan had made her a promise, a pledge that she would one day belong to him, however ephemerally, and she knew he meant to keep it. She also knew that if she made love with him, she would never again belong to herself. He continued to gaze into her eyes, silently telling her what she wanted to hear, but feared knowing, and he struggled helplessly against the tide that engulfed her.

When he looked at his Rolex and announced that they had time for a visit with her foster mother, she resigned herself to the inevitable.

"You want Clifford to meet her," he said, "but I also want to get to know her."

She wanted to ask him why, but thought better of it since she knew where such a question would lead. "In that case, prepare to eat. For her, being hospitable and feeding you amount to the same thing.'

Clifford wanted to know what she would feed him.

"You'll like it," she told him, "because it's bound to be sweet.'

She didn't feel like being jovial. If Faron Walker still hung around the Haynes place and saw her with Jordan, he'd have no doubt as to where he could find her, and that was why she hadn't wanted them to visit her foster mother. Jordan turned the Town Car toward the Chesapeake Bay Bridge and headed for Westminster. He flipped on the radio and, when sounds from Chet Atkins' magic fingers filled the car, Clifford leaned over Leslie's shoulder.

"The guitar is my absolute most favorite instrument. You think I can learn to play it, Leslie?

"What kind of music do you want to play?" Jordan asked him.

"Every kind. I just love the guitar, Unca Jordan. I wanna play like Wes Montgomery, Chet Atkins, and Segovia. My dad had a lot of their records. That's Chet Atkins playing right now."

"I know it is," Jordan said. "And I remember that Haskell loved the guitar. Both of us did, and when I was your age and a little older, we used to play together. As I recall, he was very good."

Clifford shifted toward Jordan and braced his hands against the driver's set. "Do you think you could teach me to play?" Just a little bit, Unca Jordan. Can you?"

"Sure I can, and I will. Now sit back and fasten your set belt."

"Yes, sir."

How much more was he keeping to himself? She glanced at him from the corner of her left eye. "You're full of surprises."

His long fingers rested on the wheel, and the strength she saw in his hands crammed her head with things that she wouldn't have confessed to any human being. The sudden self knowledge bruised the image she'd had of herself, and she blanched, the way a morning glory wilts after gazing too long at the sun it adores. She could almost feel the tips of his fingers on her flesh, and it cost her some restraint not to stroke the black hairs at his wrist. To her, they said power, male energy, and she squirmed at the pictures her mind conjured up. Pictures of him. And of herself enraptured in his arms. She bit her lip and glanced at him just as he looked her way and winked. Controlling the urge to clutch at her chest required concentration, and she focused on the next chapter of her thesis.

"If you think I'm full of surprises, stick around," he said, his white teeth flashing behind a wide grin. "There're a lot more. Some goodies too," he added, glanced at her and winked again.

She figured she'd gain more by keeping her mouth shut than by commenting on his loaded statement. She'd never met anybody who responded more quickly with provocative, double meanings.

"Turn left into Bush Street. It's number seventy-seven," she said when they entered Westminster.

He parked in front of a neat green and white bungalow and cut the motor. Leslie got out of the car and started up the bricked walk that she'd traveled so many times. Not

even a blade grass defaced its symmetrical design. A slim, dark, middle-aged woman with a big smile threw the door open and rushed out of it, her arms flung wide as though to envelop all that she saw.

"Leslie. Leslie. Honey, it's so good to see you."

Leslie hugged the woman who'd mothered her since she was eight years old. "Mom, I'm glad to see you."

They scrutinized each other as though searching for deeds done by the passage of time. Apparently satisfied with what she saw, Minnie Haynes looked over Leslie's shoulder and back at her foster daughter.

"Who are your friends, honey?"

Leslie turned toward Jordan and Clifford and introduced the three of them. She heard the pride in her voice, and a glance at Jordan and his smile of approval confirmed that he'd detected it. Minnie extended her hand to Jordan, and he enveloped it in both of his.

"I'm glad to meet you," he told the woman, adding that Leslie has spoken often and well of her.

"Well," Minnie replied, dusting her sides with her hands, "she hasn't said one word about you, but I expect she's going to." At Jordan's raised eyebrow, she went on. "And a good bit more, too. Y'all come in."

As they followed her onto the porch, Leslie spoke to Jordan in lowered tones, "I should have told you she doesn't bite her tongue."

He pushed Clifford in front of him and strolled into the house. "Thanks, but I've figured that out for myself."

"Pop's downtown taking a physical." Minnie said, explaining her husband's absence. "He just got a job. I tell

you, it's been a long spell between paychecks. When you get older, you're the last hired, the first fired and the one to spend the longest time looking for work after they let you go. I sure was glad to see him go out of here all dressed up this morning. Nothing hurts a woman more than to see her man without the thing that gives him his pride. And especially if it ain't no fault of his."

She excused herself, went to the kitchen and returned with a try of cake, coffee and a glass of milk.

"Miss Minnie, did you teach Leslie how to make chocolate cake?" Clifford asked. "Hers tastes just like this."

Minnie assured him that she had and took a seat facing Jordan. Knowing her foster mother, Leslie decided she didn't want to be present while Minnie grilled Jordan, and took the soiled dishes into the kitchen and washed them by hand. She was about to dry them when Minnie joined her.

"What's going on between you two?"

Leslie nearly swallowed her tongue. "Uh....Nothing," she answered when she could breath.

Minnie's hands went to her hips. "Then I suppose he's lying."

"You... you mean you asked him—"

"Didn't take much courage," Minnie assured her, "considering the way he was looking at you."

"But Mom! You shouldn't have done that."

Assuming an expression of child-like innocence, Minnie told her, "He didn't mind. Said he was working on it, but you were loaded with hang-ups about his being white. Then he asked me where I stood on the matter. I

told him snakes come in a lot of different colors, and so do flowers."

Leslie stared openmouthed at Minnie. "Who told him I had a hang-up about him? I didn't."

Minnie shrugged. "Guess he's going on the way you act. 'Course I don't blame you none for keeping your head, not that I can figure out how you manage it with that man. He's something to look at, and Lord don't let him smile. Still....It pays to be careful. Ain't nothing wrong with it, though I suspect it's a hard row to hoe if you got half the country set against you."

Leslie didn't try to hide her shock. "You mean if it was you, you'd...you'd go for it?"

Minnie looked toward the ceiling as though asking for help. "In the first place, it ain't me. And then... Well, depends how you feel. One thing's for certain. He'll get you over your petrified fear of good-for-nothing men like Faron Walker. That's a forty-carat man out there." She let out a deep sigh. "I wouldn't mind if he was chocolate brown, but he ain't, and I don't plan to get the hives about it. You hear?"

Stunned, Leslie groped for a chair just as Clifford bounded into the kitchen. "Miss Minnie, I sure enjoyed that cake, and my Unca Jordan said I could ask you for a piece to take home."

Minnie leaned over and hugged Clifford. "And I'll give you a big piece, too."

Leslie made herself go back into the living room and join Jordan. She's rather had done anything than look him

in the eye, and it didn't please her that he guessed the reason.

"I suppose she told you she cut straight to the chase and asked me if I was more to you than your boss, as you'd phrased it when you introduced us."

"Yes, and she also repeated your answer."

He sat forward, signaling his readiness to challenge her. "And that annoyed you, didn't it? Too bad, Leslie. The truth is liberating. Immensely so, and I feel a hell of a lot better for having told her. I'm thirty-six years old. This is a free country, and I'm not keeping what I feel for you a secret. Don't ask it, and don't think it. Would you please drag Cliff away from that cake and tell him we're ready to go?"

Clifford saved her the trouble. "Look, Leslie," he said, holding a box. "She gave me half a cake and said I could come spend the weekend with her any time my Unca Jordan lets me. She said all her kids are grown and on diets because they want to be skinny." He looked at Leslie for the truth of that statement. Satisfied with its veracity, he went on. "Can I come back, Unca Jordan? She's nice."

Jordan stood and, in a gesture of affection, skimmed his fingers through Clifford's wavy black hair. "Sure you can." He extended his hand to Minnie. "I'm glad we met. Do we understand each other?"

She looked him in the eye. "Yes, we do, Mr. Saber. Now you—"

"Call me Jordan. You were saying?"

"Bring Clifford back to see me. And Leslie, I'm praying that everything will …will."

When she seemed at a loss of words, he filled the silence. "I'll do that, and I'll stay in touch with you. And don't worry about Leslie. I probably need your prayers more than she does."

She studied his countenance, glanced at Leslie and replied, "You may be right."

Minnie walked with them to the car and told them goodbye amid Clifford's promises that he'd see her soon. She and Jordan looked at each other, both of them nodding their heads. They'd reached an understanding all right, but they weren't making her privy to it. She shrugged, unconcerned and secure in the knowledge that both of them cared for her.

As the Town Car sped toward the Estates, Leslie replayed the visit in her mind. She loved her foster mother and valued her judgment, but she had no intention of allowing such lopsided encouragement as Minnie had offered to derail her course. Fate had brought Jordan Saber into her life, but that didn't mean she had she had to close her eyes to all but him and abandon her dreams. Still, all the way to the recesses of her soul, she longed to know him as a man, to come alive in his arms and know herself. Shivers coursed through her as pictures of him loving her crowded her mind.

His hand covered hers, and she looked up quickly see the smile that molded his face. Had she somehow communicated to him her thoughts?

"Where were you?" he said. "I think you were miles away from me."

"Uh...I was..." She inclined her head toward the back seat. "Silence sometimes has big ears."

Jordan glanced at the rear view mirror. "Don't worry. He's fast asleep. So. Planning your escape, huh? That'll take a lot of skill, honey. And I'm warning you, if you're not sweet to me, I'm going to wreck your dreams."

She stared at him, agape at his perceptive remark. "So you're a dream smasher? I'd started to think you were a mind reader."

He stroked the back of her hand until, pulled by a force greater than herself, she capitulated and turned her hand over to unite with his palm.

"So you were thinking about me. Good. I'd be upset if you told me that soft dreamy look was for another guy. Might as well stop fighting me, Leslie. Walk away from me, from us, from this," his fingers wrapped around hers, "and fifty years from now, you'll still wonder how it might have been. No matter what man comes into your life, you'll believe you would have found more with me. And that's because your intelligence tells you that I aim to knock down every wall you put up and cultivate every nerve in your body to satisfy myself and you that I've completely fulfilled you as a woman. You know that, and you long for it. That's why you'll remember me as long as you breathe."

Her nerves quivered at the husky sensuality of his voice and the drugging meaning of his words, and her heartbeat quickened erratically. But she refused him the assurance that he'd called her number.

"I read that some modern-day prophets moved themselves and their families half-way across the world to await

the Second Coming. A week after the date passed without incident, they drifted back home. You may be better at foretelling the future, but I'm keeping an open mind. So don't package my life for me, Jordan, because you can't foretell my future. And if you could, I wouldn't want to know it."

His shrug belied the seriousness of his tone. "All right, if you don't believe me. But you remember this, Leslie. I go after what I want. And when it's something that I need, I leave no stone unturned." His long fingers claimed hers with warm strokes of affection. "You're my partner in this, honey, because you and I want the same thing."

"Let's stop and get some ice cream, Unca Jordan," Clifford sang out, calling attention to himself, oblivious to the drama in the front seat.

"So you're awake. All right. Soon as we get to the next rest stop."

A few minutes later, Jordan turned off the highway and parked. Leslie didn't want anything, so she gave Clifford a five dollar bill.

"Get yourself two scoops in a cup and bring me the change."

"Yes, sir."

As Leslie watched the boy in the dash for Howard Johnson's, Jordan's arm around her shoulders wasn't what she would have expected. His fingers caressed her back, shoulders and her right arm. As if on automatic pilot, she moved to him, and his lips claimed hers, thrilling, heating and possessing her until she clutched at his chest and parted them for his kiss. He dipped his tongue quickly into her

mouth. Then, with his fingers stroking her face, he began to speak.

"You promised to give us a chance to be friends, to get to know each other and to discover our own selves. But you renege whenever you get cold feet. I didn't park here because Clifford needed ice cream after eating all that cake. I drove in here and stopped because you needed a reminder. We want each other, and I have no intention of letting you forget it."

She didn't like hearing it form his mouth, even if it was true, so she slid away from him, sat back in the bucket seat, and strummed her fingers along the dashboard.

"Jordan, you don't need to say everything you think, and a little downsizing of your ego wouldn't hurt you one bit. Did it occur to you that our goals may not be compatible? That we may not be after the same things? You've got it made, and I'm still trying to make it."

He slapped the steering wheel with his left hand and turned fully to face her. "Those are just words, Leslie. You and I are completely compatible, and I want for you everything you want for yourself. So don't hand me that line. I'm not swallowing it."

She flung the dart that she knew would irritate him the most. "I suppose you've forgotten that I'm your cook."

He grabbed both of her shoulders. "No, I haven't, and you're holding that over my head like the sword of Damocles. If I fire you, you'll leave the Estates, and I won't know where you are. If you stay, you'll use your job against me. But I'm not giving up. Because I know you care for me and that you need Saber Estates."

Alarmed that he might have learned Faron Walker's identity and that Faron might have been to the Estates, she jerked away from Jordan. "Of course, I need the Estates. I'd looked for a job for weeks before you hired me."

He looked at her with eyes that seemed dim with unhappiness. "And what about me? Do you or don't you need me?"

He had no right to pressure her, to back her into a corner, and she yielded to her temper, finding that her most reliable shield. "Now you're breaking your promise. You said you'd be patient, that you'd nurture a friendship with me. But you're pushing me, and I want you to stop it."

His arms snaked around her shoulders caressing her, warming her and scattering marbles around in her belly. "I will be patient if you'll give me one modicum of encouragement.'

She stared at him. He couldn't be serious. "I kissed you, didn't I? More than once, in fact. If that's not a modicum, I wish you'd define the word for me."

His green eyes flashed sparks, as if he dared her not to care for him. "Yeah. But you'll do that any time I get my hand on you. That's your body talking, not your head. I'm after your heart and your head."

She sat back in the soft leather seat and folded her arms. "A gentleman doesn't hit below the belt."

He ran his fingers through his hair in obvious frustration. "Listen to me, will you? Mutual caring and electricity between a man and woman are rare and precious, Leslie, and I can't let you throw it away and ruin it for both of us."

She refused to yield to what she felt because one day soon, it would all be over. "Aren't you taking a lot for granted? How can you be so sure that it's mutual?"

He turned to face her fully, resting his right elbow on the back set of his seat. "Isn't it? Are you saying you don't feel anything for me? Well, if you told me that, I wouldn't believe you. Get over your hang-up, and let me show you what we're missing. Sweetheart, you have no idea how bright the sun can shine." A grin creased his tantalizing mouth. "Give me a chance, and I'll light up your world."

She believed his every word, and if she had any sense, she'd get away from him, and fast. But go where? She had to finish her degree, and she had to be safe from Faron Walker. She feigned nonchalance.

"You want too much right now."

His grin was meant to tantalize her, and as if to rub it in, he pulled the curl that dangled beside her ear. "Shouldn't be much of a stretch, sweetheart. Two down, one to go."

She tossed her head and smothered a grin. Doggoned if she'd let him get the better of her. "You haven't counted on my time. Your head's my problem. I have to get you thinking Saber night and day."

Laughter bubbled up in her, and she let it fly free, a magical release of the tension that had lodged in her for most of the day.

"Let me in on the fun," he said, the mesmerizing grin noticeably absent.

When she could stop laughing, she said, "Jordan, you are the fun. You are no stranger to my head."

"I don't get it. You mean…?"

She nodded. "Uh huh. So, like I said, it's my willpower we…I mean you have to deal with."

It was his turn to laugh, and he let it out. "Long as you and I both have to worry about it, I've got a sporting chance. For starters, you're due another riding lesson. How about supper today?"

When she agreed, he checked the time and look around. Clifford sat on a bench not far away, and Jordan patted Leslie's hand, got out and went to the boy, who stared into space.

"Why did you sit out there?" Leslie asked him when they returned.

He bunched his shoulders in a shrug. "I didn't think you and Unca Jordan wanted to me here. I mean—"

Jordan interrupted him. "I kissed Leslie. Men and women do that sometimes. Just because we're not concentrating on you doesn't mean we're rejecting you. We kiss you, don't we?"

"Yes, sir," he replied, but without his usual assertiveness.

"All right. You and I belong together," Jordan told him, "and I don't want you to feel left out again. Got it?"

Clifford leaned forward and put his arms around Jordan's neck. "No, sir, Unca Jordan. I won't. Not as long as cats scratch."

Jordan paused in the process of inserting the key in the ignition, turned and stared at his nephew. "Where'd you get that?"

"Gee, I don't know."

Jordan started the motor, switched into drive and headed home. "Creative, aren't you?" he said to Clifford. "I see I'm going to have to channel that. By the way, don't let me forget to buy you a guitar. Nobody plays mine but me."

"Don't worry, Unca Jordan. I won't let you forget. Not as—"

"—long as cats scratch," Jordan finished for him.

Leslie let the moment, the conversation, the feeling of belonging and the love seep into her being. She closed her eyes and gave her mind free rein. The more time she spent with Jordan, the more her distrust of men receded. He inspired confidence and so much more. He'd said he wanted for her all that she desired for herself. If she could lose her misgivings about herself and Jordan as a couple, if she could let nature lead them, she knew she'd make her happy. If.

CHAPTER SEVEN

Deep in thought, Leslie let her gaze sweep her surroundings, while Jordan parked the car and Clifford dashed into the house to show Julia his cake and tell her about his visit with Minnie Haynes. She entered the house and realized that she was loathing resuming her role as cook and maid. For most of the day, she had been her old self, unencumbered by concern for her safety, enveloped in the affection and that Minnie always showered on her and toe with Jordan while they bantered as equals.

"Pull yourself together, girl," she told herself and headed for the kitchen, where she knew Julia would be preparing supper.

"You cooked dinner today, so I'll do the supper," she told Julia.

"Shucks, you'll do no such thing. If Jordan had wanted you to help with dinner, he wouldn't have taken you with him and Clifford. We'll do it together."

Leslie thanked her, hurried over to her apartment and changed her clothes.

"You sure do know how to tone yourself down," Julia said when Leslie walked back into the kitchen. "You came in here glowing, fresh as spring dew. Honey, you're a genius. Didn't take you but fifteen minutes to get rid of your sex appeal."

Leslie knew she was in for a lecture on Julia's favorite subject when the woman braced her lips with her hands and put an expression of impatience on her face. "Tell me why you don't take advantage of your God-given attributes.

Sex appeal is no disgrace. If you ask me, it's a disgrace—no, it's a curse—not to have it." She patted her perfect coiffeur. "You won't catch me looking plain and sexless and my Cal starting to get a roving eye."

Leslie didn't take offense. Julia wanted every man to look at her, but only Cal should touch her. "You're hopeless, Julia. I'm not getting dolled up to peel onions and scrape potatoes."

"No? Men don't go blind just because they walk into the kitchen. Always put your best foot forward, my mother used to say."

She heard footsteps on the back porch, and in a few seconds, Jordan stepped through the door. When he looked at her, his face brightened, and he walked over to her and slung his left arm around her shoulder.

"Jordan, I'm... I'm busy," she stammered and glanced toward Julia to gauge her reaction to Jordan's familiarity. But Julia pretended not to see them and concentrated on slicing ham for the men's supper.

When Jordan hugged her, Leslie knew he was telling both her and Julia what he thought of Julia's attitude toward his feelings for a woman in his arms. She wiped the onion-induced tears from her check, and Jordan, misunderstanding their source, folded her into his full embrace.

"What's wrong, Leslie? Tell me what's the matter."

She resisted snuggling up to him and letting herself enjoy the sweetness of his caress. "It's nothing. Honest. I always cry when I slice onions."

He didn't release her, and while she stood sheltered in his arms, Julia walked over to them. "Cut the onion in half,

lay the cut side down and then slice. You won't shed a tear."
She walked back to the other side of the kitchen and continued slicing the ham.

His arms tightened about Leslie. "She's important to me, Julia. I don't know how much. I only know that she is."

Leslie released her breath and waited, but she discovered that she needn't have been anxious, that whatever Julia's sentiments about male-female interracial relations, she loved Jordan and either wanted his happiness or wouldn't risk the consequence of stepping out of line with him.

"I can see that, Jordan," Julia said, "and I'm aware that it's mutual. I just hate to think of the two of you struggling against everybody and everything like two sparrows, flapping around in a hurricane. Life's tough enough when everybody wishes you well."

He held her closer as though to punctuate his statement. "I've stopped fighting it, Julia, and you may as well do the same. If I have a problem with this woman, it's because she works for me."

Julia leaned against the refrigerator and waved the knife with which she'd been slicing ham. "When we were trying to save those peaches, Leslie kept us at it until we finished at a quarter of two in the morning, and she would have worked until daylight. We all need someone like that, someone who'll go to the wall for us. I can't begrudge you such a woman. But I won't lie and say this makes me jump for you. Still, you won't get any interference from me. I just thank God it's not Joan you want.'

Leslie moved out of Jordan's arms. "Don't travel so fast, Julia. We're only trying to find out if we can be friends. Nothing's set with us. We—"

Julia's arched eyebrow foretold her sentiments, and Leslie knew the woman would tear her words to shreds. "If I didn't understand Jordan as well as I do," Julia informed her, "I'd probably believe you. But I know that when he sets his cap for something, he's like a thoroughbred with blinkers on, headed for the winner's circle. So go ahead and work on that friendship, if that's what he tells you you're doing."

Jordan stared at Julia for a second, shoved his hands in his pants pockets and gave the tiled floor a few kicks with his left foot. "I'm out of here. See you at supper."

The door had hardly closed before Julia pounced. "I hope you'll put on some makeup and let your. hair hang down the way he likes it before he gets back here."

Leslie cocked an eyebrow, but managed to keep her tone impersonal. "I'm not giving him any more encouragement than he needs, and right now he's moving along too fast under his own steam. Besides," she said, mostly to herself, "as Yogi said, 'If it ain't broke, don't fix it.'"

Julia shook her head as though bemoaning human ignorance. "Maybe not, but it makes no sense to buy insurance after the house burns down; now, does it?"

They finished supper and Jordan, ignoring Julia and Cal's raised eyebrows, carried the dishes to the sink after telling Leslie, "Put on a warn sweater and a jacket and meet me at the bottom of your stairs in fifteen minutes. Okay?"

"And don't forget the girl stuff," Julia called after Leslie.

Leslie couldn't get used to Jordan's public show of affection. She was at once ill at ease and proud as they strolled hand-in-hand to the stables.

Jordan saddled Serenity and held the reins while Leslie mounted. "You do that so gracefully. Serenity's going to love you."

That wasn't Leslie's main concern. "But will I love her?" she asked him, voicing anxiety.

He shrugged. "Good questions. I hope she fares better than I have, though you may be more adept at communicating your feeling to her than me."

She looked down at him from her perch on the big bay. "I wouldn't dare comment on that. Where're we going?"

He swung up on Casey Jones, grinned at her and winked. "Out back of the pecan grove where nobody can hear your cries when I'm ravishing you."

Her face must have expressed her momentary panic, for his whole demeanor changed. "Leslie, what it is? What happened? Wait a minute. You don't think I was serious?"

She shook her head with all the energy she could muster. She wasn't afraid of Jordan but of... .Would she never forget Faron Walker and that horrible night! "No. No, of course not. It was the...the moment...is all."

She knew he didn't believe her, but at least he didn't probe. As though to test her, he headed them straight for the pecan groves where he informed her that her dismounts needed improvement.

"I thought I'd made progress."

"You have, but you need more practice, and I suggest we do this every evening after supper till you get the hang of it."

What was his game? Her dismounts weren't bad. "I swung my right foot over Serenity's back until it touched the ground, then moved my left foot out of the stirrup. What else should I have done?"

She noticed that he didn't look at her, but busied himself tethering the horses. "You could have done it more smoothly. Handling a horse isn't child's play."

She controlled her annoyance. If he needed an excuse to be with her, she could suggest something that didn't involve a cold wind blowing in her face. His smile abated her frustration. And when his hand found hers, she forgot about the wind, for his fierce stare provoked a flurry of sensation in her.

"Let's walk a little," he said.

Right then, he could charm her into doing most anything and, realizing it, wariness settled over her. "I'm...it's chilly," she stalled. "May we should go back."

His fingers entwined with hers, warming her. "All right, if you'd like, but if you're cold, I can take care of that. Come here to me."

He stopped, but she continued walking. "You're after my head, remember?"

His laughter wrapped around her, battling the rising wind entrapping her thoughts the way a smart lawyer cages an adversary. "Do I remember? You bet I do."

They reached a grove of large Schenley trees that Cal said bore the sweetest nuts he'd ever tasted, and Jordan

picked up a handful of pecans from beneath the tree, put two of them together in the palm of his right hand, pressed and cracked them. He picked out the meat, put it to her lips and watched her sensual act of chewing while she stared into his eyes.

Swallowed. "You're making putty out of me."

He wanted to smile, but somehow, it didn't come off. "Maybe that's the idea, but you don't mold easily. I'm not making much progress."

"Why are you so sure of that?"

"If I was going anywhere, you'd have your arms around my neck right this minute anywhere; you'd have your arms around my neck right this minute hugging me."

He wasn't used to deviltry in her, so the twinkle in her eyes didn't warn him, and he gaped when she said, "Hug you? What, for two pecans?"

Her countenance mirrored the smile that he knew had taken possession of his face. He said, "You're so irreverent. I want you to be free. I want to be with you when you let it all pour out. The fun, wickedness, wit…" He sobered. "And the secret you still keep. Here." He cracked another pecan, shelled it and fed it to her for the pleasure of watching her chew it. It hadn't occurred to him that chewing could be so sensuous.

"Some of that fun stuff is as new to me as it is for you," she told him.

"You mean the wickedness? Surely you know about that sharp little tongue of yours."

She shrugged. "After years of being straight-laced, I've discovered that I like feeling wicked."

"Feel devilish enough to...to kiss me?"

"We're supposed to be giving me riding lessons and finding out if we like each other."

She couldn't be serious. "I suppose I spend every minute I can with you because I don't like you. Unless you're dead set on pulling my chain off its hook, woman, put your arms around me."

Her fingers brushed his cheek, and he thought he saw love in the tender expression of her eyes. Her smile lighted the dusk-encroaching world around them, and when she raised her arms, his heart thundered in joy. He'd never know how or where he got the patience to wait as she tiptoed, grasped the back of his head with her hand and brought his mouth down to hers. Her lips, eager and warm, sweet and tender, touched his mouth, taking from him something that he'd always guarded and held apart and, in that instant, he knew she was in him forever. He reeled beneath the knowledge. Sobered.

Leslie didn't question his thoughtful manner as they headed back to the house, and he was glad. He'd have told her the truth, unvarnished, and demanded the same. He waved at Ossie in passing, helped Leslie dismount, stabled the horses and walked home with her. He knew she expected a kiss, but he didn't feel like punishing himself. He loped down the steps that led from her apartment to the garden and paused on the bottom one. Ossie hadn't moved and seemed to stare in the direction of Leslie's door. He wished he'd kissed her.

Leslie showered, put on a gown and robe and sat down to work on her thesis, but his smile shrouded the pages of

her notebook. She knew she'd come a long way in the seven months she'd been at the Estates, that she'd changed, grown as a person. But had her metamorphosis been so complete that she could ignore the consequences, the censure of ordinary people, because of a liaison with Jordan and let nature dictate their dance? She wanted to. A sheen of perspiration covered her arms as he mind teased her with images of him lying above her, loving her. Embarrassed by her thoughts, she switched off the lamp and began counting sheep.

Jordan extinguished the light on his night table. Two o'clock. If he didn't get some sleep, he'd be useless the next day. When had he last slept uninterruptedly for eight hours, or even six? He could answer that question; if he could name the day he'd begun to want Leslie. He dozed off, and the intercom buzzed. He sat up, got his bearings and pushed the button, praying nothing was on fire.

"Saber."

"Jordan! Jordan, can you hear me? Somebody's coming up the stairs to my apartment."

He was on his feet. "I'm coming. Lock your bedroom door." He hung up, stepped into his pants and boots, didn't bother with a shirt, grabbed the .45 with its holster from his night table drawer, slung it around his hips and flipped on the flood lights that lit up the back of the house and the entrance to Leslie's apartment. Then he punched Baker's intercom and alerted Cal. A minute later he was running toward the stairs to Leslie's apartment. He reached the bottom step just in time to see a man's silhouette disappear around the side of the garage, obviously scared off by the brilliant lights.

"If I get my hands on you, I'll break you in half," he yelled in frustration, knowing the man had escaped. At his knock on her doors, Leslie screamed. He started to kick the door in, but thought better of it, as he realized that would frighten her more. Instead, he used his passkey, calling her name as he did so. He walked into her bedroom as she scrambled out of bed and grabbed the lamp for a weapon, tears streaking her face. He hurt her, knowing that she was reliving the fear that had haunted her since she'd barely escaped rape five years earlier. Without a word, he lifted her into his arms, threw the covers back, crawled into bed with her, shoes and all, and gathered her into his arms. Her wrenching sobs sent chills through him, tearing at his heart. He knew he was probably back to square one with her, but he didn't bother with self-interest; his only concern was the well-being of the woman who had come to mean everything to him.

"It's alright sweetheart. I'm here, and nothing and nobody can harm you." Kissed her eyes, her nose and her forehead and whispered comforting, soothing words. But still she sobbed.

"Baby, don't. I can't bear to see you this way. Talk to me." She stirred, her deep breaths telling him that she struggled to bring herself under control. As she moved into his arms, his passion awakened. But he banked it quickly, knowing that what she needed right then was not lust but tender caring.

Silently, Cal observed them from the doorway, turned and left. Julia had told him something of Leslie's past, and

he couldn't help wondering if Jordan would ever be able to banish her fears, especially after tonight.

Jordan had similar thoughts. "Leslie, darling, you have to talk about it. I know you're hurting, but don't hold it in. Let me help you." He continued to talk to her, soothing her with his voice. "Hold on to me, Leslie. I've got strength enough for both of us, and I won't let anything happen to you. Not now. Not ever. Just trust me, sweetheart."

She turned in his arms and sought his face with her fingers. "He...it reminded me of that night...the night... Oh Jordan, I thought he was going to... that he would manage before you got here. There's never been anyone. If there ever is, I want it to be you."

Gentle now, he silently cautioned himself, cradling her while her soft sighs grabbed his heart. "Shhhhh, sweetheart. It's over now." He stood abruptly, pulled the blanket form the bed and wrapped it around her. When he lifted her and cradled her close to his shirtless body, she slid her arms around his neck.

"Where are we going?"

"I'm taking you where you belong, where I can take care of you; protect you, where you should have been all along. I know you love this apartment, but I have to know you're safe and that you're not afraid. From now on, you stay at the house with the rest of the family. Tomorrow, we'll move your things. You may come over here and work on your thesis or whenever you feel the need for privacy, but you'll live under my roof. Can you accept the conditions?"

She nodded, and he carried her into the house and up the stairs to the spare bedroom across from the master bed-

room. As he walked into the room, she brushed his lips with her own innocently, he knew.

Nonetheless, he froze in his steps. He wasn't in any shape or mood to have his control tested, and he didn't want to be reminded of her softness, nor of her near nakedness under that blanket. He looked at her and saw that she, too, had felt the electricity of that sweet little kiss. Glancing quickly away, he laid her gently upon the bed and reached to turn on the Tiffany lamp that graced the night table. The room was immediately suffused with a hazy glow, reflecting soft blue walls and the rose, sand and blue furnishings. She lay where he'd placed her, looking up at him with all that she felt shinning in her eyes.

Don't even think it, he commanded himself. Don't go near there, man!

"Sweetheart, you've been through a lot tonight. You'd better get some sleep. We both need it. I'll see you at breakfast." He slipped off the holster and turned to leave, knowing that if he spent another minute in there, he'd be in serious trouble. But she grasped his hand and clung to it, her voice soft, and her expression wistful.

"I don't know how to thank you. I mean, I don't know what to say to you. Nothing that I can possibly say will reflect what I'm feeling." She was rambling. He stood over her, his hand wrapped tightly in both hers. This wasn't the time. This wasn't the place. But God in Heaven, she'd come damned close to asking him to stay with her. He wasn't a saint, he thought, ruefully. He was human and the heat in his loins simmered like time bomb. He had to get out of

there, and he turned again to leave but, suddenly, she squeezed his hand.

He flung the holster on the chair beside her bed and, moving with lightening speed, he was beside her in a second, jerked the blanket off of her and pulled her to him. She met his kiss with her own eager, open mouth. She's a fast learner, he thought, as he plunged his tongue into her. He'd known that Leslie was basically uninhibited, at least with him. But he was unprepared for the power of her passion, when she threw her left leg over his lap, leaving her hands in his hair. Not satisfied with that, she began to caress his face, whimpering in the fashion of a woman wanting more. Much more. He knew she was in shock and only barely aware of what she was doing or of it effect on him.

"Baby, slow down her. We can't do this. "She pulled him over her, burrowing beneath him. He knew he had to stop it, but her passion, her heat, lured him as nectar entices a bee. And he had wanted, needed, gone half-mad with desire for her for so long.

She wrestled him for his hand and placed it on her breast, and with a groan of resignation, he capitulated. She arched her back and, cursing himself for his weakness, he lowered his mouth to her breast and sucked it through her sheer grown. He heard her cries and whimpers and it occurred to him somewhere in the far reaches of his mind, that they were not alone in the house. But he couldn't stop himself. He wanted so badly... needed what she offered. If he could just hold her forever! His common sense returned

like a blast of arctic air when she tried to wrap both her legs around his waist and began to undulate beneath him.

He didn't want to hurt her, but it wasn't the time or the place for them to make love. He first eased away from her and then cradled her to him. Best to talk about it, he decided.

"Leslie, honey, I want to make love with you more than anything. I want you more than I have ever wanted any woman, but after what you've just experienced, this is the wrong time. You're reacting to shock. I don't want you to associate our first time with that accident. And another thing. When we do make love, we will need more privacy than we have here and plenty of time. Leslie, tell me it's all right! Tell me what you're feeling."

He'd swear that she withheld the truth, or told only half of it, saving face, when she said, "What I'm feeling is, I'm scared.'

His laughter wasn't honest either. "You just think you're scared. If I hadn't put the brakes on, I'd be inside you right this minute." Where I want to be, he finished silently.

"Don't be so smug, Jordan Saber. I've always heard that talk is cheap; it takes money to buy land."

"Hell, there's nothing on earth that feeds a man's ego like having his woman want him, to the point where she's willing to take what she needs. Damn straight, I'm smug."

"I fattened your ego? I dread the thought of what would happen if I put some effort into it. What's with you anyway?"

If she only knew what it cost him to keep his hands off her. He leaned toward her. Exasperated. "Listen here. It's a

foolish man who runs with the ball when he doesn't have a hope in hell of scoring. Sometimes you have to punt, to give it up and wait for a better chance."

"Jordan—"

He interrupted her. "Can't you ever address me with an endearment? Must it always be 'Jordan'?"

She looked up at him and shook her head as though denying an unwanted truth, but her silence didn't fool him and it didn't please him either. He suspected that the old, self-protective Leslie was trying to emerge. Another setback. He told her good night and stepped across the hall to stare at the ceiling for the remainder of the night.

It wasn't fear of an intruder or lack of comfort that kept Leslie awake. Pondering the night's happenings, she figured she didn't and never would understand men. She'd bet anything that if Jordan had caught that man, he would have been merciless. He cared. He had to, because she showed it. Yet she'd had powerful evidence of his desire for her, and he'd still walked away, even though she'd all but begged him to stay with her. She didn't care one bit for that philosophy about knowing when you could score. By damn, she'd given him a clear field. What else did he need?

She thought about his chest, thick and hard, shirtless, its hairs teasing the tips of her breasts through her gown. She turned over and crossed her legs in frustration. And he'd had the gall to ask her to call him by some sweet name. He was lucky she hadn't socked him. She'd touched his bare flesh for the first time, and he'd squeezed her to him, his arms so strong and his body so hot. She fell over on her stomach, almost choking on her breath at the memory of

his mouth on her and the fire he stoked in her. A blaze that still threatened to roar out of control. She closed her eyes and tried to sleep, but her mind had latched on to Jordan and imprisoned her with images that made her wish she had the courage to get up and walk across that narrow hall.

On the one hand, she wanted him but, at the same time, the ultimate intimacy that lovemaking with him would involve made her uneasy. Yet, when he'd walked away form her, she'd felt that he'd rejected her. She couldn't figure it out. Get away from here, girl, while you head is still above the water. Pounding the pillow in her fist, she vowed, Come January and I'm gone.

Leslie managed to greet Julia warmly when she walked into the kitchen the next morning at precisely six-thirty, though she'd lost her sense of belonging with Jordan's "family." She wasn't one of them, and she meant to carry that fact boldly before her the way the Crusaders had carried their flags and crosses. But Julia's warmth and sympathy tugged her heart, threatening to demolish her hastily established defenses.

"I'm so sorry about last night, honey. We can be thankful that he didn't succeed and that Jordan chased him away." She walked over, put both arms around Leslie and spoke to her in soft soothing tones. "I can imagine how you felt, because that's something all we women fear. But let it go. Won't do you any good to remember it."

Deeply touched and chastened for having decided to separate herself from Julia, Cal and Clifford, she shook her head sadly, reached out and took Julia's hand.

"I....Thanks... I...I was scared, Julia. Nobody will ever know how scared I was."

Julia hugged her. "Let's just thank God Jordan was here."

Leslie did what she'd always done when she was distressed; she got busy. After she drove herself mercilessly for an hour, Julia stopped her. "The way you're going at it this morning, anybody would think you're dodging a pack of demons."

Energy that didn't belong to her had stolen into her being, an invader, driving her, and she had to expel it, to cleanse her soul of it. Impatient with Julia's remark, she said, "Will the sun shine brighter if I drag my feet?"

"Oh, oh. Well, 'scuse me."

When Jordan and Cal arrived form the fields for breakfast, Leslie's "good morning" lacked enthusiasm.

Evidently giving notice that he wouldn't react to her coolness, Jordan chewed with relish as though savoring the morsels in his mouth. "These waffles are wonderful, Leslie."

Why pretend what she didn't feel? "If they are, it's not because I tried."

Everyone present knew that Jordan loved waffles, and her comment confirmed for them the coolness of relations between Jordan and her. She knew she'd gotten to him when she remained quiet during the remainder of the meal. And she was barely chastened when he didn't eat much, his taste for the food apparently gone. All of them knew that for Jordan, food and conflict didn't mix.

Jordan was about to leave the house when it occurred to him that Leslie might have misunderstood his actions the night before. He reasoned that he'd better clear it up right then. "Leslie, May I see you a minute?"

"You're the boss." Taking her time in a show of insolence, she walked slowly to his office and knocked.

"Come in, Leslie." She closed the door, but didn't move from it.

"Leslie, I tried to explain to you last night, but I see I didn't succeed."

"It's best we limit our exchanges to my work. There's nothing else between us."

He breathed deeply, but the pain that has settled around the heart wouldn't move. Why couldn't she understand? He rounded the desk, braced his hands on either side of her head and pinned her between the door and him.

"Now you listen to me. A man would be less than a rutting bull if he took advantage of a woman's fear and vulnerability after she turned to him for help. You don't know what it cost me to walk away from you last night. I didn't want your memory of such a precious experience tarnished by thoughts of another man's monstrous intentions."

She braced her hand against his chest, and he gave her the space she demanded. "If you say so."

"What the devil does that mean?"

She looked him up and down, and her wide brown eyes were not soft. Nor were they wet. He saw only fury, which he suspected she aimed at herself for being susceptible to him. And he saw sadness too. And a lot of spirit.

Her level stare wasn't what he'd have expected from a woman who could be as soft and as yielding as she. She stepped closed and squinted as though searching for something in him that she couldn't find. "Men are…Men are…" Apparently at a loss for a suitable word, she whirled around and walked out of the room.

Julia stopped Jordan with a hand on his arms as he hurried past her, looking straight ahead.

"Yeah?"

"Did you put Leslie in your bed last night?"

He meant his scowl as a warning that she should back off.

She didn't heed him. "Did you?"

"Look, Julia, I'm thirty-six years old. You don't ask me that."

"I don't care if you're one hundred and thirty-six. I've looked after you since you were nine years old, and I'll ask you anything I want. Did you?"

"No."

The contours of her lovely face changed into a brilliant smile as understanding dawned on her. "That's why she's so mad at you. Mad at the world, in fact. She feels rejected." Julia patted his shoulder and turned to go about her work. Noticing that he remained standing there, uncharacteristically subdued, she spoke softly.

"Don't make it too easy for her. But don't make it too difficult, either. She's had a hard life. I know she's strong, and in some ways she's tough, but every woman can hurt."

He rubbed the back of his neck and blew out a long breath. "She doesn't want to need me or anybody else.

Anyhow, I think she's taken a few steps backward where I'm concerned."

Dinner later that day was not the occasion for happy camaraderie and arm twisting those meals had been in the recent past. Leslie bare spoke to him, and while he didn't reciprocate outright, he showed his displeasure by refusing to look at her. Clifford was uncharacteristically quiet and subdued, sensing something amiss between his two favorite people. It was he who finally brought it to a head.

"Leslie, are you mad at my Unca Jordan?" When she didn't reply, he looked fearfully at his uncle. "Don't you like Leslie any more?"

Jordan answered Clifford, but he looked at Leslie. "You don't stop liking somebody just because they turn out to be stub—" He caught himself, and it was well that he did.

"Now, you just look here, you… you…," she sputtered, obviously too annoyed to express her ire as she would like.

That finished the meal for him. He had already decided after speaking with her that morning to give her plenty of space. And in his present mood, he reckoned she'd better do the same for him. His annoyance was at such a pitch that he left the table.

"Excuse me," Julia corrected him, something he'd been required to say when, as a child, he left the table with everybody sitting there.

He automatically repeated the words after her, indicating that anyone who knew him that he was in one fit of a temper. He started out of the kitchen door, turned and looked at Julia.

"When you've finished polishing my manners, see what you can do for adolescent immaturity around here."

As the screen door closed behind him, Leslie was on her feet and headed for the door. He heard it when she slammed it, but he accelerated his pace. Just as he reached the barn, he felt her hand grab the back of his shirt.

"How dare you," she fumed. She had to have some contact with him. Any contact.

He turned around to face her, the heat of wrath burning his face, and pinned her arms to her sides.

"What's the matter with you? Try and get a grip on yourself. I won't tolerate this from you."

She twisted out of his grip. "I suppose you're going to send me to bed without my supper."

He reached for her, and she pushed at his chest. "That's right," he said. "Get rid of your sexual frustration by attacking me. You and I both know what your real problem is. Well, I am my own man, and neither you nor any other woman can budge me one way or another until I'm ready to move. And I move in your own sweet time."

Incensed, she jerked away from him. "Somebody sold you on your importance."

She started back to the house, but he was faster, bringing him so close to him that he could feel every line of her body, from her bosom to her hips to her thighs. His reaction to the contact shocked him.

"Damn you, Leslie. Damn you!" He didn't want to think about how vulnerable to her he was. Galvanized by his mounting frustration, he put his right hand behind her head and on her buttocks, pulled her tightly to him and

lowered his mouth to hers in a seething kiss. He knew she shocked her, because his kiss lacked the tenderness with which his mouth had always cherished her, and he wasn't trying to make her feel as it she were precious to him. She tried to move her lips from his plundering mouth, but he would have none of it. Her whimpers and trembling told him he'd begun to get to her, to expose her seemingly natural tendency to respond to his body.

She began kissing him, caressing him and, so his amazement, he experienced sudden and total arousal—the first time he remembered being unable to control it. Powerless to conceal it, he had no choice but to let her feel the full force of it against her belly. To his surprise, furious with him as she'd been, she tried to get closer to him. Hugging him. Loving him. He plunged his tongue into the sweet cavity between her parted lips and took what she offered. Her groans reminded him of their surroundings, and he set her away from him, chastened and also frustrated by her ability to bring him to heel without knowing it.

With a few deep breaths, he restored his equilibrium. "You said there's nothing between us, so don't play with me." He strode into the barn and left her leaning against the tree trunk for support.

Belatedly, he realized that they'd had a sizeable audience, as the men were just headed back to work. But there was one onlooker that he'd as soon hadn't been present. From the barn window, he saw Clifford run to put his arms around Leslie, and he surmised that what the boy had just seen had reminded him of what he witnessed at home. He made a mental note to talk to Clifford that night. Then he

propped a foot on the bottom rung of a ladder and tried to get a grip on his emotions.

Leslie trudged slowly back toward the house. The waning sound of horse's hooves let her know that Jordan had saddled Casey Jones and headed toward the brook. If she dared risk it, she'd get on Serenity and follow him, but she'd never ridden alone. She picked up a dry stick and knocked a few pebbles from the cemented path, stooped down and examined them. Could they have been the ones tossed at her windows? She dropped the stick and leaned against the railing of the stairs that led to her apartment. In spite of the chilled weather, thoughts of the incident with Jordan brought beads of perspiration to her forehead. She'd gone too far with him, pushed him and forced him to defend himself in the presence of his employees.

His kiss had awakened her to the truth. All she had wanted was passion in his arms; her audacity had been a poor substitute for the contact with him that she craved. She pulled air through her teeth, disgusted with herself.

"Well, miss, I've been wanting to speak with you."

Her head jerked up at the sound of Ossie's voice. "About what?"

He knocked his hat back and looked hard at her. "About a scruffy-looking white man who offered me fifty dollars last night to tell him which room in the house was yours. He didn't look like a man you'd give the time of day."

Her right hand went toward him involuntarily, as though to beseech him, but she quickly dropped it to her side. "And I suppose you're fifty dollars richer.'

He glared at her and stood straight. Taller. Proud as a consummate actor displaying his power with words or a successful CEO in the presence of his stockholders.

"What kind of a man do you think I am? I sent him away from here." He looked into the distance, then back at her. "You and I haven't hit it off from the beginning, Miss, and you'd be right if you said it was my fault. But I'm not evil. I suppose it'll surprise you, but I've always prided myself in being a gentleman, and I try to do what's right as I see it. I sent that man off because it was the decent thing to do, and for Jordan because he told me you're important to him. I'm beginning to see that what's going on between you two isn't a bit casual, and I...may be I was mistaken." He put his hands in his pockets, brushing back his leather jacket and exposing his trim physique. "Jordan gave me a chance to recover my life, and there's nothing I wouldn't do for him. So you needn't thank me."

She looked him in the eye. "If you didn't tell him, how did he find out? Jordan stopped him from breaking in on me."

He stared back at her. "Every man here knows about you and Jordan, and not one of us would betray him. It's impossible to police a place this size, so you'd better watch how you walk around here. There are acres on the Estates that I've never set foot on. And I doubt Jordan ever travels part of it. So you be careful." He moved on.

"Thanks anyway," she called after him.

He stopped, turned and looked at her. "Having somebody like that asking about you won't help your reputation. That guy's not so much of a man."

"Did you tell Jordan?"

"No, but I will." He tipped his hat and walked on.

She could hardly believe he'd held a civilized conversation with her. Would wonders never cease!

At supper that evening, Leslie sought to restore the warmth that usually prevailed among them at meals and which her actions at dinner earlier in the day had undermined.

"I was out of line today, Jordan. I'm sorry."

His lip dropped as if he didn't believe she'd said it. After long minutes, he replied. "Once in a while, we all lose sight of what's important."

She had hoped for more. At least a smile. She looked into those eyes that she loved and told him, "I got up wrong and stayed that way. It won't happen again."

He leaned back in his chair, and she noticed that the other three people at the table had stopped eating and looked at Jordan. "I'm still sore at you, Leslie, but I appreciate your effort to straighten things out. I'd like us to talk after we finish supper. If you wish we could ride out to the brook."

She let herself breathe normally. "I'd like that."

Clifford ran around the table to Jordan and pulled on his arm. "Unca Jordan, you promised to start me on my guitar lessons right after supper today. You did. Honest."

Jordan placed an arm around the boy's shoulders, slim, as fragile as youth itself. "Yes, I did." He looked at Leslie. "I promised him, and I want him to know he can rely on my word. Can we postpone our ride till tomorrow?"

She had welcomed the opportunity to make peace with Jordan, but she smiled to hide her disappointment. "Of course, I can't wait to hear Clifford play his first notes."

Still burdened with the weight of their cooled relationship and troubled by her reaction to it, she decided to risk another visit with her foster mother. But she knew that every time she left the Estates, the danger existed that Faron Walker would find her. Maybe Cal would take her; she couldn't ask Jordan.

With Jordan giving Clifford music lessons and Julia making it clear that she wanted to be alone with her husband, Leslie went to her room to work on her thesis. The phone rang, and she answered but let the fingers of her right hand remain on her laptop computer.

"Hello." She let the tone of her voice discourage the caller.

"Hey, girl, don't you know how to make a telephone call?"

Leslie hit the button to save what she'd typed, put the laptop aside and leaned against the headboard of her bed. "I've been meaning to call you, Berle, but just about everything got in the way of my good intentions."

Berle snickered. "'Everything' meaning that green-eyed hunk you work for?"

"Why do you say that?"

"Last time we spoke, your voice turned to honey every time you mentioned him."

Leslie thought about the way he'd pinned her to that walnut tree and kissed her into submission. "He gets to me, Berle, and he wants the whole nine yards. If I could get him

out of my head, I'd finish this thesis in a couple weeks. But that is definitely not likely."

"Hold on, honey. You're courting trouble.'

"But you said you'd be on him like... like white on rice was the way you put it. Don't tell me—"

Berle interrupted her. "Child, I was just running my mouth. He's carrying too big a load. You're not out in Minnesota, where people do as they please. A lot of these folks down here in Maryland belong to the we ain't ready club?"

A sudden sensation of tiredness seeped into her. "Which folks are you talking about?"

She heard Berle suck air through her teeth and wondered if she had another Doubting Thomas on her hands. "I'm taking about the black ones, the white ones, and the ones you can't distinguish." That brought a laugh from both women. "I'm not saying I wouldn't be tempted. Lord knows any breathing woman would fantasize about the man who looks like him would give me a complex."

"Well, he doesn't give me one. He makes me feel like... like... as if I'm the most precious person on earth."

She could imagine Berle's shock when her friend said, "You're joking. I hope. A man with his unbelievable good looks, a country-wide reputation as Mr. Great Guy and white to boot wouldn't make me feel secure. My ego's not that fat."

"I don't think about what color he is until somebody mentions it. My foster mother said she didn't see anything wrong with Jordan and me."

"Separately, I don't either. Girl, you'll be bucking the tide. Adventuresome as I am, I'm not sure I like the idea. Did it occur to you that there are places in this country he can't take you?"

"Haven't thought about it. Why would I want to enter such a place? I don't go there now."

"Well," Berle insisted, "try this one. He can have his pick of women in this world, including royalty. You comfortable with that?"

Leslie smothered the sigh of impatience that threatened to release itself. "Maybe he's chosen me."

Berle's whistle irritated her eardrum. "Way to go, girl, I just hope he's as straight as his reputation says he is."

"I trust him, Berle."

"Well, honey, if he floats your boat, go for it. But keep at least one eye open."

Good advice, she knew. But she feared it was too late for caution. Much too late.

"You want me to drive you to Westminster this afternoon to visit you foster mother?" Cal wasn't sure of the motive behind Leslie's request.

"If you don't mind, I'll only spend about three-quarters of an hour there."

He cocked his head to one side and pierced her with a blue eyed stare. "Did you ask Jordan to take you?"

"No."

"Why not?"

"Things aren't quite right with us and, until we patch up our differences, I'd rather not ask favors from him."

"I see. Well, be ready in half an hour." He went into the office and told Jordan that he was taking Leslie to Westminster at her request.

"Take Minnie a bushel of pecans and a sack of apples with my compliments."

"Sure thing, boss." He winked at Jordan and left the room.

They rode in silence. It worried Cal that the relationship between Leslie and Jordan had deteriorated badly after he'd thought they'd get together, and he didn't like it. Leslie hadn't looked that glum since her earliest days at the Estates.

"Leslie, you may think it isn't my business, but I look on you as I would my own daughter, and I want to know what made you mad enough to go after Jordan."

"It's better left unsaid, Cal. Suffice it to say, I'd be more comfortable in this relationship if I was certain of his feelings."

"He cares, Leslie."

"I know he believes he does, and he acts the part. But maybe I'm a novelty. Haven't done that. I'm beginning to wonder if what's between us goes beyond this… this fire that has engulfed us."

He turned off the highway, drove into a truck stop, parked and turned to Leslie. "Jordan Saber is a mature man, and you're anything but a curiosity to him. I know him like the back of my hand. If he says he cares, put your life on it. Why don't you believe him? And why have you been so…so down on him? Tell me. Maybe I can help."

"He... Well..." She turned away from him and faced the window.

"Now, now. No need for shyness. I work for Jordan, but I regard him more as my son than my boss. Everybody concerned here is family, and we're going to get this thing straightened out."

"He...he took me to the house the other night, put me in bed and left me there."

"And? That's all?"

"I... I asked him to stay with me, but he didn't."

"And you're upset with him because he didn't..." He looked for words. "...didn't stay the night with you? Let me tell you it must have cost him the better part of his mind to leave you. Only a man who loves you would have done that. If he'd touched you after what you'd just experienced, I wouldn't give him credit for being much of a man. Instead of being furious with him and feeling hurt and rejected, you should be admiring him for it."

"I do admire him, but I can't imagine that any woman would be dancing for joy because a man resisted what he walked away from." She turned toward him, her eyebrows arched. "In the six, almost seven months I've known you, I have never heard you speak this many words."

He shrugged. "I talk when I have something to say, and what I'm telling you is important."

She shook her head. "I wish I could be as certain as you seem. And another thing, Julia and Ossie are opposed to my romantic involvement with Jordan, though Julia has said she won't interfere. But you seem to support us."

"Why shouldn't I? I'm fond of both of you, and I can see that you care for each other. They know it too, and they can't stop it any more than you and Jordan can."

"I made him mad, and I don't know how to straighten it out. I've apologized, but he's still irked, and I'm not going to apologize any more."

Cal couldn't help laughing. "He said the two of you would talk, didn't he. And anyway, it's simple, Leslie. When a man loves a woman and wants her as badly as the man wants you, there's little that she can't get him to do. You hardly have to try, Leslie. Just let him know you need him."

"I have another problem. I'm going back to school next semester to finish my graduate degree. I won't be here after the first of the year."

Julia had told him that, and he had already decided that leaving wasn't in Leslie's best interest. Yet he wanted to encourage her to complete her education.

"My advice to you is that you sit with Jordan and tell him your plans. Don't ever let him think you've pushed him into a corner. If you want that man, you'd better open your heart to him and stop worrying about being rejected and what people think about the racial difference. That's nobody's business but yours and Jordan's, and believe me, it doesn't matter to Jordan. Is this what you're going to talk about with your foster mother?'

"Yes. Also, I haven't seen her for a while. But I guess we don't have to go. Talking with you has helped."

"Oh, we've got to take this stuff that Jordan's sending to her."

She blinked. "How'd he know we were going there, and why's he sending her anything?"

He let a smile creep slowly over his face. "Leslie, I wouldn't be taking Jordan Saber's woman anywhere without telling him first. I've known him since he was eleven years old, and I know just how far to go with him. And as far as the pecans and apples were concerned, he's sending them to her for the same reason he took her three bushels of peaches and later sent a couple of men over to clean her drain pipes when the roof of her house started leaking." She gaped at him, but he nodded and continued talking. It was something she needed to know. "He looks after her now, because you told him that the Haynes are your family, since they took you in when you had no place else to go, and they'd had no income for months until a few weeks ago when Minnie's husband got a job as a shipping clerk. He asked them not to mention it to you. Still think he doesn't care? You digest that."

Leslie dug into herself for the truth, but hated to face it. She closed her eyes and leaned back in her seat as Cal started the engine to continue the drive to Westminster.

"I don't really want to leave the Estates, Cal." At his quizzical look, she thought over that statement. It was time she faced what was happening to her and acknowledge to whom she loved.

"The truth is I don't want to leave Jordan."

"Does he know that?

"I don't know. Maybe. We've never really talked about it."

"I'll never understand how two people can care so much for each other and keep it to themselves. Leslie, the problem between the two of you isn't sex. It's a lack of understanding. You haven't shared your true feelings. When there's genuine understanding between a man and a woman who care for each other, everything else falls into place."

"I know that, or I imagined it. My first priority is finishing my degree. I promised myself that I would have choices in life, that I would educate myself. And I'm going to do it."

Cal slowed down to the speed limit and glanced at her. "I agree you owe yourself that much, and you can do that without leaving the Estates. Just remember that when you get your degree, you'll still want Jordan. So you'd better be careful of your actions. If he ever starts to doubt you, you can count him out of your life completely. Any way you figure it, if you leave here, if you leave him, he may not be here for you when you got your MBA and your life fixed up and decide you can afford to take a chance on him.'

Leslie looked out at the passing scene, remembering how Jordan had crawled with her into her bed, not even bothering to remove his shoes, to hold her and comfort her when she'd been afraid Faron Walker would finally achieve his goal. She could hear him whispering those words of comfort, of sweetness, could hear him telling her that he would never let anybody or anything hurt her, that he'd take care of her. She didn't want to need him, but she did. She cupped her face with her hands and worked at positive thinking.

"Go to him, Leslie. Even if you're going to leave him, tell him how you feel. He's hurting and needing just like you. I'm a man, and I know what he's going through.'

"I hear you, and I'll think about what you're saying." Her glance darted to the side mirror at her right, and her hand clutched at her chest. The old brown car tailing them looked exactly like the one that had trailed her from Westminster to the Eastern Shore the day before Jordan had hired her.

CHAPTER EIGHT

Jordan watched Cal stride out of his office. With his hands jammed in the back pocket of his jeans—he hated them, but Julia had said Leslie didn't like his overalls—he stepped over to the window, leaned against its frame and let his thoughts raise havoc with his heart. Leslie didn't want to need him, not even to drive her to the city. If he wasn't certain he'd hurt her, he'd ask her what she saw when she looked at him, a man with a white face, or a man who loved her?

"Come on in, Julia," he said in response to the knock on his office door. "I suppose Cal told you he's driving Leslie to Westminster this afternoon."

"He told me, and I wondered why she didn't ask you. Look. I know I said I'd leave this alone, but I can't help thinking maybe you haven't considered all the implications."

He held up his hand as though to ward off more words. "We'd better not go into that, Julia. I know you want what's best for me, but I'm capable of judging that for myself."

She walked to him, seemingly measuring both her steps and how far she could go with him. He took a deep breath and waited. He loved Julia and had since his childhood, and he understood and appreciated her dual role in his life, but she had to know where he drew the line.

A frown marred her lovely face, and he knew her next words weren't likely to please him. But he didn't try to stop her. "Suppose you... I mean, it looks like you might be in real deep—"

"You don't have to guess. I am in deep." He rubbed the back of his neck, trying to be patient. "If you want to tell me to leave her alone, you're wasting your breath."

Her eyes widened in obvious alarm. "But...Jordan. What about children? They'll be—

"They'll be one-half hers and one-half mine...that is, if I'm so lucky.'

She stared at him, "You've gone that far?"

He turned away and faced the window again, the sleepy trees and foliage that met his eyes now appearing less bleak, their late autumn cloak less dreary. "You gave me some help."

And she had. For the first time, he appreciated that Leslie, too, might have misgivings about the problems of rearing interracial children. And who could blame her? He turned back to Julia.

"It isn't a problem unless we make it one. Anyway, your worries are premature. Leslie has given me no indication that she'll go that far with me."

"She cares for you."

He shrugged. "I know that, and she does too, but she's a woman of iron will and purpose, and completing her education and making certain she'll never need anybody are her priorities. I'm not sure where I fit in."

Her hand reached his shoulder in a gesture of comfort. "I'd say the same of you. I guess you know that when a woman cares deeply for a man, tenderness will get her every time."

He couldn't help laughing. Julia was quintessential woman: she didn't approve of what he was doing, but she

loved him enough to help him do it if it would make him happy. He tugged her closer and wrapped her in his arms in an affirmation of his love from her.

She stepped back and wiped moisture for her eyes. "Nothing but good's gonna happen to you, so I'll quit worrying. Considering all you went through as a child, I marvel at the man you've become."

He walked back to his desk and sat down, terminating the conversation in the gentlest way possible. "Pat yourself on the back. You can take a lot of credit for whatever you see in me."

He reached for the phone as she closed the door. "Turner Baker, please." He had to know whether Turner had seen or heard any more of that man who was after Leslie.

Cal stopped in front of the Haynes house and parked, but Leslie didn't open the door. "What's the problem, Leslie?"

She wasn't certain, so she didn't answer. Apparently following her gaze, he looked into the rear view mirror.

"You see something?"

"I'm not sure."

"Then let's get out, unless... Why are you looking in that reflector?" He turned around and looked at the rear window. "Is anybody following us?"

She didn't know how much Jordan had told him. "I don't know. A car tailed us on Highway 695, but I didn't see it after we exited into 140. I just don't know."

"What did it look like?"

She told him and he got out, surveyed the area, and opened the door. "I don't see any such car, but we have to consider that he could have parked around the corner. I assume he knows where we're headed."

"He knows."

He reached in the car and got the cell phone. "Go on in. I'll stay out here for a while."

"Aren't you coming in?"

He hooked the phone belt. "Eventually. Am I looking for short or tall?"

"Medium," she said and realized she'd told Cal more than she had admitted to Jordan.

"Where's tall, dark and handsome?" Minnie asked her when she opened the front door.

Leslie hugged and kissed the woman who'd mothered her. "Back at the Estates. He's busy."

Minnie raised an eyebrow, a gesture Leslie knew meant disbelief. "He's busy, eh? And birds fly north in the winter. Who drove that Town Car that's out there?"

"Cal. He's—"

"I know who Cal is. Go tell him I said bring himself on in here."

Leslie cleared her throat and immediately regretted it. Minnie usually became skeptical when she cleared her throat before she started talking. "He's uh...Mom, I think Faron followed us along 695. I had to tell Cal, and he's making certain that dreadful man isn't out there somewhere."

Minnie sat down. "You told them about Farron Walker?"

"He's been snooping around the Estates, so I had to tell Jordan something, though I didn't mention Faron's name. You know he swore that if I did, he'd kill me."

Minnie sat forward. "I know he threatened to do something to you if he found out you'd breathed his name to the authorities or told anyone who would, but this is too much. Maybe you should tell Jordan, honey, because Faron Walker cases this house three or four times a week to my knowledge." She rushed to answer the doorbell.

"What color's that car?" Cal asked Leslie when he walked into the living room.

It didn't take a keen observer to know that Minnie held her breath as though fearing what her ears would hear, but Leslie had no choice except to answer truthfully. "A weather-beaten brown and it has four doors."

Minnie let out a long sigh as Cal nodded. "Yeah. He circled the block a couple of times, but he didn't see me. I expect he recognized the car, though. No point in worrying, Minnie. We'll keep him away from Leslie."

Minnie clasped her hands together. "Lord, I sure hope so, 'cause he means no good. That is an evil man."

Cal pointed to the bags of pecans and apples that rested near the door and inclined his head toward Minnie. "Jordan sent you those. Leslie, I'd like to get back to the Estates before dark. Never know what that fellow's carrying." At Minnie's gasp, he added. "That buggy of his won't make half the speed of the Lincoln Town Car, but you never can tell; he may test me."

When Cal turned onto 695, he opened the subject, as she'd known he eventually would. "How much of this does Jordan know?"

She folded her hands in her lap so that he wouldn't see them trembling. "He knows some, but less that you do."

"Why can't you tell him everything?"

She shrugged. As much as she liked Cal and appreciated his mature thinking, she didn't believe he'd understand. Neither the lawyers nor the judge had been sympathetic to her. Her own lawyer had merely done what Mom and Pop Haynes had paid him to do, but he hadn't believed that she wasn't in some way culpable. And if she identified Faron to Jordan, he'd go after him, and she didn't want to be responsible for what might happen. Besides, Faron had sworn that if she accused him again, he'd get her.

"I've tried to tell him, but it's too painful. I just can't go over all that. Jordan knows that I'm innocent of any wrong doing."

He checked the rearview mirror and as though satisfied with what he saw, put on the cruise control, flicked on the radio and headed for the Estates. "That's good enough for me, and I hope it satisfies Jordan."

At the moment, Jordan was questioning Cal's brother, Turner, as to where and when he'd last seen their mystery man.

Turner didn't think the man a threat. "If he planned to hurt her, Jordan, he'd have caught up with her by now."

Jordan weighed the wisdom of telling Turner that the man had almost done that, decided he needed all the help he could get and confided the minimum, "She's staying in

my house from now on, because some guy tried to break in on her night before last."

A sharp whistle flew to him through the wires. "If it was me, I'd ask her right out who he is and where he lives. But I've got a hunch there're two guys in this scenario: the one you described to me and the one I met. Get her to talk, man."

"When she trusts me sufficiently, I won't have to ask her. She's been through a lot, Turner. I appreciate any clues you come across."

"All right, pal. I'd keep her close to the Estates if I were you."

"Bet on it." He hung up. Nothing new there. He put on his black leather jacket, grabbed his hat from its hook over his desk and headed for the barn.

"What is it, Rocket?" The man opened the back door just as Jordan stepped out on the porch.

"I found these in the barn," he said, pointing to three baby raccoons, "and I wanted Miss Leslie to have one. When we worked on the peaches, she said she'd never had a pet. Could you give her these and let her take her pick? I'll come back tomorrow for the other two."

Jordan gazed at the creatures, then back at Rocket, a mentally challenged young man, the soul of kindness, but capable of trying his patience as no one else could. "Thanks, Rocket. I'll give them to her as soon as she gets back here."

Rocket embellished his thanks with the smiles of a simple, guileless person." There's a baby bottle and some milk in this bag." He handed Jordan a bag that bore a super-

market logo. "If she needs anything else for the little pup, you just let me know."

He thanked Rocket again, took the animals back in the kitchen and set the basket on the table. Nobody had ever tamed a raccoon, and by the time one got to be six weeks old; he could destroy every piece of furniture in the house. And few animals were more vicious. He still hadn't decided what to do with them when Cal and Leslie returned.

"It's against the law in this state to keep those things," Cal said.

Jordan saw Leslie's expressing of longing, and couldn't help wondering if he'd have to lobby the state legislature to get the law changed. "They're cute now," he told her, "but in a few weeks, they'll scratch and bite, and they carry rabies and pests."

"But couldn't we keep them till we find their mother?"

He shook his head. "If their mother were alive, they wouldn't be here." A sensation of icy prickles squeezed his heart when her face seemed to sag in obvious disappointment. "Look. If you'll let me take these...uh...back where they came from, I'll get you a puppy."

Her eyes glittered so brightly that he could have been looking at a star-filled sky. "You'd do that? I'd love to have a puppy, but I...I don't think this is the time."

The door closed softly, and he didn't have to turn his head to know that Cal had left in order to allow them privacy. "When would be the time?" He stepped closer to her. "When, Leslie?"

She backed away a few paces. "Don't you remember my telling you that I'm going back to school? I'll hardly be able to feed and care for myself."

Keep a lid on it, buddy, he silently admonished himself.

"And don't you remember my telling you that you don't have to leave the Estates to complete your education?"

"Jordan, please don't make it difficult for me to say this. I have to leave here and finish school."

"You can stay here and..." What was the point in arguing about it? He changed tactics. "It's time I closed up my boat for the winter. How about going over to St. Michael's with me Sunday?"

The look on her face was proof that he'd chosen the wrong time to suggest that she accompany him out on the Chesapeake Bay. He quickly added, "I'd planned to mention it to you, but you left with Cal before I got the chance. How was your visit with Minnie?"

"Wonderful, but we didn't stay long. Somebody followed us."

He grabbed both of her arms, caught himself and took his hands off her. "Did Cal see the man?"

"I'm not certain. If he did, I'm sure he'll tell you."

He watched her run up the stairs, away from him, her beautiful hips young, lush, and tantalizing. He stopped his fist just before it crashed into the gold leaf framed mirror that had belonged to his mother long before his birth. Appalled that his frustration had nearly shattered his self-control, he headed for the barn, intent upon giving Casey Jones the ride of his life.

Ossie sat on a high stool in the corner of the tack room, mending a western saddle while he whistled a Mozart tune, and his hands moving in a rhythm counter to the sounds that passed through his lips. Jordan watched his employee and friend, marveling as he always did at the difference between the Ossie before his eyes and the one who, almost four years earlier, had yanked his arm as he'd walked a Baltimore street and wanted to know if he had a sharp razor. He'd asked the disheveled man what he planned to do with it and had been told that that depended on how much nerve he could muster. Impressed with the man's speech and the unmistakable dignity that his rock-bottom misery failed to hide, Jordan had offered the man a new life, and he'd grabbed at it. When he'd decided to build lodging for his workers, Ossie had revealed his background as an accomplished architect, had designed the structure and refused compensation.

Jordan walked over to Ossie and sat on a bench nearby. "Whose saddle is that?"

"Cal's. If he's as hard on his horse as he is on his saddles it's a wonder you don't have a horse cemetery back there somewhere."

Ossie couldn't know he'd said the one thing that could make him laugh right then. "Cal's riding's fine, once he gets on the horse, but it's getting up there that busts up his saddle. I don't let him near Casey Jones, because Casey wouldn't stand for it."

Ossie pulled out a screw and found a more solid home for it. He dropped the pliers on the floor, rubbed his chin and looked Jordan in the eye. "I'm not talking out of turn,

because I told Leslie I'd mention this to you. Thursday night, I found a fellow loitering around the gate, and he offered me fifty dollars to tell him which room in your house Leslie slept in.

"Like I told Leslie, he was a scruffy-looking white guy down on his luck. Had to be about five feet nine and ...I'd say... a hundred seventy pounds. I've met all kinds of men, and I'm convinced that one wasn't Romeo chasing Juliet. He's up to no good."

Jordan pounded his left fist into his right palm, walked to the other end of the tack room and back again. "He or some other guy almost got to her that night. I moved her over to the house because the guy's getting too bold for my comfort. He followed Leslie and Cal to Westminster this afternoon. I have to take solace in the fact that he's losing patience and getting reckless—a sure sign that he'll walk right into a trap."

"He's got gall, all right."

Jordan turned to leave, because his frustration had abated, and he no longer needed to test his horse.

"Jordan."

He stopped and walked back to Ossie.

"Thanks, man, for knowing I didn't want that guy's fifty bucks and that I ran him away."

Jordan stared at Ossie, frowning as he did so. "You take a bribe? That's the last thing that would have occurred to me."

His steps didn't quicken with surplus energy as they had when he'd left the house. Leslie knew a man had offered Ossie a bribe for information that would enable him find

her, but she hadn't mentioned it to him. Why the hell did she insist on protecting an attempted rapist—if, indeed, he was her pursuer—one bent on hurting, maybe even killing, her? He stopped, because the squirrel who stood in the walkway eating a pecan refused to move. He had to laugh. None of the squirrels feared him, and most would eat from his hand or even crawl up his pants leg if he stood still long enough. A lot of pecans remained on the trees, and he'd have to remind Cal to have the men gather them before the first frost. Julia liked to bake with nuts right off the tree, so he left some there, but he didn't want to risk losing several barrels of them.

He opened the kitchen door seconds before Julia broke out of a steaming embrace with Cal, whose hands seemed to have covered every part of his wife's body in the second before Julia realized he'd walked in on them. He ducked out of the kitchen as quickly as he could and headed up the stairs. Leslie's voice filled the space around him with song, as she let it flow, happy as you please, and unaware of the hurt that had started to seep into him the way water inserts itself into a sponge. He listened to the end. He'd had no idea that she possessed a beautiful voice. In seven months, she hadn't sung in his presence. For the first time, he was tempted to go into her room and have it out with her, but he couldn't. He needed, valued, her trust.

He went into his bedroom, closed the door and walked over to the window. Would he ever know the completeness with a woman that Cal and Julia had found with each other, ever have a love like that? He'd just begun to realize how much he longed for it. To be loved for yourself alone,

not because your uncle had willed you some property or because you'd gotten promoted on your job. Not because you could keep a woman in Paris perfume, Italian shoes and silk teddies. But to know that you were always wanted, always loved, always needed for yourself alone by that one woman who was your whole life. His mouth watered with hunger for it. He knew that he could have it with Leslie, if only she would open up to him and let him love her, really love her. He wanted to give her so much—the security that she had never known, the love and caring that would bind her to him. She would stand shoulder to shoulder with him in any endeavor, through adversity as well as good-fortune. He'd bet his life on it. And if she ever slew her demons, what a lover she would be!

Get off that subject, he admonished himself and went into Clifford's room to check on the boy's Internet viewing habits. He'd discovered that his nephew obeyed him, but he checked on him nonetheless and found him looking at lighthouses on the coast of Maine. "Come down to the den in a few minutes and get your music lesson. Did you practice?"

Clifford scrambled up from his position on the floor. "I sure did. I know everything you taught me. I even learned some jazz licks."

Jordan raised both eyebrows. "I want you to unlearn them as fast as you figured them out. Music is learned in steps, building knowledge on knowledge. You don't start on the roof of the house before you've built the sides."

"Yes, sir."

"You still planning to go to St. Michael's tomorrow?" Leslie asked him, as he left Clifford's room.

He nodded. "The forecast is great. Just put on something warm. Okay?" She smiled her agreement, and he relaxed. Maybe they settle a few things.

Leslie stood alone at the ship's bow, unwilling to take her gaze from the water that seemed to rock and roll past them, though she knew it was only a sensation that the boat didn't stand still but sped through the water. She opened herself to the pure bliss of being in Jordan's care and to the drama into which nature enticed her. A sense of calm pervaded her whole being as the chilly wind whipped past her, the churning waters charmed her and the sun shone on her, telling her that she belonged to nature, existed as a part of it, unabused by life's artillery. She had to share it with him.

"Jordan," she called, "Jordan." But the wind whisked away her words. She turned to go the cabin and saw him standing at the door, watching her. Her bottom lip dropped at the sight of him in a red woolen crew neck sweater and tight black jeans, with a smile on his face and the wind frolicking in his hair.

As if to cement the imprint, he grinned. "Wonderful isn't it? I want to join you out here in this awesome peace and beauty, but I have to run this thing."

"Then I'll stay in there with you."

He reached for her hand as she neared him, "I ought to be unselfish and say you should stay out here and enjoy the elements, but I..."

His words trailed off, and he seemed content to let his eyes speak for him. She didn't care. She'd never felt so total-

ly alive in her life, and she knew her eyes communed with his. She grasped his hand and walked inside with him. He seemed relieved, and she searched her mind for reasons as to why he should have been anxious, but found none.

He placed her hand on the wheel. "Want to take the helm for a while?"

She grasped it eagerly. "I'd love it. Since I'm in fairyland, I might as well live another fantasy."

He moved to stand behind her and let his hands slide down her arms. "What other fantasies are you living right now?"

With abandon, she spread her arms wide and voiced the rapture that buoyed her spirits. "I'm queen of all I see, and I'm reveling in it."

He squeezed her arms, "And queen of what you don't see, though you could, if you'd turn around."

Needing greater intimacy with him, she leaned back in his arms and let him take her weight, and it didn't escape her that she'd become more comfortable in their relationship. She didn't dare turn and feel herself locked in his arms, for she knew she wouldn't let him release her until she belonged to him. Alone with him, away from the world, the real world, she almost believed they could have a future.

They spoke of impersonal things—her thesis, problems he encountered in his efforts to start breeding thoroughbreds, their college days, Maryland politics, what they feared most, his brother's ultimate death—but nothing of their relationship. She learned that he had a passion for music, and he discovered that, as an undergraduate, she'd been the women's fencing champion. He docked and

together they secured the cruiser, after which two attendants covered it with tarpaulin to preserve it through the winter.

On the pier, he buttoned her storm coat and tied her scarf around her neck. "Let's get something to eat, I'm hungry."

She locked arms with him, the first time she could remember doing that. "Can we get into a decent restaurant dressed as we are?"

His shrug expressed his lack of concern for that problem. "A fat tip buys more than the meal, honey. If you want to see perfect genuflection, press a few big bills in the hand of a maitre`d.'

They feasted on mussels in wine sauce, Maryland-style crab cakes, hush puppies and asparagus, but Jordan rejected the chef's special. "I get the best apple tarts in the world at home three for four times a week," he told the waiter, "and I don't tempt my taste buds with any others."

A slow wink sent her heart into a tailspin, and she had a mind to tell him he'd done it deliberately to drag her further into his orbit. "Better have some," she teased. "You may not get any more any time soon."

The waiter left to get their raspberry sorbet, and Jordan leaned forward. "What did you mean by that remark? I take my ration of apple tarts seriously."

She let her fingers trace his jaw, and she did so, her glance caught the two men who sat at a table opposite them, two handsome African-American men clothed in their badges of success.

"Sometimes I get an urge to broaden my expertise and another specialty. Fudge-covered brownies or maybe Napoleons.'

"If it's working, why change? I'm so used to your apple tarts now, that I think I'd be lost wi…" His gaze followed hers. "Would you be happier if I looked like those guys?"

Stunned at the audacity of the question, she asked him, "Wouldn't your life be simpler if I didn't look like them?"

One of the men signed the check, and they rose to leave, but the younger of the two paused briefly but deliberately and let her see his displeasure. She refused to let him know he'd rattled her and tossed her head, shrugged and focused her attention to Jordan.

Jordan left his seat opposite her, slid into the booth beside her and put his right arm around her shoulder, drawing her close to him. "I don't ever want to have to tell you this again. What matters most to me is not the color of your skin, the texture of you hair, your flawless complexion or even what happens to me when you fix your big brown eyes on me. All of that made me notice you. But what matters to me is what hurts you, what makes you laugh, cry, and fight for your rights. What matters to me is your goal and what I can do to help you reach it, what you need and how you need it, what makes you want to dance and shout for joy. Whether you love me and the way you love me. I don't care about the frills, the fashion, and the trappings of success. Been there and done that, and it left me with a hold inside. On my boat this afternoon, we talked for four hours about things… some of which I've never discussed with anyone, but talking about them with you seemed so natu-

ral, so enjoyable. Can't you accept that I want you for yourself?"

She leaned back so as to look him fully in the face. "You said a lot just now, Jordan. I remember asking you not to toy with me. What I meant was, try not to lead me further than you've already gone. I mean—"

"I know what you mean, and believe me, I haven't brought you as far as I am. "I'm not sure you're able to handle it yet."

She let her eyebrows rise slowly. "I can handle any ball you pitch."

He imitated her gesture. "I wish I thought it." Vision of her locked in his arms meeting him thrust for thrust lodged in his mind. He narrowed his eyes. "Be careful how you boast, sweetheart, because you haven't seen my fast ball."

She smiled at him in a deliberately patronizing way. "Take your own advice, mister. Your fast ball can let you down."

She watched the messages that darted across his face and wondered if he thought she'd stepped out of line. He gazed at her for a while before a grin curled around his bottom lip. As though against his will, he began to laugh. When he finally brought his laughter under control, he put his right index finger against her lips and told her, "If you had any notion of getting away from me, forget it. That last crack you made was as good as an invitation, and I promise you I'll leave you with no doubts as to the reliability of my pitching strengths."

His words found their target, and her mind's eye teased her with pictures of him banishing her fears and misgivings

and driving away her demons with his masterful possession of her body. He must have read her thoughts, for he squeezed her to him and dared to let her see in his fiery gaze his carnal craving for her.

I'm in your heart, and I think I'm getting into your head. If you'll quit imagining problems, I'll create a magical world for you. For us. Trust me, and I'll strip away every layer of your emotional baggage, rid you of it. It's cluttering up your life. It's like a lot of old, worn-out clothes littering your closet and turning it into a refuse bin. Give me a chance?"

"I already promised, didn't I?"

He shook his head, as though bemused. "Yes, you did, and I'm telling you what you need to do in order to keep that promise."

She'd always kept her own counsel, never tried to run another person's mile, and she wouldn't start that now. "It's all clear to you. This is your world, and even if you saw some roadblocks, you know you'd easily hurdle them, because that's been your life. Mine has taken a different course. So slow down until I catch up with you. Okay?"

His half closed eyes and sheepish grin sent darts of excitement rollicking through her, but she didn't backtrack. "Okay?" she repeated.

He nodded. "Some people spend a lifetime searching for that person, that one individual who completes them and to whom they entrust their life. Deny it all you please, but you and I have it within our grasp. I know it, and you know it, too." He poked his right jaw with his tongue, gazed up at the chandeliers that blinked form the ceiling

and finally looked into her eyes. "I'll be as patient as I can, but don't expect perfection."

CHAPTER NINE

The following Sunday morning, Cal took Julia and Clifford to Jordan's cabin on the Chesapeake Bay for what Cal considered the last fishing weekend of the year. Jordan waved them off, saddled Casey Jones and headed to the far reaches of his property to inspect fences. He tethered the stallion and jumped across a wide ditch as he always did to avoid a long trip around the fallow area. But when he attempted to avoid stepping into a deep hole on the banks of the ditch, he missed his footing and landed on a roll of barbed wire that lay partially hidden in the trench, and which shouldn't have been there.

He groaned as his two hundred and five pound weight pressed the sharp wires through his leather jacket. When he extricated himself, pain plowed through his shoulders. He whistled for Casey Jones, mounted the horse with difficulty and headed home.

The footsteps that plodded slowly up the stairs didn't sound as if they belonged to anyone who lived there. Cold sweat poured from Leslie. Quickly she told Berle goodbye, slammed down the telephone receiver, raced to the hall and let herself breathe. But her relief was short lived when she took in Jordan's demeanor.

"Jordan, it's you. What happened? What's the matter?"

He seemed to drag the words out of himself as he told her. "I've got to give myself a tetanus shot."

"Where will you get it?

"We keep a supply. In an operation like the Estates, we have to."

She followed him into his room and, to her surprise, he let her help him out of his jacket and shirt. She thought her heart would stop beating when she saw the punctures on his shoulders.

"Cal keeps some ointment in that cabinet on the back porch. Would you get it, please?"

She didn't want to see him give himself that needle and was glad for a reason to get out of his room. When she returned with the salve, he lay across the bed on his side, breathing hard.

"Turn over."

He let her know that he planned to be uncooperative. "What for?"

"I want to take care of those wounds, so please—"

"I already did that. I gave myself that lousy shot. Just put that stuff over there." He inclined his head toward his night table.

She looked at his long broad back, smooth but for the punctures, his trim hips advertised to perfection in his tight jeans, and was grateful that she'd never learned how to whistle. "These places on your back have to heal," she told him. "So come on. Lean over further."

"That stuff stings."

"Will you lean over?" she asked him in the tone of one exasperated.

He gazed at her. "You don't like my face?"

"Fishing for compliments?" she asked, teasing him, "With your mug, you should be glad to turn over."

She had intended her joke to distract him from the pain and to ease the rising tension, but he wasn't amused.

It hadn't occurred to her that he could be uncertain about his looks.

She blurted out, "Don't you know what you look like, for Pete's sake? It's a wonder half the women in Washington County aren't camped out there at the gate." Horrified at her careless comment, she pushed his shoulder.

"Lean over, Jordan. If I don't tend these cuts, they may become infected. If it stings, it'll only last a minute."

Mom Haynes always said men couldn't stand pain and that if they'd been responsible for the babies, there wouldn't have been two infants born after Eve died. She attempted to push him over, but he must have anticipated her move, for he fell over on his back, reached up and pulled her to him. She struggled to keep her balance, but lost it and landed in his arms, her legs entwined with his like freshly plaited hair and her breasts pressing his chest. A mistake! She gasped at the fire, the undisguised hunger and need shimmering in his hypnotic green eyes, and in the space of one second, she knew her answering passion leaped into her own eyes, telegraphing to him her desire.

She supposed he thought he'd made a mistake when he didn't disguise what he felt, because he pasted a cool, impersonal expression on his face. "I didn't know you liked the way I look. You've never told me how you feel about me."

She didn't want that or any other small talk. She wanted his lips on hers, his velvet tongue in her mouth. With shocking clarity, she knew that she wanted from him what she had never before wanted from any man. Surprising

him with her strength, she loosened her left wrist from his grip, held his head and poured all she felt into her lips as she kissed him. Wantonly. She knew him uncharacteristic aggressiveness startled him, but she didn't care. Not about that or anything but what she felt.

An unfamiliar peace—like sensation of a gentle spring breeze—stole over her when he broke the kiss and gently cradled her head to his shoulder. She raised her head, and when she gazed into his eyes, she recognized the expression of triumph on his face. In any language, it translated into sweetheart, your days are numbered.

But he didn't voice it. What he said was, "Get up, woman, and do whatever it was that you were going to do to my back."

He turned over with care, his discomfort obvious, and she soothed the salve over his raw cats, hurting for him as she did so.

She patted his hand. "I'll be in my room. Yell if you need anything."

"You could read me something. I don't feel like staying up here by myself."

She walked over to him. "You must have been a grand rascal when you were Clifford's age."

"I'm still a grand rascal."

"Yes," she acknowledged, he was. And he had it all. Everything. She wanted to stay with him, but she didn't. She knew him well enough to appreciate that, strong though he was, his pain could lessen his self-control and they'd both be victims.

"'Scuse me," she said, and rushed across the hall to her room to answer the telephone. "Hello. Hello. Hello!" Silence. Berle wouldn't play that kind of trick on her. Who on earth…? Oh, Lord. He'd gotten her phone number. She slammed down the receiver and sat down, defeated. Damn him. Damn Faron Walker. He'd turned her life around. Every time she got her footing, he pulled the rug from under her as it were, and she had to pull up stakes and start all over again. But not this time. This time he wouldn't win. She refused to be his victim.

Thanksgiving in the Saber household was a day that no one present would ever forget. Jordan observed the rapture, the pure exhilaration that glowed in Leslie and Clifford throughout the day, and his ability to fill the lives of those he loved with pleasure humbled him. Never had he been more aware of his good fortune in having had Julia's love and nurturing when he was a boy. Leslie and Clifford hadn't been as lucky as he, though Leslie had at least known love. Their excitement and childish merriment over the feast thrilled him. Julia and Cal hovered over them, caught up in the joy of shaping love and in the thrill of making the occasion a special one for all of them.

He tried to make it a memorable day for all of his workers as well, setting makeshift tables in his living and dining rooms so that they, too, could have a home-style Thanksgiving. Jack had prepared two twenty pound turkeys, while Leslie and Julia cooked the remainder of the meal. One of the hands roasted fresh chestnuts, Rocket brought an armful of fresh holly, and Sanchez candied a bucket of Red Delicious apples. Zeke brought along his

guitar, and his memorable jazz renditions raised questions in the mind of every person present, for none could doubt that he had known fame, if not fortune. At Clifford's urging, Jordan played "Bring in the Clowns" on his guitar, and then joined Zeke in a stunning jazz interpretation of "Lover Come Back to Me."

Clifford startled them all when he said, "If I get to be president, we'll have Thanksgiving every day. It's awesome."

Gradually, the men left, expressing their thanks, though they knew none was needed. When the last had departed, Jordan went into the living room and took a seat in the overstuffed leather chair beside the crackling fire. He should have felt good, but contentment eluded him, and he knew why. He needed to be able to put his arms around Leslie, take her up to his room, his bed, and claim her for his own with the full knowledge of anybody who cared to know it, and he needed the legal right to do it. That and that alone would complete his day. He was hanging out there, way out, and he might be out there by himself. Leslie's goals came first with her. He knew it. And she was right then stirring around in his kitchen as contented as a cat with her first kittens. If she'd been agitated because the two of them hadn't so much as touched fingers all day, she'd given no evidence of it. She seemed to be sexually unaware of him unless he touched her. He allowed himself a satisfied male grin. But when he touched her, she practically exploded. No doubt of that. But their day was coming, and soon. Clifford barged into the room, and he put

his arm around his nephew's shoulder when the boy leaned against his knee.

Jordan eased back in the big overstuffed chair, just as the telephone ring shattered the peaceful silence. He reached for it, disgruntledat the interruption.

"Saber." Getting no response, his antenna went up, and he sat forward, immediately alert.

"What do you want?" He spoke roughly and impatiently.

"Mr. Saber, Turner Baker told me to get in touch with you. I'd like to talk with you today, if possible."

"What about?" A heavy curtain of wariness settled over him. Still, he reasoned, it wasn't like Turner to let him walk into a trap. They weren't bosom buddies, but they got along and they respected each other. And Turner was honorable. He waited.

"Leslie Collins, Mr. Saber. It's about her."

His heart took off in a wild beat, pounding with the rhythm of a back bush African drummer. "Do you know where I live?" He already knew the answer.

"Yes. It'll take me thirty minutes to get there."

"I'll be there."

Then he remembered to ask the man's name, but he heard a dial tone. "Damn!"

He found Cal, spoke briefly to him, sent Clifford to keep Leslie occupied and tried to prepare himself for the long-awaited confrontation. If he only knew what he was preparing for! He went into the den, closed the door and checked the top right hand drawer of his desk for the revolver that was always there. He left the drawer unlocked

and sat down. He needed to concentrate. Something didn't tally, and he had thirty minutes in which to figure it out. Still at a loss after ten minutes, and realizing that the answer was just barely beyond his grasp, he flipped on the radio, hoping to distract himself momentarily. One of the country singers wailed about his longing to see a girl's face and to hear her voice.

Jordan stood, almost knocking over his chair as he did so. That voice! It wasn't the voice of the man he'd confronted at his garage. He had never heard that voice before. A refined voice, one that belonged to a genteel man. So there were indeed two of them. Now, what? Well, he'd know at least part of it shortly.

Jordan opened the front door to find an ordinarily-dressed, ordinary looking African-American man about sixty years old. Not affluent. Not shabby. Just ordinary.

"I'm Jordan Saber." He was neither friendly nor unfriendly, and he didn't ask the stranger to come in. He just waited cautiously, aware that the man seemed perfectly at ease as he extended his hand.

"Thank you for letting me come, Mr. Saber. I'm Franklin Collins." Jordan hoped the shock of hearing the name didn't register on his face.

"Leslie told me her father was dead."

"I'm her father's brother. I've been searching for my brother and his family for years. About six months ago, I finally got track of Leslie and also learned that Frederick was dead. Until then, I hadn't known that he had a daughter." Jordan observed him silently for a minute. Franklin Collins was neither defensive, hostile, nor threatening in

any way. He stepped back and invited the man into his home.

Jordan sat at his desk, seating the man in a comfortable leather chair that sat at an angle facing him. The man refused the offer of a drink.

"What is your connection to Turner Baker? First things first."

"None. I followed him from here one day. When I caught up with him in a bar, he declined to give me any information. So I traced him through his license plate and finally went to see him. I told him who I am and why I've been looking for Leslie. He said the simplest thing would be to call you. Frederick was my twin brother. So if you doubt that I'm Leslie's uncle, we can set aside your concern as soon as she sees me. Frederick always swam against the tide. Against our parents, the schools, the community. Everybody. He left home on our eighteenth birthday, and in the thirty-nine years since, there was never a word."

For a while, Jordan said nothing, and the man left him to his thoughts. Finally, Jordan questioned him. "Do you drive a brown sedan?" He nodded. "And did you inquire about me at the university?"

Franklin Collins smiled. "Yes, I did. I wanted to know who I was dealing with and what kind of man my niece was living with."

Jordan bristled. "Leslie is not living with me. She works here. Everybody who works for me lives on the Estates." He noted what was clearly satisfaction and approval on the face of Leslie's uncle.

"What do you want from me?" He was putting the man on the spot, but he considered it a fair question.

"My parents are long dead. My wife died two years ago after a long and very difficult illness. She was always very frail. We wanted children, but we were not fortunate. Leslie is the only surviving relative that I have, or at least that I'm aware of. I want to know her. That's all. Is it too much to ask if I may meet her?'

Jordan saw nothing wrong with that, but he couldn't speak for Leslie. And considering her wariness of strange men, he couldn't anticipate her reaction to meeting a long-lost uncle. Best introduce her to the idea slowly.

He observed Franklin closely, making up his mind. "One more thing. Why did you contact me rather than speak directly to Leslie?"

"Baker advised me to speak with you, and he's a no-nonsense man, so I took his advice."

"You were right to do so." He related enough of Leslie's life to prepare her uncle for rejection. This time, the offer of a brandy was accepted. That his guest warmed the sniffer of fine brandy slowly between the palms of his hands before inhaling it gently, then taking a small sip and swirling it on his tongue, was not lost on Jordan. The man had some class.

"Tell me about yourself."

He learned that Franklin Collins was a lawyer, born and raised in Nashville, Tennessee, and had graduated from Duke University in Durham, North Carolina. He'd studied a year in England as a Fulbright Fellow   , gone back to Duke and gotten his law degree. His wife's

eight-year illness had left him nearly broke, partly because
he'd quit work in order to spend the last year of her life at
home with her. He told it without any expression of bit-
terness or self-pity, and Jordan couldn't help admiring the
man.

"Where do you live now?" he asked him.

"For the past two years, I've been living wherever my
search had taken me. Now that I've found Leslie, I hope to
go back to my job in Nashville, if it's still there. If it isn't,
I'll find another one or go into private practice. I've some
contacts there."

Jordan liked what he'd seen and heard. He nodded
thoughtfully. "All right. I'll ask her if she'll see you."

Jordan asked Cal to entertain the visitor, excused himself and went to speak with Leslie. Her initial disbelief did-
n't surprise him. As she explained, her father had never
spoken of a brother, had in fact claimed that he didn't have
a family.

"He says you can verify it by looking at him, that he's
your father's twin." He couldn't say why he felt such relief
when she agreed to meet Franklin Collins.

"Give me a few minutes." Her nervousness stabbed at
him and, in a gesture of support, he draped his arm around
her shoulder.

"I think you'll like him. I do. But how I feel is irrele-
vant. The minute you want him to leave, he goes."

Leslie's gasp when she saw her uncle told Jordan what
he needed to know. Her face ashen, she leaned against the
door jamb for support. Boldly, he placed his arms around
her shoulders to steady her and to remind her that he was

there, and there for her. The man who claimed to be her uncle stood as Leslie entered the room and waited for her to make her first move. Jordan saw the gesture as one of consideration for Leslie, and he walked slowly to Franklin Collins, his arm still snug around her. She regarded the man before her the way a woman scrutinizes her nylons for runs before dressing for a special date. Not with apparent curiosity, but with an almost impersonal hope.

She spoke first. "I'm glad I didn't just happen upon you some place. You and my father must have been identical twins."

He smiled. "Yes, we were. And I'm sad to say Frederick resented it every day that I knew him."

Jordan would have left them alone, but Leslie clung to him as one clutches a life line. He stayed with her, knowing she'd had an emotionally crippling shock. When Julia and Clifford joined them, bringing tea, coffee and cookies, Clifford greeted Franklin with exuberance.

"I'm glad to meet you. Now Leslie had some family, too." He grabbed Leslie's hand, looked up at her, his face shinning with joy, and wrapped his arms around her waist. "Leslie, this is our absolute very best day in the whole entire world."

His smile blessed them all, and he said to his uncle, "Isn't it just awesome, Unca Jordan? Now me and Leslie both have a family."

"Yeah, it's awesome all right."

He corrected his nephew's grammar and regarded their guest. "Will you stay for supper, Mr. Collins? That'll give us all a chance to get better acquainted."

Franklin Collins smiled, his demeanor that of a man contented with himself and at ease in his surroundings. "Thank you. I'd like that very much."

Leslie wasted no time getting answers to questions that had nagged her. Her uncle informed her that he drove a brown Buick, not the brown Taurus that had followed her form Westminster to the Eastern Shore and along Highway 695 when Cal drove her to Westminster, and that he had never thrown pebbles at her bedroom window. And he made it clear that her question about the pebbles didn't sit well with him.

Jordan grabbed her arm. "When did this happen?"

"Several times. Maybe half a dozen."

He released her hand and began pacing the floor. "And you never told me? Not even after I damn near caught a man trying to break in on you? How can I protect you when you insist on withholding this kind of information?"

"That night was the last time it happened. Since then, I've been staying over here in the house, and I figured that there was no point in telling you."

"No point?" He turned first to Cal and then to Franklin. "Does either of you understand how the female mind works?' He threw his arms up in frustration. "That settles it. I'm going to find that man whether you help me or not," he declared, drawing an inquisitive stare from Franklin Collins.

Later, they all sat around the living room fireplace swapping stories, singing and enjoying the music that flowed from Jordan's fingers as he demonstrated his skill as a guitarist. When he glanced at Leslie and coaxed from the

strings the haunting, "If I Loved You," she had to blink rapidly a few times to hold back the tears. How could he know she loved that song, that when she'd first heard it as a teenager, she'd wept for her loneliness?

Did he know the words, and did he mean them? Words that spoke of love for all time. Endless love. She thought her heart would burst with love for him. The song held deep meaning for him too, she realized, when his voice floated to her on the air, and she thought he'd asked her to come to him, that he'd whispered "I love you." But he hadn't parted his lips, though for that second, his eyes must have telegraphed that message from his soul to hers. How else could she have heard it? He glanced up at her as he neared the song's end and mounted the words reminding her that she would soon leave him. She couldn't bear the distance between them and, as his fingers teased out the closing noted, she walked over to him and sat on the floor beside his chair. He finished the song, stood, helped her to her feet, looked into her eyes, and all else around them faded into oblivion.

"Anybody want some more coffee?"

Only Julia would have realized how close she'd come to putting her arms around Jordan and losing herself in him right then and there. She expressed her thanks in a smile and nod of her head, and she could tell that it cost Jordan something to snap out of it. A sober expression eclipsed his earlier warm demeanor, he didn't have to tell her that, for him, the evening was at an end.

Jordan said to Franklin Collins, "It's getting late, and I don't know where you're headed. We'd all be pleased if you would spend the night with us."

"I appreciate your hospitality." Franklin said, "Thank you."

Jordan rubbed his chin. A man with good manners appealed to him. "Leslie and Julia will show you to your room," he said. "Breakfast is at seven-thirty."

He glanced at her and briefly closed his eyes, a gesture that betrayed to her his longing. The he shook hands with Franklin, let the fingers of his right hand graze her cheek and told them all good night.

After breakfast, Franklin Collins bade them goodbye. Leslie didn't want him to leave with nothing because, she realized, she liked him and wanted him to be a part of her life.

"You're welcome here as often as you care to come," Jordan told the man, who seemed touched by Jordan's generous gesture and looked to Leslie for confirmation. She hesitated for a second and then stepped forward and embraced her uncle.

"Come back soon, Uncle Franklin, and keep in touch."

Jordan watched as they smiled through their tears. This had been a healing experience for Leslie. At least he hoped so. A paternal uncle was a close relative, and this one gave every indication that he was worthy of trust.

Leslie announced at supper the next evening that she had to be in College Park early Monday morning to register for the coming semester.

Before anyone else could react, Jordan took the moment. "I've got to be there, too, to register my students. And I'm changing from one class on Tuesday evenings to two classes on Tuesday afternoons. My department secretary will make our reservations. You can ride in with me Sunday evening, and if you've finished by noon on Monday, we can be back here by three o'clock."

He wanted to hug Julia when she moved quickly to forestall any objections or excuses that Leslie might offer. "That's great. We'll all have Sunday night out. Clifford wants to see the new Disney movie, and Cal and I can take him Sunday afternoon. Then the three of us can have supper at Tandy's. A little time away from this kitchen won't hurt either one of us, Leslie."

After supper, he went into his office and closed the door. Leslie hadn't uttered a single word in response to his suggestion that they go together to the university. But he had no intention of backing down. It was D-Day for them, and if she didn't know it, she would, and soon.

"Come in," he said in response to the knock.

Cal walked in and closed the door. "This step you're talking could torpedo your relationship with Leslie."

"Or cement it," Jordan said. Cal had struggled with him through his adolescent years, and didn't resent his remark any more than he would frowned upon advice from his father.

"I just hope you know what you're doing, son."

"Yeah. I can appreciate your concern, because I feel like I'm stepping on hot coals. But I love her, and I have to deal with it."

"I know you do, and I know how important this is to you. Just think of her first and yourself last."

Jordan shoved his hands in his pants pockets and leaned against the edge of his desk. "I've never done otherwise."

CHAPTER TEN

Leslie threw her suitcase on the bed, unopened, and walked out on the balcony that adjoined her hotel room. The evening glowed with an awesome beauty, not quite as cold as it had been, and but eerie in its dusk-gathering quiet with the lingering reds and purples of the sunset. Jordan had registered, and, they'd gone to their separate rooms without speaking, and she was grateful that he seemed to have sensed she needed time to herself. She hadn't bothered to determine where his room was, though she suspected he was also on the fifth floor. Her nerves had begun pitching throughout her body as soon as Jordan suggested they travel together and stay in the same hotel. Filled with anticipation, and maybe even a little dread, she'd been too nervous to eat much dinner, and now, hunger pangs gnawed at her belly. She stepped back into her room and began to unpack the few things she'd brought, a dress, robe, gown, cosmetics, stockings and a pair of dress shoes.

She answered the phone, knowing it was Jordan. "Are you about settled? I'd like to have supper pretty soon. Meet you in the lobby in, say, ten minutes?"

Ten minutes? She hadn't even finished unpacking. "Could I have half an hour?'

Jordan agreed and hung up. He stood gazing down at the telephone resting in his cradle. What had she been doing since they'd separated an hour and a half ago? Hadn't she expected them to share the evening meal? He ran his fingers through his hair in frustration.

"I'm not backing down," he told himself and stepped out into the corridor.

Leslie wondered why she was taking a shower when she'd had one that morning—especially since she'd told Jordan that she'd meet him in 30 minutes. At least she had had the presence of mind to wear a shower cap. She dried off quickly, applied some body lotion and began to dress, reaching for the burnt orange woolen knit dress she'd decided to pack at the last minute.

She gazed at the curves of her body that the dress exposed. What would he think seeing her dressed that way? Well, she hadn't brought anything else, so she had no choice. She found a matching color lipstick in her makeup kit, put on the big, gold-toned ear hoops that she'd brought on a whim and bushed her hair until it shone, floating free well below her shoulders. Where was the perfume that her foster mother had given her when she'd graduated from college? She searched her handbag frantically, annoyed with her nervousness and intuitively feeling the age-old feminine need to arm herself with a delicate, luring scent. Relieved to find it, she dabbed some on numerous spots on her body.

She sat down on the bed to put on her slipped, simple, black suede pumps, and a feeling of weakness, akin to a delicious wickedness, permeated her body. She stretched the way a young lioness does when she hears the fierce roar of her mate. A vision of the way he'd looked at her when he left flashed through her mind, and frissons of heat went arrow straight to her loins. She ignored the ringing telephone, got her handbag and reached for the doorknob. Her

glance took in the full length mirror attached to the door, and she did a double take and stared at herself.

Was she that woman? The transformation from the girl of over seven months earlier into the stylish woman in the mirror stunned her, but heightened her confidence. She said a silent prayer and left the room.

As the elevator descended, Leslie wondered how he would react to her. "Where the hell is she," she heard him wonder aloud, pacing the floor beside the elevator as the door opened. His long, smoldering look told her she needn't have worried about his reaction to her appearance.

He had a sense of immense relief. He didn't know what he'd expected her, but... Well, she was there! It wouldn't have surprised him if she'd locked her room door and gone to bed. They had hardly spoken since leaving Dexter, and he couldn't figure out why she'd withdrawn so completely. He could have told her that he'd never touched a woman who wasn't willing, but he hadn't. She ought to have sense enough to know that, he reasoned. Besides, he was damned well going to make her willing. She was something of a shock, though. He had always liked the way she looked, even when she was working, and he'd certainly seen her dressed up. But he hadn't ever seen her looking the personification of sexiness. He was glad he'd had the presence of mind to discipline his tongue as well as his physical reaction to her.

"You're worth every second that I waited." She'd faint if he voiced the rest of his thoughts. He took her elbow, looked down at her and softly breathed the words. "You're beautiful, Leslie. I'm proud to be with you."

Something approximating a smile crossed her face. "Thanks. You're not bad yourself."

Her facial expression told him her nerves were on a rampage, and he was going to avoid doing and saying anything that would make her skittish. He led her across the lobby to the entrance of a very nice restaurant that adjoined the hotel.

As taut as a marksman's bow, she concentrated her energy on quieting her nerves. Jordan not only wouldn't make a move that would cause her distress, he'd take to task anyone who did. Yet, she couldn't banish the feeling that she was about to take a proverbial walk into outer space.

"Leslie?" He held the chair for her, waiting for her to sit. His gentle, almost impersonal smile should have reassured her, but when his hand casually caressed her shoulder, she nearly jumped. And she knew he'd notice, because nothing escaped him. He was by nature perceptive and, when it came to her, he seemed doubly sensitive.

After they'd given their orders, the waiter brought the wine, a fine California Chablis, and Jordan raised his glass. "To the loveliest woman I've ever known."

Butterflies had joined the marbles in her belly. "Th…Thanks."

"What about me? Aren't you going to toast me?"

She opened her mouth for a snappy retort and closed it mutely, at a loss for words. He grinned, a heart-stopping breathtaking grin that sent her spinning.

"I didn't think I'd ever see you speechless," he taunted. You gave me 'what for' before I even hired you. What's come over you, Leslie?"

She'd become impatient with her nervousness, so she let his innocent words stoke a fire in her.

"You're playing with me, and I want you to stop it."

"Me? I'm just trying to give you a shot of emotional involvement. The Leslie I know I would have teased me right back."

"You don't want to tangle with me. Shove and I'll shove right back."

That was what he wanted. Some fire. Spirit. The ready boiled that was part of his attraction to her. "I want to tangle with you, all right, but definitely not here," he said, and dropped a quarter into the juke box selector at their booth.

Heat sent the blood rushing to her face when she heard the country group. Alabama, launch into "If I Had You," but she forced herself to look him in the eye. With his A-1 gin, he as much as told her knew that it cost her not to back down. Then as though weary of needling her, he switched the subject and the mood, and they were soon speaking of the coming semester and what she hoped to accomplish.

After some minutes, she asked him, "What was your childhood like before you lost your parents?"

"Normal, I suppose. Our parents were university professors, devoted to their work and to each other. That didn't leave them with a lot of time for Haskell and me, but what time they had to spend with us, I guess you'd say was quality time. They weren't always kissing us, but whenever we talked to them, they stopped whatever they were doing and listened, really listened. I always felt that we were really important to them. They loved to gather wild mushrooms during their walks in the woods. One day they got

some bad ones, and, well…it took them both. I think it was natural for them to go together, considering how close they were.

"It took me a long time to accept that Haskell just walked out of my life. He was almost ten years my senior, and I practically worshipped him. Looking back, I realize that he wasn't cut out for a rural, farm existence. He just said goodbye and left. I never heard from him or about him from the time I was nine years old until Clifford came to me. I hope he found what he was looking for. You might say Julia has been my family, my mother, and when she married Cal, I got a father as well. I care a lot for her. Uncle Riddick showered me with kindness, and I know he loved me, but he had no idea what to do with a child. Julia was so full of energy, fun and love, always filling the place with happiness that I, well…she was everything a small boy needed."

"You're fortunate. I suspect she needed a child to care for just as you needed a mother's love. The age of nine must have been a terrible time to lose both parents and the older brother, whom you idolized. It's no wonder that you love Julia."

He couldn't risk getting mired in nostalgia, so he dropped quarter in the tune selector and without shifting his gaze from her, rose to his full six feet, five inches. "Dance with me, Leslie. I need to hold you."

"R…Right her?" She stammered. "I mean, I'm not much of a dancer."

The stood so close that air could barely pierce the distance between them. He didn't want her beguiled, but fully

knowledgeable of every move he made. He didn't believe in seducing a woman.

He stepped back and looked at her. "You don't need to be expert at it. Just move with me."

"Said the spider to the fly," she murmured.

"What was that?"

"Nothing important."

"I'm not spinning a web or any other trap for you." He led her in a gently swaying two-step, his right hand splayed lightly at her lower back and his left one firmly grasping her right hand. She missed a step, and he drew her closer, so close that the pressure of his chest caused her nipples to harden, she stifled a gasp and lowered her eyes. The song ended, but he didn't leave the floor.

Someone had spent a quarter on a song about pleading unrequited love. She knew the words implied his heed of her, but she couldn't resist resting her head on his shoulder and letting the music and his sensuous rhythm sweep her away. She gave in to the music as she danced, relaxed in his arms, not thinking that she was stirring the coals of a fire that he might be struggling to contain, but responding to the sensual pleasure of moving in the arms of the man that she loved. She felt free, even a little wild, and she suspected that he sensed it. Her heart sang a new tune, but would understand that?

Jordan decided that it was then or never; he had to put his life, his house, in order. If he didn't reach our and take her, he'd never get her. Her head was full of him right then, so he was moving while he had the wind at his back.

"Let's go."

"It's early yet, only eight-thirty."

"Believe me; it's not all that early." He led her from the dance floor, signed the check and headed them toward the elevator. As they ascended to their floor, he held her hand and could feel her tremble when he drew her close.

"I guess I had too much to drink."

That was one excuse he didn't intend to accept. He'd take nothing less than honesty. She wanted to or she didn't want to. "Come again, Leslie. You didn't drink half a glass of wine. You're sober as the head of the Women's Christian Temperance Union ever was."

They stopped at her door, and she looked up at him inquiringly. He was calling a spade a spade, and he was through tiptoeing around the issue, "We can enter from your door or from mine," He told him bluntly. "There's a connecting door between our rooms,"

Her eyes widened in surprise, he didn't hesitate. He stepped inside her room; his hand splayed lightly at her back, closed the door and pulled her to him. She opened her mouth, but her words that she would have spoken were lost on the tip of his tongue as he closed in on her, thrilling her, setting her afire, taking possession of her senses. But as she relaxed and melted into him, he released her.

"I want you, Leslie," He gazed intensely at her. "I want to make love with you. Here. Now. I told you that I haven't touched a woman since I laid eyes on you. Oh, they are not there, all right, but I have wanted only you. It's time for us. It's long past time. We have to know what there is between us, Leslie, and we have to know what where it's going. I know what I want, but I'm not sure that you do. I told you

that our relationship isn't normal, and isn't. I am a man, Leslie, a young healthy man, and I need you in my arms, in my bed. I want to love you. I want to know the glory of your body, to give you the supreme pleasure that a man can give a woman, and I want to feel it myself it myself, nestled deep inside you. I know you want me and that you care for me. But I will not continue the way we are now. I can't stand it!"

Leslie moved toward Jordan, as if his nearness would guide her, but he stepped away, making it clear that he would not pressure her.

"Don't let your demons rob you of your womanhood. If you'll trust me, I'll give you're your birthright. I'll set you free, Leslie."

She looked away from him. Maybe she was trying to come to terms with her feelings, with what loving him would cost her. But she should already have done that. He'd done the sweating, tossing and weighing of consequences, had first accepted and then embraced what nestled in his heart for her. He needed her, and he had to have a resolution of their relationship one way or the other.

"I won't come to you. Not here, not ever, if you want me, you'll always know where I am. But make certain that you don't wait too long. Maybe I'm doing the wrong thing leaving you right now, but I'm human, and rejection hurts me as much as it does the next man." He turned and entered his room through their connecting door.

Had he looked, he would have seen her reach out to him, seen the desperation in her eyes. In her room with the doors closed she clung to the foot of the bed for support.

He had challenged her, and he had the right to do it. Hadn't she encouraged him with her response to his kisses and caresses even as she'd said there could be nothing between them? Shaking her head as if to clear it, she walked to the closet door, opened it, reached for her robe and paused, as a pain settled in the region of her heart. She leaned against the door.

"Oh, God, please, don't let him walk away from me." She'd always reached out for what she wanted. So why did she fear what she wanted so badly? She reached for her robe, and her glance feel on the gown that hung beside it. She'd never worn the dusty-rose lace garment, because it demanded male companionship.

Since her father's death, she had feared intimacy, had feared the loneliness that came with the loss of someone you loved. And her nearly catastrophic experience with Faron Walker has saddled her with a dread of physical intimacy. Strangely, she hadn't dwelled on it in recent months. Yet it troubled her now. Panic began to suffocate her, but with it came anger. Anger at Faron for his beastliness and at herself for her inability to shed those omnipresent, crippling demons. She forced herself to see that the fear of intimacy with Jordan was groundless, robbing her of something precious. He had said that he would give her birthright, and she wanted, oh how she wanted, to believe him. She didn't want to go through life without having known love in Jordan's arms. It could blow up all around her and leave her with the ashes of a foolish heart, but if she gambled and lost, would she hurt more because she'd become a woman in his arms or because she hadn't? She

remembered how she had felt every time he kissed her, that she never wanted him to stop, and her mind replayed Jordan's words: I will not continue the way we are, I can't stand it. Neither can I, she thought, and reached for the lacy gown.

Jordan undressed slowly. He knew he wouldn't sleep, but he'd reconciled himself to it. "Just another sleepless night," he muttered. But it wasn't just another night. All he had to do was open the door and crawl into her bed and he'd have what he needed. But he didn't want her that way. He wanted Leslie to open up to him, to come to him, because she needed him and because she cared for him. He didn't want her to give in to him, because she couldn't control her body's reaction to him. He wanted, needed her heart and mind, as well as her body; he wanted her to love him.

What a laugh! He'd never been inconsiderate where women were concerned, and he had never taken unfair advantage of them, but he hadn't ever had to ask the second time, either. Sure to God, he'd never pined for a woman. Maybe he'd made a mistake by walking away from her. But it had been that or lose control, and to lose mastery of himself where Leslie was concerned was unthinkable. He cherished her as he'd never treasured any other human being, and he would protect her even from himself. He undressed down to his briefs—a yellow thing that was barely more than a G-sting—and protected by the darkened room, walked over to the window. He propped his right foot on the chair, rested his right elbow on his right knee and looked out at the millions of stars and the moon cradled in

their midst. Through a window across the way, he saw a woman by the hand just before he switched off the light. He swore harshly and rested his chin on the back of his hand. How would he get through the night?

"Jordan?"

He didn't respond, but continued massaging his temple.

"Jordan?" She said it more softly this time, anxious because he hadn't answered. She longed to move closer to him, to touch him, but how could she when he didn't acknowledge her presence.

"Jordan?" She barely whispered it.

He raised tortured eyes, looking at her but appearing not to see her. Deflated, she turned to leave, and her sudden movement must have caught his attention.

"Leslie. Leslie!" It was a hoarse shout; one that she knew was wrenched from deep inside him.

She stopped, but didn't speak. Couldn't speak.

"Don't leave me. Please don't leave me!"

She could feel his pain, could almost touch the need that vibrated from him. She hated her inexperience, hated her lack of knowledge about men and how to deal with them. But her intuition told her that he was as vulnerable as she, that he was hurting as she was. With instinct alone to guide her, she turned slowly and raised open arms, wordlessly letting him read in her face all that she felt for him.

Oblivious to his near nudity; heedless of his six-year vow to avoid vulnerableness to any woman, and propelled by his consummate love for her, he moved with lightening speed into the sweet haven of her arms. She clasped him

tightly, and he didn't try to control the tremors that shook him as he buried his face in the warm curve of her neck.

"Leslie! Oh, Leslie!" He wrapped her in his arms and held her silently, nearly unstrung by his overpowering emotions. For over seven months, they had headed for this moment, and for just as long, he hadn't known where he stood with her.

When he was able to dampen his feelings, he stepped back from her, his hand resting on her slight shoulders. He didn't want any misunderstanding now; it wasn't time for mistakes, neither his nor hers. The gravity of the moment made him tense, cautious. He was looking at his life and, whether she knew it or not, she was facing hers. His heart seemed to seesaw back and forth in his chest as he gazed at her, almost unable to believe that she'd come to him.

"Why are you here, Leslie?" He spoke softly, because he didn't want to undermine her confidence.

"I'm here because it's where you are?"

Her answer didn't satisfy him, but he had to be patient. "This isn't the time for mystery or misunderstanding, Leslie. It's time for plain truth between us. We've already blundered too much. Why have you come to me?"

She looked at him intently, searching, and he had to force himself to smile and to appear relaxed, although he could hardly breathe while he waited for her answer. He supposed she was still troubled by what she had to lose, and he didn't blame her.

He could tell the minute she came to terms with their moment of reckoning, for her face suddenly bloomed. "You told me that you can't stand it any more. I can't stand it

either. For reasons I've told you about, I've been wary of men. I've gone further with you in many ways than I have with any other man. You held me and caressed me, and wanted more. I...I thought I could sacrifice my feelings for you the way I've shelved so many other things I've wanted."

When he didn't speak and held his breath in anticipation, she continued. "I ached. Some nights, I couldn't sleep. I knew what I needed, but I was scared to take that step. Not afraid of you, but of the unknown; wary of all the social ramifications, and of the chance that I might forfeit my degree. But I'm not afraid now."

At those last words, he let out his breath and crushed her to him. Then he held her away, searching her to face his answer.

"Yes. Oh, yes, Jordan."

"Do you realize what you're saying sweetheart? Do you? Are you telling me that you want me here and now? That's what I'm asking, Leslie."

"Yes."

He found her mouth then and, for the first time, she knew what it was to have Jordan kiss her, really kiss her. He had his control, but he unleashed his passion. She felt his velvet tongue deep in her mouth, teasing every crevice in it, simulating the act of love. His big warm hand went inside her gown, gently grasping one breast and softly rubbing its nipple between his thumb and fore-finger before he caressed the whole globe. His full arousal rose against her belly, and she stiffened, even as her breath quickened, but he pulled her closer, and gripped her buttocks tightly. He

held her to him until her blood accelerated its pace and sped wildly through her veins.

"Don't hold back on me, sweetheart. If it feels good to you, let me know it. I'll take care of you. Don't resist me. Give in to me, Leslie. Nothing that we do here is cause for shame. Open up to me." She looked up at him, stared into the hot fire of his smoldering green eyes and slumped against him in surrender. He eased the negligee and gown from her shoulders and let them fall to the floor.

She had barely been aware of his near nudity. But while he gazed at her, appreciating her womanliness, she finally saw him as he was. Mesmerized by what her eyes beheld, she stared and stared, unaware that she ogled him. Her first lust-inciting look at a fully aroused man.

"My God, Jordan. Your are... You are..."

Captivated, she stepped forward and placed a palm on his chest, while her other hand touched his left biceps. Then she sent her gaze slowly downward, coming to rest at the apex of his thighs, where his proud sex stood in full readiness. She looked and looked, her gaze finally roaming slowly up to his tapered waist and iron-tight belly. As though in a trance, she smiled and licked her lips, as one savoring the prospect of a grand feast, before stepping back for enough to see the whole man, to take him in form head to foot. Almost stupefied, she ran her tongue slowly around the rim of her top lip, bit on her bottom one and then bathed it generously with her tongue. Her senses had taken possession of her.

It was too much. He let out a harsh groan, reached for her, lifted her until she was eye to eye with him and kissed

her hard. Then he lifted her higher, clamped his lips over her breast and suckled her vigorously. She clasped his head to her and cried out from the pleasure that he gave her. He carried her to the bed, turned back the covers, laid her gently on it and leaned over her, burning her with his plundering mouth, searing. He tortured her neck, kissed the valley between her breasts and then took each nipple into his mouth to tease and suck. She squirmed and thrashed against the sheets, but he had only just begun. He intended to adore her in every way a man could love his woman, and though his hunger for every part of her body tempted him, he knew that she wasn't ready for the ultimate kiss. But he didn't spare the rest of her.

"Jordan!" She moaned. "Please."

"Be patient, baby. We've got all night." He climbed into bed and pulled her to him, her skin to his skin from shoulders to knees. When her breast touched his massive chest, she shivered from the thrill of it, and her body jerked like a hand unexpectedly exposed to a flame. He placed his right hand behind her head, lowered his mouth to hers and ran his tongue around her lips, asking for entrance. She parted them for him and took his tongue into her mouth. He caressed and soothed and stroked, and she was a sapling in a storm when his fingers began their torrid dance at the threshold of her love nest.

He felt her tense, but he didn't stop, understanding her virginal hesitancy. Then he parted her delicate feminine folds and she cried out, shifting closer to him, hugging him. He loved the currents that her soft hand sent speeding along his spine as she caressed him, though he felt her fin-

gers tremble. He spread kisses all over her face, enjoying the feel of her delicate hands as they roamed over his back, adoring him.

He opened his mouth above her lips and kissed her, unleashing his passion, letting her know the urgency of his need, the power of his desire for her.

She threw her right leg across his hip. "Jordan, please. Honey, I can't stand this. I ache deep inside. Can't you... fill me? Fill me!"

Her voice rose as her passion escalated, and he had to struggle to stifle his need to explode within her. He let his hand learn her body while he bent to her breast, kissing and sucking until she begun to undulate wildly beneath him. He skimmed her inner tights with his palms, wanting to heat her to boiling point, to make her certain that he could bring her to the pinnacle and give her all that he'd promised.

Out of control now, she screamed, "I want to burst, I need....."

He swallowed her words, reached down, checked for her readiness and, finding what he wanted, raised himself on his left elbow and slid his right leg across her thighs. With his right hand cupping her mound, he eased his left arm beneath her shoulder, lowered his mouth to her swollen breast and rose fully above her.

"Stop! Oh. God, please stop!"

He froze. Raising his head, he looked into her petrified tearstained face.

"For the love of God, sweetheart. What is it? What is the matter?" He rolled away and sat on the edge of the bed

with his back to her, shocked. One minute she had been begging him with every frantic twist of her hips to take her, and the next she was pushing him away, panic-stricken. His first thought was that he'd had torture aplenty, that he couldn't take anymore. Then he thought of her and of the pain that she must surely be suffering, turned and saw that she'd covered her face with her right forearm. Gently, he moved it so that he could look into her eyes. There were squeezed tight. Seeing that, he was glad he hadn't moved away from the bed, deserting her.

"Honey, can you tell me why you stopped me?" When she didn't reply, he made up his mind to know the truth no matter how merciless he had to be. He was entitled to an answer, dammit, and he was going to get one. He took a deep breath and calmed himself.

"What happened the minute I rose above you?"

Tears from her tightly-closed eyes rolled down her checks. Damn! He reached over and took her left hand in both of his. Be gentle, he told himself, but be firm.

He tried a different approach. "Leslie, I've never had an experience like this before in my life, and I'm going to keep you here until you explain what happened even if it takes until next week. If I don't register my students, hell, if I don't teach. I don't care. What matters to me is us, you and me, and the burden you're carrying that's destroying what we could have together. Why are you afraid to let me make love with you? Why, Leslie? Don't you trust me? Don't you know that I'm just as vulnerable to you as you are to me?" He got up, walked over to the well-stocked bar and got her a glass of club soda.

"Sit up, sweetheart, and lean on me."

She did as he asked, clutching the sheet to cover her breast, and he held the glass while she sipped.

"Talk to me, baby." He tipped her chin up, forcing her to look into his eyes; eyes that he knew mirrored his anguish. Each of them tried to give the other a reassuring smile, and neither succeeded. He watched her fight the tears and grasped her hand to give her the strength that she seemed to need, all the while wondering what could have had such a damaging effect on her. He waited.

As though touching him made it easier, she put her free hand on his arm and begun to speak. "I worked as a clerk for a shipping company the summer after I graduated from college. I needed the job badly, and in my naiveté`, I ignored my boss's suggestive remarks. He started touching me, and I asked him to keep his hands off me, but he wouldn't take me seriously. He said…he said…"

Jordan squeezed her hand. "Go on."

"He made me work late one day and, about six o'clock when the office was empty except for us, he walked over to my desk and sat on the edge of it. He said ever since I'd gone to work there, he'd wanted to know…what it would be like with me and that he was pretty needy. I'd always thought him boorish and contemptuous of simple courtesies, but I stayed late as he asked because I needed the job so badly. Anyway, his wife was in the hospital having their third child, and I had sense enough to know what that meant. My senses told me to get out of there, and I jumped up and started for the door, but he grabbed me. He had me on the floor and was on top of me and sent him into shock

long enough to get away. Mom and Pop Haynes insisted that I bring charges against him, and I did.

"His lawyer tried to bargain with me, claiming that no jury would believe me. But the man had raped two of his female employees, both white, and threatened them into silence. When they read about the trial in the newspaper, they volunteered to witness for me, and the jury found him guilty.

"His lawyer had interrogated me for days, claiming that I had led the man to think I wanted him. My own lawyer told me I was lucky, that he didn't believe a man deserved a conviction for something like that. He hadn't believed me, and the judge hadn't shown much interest until those women came to my defense. You can't imagine the humiliation of that trial."

"Was that man white?"

She nodded. "Yes."

Jordan said nothing, but he understood more than she'd told him. For several minutes, he didn't trust himself to speak, but rocked her gently, stroking her, reassuring her as best as he could, as the magnitude of her near tragedy intensified his mounting fury. With one hand at the back of her head and the other cradling her shoulder, he told her gently, "You've come so much. I'm humble."

"You don't think I led him on? You're not, not ashamed of me, I mean—"

He interrupted her, more sharply than he'd intended. "Why should I be ashamed of you? That's the most ridiculous thing I've ever heard. You're the victim, not the offender. I'm proud of you and proud that I'm the man to whom

you've given your trust." He wanted to ask her why she still hadn't told him of the man's name, but decided she didn't need any pressure at the moment. So he wouldn't ask.

"You testified in court for how many days?"

"Four. But the worst of it all was that I had to take a physical examination to ensure the conviction. It was humiliating for strangers to have such personal information about me."

"How do you feel right now?" He held her a little closer, his lips barely grazing the top of her head. "Are you afraid?" He wanted to get the conversation back to their intimacy, and he knew it would be disastrous to linger over that calamitous experience. But he didn't want to give the impression of minimizing its importance, either.

"Talk to me, sweetheart. Don't you know that I'll protect you, even from my own need for you?"

"I know." She smiled, and he released his breath, unaware until then that he'd been holding it. She slipped her arms around his waist and leaned into his bare chest. The she begun to giggle, and he shifted her position to look into her face, his first thought being that she'd become hysterical.

But her face held a broad grin. "Do you know we're both setting her without a stitch of clothing?" He smiled. Though mirth was not what he felt, he figured that a little humor right then wouldn't hurt.

"Then let's get in bed. When I take off all my clothes, I'm either going to swim, take a shower or go to bed. And right now, I want to go to bed and take you with me."

"Don't you usually…you know?"

Then he did laugh. "Leslie, I can make love in the shower, in the bed and in the water. On the few occasions that I've done it anywhere else, I was in too big a hurry to take off anything."

Time to stop fooling around, lest he lose her. He focused into his longing and frustration. She'd curled into the bosom of his embrace, and he wondered if he was back to square one. Maybe. But he wasn't ready to give up.

He caressed her forehead, and she let him. "Leslie, did you have your eyes closed when I attempted to cover you with my body?" When she didn't respond, he persisted with the question.

"Yes."

She had relived the horror, the terror of that long evening. The man above her had no longer been the one so dear to her, but the brute who's almost taken her against her will. She had wanted so badly to come alive in Jordan's arms, to know at last what it was to have a man who loves her. But that repulsive ordeal of five years earlier had returned to haunt her, an ominous cloud. She vowed that she wouldn't let it deprive her of what might be the only joy she'd ever know with this man. She just wouldn't.

He spoke with a gentle but firm voice. "Leslie, if we separate right now, it's the end. I ache, Leslie. I'm hurt. And it isn't only physical pain, though there's that. I love you. I have never loved another woman the way I love you, and I've never needed one like I need you. But if it's what you want, we'll agree that my bringing you here was a mistake. We can remain friends. It's up to you."

Her silence must have fueled anxiety in him, for he urged, "Talk to me, Leslie. I don't have much more to give."

She pushed aside her misgivings and looked him in the eye. "I would as soon hurt myself, Jordan, as hurt you."

He shook his head, telling her it wasn't enough. "I need the answer to two questions, Leslie. Tell me in plain words, what do you feel for me?"

She didn't hesitate. "I love you; I've loved you for months."

As though careful not to appear threatening, he stroked her cheek with the back of his hand and asked the other questions. "Do you want me to make love to you? Here? We can't continue as we have been. This is it. Tell me."

He might as well know that, although what she'd just experienced might have drained her emotionally, the fire hadn't gone out of her. "I want us to make love right now, Jordan, but you stop dictating to me and giving me ultimatums."

He stared at her for a second, then threw his neck back and laughed uproariously. This was a funny way for them to say that they loved each other, barely touching, though there was sweetness about it. And it was even more comical that she should choose this moment to tell him off. But he got her point. She had her fire back, and she was ready for him.

CHAPTER ELEVEN

Jordan crawled up on onto the bed, easing her on to her back and stoking her long, enticing neck as he pulled her to him. "Kiss me?"

He'd never asked her before. She parted her lips and lifted her face to his. He began the kiss as an expression of what he felt, caring, tenderness, but it rapidly exploded into seething passion. His body pitched forward, intimidating the act of love, and she curled into him opening her mouth wider for more of him, her nails scoring his flesh and her nipples rock hard against his chest. Quickly, he harnessed his fervor and pulled back, all the while teasing and taunting her, plunging her further into a whirlpool of feverish desire.

"I love you, Leslie. Tell me right now that you trust me, that you know I'll take care of you."

"Yes. Yes. Just love me. Love me. I love you so much. So much!" Her voice, her body begged for action, but he wanted to give her everything, to make her certain that she was fulfilled and, for that, he needed to bring her to fever pitch. Instinctively, he knew she ran her hands down his long back and gripped his hard buttocks in an aggressive demand that surprised him. Impatient now, she found him and began to stroke him, but he jerked away. Nearly trembling from the force of the need she'd intensified in him, he tried to find something else to occupy his mind. But he could think only of her, so he corralled his thoughts and methodically kissed every inch of her, all but the sweet center, that gate of heaven that he so longed to enter. She

squirmed, urging him with her cries and the dance of her hips, but he denied her. He went back to her breast, kissing and sucking while his educated fingers danced on the nub of her passion. She cried out, begging him for release.

"Honey, I'll die if you don't do something to me."

He pressed his rigid instrument of love against her mound and le this tongue frolic in her mouth, loving her, tantalizing her.

She reached for him. "Get in me. In me!"

He took a minute to protect her. "All right, sweetheart, but I want you to look at me. Open your eyes and keep them open. I want you to know that it's me, Leslie. I want you to know that you're in the arms of the man you love. Look at me, baby. Don't close your eyes! It's me holding you, and it will be me inside you." He had never stopped caressing her and, as the signal of her readiness flowed over his finger, he knew that he had to move. She gazed at him expectantly as he rose above her.

"Now, sweetheart. Now. This is not something that I do to you, love; it's something that we do together. Raise your knees a bit and let me in."

She nodded, still wide eyed. Suddenly she smiled at him, and his heart kicked over.

"Ahh, sweetheart, I love you so!" He took her hand and clasped it around him. She gasped, but she didn't turn loose. He tried not to think that she was actually holding him in her fingers, as he guided her hand. When at long last he touched her portal, she stiffened.

"Relax, honey, and give yourself time, just like I'm giving myself to you." He reached the barrier. "This is the

most important thing that can happen to us, Leslie. But I have to hurt you now. I hate it, but it will only hurt just ones."

Her gaze didn't waver. "I know it's supposed to hurt." When he didn't press as fast or as hard as she thought he should have, she raised her hips to force his entry and experienced an excruciating flash of pain. She squeezed her eyes shut to stop the tears.

"Don't baby. It'll be over in a minute. Open your eyes." He pushed gently, and she clutched at him, wrapping her legs around his hips and pushing herself up to him, heedless of the pain. Tears of joy streamed from her eyes when, at last, she held him within her body.

He could hardly stand it. If he had known what awaited him, he would have gone mad wanting it. Almost immediately, he felt the sweet quivering of her hot velvet sheath. Forget it, he told himself. This is not for you. It's for her. Get hold of yourself.

"Are you alright, Sweetheart?" He kissed the tears that lingered at the corners of her wide brown eyes. The smile that fairly split her face told him everything. She nodded, but he hesitated, because he had to be sure.

She looked at him quizzically. "Who is supposed to move, me or you?" Next week, he would laugh like hell about that. Anxious to get started, was she? He merely grinned.

"Both of us, sweetheart. Both of us." And he began a gentle thrust.

She quickly caught his rhythm and, as he increased the pace, she kissed him wantonly, letting herself flow with the

passion that the excited her. He gloried in her passionate movements beneath him, meeting his thrusts as if they'd been making love forever. She locked her long sleek legs around him, grasping his buttocks with her hands, and her rhythmic spasms gripped him while they rippled through his body. He wanted her to reach the moon, and he thrust, teased and rotated his hips to see the she got there. But he was running out of time. The throbbing had begun. Her approaching climax squeezed and pinched him, sucking him in like quicksand. He had wanted to give her pleasure she'd remember forever, to remove any doubt that she belonged to him. But it was getting to him. He thrust powerfully again and again, as she called his name and let him know the indescribable joy of it. Control. He wanted more control so that he could give her everything. But he'd never experienced anything like the electrifying power of her passion and as she cried out, "Oh, Jordan. Jordan. I love you. I love you," he stumbled with her into the sweet, mindless oblivion of ecstasy.

When he finally was able to get his bearings. He levered himself to rest on his forearms and looked down at her. He wanted to smile, but he couldn't. She had shaken him to the very depths of his being. He wanted to tell her how he felt, but he couldn't describe it. Her face bore one enormous question mark but, for once, she seemed tongue tied. They simply looked at each other, drowning in each other, but unable to articulate their feelings. He saw tears glistening in her eyes and, without speaking, he bent forward and kissed her mouth, her eyes, and her whole face. As though sensing that the intensity of his emotions matched her own,

she curled into him and kissed him feverishly. He rolled to his side then, holding her tightly to him, while still buried deep within her. She had taken him out of himself, moved him beyond words.

Leslie awakened several hours later, still locked tightly to Jordan. His strong arms around her gave her the feeling that she floated somewhere in heaven, and she snuggled closer to him. She never wanted to leave him and never wanted any other man to touch her. She thought of how he'd made her feel, his tenderness and gentleness. And his patience. He'd made it seem so right, and it was right. She wasn't ashamed of her freedom with him. She thought of that moment when he'd slid fully into her for the first time. The feeling of him inside her, moving, stroking, while he kissed her lips and her breasts, setting her a fire and loving her. Even as he drove within her, mercilessly drowning her in sensation after sensation, he'd been tender and caring. The memory of it sent shocks plowing throughout her body, and involuntary spasms gripped her love tunnel. She swallowed the fluid that accumulated in her mouth and squeezed the fluid that accumulated in her mouth and squeezed him to her, kissing his beloved face and whispering endearment as she did so.

He opened his eyes and smiled. "Hi."

"Hi." A pulsating knot tied up her stomach when she realized that he hadn't been asleep, that he must have felt the evidence of her desire for him.

"You're a cheat." She punched him gently in the ribs. "You were playing possum."

He grinned and joined their lips in a passionate kiss. "Are you happy right now?"

"Happy? If I was lost in the middle of a dense forest and you found me, would I be happy? I can't explain what I feel? You made this a wonderful experience for me, and I doubt it can ever be duplicated."

He raised an eyebrow and smiled in the way of his that always made her think her blood had started flowing backward. "Can't be duplicated, huh? Let's see about that." He bent to her mouth, braced himself on his forearms, shifted his hips and took her on an ecstatic, whirlwind ride into sweet paradise.

With the traffic lighter than usual Monday afternoon as they headed back to the Estates, Jordan put the car on cruise control, got some chamber music on the radio and raised the question she'd expected since announcing her intention to go back to school.

"Why do you have to move to Baltimore just to write a thesis?"

"The graduate campus is there. I've asked the dean's office to look for small housekeeping apartment for me."

"I know the campus is there. After all, I've taught there full time. But if you've finished your classroom work and only have to write the thesis, why can't you stay home and dot it? Why do you want to move into a...a...What you'll be able to afford won't be bigger than a shoe box."

His reference to this home as being hers stunned her, and she took a minute to retrieve her balance. "I have thesis seminars on Tuesdays and Thursday afternoons. I don't have a car, and the bus is inconvenient. Also, I don't know

which professors will be on my committee. If they live on the campus, I need to be nearby, because they'll call meetings for their convenience, not mine."

She suspected that if he'd decided he didn't want her to leave the Estates, he'd use every legitimate means at his disposal to prevent it.

"You can ride in with me on Tuesdays, and either Cal or I will take you in on Thursdays and pick you up whenever you have to stay late, and you can live at home where you'll be comfortable." And that settles it, his tone implied.

And she would be dependent on him. But if they were to have a chance, she had to meet him as her own woman, not as a recipient of his benevolence. "I appreciate your offer more than I can say, but I think Baltimore is best. Anyhow, we'll see."

She didn't want to deviate from her course, but she was so full of him, and he'd completely captivated her that she wasn't sure she had the ability to deny him anything.

"Let me out at the front door, please," she asked him when they reached the Estates.

Jordan drove the car into the garage, got out and stood beside it, his mind warring with his common sense. He was damned if he'd ever understand Leslie. Why would a twenty-nine year old woman want to keep it a secret from the people closest to her that she slept with the man whom every one of them knew she loved? For what other reason would she have asked him to let her out at the front door? She was in for a surprise. Nothing escaped Julia. She'd validate her suspicions with one look at either one of them. He shrugged. If Leslie wanted it that way, he'd try not to expose

her. But hell, he felt like Sir Edmund Hillary must have felt when he reached the top of Mt. Everest, if he wasn't careful, he'd crow.

He caught up with her at the top of the stairs. "Why do you want to keep the fact that you spent the night in my bed? Are you ashamed of me?"

"Ashamed of you? How could I be? You have to understand that Mom said this sort of… of thing is private, and that it's bad taste to flaunt it even if you're married."

His irritation eased a little. "I see. I don't like it, but if that's what you've been taught…..Hell, how's a guy to crow? Where's the pleasure in winning a lottery if you can't spend the money?" He grazed he cheek with his left hand. "See you at supper."

Right after dinner the next afternoon, Leslie worked with Julia in the kitchen, and Jordan leaned against the doorjamb with his ankles crossed, his arms folded and his eyes on her. "I'm going to Dexter. Be back in time for supper."

He appeared to speak to both women, but his gaze didn't waver from her, and his knowing smile made her pulse skip. She tried not to focus on him because Julia watched her like an owl. Surreptitiously, of course.

Ever the mother, Julia handed him a cookie. "More where that come from."

He bit into it. "Glad to know it, `cause this is wonderful. But don't you put pecans in them any more?"

She told him she didn't have any fresh ones in the house. Leslie sensed his nearness, turned her head, and the kiss he'd aimed at the check caught her mouth. He held her

face in his hand, increased the pressure, and her arms wound themselves around his neck.

"Love me?"

She nodded. "Uh huh."

He rubbed his right index finger over the tip of her nose. "Me, too."

Minutes later she heard the motor of the Town Car taking him away. Julia patted her hair and walked over to where Leslie rolled out dough for pie crusts. "You look so pretty today. You're just blooming. Why don't you let your hair down around your shoulders the way he likes it? When I told him you didn't like his overalls, he bought some jeans, and that's all he's worn since, I tell you that shocked me, because Jordan always hated jeans."

"You mean you actually told him I said he looked ridiculous in—"

Julia laughed. "I thought it was funny, but he didn't. I do everything to please my Cal."

Leslie let out a long breath of exasperation. "Face it, Julia. You wouldn't mind if every man on this planet wanted you.'

Julia stared at her for a second before smiling at some unseen wonder. "You're right. It wouldn't hurt me a bit, because Cal wouldn't think of leaving home."

"You're a case, friend. I'm going to the groves for some fresh pecans. Call Cal and ask him to saddle Serenity for me."

She grabbed her coat from the hall closet and stopped as a recurring thought presented itself. She walked back into the kitchen. "I know you'd rather Jordan wasn't inter-

ested in me, and I know why. So I can't understand why you encourage us, why you urge me to look the way you think he wants me to look."

Julia stopped chopping celery. "I've got shortcomings, honey. Plenty of them. But I'm honest. I still think you'd both be better off with your own, but I love Jordan, and I want him to be happy. And the more I see of you, the more I understand why he cares for you. Besides, I've grown to like you a lot. I'll never move against you, unless you do something awful."

In for a penny, in for a pound. "And you wouldn't get out of joint if he married me?" Not that she'd do it, but it wouldn't hurt to get the issue out in the open.

Julia's shrug has been more assertive and definitely more nonchalant on other occasions. "In that case, I'd help you take care of your little café au lait babies."

Leslie sucked in her breath and decided to quit before one of them crossed a boundary. "Thanks. I think. I'll be back shortly."

When she got to the barn, Ossie awaited her, and he didn't seem pleased. "I thought Cal was—"

He interrupted her, "Cal is the ramrod. He doesn't have to play groom for anybody." He led the horse out of her stall, saddled her, folded his arms and waited for Leslie to mount. "Let's see how you handle this little exercise."

The blood rushed to her head, her breath came in pants and she shook in anger. She'd show him. She grabbed the reins, put her foot in the stirrup and slid onto Serenity's back, but as she did so, she tightened the reins, and the horse plunged into a gallop. Shards of ice pummeled her

heart and perspiration poured from her forehead. She heard his shout, far away like a shadow on the wind, but Serenity galloped on as though fleeing something supernatural.

"Whoa. Whoa."

She sensed a rider alongside her, but didn't see him, for she'd glued her gaze to the grove of trees that rushed toward her. His horse brushed her leg, and he grabbed the reins for her and brought the panic-stricken Serenity to a halt. She leaned forward, too exhausted and too frightened to speak. To her astonishment, he lifted her from the horse.

"I'm sorry, Leslie. I was needling you, just testing your mettle. I would never... Look, I'm... I'm ashamed that I almost got you injured or maybe worse. I thought I'd go crazy when Serenity took off like that. A spooked horse is dangerous. I...I hope you forgive me, because I would never intentionally cause you any harm."

She walked over to the nearest pecan tree and leaned against it. "At least you didn't let the horse kill me." She looked at him for a long time. "Do you know this is the first time you've addressed me by my name? Why do you dislike me so?"

He looked into the distance. "I don't dislike you. I just hate the idea of African-American women with white men."

She glared at him. "What about all these filthy rich African-American guys in sports and entertainment and some not-so-rich ones who have white wives and girl-friends? If that puts you out of commission, you must be a perpetual wreck.'

"Look, I'm not a bigot, and I don't feel like digging into myself to figure out why I think the way I do. I know his head as them bemused. "Why did you decide to ride out her alone?"

"I wanted to pick up some fresh pecans so I can make Jordan some brownies tomorrow, but I left the basket back there at the barn."

His white teeth flashed against his dark skin. Another first. He'd smiled. "Okay. Stay put. I'll go get it."

Minutes later her jumped off his horse and handed her the basket. "Come on, I'll help you."

They'd picked up about a quarter of a bushel when she decided to satisfy her curiosity about him. "How'd you get here, Ossie? I've learned that Jordan collects wounded people, including me. What was your situation, if you don't mind telling me?"

"Why should I mind? I'm an architect. A commercial building that I designed buckled beneath its own weight before the interior could be finished, killing several people. Up to that point, I was a corporate giant. The builder cut corners and used sub-standard materials, but I got the blame. I lost a class action suit and with it, my wife and everything I owned. Two years of scuffing from hand to mouth on the streets of Baltimore just about did me in. I stopped Jordan on the street one day with my hand out. He asked me what I'd do if I got a second chance. You know the rest. There's nothing on earth I wouldn't do for him."

"Will you practice your profession again?"

"I hope so. I've saved enough since I've been here to get that case re-opened. I don't want any money, just my name cleared."

She patted his hand. "I hope you succeed."

"What about you?"

A week earlier, she would have been ashamed to tell him, but knowing Jordan loved her in spite of what she'd experienced had freed her from unwarranted guilt. She gave him the essence of the story, adding, "I'm sure that being here has saved my life."

"No doubt about it. I get the impression that you're well educated. Am I right?"

"When I finish my thesis, I'll have earned my MBA."

He whistled. "Is that going to cause a problem with Jordan? Finishing the degree, I mean?"

She lifted her right shoulder in a shrug that was part hopelessness and part frustration. "I know what you're asking, but I don't know the answer. But you can bet I won't stop till I have that degree. Without it, I won't be able to take proper care of myself. A bachelor's degree doesn't get you far these days."

"Tell me about it." He cleared his throat. "Uh... I wouldn't take Jordan for granted. You'd regret it sure as I know my name." He stood and picked up the basket of nuts. "I'll carry these."

When she glanced warily toward Serenity who stood nearby, Ossie said, "Just don't jerk the reins when you get up. She'll be gentle as ever."

She couldn't help smiling at the concern in his voice. "Thanks."

He gazed up at her as she sat on the big bay mare. "Friends?"

"Friends."

She left Serenity for Ossie to groom and walked on to the house. One thing was certain; Ossie had not thrown pebbles at her window. She'd thought Faron the culprit, and now she'd bet on it.

She walked into her room after dinner the next Thursday afternoon as the phone ran. "Hello."

She listened, dumfounded, as the clerk in the dean's office told her she had a two-bedroom apartment in Embassy Suites on Charles Street.

"But I told you I couldn't afford more than four-hundred a month."

"It's been paid for full term, Mrs. Collins," the woman assured her in a dry, cracked voice that grated on Leslie's ear.

She didn't like the sound of it. She wouldn't put it past Faron Walker to go to that extreme to get her in his clutches. "I couldn't accept such largess from an anonymous benefactor, Miss Crane."

What sounded like someone clearing a throat reached her through the wires. "Well, it's a gift most of our students would give their eye teeth for. You're fortunate."

"I'm sorry, but I can't accept it not knowing who's giving it to me. So, would you please continue to look?"

She hung up and sat on the edge of her bed fighting a sense of doom. If Faron... She jumped up and walked from one end of her bedroom to the other and back, rubbing her hands up and down her thighs as she did so. Then she sat

down and collected her thoughts. Faron... But he'd lost his job, so how could he afford to? "That's it," she said aloud. Not Faron. Jordan. She grabbed her jacket and headed for the stables when she found Jordan saddling Casey Jones.

His smile nearly sapped her will, but she had to tell him, "I know you meant well, Jordan, but I can't accept it. I can't let you pay my rent."

He didn't pretend not to understand her. "I couldn't let you flounder around in a blighted area, dodging God knows what or who. You're bent on leaving here, and I... well, I want to take care of you."

"I appreciate that. I really do. But Jordan, where does that put me? You'd visit me and, who knows...you might even spend the night sometimes. Right? And how does that add up? Not so good, huh? And what will the dean think of one of the university professors is footing my bills? As much as I love you, Jordan, I think I'd better leave now and not wait for January. I can't let you take over my life."

The color drained from his face, but his words belied what that implied. "Think carefully before you make the move. I am not trying to get on my knees and beg you to take that apartment. I told you that this is your home for as long as you want it. Let me know your plans." He jumped on the stallion and headed toward the ravine.

Halfway to the house, she passed Cal, seeing and not seeing him. In her bathroom, she washed her tears from her face, though she hadn't known that she'd been crying. She went to her window and stared out at the rolling hills of Saber Estates, beautiful even in the absence of the foliage, flowers and green grass that made it to magnificent from

spring through early autumn. And once again, she knew that she had to face the peril of leaving home. Home! That's what the place has become to her. Home.

She dragged her old suitcase out of the closet and threw it on the bed. Then she phoned the YWCA in Baltimore and reserved a room for a week. In that time, she should be able to find a more suitable place. More dejected than she'd ever imagined she could be, she began to pack.

She barely noticed when the door sprang open. "Leslie. Leslie, can you check my math. Unca Jordan said I could get a riding lesson soon as I finish it. Leslie, where are you going?" She whirled around just as Clifford reached her. Oh, Lord! She'd forgotten all about him, she stood staring at him the way a guilty shoplifter eyes a store detective. And in her mind, she was guilty. She opened her mouth, but no sound came out. What could she say to him?

"Leslie, where are you going, Leslie?" Are you going to visit your Unca Frederick? Are you, Leslie? He rambled on, hopefully. "Maybe we could ask my Unca Jordan if I can go too. Can we, Leslie?" She sat on the bed and tried to gather her wits. Clifford struck one of his favorite poses, as he leaned against her with his elbows on her lap and his palms cupping his face as he looked up at her, full of love for her and confident in hers for him.

"Yes. Where are you going, Leslie?" They both looked up sharply as Jordan entered the open door. "I see you're packing." He commented, in a strangely soft voice.

Stung by his harshness, she nearly choked on her breath. She didn't want to leave him-not ever, but if she let him support her and be her lover, would she be better than

a kept woman? That wasn't the free and independent life which she had struggled so hard to achieve. She opened her mouth to speak, but no sounds came from her lips. She fought to retain her composure, and in her despondency, her weariness, she closed her eyes to the two precious beings that tempted her with treasures she couldn't accept.

"Unca Jordan, I think maybe she's going to visit her Unca Frederick. Aren't you, Leslie?" Jordan ignored Clifford, who had become agitated by Leslie's silence and her failure to answer him, even as the child ran to him for reassurance. Jordan walked to where Leslie sat, her hands folded almost as if in supplication.

"I don't think so, son. Where's you tongue, Leslie? Don't have the guts to tell him that you're leaving us, do you?"

The boy ran to Leslie, an expression of terror on his youthful face. Yet, he spoke with an icy calm. "Where are you going, Leslie?" His tone was that of one who has the right to an answer and knows it. She didn't look at either of them.

"I love you, Clifford," she said, her voice dull and hoarse, "but I have to leave. If someone will take me to the bus station, I'm going to Baltimore." He might have been programmed to do it, so rapid was Clifford's move from Leslie to stand beside Jordan, taking his uncle's hand in an unconscious groping for support.

"When are you coming back?" was the boy's next question.

"I..."

"She isn't." Jordan answered for her. Without another word, the boy bolted for the door. She reached blindly for the child as he disappeared down the hall.

"Clifford! Clifford! Honey—"

"Leave him alone. Nothing you can say will erase what you've just done. You've shattered his empire. Destroyed his security. Didn't you know that his world revolves around you?" His frigid voice chilled her. This was a different Jordan. A man who had distanced himself, who'd re-erected a solid wall between himself and her. If he cared, no one would have guessed it.

"Let me know when you're ready to leave." He turned on his heel and left.

She stared into space, confronting the onset of her loneliness. Why had they, both of them, behaved as if she'd done something wrong? Why hadn't they tried to understand? If she didn't do all she could to get her MBA on her own terms, she would not be a whole person. And if she let Jordan take care of her while she did it, she wouldn't respect herself. She blew out a deep breath and began to pack.

Leslie glanced around at the surroundings. Not the elegant Saber house, the big white Georgian with its high ceilings, numerous windows and spacious rooms. Slowly, she unpacked in the terrifying silence that brought sharply to the fore the magnitude of what she had done. There would be no tears and no regrets; she'd hammered into her mind during the silent ride with Jordan to Baltimore. The longest ride she'd ever taken. When she'd told him she preferred Cal to drive her, he had advised her that he'd take her. Acting the part of the powerful boss of Saber Estates for the

first time since she'd known him, he had coolly and dispassionately called her attention to his status.

"Cal is not available to drive you anywhere," he'd informed her in a frigid voice. When they had arrived at the YWCA, he'd taken her suitcase to the reception desk, placed it on the floor and turned to her.

"I gave you a home at Saber's for as long as you wanted it. I want you to remember that you were the one who decided to leave." He didn't give her time to answer, just turned and strode quickly away.

She tried not to reminisce, but she couldn't help it. She'd thought she knew how much all of them meant to her, but she hadn't. She hurt Clifford, and she doubted that he would forgive her. He had refused to tell her goodbye, locking himself in his room. So she had written him a letter and stuck it under his door. She hadn't been able to find Julia and Cal and realized that they, too, were avoiding having to say goodbye.

"What a mess I've made."

A week had passed, and she had to fight an encroaching feeling of desperation. She hadn't found better accommodations, hadn't done one bit of work on her thesis, hadn't gotten a part time job and hadn't been able to suppress her yearning for Jordan. She had written three letters to Clifford and one to Julia, thanking her for her friendship and kindness, but what she wanted most was contact with Jordan, and she could forget about that. By the end of the second week, she realized that she was developing a pattern that wasn't healthy; whenever she got into a deep blue funk,

she sat down and wrote Clifford, though she tried not to communicate her misery to him. He still hadn't written.

Jordan had spent hours going over every facet of his relationship with Leslie, and he'd concluded that her departure sprang from something far more crucial than his having paid her rent. He couldn't dismiss the gnawing certainty that Leslie had a reason for withholding from him the name of the man who pursued her.

Six days had passed, and his restlessness intensified. After dinner on a mid-week day when he'd normally have been working, he dressed and drove to Westminster. She'd given him enough information to enable him to estimate the time of that attempted rape, but his search at the library proved fruitless. Glancing at his watch, he figured that he had about forty minutes in which to chase a long shot. Using his name like the official passport that it was, he got to see the county clerk immediately, and an hour later, he had the information that he wanted. He thanked the clerk and headed back home.

He closed the door of his office because he didn't want to be disturbed. But now that he had the facts, did he really want to know them? He spread out the papers and saw at once what he looked for, a mug shot under which was printed Faron Walker, the man he had confronted at his garage door more than five months earlier. The man who was Leslie's attacker and who, the records said, had spent three years in jail for it. What did he want with Leslie? Certainly not to finish what he'd started? No. Vengeance! The man wanted revenge, because she'd had the guts to bring charges and testify against him. He'd been paroled

after having served three years of a five year sentence. The parole officer's note showed that, after the sentence, Walker lost his job, and his wife was granted a divorce and sole custody of their children. The man had haunted Leslie ever since his release. No wonder she'd had four addresses in the last two years. What he couldn't understand was why she had to refused to give him the man's name when she had most certainly known that he was her pursuer. And has surely known that after her uncle's visit.

He didn't want to care about Leslie, but he did. He read the trial records, noting that the defense attorney had been harsh and accusative with her, had attempted to portray her as a disputable woman. That explained why she didn't trust him fully and had been hell bent on protecting herself even when there no need. He went to find Cal. He needed to talk, but not to Julia. She was too judgmental and too biased in his favor.

Jordan sat staring at the man who for years had been his closest friend. "You're telling me that I ought to go to Baltimore and get Leslie? She left of her own accord, and she hasn't called or written me. The move is hers. Loving her doesn't mean that I have to be her doormat."

Cal snorted. "What's done is done, Jordan, and you can't change it. That woman is the one you want, and you're not going to be happy with any other. And I know you know it. Besides. Hasn't it occurred to you that if he followed her here, as remote as this place is, he'll find her in Baltimore where she has no protection?'

Jordan stiffened. "Of course it's occurred to me. But she doesn't want my protection or my help. That's why she left here. To avoid both."

"You're your own man, Jordan, but you're being pig headed right now. And you may be sorry."

CHAPTER TWELVE

Clifford was quieter than usual at supper that night, though he hadn't been his joyous self since Leslie had moved. Julia tried without success to make up for the shock of Leslie's leaving, but the boy rejected affection from any source.

"What's troubling you, son?" Jordan was as attentive as possible to Clifford, short of babying him. The child didn't answer, and Jordan patiently repeated the question.

"I don't think you want to know, Unca Jordan."

"Why not? I want you to tell me whenever anything bothers you. I may be able to help."

"You can't help this."

Jordan stopped eating and rested his knife and fork on the plate, suspicious that whatever was troubling Clifford had to do with Leslie. And he thought that strange, because the boy had barely mentioned her in the three weeks since she'd left.

"Try me."

"Unca Jordan, I think something must be wrong with Leslie. She was writing me every other day, but I haven't had a letter in almost a week. Could you call her and see if she's okay?"

Jordan stared, his eyes wide. He knew Clifford loved to get the mail and distribute it among them, but the boy hadn't mentioned any letters from Leslie. He'd almost pretended that she'd never existed.

"You want to talk with Leslie? I don't have her number."

"That's okay. I have it. She sent it to me."

"Then why don't you call her if you want to talk to her? There's a phone in every room, and you know how to dial."

Clifford's chin went out in defiance. "I don't want to talk with her; I just want to know she's all right." The adults looked at him. They had known that her leaving had hurt him but, until then, none of them had realized the depth of his grief. Trying desperately to control his quivering lips and nearly collapsing face, he spoke without looking up. "Aunt Julia, May I please be excused?" he asked, and left the table without waiting for permission.

"Damn!" Jordan was right on his heels. He'd had thirty-six years in which to learn how to take hard knocks, but Clifford was only eight. He put an arm around Clifford's shoulder, walked him into the den and got a second shock. The boy had memorized Leslie's number.

Jordan waited as the phone continued to ring. Uncomfortable. What would he say to her?"

"Miss Collins, please."

Clifford watched as his face must have registered his concern.

"Where is she?" He scribbled on a handy pad. "Thanks." Uncharacteristically disconcerted, he turned to the boy and spoke barely above a whisper. "Get your jacket, Son. We've got to go to Baltimore."

"What is it, Unca Jordan? What's happened to Leslie?"

Jordan clasped the child to him and hugged him tightly, knowing that he probably frightened Clifford even more.

"She's had an accident. That's all I know. Get your jacket, and let's go."

When Jordan arrived at the garage, Cal and Julia were waiting there along with Clifford, who had remembered to tell them, even if he hadn't.

They found Leslie in a hospital room for four, but two of the beds were unoccupied. Clifford rushed to her. "Leslie. Leslie, are you alright? What happened?" She reached out and hugged him as best as she could with one arm. Jordan stood over them, shocked at seeing her bruised and bandaged, unprepared for the pain that surfaced around his heart. He thought he'd suffocate. If only he hadn't let her go.

"Did the car run a light? The guy must have been speeding. Why couldn't he stop?" Useless questions, he knew. But he felt so helpless, seeing her like that. Her reply shook him to the core.

"Somebody pushed me from behind, Jordan. I'm sure of it. I was standing on the curb, when…"

"What?" All four of them spoke at one. Jordan sat down, it wasn't even a riddle. He'd get her out of there, and then he'd take care of everything.

"How much damage?" her asked her softly, preparing himself for the worst. She told him that she had a sprained left wrist, two broken ribs, a dislocated shoulder, a mild concussion and assorted bruises.

Clifford's face mirrored his grief. "Will you come back home with us, Leslie?"

She longed to tell him what he wanted to hear, because she had missed them all so terribly. She wanted to go back to the sweet haven of Jordan's love, to the warmth and security that she'd known among these people, but hadn't

known how to make the first move. She looked up at Jordan, who was waiting for her answer. She needed to know how he felt.

"Well?" Jordan asked her, his voice soft and his thoughts concealed. She nodded as her tears broke loose. Julia walked over and took Leslie in her arms.

"No need for tears. We all make mistakes, and you haven't missed us any more than we've missed you." She turned to Cal. "Honey, let's go down to the cafeteria. I want some coffee. Come along, Clifford."

But he wouldn't move. "I'm going to stay here with Leslie and my Unca Jordan."

"Would you please close those blinds?" Leslie asked Jordan. "The lights hurt my eyes."

Jordan moved to the window, closed the blinds and worked at getting his emotions under control. The minute he'd looked at Leslie, his feeling for her had almost over-whelmed him. He wanted to caress her and love her, to love away the hurt and bruises; he needed to hold her, protect her. Disconnected and unsettled by the force of his need, he squeezed her hand, walked back to the window, took a chair near it and calmed himself in the dark silence. She wouldn't get away from him again. Not ever.

Curious as usual, Clifford went to inquire about his uncle's mood. Almost immediately after the boy moved away from Leslie, a figure stealthily entered the room and moved toward Leslie's bed. Jordan was on his feet instantly and knew with certainty that he had his man.

He whispered to Clifford, "Tell the nurse to get the police. Go." And the boy went!

"Don't move another step, Walker." The man whirled around and, recognizing his adversary, lunged, but Jordan sent him to the floor with one solid uppercut.

"If you move a muscle," he told the man, "I'll finish you right here, right now. You weren't satisfied with trying to rape her, lying in court and causing him to be subjected to virginity test, following her around and even attempting to break in on her. You had to try to kill her." He glanced at the knife lying on the floor, as Leslie's blood-curdling scream rattled his eardrums, but he kept his attention on the man he'd wanted for so long.

"When that car didn't do the job for you, you came here to finish her off. Well, you'll be too old to hold a knife when you leave prison this time. If I have to use every dime I've got, I'll see that you rot behind bars."

His gaze shifted briefly to Leslie, who sat up in bed staring catatonic-like, her mouth open in a silent scream and her face awash with tears. He resisted the urge to give the man the beating of his life. Cal and Julia returned just as Clifford arrived with the hospital police.

When the officers took Faron Walker away in handcuffs, he screamed at Leslie. "I told you that I'd get you when I got out, and I will."

Jordan checked Leslie out of the hospital, hired an ambulance to take her back to the Estates and left the Town Car with Cal. Though Clifford wanted to ride home in the ambulance with Leslie and Jordan, Julia and Cal took him with them to collect Leslie's belongings and settle her bill at the YWCA.

Jordan carried Leslie up the stairs to her old room, laid her on her bed, knelt beside her and gathered her into his arms. "You're home now, and I want you to stay here."

Her lips quivered, and her eyes blinked rapidly, but a smile, weak though it was, claimed her face. God help him; he'd almost lost her. He took her mouth urgently but gently, sweetly and then hungrily, his desire sending fire at lightning speed through his body. But he put on the brakes and busied himself making her comfortable. As soon as he got Leslie settled, Jordan telephoned Franklin Collins, gave him a full account, and invited him to join the family for the holiday festivities.

Four days before Christmas Eve, Leslie was able to have her meals at the table, but she had energy for little else, and she still had not regained her sense of belonging in the household. She could see that they were happy to have her back, but she felt guilty for having left them and undeserving of their affection and caring. And Jordan. Not once since he'd kissed her after bringing her home had he so much as touched her finger. Cal's words jarred her brain: *If you leave him he may not be here for you when you've got your degree and your life fixed up and you decide you can afford to take a chance on him.* She needed Jordan desperately and wanted to reach out to him, but felt she had no right. What was she, anyway? Houseguest? Servant? Kept woman? She hated the position she'd put herself in. So she kept her distance, as much as it pained her to do it. If he had just once looked into her eyes and smiled a lover's smile, she would run to him.

After supper that evening, she went to her room. She hadn't wanted her little apartment anymore, though she was no longer in danger, and Jordan hadn't mentioned it. She wanted to be with them, a member of the "family." She took a leisurely bath, patted herself dry, put on a pair of red cotton pajamas and crawled into the bed. Minutes later, her nerves began a wild dance; only Jordan knocked with authority.

"Come in." She couldn't believe he'd come to her, for he'd paid her little attention since he'd brought her back to the Estates.

As usual, he didn't waste his breath on small talk when his mind was on a serious matter. "Leslie, we have to talk."

Those words unsettled her, because conversations beginning with the phrase more often than not involved something unpleasant. He ignored her frown and continued. "Let the past go. We care for each other and you know it. I'm not going to permit you to pretend that I'm nothing to you. And I'm through acting as if I don't want you and you don't want me. You haven't fooled Cal or Julia, and you're causing unnecessary discomfort for everyone around us. Hell, I'm just going to tell them we're lovers. They know it, and they'd be happy about it, if you'd just act normal. Every one of my workers knows how we feel about each other."

"Don't. Please don't."

He stared toward her then, and or his scowl, it wouldn't have surprised her if he shook her, and said, "I'm not asking your permission. Julia and Cal have been like parents to me, and if you think they can figure me out in a flat

minute, you're fooling yourself. They've had over a quarter century of practice. Make up your mind to accept it. If you were going to be ashamed of having made love with me, you shouldn't have done it."

She pulled the bedspread all the way up her shoulders. "A gentleman doesn't kiss and tell. And he doesn't go around bullying women, either." She'd gotten it out, but it sounded weak, because her heart wasn't in it. Yet if she didn't participate in the argument, he wouldn't have a reason to stay, and she didn't want him to leave.

"I told you. I'm a gentleman when it suits me. I won't have my household turned inside out because you won't accept the fact that you're a grown woman entitled to make love with an unattached man without anybody's permission except his. And another thing: you're not sweeping me under any carpet. No woman has ever tried it, and if you attempt it, I promise you faithfully that you will regret it."

He had reached the bed and was leaning over her, a scowl marring his handsome face. She scrambled quickly to the other side of the bed.

"Don't come near me. D… don't touch me, Jordan."

"Afraid I'll see you through that curtain you've thrown up? Afraid I'll show you that all I have to do is touch you and you'll melt in my arms? You're mine, Leslie. Mine! Just like I'm yours. And don't get any notions to the contrary. I didn't get where I am by lying down belly up and letting life screw me. So you level with me right now. If you plan to continue this farce, just say so and you'll be free from me. Permanently!"

He was making it easy for her. She looked at him and saw that his scowl had become something akin to naked pain. Impulsively, she reached toward him. But she knew that he wouldn't welcome such a gesture and let her hand fall weakly to the bed.

"You don't understand…"

He cut her off. "Don't I? I… Look…" He turned as if to leave.

She has to maintain some contact, to detain him, and she didn't stop to figure out how best to do it. "Jordan, please listen to me. It's not your reputation that's at stake. Or your independence. Or your self-respect that's…." He jumped across the bed and grabbed her, as furious as she'd ever seen him.

"What do you mean by that? Are you telling me that I've compromised you? Are you saying that having me inside your body damaged your self-respect? Is your memory so short that you've forgotten how you went wild beneath me? How you lit up like a ball of fire? Is that what happened to your self-respect? Damn you, woman. Damn you! You gave me a taste of paradise, and then you curse me for accepting it."

He leaned over her, his elbows on either side of her, trapping her. But she didn't feel trapped. What she felt was the heat from his nearness spreading through her, reminding her of what his body could do to her, how it could make her feel. Bathing her lips with her tongue, she raised desire-glazed eyes to him, vaguely groping for words that would deny his charge. She knew he saw her fire and that he rec-

ognized it for what it was—her need to have him locked himself inside of her.

"Oh, Leslie, baby, how can you be such a fool?" He bent to her mouth and when he touched her, she met him with lips parted and hungry. Already out of control, she reached for his belt as his hands dragged her pajama top away from her simmering body and claimed her turgid nipples. He raised his lips when she tugged his jeans out of the way. And then she found that already tumescent, sweet instrument of rapture and began caressing him lovingly and sending him to the edge. Her hands were magic on him, intuitively drawing fire with each knowing stroke. He had to stop her. If he didn't, he wouldn't last another second. But he didn't want to stop her. He wanted to let her take him all the way, but that kind of selfishness wasn't in his make-up. He was a giver. He pulled himself together and gently moved her hand.

Her shy glance reminded him that she was still a novice in the ways of loving. "Didn't you like that?"

"I loved it, sweetheart, but you were bringing me to the point of no return, and I want us to reach that together." He removed her pajama bottoms, his shoes and the remainder of his clothes, got up and locked the door. She gazed hungrily of him as he walked back to her in that well-lighted room, and let the sheet drop to her naked waist as she raised her arms. He trembled with need, and when she lay back and opened her arms to him, he'd never loved her more. Caught up in the maelstrom of their desire, he stumbled to the bed and took her to him.

Whether they'd wanted to give tenderness and sweetness along with their passion was no longer an option. They had been starved for each other, their needs for sharing themselves ignored: his rejected; she denied. Wanting, needing and demanding fulfillment, they went at each other as if only they existed, as if it were to be the last time. Her body shook, out of control, as it lifted itself to him, bobbing and weaving, jerking and swaying. She grabbed his buttocks and forced him to hold back on her account. To let himself go. She willed him to release himself to her, demanded all of him. He opened up, and their tumultuous coupling stunned them, a thing out of time—untamed and frenzied like wild waves crashing against an empty sound, boisterous thunder announcing a coming storm. He commanded her surrender, and she gave him everything. He covered her lips with his own and silenced he screams as the voluptuous pumping began. As they took. As they gave. And as they pushed each other over the edge until, at the apex of it, touched the sun.

When he squeezed her to him and pressed soft kisses to her face, she knew she no longer belonged to herself, but to him. Then and always.

They hadn't spoken. Stunned by the awesome power of his release, he lay above her holding her, wondering if he should simply get up and walk away. Never had been so completely at the mercy of his feelings. If there had been an immediately impending disaster, no matter how ominous, he wouldn't have been able to save himself or her. He had been immersed in her, totally besotted. He wasn't sure he relished losing himself so completely, even in the woman he

loved. She had dragged him out of himself, shown him a man he'd never known. She had rocked him, shaken him up, and he would never be whole without her.

Lying in Jordan's arms, Leslie, too, was unstrung. She loved him. God knew she did. But when she'd come tumbling down from that swirling cloud that he'd put her on, she had been scared senseless. She wouldn't take anything for the experience. But he'd had her on a rack, feeding her tantalizing little morsels of ecstasy, while she'd shamelessly evidence that, so soon after he'd given her all a woman could desire in a lover, she wanted him again. Embarrassed and too shy to ask for what she wanted, she slid out of his arms and went into her bathroom, hoping to get herself under control.

She walked back into the room to find Jordan sitting up in the bed. He didn't wait for her to speak. "What's wrong, Leslie? Having trouble coping with what just happened?"

She knew that he was covering his flank, and she didn't blame him. But she was too weary, too drained to care about face-saving. She shook her head slowly, indicating the muddled state of her thoughts.

"I feel as if I've been pole axed. And I feel like I've just left another world. Jordan, I want to run like the devil, but I don't want to leave you. And if I don't leave you, well..." She let her hands drop to her sides in a gesture of frustrations.

Her eyes were on him as he looked to the distance, seemingly seeing what wasn't there. He spoke softly, like a man who'd been humbled.

"It was like being in the tail of a tornado. And it was like having the gates of Heaven open wide and let me in. I may never recover from it. I certainly won't forget it. What are we going to do about it? Are you saying that you want out?"

"No. I don't think I could handle that. But Jordan, I don't feel right. I work for you and live in your home. I can't have an affair with you, and unless I move out, I'm not sure how that can be avoided."

"I haven't asked you to have an affair with me, Leslie. I don't want that with you. And I don't want you working for me as a cook or housekeeper, either. I want you to trust me enough to stop worrying about your independence. Enough to stay here, write your thesis and commute to the university for consultations and exams. If you insist on working, then be my business manager, my partner. Stop putting up barriers between us." He looked at her now and saw her hope, her fear, and her anxiety. It was risky, but he had to ask it.

"Why wouldn't you give me Faron Walker's name? You knew he was the one stalking you. Why?"

"I wanted to tell you. But he had called me several times before I came here and threatened me, and then he'd say that if I ever told anyone and he found out about it, he'd kill me."

"I wish you'd told me. Never mind. That's behind us now. He has twenty years to think about it. Come over here, Leslie." She moved closer and he took her hand in his.

"Sweetheart, I'm thirty-six years old, and my life still isn't on track. I've got everything that I want and need,

except my woman and the children I want with her. Marry me. Be my partner and the mother of my children. Build a life with me, Leslie. If you don't like this house, we'll build another one and give this one to Julia. I love you." He cupped her chin. "Look at me, baby. Will you have me for your husband and the father of your children?"

She stared at him. "Marry you? I... I want to, but..."

"But what?"

"I... don't know if I can handle the pressure, the animosity from total strangers. I'm honored that you want to marry me, but...I... I have to get used to this."

He got up. "All right. I'll give you a couple of days to get used to it, but Christmas Eve, I want to tell your uncle Franklin and everybody else that I want to marry you. While you're thinking, Leslie, ask yourself what's more important to you, society's blessing or living with me as my wife."

She reached toward him, involuntarily, he thought, but let her hand drop to her side without touching him. "What about children? Have you thought about them?"

He walked back to her, ready to knock down any barrier that she erected. "I'll take as many as you'll give me. I want to be a father. You understand? I want a family."

She nodded in an absentminded kind of way, and he looked at her for a long time, giving her an opportunity to react. When she said nothing, he tipped an imaginary hat. "See you at supper."

Jordan told her that he didn't want her to cook and clean, but she couldn't allow Julia to handle the work alone, especially at Christmas time. She stood at the kitchen sink

polishing silver and marveling that, at four-thirty in the afternoon, night had already fallen. A splash of rain hit the windowpane and a gasp escaped Julia, who worked nearby.

Leslie looked at Julia and didn't like the slump of her shoulders, not for a woman who prided herself in her figure and carriage. "What is it? Julia, what's the matter?"

Julia shook her head and wiped moisture from her cheek with the back of her hand. "Don't you think it's unusual that Cal's been out there since one o'clock in this weather? I can't call him. 'cause he forgot his cell phone. He's not out there in the rain because he wants to be."

Leslie draped an arm around Julia's shoulder. "I thought you were quiet because I'd displeased you in some way."

"No. I've just been...waiting to her his footsteps on the porch."

"If you think something's wrong, shouldn't you tell Jordan?"

"I didn't want to upset him, but—"

"Tell me what?" Jordan asked as he entered the kitchen.

Leslie's answer had barely passed her lips before he'd headed for the hall closet and his coat and hat.

"I'm going with you," Julia said, following close behind him.

When he saw that she wouldn't be discouraged, he gave in. "In that case I'll take the pick-up."

He helped Julia with her coat, pressed a kiss to Leslie's cheek, and left holding Julia's hand. Leslie telephoned Jack at the men's quarters and alerted him that Jordan might need assistance, put the silver away and got busy preparing supper.

Three-quarters of an hour later, the phone rang.

"This is Jordan. We're taking Cal to the hospital. His horse cracked his leg and fell, and Cal couldn't extricate himself. He's hurt, but I don't think it's too serious. Call you when I have more to tell."

It was almost midnight when she got Clifford to sleep. He'd eaten very little supper and had cried throughout the evening. Exhausted, she showered and got ready for bed.

"Where are you?" she asked when Jordan finally called.

"At Johns Hopkins Hospital in Baltimore. He's got three broken ribs and a sprained ankle. Go on to bed; we probably won't get back for another two hours. Stay sweet."

Leslie walked into the kitchen the next morning and stopped. If she'd been pole axed, she wouldn't have been more immobile. She hardly recognized the woman before her. Julia couldn't have slept one minute the previous night.

"I know what you're thinking, Leslie. I make a fuss about always looking good. Being perfect. And I know I look a mess, because I haven't washed my face since yesterday. But I don't care. What's important is my Cal. I like to look good for him, but it's more than that. If I lost him..." she spoke with difficulty. "I...I wouldn't want to live. He's my life. When we found him out there on that soggy ground trying to drag him back to me, do you think I thought about the mascara dripping into my eyes and down my cheeks? When I saw him half under that horse, I nearly died. Later maybe I'll fix myself up, but right now he needs me to look after him,"

She put some alcohol and water in a basin. "If you've got a man who loves you like my Cal loves me, you've got

the whole world. I've always known he doesn't care if my hair is stringy and my face looks as if somebody walked in it. He loves me, and I know it. It's a blessing from God, and that's the way I treat it. Don't be foolish and let it slip through your fingers."

Leslie prepared the breakfast, careful to cook the grits exactly as Cal liked them. She took a breakfast tray to him and Julia. It distressed her to see the big man propped up in bed and swathed in bandages.

"Don't look so sad," he told her. "I'm in this bed because my wife wants me to look after her. I'll be out of here Christmas Eve morning. If I'm not, we may have to take Clifford to the hospital."

Julia raised an eyebrow as though to gainsay his words. "Hump. That's not the way I heard it. The doctor said you're to stay in bed the next two days."

He held up a hand. "Okay. Okay. I have no aversion to your tender, loving care. With you to fuss over me and Leslie to feed me, maybe I ought to thank my poor old horse."

Leslie left them, pondering the love that she could feel flowing between them, a love that had bound them for over twenty-five years.

She needed to be away from all of them—Jordan, the Bakers and Clifford. She had to look at herself without blinds. Without ego. Jordan would stand by her, no matter what, but she wanted to be able to fight her own battles. Her chest nearly burst with pride. He loved her and wanted him for his wife. Would she care if somebody else didn't like the idea?

When she'd told Berle, her friend had vacillated, skirting the issue with the comment, "Well, if he's the one that rings your bell…Still, maybe you ought to look around and be sure."

She'd replied that, ninety years hence, she would still want Jordan Saber, and Berle had backed off. They would remain friends, but Leslie knew that their conversation wouldn't include Jordan. She buttoned her coat collar. Colder air was expected from the northeast that evening, and the change was already noticeable. She looked up at the dark clouds, tightened her scarf to ward of the damp cold and wondered if she'd soon see the first snow of the season. She peeped into the stable, saw no one. At least she could be alone and warm there. She sat on a bench with her back to the window and tried to imagine how she would have felt had it been Jordan rather than Cal who'd gotten trapped beneath his horse.

She could imagine Julia's alarm when she found her husband that way. Julia. Had she at last seen the real Julia? Not the femme fatale who had seemed to focus on outward appearances and to regard men as sources of ego enhancement. The Julia who'd braved cold, wind-blown sleet to find her man, who'd spend the night nurturing and caring for him with no regard for her soggy hair and mascara-mottled face and disheveled clothing. The woman who had discarded the outward trappings of femininity that she so staunchly touted, who had forgotten herself and her vanity and been there for her man when he needed her. The woman explained the Julia who could rise above her bias to embrace those for whom she cared. That woman who knew

the meaning of love. Did Julia love Cal more deeply than she loved Jordan? She didn't think it possible. Julia's words had shaken her to the depths of her being, and still they droned in her ears. Don't be foolish and let it slip through your fingers. If Jordan needed her, and she wasn't there....

She'd sat on the wrought iron bench in the encroaching darkness for more than an hour when the door opened.

"What're you doing sitting out here by yourself?"

She didn't want company, not Ossie's or anyone else's, for she still hadn't solved her quandary. "Hi, Ossie. It seemed a good place to sit and deal with ...with things."

"You must have some heavy duty thinking to do. Mind if I sit down for a minute?"

She shrugged. "I don't mind."

"It gets dark early these days, so you want to be careful about timing your moments of solitude out here in the stable. How're things, with you and Jordan? He seemed pretty preoccupied all day."

She picked up a handful of hay and let it fall like chaff through her fingers. "We're the same, except more so."

His hearty laugh did little to cheer her. "That's doubletalk. You mean the two of you are getting no place fast?"

She released a long breath and decided to spill it. He could be trusted for Jordan's sake, if not for hers. "He asked me to marry him, Ossie, and I don't know, I just don't know."

His whistle split the silence. "He asked you to marry him, and you don't know what? Do you love him?"

What a time for tears to want to spill out of her eyes! "Yes, I love him."

"He loves you, too. So what's the problem?"

"I've got one girlfriend, and she doesn't think it's such a hot idea. You were against it, and so was Julia. I want people to be happy for me when I get married, not frowning and causing problems. I've weathered my share of storms, but going up against half the country on something this important... I don't know."

"I'm surprised at you. You'd impressed me as a woman with spunk. What the hell do you care what people think as long as you love the man and you know you're his world. Get yourself another girlfriend, or walk down the aisle without a maid of honor. Let him go, and you'll down on the inside long after your tears stop falling. Been there, friend. Hell, I wouldn't spend thirty seconds worrying about it. Come on, I've got to close up, it's get—"

"What's going on here? What are you two doing huddled up out here in the damned stables?"

Ossie knocked back his hat and looked up at Jordan.

"You're kidding, man. Get it together. If you don't know you're head honcho with this woman, you need your head examined. You gonna lock up, or you want me to wait and do it?"

Jordan shoved his hands into the pockets of his jeans. "What's this about, Leslie? Are you interested in Ossie?"

Ossie stood. "I'll see you two later. Good luck, Leslie."

"See you, Ossie." She patted the portion of the bench that Ossie has just vacated. "Want to sit down?"

"You're not planning to answer my question?"

She lifted her left shoulder and lowered it, reflexively. "Do you need an answer?"

He didn't sit. "He's a good looking man, intelligent and competent. I'm sure lots of women have wanted him."

"And I suppose you're not good looking, intelligent and competent. Huh? Don't you realize that in my life, I have loved only you?"

"But not enough to be my wife?"

She stood and clasped his precious face in her hands. "I love you to the recesses of my soul."

His hands went to her waist, and his heat began to furl around her, to draw her into him. She heard the rain stabbing at the window, or was it her blood pounding her head? He backed off and gazed at her with eyes fiery and wanting, mesmerizing, drawing her to him, a flame seducing a moth. She sucked in her breath, wanting him to touch her. Anywhere. Just put his hands on her. Her nipples itched for his fingers, and she rubbed them. He grabbed her, lifted her and she locked her legs around him and pressed herself to his bulging need. But when she thought he would kiss her, claim her, shudders seemed to pass through him, and he gently set her away for him.

Thunder screamed and played its loud games above them, and she sought the shelter of his body but, again, he placed gentle hands on her shoulders and moved her from him.

"What is it? What's the matter? You don't believe Ossie—"

"No. I don't believe it. I'm trying to tell you that I am not interested in crumbs, little pieces of you. I want all or nothing. If we're not going to spend our live together. I

don't want any more teases, mind-blowing tidbits of what I'd have if you were my wife."

Icy splinters darted around her heart. "I won't let you walk away from me. I won't. Hold me. Honey, hold me. I need you. I need you!"

His hands went around her, and she reached up and locked her hands behind his head. "I want a lot of things, but I need you." She swallowed the sobs that nearly poured from her throat. "I don't want to live without you."

He stepped back from her. "Whatever you'll face. I'll face with you. If it hurts you, I'll feel the pain. I'll always be there for you. For the last time, will you be my wife?"

The window blazed with the dazzling display of lightning and the sound of thunder roared through the darkness, but she looked only at him, thought only of him. If he walked away from her, her soul would go with him. She didn't hesitate. "I'll marry you whenever you're ready. Tomorrow, if that's what you want."

He pulled her into his arms and locked her to him. "You're sure? We're dealing with our lives. You won't regret it. I promise you that."

She nodded. "As sure as I am of my name.'

At last she felt his mouth on her, and she didn't hold back. It was a though he hadn't banked her fire, but had stoked it to brilliance. She let her hands roam over him, stopping and fondling wherever they chose. His tongue circled her lips asking for entrance, and she opened to him and let herself succumb to the inferno he built in her. His left hand went to her right breast, stroking and squeezing until she ripped the snaps from her denim shirt and gave

him her treasure. He suckled her until she couldn't control the moans that rose in her throat.

"Do you want me?'

She tried to climb his body…"Yes. Yes"

He stripped off most of her clothes, spread their jackets on the hay at his feet, and laid her there. He gazed toward the door, rushed over and slipped the latch. He stood over her for a minute, a half wild expression on his face. But when he lowered himself to her, the flashes of lightning revealed only love. He removed the remainder of their clothes.

"I don't have any protection for you. When did you last have your period?"

"Due tomorrow. It's safe."

She found him and began the magic strokes, but he stilled her, held both of her hands above her head and bent to her breast. Flames seemed to shoot straight to her lover's tunnel. She writhed beneath him, wordlessly begging for relief. His hands replaced his lips; she bucked beneath the feel of his mouth on her belly.

"Jordan. Oh, Lord, honey, I'm going crazy. Please."

For an answer, he parted her secret folds and kissed her. And kissed her. Her screams mingled with the pounding rain and the never ceasing thunder. He kissed her belly and let his fingers play her lover's lyre until he knew she was ready for him.

He found his home inside her, and she wrapped her arms and legs around him, and immediately he swept her up in a tidal wave of heat and passion. She couldn't bear the pleasure. Hew as deep in her, over her, under her, all around

her. The thunder roared above their head, lightning became a neon light letting them stare into each other's eyes, and the wind and rain howled and pounded all around them. Through it all, he stormed within her, loving her, branding her until the pumping and throbbing caught her. Thunder crashed around her and in her until she erupted in ecstasy and sand with him into sweet delirium.

"Jordan. Jordan. My darling. My love, I love you so."

She'd drained him once more, he thought to himself, as he lay there on the straw locked in her arms. But this time, he revealed in it. This time, he didn't feel as though he'd just been rationed a portion of her loving.

"I didn't know I could be so happy," he told her. But you know, I'm thirty-six. This sort of thing may be too much for a man my age."

"Are you serious?" She put her hands over her head and stretched like a sated feline. "First time we did this, you were busy again ten minutes later."

He grinned in that devilish way that she loved. "I was stating my case. We've got all night for that. I'll help you get supper and clean up so we can get started early. Come on."

"Are you going to tell the others?"

His expression suggested that he might not have heard her correctly. "Soon as I step into that house. And another thing, figure out how soon we can get married. I don't want to wait."

She reached for her shirt. "No problem. I don't either. By the way, Ossie was telling me how stupid I was to worry about what people would say if we got married. He said I only had to know that you love me and I love you."

He laughed. "I figured that out even before he got his back up."

He helped her dress, locked the door, took her hand and sprinted home.

"Julia, we're getting married," he said as they entered the kitchen.

She looked at Leslie, "I see you came to your senses. And about time, too." She hugged them. "Take care of each other. I can't wait to tell Cal."

He got a bottle of Veuve Cliquet from the refrigerator. "Could you get us a couple of stem glasses, honey?"

He eased the cork from the bottle of champagne, filled their glasses and held up his own. "I'll love and care for you 'till death do us part, and maybe after that."

She raised her glass. "To my only love."

He got two more glassed. "Let's drink the rest of it with Julia and Cal. Supper can wait."

Dear Reader,

I hope you enjoyed Leslie and Jordan, their struggles to overcome the impediments and adversities that threatened to torpedo their relationship, and their battle against a hostile society and with their own feelings and prejudices. I found in Jordan Saber the decency, sweetness and tenderness that only a truly strong man can evince and in Leslie Collins the strength and determination that characterize so many of our women. I believe Ossie Dixon offsets Jordan perfectly, because he shows that decorum is not a monopoly of the privileged, that when dignity is an inmate part of a man, nothing—including poverty, misfortune or the position he occupies—can hide that dignity.

Thank you for you support of all my books, including *Naked Soul*, my first one for Genesis Press. I treasure the letters and e-mails that I have received lauding this book. If you have not already purchased a copy, you'll be glad to know the Genesis Press released *Naked Soul* in trade paperback in August 1999.

Don't forget to keep my mailbox full or to e-mail me if you have access to the Internet. I love hearing from my readers. If you enclose a self-addressed, stamped envelop, I'll answer within three weeks and enclose information about what I'm up to. You may write me at P. O. Box 45, New York, New York 10044-0045 or e-mail GwynnelF@aol.com You'll find lots of information about me and my books on my web page at http://www.inofkart.com/gwynneforster.

Best Wishes,
Gwynne Forster

ABOUT THE AUTHOR

Gwynne Forster was born in North Carolina and grew up in Washington, D.C., where she lived before going to New York to work as a demographer at the United Nations. When she left the United Nations to form a working partnership with her husband. She was chief of the Fertility Studies section of the Population division. As such, she she was responsible for research and analysis of social, economic, cultural and demographic factors and conditions that influence fertility levels and trends throughout the world. The studies were published under the United Nations imprimatur and in the name of its Secretary-General. She lives in New York City with her husband (who is also a demographer) of twenty-five years. She hold bachelors and masters degrees in sociology and a masters degree in economics/demography as well as graduate credits from Columbia University. As a demographer, she has been widely published. Her extensive travels for the United Nations and later for the International Planned Parenthood Federation (London Office) have taken her to Brazil, Mexico, most European countries and throughout Asia, Africa and the Caribbean. Her work on these trips includ-

ed representing the Secretary-General of the United Nations, lecturing, conducting workshops and delivering research or policy papers at conferences. She has acted as president of the Board of Directors of the volunteer library that serves the eight thousand people who live in her community. She is currently a member of the board, and occasionally volunteers at the library. Since becoming a published author of romance novels, Gwynne has lectured on various phases of the writing business. At the 1995 *Romantic Times* (RT) Conference in Dallas, she lectured on techniques of selling a manuscript, including writing query letters and synopses and relating the story orally and in writing to agents and editors. She also spoke on these topics at Howard University Seminar in June 1995, and also at the March 1996 annual conference of Romance Writers of America/New York City Club (which was convened in Melville, Long Island). She held a workshop on the subject on the subject at the 1996 Romantic Times conference in Baton Rouge, Louisiana. She also lectured on fiction writing at the African American Women Writers Conference. This was held at the University of the District of Columbia in April of 1997. Since February 1998, Gwynne has lectured on all aspects of fiction writing at the branch libraries for the Queens Borough Library System. She is also a freelance non-fiction writer. Her last article is a profile for Kofi Annan, United Nations Secretary-General, the cover story

of the April/May issue for *Crisis Magazine*. Crisis is the media organ of the NAACP. Pinnacle/Arabesque published her second novella, A Perfect Match which is part of the *I Do* anthology (a Valentines Day anthology in February 1998 and released her fourth full length novel, *Obsession*, in April 1998. Genesis/Indigo published *Naked Soul*, Gwynne's first hard cover romance, in June 1998. Gwynne's previous books include *Sealed with a Kiss* (October 1995), *Against All Odds* (September 1996) and *Ecstasy* (July 1997). Her first novella, Christopher's Gifts, is included in the *Silver Bells* anthology. All were published to wide acclaim by Pinnacle/Arabesque. She is represented by the James B. Finn Library Agency, Inc., P.O. Box 28227 A, St. Louis, MO 63132. Readers may right her at P.O. Box 45, New York, NY 10044-0045. Or by the web at http://www.infokart.com/forster/tgwynne.html or by email GwynneF@aol.com.

January

A Lover's Legacy
Veronica Parker
1-58571-167-5
$9.95

Love Lasts Forever
Dominiqua Douglas
1-58571-187-X
$9.95

Under the Cherry Moon
Christal Jordan-Mims
1-58571-169-1
$12.95

February

Second Chances at Love
Cheris Hodges
1-58571-188-8
$9.95

Enchanted Desire
Wanda Y. Thomas
1-58571-176-4
$9.95

Caught Up
Deatri King Bey
1-58571-178-0
$12.95

March

I'm Gonna Make You
Love Me
Gwyneth Bolton
1-58571-181-0
$9.95

Through the Fire
Seressia Glass
1-58571-173-X
$9.95

Notes When Summer
Ends
Beverly Lauderdale
1-58571-180-2
$12.95

April

Sin and Surrender
J.M. Jeffries
1-58571-189-6
$9.95

Unearthing Passions
Elaine Sims
1-58571-184-5
$9.95

Between Tears
Pamela Ridley
1-58571-179-9
$12.95

May

Misty Blue
Dyanne Davis
1-58571-186-1
$9.95

Ironic
Pamela Leigh Starr
1-58571-168-3
$9.95

Cricket's Serenade
Carolita Blythe
1-58571-183-7
$12.95

June

Cupid
Barbara Keaton
1-58571-174-8
$9.95

Havana Sunrise
Kymberly Hunt
1-58571-182-9
$9.95

July

Love Me Carefully	No Ordinary Love	Rehoboth Road
A.C. Arthur	Angela Weaver	Anita Ballard-Jones
1-58571-177-2	1-58571-198-5	1-58571-196-9
$9.95	$9.95	$12.95

August

Scent of Rain	Love in High Gear	Rise of the Phoenix
Annetta P. Lee	Charlotte Roy	Kenneth Whetstone
158571-199-3	158571-185-3	1-58571-197-7
$9.95	$9.95	$12.95

September

The Business of Love	Rock Star	A Dead Man Speaks
Cheris Hodges	Rosyln Hardy Holcomb	Lisa Jones Johnson
1-58571-193-4	1-58571-200-0	1-58571-203-5
$9.95	$9.95	$12.95

October

Rivers of the Soul-Part 1	A Dangerous Woman	Sinful Intentions
Leslie Esdaile	J.M. Jeffries	Crystal Rhodes
1-58571-223-X	1-58571-195-0	1-58571-201-9
$9.95	$9.95	$12.95

November

Only You	Ebony Eyes	Still Waters Run Deep – Part 2
Crystal Hubbard	Kei Swanson	Leslie Esdaile
1-58571-208-6	1-58571-194-2	1-58571-224-8
$9.95	$9.95	$9.95

December

Let's Get It On	Nights Over Egypt	A Pefect Place to Pray
Dyanne Davis	Barbara Keaton	I.L. Goodwin
1-58571-210-8	1-58571-192-6	1-58571-202-7
$9.95	$9.95	$12.95

Other Genesis Press, Inc. Titles

A Dangerous Deception	J.M. Jeffries	$8.95
A Dangerous Love	J.M. Jeffries	$8.95
A Dangerous Obsession	J.M. Jeffries	$8.95
A Drummer's Beat to Mend	Kei Swanson	$9.95
A Happy Life	Charlotte Harris	$9.95
A Heart's Awakening	Veronica Parker	$9.95
A Lark on the Wing	Phyliss Hamilton	$9.95
A Love of Her Own	Cheris F. Hodges	$9.95
A Love to Cherish	Beverly Clark	$8.95
A Risk of Rain	Dar Tomlinson	$8.95
A Twist of Fate	Beverly Clark	$8.95
A Will to Love	Angie Daniels	$9.95
Acquisitions	Kimberley White	$8.95
Across	Carol Payne	$12.95
After the Vows	Leslie Esdaile	$10.95
(Summer Anthology)	T.T. Henderson	
	Jacqueline Thomas	
Again My Love	Kayla Perrin	$10.95
Against the Wind	Gwynne Forster	$8.95
All I Ask	Barbara Keaton	$8.95
Ambrosia	T.T. Henderson	$8.95
An Unfinished Love Affair	Barbara Keaton	$8.95
And Then Came You	Dorothy Elizabeth Love	$8.95
Angel's Paradise	Janice Angelique	$9.95
At Last	Lisa G. Riley	$8.95
Best of Friends	Natalie Dunbar	$8.95
Beyond the Rapture	Beverly Clark	$9.95
Blaze	Barbara Keaton	$9.95
Blood Lust	J. M. Jeffries	$9.95
Bodyguard	Andrea Jackson	$9.95
Boss of Me	Diana Nyad	$8.95
Bound by Love	Beverly Clark	$8.95

Other Genesis Press, Inc. Titles (continued)

Other Genesis Press, Inc. Titles (continued)

Falling	Natalie Dunbar	$9.95
Fate	Pamela Leigh Starr	$8.95
Finding Isabella	A.J. Garrotto	$8.95
Forbidden Quest	Dar Tomlinson	$10.95
Forever Love	Wanda Y. Thomas	$8.95
From the Ashes	Kathleen Suzanne Jeanne Sumerix	$8.95
Gentle Yearning	Rochelle Alers	$10.95
Glory of Love	Sinclair LeBeau	$10.95
Go Gentle into that Good Night	Malcom Boyd	$12.95
Goldengroove	Mary Beth Craft	$16.95
Groove, Bang, and Jive	Steve Cannon	$8.99
Hand in Glove	Andrea Jackson	$9.95
Hard to Love	Kimberley White	$9.95
Hart & Soul	Angie Daniels	$8.95
Heartbeat	Stephanie Bedwell-Grime	$8.95
Hearts Remember	M. Loui Quezada	$8.95
Hidden Memories	Robin Allen	$10.95
Higher Ground	Leah Latimer	$19.95
Hitler, the War, and the Pope	Ronald Rychlak	$26.95
How to Write a Romance	Kathryn Falk	$18.95
I Married a Reclining Chair	Lisa M. Fuhs	$8.95
Indigo After Dark Vol. I	Nia Dixon/Angelique	$10.95
Indigo After Dark Vol. II	Dolores Bundy/ Cole Riley	$10.95
Indigo After Dark Vol. III	Montana Blue/ Coco Morena	$10.95
Indigo After Dark Vol. IV	Cassandra Colt/ Diana Richeaux	$14.95
Indigo After Dark Vol. V	Delilah Dawson	$14.95
Icie	Pamela Leigh Starr	$8.95
I'll Be Your Shelter	Giselle Carmichael	$8.95

Other Genesis Press, Inc. Titles (continued)

Other Genesis Press, Inc. Titles (continued)

Naked Soul	Gwynne Forster	$8.95
Next to Last Chance	Louisa Dixon	$24.95
No Apologies	Seressia Glass	$8.95
No Commitment Required	Seressia Glass	$8.95
No Regrets	Mildred E. Riley	$8.95
Nowhere to Run	Gay G. Gunn	$10.95
O Bed! O Breakfast!	Rob Kuehnle	$14.95
Object of His Desire	A. C. Arthur	$8.95
Office Policy	A. C. Arthur	$9.95
Once in a Blue Moon	Dorianne Cole	$9.95
One Day at a Time	Bella McFarland	$8.95
Outside Chance	Louisa Dixon	$24.95
Passion	T.T. Henderson	$10.95
Passion's Blood	Cherif Fortin	$22.95
Passion's Journey	Wanda Y. Thomas	$8.95
Past Promises	Jahmel West	$8.95
Path of Fire	T.T. Henderson	$8.95
Path of Thorns	Annetta P. Lee	$9.95
Peace Be Still	Colette Haywood	$12.95
Picture Perfect	Reon Carter	$8.95
Playing for Keeps	Stephanie Salinas	$8.95
Pride & Joi	Gay G. Gunn	$15.95
Pride & Joi	Gay G. Gunn	$8.95
Promises to Keep	Alicia Wiggins	$8.95
Quiet Storm	Donna Hill	$10.95
Reckless Surrender	Rochelle Alers	$6.95
Red Polka Dot in a World of Plaid	Varian Johnson	$12.95
Reluctant Captive	Joyce Jackson	$8.95
Rendezvous with Fate	Jeanne Sumerix	$8.95
Revelations	Cheris F. Hodges	$8.95
Rivers of the Soul	Leslie Esdaile	$8.95

Other Genesis Press, Inc. Titles (continued)

Rocky Mountain Romance	Kathleen Suzanne	$8.95
Rooms of the Heart	Donna Hill	$8.95
Rough on Rats and Tough on Cats	Chris Parker	$12.95
Secret Library Vol. 1	Nina Sheridan	$18.95
Secret Library Vol. 2	Cassandra Colt	$8.95
Shades of Brown	Denise Becker	$8.95
Shades of Desire	Monica White	$8.95
Shadows in the Moonlight	Jeanne Sumerix	$8.95
Sin	Crystal Rhodes	$8.95
So Amazing	Sinclair LeBeau	$8.95
Somebody's Someone	Sinclair LeBeau	$8.95
Someone to Love	Alicia Wiggins	$8.95
Song in the Park	Martin Brant	$15.95
Soul Eyes	Wayne L. Wilson	$12.95
Soul to Soul	Donna Hill	$8.95
Southern Comfort	J.M. Jeffries	$8.95
Still the Storm	Sharon Robinson	$8.95
Still Waters Run Deep	Leslie Esdaile	$8.95
Stories to Excite You	Anna Forrest/Divine	$14.95
Subtle Secrets	Wanda Y. Thomas	$8.95
Suddenly You	Crystal Hubbard	$9.95
Sweet Repercussions	Kimberley White	$9.95
Sweet Tomorrows	Kimberly White	$8.95
Taken by You	Dorothy Elizabeth Love	$9.95
Tattooed Tears	T. T. Henderson	$8.95
The Color Line	Lizzette Grayson Carter	$9.95
The Color of Trouble	Dyanne Davis	$8.95
The Disappearance of Allison Jones	Kayla Perrin	$5.95
The Honey Dipper's Legacy	Pannell-Allen	$14.95
The Joker's Love Tune	Sidney Rickman	$15.95

Other Genesis Press, Inc. Titles (continued)

The Little Pretender	Barbara Cartland	$10.95
The Love We Had	Natalie Dunbar	$8.95
The Man Who Could Fly	Bob & Milana Beamon	$18.95
The Missing Link	Charlyne Dickerson	$8.95
The Price of Love	Sinclair LeBeau	$8.95
The Smoking Life	Ilene Barth	$29.95
The Words of the Pitcher	Kei Swanson	$8.95
Three Wishes	Seressia Glass	$8.95
Ties That Bind	Kathleen Suzanne	$8.95
Tiger Woods	Libby Hughes	$5.95
Time is of the Essence	Angie Daniels	$9.95
Timeless Devotion	Bella McFarland	$9.95
Tomorrow's Promise	Leslie Esdaile	$8.95
Truly Inseparable	Wanda Y. Thomas	$8.95
Unbreak My Heart	Dar Tomlinson	$8.95
Uncommon Prayer	Kenneth Swanson	$9.95
Unconditional	A.C. Arthur	$9.95
Unconditional Love	Alicia Wiggins	$8.95
Until Death Do Us Part	Susan Paul	$8.95
Vows of Passion	Bella McFarland	$9.95
Wedding Gown	Dyanne Davis	$8.95
What's Under Benjamin's Bed	Sandra Schaffer	$8.95
When Dreams Float	Dorothy Elizabeth Love	$8.95
Whispers in the Night	Dorothy Elizabeth Love	$8.95
Whispers in the Sand	LaFlorya Gauthier	$10.95
Wild Ravens	Altonya Washington	$9.95
Yesterday Is Gone	Beverly Clark	$10.95
Yesterday's Dreams, Tomorrow's Promises	Reon Laudat	$8.95
Your Precious Love	Sinclair LeBeau	$8.95

Contents

MAPS

Acknowledgments

THIS BOOK came into being through the efforts of a number of generous people. To the following scholars, all of whom made at least one vital contribution, I extend my warmest thanks: Morris Opler, Fred Eggan, Harry Hoijer, Emil Haury, Bernard L. Fontana, and Dan L. Thrapp. During the early stages of planning, when it was by no means certain that all the necessary arrangements could be made, I was aided repeatedly by Raymond H. Thompson and Harry T. Getty. I am very grateful to them, and also to Edward H. Spicer who kindly consented to provide a biographical sketch of Grenville Goodwin for inclusion in this volume.

I am equally mindful of the assistance provided by William Kessel and E. W. Jernigan. Working with Goodwin's original notes, Kessel spent many hours locating on contemporary maps places that were of significance to the Western Apache over a century ago. The work was difficult, tedious, and not always rewarding. Had it not been performed, however, the geographical dimension so vital to a full appreciation of Goodwin's materials would be lacking.

The information obtained by Kessel was transformed into the maps that accompany Part I by E. W. Jernigan. In my opinion, these maps reflect not only the skills of a highly talented draftsman but also Jernigan's sensitivity to the importance that land and travel had for the pre-reservation Apache. Jernigan also helped select the photographs which illustrate the book and chose the basket design for the jacket. It should be obvious that my debt to him and Kessel is a very substantial one.

Grenville Goodwin was a linguist, as well as an ethnographer, and his field notes on raiding and warfare were liberally interspersed with Western Apache words and phrases. In order to disclose as fully as possible the morphological and semantic structure of these native terms, linguistic research was conducted for ten weeks on the Fort Apache and San Carlos reservations in east-central Arizona during the summer of 1969. Funds for this work were provided first by a grant from the American Philosophical Society and later, when the data were being processed and re-analyzed, by the American Indian Oral History Project, at the Arizona State Museum, University of Arizona. I am deeply grateful to both these institutions for their support.

Many Apaches helped me during this "linguistic" phase of the project, and I thank them all—not only for the information they so willingly provided but also for their quiet encouragement to make public a view of history they consider their own. I am especially indebted to Morley Cromwell, Annie Peaches, Nashley Tessay, Ernest Murphy, and Francis Dehose—all of Cibecue on the Fort Apache Reservation—and to Ned Anderson and Philip Casador of Bylas and San Carlos respectively.

While at work on the manuscript, I had access to the manifold resources of the Arizona Pioneers' Historical Society and the benefit of full cooperation from its talented staff. Sidney Brincker-hoff, director, gave freely of his enthusiasm and knowledge and was extremely helpful in other ways as well. I also want to thank Carol S. Baker, who prepared an excellent preliminary typescript and made valuable suggestions concerning matters of style. The final draft was typed in expert fashion by Melody J. Brancato.

From start to finish, Marshall Townsend, Douglas Peck, and editor Elizabeth Shaw—all of the University of Arizona Press—gave counsel that was unfailingly relevant and consistently helpful. Each made a special contribution and each deserves special thanks.

My greatest debt and final acknowledgment is to Mrs. Janice Goodwin, who graciously presented her husband's Apache materials to the Arizona State Museum and (probably with some misgivings) agreed to let me edit them. Mrs. Goodwin did a great deal of work organizing the field notes and supervised entirely their initial typing. I am deeply grateful for her help, friendship, and cooperation, and I hope that in her eyes, as well as in those of others who knew and admired Grenville Goodwin, this volume gives testimony to his accomplishments and the spirit in which he worked.

KEITH H. BASSO

WESTERN APACHE
RAIDING AND WARFARE

Grenville Goodwin—1938

Grenville Goodwin: A Biographical Note

by Edward H. Spicer

To Grenville Goodwin we owe most of what understanding we
have of the way of life of the Western Apaches. Few have tried
seriously to learn what that way of life was, and even fewer have
written effectively about it. The abundant literature on the Western
Apaches, inspired in great part by the spectacular forays of
Geronimo and his predecessors, is largely a literature of the white
men who fought the Indians and participated in the final, relentless
roundups. It is not a literature from which emerges a view of the
values by which Apaches lived. But for the work of Goodwin,
we would have lost almost all opportunity to participate in the
Apache world.

There was Cremony, of course, and there was Crook's
chronicler, Captain John G. Bourke, both of whom were writers
of vivid prose and both sympathetic to Apaches. But skill and
good intention were not enough. To learn the way of life of others,
and to present one's understanding successfully, requires more
than literary art. It requires first a kind of selflessness, a willingness
to suspend one's own existence temporarily while coming to
appreciate another view of the universe. Cremony's capacity for
this was extremely limited, and he was in a good deal of a hurry
anyway when he wrote his memoirs. Bourke, a gifted writer who
told good stories, became deeply interested in observing and in
seeking to understand the premises of Apache life; but his own
life was too full of other things by the time he started. Thus the
period of transition from free to reservation life remains in-
adequately interpreted. In contrast with the Plains Indian the
Apache had no interpreters of culture who looked from the inside
outward—no squaw men, articulate war chiefs, or others to give
us an interpretive literature of that other Indian-way. It is perfectly
true, as modern Apaches insist, that there is no written Apache

This is an expanded version of a biographical sketch that first appeared in *Arizona and the
West*, Vol. III, No. 3, Autumn, 1961, pp. 201–04.

history, only white men's history; Geronimo is the only Apache autobiographer, and his ghosted story tells little of Apache life. Goodwin almost singlehandedly learned enough to put us on the right track.

How did Goodwin get beyond the externals which have become familiar in works like those of Lockwood, Wellman, and others who have portrayed Apache life from the viewpoint of the white military campaigner? It was not through an elaborate training in any school of anthropology. Goodwin studied little formal anthropology before beginning his Apache work. He was not armed with course notes on field techniques or on theories of primitive society. He later made an effort to gain such special knowledge because he learned as he went along that this could be a source of deeper understanding of what he had found out by his own methods. He began with little more than that basic essential—a humble desire to know what it was like to be born and raised an Apache. The techniques for learning were instinctive in his make-up.

Goodwin began simply by going to live for the greater part of three years with Apaches at Bylas, Arizona, on the San Carlos Reservation. He knew that he could not push himself at people, and so he got a job—assistant to the trader in the Bylas store— which gave him a place in the community. In this capacity he came to know many families, most of whom were of White Mountain Band origin, in the eastern part of the San Carlos Reservation. He came to know them; they came to know him. Quiet and reserved, he made acquaintances rather slowly. He gathered information in a way which suited the people with whom he worked. He plied no one with a stream of questions. He visited and chatted. He sought older people who wanted to talk about old times. He was a master listener. Today Apaches on the San Carlos Reservation often mention Grenville Goodwin. They say: "He used to come and sit around on the ground in the evenings. The old people liked to talk with him." On this basis his friendships developed and he was invited to every kind of gathering—whether medicine sing, puberty ceremony for girls, or tulapai party. He went, and his knowledge deepened. Anthropologists call this "participant observation"—for Goodwin it was "getting to know people."

Goodwin was born on Long Island, New York, in 1907. For his college preparation he was sent to the Mesa Ranch School in Arizona. From that time, he was a dedicated Southwesterner. While at the Mesa Ranch School he became acquainted with Dean Byron Cummings, who encouraged him to come to the University of Arizona to study anthropology. Dean Cummings was an important figure in Southwestern archaeology, but it was the Dean's humanism and attitude toward Indians which attracted Goodwin. At first he followed the lead of Dean Cummings and made some trips among the Navajos, but from the start his interest in the Apaches had been deep. At this time, in 1931, Dean Cummings was beginning his first excavations on the Fort Apache Reservation Kinishba, and he gave Goodwin steady encouragement. Goodwin was not interested in earning an academic degree and, once he had decided what he wanted to do, he did not continue in classes. He went to live at Bylas, and from then on throughout his short life his whole attention was devoted to the Apaches.

For the next ten years Goodwin extended his acquaintance throughout the Fort Apache and San Carlos reservations. Besides Bylas, he studied the communities of Fort Apache, Canyon Day, and Cibecue. His specialty in ethnology became the White Mountain rather than the San Carlos people. Nevertheless he travelled with Apache companions to all parts of the Western Apache territory, including the Tonto area; and at the time of his death he had visited many places in Sonora and Chihuahua, as well as in the United States, which figured in important ways in Western Apache history. He never claimed more than twenty-two months in the field, but this was undoubtedly an understatement which referred to periods of continuous residence only.

Goodwin never bothered to earn a degree of any kind, although he carried out some graduate work at the University of Chicago just before he died. In his fieldwork he had become acquainted with professional anthropologists, particularly those from the University of Chicago who were studying the language and ethnology of the Eastern Apaches. In 1931 he met Morris Edward Opler, student of the Chiricahuas, and gained much inspiration and practical advice from him. At the same time he gained acquaintance with Harry Hoijer of the University of Chicago, and learned from him methods of transcription of unwritten languages. Without Goodwin's knowledge of the Western Apache language and his ability to transcribe phonetically the native names for what he was studying, much of the value of his work would have been impaired. These and other friendships, such as with Leslie Spier and with John Provinse in Tucson, brought him increasingly into contact with the whole field of anthropology and greatly enriched his work.

The first publication by Goodwin came in 1935 with a paper in the *American Anthropologist*, and through the late 1930s he published occasionally in various journals. He was determined to prepare himself, by further study, to analyze and publish his extensive store of field notes. In 1937 he was asked by Scudder McKeel, social anthropologist in John Collier's Bureau of Indian Affairs, to advise in connection with laying foundations for a tribal government organization among the San Carlos Apaches. Goodwin's report, still unpublished but available in the files of the Bureau of Indian Affairs and the Department of Anthropology of the University of Arizona, was a pioneer effort in applied anthropology.

In 1939 Goodwin went to the University of Chicago for graduate study in anthropology, and to complete a monograph on which he had been working under the guidance of Professor Fred Eggan. In the same year he was appointed Research Associate in the Arizona State Museum. Goodwin's work with Eggan and Hoijer at the University of Chicago resulted in his major contribution, the widely known monograph entitled *The Social Organization of the Western Apache*. One of the most detailed and best-documented studies of Indian social organization, this volume has made its author a major figure in North American ethnology.

The book was published posthumously. As he completed the last pages, Goodwin contracted a brain tumor and died suddenly in June, 1940. He was buried in Tucson, where he had decided to take up permanent residence with his wife and a child named for one of his Apache friends. It was to have been his headquarters for a projected lifetime of work to be devoted to interpretation of the Western Apaches. Goodwin had planned a series of monographs. He had hoped to follow his study of social organization with one on religion, and had taken the notes with him to Chicago. This monograph was never written.

Grenville Goodwin's death did not, however, cut short his contributions to the understanding of the Western Apaches. His field notes turned out to be voluminous and recorded in great detail, with careful attention given to the transcription of Apache words and phrases. It became clear that the excellence of the monograph on social organization rested on meticulous field techniques and that his notes covered far more than the area of social organization which he had chosen for first publication. During the years following his death, the extensive notes on religion and other topics were transcribed by his wife, Janice, from the many pages of longhand. And graduate students at the University of Chicago, under the direction of Fred Eggan, began the task of editing the notes for publication.

It was not, however, until 1969 that the right combination of circumstances was realized for making Goodwin's materials available. Mrs. Goodwin, the Department of Anthropology of the University of Arizona, and the University of Arizona Press arranged for the careful editing and publication of the whole body of notes. The editing is being carried out by Keith Basso, who has done intensive fieldwork among the Western Apaches throughout the past decade. The project will extend over several years, so great is the volume of notes Goodwin left behind.

The present publication dealing with raiding and warfare is primarily based on the personal narratives of six Apache men and women whose life experiences included the last phase of Apache life when raiding was still an important aspect of their adaptation. Although some of the informants did not themselves take part in raids and war parties, they were well informed through parents or grandparents who did participate. The information was gathered by Goodwin over several years and was widely checked with other Apaches. The high quality of this material is similar to that which characterizes his notes and publications on religion and social organization. In this and subsequent publications solid knowledge of Apache life during the period preceding reservation conditions will be steadily rounded out.

The Western Apaches are fortunate in having a student of their way of life as talented and dedicated as Grenville Goodwin. We are all fortunate that his contributions will continue even after his too-early death.

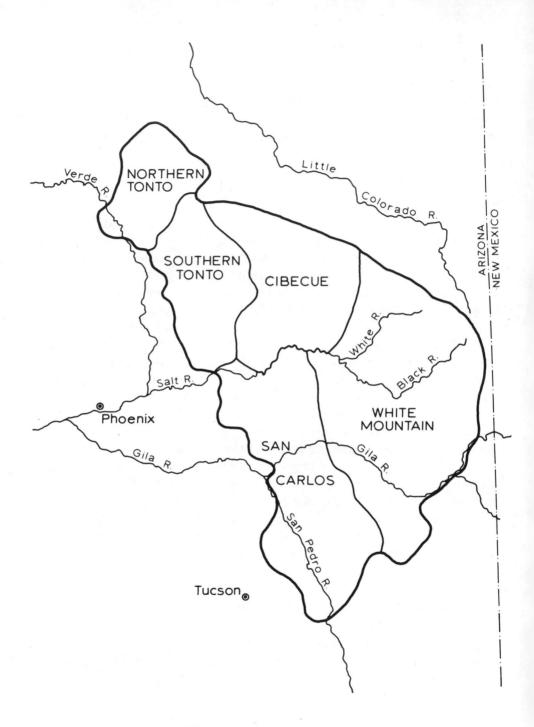

Western Apache Subtribal Groups

Introduction

OF THE MANY GROUPS of American Indians whose subsistence
activities formerly included raiding and warfare, few are as familiar
to the general public as the Apaches of Arizona and New Mexico.
Widely renowned for their tenacious resistance to U.S. military
forces in the late nineteenth century, these people have been
glorified by historians, glamorized by novelists, and distorted
beyond recognition by commercial film-makers. Apache war
leaders such as Cochise, Geronimo, and Victorio have become the
victims of exaggeration and caricature, a fate which has left them
enshrined in contemporary folklore as the epitome of bellicosity
and brutality. Indeed, one is led to conclude that "the Apache" —
and just who or what this might be is often difficult to tell — has
been transformed from a native American into an American myth,
the haunting symbol of a vanished era in the history of the Southwest.

Given the popularity of the myth and the basic validity of the
symbol, it is interesting to take note of a statement made in 1931
by the anthropologist Alfred L. Kroeber:

In terms of precise knowledge, the Apache are, with the possible exception of the Objibwa, the least known surviving North American group
among any of like areal extent or historical importance. [1931:35]

At the time Kroeber was writing, virtually nothing was known
about the Apaches ethnographically. P. E. Goddard, one of the
founders of American anthropology, had collected several volumes
of Apache myths in the vicinity of San Carlos in 1915–16 but,
for reasons that are not entirely clear, his investigations ended
there. Of course, the reports of Army personnel were available to
scholars, as were journals of travellers and missionaries, but in the

[9]

main the cultural information contained in these sources was meagre and superficial. It was not until the 1930s, by which time the several remaining Apache tribes had been settled on reservations, that ethnographic fieldwork began in earnest. Almost entirely through the efforts of three men—Morris Opler, the linguist Harry Hoijer, and Grenville Goodwin—the cultures and languages of the Chiricahua, Mescalero, Jicarilla, Lipan, and Western Apache were described and rendered intelligible.

Although these scholars presented data about raiding and warfare that frequently contradicted the Apache myth, few of their publications treated the subject in isolation. Opler, in particular, was concerned to show that raiding and warfare were elements in a total cultural system and should be studied in context, that is, in relation to other elements. Consequently, emphasis was placed less on the development of raiding and its adaptive consequences than upon the manner in which it articulated with other social institutions. This approach made sense to anthropologists, especially those interested in functional models of society, but it was essentially synchronic in character and therefore had limited utility for students of ethnohistory and culture change. This may help explain why, as late as 1962, Edward H. Spicer was able to observe:

There is simply no book which tells the story of changing Apache life during the past hundred years. Even less is there represented in the literature anything which relates the facts about the crystallization of the raiding complex during Spanish times to the sequence of later events. [1962:593]

If southwestern ethnologists can be faulted for paying insufficient attention to Apache history, professional historians have been equally guilty of an almost total neglect of what is known about Apache cultures. For purposes of illustration, let us consider a single tribe, the Chiricahua. What was the political organization of these people? And how did their division into three subtribal units affect the conduct of military activities? How were raiding parties organized? And how did these expeditions, which were bent on the capture of livestock, differ from those whose objective was to avenge the death of a warrior killed in battle? What qualities did the Chiricahua consider necessary for leadership in war? To what extent did ritual considerations influence the planning and implementation of military strategy? How were new warriors recruited from the ranks of adolescent boys? And what became of captives?

The answers to these and other seemingly relevant questions have been available since the publication in 1941 of Opler's classic Chiricahua ethnography, *An Apache Life-way*. Yet, for some reason, they seem never to be asked by non-anthropologists and, as a consequence, find no place in chronicles of the developing Southwest and the so-called "Apache wars." This does not necessarily result in bad history. But it has led to an unfortunate situation in which, as B. L. Fontana (1968:447) aptly observes, ". . . Apaches are essentially an 'x' in the historical equation."

The trouble with too many "x's" is that they foster myths. All too often, "the Apache" has been portrayed as a figure barren of ideology, devoid of values, and somehow—miraculously— exempt from the inevitable constraints imposed by membership in a society. He is a man without culture and therefore he is an impossible man. Is it any wonder that the survivors, the Apaches who live today on reservations in Arizona and New Mexico, ". . . complain constantly that all the history which is in print misrepresents them." (Spicer 1962:593)

The remarkable documents that comprise this volume—all of them verbatim narratives by Western Apaches—provide detailed information about raiding and warfare that is simply unavailable from any other source. As such, they stand as a major contribution to the data of North American ethnography and the history of the American Indian. More important, these narratives give extraordinary insight into the Apache themselves who, once divested of their acquired mythological trappings, become instantly more believable and altogether human. It is entirely fitting that the work of Grenville Goodwin has given the Western Apache an opportunity to be their own historians and autobiographers—a right and privilege that should have been accorded them long ago.

MANY OF THE NARRATIVES in this collection can be read and appreciated without reference to ethnographic and historical facts, but the majority call for supplementation in the form of a statement which describes (1) the basic components of Western Apache culture and social organization as it existed prior to 1850, and (2) the major events that took place after the Western Apache came into sustained contact with U.S. military forces and were drawn into the Chiricahua campaigns of the 1870s and '80s.

Linguistically affiliated with Athapaskan-speaking peoples in Alaska, Canada, and northern California, the Apacheans (or Southern Athapaskans) were intrusive to the American Southwest. Prehistorians place the time of their arrival in this region between A.D. 1000 and A.D. 1500, but the exact routes they travelled and the chronology of their migrations from the north have yet to be precisely determined (Hall 1944).

By the late 1500s, the Apacheans had separated into several smaller groups and spread over a vast region extending from central Arizona to northwestern Texas. In the centuries that followed, these groups became progressively more isolated from one another and, adapting to local ecological conditions, developed the linguistic and cultural characteristics which were to distinguish them in historic times. On the basis of these characteristics, anthropologists have divided the Apacheans into seven major tribes: the Jicarilla, Lipan, Mescalero, Chiricahua, Navajo, Kiowa-Apache and Western Apache.

Grenville Goodwin (1935:55) designated as Western Apache: "Those Apachean peoples who have lived within the present boundaries of the state of Arizona during historic times, with the exception of the Chiricahua Apache and a small band of Apaches, known as the Apache Mansos, who lived in the vicinity of Tucson."* The totality of people thus designated—Goodwin estimates that between 1850 and 1860 there were approximately four thousand—were divided into five subtribal groups that occupied contiguous regions in the eastern and central portions of Arizona (See Map I).

The White Mountain Apache, easternmost of the subtribal groups, ranged over a wide area bounded by the Pinaleño Mountains on the south and by the White Mountains on the north.

---

*Most of the data presented here on pre-reservation Western Apache culture come from Grenville Goodwin's ethnography, *The Social Organization of the Western Apache*. For additional information, the interested reader should consult Goodwin 1935, 1937, 1938, 1939.

To the southwest, near the foothills of the Santa Catalina Mountains and on both sides of the San Pedro River, lived the San Carlos Apache. The territory of a third group, the Cibecue Apache, extended north from the Salt River to well above the Mogollon Rim; its western boundary was marked by the Mazatzal Mountains, homeland of the Southern Tonto Apache. The Northern Tonto, which of all the Western Apache subtribal groups lay farthest west, inhabited the upper reaches of the Verde River and ranged north as far as the present community of Flagstaff.

Altogether, the Western Apache occupied a territory of nearly 90,000 square miles (Getty 1964:27). Characterized by great ecological diversity, it is a region of jagged mountains and twisting canyons, of well-watered valleys and arid desert. Elevations rise from 2,000 feet above sea level to slightly less than 13,000, and temperatures fluctuate from near zero in the winter to well above 100 degrees during the months of July and August. Precipitation ranges from about ten inches at the lower elevations to twenty or thirty at the higher altitudes. The flora varies correspondingly, from essentially desert types, including a large number of cactus species, to heavy stands of conifers, cottonwood, and oak. Wild game in the form of deer, elk, wild turkey, bear, and javelina is plentiful.

Although the Western Apache engaged in subsistence farming, their economy was based primarily on the exploitation of natural resources and the spoils of raiding. Goodwin (1937:61) estimates that agricultural products made up only 25 percent of all the food consumed in a year, the remaining 75 percent being a combination of undomesticated plants, game animals, and stolen livestock. Because they could not rely on crops throughout the year, the Western Apache did not establish permanent residence in any one place. In fact, except for early spring, when farm-plots were seeded in the mountains, and early fall, the time of harvest, they were almost constantly on the move.

Despite the fact that the five Western Apache subtribal groups —the Cibecue, San Carlos, White Mountain, and Northern and Southern Tonto—spoke a common language and intermarried to a limited degree, they considered themselves quite distinct. Open conflict among the different groups was rare, but it should be emphasized that they never formed anything like a unified political body. The territorial boundaries of each group were clearly defined, and it happened occasionally that trespassers were forcibly expelled or killed.

Each of the subtribal groups was divided into from two to four smaller units which Goodwin termed *bands*. Band distinctions were not as marked in some groups as in others, but each had its own hunting grounds and, except when pressed by starvation, did not encroach upon those of its neighbors. Using military censuses, it is possible to compute a mean size for Western Apache bands between 1888 and 1890. This figure comes to 387 individuals, but there was considerable variation in both directions. For example, the San Carlos band of the San Carlos subtribal group had only 53 members, while the Eastern White Mountain band of the White Mountain group numbered 748. Although bands were characterized by an internal unity somewhat greater than that of subtribal groups, they did not participate in any form of joint political action. As Goodwin (1935:55) put it, "Bands were units only in the sense of territorial limitations and minor linguistic similarities."

Bands were composed of what were unquestionably the most important segments of Western Apache society, what Goodwin referred to as *local groups*. In his words: "These were the basic units around which the social organization, government, and economic activities of the Western Apache revolved" (Goodwin 1942:110). Local groups varied in size from as few as thirty-five persons to as many as 200, but each had exclusive rights to certain farm sites and hunting localities, and each was headed by a chief who directed collective enterprises such as food-gathering expeditions, farming projects, and activities involving other local groups and tribes.

The lack of solidarity characteristic of subtribal groups and bands was replaced at the level of the local group by a high degree of cohesiveness, primarily because most of the individuals who comprised these units were related by blood or marriage and, as such, felt obligated to aid each other in any way possible. A substantial number of marriages took place within the local group and, in fact, this seems to have been the desired arrangement. Charles Kaut gives what is probably a sound explanation:

Basically, people who had grown up in the same area could operate
together as a better economic team. . . . Gathering activities, especially,
required a very specific knowledge of rough terrain which could only
be gained over a period of many years. The man's main economic
activities were centered around hunting and raiding, which also required
extensive training and integration into a tightly organized group. A
man hunted best on his home ground, both because he knew it so well
and because he garnered power from the very ground itself—a power
which he lost when he entered other hunting grounds. He was trained
for war and raiding by his mother's parents, his father, his elder brothers,
and his mother's brothers. . . . For these reasons, a local group which
drew its members from the same general area could operate more effi-
ciently than one which contained many men who were strangers to its
territory. [1957:63–64]

In order to understand some of the important differences
between raiding and warfare, it is essential that mention be made
of the Western Apache clan system. Unlike bands and local groups,
clans were not spatially distinct. Members of the same clan lived
scattered throughout Apache country, thus creating an extensive
network of relationships that cut across bands and local groups
but at the same time joined them together.

Let us suppose, for example, that a man who lived in a local
group of the Western White Mountain band belonged to the clan
dɛsčidn ('horizontally red people'). Such a man was almost certain
to have clan relatives in the Eastern White Mountain band, the
San Carlos band, and several others as well. He could travel
throughout the territories of these bands and, having identified
himself to his fellow dɛsčidn, expect to receive food and lodging.
In this way, the clan system served to extend the benefits of kinship
far beyond the local group and establish viable ties between
individuals who normally lived at great distances from each other.

All told, there were sixty-two Western Apache clans. The
members of each considered themselves related through the
maternal line, the descendants of a group of ancestors who established farm sites at the clan's legendary place of origin. Although
persons belonging to the same clan were forbidden to marry,
they were expected to aid each other whenever the need arose.
Beyond these obligations, however, and the important but somewhat restricted influence of clan chiefs, there was little in the way

of clan government or law. The clan's main functions were to regulate marriage and facilitate concerted action in projects requiring more manpower than was available in a single local group.

All but a few Western Apache clans claimed affiliation to one of three mythological clans and, on this basis, were grouped into phratries (Kaut 1957:40). Phratry members were not allowed to marry and, like persons belonging to the same clan, were bound by obligations of mutual support. For this reason, the phratry, like the clan, served as an indispensable means for recruiting participants in activities—most notably war parties—that required the cooperation of large numbers of people.

THE WESTERN APACHE drew a sharp distinction between "raiding" (literally: "to search out enemy property") and "warfare" ("to take death from an enemy"). As translation of the native terms suggests, raiding expeditions were organized for the primary purpose of stealing material goods, preferably livestock. War parties, on the other hand, had as their main goal to avenge the death of a kinsman who at some earlier time had lost his life in battle. The differences between raiding and warfare went considerably further than this, however, and it will be helpful in orienting the reader to discuss briefly other characteristic features of each.

Raids were organized in response to a shortage of food. Whenever it became apparent that the meat supply of a local group was running low, some individual, usually an older woman, would publicly draw attention to the fact and suggest that plans be made to capture enemy livestock. Within a few days, it was expected that a man with previous experience in raiding would step forth and volunteer his services as leader. Having announced when he intended to leave and against whom the raid would be directed he issued a call for followers. All able-bodied men were eligible to go, providing they had participated successfully in the so-called "novice complex," an extended period of instruction during which adolescent boys were introduced to both the practical and ritual aspects of raiding.

Raiding parties were normally composed of from five to fifteen men. (Larger numbers were discouraged because the success of a raid depended almost entirely upon being able to travel without being seen). The party proceeded slowly until it moved into enemy territory. Here the pace quickened, special measures for conceal- ment were taken, and a number of taboos went into effect, including the use of a special "warpath language." More than anything else, Western Apache raiders were anxious to avoid armed conflict— not out of fear, but because it would reveal their position and numbers, alert the enemy for miles around, and increase the chances of being intercepted on the way home.

Raids usually took place in the early hours of the morning. Two or three men approached the enemy's herd on foot and moved it as silently as possible in the direction of an open trail. Here the livestock was encircled by the remainder of the party and driven off. Speed was imperative on the journey home, and it was not unusual for returning raiders to go without sleep for as many as four or five days. As soon as the party was secure within the borders of its own territory, a messenger was sent ahead to inform those who had stayed behind in the local group that the venture had been a success.

Men who had captured livestock were entitled to give it away to whomever they chose, in most cases to close maternal kinsmen. In addition, however, they could be prevailed upon by female non-relatives who, either by singing for a raider, or dancing with him in the context of a ceremonial called *inda kɛ ʔho ʔndi* ('enemies their property dance') obligated him to present them with at least one animal. These customs had important economic consequences for they helped assure the even distribution of livestock throughout the local group and not just among the families of raiders.

Whereas raiding parties drew their personnel almost entirely from the men of a single local group, war expeditions were recruited primarily on the basis of clan and phratry. It was up to a warrior's maternal kinsmen to avenge his death, and this responsibility applied to clan and phratry members as well as to those more immediate relatives who resided in his local group. Although the latter took it upon themselves to sponsor the expedition, the former were always asked to participate and, apparently, never refused.

When the decision was made to prepare for war, the chief of the slain warrior's local group sent messengers to clan chiefs in other local groups inviting them to convene at an appointed spot. Here, all the men who planned to take part in the expedition joined in a ceremonial called *ʔikałsita ʔ* ('going to war'). Warriors from each clan were called upon to dance and speeches were made encouraging them to "think of angriness, fighting, and death." This was in sharp contrast to the members of raiding parties, who were instructed to avoid combat unless it was absolutely necessary.

War parties were composed of as many as two hundred men under the direction of a single leader. In addition, they contained at least one shaman, or "medicine man," whose primary task was to encourage proper conduct on the journey to enemy territory and, through the use of supernatural power, to look into the future and predict the outcome of the impending conflict.* Prior to battle —if chances for victory appeared good—the shaman might also perform a short ceremonial which was believed to give protection against the enemy and instill the will to fight.

Warriors preferred to attack the town or settlement where their kinsman had lost his life, and sometimes it was possible to single out in battle the individual who had actually done the killing. Ordinarily, however, the identity of the slayer was not known and the expedition attacked any encampment they came across in enemy territory. In either case, the basic strategy was the same: send out scouts to locate the target, surround it in full force during the night, and then, in early-morning ambush, kill as many of the enemy as possible. When the fighting was over, the expedition's leader might suggest that his men keep going and attack elsewhere, but in most cases a single victory was considered enough, especially if moving on meant the forfeiture of captured livestock.

The return of a victorious war party was celebrated with a performance of 'enemies their property dance' and, if adult captives had been taken, with their torture and eventual execution by close female relatives of the warrior whose death the party had been sent to avenge. On most occasions child captives, especially young girls, were not harmed.

---

*In the event that a victory seemed unlikely, the shaman would so advise the members of the war party and suggest that they return home or, alternatively, select another target

THE EARLIEST EVENTS described in the narratives contained in this
collection probably took place in the 1850s.* At this time, of
course, Mexico's control of her northern frontier had been weak-
ened, and Anglo Americans, though still relatively few, were
appearing in greater numbers than ever before. Concomitantly,
Western Apache raiding had reached its highest peak since the
collapse of the so-called Galvez policy in the 1830s (Spicer 1962:
239–40).

It was a time of uncertainty, fear, and turmoil. The presidios
on the borders of Apache territory had ceased to function effectively, and the local citizenry was desperate for a reliable and
organized means of protection. Volunteer armies met with limited
success at best, and bounty hunters—the going rate was one
hundred dollars a scalp—rarely ventured north of the Gila River.
Taking advantage of the situation, the Western Apache struck
deep into eastern and northern Sonora. Mexican settlements seem
to have been their favorite targets, but throughout this period of
heightened predatory activity, raids were also staged against
peoples closer to home: the Pima and Papago, the Navajo and,
less frequently, the Yavapai.

It is important to understand that the Western Apache did not
organize raids for the purpose of increasing their already vast
territory; nor was their aim to drive away or exterminate the
Mexicans and Indians who had settled along its margins. To the
contrary, these populations had become extremely valuable
economic resources which could be counted on throughout the
year to produce substantial amounts of food and livestock. It was
to the Apaches' obvious advantage that such resources remain
viable, and this may help explain why mass killing and the destruc-
tion of enemy property never formed a part of the raiding complex.

---

*In preparing this brief summary of Western Apache history, I have relied most
heavily on Dan L. Thrapp's excellent military history *The Conquest of Apacheria* and
Edward H. Spicer's *Cycles of Conquest*. Other works of immediate relevance include
Betzinez (1959), Bigelow (1958), Bourke (1886, 1891), Clum (1936), Crook (1946), Cruse
(1941), Davis (1929), Forbes (1960), Moorhead (1968), and Thrapp (1964).

Although the Western Apache raided continually throughout the 1850s, Anglo attention was focused farther east where the Chiricahua Apache had become a major obstacle to the settlement of the newly formed Territory of New Mexico. Treaties were made with several Chiricahua bands and an agreement was reached whereby they promised to give safe passage to the Overland Mail. It looked for awhile as if a durable peace might be achieved. But peace was not to come. In 1861 a young cavalry officer attempted to recover a Mexican captive from the central Chiricahua band by holding hostage its leader, Cochise, and several of his sub-chiefs. Cochise was able to fashion an escape but his companions were murdered. The Chiricahua leader retaliated quickly by killing an Anglo trader, and war was on. Treaties were forgotten, attacks on the Overland Mail resumed, and the U.S. Government declared its intention to exterminate the Apache as quickly as possible.

At first, the struggle was confined to western New Mexico and southeastern Arizona, leaving all but one or two of the Western Apache bands unmolested and free to continue their raids into Mexico. But in 1863, the year Arizona became a territory, gold was discovered in the heart of Tonto territory and hostilities flared. Soldiers stationed at Fort Whipple near Prescott killed indiscriminately, and private citizens organized frequent "Indian-hunting expeditions." On one infamous occasion, a group of Apaches was fed poisoned food while participating in what they believed to be a peace conference. Predictably, the Indians responded with massacres of their own, and for a time it seemed that the Anglos would be forced to abandon central Arizona.

In 1864, Camp Goodwin (named after the first governor of Arizona) was established on the Gila River in White Mountain territory. This was an event of major significance, especially for Apaches living to the north. Sandwiched between Tonto country and Chiricahua country, the northern White Mountain groups were geographically isolated and had remained comparatively undisturbed by Anglo military operations. Led by the powerful chief Diablo, they were anxious to avoid the fate that had befallen their neighbors to the east and west and so, when the soldiers arrived at Camp Goodwin and made offers of peace, they accepted. In the years that followed, White Mountain raiding parties continued to make forays into Mexico but, with the exception of minor skirmishes, open conflict with the soldiers was avoided. The result was the development of an uneasy friendship that was to have two very important consequences. One was the unresisted establishment of Ford Ord (later Fort Apache) on the White River in 1868; the other was the willingness of White Mountain and Cibecue Apaches to serve as scouts for General George Crook in his later campaigns against the Tontos and Chiricahuas.

By 1870, it was becoming increasingly clear that the Territory of Arizona lacked the military means to exterminate the Apaches. The number of forts continued to grow, but the Army was undermanned and, more important, unable to formulate a clear and consistent plan for dealing with the problem. Following the Camp Grant Massacre in 1871, during which a body of enraged citizens from Tucson and a group of Papagos slaughtered more than seventy-five Western Apache women and children, the federal government implemented its new "Peace Policy" in Arizona. This policy was intended to put an end to the Army's fumblings and to curtail the activities of corrupt civilian agents.

The Peace Policy called for the collection of all Apaches on reservations as a first step towards promoting "peace and civilization" among them. The Indians would be settled on their own lands, given protection against Anglos, and encouraged to make a living through agriculture or the raising of livestock. Four areas were hurriedly designated as Apache reservations. A large tract of land was marked off around Fort Apache, this to be the home of the Cibecue subtribal group and the northern bands of the White Mountain group. In central Arizona, Camp Verde became headquarters for the Northern and Southern Tonto, as well as the Yavapai. An area around Camp Grant was set aside for the San Carlos subtribal group and the southern White Mountain bands. And in western New Mexico, near Ojo Caliente, a reservation was created for the eastern, or Warm Springs, band of the Chiricahua.

Meanwhile, General George Crook assumed formal command of U.S. military forces in the Department of Arizona. More than any other single individual, Crook was responsible for engineering the Apaches' final defeat; but at the same time, he developed great admiration for their knowledge and endurance, and consistently treated them with intelligence and understanding. Even in defeat the Apaches respected Crook and, like all who have known good enemies, he responded in kind.

Crook was skeptical of the new Peace Policy. Many Apaches had come in to the reservations but a large number, obviously uninterested in peace, stayed away. Everywhere the Indians were fearful, restless, and uncertain. Camp Grant was abandoned when trouble arose, and new headquarters were established at San Carlos on the Gila River. Sporadic raids continued to occur, and the suspicion grew that a massive outbreak was imminent. Crook saw that something had to be done and toward the end of 1872, when attacks intensified in the Prescott region, he embarked upon a campaign to round up all Apaches who had not yet settled on reservations.

In the winter of 1872, Crook began a series of vigorous operations against the Tonto Apaches and, within a few months, succeeded in dealing them a resounding defeat. Several hundred Tontos lay dead, and the remnants of their shattered families were taken captive and placed on reservations. The survivors were warned not to attempt escape and urged to cooperate with Indian Bureau personnel in the development of agriculture. A measure of peace had been restored to central Arizona, and General Crook was hailed as a hero.

But trouble was on the wind. In 1874, the Department of the Interior embarked upon a "program of removal" which had as its main objective the concentration of all Western Apaches, Chiricahuas, and Yavapais on a single reservation—San Carlos. Centralizing the Indians, it was hoped, would make them easier to control and thus reduce the threat they posed to the Anglo citizens of Arizona. From Washington the removal strategy looked sound, but its implementation had unforeseen consequences—none of them altogether surprising—that probably did more to prolong the "Apache wars" than bring them to a close.

In February, 1875, more than 1400 Tonto Apaches and Yavapais were brought to San Carlos from Camp Verde. They were followed there several months later by a large body of White Mountain and Cibecue people from Fort Apache. In 1876, a body of 325 Chiricahuas came in to the reservation, although the most hostile factions, under the leadership of recalcitrants such as Juh and Geronimo, remained at large. With the removal in 1877 of the Chiricahua chief Victorio and some four hundred of his followers from Warm Springs, the total number of Indians at San Carlos rose to above five thousand.

There were problems from the start. Many of the groups living at San Carlos had never before been associated with one another, and their new proximity gave rise to mistrust and suspicion. Then, too, factional disputes developed within single groups, especially the Chiricahua. Some elements, tired of war and constant travelling, seemed to be in favor of peace. Others found the conditions at San Carlos intolerable and waited for a chance to escape. Among all Apaches there was the feeling that the future was uncertain and that, despite attempts by Indian Agent John Clum to give them some control over their own affairs, anything could happen at any time.

Victorio bolted from San Carlos six months after he arrived, taking with him 310 followers—men, women, and children. He surrendered voluntarily at Ojo Caliente in the fall of 1879, only to break again and embark upon a series of depredations that threw the entire southwest into a state of panic. In 1881, after a number of Anglo troops were killed at Cibecue while trying to arrest an Apache shaman, more Chiricahuas fled from San Carlos, and it appeared that the removal program had backfired completely. Two years went by before the nearly one thousand Indians who had escaped were hunted down and returned to reservations. The most significant blow was struck by Crook himself who, in 1883, led a force composed largely of Indian scouts deep into Sonora's Sierra Madre and there entered into negotiations with Geronimo that ultimately resulted in the surrender of nearly four hundred Chiricahuas.

By 1884, peace had been restored and several groups of Apaches, including Geronimo and a small band of Chiricahuas, were taken to Fort Apache. Here, under strict military control, they set about the construction of irrigation dams and the planting of crops. Crook relied heavily on Indian police to preserve order and, like John Clum before him, favored a policy of trial by native juries. Most of the Indians at Fort Apache attempted to adjust to the new conditions as best they could. Internal strife was kept to a minimum and there were no outbreaks.

The calm was shattered in the spring of 1885 when a group of Chiricahuas, led by Geronimo and other seasoned fighters like Natchez, Mangus, and Chihuahua, became disturbed at Crook's refusal to allow. the production and consumption of native liquor. Confronting Lieutenant Britton Davis, then the commanding officer at Fort Apache, they explained that they were tired of restrictions and demanded the right to brew their own intoxicants. Davis, sensing the delicacy of the situation, wired Crook for orders, but the request was short-circuited at San Carlos and never received. Three days later, on May 17, Geronimo, thirty-three men, eight boys of fighting age, and ninety-two women and children broke from Fort Apache and headed south. The Chiricahuas avoided capture for sixteen months but finally, having once again been pursued into Mexico, they agreed to surrender. Shortly thereafter, on September 7, 1886, they were taken to Holbrook, Arizona, loaded into boxcars, and shipped to Fort Marion, Florida. The next few years saw scattered renegade action around Fort Apache and San Carlos, but no more large-scale outbreaks occurred and the Indians on both reservations became conspicuously less restive. By 1890, the "Apache wars" were over.

Throughout the conflict, the Western Apache suffered less severely than the Chiricahua. Fewer of their people were killed, and except for their confinement at San Carlos during the middle 1870s, they were never uprooted from their original territory. Of all the Western Apache groups, the Tontos were unquestionably the hardest hit, but even they recovered and managed to survive in rather substantial numbers at Camp Verde. From the outset, the Cibecue and White Mountain Apaches were inclined towards peace and adjusted comparatively well to living on reservations. More important, these groups supplied the Army with skillful and dependable scouts whose aid, as Crook himself stated on numerous occasions, was absolutely indispensable in bringing about the Chiricahua's final defeat.

Grenville Goodwin was acutely aware of the contribution made by the Western Apache scouts and was anxious that their exploits become more widely appreciated. As he himself stated, he recorded their reminiscences ". . . in the sincere hope that the people of this country will come to understand more fully the great part that the Western Apache people played in the settling of a wide area of the present state of Arizona through their willingness to help the U.S. troops." (1936:32)

Goodwin's sentiment is completely justified, of course, but the passage of time has given to his Western Apache materials a much deeper significance. Many of America's Indians, including the Apache, are currently engaged in a search for their own history —not as it has been depicted and all too frequently biased by Anglos, but as it relates to their own knowledge of who they have been and who they have become. Ideally, such a history should come from the people themselves, and it is Goodwin's great and lasting contribution that he helped make this possible. In every meaningful sense, this book was written by the Western Apache. For this reason, and because Grenville Goodwin would have almost certainly done the same, I have taken the liberty of dedicating it to them.

The present volume is divided into two sections. Part I is made up of six autobiographical narratives. These have been arranged chronologically, the first, by Anna Price, dealing with events that occurred during the 1850s and '60s. Part II is composed of briefer statements which have been organized under the topical headings—"Weapons," "Taboos," etc.—that Goodwin used to order his field notes. The Western Apache terms which appear scattered throughout both sections have been checked with informants living today on the Fort Apache and San Carlos reservations in east-central Arizona. English translations have been provided for the Apache terms, but it should be emphasized that these do not always correspond exactly with the native semantics. The orthographic key on the following page will facilitate pronunciation of Apache words in the text.

KEITH H. BASSO

KEY TO THE PRONUNCIATION OF APACHE WORDS

The orthography employed in this study is strictly phonetic. To facilitate printing, vowel length, stress, aspiration, and tone have not been indicated.

Vowels:

/a/	as in English father	/o/	as in English mow
/æ/	as in English bat	/u/	as in English boot
/ɛ/	as in English met	/ɔ/	as in English claw
/i/	as in English bead	/ə/	as in English but
/ɨ/	as in English hit	/e/	a diphthong, as in English may

Vowel nasalization is indicated by a subscript hook, for example /ą/.

Consonants:

/b/ voiced bilabial stop
/t/ voiceless alveolar stop
/d/ voiced alveolar stop
/k/ voiceless velar stop
/g/ voiced velar stop
/n/ voiced alveolar nasal
/m/ voiced bilabial nasal
/č/ voiceless alveopalatal affricative
/ǰ/ voiced alveopalatal affricative
/s/ voiceless alveolar fricative
/z/ voiced alveolar fricative
/š/ voiceless alveopalatal fricative
/ž/ voiced alveopalatal fricative
/h/ voiceless glottal fricative
/l/ voiced alveolar lateral
/ł/ voiceless alveolar lateral (usually spirantal)
/x/ voiceless palatal spirant
/γ/ voiced palatal spirant
/ƛ̓/ voiceless lateral affricative
/λ/ voiced lateral affricative
/w/ voiceless bilabial semi-vowel
/ʔ/ the glottal stop

[26]

Part I

PERSONAL NARRATIVES

Grenville Goodwin photo, courtesy Arizona State Museum

Anna Price

1

ANNA PRICE

Anna Price was one of Grenville Goodwin's most trusted informants. Her real name was 'Her Eyes Grey' and in 1931, when the following narrative was collected, she was close to one hundred years old and blind. Anna Price was the eldest daughter of Diablo, probably the most influential chief ever to appear among the White Mountain Apache, and most of her recollections deal with the exploits of her father.

In the old days when a person got ready to be told a story, from the time the storyteller started no one there ever stopped to eat or sleep. They kept telling the story straight through till it was finished. Then when the story was through, the medicine man would tell all about the different medicines. There would be a basket of corn seeds there, and for each line that was spoken, that person who was listening would count out one corn seed. This way there would be sometimes two hundred corn seeds. Then that person would have to eat them all. If he could eat them, then he would remember all the words he had been told. If you fell asleep during this time, then the story was broken and was no good. That's the way we used to do.

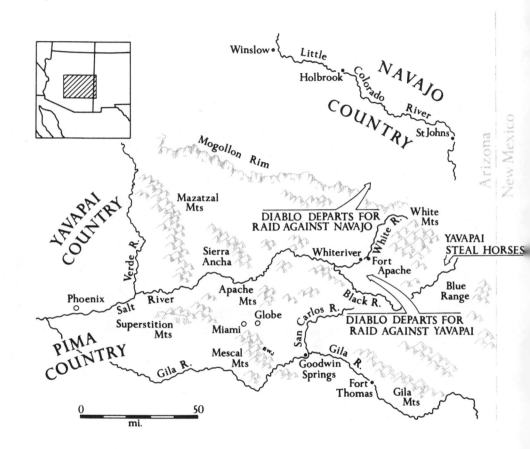

Anna Price Narrative

This is a story that I heard when I was a young girl. I don't know when it took place, but it happened before I can remember. One time some of our girls got captured someplace by some Mexican soldiers. The Mexicans took these girls off down to Mexico. There where they were holding them prisoners this happened. There was one of the girls who always stayed apart by herself from the rest and when they gave her food to eat, she went aside and cooked it by herself. One day while they were cooking, this girl cut a strip of meat off the leg of a beef. Then she went to one side and built a fire and laid her meat on it to cook. The Mexican officer was standing close by watching her. She said to him, "This meat I have cut here will turn over by itself on the fire." The Mexican officer laughed and said, "If that meat turns itself over, then I will send you back to your people."

They sat there watching the meat, and when it got cooked on one side, it turned over by itself. "All right, I have promised you already, so you can go back to your home. You were living over there to where that big mountain is. In the daytime don't cross over any open country, but stay in the mountains. Don't try to walk fast—go easy for two days. This way you must cross the open country at night," the Mexican officer told her. Then he gave her some meat and bread and started her off.

While she was on her way she lived on mescal, roasted, and what acorns she could gather. These she tied up in her blanket and carried along with her. She must have been very far off because it took her three months to reach her home again, near Fort Apache —where it is now. The person who told me this story said she heard lots of Indians crying over something one day, so she went to find out what it was. When she got there, she found they were crying over that girl who had made her way back from Mexico.

入入

One time we left White River for the Blue Range, where we intended to gather piñon nuts. We traveled on horseback and on our arrival turned our horses loose for the night. I had two horses of my own now, as I was a big girl. My father had four geldings and my father's brother had three. There were more horses belonging to other people, but I can't remember who all came with us. The next morning we went out after the horses, but no one could find them. Finally they found the tracks of Yavapai. They had taken our horses. Our men knew they were Yavapai because their moccasins were a little different from ours. They had a habit of sewing the buckskin uppers to the rawhide sole with thin strips of hide. It was possible to see the mark which these seams left in the dirt.

The men returned to camp with one moccasin which the Yavapai had lost. No one tried to follow the Yavapai immediately. "We'll go after them when we get home," they said.

When the boys returned with some more horses from Black River we were feeling pretty angry about it all. We didn't get many piñon nuts because we had no horses. That same day we left the Blue Range and went home, traveling light and fast. My father gave orders for one cowhide to be placed in the water to soak, in order that horseshoes might be made from it.[1] "Tomorrow we will shoe the horses. The next day we will go after those who took our horses from us. Put up a sweat lodge and kill one cow.[2] We'll eat the meat while we take our baths," he said. While they were at the sweat bath, my father spoke: "I'm going after the ones who stole our horses in two days. Every one of you tighten your bowstrings." Some of the men said, "I have my bowstring tied already, prepared to leave." "Have you fixed all the shoes for the horses and put them on?" "Yes, it is done already," they said. "How about your moccasins? Do you have them all sewed up?" And they answered, "Yes."

My father said, "Come over to my camp in two days. Count yourself out about thirty strong; I want some thirty of us to go." So that's the way they did it, counted out thirty of them and at the end of two days were ready to start. "Saddle your horses. This is not our fault; they did it. We didn't steal their horses but they have stolen ours, so we will go over there and let them see what we are like. It is just as if they are asking us to come over after them. They did it first, not we, so we'll go over there and see what they are able to do. We may be back in ten or twelve days," my father said.

Three of the men who were going took along war shields with them. These were all white. Just before starting they sang a song in which they spoke of my father as being their leader. They were in a big hurry to go. They were very mad and wanted to get it over as soon as possible. Leaving in the morning, they traveled steadily all day, all night, all the next night, all the third day and night, and on the morning of the fourth day they arrived there.

First they came to some Yavapai women who were putting mescal into a roasting pit. Our men killed all the women except one old woman who asked that she be spared. I don't know exactly where this took place. My father talked to the old woman, "I have a family back there I live with. I never go anyplace or do anything. It's as if you people had wished that I be here and so I am here for you. I have you now. If you hadn't bothered me and had let my horses alone, I wouldn't be over here. I was taking my people to gather wild fruit and that was where your people stole our horses. You can tell this to your people when you get home," and he released her.

After they had killed the women they went to a place where Yavapai were living. Here they had a big fight and shot at each other. My father's brother was riding his horse in the battle and the horse was killed under him. They only fought in the open for a little while, then all took cover among the rocks. Our men didn't know how many they had killed at the camp. They only knew they had killed those at the mescal pit. My father said he knew he had killed at least one at the camp and after that our men left because the Yavapai were in the rocks. The man my father shot must have been off gathering horses and returned not knowing that our people were there. As he ran to the camp, he was motioning with his hand and talking, but our men couldn't understand his language.

The war party had been gone six days when two of them arrived home, sent ahead to tell us the rest were safe. That is how we knew. They brought no horses back with them because the Yavapai only had a few at the camp, though they got two of the horses stolen from us. All the rest had been driven off to a big mountain which could be seen from the Yavapai camp. Two youths from the war party were sent on ahead to tell us how they had succeeded and that we had gotten back two of the horses. The first thing they said on arriving was, "We have killed the Yavapai." The rest of the men were one day behind them and the youths said they would be in in two more days.

The following day the women started to boil *tuɫpai* [a mild liquor made from fermented corn]. When the war party arrived, some of the old women who had horses stolen from them in the Yavapai raid danced about for joy. They called my father's name, "*Haškɛ dasila* ['He Is Constantly Angry'] always does this way. He has killed some Yavapai and brought horses home." Women who had had their horses stolen were drinking *tuɫpai*. They became intoxicated and cried and danced about.

My father said, "I am satisfied now. I have done this last and they did it first. It was just as if they asked us to come over to their country." The Yavapai never came back after our horses again; they were scared of us, I guess. It was the first raid like that they ever made and it took place before the soldiers came to Goodwin Springs [1864].

This happened when my father was living on the East Fork. Some Navajo came to us to get mescal. They brought sheep hides and blankets to trade. My father and some of his men had gone hunting. These Navajo surrounded them at nighttime and started to fight just as our men were eating their supper of deer meat. Two of our men were killed. Another man shot at the Navajo, even though they could not be seen, and managed to kill one. Two days after the hunters returned home they sent word among all the people to assemble. They made a dance there, a war dance.[3] They used shields to dance with, made of hide.[4]

My father talked to the men before they left, "We are going after the Navajo. I don't know why they attacked us. We always treated them right before, but now we might just as well go and see them—fight them all."

They started and in two days arrived in the Navajo country. The Navajos had not gone far from where they killed our men on the other side of the White Mountains. Our people surrounded the camp and started the attack before dawn, while the Navajo were still asleep. All of them were killed. They tried to run off, leaving their guns and bows and quivers behind them. Our people set fire to their houses and burnt them up. They also set fire to the sheep corral.

During the battle my father talked to the Navajo, "This is

what you want. You have asked me to come over to fight you. That's just the way it is. It used to be as if we ate together, but now I have come to fight you."[5]

They captured one Navajo boy. He knew of another Navajo camp above this one, so they took him to guide them to it. The same day they arrived there at noon and started to fight immediately. The Navajo in the camp were all killed. A few who were herding sheep in the mountains not far off saved themselves. Thus they had fought in two places the same day, one in the morning and one at noon. We were lucky and not one of our people was killed. Whenever my father went to war a lot of men always accompanied him, lots of them, just like ants.

They had captured a second man at this Navajo camp who told them, "Some Navajo have been gone on the warpath for a long time. They went against the White people.[6] One man has just returned ahead of the rest and has said the others will be in tomorrow and that they are bringing lots of cattle in two great herds, one in front of the other."

Two of our men were sent in search of them. The returning Navajo had sent two of their boys ahead to stop at a spring and prepare some meat for those who were coming behind. Our two men saw these boys, who went ahead and built the fire to prepare the meat. Our men knew that all the Navajo would be eating at that place. They set an ambush for them. It was almost sundown and they placed themselves about the spot where the cooking was going on.

Just about an hour later the cattle came up over the hill. One Navajo was riding in the lead, the chief of the party, I guess. They arrived and our men could see many Navajo gathered together by the fire. They started to eat all in a bunch and our men began to shoot. The Navajo got scared and not one fired a shot. A few of them who were herding the cattle saved themselves, but those who had been eating were slain. One Navajo spoke, ". . . you have killed us all."

My father spoke to his men, "Fifteen of you take those cattle home. We want to fight more. There is another herd of cattle coming. The rest of us will go and fight them again." A Navajo had told them these springs were the only ones in the region and that the second herd would certainly stop there in two days. They stayed only one night at the springs.

The next morning fifteen men took the cattle toward White River. The remainder went on ahead to intercept the Navajo. They kept the boy they had first captured. He wanted to show our men where a spring came out between two adjoining hills. At the foot of the one to the west was a little spring. When our men arrived there, the Navajo were bringing in their cattle at the same time and the two parties ran into each other. They saw the cattle coming and so formed a semicircle about the spring so that the Navajo might drive the cattle right into them. There was a bluff on one side and at its foot the spring. It was just like a corral and they had only to arrange themselves on one side because nothing could escape on the side of the bluff. A few were on top of the bluff.

The Navajo arrived and started to water. There were a lot of them. Just then, one of our men started to shoot. They were cut off on one side by the bluff and not one of them escaped—all were killed. At the end of the fight, two Navajo were still alive, one of them having had his side shot away, and the other shot through the leg. They both were sitting there and talked even though shot down. The one wounded in the leg said, "I have killed your men many times and left their bodies for the coyotes. But now you have done the same to me."

All our men gathered about them and my father, being chief, talked to the Navajo. "You have asked for me and for this fight. We used to be friends just as if we lived in the same camp. I don't know why you want to fight my people, so I fight you. The cattle herd ahead of you has been taken down to White River for me; the herd you were bringing home I'm going to take to my home also. You have done well for me and brought lots of cattle from the warpath. You can just sit there and tell your people. I want you to tell them about me. But you who are shot in the leg, side, arm, I am going to kill you." So he killed one, and the one who was left, the one who still sat there, said, "If any of you have some mescal, I wish you would give it to me. I want it. Then I will eat it up. Maybe that will bring me home to tell my people about you. I have had a hard time from your people. Give me some water." My father gave the Navajo some water. "Here," he said, "this will take you home to tell your people about us." Then the Navajo said, "All right, take your cattle home and I will talk to my people about you and also you tell your people about me. Put me in the

Courtesy Arizona Pioneers' Historical Society

Diablo

shade. You have killed me. Put me in the shade of that pine."
So they did. My father told him, "When you get home, tell your
people about me and call my name. Tell them I am the one who
got your cattle."

The fifteen men who took the first herd home got there first.
The second bunch had been gone seven days when they got home
with the cattle. They killed the Navajo boy when they left the
spring.

My father had said when he started to war, "My heart is
moving within me just as the sun moves overhead. That is the way

the killing of my relatives makes me feel." When a man gets mad his heart beats fast and hard. This is what he meant.

¡¡¡¡

At Turkey Creek near Fort Apache, we were camping. Three young men went to hunt deer. While they were out they were attacked by Navajo. Two ran off and were saved; one was killed by the Navajo. When the boys got home they spread the news among the people. So all the older men who were left at home gathered. They met at one place and had a meeting. They decided they should follow the trail while it was fresh.

Diablo was the big chief then. He made a speech there. "We are men also. The Navajo are men also. They have life just as we do. Tomorrow we will wash up at a sweat bath and the next night we will have a war dance. While they were having the sweat bath, all the women gathered wood.

While the dance was going on, a woman talked to the men to make them brave. "They killed one of our men. You will try to do the same thing, too. They have the same life we have; they have blood like us. They die just like us also," the old woman said. They danced all night. They said if anyone had a good horse, to take it, but some went on foot.

They started off the next morning. They sent two men ahead of them as scouts. They were on the way about four days until they got to the Navajo country.

When the Navajo killed that boy they knew that they would be attacked back by our people, so they moved away from their homes. Our people got to their old camps soon. When they got there they started to follow the trail. The Navajo had taken the horses and sheep out of the corrals and driven them along. They followed the trail and sent two men on foot ahead. These two men saw the smoke from the Navajo camp ahead. When these two men got back and met the rest, they made camp there. Then they sent those two men out again to see just how the camp was located. They found the camp to be right in a valley at the end of a mesa.

About sunrise Diablo made a speech, "We should attack those Navajo before they see us, while their women and children are still together." But some of the men said no. While the chief made the speech, these said, "No, we can attack these people tomorrow morning, in the early dawn while they sleep." But they stood by the chief's word that they were to attack right away. The chief said, "Hitch up your horses tonight, and string your bowstrings to fit."

Diablo made a speech when they started to attack. "Don't any of you men run off when the fight starts. Try to be brave." So they all divided up into three companies. They were in a line, and then on the left side of the line they gave the signal to go, then on the right, then all rushed to attack. All at once the men rushed among the Navajo camp and killed them. Then all the Navajos together rushed out of the camp. Some of our people used arrows, some guns, some spears, and started to kill off the Navajos. They chased the Navajos across a river. The Navajo women and children were in front. The Navajo men formed a line behind. Not one of the Apache got killed.

While the fight was still going on, one of the head men sent his men among the others and said, "Let's stop it. Let's stop it and gather together in a bunch again."

After the fight was over they went back to the Navajo camp and looked for all they had—bridles, bits, silver, blankets, all they had. The men who had come on foot got horses here and some rode off with Navajo saddles and Navajo blankets tied up behind. When they had cleaned out all the camp, they started as fast as they could, because they knew that the Navajo would follow them.

On the way to the Navajo they spent four nights, but on the way back they took three days. They traveled all day until sunset, and the next morning they would get up early before sunrise. That way they got back home again.

Grenville Goodwin photo, courtesy Arizona State Museum

Palmer Valor

2

PALMER VALOR

When Palmer Valor related the following stories in 1932, he was over ninety-five years old. Goodwin notes that "Valor's accounts of the old days are unique since he was almost the only Western Apache left who had taken an active part in the life of the people prior to U.S. Army control. Among his own White Mountain Apache, he was known as a widely traveled man and an authority on the earlier life and times." Valor describes a number of raiding expeditions in which he himself participated, most of them directed against Mexican settlements. Of particular interest is his account—the only one collected by Goodwin—of a raiding party that reached the Gulf of California.

I was born long ago at Canyon Day.[1] Then the earth was like new, and there were lots of animals and plants. There were four kinds of grass we used to live off that were growing all over this country then. There was red grass, yellow grass, blue grass, and white grass. When the wind blew through these grasses as it is blowing now, the air smelled sweet. Now it is different.

In those days, there were no White people in the country whatsoever, and only the Mexicans lived south in their own country. We always used to cross this valley of the Gila on our way to Mexico. I can remember once being gone to Mexico for twenty-

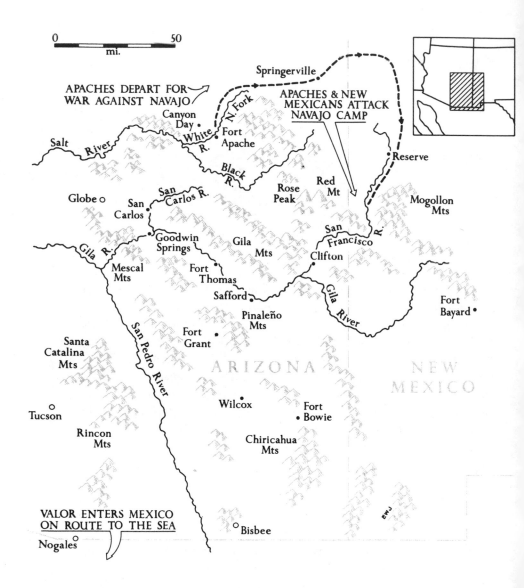

APACHES DEPART FOR
WAR AGAINST NAVAJO

Springerville

Canyon
Day

Fort
Apache

N. Fork

White
R.

APACHES & NEW
MEXICANS ATTACK
NAVAJO CAMP

Reserve

Salt

River

Black
R.

Rose
Peak

Red
Mt

Mogollon
Mts

Globe

San
Carlos

San
Carlos R.

Goodwin
Springs

Gila
Mts

San
Francisco R.

Clifton

Gila R.

Mescal
Mts

Fort
Thomas

Safford

Gila River

Fort
Bayard

Pinaleño
Mts

Santa
Catalina
Mts

San Pedro River

Fort
Grant

ARIZONA

NEW
MEXICO

Tucson

Wilcox

Fort
Bowie

Rincon
Mts

Chiricahua
Mts

VALOR ENTERS MEXICO
ON ROUTE TO THE SEA

Nogales

Bisbee

Palmer Valor Narrative

five days and only seeing one White man that whole time. There were people living in Tucson then, but that was the nearest.

All this country here belonged to us alone. All the mountains around here had names and now they have none. In those days there were lots of us and the trails around through these mountains were well traveled, like roads. Now they are all faded out and hard to see.

When the White people first came we used to fight with them, but later they gave us presents and that way we got to be friends with them. Now we are making our living from them.

Long ago when we made camp, we just put up a circle of brush around us for a shelter and kept warm. Now we have good tight wickiups, but even if we keep the doors closed, we are cold. In the old times there was no sickness among us and it seemed as though people didn't die. Now we have lots of sickness and many of us die from it.

Our people used to go on raids down into Mexico to bring back horses, mules, burros, and cattle. This is the way we used to take the property of the Mexicans and make a living off them. There were no White people to take things from in those days. We never used to travel around with the Mexicans because we were always fighting with them. This way, when we fought with them, some of us would get killed and some of them would get killed. It was hard living in those days, and sometimes a raiding party would get nothing in Mexico and come back empty-handed.

I have been many times to Mexico on raids and twice as far as the sea.[2] There on the edge of the sea we could see out over the water, and it was as if the sky ran right down into the sea and the top of the water kept moving up and down. There were abalone shells and other shells there, but we could not touch them as this would be a bad thing to do.[3] We just sat there and made a prayer to the water; "I am here, far from my home and I want to travel safely back to my home without anyone seeing me," we prayed.

Besides going to Mexico, sometimes we went over towards Mogollon Mountain where we fought with the Navajo and took their sheep and horses.[4]

There are no people left from those old times now, except me, and an old man living up at Fort Apache, who was raised as if with me. He went on the first raiding party that I ever went on. Besides us there are two women left from those times and they are 'Her Eyes Grey' [Anna Price] and her sister, 'Her Eyes Brown.'

These people that you see around here who look old and have gray hair, their mothers were my sweethearts when I was young. I have lived a long time and I have had lots of trouble all through my life, but I always have kept my head. I guess that is why I am still alive.

One of the first things that I can remember is when I first started to use a small bow and arrows. Then my mother said to me, "My boy, go out hunting and kill lots of birds and rats and that way you will make a living." I kept on growing and after awhile my mother said to me, "Go out and hunt deer now. Kill a deer with your arrows," and this is the way that I was doing.

We used to kill bear in those days. My heart was not afraid and even if a bear had run at me, I would have killed him with an arrow. My mother also used to make me swim in the early morning and she used to say, "If Mexicans or other enemies should come here, you will get scared and be no good if you don't make yourself brave by swimming in the cold water."[5]

My mother used to tell me about the old times and the things that she had seen in her time. She told me about the time when our people first brought cattle up from Mexico. They drove them to Oak Springs and lots of people went together to this place to see them. Many of them had never seen cattle before, and so they sat there and watched them eating the grass and chewing their cuds. They didn't know what the cattle were doing when they were chewing their cuds and so they said, "What's the matter with them?"

Another time my mother told me how she had seen the stars rain down in a straight line over to the west.[6] This was very long ago and not long after it happened, there were lots of our people traveling over near Klondike and my mother was with them. They made camp in a canyon and were gathering wild daisies at that place.[7]

One day while they were there the sun started to go dark. In a little while it got so that only half of the sun was showing, like the moon does. The people started to call each other and it got so dark that they built a fire at the camp so the people could see to get back to it.

Now they could see the Pleiades up in the sky and it was way over to the west. All the people started to sing so that the sun would come back. They had all come together now. Finally when the sun was way low in the west, it came out again and was all right once more.

Later on an old man that I talked with when we were living at Calva told me that during that same time the sun got dark, a girl had gone out to look at a trap that had been set for coyotes. She saw a rat in the trap, and when she tried to take it out, the trap fell on her and broke her back. When all the people got to camp they found that this one girl was missing and when they went to the trap to look for her, they found her there dead. The old man said that this had happened when he was a boy.

I have just heard about how they used to make these traps for coyotes, but I have never seen one made. They built a kind of little house for the coyote to go into and fixed a big flat rock in front of the house and had it set up with a set-stick that had a rat for bait on the end of it.

I can remember the first time that I ever went on a raid to Mexico. I was only a boy then and not very big, but I thought that I would like to go to war and so I joined in with a party. All the men said, "What's the matter, little boy? We are going a long way, and we will be gone for fifty-nine days. You are too small to go with us." But all the same I went with that party.[8]

We carried packs on our backs with our food in them and as we traveled along we were careful to keep ourselves hidden. After we got to Mexico we met up with a bunch of Mexicans and killed one of them. The rest of them got away, but we got all the stock. All this happened very long ago.

While we were camping at one place the Mexicans came on us in the morning and started to fight. They killed two of our bunch, both good men, and for this reason we started off back home. On our way we went by a big town. There was a big pasture at this town with lots of horses in it. So that night we went to this pasture and took out all the horses.

That same night we started on with them and traveled all night till early morning when we stopped to rest. Now we had the horses and so we went on home with them. We had been gone for twenty-three days on this raid.

We had lost two men on this raid and on account of this the people were all notified that there was to be a council about it. This was some time after we had gotten back.

Some horses were butchered to feed the people, and they put up a dance which lasted for about two nights. Right after the dance was finished, about two hundred of us men started off on the warpath to Mexico. They said that we were going to kill every Mexican that we met.

When we got to Mexico we killed about twenty Mexicans and captured one Mexican man. Then we started back home, taking the prisoner with us. When we got back home to where our people were at Ash Flat, we made a victory dance.[9] That night they made the Mexican dance with them.

The next morning an old woman there took up a spear and ran at the Mexican and stuck it right through him and killed him. This old woman was the sister of one of the two men who had been killed by the Mexicans and this man, her brother, had been a chief. That's the way that they did—one night they danced with the Mexican and the next morning they killed him. Now the dance was finished.

One time we set out for Mexico to a great big town. This was the place that we were coming to to steal stock, so we waited not far off till it got dark.

When it was dark we went in near the town and started to round up all the gentle horses that we could and when we got through we had about fifty-three head. We started off and herded these fifty-three head of horses that same night and all the next day. We left the horses in a place and then when it was dark we turned around and went back to the town. There we got twenty-one more horses out of the pasture and took them back and put them in with the bunch that we had already taken.

Now we started out for home by a trail that we always used to take when we were going through this part of the country.

While we had been away some enemies had attacked the place where our people were camped waiting for us, and had broken up the whole camp.[10] When we got there, I gave away the four horses that were my share of the trip. I gave these horses to my mother, my sister and my maternal uncle. They butchered them and used the meat to eat. This way we ate those horses all up.

We were down at Goodwin Springs and that is where we started from. There was a big bunch of us, but we didn't all travel together. That's the way we used to do—two or three, or maybe five, or anywhere up to eleven of us would get together to go to Mexico.

This time there were eleven of us, but two of the men came back home as soon as they had captured some stock. We used to do this quite often also; when some of the party had taken some stock, they would turn back and go home because they would be satisfied. But the others who had taken no stock would keep on till they had captured some horses or cattle.

When the party set out for Mexico I was out hunting birds. I saw them setting off and so I ran after them and caught them up and joined them. We traveled for seven days and nights and then came to a dangerous spot where we had to walk on our toes to be sure that we left no tracks and be sure that we hid all our tracks.

This place is a great plain, all open, and if the Mexicans had ever found our tracks on it, they could have run us down for sure because we were all on foot. There is only one mountain on this plain, and it is so far from any other mountain where we could have taken cover that we could have easily been caught.

We kept on across the plain and after some time we came to a place from where we could see a mountain which is right close to the sea.

Down at that place the country looks like this across the Gila River here with lots of brush growing and a great many giant cactus and lots of creosote bush. In all this brush there were lots of quail.

Now we went on to a small mountain and on to the southeast side of it. The sea was not far off now, only about ten miles. It looked like the sky is today and on the other side of it there were no mountains, but instead the water as if it ran clear out and into the sky itself. We stayed two days there and looked around.

At the end of the two days we saw lots of dust way below where we were and it looked as though it was made by horses. From where we saw the dust it kept on coming towards us and right into the valley below us where we could see it. The other men in the party knew that there used to be a corral on the other side of this mountain that was built with a stone wall. They had been there before and so they said that we would go to it. Some of our party thought that what was making the dust was heading for this stone-walled corral. Then the rest of us set out for the stone corral.

This corral had two big posts set one on each side of the entrance and between these posts were bars that could be set up to close the entrance. This was the only place that you could get into it, and there was no way to get in by tearing down the stone wall, as this was too hard.

There is one old woman still living whose husband was in charge of us. This man told two of us to go to the gate of the corral and watch there. A little while after these two had been sent over to watch the gate, one of them came back and said that the horses had gone into the corral by themselves and that there was no one driving them. There were some men in our party who understood about horse medicine, and it must have been these who made the horses go into the corral like that by themselves.[11]

Now the one in charge sent the man who had come from the gate back there and told him to get the gate closed. The sun was above us and it was just about noon then, so we waited till evening before we went to the corral to get the horses.

In one direction from the corral there were some Mexicans living about six miles away, and in the other direction there were some living about fifteen miles away. We were all very anxious for the sun to go down so that we might go to the corral. Pretty soon there was only a little time left till the sun would set, and we thought sure that no one would be there now and so we went to the corral.

When we got there we saw that there were lots of horses in the corral and they were big ones like soldiers' horses. Now the man in charge of us said, "I don't think that the horses will get out of the corral and so you can all go ahead and rope the ones that you want. You have your ropes, so go and do it."

The man in charge of a raiding party like this was just like an officer and when he said something he meant it.

So now we all started to rope the horses that we wanted. I caught a good gray horse right away and after him I caught two others. Some of the men got three and some got four. We were still roping horses when our chief told us to stop. There were eleven of us and no one of us had two horses; we all had from three to five apiece. We left about eleven head still in the corral. There must have been lots of horses in that bunch because we all had so many. The eleven that were left were for the chief.

Then the chief said to us, "If you take your horses out of the corral before you get on them, they will be likely to run away and drag you after them till you let go. So you all better get on them in the corral and gentle them there."

Our chief picked out his men just as if they were out on a cattle roundup and set them at different jobs. We got on our horses in the corral and then he told us to open the gate. Two of us he set to lead, and two he told to go on each side of the herd, and the other five of us rode behind and drove.

Now we started out of the gate and the chief told us to drive easy at first. We drove the horses slowly till we got across the river there, and then we started to drive them faster.

"For two nights we will travel till dawn steadily," our chief said. And he meant what he said, for the next two nights we traveled all night till morning.

There was a big open level plain that we had to cross, but there was lots of heavy brush growing on it so that we could cross it in the daytime safely without anyone seeing us. We set out and crossed over it that day and stopped by a little mountain on the other side. There our chief said that we had better keep on going and that if we traveled all night we could get to a stopping place by early morning.

Now we had been traveling steadily for three nights and three days since we had left that stone corral near the ocean, and again this day we traveled all day, keeping on the mountain. That night we drove the horses on, and at the foot of a mountain we herded the horses all day.

While we had been coming on our way all this time, we had not stopped to eat anything at all. Now they said that we would start for the top of another mountain and that we should get there by early morning of the next day. So we started off and by the time that it got light in the early morning, we had got to the foot of this mountain and then climbed it, almost to the top, to a level place.

"I don't think that any Mexicans coming after us could have caught us unless they had flown, so let's stop here and butcher one of the horses," the chief said. We had been going steadily for five nights and days now. The night that we left the stone corral we had only a small piece of meat left from the food that we had brought with us, and we had eaten this up that same night.

The chief had a good sorrel horse and he told us to kill it. We did, and cooked some of the meat, not much though, and ate it. Some of the men, while they still had meat in their mouths and were sitting there chewing it, went to sleep right there. This was because we had been traveling steadily for five nights and days now, never stopping to sleep or eat.

In those days they knew what ones were the men, and even if he was still young, only a boy, it didn't matter if he could stand it. This way some boys went along and were able to stand these trips, just like the men.

The chief said that we would stay here and sleep for a while. But he told me and another of the party to go and watch back over our trail to see if anyone should be coming. "Don't go to sleep while you are watching," he said to us. In those days long ago I used to have a great power, and that's why I began to be different.[12] They always used to put me in the most dangerous places to do things.

I and the other man stayed and kept a lookout over our back trail till mid-afternoon, and then we came back to sleep. The chief told the others to cook some meat for us two right away and then he said to us to go to sleep, and when we woke up we could eat. We had no water with us at that place. We two slept for about two hours, I think, and then we woke up and started to eat the meat.

The chief said, "We will cross right above here." Then we went to the top of the mountain that we had been camped on, and herded the horses right out to the end of it. By the time we had got to the end it was dark and we were close to a town. From here we set out and traveled all night. We had been going six days now and six nights and there was one night left during which I couldn't sleep.

That day we kept on and when night came we crossed over some open desert country, about as far as it is from here to Point of Pine.

Now it was seven nights and days since we had had a real sleep, and that's the way that we used to do when we were on the warpath or on a raid. A man had to be mean and smart so that he would never be caught by the enemy.

Now the chief said, "We have been driving these horses for seven nights so we might as well turn them loose in this canyon here, and we will sleep at the mouth of it so they can't get out." We knew that we had herded these horses—there were fourteen of them left—steadily for seven days and seven nights, and we had been coming as fast as we could. But from here on it was almost like home, and there was only one more Mexican town to pass. We rested there all that day and the next day we went on.

I have been all through this country many times and that is why I remember all these places so well.

This is the way that we used to live in the old days. One time a party of Navajo came down into our country and attacked a bunch of our people who were living on Turkey Creek. They killed a lot of our people at that place.

Some time after that two Navajo men came among our people on the White River. We didn't know just where they came from, but we knew that both these men had been in the party of Navajo who had killed some of our people on Turkey Creek. These two Navajo said that they had come to visit our people, but I don't know why they had the nerve to come back this way.

When they came there our people notified each other that a sweat bath was to be set up and that we would get these two Navajo to go inside to take a bath and then kill them in there.[13]

So they made the sweat bath and then invited the two Navajo to come there and take a bath. They came to the sweat lodge all right, but wouldn't both go in to bathe at the same time. Only one of them would go in and the other stayed outside and sat in the shade. When the other one went in the sweat lodge, some of our men went with him and right in the lodge they grabbed hold of him. But at the same time, a little before, some of our men grabbed the one who was waiting outside. He must have said something to the other in the sweat lodge, because before they had a chance to really get hold of him, he jumped out of the lodge and got away. Our people killed the one outside, but the one who jumped out of the lodge got away and we didn't kill him. He ran off in the brush just as he had stripped to take the bath, without any moccasins and no clothes at all.

Not long after this took place an officer received a letter from the Navajo country saying that all the White Mountain people were to go on the warpath against the Navajo and that we were to meet the soldiers at a certain place and help them against the Navajo.[14] This was just two days after we killed that Navajo.

At the time that the one man got away from us, our people had said that we better follow him and see if he went back to his people, that we had better catch him or he would go back and tell his people that we had killed the other man. So because we had received the message about going to war with the Navajo and on account of the man who got away from us, we set off.

There were about two hundred of us, but we were not like enlisted scouts. We were on our own and only helping the soldiers who we were to join. The first day we got to the upper part of North Fork and camped there. The next day we went up on top of a mountain and made camp. From here we went on by the regular way that we always took in going to Fort Wingate and Albuquerque.

The day after that we met some New Mexicans.[15] There was only one White man with them and the outfit must have been New Mexican soldiers. There were five companies of them. While we were there we had a talk with the officer in charge of the New Mexicans and he said that a fight had once started right there. They were not allowed to travel through this place or near it.

This place was like a holy place and there was a power here. These New Mexicans that we saw here tied some strips of yucca around their heads, arms, and legs. Then they made a sort of big basket out of brush about twelve feet long. Two men took this basket, two at each end, and waded with it out into the water there and dragged it along under the water so that they could gather the salt up on it. As they waded along, the water only went as far up their legs as where the yucca strips were tied and it wouldn't go beyond these strips.

Right there in the middle of this place there were two hills, and right between them the water is a black color, and on the other side it is a green color, and on the other side it is a yellow color, and on the other side it is a white color. Right in the center you throw beads of four colors, and if you throw them in like this, you can swim in this water here. If you swim in this water you can never get sick. All this the officer in charge of the New Mexicans told us.

We stayed at this place for three days. We asked the New Mexicans if all of them were going on the warpath, but they said no, that some of them had just come here to get salt and that they would be going back home soon. "Only some of us are going to help you fight," they said.

The White officer said to us, "We have met here for a reason and not for nothing. That's why I shake hands with all of you here," and he now shook hands with all of us. Then he got out about five yards of red cloth and divided it up among us so that each one of us got some. The next morning we started out with the soldiers. There were ninety-nine of our people there.

We camped on the east side of a mountain, and from here it is straight to Mogollon Mountain. The next day we set out and crossed a big flat and stopped to camp. From here we went on and camped where there were lots of pines growing. Next we came to a river and that is the next place that we camped.

Then we went on down the canyon from here, and while we were going one of our chiefs came and told us to go over to a big black mountain that was there, and go up on top of it to see if we could see any fires that would be Navajo camps. He told six of us to go and I was one of those who went along.

We started out and on our way we met lots of bears. We got to the top of that mountain the same night and looked for a fire, but we couldn't find any. We stayed there all that night and the next morning, far off, there was a mountain spotted with timber and on a point just below this mountain we could see smoke spreading out. So now we went back to the camp and joined the rest and told them that we had seen some smoke far off, behind the mountain. Then the White officer said that we would all stay where we were till it got dark, and then we would set out for where the smoke was.

There was lots of timber growing out in patches in the open country just this side of where the smoke was. Some of those men were not very smart. Only some of us knew what to do, and it was some of our people who said that we should stay here till it got dark and then go to the smoke. It was not far to the smoke, but we should always travel to it at night.

That night we set out and got pretty close to the smoke but could not see it yet. So they told us to go up on the mountain there and see if we could see any smoke. I and two other men went up and looked for the smoke. When we got up there we saw a camp right below us and we could see lots of sheep being herded by the camp. This was a Navajo camp all right, and so we went back to the others and told them. We had waited at that place the rest of the night and when the dawn had come was when I and the two others had gone up on the mountain and seen the camp.

Now when we got back we all got ready to fight. The New Mexicans said that we should all wear something in the fights so that we wouldn't look like the Navajo and have the New Mexicans shoot at us by mistake and kill some of us. Then we all lined up with the soldiers that morning. When we started out we all went in front and the New Mexicans came behind us to the west. Where the pack outfit was being driven along, they put one company of the soldiers so that some were riding on each side to guard. The horses were divided up so that they were in four parts on the side in a line.

Then the White officer called the father of Anna Price [Diablo] to him and said to him, "You are the chief of these White Mountain people and I understand you are a good fighter. Today we are going to fight and we will find out about you." "All right, you will find out about me. All these men here—they know me. I have always fought together with them. These New Mexicans here are your soldiers. I don't know which will do the best, your men or mine," our chief said.

The officer in charge of the New Mexicans said, "For what happens from now until sundown, we will want to know who will

be named the best. If you Indians do the best, you will be named
well. If it is that way, it will be good. But if these soldiers of mine
on their horses do not do much good, my name will not stand for
anything."

Now it was all right, and we went in a line. We went in front
and the ones who were our chiefs rode at our head. While we
were on our way, our chief rode around among us and told us to
go slow. Just before we started, the earth shook and trembled.

Before we got to where we could see the dwellings of the
Navajo, we saw some Navajo herding in some horses to their camp,
just this side of it. They were good horses, all of them like cowboys'
horses, and one had a saddle on and another had a pack on.
The Navajo was driving them on foot. He had a six-shooter with
a white handle with him, but it was not loaded, and he also had a
rifle, but this was not loaded either. He tried to load it now, and
if he had had it loaded he would have killed one of the soldiers
for sure.

One of the New Mexicans, a tall slim fellow, rode fast on his
horse at the Navajo. The Navajo was at his horse's tail, and he had
his gun loaded by now, and so he shot at the New Mexican but he
missed. The Navajo kept moving fast and the New Mexican did
not kill him. The rest of the New Mexicans rode to the Navajo
camp, but we didn't pay any attention to the camp and just tried
to get hold of the Navajo horses. Some of our people got some of
the horses and got on them.

I tried to help catch the horses. I was on foot like a great
many of us were, but in those days my legs were like automobiles
and they amounted to a great deal, and the other men knew this
because when we had had hard times I always had helped out
with my legs. My legs were a great deal then. I roped on foot and
caught one of the horses by the forefoot. There were lots of sheep
at this camp that the Navajo had there.

Only one Navajo got killed at this fight and he was the only
one killed in the whole fight. The soldiers ought to have helped us
to get all their horses instead of going to the camp after the Navajo,
and if they had done this we would have killed lots of the Navajo.[16]
But instead of that, all the Navajo got away on their horses from
their camp and they took their guns with them.

Right on top of a rock bluff there they left two of their horses, and a little farther on they stopped and all lined up ready to fight, standing with their guns. Now they started to shoot and they made so much smoke that we couldn't see them at all. Then some of us started to them to fight, and this was when I captured one good horse with a saddle. All of our people captured lots, but the White officer and his New Mexican soldiers captured nothing at all. We also took one of the Navajo prisoner.

Later on the officer in charge of the New Mexicans wanted to know what kind of an outfit the Navajo was wearing who had been killed. This Navajo was wearing a belt with silver all the way round it. He had a pouch for bullets and a steer horn to keep his gunpowder in. Someone had taken all the things from the dead man, and so now the officer said that he wanted all these things brought back.

He spread a blanket on the ground for the things to be put on —rifles, pistol and all. Then he asked again who had killed the Navajo. They told him that a certain one of the men had done it. "Well, let him come here. He killed this Navajo, and so all these things that the dead man had will go to him, no matter if some of you have already taken them for yourselves. He has done this and so he gets it all," the officer said. So the things were brought and laid on the blanket for that man who was standing near, but he said that he didn't want all these things for himself, and that he would give some of them to our people.

After this, that officer in charge of the New Mexicans told us, "I have fought lots of times with the Navajo, and they are like coyotes. I think that tonight they will try to come to where we camp and surround us. For this reason we had better leave here and go back over that open level country the way we came, so that they won't have a chance to come up on us. We will camp out in the open and make a corral to put the stock in."

So then we started to herd the stock out into the open country. When we got lined out we could see that we had a lot of horses, goats, and sheep—about five hundred in all. Our men herded the horses and pack horses. It looked good to me to see so much stock that we had captured from the Navajo.

About dusk we stopped out in the open country to make a corral, and to camp. All the soldiers formed out into a great circle, each man about four feet from the next, just like posts all around the stock. They made the soldiers stay like this all night, and that's the way we made our corral.

The next morning we gathered up all the horses and started on our way. They said we would make our next camp where there was lots of water, and we did this when we came to a canyon that had water in it. From here we went on to the other end of the same canyon and made camp again. The next day we moved on, and just before sundown we stopped and made camp right below Mogollon Mountain where there are lots of trees at the end of the mountain.

As soon as we had made camp the officer in charge of the New Mexicans said, "Come, we will eat right away, for after we eat I want to hold a talk with you." So we ate, and after we were through the officer called us to come.

When we got there he said to our chief, "That was true, that which I told you about just before we went to fight the Navajo. I said that you were the chief of the White Mountain people and that you, as a chief, were a great fighter. I understand now, and know that you are a great fighter. Everyone is afraid of you. I know that it is true. You are my brother, Diablo, and you have done well. All your men captured the sheep and goats and the horses, but my men have captured nothing at all. My name is no good and your name is best now. I figured that my soldiers were good fighters, but here they have taken only one old sheep hide in this fight.

"We will stay here at this place tomorrow, and I want you to divide up all this stock that has been captured, and give half of it to our party. I and my men have had a hard time fighting and driving this stock as well as you all, and for this reason I want you to do as I ask."

The next morning we got ready and rounded up all the horses. It was agreed that our chief and another chief would go on one side of the captured horse herd, and the White officer and another New Mexican officer would go on the other side. This way each could cut a horse out of the herd one at a time, so that two men working together would cut out two horses at a time. First the two officers would cut out two horses, and then our two chiefs would cut out two horses. As the horses were cut out they were driven into two separate herds, and in this way our people and the soldiers divided up the horses into two equal bunches, one for us and one for them.

This took a long time, and as the horses were being cut out we joked and said that we felt good and that maybe the soldiers had something to drink with them. When we said this the New Mexicans got out a gallon jug of whiskey that they had there. Our chief said, "This way, we will all have a good time. There will be fun for all of us."

When we had got through cutting all the horses, there were three left and the White officer said that these three horses that were left we should take for ourselves. We had started to cut out the horses in the morning, and it took a long time to finish it, but finally it was done.

Then they brought all the sheep and goats to the same place to divide them up also. All the New Mexicans and all of us lined up around the sheep and goats in a big circle. Then we cut out the goats from the sheep and stood around the sheep in a big circle like a corral. Some of the men went in the circle that we made and stood across it so that they divided the circle into two halves.

Now we drove one half one way and the other half the other way so that we had a herd and the New Mexicans had a herd, both of the same size. They had been careful to stand so that they cut the circle of our corral just in half, and had moved one way and then the other way till they had got it just right.

Then they brought up the goats. We stood all around them, alternately, first one of us and then one of the New Mexicans. Now the White officer rode up on his horse and said, "I don't want us to get into an argument over this stock, and so I don't care who gets the most, your people or my people. I have a white cloth in my hand and when you see me wave it up and down four times, then everyone start in and grab a goat. This way we will see who gets the most goats."

So then he got ready and waved the white cloth up and down four times and we all started in to grab goats. It sure was a scramble, and the dust that we raised was so thick that we could hardly see at all. Some of the men tried to take away goats from those who already had hold of them.

At last when it was all over, there was one man lying there on the ground, and he was unconscious. The goats had trampled all over him and his mouth and throat were full of dust. He was one of the New Mexican soldiers. When we came to him he was still breathing, and so they got a piece of canvas and soaked it in water and rolled the New Mexican all up in it. In that way he got all right and came to. Then they took him back to camp, holding him to both arms. It had been almost as if he had drowned from the dust.

It was about mid-afternoon when we got all through dividing up the captured stock, but as soon as we had got our share separated from the part the New Mexicans took, we left the New Mexicans and started off for home. That night we stopped to camp where there were lots of pines at a place near Springerville. From there we went on for three days to a place not far below where Fort Apache is now. There are lots of farms at that place now. From here we went on and the next day we were home again.

I had seven goats and twenty-three sheep, which all together with the goats made thirty head. I had one horse also, and so I really had thirty-one head that I had captured from the Navajo.

IIII

The first time that our people had anything to do with the White people was when we went to meet a White officer who issued some clothes to us. He also gave us some big brass kettles, red blankets, and some copper wire for making bracelets. A whole pile of things he gave to us. Besides these things he gave us about thirty head of cattle. That's the way the White people first started to make friends with us.[17]

Then the White people came to Goodwin Springs [1864] and started to live there.[18] One of our great chiefs, Diablo, came to have a talk with the White officer at Goodwin Springs. There were lots of White people and lots of our people who met at that council. During the talk some of our men carried a hard rock to the meeting and put it right where they were talking. "We will be friends together as long as this rock lasts," they said. That rock there meant that an agency was set up for us and that we were friends with the White people. That rock is still there and we are still friends. After the council was over the White people gave out some coffee, sugar, and flour to us, and they are still doing that way today. From then on the White people tried to make us understand things, and that if we were traveling along a trail and we saw something that was not ours, we were not to pick it up and take it.

While we were at Goodwin Springs that time they talked about setting up an agency for us at Fort Apache. The main chief who lived on White River agreed to this, and that's how the White people came to move up there and build Fort Apache and live close to our people. Up there around Fort Apache it is good country with the mountains and the river. The water is colder up there and the weather is colder too, so that when we were all living up there we were well off. We were all well off then and lived well.

➤➤

One time, we made a thirteen-day trip to a place where our party agreed to split up into three parts, and each part was to go to a different place and make raids on three Mexican towns. We were going to split up the next day but that night we all started on together and went on for about a quarter of a mile that way. We did this because we knew that the Mexicans who lived around here were bad and mean. Even in the nighttime they would look for our tracks if they thought we were around. They used dogs to track us with. For this reason we all stuck together when we went past this town, and when we got by they sent three of our men back to see if we were being followed.

We had gone on a little way and up onto a little ridge, and then we knew that lots of Mexicans were following us. It was a good bright moon that night and we stopped there to look back. There we saw way back on our trail, a big white dog. He was going on in the lead and there were some other dogs in back of him, following. Pretty soon the three men that were sent back to watch our trail and see if anyone was following us, came back and said that the Mexican soldiers were following us.

We kept on traveling that night and went about ten miles further. Then we thought that we were safe and so got ready to stop for the night and sleep. But before we went to sleep they said that we had better send someone back to see if the Mexicans were still following us. So they sent one of the men back to look. In awhile he came back and said, "The Mexicans are following us right up along the top of that mesa there." We had been gone from the Mexican soldiers for quite some time, but they were coming up on us again and so we started out and all ran away from them. As we went our feet sounded like drums on the ground—there were so many of us.

That same night we went on about ten miles farther, and by that time it was near morning and so we stopped again. We had a little food with us and also some blankets, and so we spread these out and lay down in a line to sleep.

About a quarter of a mile away there was a little hill, and in a short while we saw the Mexicans come out on top of this. We could see that they had two dogs there, and one of them was white and the other was black. They both had long ears. While the Mexicans stood there and looked at us we crossed over the canyon and looked back at them from the other side. There they were, still standing on the rocks and we counted twenty-six of them. Then we hollered back to them and they hollered back to us. We could see that they were drinking some liquor out of bottles and that when they had drunk all there was they threw the bottles away. After that they started to shoot their guns up at the sky. We knew that these Mexicans always did this, and so when they shot at the sky we understood it.

When we saw that there were only twenty-six of them, we thought that we might as well go on ahead and lay an ambush for them and fight them. We all agreed about this and we were mad because we had been chased by these Mexicans all last night. So we started on ahead, and farther on we came to a big canyon through which there was only one way to go, and there we stopped.

There were lots of us, eighty-seven, and we were ready for the Mexicans. Soon they came up and we ran out at them as fast as we could. I was out in front. The Mexicans had got to this canyon almost the same time that we had. As soon as they got to us they started to shoot at us right away. Now when they had shot at us this way we all said, "Don't anyone run off. Everyone must go for the Mexicans now." Some of the older men kept telling the younger ones not to run from the Mexicans, but to stay there and fight them. Now we started to shoot, and when we fired we could see three of the Mexicans fall. Those Mexicans were drunk, but anyway they kept on coming and didn't care because they had drunk so much of their liquor.

The father of John Rope was the chief who was leading us. During the fight he got shot in the hand but he didn't get scared. Before the fight had started, when we had first got to the canyon, our chief had told us, "We better go in the canyon, and then some of us go up on each side of the slopes. If we all go in a line down the creek here, then if the Mexicans shoot at us they won't be able to help hitting some of us."

In this fight we killed six of the Mexicans. Of our party, one got shot in the hand, one got shot in the neck, and one in the sole of the foot, and some of the others were wounded a little also. None of us got killed, but there were about twelve who got wounded.

After the fight we stayed there for two nights and then split up. The twelve men who were wounded started for home. The six Mexicans who had been killed were packed off on mules to the Mexican town by the rest of the soldiers. The time of that fight was the only time that we saw any Mexicans on this trip.

From the place where the fight had been, we set out. We got to a mountain and right on top of it we met three Chiricahua. They told us that they had seen the Mexican soldiers pass close by them. They said that they had wanted to meet the Mexicans and start a fight with them and shoot at them. But the Mexicans had looked so mean that they had not bothered with them, and had been afraid to shoot at them. When the Mexicans had seen them, four of the soldiers had grabbed their guns as if they were going to shoot at the Chiricahua, and that's why the Chiricahua had left them alone.

On the top of this mountain our bunch split up, and part went to the west and part to the east. Later on we came together again, and right above there is a big town for which we headed. This was the same town that we had been to before and that night we intended to go to this town and try to get some horses. On account of this we sent six men on ahead to look around.

Late that night we all went to the town and there were seventy of us all together now, but even so we got scared on account of something and all ran off from that place. We camped at the foot of a mountain that night, and the next night we got to the only springs which come out in that part of the country and made camp there. While we were near these springs we captured some horses, and then started off driving these horses for four days, going steady. We traveled always at nighttime, and after we had gone for four nights we traveled by day.

After eight more days we were back with our people once more, and there was lots of dancing because we had been successful. They put up a dance which lasted all night and till morning. That dance was given on account of the six Mexicans that we had killed. We had just seen those Mexicans fall and had never gone to them, but all the same we made a dance over it. That's the way we used to do when we came back from raids and the warpath.

I have been many times to Mexico this way when I was a young man. It is almost as if I had grown up in Mexico. From Mexico we always used to bring back lots of horses and cattle, burros and mules. In the old days some Mexicans and also a few White people used to come from the north to get horses, mules and burros from us that we had taken in Mexico. They used to trade us blankets, guns, and gunpowder for them.

ⅢⅠ

The next time that I went to Mexico, at one place we stopped to camp we got some liquor from the Mexicans and became drunk on it. It was mescal. The mescal that they used to make the liquor grew quite a long way off from that place.

When they made the mescal, the Mexicans would get a cowhide and make a sort of vat out of it. This cowhide they would set on a hard cement floor there. There was a little pipe which ran down into this hide and drained the mescal into it. When they were making it they had to sprinkle the mescal with something. On the other side they had their pit to roast the mescal in. After the mescal was cooked they ran the pipe from it into the cowhide. When they ran the liquor off out of the cowhide, it was then mescal and ready to drink.

They had lots of bottles and barrels there to put the liquor in. When we got to this place some of our bunch drank the mescal and some got a cow stomach and filled it with the mescal. After we filled the cow stomach we went with it up to the top of the mountain there and had a good time drinking the mescal in it. We all got feeling good.

From here we went on to a big town. We went up on top of the mountain there and sat looking down at the houses in the town. Then while we were sitting there it started to rain a little. About a quarter of a mile off we could see a small corral and it was built of stone. It was about as big as the shade of this cottonwood that we are sitting beneath here, and on account of its being built of stone it was hard to get into by tearing down the walls. There was a gate made of big poles set in the ground on one side but this was on the side facing toward the house near the corral. We could see a lot of mules in the corral, and in with them there was one white horse with a bell around its neck. "That white horse will be mine," I told the other men.

While we were still sitting there it got dark and then we started for the corral, going on down the hill to it. There were eleven of us. When we got there the father of Francis Drake roped the white horse and it was a good one. He said to me, "This horse is not mine, but I will just ride her in front of the mules so that they will follow her. I will take off the bell and just rattle it once in a while, so that the mules will hear it." We took all those mules out of that corral that night and started out to go by another big town that was about eight miles away. About two days before this some other Apache had taken some horses from the town, and the Mexican soldiers had chased them. On account of this the Mexicans were on the lookout for more of our people.

The only way that we could take our stock through that part of the country was through a pass, so we had to try and get through this pass. When we got to the pass the Mexicans cut us off there. We had about eighty mules in the bunch that we had taken from the corral and we were herding them along to get through the pass.

It was just about early morning when the Mexicans struck us and got the mules from us. Then when they had the mules they started for us. We got away on the mules that we were riding, but these were the only ones that we were able to get away with.

All the rest the Mexicans took back from us. I was riding a good brown mule, and my father-in-law, the father of Francis Drake, was still riding the white horse that had had the bell. He said to me, "Tomorrow I will give the horse to you."

When we got away from the Mexicans we all went to the top of a big mountain there and stopped to talk. We said that we had only a few mules and so there was no use going home yet—we might just as well go on and try and get some more horses. So we left the mules and the horse on the top of the mountain with three men to look after them, and told them that we would be back in three days. Then, eight of us started off on foot.

Just about sundown we got near a big town in the valley and struck an old road there which we followed along. As we walked along the road we saw some Mexicans coming with some burros. Pretty soon we would meet them. As soon as they saw us they started to run for us. My father-in-law who was in charge of us said, "Don't run from them. We will go at them. There are only about sixteen of them."

Now the Mexicans were close to us and they started to circle around us on their horses. My father-in-law shouted to me not to run off but to go for the Mexicans. There was one Mexican who rode by me, and as he rode he hung down on the other side of his horse so that he wouldn't get shot.

I had a bow and arrows with me and now I shot at him. The arrow went over him, but the next time I shot and the arrow hit the horse in the neck, just below the mane. The horse started to pitch with the Mexican and he jumped off to the ground. He ought to have waited till he was bucked off. The other Mexicans saw the man on the ground and one of them grabbed him up and they ran off with him.

Now we all agreed to shoot as many of the Mexicans' horses as we could and this way we killed two horses. Then the Mexicans got scared and ran off and left us. One of our men had been scared in this fight also and had run away. We looked for him till it got dark, and as we didn't find him it looked to us as though he had been killed. "We will look for him some more tomorrow," we said.

Then we struck out for the foot of a mountain there, and when we reached the base that man caught up with us. That's the way some of our people do; they get scared in a fight and run off and hide. Men who understand about fighting never get lost or hide themselves. They stay and fight no matter how hard the fight is. They never run off and leave their guns behind, but they stay right there and keep on fighting. I did this way one time and I will tell you about it later on.

That same night we went back to where we had killed the two horses and we butchered them for some meat. Each one of them had a good saddle on, new ones, and we took them off. Our leader said that we would pack them back with us. I took off one of the saddles and was going to pack it back but one of the other men, my cousin, said to me, "Give me that saddle for myself, my cousin," and so I gave it to him, and he carried it back to where we had our horses on top of the mountain. Another man took the other saddle and the two of them started off with the saddles. That left only six of us there and so we decided to go and try to get some more things from the Mexicans.

We set out and went to the top of a mountain and camped there. There was a big town with mountains near it and we went there to look around. There we saw some horses, twenty-one head, all gentle, and so we went to them. One of the horses was a gray roan with a long shaggy mane, and on account of this we knew that he was a broncho. Our leader told us, "That horse is a broncho so don't try to catch him. When a horse is too wild like that, leave him alone and don't try to rope him. If you rope him he might run off and take your rope with him and the other horses would follow him."

So we started to catch up the other horses and I roped a big black gelding. One of the men roped the gray roan anyway in spite of what our leader had said. The broncho started to pull him off and there were three men holding onto the rope. But all the same the horse got away and took the rope with him. He ran around us in a circle and all the other horses that were loose followed him. There were two horses that we tried to rope who got away and all the others ran after them. They ran for the town which was about two miles away, dragging two ropes after them. Pretty soon they reached the town, and the Mexicans saw them come in with the ropes so they knew that someone was trying to catch their horses.

There were some Mexican troops in the town and right away they came out and made for the place where the trail that we had to take went into the hills. It was the only way that we could get out of there, and that way they knew they could cut us off. We tried to hide ourselves but the Mexicans had seen us already.

One of our men said, "I don't want the Mexicans to get their horses back from us," and he took his spear up and killed the horses that we had with us. Our leader spoke to us now and said, "All these Mexicans, when they were babies, were nursed at the breasts of their mothers and that's why you can get away from them.[19] They have hearts, but they are soft."

When he said this to us we all started for the only place that we could get through, and at the same time the Mexicans came at us. They all came on foot and there was only one of them mounted. He rode a gray mule behind the others as if he was driving them to us. This is the way that we had a hard time that day.

When the trouble started I got down behind a rock and hid there. The Mexican bullets hit the rock and knocked off splinters from it. These splinters hit me and made me mad. They stung when they hit my body. We were ready to fight now, and no matter if the Mexicans were shooting their guns at us or not, we didn't think that the guns would kill us. The bullets went "*lu, lu, lu,*" and they kicked out clouds of dust from the ground about us.

We were in a bad place there, and we couldn't fight from where we were sitting behind the rocks so we got out around the shoulder of the hill, and then made straight for the hill where the Mexicans were. As we came we kept shooting at the Mexicans, and this time they all ran away from us, even though there were only six of us. One of the Mexicans we chased for a long way and shot him in the legs. He fell to the ground, and when he did this all the other Mexicans went to him and grabbed him up and carried him to the top of the hill.

Now we could get through the gap and by the Mexicans. That's the way with our people; if a fight starts and if a man fights hard and doesn't lose his head he is all right, but if he gets scared then he is likely to be killed. It's the same way with Mexicans or White people. Even if two men get caught by a lot of others they will come out all right in the fight if they are brave and are good fighters. They will talk to each other and tell each other to fight well.

This way, if there was a party of our people traveling out in the open country and they were attacked by some Mexicans, then the men who would understand about war would tell the others, "Don't run off. Stay here and fight. Don't go and leave the other poor men to do all the fighting. If you do this your name will not be good, and there will be bad stories going around about you back home."[20] It was this way that our leader spoke to us during the fight, and that was how we were able to get by all those Mexicans.

After we got through the gap where the Mexicans were we kept on till we came to where there were two big mountains, and between these two mountains we went, down a valley right in the middle to a place where we were going to hunt for more horses. Sometimes as we traveled along the Mexican troops saw us but we were never stopped. The Mexicans themselves always saw us but they didn't bother with us.

When we got to that place we caught up seven head of horses that we found. There were six of us so that we only had to lead one of the horses and rode all the rest. There were lots of bronchos at that place also and we were going to wait till night and drive them all off with us. But just before we were going to do this the Mexicans saw us and we had to get away from them. This way we only got off with the seven head that we already had. We decided to ride all night and get back to that big mountain where we had been before. So we set out and got there at sunrise. It had been two days ago that we had last eaten and we were very hungry now.

The horse that was being led was a good horse and so the man who was leading him said to me, "You kill that bad horse you are riding and I will give you this good horse that I am leading." The horse that I was riding was a good one all right but he kept switching his tail, and on account of this I didn't like him. So I killed him and took the other horse.

There was a town about eight miles ahead of us, and the Mexicans had sent word on ahead to the people in the town telling them about us taking the horses, and it seemed as though we were to have more bad times again, though we didn't know it then.

We said that we might just as well turn the horses loose and let them drag our ropes so that we could catch them up easily, and then we could take a rest by the spring that was there. So we did this and then started to cook some of the horsemeat over a fire.

While we were doing this the Mexicans came up on us without our knowing it. Right on the side in some low places the Mexicans hid themselves and surrounded us. While we were still eating they shot into our fire and scattered it all over the place. When that happened we all got up and ran off in the brush.

I was in such a hurry to be gone that I forgot my bow and quiver of arrows and left them lying there. Then I remembered them and went back to get them. Some of the other men who did the same thing just let it go and didn't come back after their weapons. I didn't get scared and never lost my weapons. At that place the Mexicans killed one of us, and so that left only five of us.

That same day we got back to the mountain where we had left the others to look after the horses several days ago. Maybe the Mexicans had come to that place and taken those horses back also, we thought. Our leader felt bad now about all that had happened and he said, "Wherever we go the Mexicans always chase us and fight with us. We have had bad luck and so we might just as well go on home."

In a little while we came to where we had left the other three men with horses, and they were still there with the two men who had taken the saddles back to them that time that we captured them from the Mexicans. So we all set out to try and get some cattle to drive home, even if we couldn't get any more horses. When we came to the place we were heading for we waited until evening, and then rounded up a bunch of cattle, lots of them, about sixty head. Then we drove them off towards home.

We had a hard time driving those cattle home but finally we reached the south side of the Graham Mountains here, and at that place we divided up the cattle. My share of the trip was four head of cattle and one horse, which together made five head. All the rest got four head of cattle apiece, too, except the two men on foot, who only got three head apiece.

We came on right through over a flat that is just this side of the Graham Mountains, no matter if there were White people and soldiers living at Goodwin Springs, which there were. I took all my cattle and joined my people once more.

9

One time, later, on another raid, three of us got close to a Mexican town, and I went on one side of the houses and the other two went to the other side of them. The man in charge of us told us what to do because he had been there before and had seen horses in the corral, and so he thought that there would still be horses there.

It was midnight now but it was bright so that we could see a big corral right in the middle of the town. This was the corral where there should have been some horses, but there were none in it. I stood there and listened, and then I heard above the big corral the sound of horses neighing. So I went right in the town and started through it. I was not scared at all and it was midnight then anyway.

In those days I was not scared of anything and so I went right on to where I had heard the horses, thinking that the other two men must be there already. Pretty soon I came to where the horses were in a small corral. There were four of them. There was only one gate to the corral on the lower side, so I went to this and crawled under the gate bars and got to the horses in the corral. They were four good big ones.

Our chief had told us to all meet him out at the end of the town, and so I went back to the end of the town there to try and find them. I walked right through the town and finally got there where we three had first split up. Now I whistled to them but they didn't answer. There was a bridge there and I looked for their tracks by it. By this time it was getting to be early morning. There was a bright moon, and so I could see their tracks there where they had crossed the bridge and gone on some place.

I knew where I had seen those four horses, and so now I thought that I might as well go back there and get one of them anyway and ride it out through the town. So I started back to the little corral where they were.

Then I went into the corral and roped one of the horses there —a good gray one. With my rope I made a bridle to ride the horse with, put it in his mouth and tied it there. Then I got on him, still in the corral, and rode him around inside there doing nothing about getting away out of the town.

There were four crossbars across the gate, and now I let these down carefully so as not to make any noise. Then I roped a bay horse, thinking that I would ride the gray and lead the other right out of the town. If some Mexicans should see me and holler, then I could turn one loose and get away on the other.

I was all ready now, and so I started to get on the bay horse and then lead the other slowly through the town. There was a wide road right between the houses. I kept to the main road, leading the other horse behind. All the other horses that I had left in the corral followed after me.

I was going along slowly when I heard a Mexican only about as far as from here to that cottonwood tree over there [approximately twenty feet] holler, "Caballos." Then someone shot off a gun and when I heard the shot I started to ride fast and get away. I made a run for it on the horse and crossed over the bridge on the edge of the town, then on over a wash there with a little water in it. The two loose horses went on in front of me now, and I started to travel slowly once more.

When I had gone about a quarter of a mile the sun started to come up. Then I made for the place where we had left the other two men. I saw one horse track going towards this place already. In the morning I got out to our camp with all four of the horses. There I found the rest of our party.

Grenville Goodwin photo, courtesy Arizona State Museum

Joseph Hoffman

3

JOSEPH HOFFMAN

Originally from Cibecue, Joseph Hoffman was living at San Carlos when he was interviewed in 1932. He did not know his age, but guessed that he was over eighty-five. Goodwin notes that Hoffman had at one time been a Reservation judge, possessed supernatural power, and knew much of the old culture ". . . with which he felt a great affinity." Hoffman's reminiscences deal almost exclusively with warfare. Especially valuable is his detailed account of a massive expedition against the Navajo, and another in which Western Apaches are joined by Yavapais in an attack against the Pima.

I am a *dziltadn* [i.e., of the Cibecue subtribal group] and I was born at *ki nandune* ['concealed houses'] where there is a mountain and where our people first settled when they came from the north long ago.[1] There were some old houses at this place, up under the bluff, and that was the reason that it was called this way. My father came from Canyon Creek.[2] In those days when I was just a baby, our people used to live at many different places.

Then when I was little I had to learn to do many things. First I learned to sit up, then I began to crawl, and finally to walk. At first when I tried to walk I fell on the ground, but later on I got better at it. When I was only two or three years old I didn't know

[73]

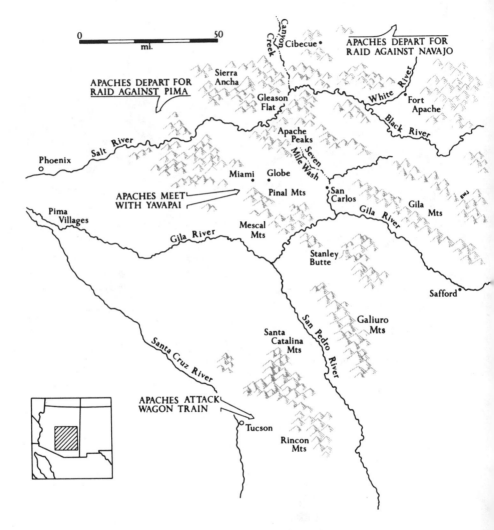

0 ──────────────── 50
mi.

APACHES DEPART FOR
RAID AGAINST NAVAJO

Canyon Creek

Cibecue •

Sierra
Ancha

Gleason
Flat

White River

Fort
Apache

APACHES DEPART FOR
RAID AGAINST PIMA

Apache
Peaks

Black River

Salt River

Phoenix
○

Miami
•

Globe
•

Seven
Mile Wash

San
Carlos

Gila River

Gila
Mts

Pinal Mts

APACHES MEET
WITH YAVAPAI

Pima
Villages

Mescal
Mts

Gila River

Stanley
Butte

Safford •

Santa
Catalina
Mts

Galiuro
Mts

San Pedro River

Santa Cruz River

APACHES ATTACK
WAGON TRAIN

Tucson
○

Rincon
Mts

Joseph Hoffman Narrative

anything, but when I got to be about six, then I began to understand things and I started in to talk. By the time that we went to *tis das ?an* ['cottonwoods, growing out'] and started to clear land there to make farms, I was able to think a little for myself.[3] This place is at the side of a mountain there. This was all long before the White people came to this country. In those days our people used to dig with sharp-pointed sticks to make a hole in the ground in which to plant seeds. We raised corn.

After awhile I came to know that our people and the Mexicans and the White people did not get along together, and that we used to fight each other, and try to kill one another. We had no guns, but we made arrows out of cane and put points of white flint on them. With these we could kill our enemies. The Mexicans used to have spears with steel points and they fought with these. We killed lots of White people and Mexicans when we fought with them long ago. In one fight that they had, our people took spears from the Mexicans, and then all our men had spears. During the fight one of the Mexicans stuck a lance clean through the chest of one of our men. Then another one of our men jumped at the Mexican and killed him with a lance, and they brought the wounded man home, still with the lance hole in his chest. He never died from this wound at all. All these things were going on around me, and I began to think about them.

When the corn became ripe at that place where our people had planted, we harvested it, and then all went on to Cibecue to where there were lots of farms. At this time of year, in the fall, there always used to be lots of our people who gathered at Cibecue. There were big farms at that place. This fall when we all went there, a certain woman whose son had been killed by the White people about one year ago went to the chief there and spoke to him. She said, "You have a bow and arrows. You know what happened to my son, so why don't you go to the White people and make war on them?"

On account of this they decided to hold a war dance there, and then start out to fight the White people. I remember that dance, and it lasted for two nights before the men left to go on the warpath. When they left they said to us that they would be back in forty days. "If we kill some White people before that time, we will be back before forty days. We will send a message back to you if we kill six or seven White people, and if we are bringing back cattle." Then they started off, and on that war party they killed lots of White people and brought back one scalp with them.

When the party came home the women got ready and painted themselves with a band, spotted, over one shoulder and under the other arm. Then they danced, wearing nothing more than a G-string. They had their hair tied up on the top of their heads so that it stood up straight. Before the war party had come into the camps, four or five of the women dressed this way, went out and hid in the brush and waited there till the chief of the party came along. When he came abreast of them they all jumped out at him, and if one of them had a spear she would kill the horse that the chief was riding on right there.[4] When I saw this I knew for sure that the White people and the Mexicans did not like us. When they got in I saw the one scalp that they had brought back with them. They held it up on the end of a stick, and this way they danced with it, around about. Our enemies used to do the same way with us.

In those days we had no flour and other food that we have now, but we had the fruit of different kinds of cactuses, corn, and mescal. We used to eat the fruit of the prickly pear cactus and lots of other kinds of plants. It was God who made the earth, and it was He who in the beginning told us to eat these different kinds of plants. This is the way that I learned how our people did.

Some time passed and then I heard that the Pimas had killed lots of our people. Then, about one year after this, three men were sent out to go all around and tell all the men to meet at the foot of the mountain at Sierra Ancha in so many days. When they all came there, they would start out against the Pimas. The women put up food for the men to take along with them on the way— dried meat and seeds. Now they were all at the place and from there they started out, some on horses and the rest on foot. Some of the men had war shields,[5] round and of two thicknesses. An arrow wouldn't go through these. They also had some breastplates made of sections of wood tied together and then fastened at the waist. They wore these so that arrows could not pierce their chests.

When they came to the Pima camp they surrounded it at night, and in the early morning they were hiding there in the brush. Right then at dawn they attacked the Pimas while they were still asleep. There were lots of our people, and they killed all the Pimas with their arrows and spears. Then they set fire to the wickiups of the Pimas, and there they caught lots of the boys and girls—all Pima children. They took a scalp there, too. After the fight they sent one of the men back to us at home to tell us about what had happened.

When the war party came home they set up a dance for them. The people whose relatives had been killed by the Pimas that time before were told to come to where the dance was. When the Pima children were brought there they were divided among the women whose relatives had been killed. This way these women got all of the Pima children in place of the ones who had been killed. This is called *gɛgodza ʔ* ['to be paid back'], and when it was done they felt all right again.

I was getting bigger now, and I knew what was going on around me and understood everything. Then it was that a Pinal Apache man came to Cibecue where we were, and told everyone to come to a place near where Miami now is—all the men—and to all meet there in a group. At that time our people used only to wear shirts and dresses of buckskin. The women dressed in buckskin also. Our people set off for that place. When we got there they made a big sweat lodge like this one here in my camp. The women had to bring food to that sweat lodge so that the men could eat while they were there. They killed a horse so that there would be plenty to eat.

At the sweat lodge the chief talked to the men, and said to them, "Our people were killed by the White people some time ago. That is the reason that I wanted you all to come here today. So now we have to kill the White people on the same day that they killed our people." The chief talked from a rocky point so that all the people could see and hear him. I was there then and I saw all this. I was a big boy now. The chief went on and said, "They got killed at Tucson and so we have to go to that place. That's what you remember, and that is what we are here for today. All right then, let's go there to fight," he said.

After him another chief got up and talked just like a sergeant. He told all the boys and girls to go and get lots of wood because there was going to be a dance that night. At that place they danced for two nights. When the dance was over at dawn, we all slept during the morning. About noon we all woke up and got ready to go on with things. I wondered to myself why it was that the White people killed our people, and I thought a lot about it.

Now we had another dance there. One of the women whose relatives had been killed by the Whites that time went to the chief who had given the talk and spoke to him. "Your face is all right and you are young yet. You have no way to go but to the White people, and so you might just as well go in the ground," she said, and that was the way that she made him brave so that he would go and fight.[6]

That morning after the dance, they made another sweat lodge for the men. Some more men had come in on horses and even though they had not been notified to come, they wanted to go on the war party when they heard that the dance was going on. These men were of the San Carlos band and of the Arivaipa band. They told the chief that they wanted to go along, and he said, "All right. If you want to help, it is good. We will go together."

That second time that we had the dance the men danced with shields and spears—all of them. There was one girl who danced on the side alone, and all the men lined up in front of her and danced there. Whichever way the girl turned while she danced, the men had to do the same way as she did. As she danced she held out her arms spread in front of the men, and they sang a song as if they were praying to the girl. This song was made so that no one would get killed, and the reason that she held out her arms that way was so that no bullets or arrows could get by her. She was holding them back.

In those days there were no White people living there at that place, and our people always used to camp up on the hills there so that if any White people should come traveling through there, as they sometimes did, they could not get at us. When the war party left they told the rest of us to wait on the mountain there for them. "We will be gone for twenty days, but if we kill some White people before that time we will be back before that," they said. I didn't go on that war party, but I heard later on what happened on it.

When they got down near Tucson they saw five or six wagons coming, and so they waited ahead of them to ambush them. When the wagons came up—there were six of them—our men attacked them and killed about half of the White people that were with them and captured all the wagons. In them they found shirts, calico, and some food. They also took two Mexicans captive. None of our people got hurt at all. Now they all started back with the two prisoners and the things that they had taken. They sent word ahead to us to meet them at a place where they were going to make a big dance. From the wagon train they had captured a big drum and also a bugle. Long ago we only used to fight with other Indian people, and not with the White people.

At that place they made one of the Mexican boys that they had taken dance. He tried to sing like one of our people, and he danced and jumped around. "Ye-ye, ye-ye," he sang. The men brought back with them three flintlock guns, and these were the first that I had ever seen of this kind. The men danced all night, and in the morning the chief spoke. "I am very thankful. What we set out to do we have done. We did to them the same that they did to us a year ago. Now we have done it to them, so you can all go on to your homes. I am very thankful." So after that we all started for home. The Arivaipa people and the San Carlos people had already gone to their homes.

After that war party against the Whites we went back to our farm on the east side of the Sierra Ancha. First of all we planted some wheat, and when this was ripe we put in corn. We had to set to work and make a dam in the stream so that we could irrigate our fields. Also we had to make ditches. First some of us dug along with our digging sticks, and then those who came behind took away the loose dirt in baskets. That is the way that we made our ditches. There used to be lots of deer in our country, and we ate the meat of them when we could get it. Near where we lived we used to hunt them. One man would go up on the top of a hill, and four or five other men would drive the deer up to him so that he could shoot them with arrows. About all that we did in those days was to hunt and fight.

I knew everything now, and sometimes I went to talk with the men. I was about ten or twelve years old. As soon as we had all the crops harvested in the fall, our people went over to the other side of where Miami is now. We went there so that we could get some mescal, and also because it was easy to start out from here to go to Mexico on raids. All of us moved down to that place, even women and children. When we got there the women and children stopped and stayed on there in camp. Only about four or six of the men went on from there to the Pima settlements to get some horses. Right away they were back with some horses that they had taken from the Pimas.

Not long after this I saw some Yavapais coming to our camp. They had come to see my father, and they talked with him in our language. When they got through talking, my father said to us that these Yavapais wanted us to go to a place where there were lots of Yavapais waiting for us to visit them. They said that they wanted us to start with them tomorrow. So we decided to go there, and the next morning we all started out so that we could get there and make a dance with them. We came to that place about noon, and there were lots of the Yavapais and many of their women as well. The Yavapais who had come to get us said that they wanted to go and fight the Pima people. This was the reason that the Yavapais wanted our people to go with them.

Now the Yavapais started to get ready for the dance. They painted their faces all black and around their eyes they made a circle of red. When I saw the Yavapais this way I got scared and ran away because I thought they were going to kill us. The Pimas had killed some of these Yavapais some time ago and that was why they were going to fight them now. That was why they had asked us to help them. All that night they danced and, in the morning, the dance was over.

Just after the dance, in the morning, the Yavapais all came around our camp. They were still painted up, and that was when I got scared and ran off. In our camp they jerked the blankets off of some of our people, and they hit the fires with sticks so that they knocked them all about. Then I saw them coming again, all in a line, and I got way off and hid behind a big rock. Right there they sang and danced some. When they were through, our men mixed with them, and they all started off for the Pima settlements.

When they went, I and the other children and the women all went on top of a small mountain and the men told us to stay there till they got back. They said that they would be back in four days. The time went on and then there was only one day left till the men were due back. Then it was four days that had gone by, and the war party came back with three Pima horses that they had captured. In the fight they had killed ten of the Pimas.

When they came back our people started back to our homes at 'cottonwoods, growing out' and got to that place after some travel. In the fight with the Pimas my father had taken a gun from them. I guess that the Pimas must have taken it from the Americans when they fought with them. It was a muzzleloader and had a stick that you had to ram down the barrel. It had two barrels and you put caps on it to fire it.

Some time after we had come back to our camp east of Sierra Ancha, a man rode over from Cibecue on a mule. He was *tseyidn* [a clan: 'in the rocks people'], chief of some of the people over there. This chief spoke to us and called us brothers. He said that a certain chief had been killed some time ago, and that he wanted our men to come and help him now. It was to the *tsečiscine* [a clan: 'rocks jutting out people'] chief that he spoke, and it was of him that he was asking the help.[7] That's the way that we used to do—always go around to help each other out when our relatives got in trouble. So on account of this chief asking our people to help him, our people moved over to Cibecue. On the way we stopped one night, and the next day we got in about noon. I was a big boy now.

The day that we got to Cibecue that same chief who had come to get us rode over to our camp to talk with us some more. He said, "One of our chiefs was killed some time ago. On account of this I want you to come and help us. We have all the food ready for you." It was only to the 'rocks jutting out people' that he spoke. That evening some women came carrying baskets with green corn in them, and they gave this to us. The chief had one cow killed for us also. Our chief told us to eat it and divide it up so that all of us would get some.

The next morning the people of the *da?izkan* [a clan: 'flat-topped people'] came in there and made camp. The same *tseyidn* chief went to them and talked to them. This time I could not hear what he said, but later on I saw them bringing food to these people, just as they had done for us. They killed a horse for them also. Now all the people got ready and made a war dance. After the dance was over we all moved over to a place west of Cibecue and stopped to camp there. The war party went on from there, but we did not follow them.

While we were camping there, two young fellows came to us. They were both of them my *sibeže* and the father of one of them had been killed and the father of the other was sick.[8] They had come to our camp to see my father, and when they spoke to him they said that they wanted to go with some other boys to Tucson to raid. My father said to them, "That is not right. You ought to have gone with these others who have gone to war. I won't let you go now." But the boys said, "Our children don't have any rawhide for their moccasin soles, and that is why we want to go and get some cattle." So my father let them go and said, "If you see any cattle and capture them, don't stop on the way when you are driving them. Come right back here. Keep on going for two days and two nights steady. That is the way that you will get away from the White people. Start from here tomorrow early."

This way these young fellows started off, and they didn't notify us when they would be back. I heard later of what happened to them on this trip. When they first started out and got to the top of the hill on their way, a great wind came up and blew downwards on them. After some time they got near Tucson, and there they took some oxen and started to drive them back home. They drove them all that day and the night. The next day they kept on till evening, and then they stopped to camp for the night. Five of them there were in the party.

The next morning at sunrise they could see about five Americans coming after them. They were about a mile away when they saw them. The Americans had guns and they began to shoot at our men. In the first volley one of the party got killed. Then two of our men started and ran up the side of a hill there. About halfway up one of them was killed also, right on the side of the hill. The one who got to the top of the hill was killed right there at the summit. This left only two of our men, but they got away all right. One of them went to the Apache Peaks, where he belonged, and the other came home to us near Cibecue. After that, we left where we were staying and went to a place not far from Sierra Ancha.

We lived there for one year, and then a chief came to see my father and said, "Why are you living by yourself here, as if you had run away from the other people?" My father told him, "I feel sorry about my relatives that I lost. I am going down there to Tucson sometime to pay the White people back."[9] The chief that had come to see us here wanted us to go to his camp, so in the morning we started out for that place and got there.

We lived there for a while near that chief who had come to get us. This chief had some cattle down on the other side of Apache Peaks and he sent down there for them. They brought the cattle in and he had one of them killed for us. All this was done because they were going to talk about those three men who got killed by the White people about one year ago. So they made a big sweat bath, and there they talked over about going down to Tucson. This way they decided to go, and so the next day we gathered wood for the dance that was to be. That night they danced all night, and the next day we all went down to a canyon northwest of Stanley Butte.

From this place they sent some men to the people at a farm site north of the present town of Globe, Arizona. At Stanley Butte we danced all night, and the next day about noon the men who had been sent to that place came back with some Pinal Apaches. They came on horseback and there were lots of them. The night of the day that the Pinals got there and joined us, they danced again and the Pinals copied the way that I had seen the Yavapai do that time before. They went among the camps and knocked the wickiups down and then came away again. They caught a dog and killed him. Then they took his guts out and hung them around their necks. This way they showed what they were going to do to the White people of Tucson.

In the morning we told the Pinals that we would go to a mountain east of where Globe is now and that we would wait for them there to join us and start off for Tucson from there. We had one more dance when we had all our bundles packed up. Then as soon as it was over we set out. One of the women came to talk to the men who were going to fight. She said, "Thanks, you boys, for going to Tucson to fight. I want you to be careful on the way and when you fight." After the talk she gave to us, we started out. I ran after them because I thought I was old enough to go to war, and I wanted to see the fight. But my father didn't want me to go. "You are too young now to go to war. When you are older, then you will be able to go. Now you better go back home," he told me. So I didn't go that time. This way the war party left us and went down to near Tucson.

When they got there they saw six wagons coming, so they stepped in front of them, and when they came up our men started to fight with the White people. Some of our men went to the wagons and pulled the White men out of them and killed them there. They were soldiers and those that they didn't kill they drove away from the wagons. One of the soldiers who was on horseback got shot in the back with an arrow. He couldn't reach it to pull it out. So he ran on his horse to overtake the other White men who had gone to get some help, but he died before he got to them. Our men killed three of the Whites and captured one preacher. They were going to kill him when they caught him, but he got down on his knees and started to pray to the sun. When they saw him do this, they knew that he was a preacher and so they let him go. They told him to take the road and not to look back —that no one would hurt him.

During the fight one of our men ran up on the side of a little hill and lay down behind it to shoot at the Whites. The White people knew that he was there and so they waited till he raised up to shoot again, and when he stuck his head up they shot him in the head and killed him. They only scalped one of the White men they had killed.

That party took lots of calico and clothes from the Whites. They also got fifty-four gallons of whiskey there. It was in lots of barrels, and they thought that the barrels had water in them. So they broke open the top of one with a big rock, and then they found out that it was whiskey. They took all that the Whites had —all their horses and teams—everything. They were going to take the things that they wanted and start for home, but that man who had been killed by the Whites was not there. "Where is he?" they said, and they started to look all around. After a time they found where he was lying dead with his gun in his arms. Right there where he was lying, they threw that White man's scalp away that they had taken. After that they all started for home with the booty.

We had sent for the Pinals to help us in this fight, but they had never turned up where we were to meet them. Now these same Pinals heard that our men had taken all these clothes, cloth, and whiskey, and so they met our men. The Pinals got drunk on the whiskey. They said that now they were going to help us and ride back to the same place where our men had the fight, but they were just drunk. My father told these Pinals, "We don't believe you would help us again because we sent for you when we started out on this war party, but you never came with us as you said you would." At the war dance that we had had, these Pinals had said that they were going to do great things, but they did nothing.

Another time eight chiefs started out from Cibecue to take some horses and mules up to the Navajo country to trade with the Navajo. They told the rest of us to stay home and said that they would be back in so many days, and this way they left. When the time was come when they were due back, they never got back. Two days after that one of them got there and said that the Navajos had killed all the other seven. These seven were all big chiefs, one was of the *desčidn* ['horizontally red people'] clan, one of the *tiskadn* ['cottonwood standing people'], one of the *tseyidn* ['in the rocks people'], one of the *tsečisčine* ['rocks jutting out people'], one of the *dziłtadn* ['foot of the mountain people'] and one of the *dušdoę* ['flies in soup people'].

Some time after this happened, a woman was talking to her brother, a *dušdoę* chief. She said, "You remember our chief who got killed up in the Navajo country. You are a man, and a man ought not to stand for that. If your relatives get killed, you ought to do something about it." That chief started to think this over, and then he decided to notify the Pinal band, the Arivaipa band, the San Carlos band and the Apache Peaks band about what was in his mind. So he set out for the country of these bands and talked with their people. They made a plan for everyone to meet at the head of the Seven Mile Wash near Apache Peaks. Then that chief came back to Cibecue and told all the people that they were to go down across the Salt River to the head of Seven Mile Wash, and that the other people who lived south of the Salt River had agreed to meet there.

So we started out, taking lots of food with us, and made our first stop at Gleason Flat on the Salt River. There were a great many people along, and the line they made would have reached almost from here to Rice (three-quarters of a mile). Some were on foot and some on horses. The next day we got to the head of Seven Mile Wash. Soon after us the Pinal band got there. The day after that the San Carlos band came. After them the Arivaipa band got there, led by a big medicine man called *mbabɨjɛyɨ ʔ* ['Hears Like Coyote']. Then everybody was there—all the brave men—and ready to go against the Navajo.

Then early in the morning a woman began to talk to all the people there and said, "I am glad you are going up there to fight those Navajos for what they have done to our chiefs." She kept on talking from then on till noontime, praising them for going. They call this talking *nagołkat* ['fighting words']. There was a very big group of men there, and they all stood still while she talked. Then they said, "All right, we will go."

Then 'Hears Like Coyote' got up and spoke. He said, "We are going to the Navajo country to help because these chiefs have been killed. That's what they want us for." Then he stepped to one side to make medicine and find out what was going to happen. He took his cap off and looked inside it. No one knew how he did this. Inside it he saw children, women, and men. Then he said to the people, "We are going to kill fifteen women and fifteen men first, but we are not going to kill the one who killed our chiefs till the sun goes down. When it does, then we will kill the one who did it."[10] Then 'Hears Like Coyote' walked right to where that woman who spoke was and told her, "All right. We are going to do the way you want and kill all the Navajos who killed those seven chiefs. More than seven we will kill. The last one we kill will be the guilty one." The woman said thanks to him. Then they said they would put up a dance here and everyone agreed, so they did.

Next day we all left and went towards the Salt River and put up another dance at another place. After that we went on to Cibecue and stopped there. There were lots more men living at that place, and they wanted to join and help the war party. 'Hears Like Coyote' said, "I am not lying. I want all the women and children to gather here." When they had come, he stepped off

to one side and looked in his hat once more. Then he came back
and said that they would kill thirty people, as before. "We are
going to have a hard time to do it, though. But none of us will
be killed if we do hard work and fight well," he said. That man
was a very good medicine man. He was to look in his hat two
more times after this. But now he said to the people, "It's up
to you. Now go and eat and if you want to dance tonight, it's all
right, but I won't go to the dance. I want you to come back at
noon here tomorrow. I want to start soon."

We had a dance that night, all night. One of the big chiefs at
Cibecue told the people next morning to get the food ready and
grind lots of corn. Also he told the people to dance again. 'Hears
Like Coyote' had talked with that chief. That noon 'Hears Like
Coyote' had the people come together for the last time. Then he
told four men to come out and line up. When they did this, he
said, "All you four men point to the north to the Navajo country,"
and as they did, he prayed. Then while they were still lined up,
he stepped to one side and looked into his cap for the third time.
Again he saw fifteen women and fifteen men, and the guilty one
was not among them, but was to be killed at sunset.

He was sitting on horseback now and he talked to the war
party. "When you get into the fight, don't run away; for if you
do, you will be killed. You must fight well, and where you see
danger, go to it and not from it. Don't ever turn back. Now we
are going to start, and you are to stop at water when you get to a
certain spring north of Cibecue. But I will not go with you when
you leave. Don't look back at me on your way," he said to the
men. "In four days we will be on the edge of the Navajo country."
He wanted to stay behind and make medicine. Everything was
all ready—the horses were in, food packed, and so they started.
'Hears Like Coyote' had been the only one to talk and give any
orders. None of the chiefs had directed this thing at all because
the medicine man had great power and knew about war.

I was only a boy at that time and so I didn't go along when
the war party left, but I heard all about what happened. In four
days they stopped on the edge of the Navajo country. There 'Hears
Like Coyote' picked four men; one was a chief of the 'cottonwood
standing people,' a brother of one of the chiefs who had been
killed, the second was a 'rocks jutting out people' chief, the third

was the brother of 'Hears Like Coyote,' and the fourth was that medicine man himself. These four were to lead the war party from now on.

They all went pretty slowly for three days. Then about mid-afternoon of the third day they were pretty close to where the Navajo were. They kept on and by late evening had come close to the Navajo camps. Here 'Hears Like Coyote' picked two men and sent them off to locate the Navajo camps. There was a big wash at this place, and they knew that the Navajo were always camped someplace along it. About midnight the two men got back and said they had found a place where there were lots of Navajo camps. So everyone started right away to go to the Navajo. When they were close, they stopped and sent two men on horseback to reconnoiter the Navajo camp. They found lots of camps together in one place.

It was near dawn now, and 'Hears Like Coyote' divided his force up into four parts, each one under one of the four leaders, and each to attack the camp from a different side. 'Hears Like Coyote' took his part right straight to the front of the camp. They were so close that when they stopped they could hear a Navajo medicine man in one of the camps singing over a baby. Right then they started to go for the Navajos and killed all of them that were in the camp with their spears. Some of them climbed up into a piñon tree to try and get away, but they killed them with their spears right in the tree.

After the fight was over, 'Hears Like Coyote' wanted to know how many of the Navajos had been killed. They looked around and found that thirty had been killed, besides which many women and children had been captured. There were four sheep corrals at that place with sheep in them, and now 'Hears Like Coyote' said to drive all these sheep from the corrals out onto an open flat close by, and to put all the captives with the sheep. This they did and drove them all out onto the flat where they stopped. Then 'Hears Like Coyote' said, "We are going to fight here for three days, but anyway we want to take these sheep back with us."

It was morning now. Some of the Navajos had got away out of the camp and run off to some other Navajo camp and told the people there what had happened. So now a big party of Navajos was coming to where our people were out on the flat. They were mostly on horseback, and as soon as they got there, started to fight. That day they fought all the time until sundown. 'Hears Like Coyote' said to his men, "Don't be afraid. You will not be killed."

That night the fight was still going on and 'Hears Like Coyote' rode around among his men on horseback, talking to them. More and more Navajos kept coming to that place. All night they came till they were as thick as these bushes growing around here. But no one had been killed since those first thirty Navajos. It was impossible to see anything because there were so many horses and so much dust. At noon the next day they were still fighting.

Now the Navajos were all around our men, but we still had the sheep and had men in three circles about them. Then one Navajo spoke. He said, "Don't shoot me. I'm coming to you." Now everyone was quiet as this Navajo rode out to meet our people. When he had come pretty close he stopped. 'Hears Like Coyote' said, "A while ago seven of our chiefs got killed up here." The Navajo answered, "We didn't do it. We are your friends up here. But now you kill all our people. The one who killed those seven chiefs we have just sent for and he ought to be here pretty soon. None of our people did it at all."

Then 'Hears Like Coyote' took off his hat and looked into it and asked something. This way he knew that the Navajo spoke the truth and that the guilty one was coming. Then he said to his men, "Shoot well, for we are going to kill the man who has done this and who is coming here." Now that Navajo wanted to know what people our men were and where they were from and who the headman was. They told him. The Navajo answered, "Yes, I have heard of those people—they are good fighters. We are all played out because we have been fighting day and night. I think all our people will go away as soon as that man we have sent for gets here. We are all hungry. If we decide to leave here, I will come back and tell you." That's all that Navajo said. Then he rode away.

Now, way far off, our men could see some dust rising up. This was made by that man coming. Pretty soon the Navajos started to leave, and that Navajo who had spoken to our people before rode up again and said, "Well, the man who has done

that to your seven chiefs is here now, so we are going to leave
him at this place. It's pretty hard to kill you people, and we are
all played out now. You can have all the sheep and what people
you have captured. We have fought three days and three nights
now, so the rest of us are going away and are going to turn the
one who did it over to you. When you start for home, don't think
that we will try to ambush you on the way. Keep on going and
no one will bother you."

Then 'Hears Like Coyote' said to take the sheep and captives
and start moving. There was still some fighting going on then.
Pretty soon a man rode out from the Navajos and held up his
spear. "This is the one [the spear] I killed seven men with, and
I am going to do it again," he yelled. He was seated up behind
another man, double, and now they rode their horse down towards
the river there where that man who had spoken jumped off. All
our men shot at him, but no one could hit him. Our people kept
on driving the sheep in three herds and at the same time they were
fighting the Navajos.

Now the Navajo who had killed our seven chiefs jumped on
his horse and rode at a run towards our men. Then when he got
pretty close he jumped off and shot at them. All of our men shot
back at him, but couldn't hit him. They kept on this way, driving
the sheep and fighting off the Navajos who still had stayed there.
Again that man rode at our people, and when he was close
enough, jumped off and started shooting. There were four fights
going on in one place—one in back, one in front and one on
each side. Our people tried to keep on driving the sheep towards
home, but they couldn't make much headway.

About mid-afternoon that Navajo rode at our people again.
A man called *haskɛkɨłnihi* ['He Calls Himself Angry'] saw him
coming and hid down behind a bush. The Navajo didn't see him,
and not far off jumped down on the ground and started shooting
again. Right there 'He Calls Himself Angry' killed him. Another
Navajo rode up and tried to pick the dead man up by his hair
from his horse, but he missed. This was the one who had been
on the same horse with the dead man the first time. All our men
ran to the dead Navajo. After that, the war party sent one man
ahead to tell our people that they were coming with Navajo
captives and lots of sheep. The sheep were getting close now, and

we could see the dust coming up from them. They were in four parts. Lots of men and women who were there started to dance. There were so many of them that they would have stretched from here to the river (400 feet about). The people were glad because they knew that soon they would have lots of meat.

When the captives were brought in, they were put in the middle where all the people were and ordered to dance and sing. There was a big fat, Navajo woman who had a baby with her, and she had to dance and sing also. Everyone did. All the people were having a good time. The sheep had been brought up close. Now one woman started to sing for some of the sheep. She was given two sheep because she sang about the man who owned them. We always used to dance when our war parties brought back things from the enemy. This way everyone was satisfied.

All the people stayed at Cibecue for quite a while. 'Hears Like Coyote' took a good rest there. The people kept on dancing every night and at these dances there were lots of girls and women who won sheep from the men who owned them by singing to those men.[11] This all happened long before the White people came here, and the men who took part in that war against the Navajos are all dead now.

Grenville Goodwin photo, courtesy Arizona State Museum

John Rope

4

JOHN ROPE

In 1936, when Grenville Goodwin published an abridged version of this narrative in Arizona Historical Review *(Vol. 7, Nos. 1 and 2), he provided the following biographical information about John Rope:*

John Rope is now an old man living among his people at Bylas, Arizona, on the San Carlos Indian Reservation. He or his people did not keep track of their ages in the old days, but as near as it is possible to figure out, he was born about 1855. His real name was tlodiłhił, *which means "black rope," and by this title he is known to almost all his people. . . . I first met the old man in the fall of 1928 at Bylas, but it was not until the spring of 1932 that he told me these stories of his adventures.*

John Rope's narrative has mainly to do with his experiences as a scout for the U.S. Army, though the first part deals with some of his boyhood remembrances. He witnessed or participated in a number of critical events, including the founding of Camp Goodwin (1864), the government's ill-fated "removal program," and General Crook's famous campaign into Sonora in 1883. Of equal or greater interest is Rope's account of his role as an Indian scout and the overall picture his narrative gives of Western Apache society at a time when it was seriously disturbed and in the process of rapid change.

I was born at a place between Old Summit and Black River, but I don't remember much till we were living at Cedar Creek, just west of Fort Apache. I can remember playing as a child there

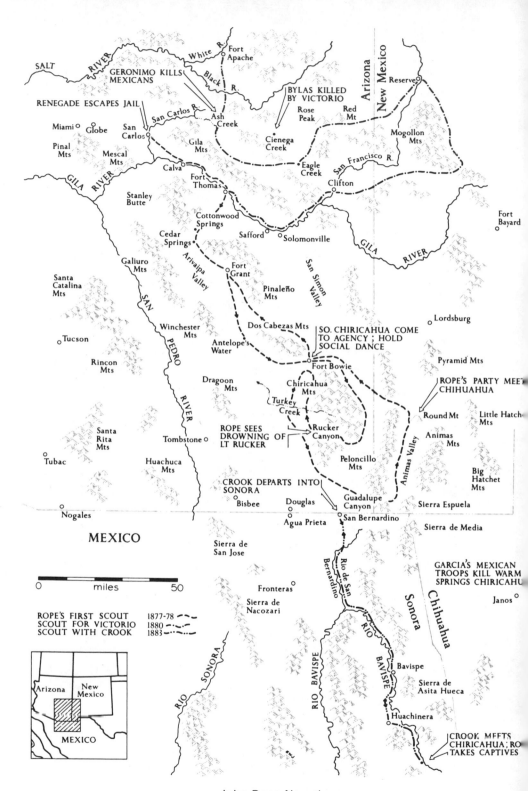

SALT RIVER

WHITE R.
Fort Apache
Black R.

GERONIMO KILLS
MEXICANS

RENEGADE ESCAPES JAIL

San Carlos R.
Ash Creek

BYLAS KILLED
BY VICTORIO

Reserve

Arizona
New Mexico

Rose Peak
Red Mt

Mogollon Mts

Miami   Globe
San Carlos

Gila Mts

Pinal Mts

Mescal Mts

Cienega Creek

Eagle Creek

San Francisco R.

Calva

GILA RIVER

Stanley Butte

Fort Thomas

Cottonwood Springs

Cedar Springs

Clifton

Fort Bayard

Safford   Solomonville

GILA RIVER

Galiuro Mts

Arivaipa Valley

Fort Grant

Santa Catalina Mts

SAN

Pinaleño Mts

San Simon Valley

Tucson

Winchester Mts

Dos Cabezas Mts

Lordsburg

SO. CHIRICAHUA COME
TO AGENCY ; HOLD
SOCIAL DANCE

Pyramid Mts

Rincon Mts

PEDRO

Antelope's Water

Fort Bowie

ROPE'S PARTY MEET
CHIHUAHUA

Dragoon Mts

Chiricahua Mts

Round Mt

Little Hatch Mts

RIVER

Turkey Creek

Santa Rita Mts

Tombstone

ROPE SEES
DROWNING OF
LT RUCKER

Rucker Canyon

Animas Mts

Animas Valley

Tubac

Huachuca Mts

Peloncillo Mts

Big Hatchet Mts

Nogales

CROOK DEPARTS INTO
SONORA

Bisbee

Douglas

Agua Prieta

Guadalupe Canyon

San Bernardino

Sierra Espuela

Sierra de Media

MEXICO

Sierra de San Jose

Rio de San Bernardino

GARCIA'S MEXICAN
TROOPS KILL WARM
SPRINGS CHIRICAHU

Janos

miles   50
0

ROPE'S FIRST SCOUT   1877-78
SCOUT FOR VICTORIO   1880
SCOUT WITH CROOK   1883

Fronteras

Sierra de Nacozari

RIO SONORA

RIO BAVISPE

Sonora

Chihuahua

RIO BAVISPE

Bavispe

Sierra de Asita Hueca

Arizona   New Mexico

MEXICO

Huachinera

CROOK MEETS
CHIRICAHUA ; RO
TAKES CAPTIVES

John Rope Narrative

with the other children. At that time we had lots of corn planted, and our people were digging a ditch and making a dam in the creek to water the ground. The men and women worked together, digging with sharp, pointed sticks. The women carried the loose dirt off in baskets. After the ditch was finished, they started to make a dam to turn the water into it. They first set up a series of four poles tripod-like, across the creek in a line. These poles were driven into the creek bed in a square of about three feet, and their tops brought together and tied. Thus the tripods stood about three feet high when finished.[1]

The men did this work and when it was done they laid bear grass lengthwise along the upper side of the tripods from one to another. Over the bear grass they packed the dry inner bark of cedar and cottonwood, the men and women both working. This inner bark was pounded up soft and wadded in. Around the tripods and between them they put piles of rock to hold them steady. Now, on the upper side right along where the bear grass had been put, they built a wall of flat red stones all along till it was as high as the posts. They took great care that this wall and dam were made straight. Between this wall and the bear grass was a space which they filled in with gravel and dirt, which the women dug out and brought in their baskets. This space was completely filled with earth. Now the dam was finished. It took about two weeks in all.

After it was made the people watched it carefully to see if it leaked anywhere. If a leak was found, then it was plugged right away. The old people used to watch them working on the dam. When the dam was finished, the water was turned into the ditch and finally they were ready to water their ground. The headman of a community was always the first to get the use of the water. After him came the others.

When the ground had been watered and had started to dry out a little, they planted corn. When planting his field the owner hired some men to help him. He paid these workers with cooked corn and would tell them to bring baskets or pots so they might divide it up and take it home. They used a metal hoe with a handle to dig the ground up. I guess they got them from the Navajo and Zuñi.

When the people saw the corn begin to come up after it had been planted, it made them happy. If there was any grass or weeds in it, they pulled them out. When the corn was up about one and a half feet, it was time to water it again. When it was up about three and a half feet tall, it was watered once more. At this time it was beginning to form ears, and when it reached this stage, our people used to go off south of Black River to gather acorns, and the corn was left to mature by itself.

We used to gather acorns all the way from Oak Springs on the west to Rock Creek on the east.[2] When the acorns were ripe, we climbed up in the oak trees and shook the acorns down on the ground where they were picked up and carried back to camp in baskets. After a while they always sent someone back to Cedar Creek who would see how the corn was getting on and return to tell the others. If the corn was ripe, all our people would pack up the acorns that had been gathered and move back to harvest corn.

In the late fall we used to go to gather juniper berries.[3] One fall (I was still a little child at the time) we started out and made camp where the White River Bridge is now. We didn't know it then but we were to have bad luck. The next day we crossed over south and camped in the pines. That evening it was very cloudy overhead. Our whole band was there, but among us we only had six or eight horses. My father had a spotted mule. My grandmother and my mother built a shelter for the night by laying pieces of dead wood up against the trunk of a pine tree and all around it. That night it rained and snowed all night. The next morning there was lots of snow when we woke up. Some of the people had not built any shelter at all. The snow was about waist deep. It was some eight miles from here to the place we were going to gather juniper berries. We dug the snow away down to the ground and made a fire with some pine wood.

Some people went to look for the horses. It was hard to find them in the snow, but they went anyway and brought them in. They were saddled up. In those days we only had moccasins which came up to our knees. We tied the tops round close to our legs. Some men started out with the horses. A mule went in front and the horses followed. This way they broke a trail up onto a ridge above us where there was not so much snow. Then they came back with the horses and we packed up and started off for the ridge. The people had to carry a lot of the stuff in burden baskets on their backs, as we didn't have enough horses to pack everything. The people on horses went in front and the others followed.

We finally got to a place and made camp there. There was not much snow here and under the trees there was none. We made our camps under blue oaks and junipers. There the wickiups were made, just like these we use today, only they were covered with grass, not canvas.[4] We made our beds out of grass, and living this way we could keep warm.

We boys used to hunt pack rats with bow and arrows. A lot of us used to start out in the morning and hunt till mid-afternoon. The way we got the rats was by one boy poking a long stick into the rat's nest. The other boy would stand near the nest entrance on the opposite side. When the stick was poked in, the rat would come to the door and stick his head out. Then the boy would shoot him. Sometimes the rats would come to the door and then go back. If they would not come out, we would tear the house down and dig them out of their hole. We would poke our stick in the hole and if there was hair on the end of it when we took it out, then we knew the rat was there and we would dig him out.

Some rats were easy to get and others were not. If a rat got away from us the older boys would make fun and say, "What did you let that rat get away from you like that for?" It was a rule that once we started to get a rat out of his nest we could never stop till we killed him. When we came home from a rat hunt, the rats would be divided up evenly among us. We used to hunt cottontail rabbits too and shoot them where we saw them sitting under brush or in the grass. The rats to be eaten were put in the fire and all the hair burnt off. Then they were skinned and either roasted or boiled. It was the same way with rabbits.

One time a boy went out hunting rats. He chased a rat into a hole and caught hold of its hind legs. When he came to pull his hand out, he could not do so. The hole was too small. He stayed there all that night, crying and hollering for someone to come. Next morning the other people decided they better look for him as he had not come home. They finally found him with his hand caught in the tree. One of the men took his knife and cut the hole a little bigger so the boy could slip his hand out. This way he got loose and got the rat too.

We had been camping by Turnbull Mountain that spring, gathering mescal, and now we started home. We moved our camp onto the Gila River. From here we journeyed on back to Cedar Creek. It took us a long time. Those who had horses packed them up and took one load on, then returned and took another load, and so on till all the mescal was brought up from camp to camp. They always made us boys carry the water bottles and sometimes the cedar bark torches.[5] When we got back the mescal shoots were stored up in the branches of juniper and oak trees around camp.

Our people were camped near the falls on Blue River when word came that there were some White men camped at Goodwin Springs [1864].[6] A bunch of people started out from our camp to go and see what these White people were doing. I was still a boy but I went along with them. We made camp at the cave on the head of Salt Creek and the next day moved on down towards the Gila River. Near where Calva now stands we came out on a hill on the north side of the river. From here we could see a big bunch of our own people and White men talking together on the flat across the river. We were afraid to go down there, so they sent one man ahead to go and see what all these people were doing. It was agreed that if this man should stand apart from the crowd, then it was safe and we all were to come on down. If he did not do so, then there was danger.

He went down and we could see him standing apart from the rest, but all the same we didn't go to him. Instead we went up the river for a way and then came down to the edge. There our man met us and told us what he had seen. Somebody found some little sticks with red points on their ends. These were matches, but we had never seen them before and did not know what they were. They had been dropped there by the White men. They smelled and someone struck one against a basket. It caught fire and that was when we first knew matches.

Our people kept on up the river along the old trail where there was lots of white grass growing. This was the south side of the river. Just the other side of Black Point some of our people were camped and we made camp there too.

I was with my aunt. She got hold of some flour from the White men, but she had never seen it before and did not know how to cook it. My other aunt was there and she knew how.

She took it, made it into dough and put it in the coals to cook. When it was done she took it out and cleaned off the ashes. This was the first time I ever saw the White man's food. The women were gathering wild hay and trading it to the White men for this new food.[7]

The next day all of us boys started over to Goodwin Springs to see the White people. We had never seen any White people before. We went up on the side of a bank and watched them. There were lots of them, all dressed the same. They wore blue pants, black shirts, and black hats. Later on we found out they were soldiers. While we were watching, they brought over a big basket of beans and meat and bread to us. When we got back to camp with this food there were some bones in the stew which had been sawed off. We thought the White people must have some kind of sharp knife with which they could cut right through a bone. The women kept on trading wild hay to the White men for grub. We didn't know what money was in those days.

In two days we boys went back to the White man's camp again. The soldiers then had the old guns, percussion locks.[8] While we were there the cook filled a sack with bread he had just cooked and threw it to the other side of a ditch where we were standing. All the boys but me got some. The White man saw this. He went back to the camp and brought back a cloth coat and some bread. He told the other boys to stay away and then he gave me the coat and the bread. I put the coat on; it was long and yellow with a cape over the shoulder. It had fine brass buttons on it. The boys didn't know this kind of coat and had never seen fine cloth like this. They gathered all around me to look. From then on we boys went every day to the White camp to eat.

One day my brother and I went to the camp and got there about noon. We met a White man riding. He was leading a white horse to where they butchered their cattle. We watched him to see where he went. When he got to the place, he killed the white horse and told us to come and butcher it. We ran up and each of us grabbed a leg, saying, "This part is for me and this part for you," but we had no knife. In a little while lots of our people were there. They butchered and skinned the horse and took most of the meat. That White man had killed the horse for my brother and me, but my brother only got a front leg and I got the neck.

After a while, when my aunt had gotten quite a lot of beans

and flour from the White men, we started back to Blue River. The headman of the Whites at Goodwin Springs had said he wanted to see *haškε dasila* ('He Is Constantly Angry'), who was the chief of the Eastern White Mountain people then.[9] So this chief, whom the Whites called Diablo, started out for Goodwin Springs. As he traveled along with some other people, he kept burning the brush along the trail and making lots of smoke. As long as we could see this smoke, our people would know that things were going all right and that there was no danger. But if the smoke stopped, we would know that this party had got into trouble with the White men. Diablo also carried a white flag in his hand. All his band was with him.

They came all right to Goodwin Springs and met the White officer. I don't know what his name was, but we called him *gušhujn* ['Wrinkled Neck'].[10] Since that time we have always had an interpreter with us. In the old days we used to have Mexicans whom we captured in Mexico as children and raised among us. These used to be our interpreters. Some of them got away and went back to Mexico.

The head officer at Goodwin Springs told Diablo that he wanted him as a friend. He said, "We White people are far from home here, but you Indians know all this country, where the water is and where are the best lands. Your people should settle down and live around here in the good places. If you keep on living your old way, you will never eat this new food that we have, but if we are friends, then we will all eat it. I see your people eating the guts, legs, hoofs and heads of horses. If we are friends we shall have lots and only eat the good meat parts."

"All right," Diablo said, and then told where he lived at a place where two streams came together [the junction of the forks of White River]. Then he and 'Wrinkled Neck' embraced and were friends. From that day on they were like brothers and had no more trouble. It has been like that with all of us since that time, and it was Diablo who made it this way with the White people for us.

All those people who were full-grown then are now dead. We don't remember our grandparents' times, just as you White people don't.

After the council the White officer gave our rations to Diablo and then this chief and his band moved back to near Fort Apache where they had lived for about a year. This chief had told the White officer he should put another soldiers' camp at the place where Fort Apache now stands, and shortly after he and his band moved back from the Gila River the White man started up to the Fort Apache location to make a camp there. They drove wagons drawn with oxen and made their road as they went.[11]

iTTi

When the soldiers' camp at Fort Apache was established [1870], they issued rations to us regularly. We drew flour, sugar, coffee and meat. There were lots of our people and it took all day for everyone to draw their rations. There were several head-men among our people. We drew rations every ten days. After awhile they stopped issuing beef and gave out the cattle for us to butcher ourselves. They allowed ten to fifteen head for each band. If the band was very large, they gave twenty head. Once they issued blankets to us, just like Navajo blankets, but a different color and lighter and thinner. Later they gave us blankets of different colors —black, red and blue blankets, three to each camp.

While we were all camped here at Fort Apache, some Eastern White Mountain people and Western White Mountain people went on the warpath. They went south to Graham Mountain and stayed there quite awhile. Then they came back and tried to make friends with the White people at Fort Apache. Most of the Cibecue people and *čačidn* [a clan: 'red rock strata people'] were camped at the fort also. They were camped on the east side of the river near the soldiers. All the White Mountain people were camped on the other side of the river. My family was living near the soldiers then.

I think the White man in charge of the fort maybe told the Cibecue and the 'red rock strata people' to kill those men who had been on the warpath down to the Graham Mountains. They started to do this. They would kill one man and in a few days they would get another. This way it kept on. One day they killed a certain Eastern White Mountain man and all the White Moun-

tain people got mad and shot back at them. They killed nine
Cibecue and 'red rock strata' men that day and three of their
own men got killed.[12]

There were lots of soldiers there at Fort Apache. The agent
there was called *ča da ʔɨzkan* ['Hat, Soft and Floppy']. The agent
at San Carlos was John Clum.[13] I guess Clum heard about the
killing that was going on at Fort Apache, as he sent a letter up
to the agent there. Whatever he said in the letter, the agent at
Fort Apache said "No" to him. He wrote again and the Fort
Apache agent still said "No." Then Clum came up himself to
Fort Apache. When he rode up to the Fort, he was riding a gray
horse and coming fast. Just before he got to where the people
were standing, his hat blew off. One of the officers picked it up
for him. Right there he held a talk with the agent at Fort Apache.
He took the letter out of his pocket and showed it to the agent.
Then he said that all of us were to come down and settle at San
Carlos, the Eastern White Mountain and Western White Mountain people, Cibecue people and the 'red rock strata people'. We
all moved down to the Gila River after that, all except the 'red
rock strata people' who never came at all.[14]

Our band used to draw their rations just the other side of
Goodwin Wash. Later we went to Goodwin Springs to draw our
rations. Again after that they gave out our rations just east of
Black Point. They made an agency there for us. 'Crooked Nose'
was the sub-agent, and we named him this because of his crooked
nose.

It was about this time they started to make up the Indian
scouts.[15] One officer and some scouts were sent down to Fort
Bowie.[16] These scouts and soldiers down at Fort Bowie captured
a lot of Chiricahua Apaches and brought them back to Goodwin
Springs to live [1876].[17] Some of the Chiricahuas they never
caught. The Chiricahuas they did catch were brought to Goodwin
Springs in big army wagons with high sides. Our band lived near
the Chiricahuas by Black Point. They issued them supplies and
blankets and sent some scouts up to San Carlos to bring back
some cattle for them to butcher. I was about eighteen years old
then.

Now they sent the scouts over east to bring back the Warm
Springs Apache [Chiricahua: Eastern band] living out there

[1877].[18] Richard Bylas's uncle was a chief then, and he was first sergeant of the scouts that went over after the Warm Springs people. After they got out to where the Warm Springs people were living [near Silver City, New Mexico], all the scouts went into a building there and hid, all except Richard Bylas's uncle, who knew most of these Warm Springs people. When the Warm Springs people came in, they lined up and the officer took their arms from them. Then all of the scouts stepped out of the building with their guns and surrounded them.

Then they started to bring the Warm Springs people back to San Carlos, some on foot, some on horse. Their grub they carried in a wagon. On the way smallpox broke out among them. Our band heard about this so all our people went off in the mountains and lived scattered in different places. When the small-pox was over, 'Crooked Nose,' the sub-agent, sent us word and we came in again. Just after this they issued us some sheep for us to raise, one to each man. But we did not want them and butchered them right away to eat.

The sub-agency was now moved to where Calva now is and 'Crooked Nose' was still our agent there. That spring we moved to Fort Apache to plant our corn but we came all the way down to get our rations at the sub-agency just the same and drove our issue cattle back to Fort Apache. When the corn was ripe and harvested, our band moved back to the sub-agency. Then I was getting older. From the sub-agency some of the men went to join the scouts. They sent them off to different places and in six months they came back again to the sub-agency.

The next time they made up the scouts a whole bunch of us went up from the sub-agency to San Carlos to try to enlist. My brother and I went along on one horse, riding double. At San Carlos there were lots of Indians gathered to enlist; Yavapais, Tonto Apaches, San Carlos Apaches, and White Mountain people were all there. We lined up to be chosen. My brother was the first one picked. My brother said if he was to be scout, then he wanted me to go as scout with him too. He told this to the officers. They asked which one I was and he took them to where I was standing. These officers looked me over to see if I was all right. They felt my arms and legs and pounded my chest to see if I would cough. That's the way they did with all the scouts they picked and if you

coughed they would not take you. I was all right, so they took
me. After they had picked about forty men, they said that was
enough. I was twenty or twenty-five years old at that time.

Our officer said we scouts would move out for Fort Thomas
the next day.[19] We made it as far as the sub-agency at Calva and
camped. The next day we got to Fort Thomas. Those scouts who
had wives were followed by them to Fort Thomas, and there they
were allowed to draw out five dollars worth of supplies from the
commissary for their families. Our next camp was at Cedar Springs
and from there we went on to Fort Grant.[20] From Fort Grant
we went to 'Antelope's Water' [a waterhole between the south end
of the Graham Mountains and the Dos Cabezas Mountains] and
camped. The next camp was at some springs just north of Fort
Bowie.

The following day we got into Fort Bowie, where we stayed
four days while they were shoeing the pack mules and we were
fixing our moccasins. Now they packed up the leather pack bags
for the mules and said we would move out tomorrow to be gone
for one month. This was the first time I was ever a scout. The
officer said at the end of one month we would come back to the
Chiricahua Mountains and camp there.

We started out and went to a big mountain southeast of the
Chiricahua Mountains, all the time looking for sign of the
Chiricahua.[21] There was lots of food with us. The first three days
I got very stiff and sore; then after that I was as though I was
getting light and it was easier.

We scouts carried a belt slung across the shoulder and chest
with fifty cartridges in it also. Besides these we carried our rifles
and a canteen of water. We used to eat early in the morning and
again late at night, only twice a day. This is the way we rounded
up the Chiricahuas and it was hard work, but we had to do as
our officer said.

We traveled every day, making our camps at springs. After
about a month we started for our new headquarters. We always
kept a guard in front and back when we traveled. We found the
soldiers camped at the southeast corner of the Chiricahua Mountains. There were scouts there from San Carlos also. They knew
we were coming and had grub cooked up for us when we got there.
The officer told us to make our camp about three miles below
where the soldiers were. There were two creeks coming together

here. The soldiers were camped on the right fork and below them was our camp on one side of the stream and a saloon was on the left fork. The day after we got there the San Carlos scouts moved out. The name of this place is now Rucker Canyon.[22]

After we had made our camp our lieutenant and the lieutenant of a company of scouts camped quite a way below us started out up the river to the soldiers' camp. Soon after they left, it started to rain very hard. The water ran off the mountain nearby and covered all the flat and filled the washes. The two officers who started up the river got to the saloon on the left fork and there met two citizens, one of whom was in charge of scouts. They all four stayed there till the rain was over.

After the rain was over, the river was high. I guess the men at the saloon were a little drunk. Anyway the two citizens got on their mules and swam across the river. Then they went up a little way and crossed back safely. Now the two officers tried it. One had a black horse, the other a sorrel horse. They mounted and started across, riding side by side, instead of going one behind the other as they ought to have done. When they got out in the deep water, the current knocked the upper horse over against the lower horse and upset both. The officers fell off in the water and the horses swam to the shore. The saloon men saw what had happened and threw a rope to the officers. They grabbed at it, but missed, and the water washed them on down.

Right below the saloon the river went through a rocky canyon and there at the end of this canyon was our scout camp. The officers got washed right into this canyon. About sundown a man rode down on the opposite side of the river from our camp and hollered across to the man who was in charge of our pack mules. We were busy moving our outfit back on higher ground. He told the packer that the two officers had been drowned and how it happened. He said they wanted all us scouts to come up the river to the saloon and also the soldiers.

Our sergeants got us together and we started. We crossed the river twice getting up there and the water was up to our armpits. When we got there, a citizen—a man named Jack—and the other men were still crying in the saloon about what had happened. They called the sergeant in and said, "Here is your officer's hat still lying here on the bench." We all started out to look for the bodies, but we couldn't find them and so went on down to our camp again. They told us we would look again tomorrow. About one hour after we got back, two soldiers came for us. They said we were to go back again and look for the bodies that night. The packer called us over to where the mules were and there he had a jug of whiskey. He poured us out each one cup.

Then we started up the river again. We met the soldiers all lined up with lanterns. They said the soldiers would search the river on both sides where it was open. We scouts were to look in the canyon. I guess they were afraid some coyotes would eat the bodies or something. They gave us long sticks to poke into the piles of driftwood and brush that had caught along the sides in the bushes. The water had run out by now and only mud lay along the banks. We started into the canyon and went all through it, but could find nothing of the officers.

On the way out one scout was behind us. Just on a little knoll over which the high water had been he found one officer. He called us all back. The soldiers and everyone gathered all around with lights. The shirt was torn, but the pants were still all right. The doctor with the troops listened to his heart with something. He said the heart was still warm. Now they said to carry the body out. It was heavy and we had to take turns carrying. They took him to the hospital at the soldiers' camp. We scouts went on back to our camp.

It was almost dawn when an officer came to tell us to start out again. The packer told us to get up. Some were too sleepy and did not want to do so. They sent twenty-one of us scouts down the river to search. The other scout company below was to work up and meet us. I did not go, as I was doing the cooking at the time. There were four of us who stayed behind. They found the other officer's body below where a big sycamore tree was growing in the wash. He was doubled around the trunk of the tree. He had two hundred dollars in bills in his pocket wallet. They took him on up to the soldiers' camp.

While we were there they used to line us scouts up every day and count our rifles and cartridges and other equipment. In fifteen days the scout company below us got a new lieutenant and started out again to travel. We did not get a new lieutenant to replace our drowned lieutenant for twenty-eight days. Then a lieutenant and two soldiers came on down from Fort Thomas to where we were camped. This officer was young and stocky. He was to be our new officer. He said he wanted to shake hands with all of us, so we did. We felt badly about the loss of our old officer and it made us sick inside.

The next day after our new officer got in we moved out to the southeast, going around the corner of the Chiricahua Mountains and on to near the Mexican border, camping at Guadalupe Canyon.[23] From here we went straight east to Round Mountain in New Mexico and made camp there for four days. There were springs there and lots of willows growing near. The officer sent us out from this camp to look around. We took our blankets and grub with us. He told us to be back in four days. We went out but found no sign of the Chiricahuas.

We all moved out at the end of four days, passing through a canyon and over to some springs and camped again. The next place we went to was on the east side of the Sierra Espuela. The sand in the wash at this place is sort of streaked with a green powder. We stayed here three days and reconnoitered. Then we circled up over the hill there and back down into a canyon on the other side.

To our next camp we moved over through a little pass to the northeast end of the Chiricahua Mountains and stayed there. Now we moved up towards Fort Bowie and camped at 'Red Standing Rocks' at the foot of a canyon. Then on to Turkey Creek to where the Chiricahua often camped. We moved on from here and finally arrived back to where the officers had been drowned. The other scouts and soldiers were still there. They had seen us coming and had our dinner already cooked for us. It was our relatives who had done this and they called us over to eat. This time we camped close to the soldiers, as this was better for us.

The day after we got in, the other scout company moved out again to travel for one month, looking for the Chiricahuas around to the southeast. Our officer told us not to bother to fix our moccasins as we would be starting back for San Carlos.

While we were at Rucker Canyon we had drawn twenty-six dollars of our pay—two months time. We still had four months pay coming to us. We were anxious to get back to San Carlos. Some of us had bought horses with our money and others had lost theirs gambling. When we started back we drove our horses and also those horses that the other scouts had bought—the scouts who were not due home yet.

The first night we stayed at a place on the east side of the Chiricahua Mountains. The next day we got into Fort Bowie. There were lots of soldiers here. That night most of the scouts got drunk. At this place my older cousin, who was a scout with me, said to me, "You have done lots of work for me, getting wood, water, building fires, and cooking. You have done the right way."[24] He had a good new Mexican straw hat on his head which he took off and gave to me for what I had done. He was the only one who gave me anything.

When we young men joined up as scouts, our older male relatives would tell us to do whatever the older scouts wanted us to do. If we didn't work hard as we should that would be no good. This way we boys who were the youngest in the company used to take turns doing the camp work. We used to kill lots of deer while on these scouts.

From Fort Bowie we went to some springs. The next camp was 'Antelope's Water.' Then we got to Fort Grant. They used to have a good time at Fort Grant and the soldiers had a band there. From here we went on to Cottonwood Springs and at this place we put on all new clean clothes, new moccasins, white drawers, new G-string, shirt and vest. Around our arms we wore copper arm bands. Some of us painted our faces red. We packed up and started out, passing to the north, then to Fort Thomas.

At Fort Thomas we stopped and drew the rest of our pay and also the money that was due us for not drawing our uniforms.[25] In all, this came to forty-seven dollars. This money we divided up among our relatives. That is the way we used to do in those days, take care of our relatives by giving them clothes and grub. The Indians around here don't do like that now.

Down on the flat at Fort Thomas our relatives were waiting for us, as they knew we were due. There were some young girls there all dressed up and wearing their hair done up at the back on hair forms with brass on them.[26] The girls were waiting for their sweethearts to come. We camped here, the next day moving on to the sub-agency [Calva]. From here they took the pack mules up to San Carlos, but they said we could do as we liked, as we didn't have to join.

§

I did not join up again right away but stayed home for a little over a year. Then I joined again. There were eight White Mountain, twelve San Carlos, and five Chiricahua men in our company.[27]

We started out from San Carlos and stopped at the sub-agency. From here our relatives followed us to Fort Thomas so they might draw five dollars worth of supplies against us at the commissary. They also issued our company four rifles here. From this place we went to Cottonwood Wash and then to Fort Grant. The next camp was at the foot of the Winchester Mountains.[28] Then we got to the other side of Willcox at 'White Man's Water' and camped. The next day we got into Fort Bowie. We stayed here for five days. They issued us wood and food. We fixed up our moccasins and the rest of us drew our rifles, ammunition belts, cartridges, uniforms, and canteens. They also gave us a black poncho and a brown blanket apiece. Our mules were packed up with four boxes of cartridges.

We started off and went to near where Bowie now is, camped here, and then moved camp out into the San Simon Valley. Then we crossed over the mountains to 'Red Rocks Standing' and camped. This way we always traveled the same places along the border, as we were afraid to go into Mexico.[29] The next camp was at Cave Creek and after that we stayed at the northeast end of the Sierra Espuela.[30] I knew this country from the last time we were scouting there. We moved on to Guadalupe Canyon and from there we had intended to go to Round Mountain in New Mexico, but one of the soldiers said there was water a little way beyond. We went there but there was no water, so we came back to Round Mountain and stayed there four days. Then we went beyond here to a canyon where we found water and made camp. From here we could see a big white mountain and the next day we set out for it. There were some springs coming out at its foot with lots of willows growing around.

We stayed here three days looking for the Chiricahuas. We thought we could see some springs on the top of the mountain and if there was water there, we would move up. But it turned out there was no water. We moved further around into a canyon and stayed there two days. At this camp some of us wanted to get to the Sierra de Media. We talked about it but the others said not to go there as it was in Mexico. We went toward it, but found no

water, so they said we might as well go to the west edge of the
Sierra de Media, which we did, and camped there. We crossed the
mountain here, looking for signs, and then circled back to camp.

Our next camp was at a place near here where some of the
scouts found water. From this place we crossed over a ridge and
made camp in a canyon. Then we moved on to the mouth of
Guadalupe Canyon and from here to near where Agua Prieta
now is. From here we went to Rucker Canyon and camped.
Then on up the west side of the Chiricahua Mountains. Then we
went on to Turkey Creek Canyon and the day after we got back
to Fort Bowie.

We stayed at Fort Bowie about one month. Then the head
officer there received word from Geronimo and a chief called
tandinbilnojui ['He Brings Many Things With Him'] that they
with their people were coming into Fort Bowie pretty soon—that
they wanted an agency put up there for them and they didn't
want any Apache scouts around when they got there.[31] Geronimo's brother was a scout at that time.

Pretty soon after we reached Fort Bowie, the head officer
there got word that the Southern Chiricahua were coming as they
had said they would. They passed by Turkey Creek Canyon and
over the level country. We could see them coming for a long way.
They made camp some distance below the fort. Then a White
man who had married one of their women and who was living
with them came to our scout camp. This man was *jelikine* ['Pine
Pitch House'].[32] A little below us camped some Tonto scouts.
'Pine Pitch House' stopped there and asked where the 'brainless
people' were camped.[33] The Tontos told him and he came on up
to us. His wife was with him. It was about noon then. *Nagutline*
['He Is Building Something'], who was with us scouts, knew this
White man well. I knew him a little. He shook hands with him.
'Pine Pitch House' said, "You scouts are all right with me." We
told him to come in and eat. "All right," he said, and he and his
wife started to eat. After he was through, 'Pine Pitch House' went
out of the tent. There we had some acorns and gave him some.
He tasted them and said, "I guess these come from Ash Flat or
Rocky Creek all right—it's good to taste them again."[34]

Pretty soon 'He Brings Many Things With Him' came to our
camp. He said we scouts were living pretty well. 'Pine Pitch House'

Courtesy Arizona Pioneers' Historical Society

Fort Bowie in 1886

told us this man was of the Southern Chiricahua band and a chief. He said the people were afraid of him. We asked him to eat and spread a canvas and put down coffee, bread and sorghum in plates. "Now eat, my friend," we told him. He did. I stood there and watched him. Then he said, "All right. I like to try the scouts' food and see what it is like. It is good food and tastes well." Pretty soon some cowboys drove in cattle to the Chiricahua camp to be butchered. They also took down some wood to the Chiricahua in wagons.

Then 'Pine Pitch House' told us that the Chiricahuas would give a dance that night and for all of us to come down. They were going to tie up a drum.[35] "Good," we said. Then they sent two more wagon loads of wood down for the dance. That evening we heard the drums begin to beat. All of us scouts, the Tontos, and the soldiers went right down to the Chiricahua camp.

Before the dance started, 'Pine Pitch House' made a talk. He said, "Some of these young girls here are wanton and they will try to make you dance farther and farther out in the dark away from the fire, so watch out for yourselves." *Haškɛnadɨltla* ['Angry, He Is Agitated'], an old lame Chiricahua, was the one who knew all the dance songs and he and the other Chiricahua singers stood in a bunch.

Now this old man talked. He said, "We are going to dance the social dance, so get ready. The right way to dance for you girls," he said to the Chiricahua girls, "is for the man to put his head on your shoulder and you put yours on his.[36] I want to see you dance this way with these Western Apache. Every song I sing you Western Apache have to pay me a quarter," he said to us scouts. He was making fun all the time.

Then they started to sing. We danced till we pretty nearly bumped into the girls and then back again. We didn't know how to do this Chiricahua dance. 'Angry, He Is Agitated' yelled again that that wasn't the right way and for us to put our head on the girls' shoulders as he said and follow the girl.

Pretty soon they started to dance differently. Two girls would catch hold of us by the shirt-sleeve.[37] They wouldn't let go, but just dragged us out, one on each side. The only way you could quit dancing was to give them two dollars credit at the commissary at the fort. Then they would go and catch another one. They started this up about midnight. There were not many girls, so the men who had young wives let them dance too. We kept on dancing till morning. I got caught twice by the girls.

The Chiricahua said that the dance was over now and that we were all well acquainted. In the morning all the girls came to our camp and made us go to the commissary with them to buy them what they wanted with their two dollars. We all went there. Those girls weren't a bit ashamed and they just pointed out whatever they wanted. We bought calico and lots of things for them.

That day the Chiricahua said they wanted to play hoop-and-poles with us.[38] I had a small Navajo blanket with me. A Chiricahua wanted to play me for my blanket, putting up a white mule against it. Another Chiricahua wanted to make the play the winning score of two games, and I was willing, but the other man said it would have to be three games, so I agreed and we started.

The first game I won on the mule. The second game I won also. Now I only had to get one more game and I would win that mule. The next game the Chiricahua won, and now I only had one game on the mule. He won the next game too and now I had no games. We stopped now. The Chiricahua wanted to play more, but I said no, because he would not agree to make the play for two games in the first place and so we would not play any more. The next day the Southern Chiricahua all set out for San Carlos, driving their cattle with them. A lot of things had been issued to them at Fort Bowie.

Two days after that a Southern Chiricahua woman came into our camp. She had her face painted. She had been following the other Chiricahua up to Fort Bowie, stopping in their old camps and living off their leavings. On a ridge just the other side of the fort, she had seen a little spotted calf. She tried to catch it for butchering but every time she had made a grab for it, it had jumped away. She had been living with her husband back in the mountains and he had been killed, so she had started out to find her people. She went and stayed with the five Chiricahua scouts in our company.

The next day two scouts went deer hunting over to the northeast end of the Chiricahua Mountains. There they saw a Chiricahua woman trying to roast some mescal. She was so poor and thin that she was like an old woman, though she must have been fairly young. Her body was as if all dried out and she was using a stick to walk with. She was starving to death. The two scouts brought her back to our camp and the soldier doctor came over to see her with the lieutenant. He gave her some whiskey and milk to drink. They gave her no food at all. The next day they fed her a little bread. She was taken over to the packer's camp near us. The day after that she was able to feed herself. In about a week she was better. Now the five Chiricahua scouts were looking after both these women who had come back.

When she was well enough they got her to make a story and it went this way. She had been captured some time ago by the Mexicans and kept in a jail. This was an adobe building with no windows in it, only a little hole or chimney in the roof in one corner. She could look up through this and see blue sky, but that was all. They kept her in there almost a year. The only way she could tell this was by watching new leaves come out on the cottonwood tree whose branches she could see above through the chimney.

This place where she was, was in a big Mexican town. She had a friend there, one Mexican girl, who used to come and see her quite often. She brought her things that she made herself. She used to come every two days or so. One day she asked her if she never thought about getting away and going back to her own country and people again. The Chiricahua woman said yes, she couldn't help but think about it, but it was no good because she thought she would never see her land again. The Mexican girl answered, "I think you will see your home again. There is going to be a big dance just outside the town in about seven days and I am going to take you to it."

A couple of days after the Mexicans made all the prisoners come out and clear a path through the brush from the town to where the dance was to be. They made the Chiricahua woman work too. They piled all the brush up in two big piles on either side of the path to the dance ground. After this the Mexican girl came back again and brought the Chiricahua woman a dress she had made of brown cloth, some matches and some bread, all done up in a package. She told her to hide it and let no one see. Then she said that the Chiricahua woman must shake her arms and legs and run around inside the building so she would not be weak. She could hardly wait for the seven days to end and the time for the dance.

The day before the dance the Mexican girl came again and said, "There is a big mountain back of where the dance is to be, but it is far away. The big mountain back of the jail on this side of the town is near. Go up on it and stay there, then start out for your country, but only travel at night, as the Mexican soldiers will be out looking for you." She brought a white dress for the woman to wear.

The next night of the dance it was bright moonlight. She could hear the drums and horns over where the dance was. She put on the white dress and pretty soon the Mexican girl came and got her. They started to walk down the path that the prisoners had cleared. There were lots of Mexicans going along the path, but it was too dark and the Chiricahua woman was dressed like the other Mexican women. The Mexican girl was carrying the parcel with her food and the brown dress under her arm. There were two girls in front of them, so the Mexican girl and the

Chiricahua woman went from side to side pretending to look at things and let the other people get ahead, as well as the two girls. Pretty soon there were only a few Mexicans behind them and the Mexican girl and the woman dodged in behind one of the piles of brush at the side of the trail. Here the woman put on her brown dress and took the food. The Mexican girl walked out and caught up with three other girls in front and went on to the dance.

When the Chiricahua woman saw there was nobody left, she started for the mountain in back of the town. She got to the foot of it just about sunrise and slept there. Later on she went on up the mountain. From here she could see the fire and smoke signals that the Mexicans were making to tell of her escape. About sundown she went down the other side of the mountain and got to the foot just at dusk. From here she crossed a big valley to another mountain and went up on top of it. Here she hid all the day again and that night started once more.

After three days of going at night, she started to travel in the daytime. She was getting into country she knew now, and also her food had run out. She lived on the inside fleshy part of a kind of small ground cactus from now on. Every time she found some of these, she would do them up in her bundle and take them along to eat. She was beginning to give out now and she was starving. She could not travel fast. After awhile she got to the Chiricahua Mountains and followed them on up towards Apache Pass. But she couldn't remember which place this was and got lost. This was the time the two scouts found her near the northeast corner of the Chiricahua Mountains and brought her back to our camp.

We stayed on for one month at Fort Bowie and just hunted deer. The officer told us in seventeen days we were to be discharged. He said we had lots of horses now and for us to take turns letting the two Chiricahua women ride our horses on the way back. The next day we started and made camp at some springs north of the fort and next on to some other springs. Now it was my turn to loan a horse to one of the Chiricahua women. We made our next camp at 'Antelope's Water' and when we got there the horse that I had loaned the woman was all sore on the withers. We went on into Fort Grant and then on to Cedar Springs and then Fort Thomas, where we stayed for eleven days, till our time was up. The two Chiricahua women they sent on to the sub-agency to their relatives. We got paid off at Fort Thomas and took our horses up to the sub-agency. The soldiers went on to San Carlos.

$$\rightarrow$$

    I had been living at the sub-agency when not on scouts, yet I really belonged at Fort Apache, so I moved back up there now. They used to enlist scouts at Fort Apache just the same as at San Carlos. About August they started to enlist scouts. That day forty Western White Mountain men enlisted. This was because the feeling was so strong about the killing of Richard Bylas's uncle. This man was a chief of the Eastern White Mountain people. He had killed some member of Victorio's band some time ago. After this he had gone down to the sub-agency to visit some relatives. Then he started back to where his farm was. Before he got there, Victorio came to that place with his men and caught one White Mountain man. Victorio said he had come after Richard Bylas's uncle and wanted to know where he was. The man said he had gone to the sub-agency, but that he was due back in a couple of days and would probably be camping at Cienega Creek on his way. The man was scared. That's why he told all this. Victorio went to Cienega Creek with his men and there ambushed and killed Richard's uncle and all his family in the early morning. This was in the spring.[39]
    Now the chief of the White Mountain people at Fort Apache said there would be a dance given that night so the scouts might start off right the next day and find the men who killed their chief. It was to be a war dance.[40] They spread a cowhide out for this dance. All the people—men, women and children, were at the dance ground standing all around. A big fire was lit in the middle. All the scouts were there, and I was one of them. We never laid down our rifles all that night.
    Everybody stands up at these war dances. The men who knew the war songs sang. As they sang, the dance leader would call out a scout's name, and the scout called would have to go out and dance around the fire with his rifle, acting as if he was fighting, pointing his rifle at the ground and pretending to shoot and putting his hand to his mouth and yelling as he would in battle. One after the other the dance leader called out the scouts. When

Victorio, war chief of the Warm Springs Chiricahua

a man was called out, the girls who were his close relatives followed in a line, dancing behind him. When all forty of us scouts had been called out and danced, we were all dancing in a circle around the fire. A medicine man, an old man who knew war medicine, led us and we followed him.

Now they took away the hide from where it was spread on one side of the fire. After the hide was taken away, they sang four more songs and we scouts danced for all four songs. Then four more songs were sung again, during which twelve men danced. They picked out the twelve strongest and bravest men who were most likely to succeed in war to dance for these four songs. After this, four of the best men were picked. One after another and only one at a time, they went out in the circle near the fire.

Everybody kept absolutely still while this was going on and only the drum was beaten for the man who danced. When one of these four men went out, he would talk and step around in different places. He would say, "I met a bear some time ago and had trouble with him, but I came out all right," and so on, telling of different dangers he had been in and come out from safely. Each time he told of a happening he would point at the ground in one place to emphasize and mark the incident. This way these four men made medicine and prayed. Now the war dance was over. This dance was given to let the scouts have war practice and to make war medicine.

Next a man who knew songs for the social dance went out in the middle and called the people to come all around him, young girls and even married women and all the men and scouts. Now they started to sing. If a woman wanted to dance with a man she went and touched him on the shoulder and then he would follow her out into the circle and dance. We scouts always carried our rifles when we danced with the women. They kept dancing and singing all night.

When the morning came, we scouts were called together and talked to. The first talker was an old woman, one who knew about war medicine. She said, "You boys are like close relatives to me. I want you to look out for yourselves and do things the right way. If you see the Warm Springs people, follow them and don't let them get away." Then a chief talked to us and said, "The Warm Springs people are born from women only. You are born from women also. If you see the Warm Springs people, go right after them. Don't run away, but go to them and stay fighting them." They talked with us that way because of the White Mountain chief who had been killed by the Warm Springs people.

That morning we scouts set out and made camp at the old wagon road at the crossing of the Black River. From here we went to Soldiers' Hole and made camp there for ten days to wait for some soldiers who were to join us. Lots of soldiers came bringing sixty head of horses to replace the ones that they were using. They spent the time shoeing the horses and breaking them, as most were broncos.

In seven days more we all started out eastward to some springs where we camped. From here we went on to Eagle Creek and got there at noon. The next camp was at the foot of Rose Peak. Then we went on over by Red Mountain to a big grassy flat.

On the way over I was off to one side hunting. I saw a big blacktail deer and shot at him about ten times and killed him. Right there I sprained my ankle. I skinned and butchered the deer, but as I had that bad ankle, I only took along the skin to our camp. My foot and ankle were all swollen up when I got there. The other scouts asked me why I only brought the hide and I told them. The army doctor looked at my ankle but could not cure it that night. The next morning the officer brought over a mule and told me to ride it. We started out, the scouts going in front. Pretty soon I saw a big deer. He smelled the tracks of the scouts who were ahead but came on anyway. I got off the mule, tied him to a bush and shot the deer. He had great big horns. I butchered him and called the packer over to get him to put it on one of the pack mules. He wanted to cut the head off but I said no.[41] We put it on one of the mules.

The next day we went on east to a place where some Mexicans had a lot of sheep. They roped one and gave it to us scouts. We butchered it. There were lots of Mexicans living there and we all camped close to them. At this place we stayed three days, and so we scouts had time to remove the hair from our deer hides.[42]

Our next camp was around on the northeast end of Mogollon Mountain on a mesa where a cowboy's ranch was. The cowboy's house was built all of rocks and had a loophole pierced in each side so the place might be defended from the Warm Springs people who used to ride by this place and try to shoot in their loopholes. There was nobody living here, and I guess the Warm Springs people must have killed them all. We could still see the bullets in the rocks about the loopholes. At this place they gave us scouts half a steer to eat.

From here we moved towards a place where there was a house with lots of cedar trees around it and which looked as though springs were likely to be there. When we got there, there was only mud in the spring holes. We all started on, intending to make camp at the first water we found. The soldiers and ourselves ran out of water and almost gave out.

On these marches they always kept five scouts out on either side as flankers. Five of us scouts went off in a canyon and there we took a rest. I fell asleep under a cedar tree and was dreaming about some White man hollering at me. Then I woke up and there were two White officers standing there, yelling at me to wake up. I asked them if they had any water but they just took their canteens out and tipped them upside down—they had no water.[43] I kept on following up the canyon behind the others. Pretty soon I came to where some willows were growing. Here there were some black rocks ahead and it looked like water at their foot. The other scouts were waiting for me there. They said not to drink much. I wanted lots of water but only drank a little.

Soon we came to a White man's ranch. There was no one here so I guess they were killed by the Warm Springs people. But there were springs here so we all made camp at this place about sundown. The pack mules were way behind and did not get in till evening. The officer made a count and there were ten scouts missing who had given out awhile back. One scout said I should go back and take water to them, as some of these missing scouts were my relatives. We filled five of our canteens and five soldiers' canteens—the officers' canteens were larger. I packed these on a mule, got on and started back, carrying my rifle. The officer called me back and said to leave my rifle behind. He gave me his pistol and a belt instead. I also led one horse and went back this way to help the scouts.

There was lots of brush in the canyon and it looked as though a bear might jump out at me. Pretty soon I met five of the scouts. They had found a burro and were taking turns riding double on it. Now I gave them some water and the horse I was leading to ride on, then went on alone down the canyon to find the other five. The mule acted as though he didn't want to go and kept shying at things. I stopped awhile under a tree and listened. The mule heard something and pricked up his ears. Pretty soon I could hear someone laugh. I knew right away it was *bešn* ['metal knife'], one of the scouts.

Then all five of the scouts came along. They saw me and hollered, "Who's there, an Indian?" I said, "Yes, it is me." The sergeant was with them. "I'm glad to see you now," he said. I had five canteens with me and I gave them these. We all started back to camp, taking turns riding double on my mule. After awhile it came my turn to ride again. There was only one of these men who did not ride—he refused. When we got to camp the officers were still up. They were playing cards. The head officer asked if everybody was in now and we answered yes.

I took the mule over to the horse herd and turned him loose. I thought, now I will get some good beef stew and other food, but when I got to camp there was only some coffee and bad soft bread left, half burnt. It was about midnight now but anyway I got some bacon and fixed up some beef with it and ate the burnt bread all the same.

There was one scout I always slept with and I went over to where he was. From here I could hear one of the scouts was sick. He was moaning and so I went over to him. He was a boy who had never been a scout before. I said, "I told you not to join the scouts, that it was too hard work for you."

The next morning they butchered two steers for the soldiers and scouts. We scouts went over to where the White man was butchering and got all the guts. These we took back and put in the fire to cook. Right then the officer called to us to start out. But we stayed and waited for the guts to get cooked. The officer got off his horse and came over to our fire, threw all the cooking guts out around and scattered our fire.

Then we all started out with five scouts on each side. In awhile we came to some springs on a mesa. There was some bitter weed growing there. We unpacked the mules and started to cook. A White soldier came over to us and told us to come and get some meat, so we went over and got two front quarters of beef. At this camp we stayed all day, eating lots and then taking a sweat bath.

The next day we started off and got lunch at a place by some springs. There was a White sergeant coming on behind and he heard two shots fired up on the mountain. Now no one was supposed to shoot his gun, as the Warm Springs people might hear it and run away. The two shots were fired by two of the scouts. They had seen a big animal at the foot of a bluff. "What is that?" they asked. It was an elk and they shot it. They were afraid to go to it because of the officers getting after them about the shooting. They came on back to camp and there the officers made them go back with a mule to get the elk. The officers did not punish these scouts. They gave the hind quarters to the soldiers and we got the front.

We stayed at this place four days looking for sign of the Warm Springs people. There was a citizen in charge of us scouts and he took all of us out to reconnoiter, except four who were left behind to cook. We traveled down by a creek where there were lots of cattle. We asked the citizen chief scout about killing one of these cattle to eat. He said no, that they had given orders not to do any shooting, and he did not see how we could get the cattle without shooting them. "All right, then," we said, "we will kill them with a knife, hamstring them and then cut their throats." All of us scouts started to surround the cattle, but they ran out and broke through us. We all ran after them. One man caught hold of a cow's tail while she was running, took out his knife and hamstrung her just above the hock. Another man caught one by the tail and hamstrung it just back of the ankle above the hoof. This way we got two.

They were fat cattle, and we butchered them right there and started cooking. The meat looked good, but it tasted bad, like bitter weed, as the cattle had been eating a lot of these plants which grew here. What we wanted most was the hide for our moccasin soles. This was divided up, enough for one pair of soles each. Then we wrapped the meat up in what was left of the hides, slung it on poles and carried it back to camp. The soldiers saw we were carrying something and all came out to see what it was. The White chief of the scouts had ridden on ahead of us and told the officer what we had done, that we had killed two cattle.

That evening the officer said he wanted to see all the scouts. We all went over after supper. The officer said, "I heard you killed two steers. You did well. You didn't shoot at all. That's the right way." The next day twelve of us went out to reconnoiter again. We saw a mother elk and her calf up on the mountain. There used to be lots of elk over at Mogollon Mountain.

We left this camp, the scouts going ahead and the soldiers behind. They always kept two of us scouts right at the head of the column of soldiers. I was one of these that day. Two horses got away from the soldiers but were finally put back in the bunch. This delayed us a little. Pretty soon we could see a wooden house. Right this side of it was standing a post. There was a slip of paper stuck in the post that the citizen scout had left. At the foot of the post were the heads of five White people. A man and his family had been living here and the Warm Springs people killed them all. There was also a bag of laundry soap here. One of the soldiers took this and packed it on a mule. It was the same band of Warm Springs people who did this that killed Richard Bylas's uncle. This was the band we were trying to find.

At this place where there was a little canyon with a creek in it, the scouts who had gone on before us found some burro tracks. They all had started out to run to where the burro was. Those same two men who had shot the elk got there first and started to argue over which one of them should have the burro. They got mad and shot the burro twice. We could hear the two shots from where we were with the soldiers. They sounded over from behind some black, rocky, brushy hills, and we didn't know if it was the Warm Springs people or not. The scout sergeant ran back from where the shooting had been done to tell what had happened. He came out on top of the hill just above us. The soldiers thought it was a Warm Springs man and pretty nearly shot him, but he yelled that he was a scout, so the officer stopped the soldiers. We made camp that day in a canyon at a place where the other scouts had already stopped. We scouts had for an interpreter a man who had been captured by the White people from the Navajo country. He was a Navajo Indian.

After supper the officer called us scouts over to his camp. The soldiers were all lined up, three companies of them. There were four officers and one army doctor. The head officer spoke. He said, "These two scouts killed an elk two days ago, but then I did not say anything about it and gave them another chance. Today the same two shot a burro. It seems to me as if they were trying to help the Warm Springs people and warn them by shooting this way. Tomorrow I am going to discharge these two, send them back home, and take their rifles, canteens and cartridge belts from them."

One of these men was related to our sergeant, so he said that he did not want these scouts sent back. The officer would not listen to him. All of us scouts felt the same way and we did not want these two men sent home, as they were far from home and might get killed by wild animals on the way back. The sergeant said that if these two men were discharged, we all might as well turn in our outfit and start back tomorrow. The officers talked among themselves, and I guess they changed their minds, because the head officer said, "All right, we will keep these two men, but from now on they will have to take the place right at the head of the column." Next morning we started out.

These last few days we had been traveling south, along the east side of Mogollon Mountain. Now we crossed over a spur on the east side of Mogollon Mountain and went up through a little pass. There was lots of brush here, and they kept the soldiers cutting away in it so the horses and packs could get through. There were lots of deer in here, but none of us shot. We scouts waited in front for the soldiers to come up.

Pretty soon we would see a tall, pointed rock standing straight up ahead of us. At the top it was smooth. Right at the foot of it there was a sort of doorway going in like the entrance to a wickiup. Right in front of this door was a low stone wall about two feet high. Some of the scouts went near this door. It smelled very bad inside. On the rock around the door and above it were drawn pictures. There was the morning star, the Pleiades and the new moon drawn there. On one side above the door was a buck deer and on the other side was a female deer with its young one. All around both of these were figures of *gan* ['mountain spirits'] holding some long things in their hands.[44] They had no headdresses on. These pictures were high up on the rock, about fifteen feet above us, and I don't see how the people who drew them were able to put them there. It looked as though the rock must have grown up since the pictures were made. The officers looked at them through their field glasses. I was talking with a Chiricahua about this place one time and he said that the Warm Springs people always used to stop here on their way by and pray to the *gan*. He said his grandmother knew about that place.

We started down from here into a canyon. The officers gave us scouts each two cartridges, one to kill a turkey and one for a deer. They made camp in the canyon and we scouts brought in lots of deer, all whitetails. We shot our own cartridges as well as those two the officer gave us. The next day we circled around into a canyon where there was water and lots of cottonwood trees. We had crossed over the hills and arrived there about dark.

At this place we stayed four days and sent and received a letter from a place quite a ways from here, an army post where there were a lot of Negro soldiers.[45]

There was a White man living near our camp who had a lot of whiskey. Some of the soldiers and scouts got drunk on it. The soldiers' cook was drunk the next morning. The four officers were together getting on their horses. A little distance away was a big soldier. He was drunk and yelling and making a show. One of the officers got off and went over to where he was and told a sergeant to tie this man's legs and arms up, to tie him to a tree because he was drunk, so they did. The officer went back to his horse. The drunk soldier was crying about being tied up and I guess he said something bad to his officer. We were there and our interpreter told us what he said. He said, "You're a bull's father and a burro screwed your mother to make you."

The officer took up a stick and went back to where the man was tied. The soldier said, "Don't hit me when I am tied up this way. Turn me loose." The officer told the sergeant to turn him loose. He did so, but the soldier still had a piece of rope tied to his wrist. He jumped on the officer, ripped his shirt and vest down and knocked him on the ground. The other officers came over and pulled him off, picked the officer up, tied his shirt together and took him away. Then one of the officers came back and with the sergeant he took the drunk soldier to the edge of a waterhole, right up on a bank, so that if the soldier moved he would fall in the water.

We stayed here and fixed our moccasins up. From here we moved on over to near where Clifton now is, towards the Gila River. We saw lots of blacktail deer on the way. One deer came near us, a big one, and fell dead. An old man who was a scout said, "There, that deer will be mine," and he went over to it. But there was a scout following the deer and he told us all to keep away from it as he had shot it.[46] The hide was big and we wanted it. The man took out his knife and slashed the hide in several places so it couldn't be used. The meat was fat and showed through the slits, but the hide was no good now, so only the meat was taken.

We killed lots of deer and antelope that day and the packs were loaded with them. When we got into our camping place there was one great big deer on a pack. Two soldiers grabbed it to take for themselves but some of us scouts grabbed the other side. Our sergeant was with us. We each wanted the deer and stood pulling at it. Finally they made us give it to the soldiers. Our sergeant got discharged on account of this later on.

There was a White man's farm at this place with milk cows and planted fields. After supper we went to see it. The White men were churning some milk and gave us a slice of what they were making. It was like cheese. [47] They had cornfields here, and the corn was already on the stalk. Just about sundown that soldier who had been drunk and was now a prisoner was brought in by two sergeants.

The next day we moved on down the river and camped at a mountain across the Gila River from Solomonville. This place is right between two bluffs, and the springs are always running there. The prisoner got in after sundown again. He always did that way. The next day we moved on down to near where Safford now is. In those days there were only a few White men living in that part of the Gila Valley and there were no towns at all. The day after that we got into Fort Thomas. Here they put the prisoner in irons and sent him off someplace. The next day we scouts were lined up. Fifteen of us quit and some more were discharged.

9

After we had stayed quite awhile at Fort Thomas, I asked for leave to go and see my people with my sergeant at Fort Apache. They granted it to us and let us have a mule to ride. Early in the morning I started out on foot, not bothering to eat anything but just putting on my best clothes and taking my rifle. When I got part way there, the sergeant caught up to me, riding the mule. He said, "You travel fast. I have been trying to catch up and have had a hard time." I got on the mule and we rode double.

We stopped at the camp of an old man to try and get something to eat. The old man said, "You scouts have lots of food. I have nothing to give you." He did not want us to stop there so we kept on, crossed the Gila River opposite Dewey Flat, to a big wash and camped there for the night. We had no food with us at all. The next morning we started early when the morning star was just a little way up. We went through Warm Springs on Ash Creek and up by Rocky Creek.[48] There were always people camped in here this time of year but now there was no one, even at Rocky Creek. We didn't know what to make of this.

Later on we saw two women grinding something quite a way off. When we got there, we saw a girl who was grinding acorns. Her mother was boiling some meat. We told them to hurry up with their cooking. They made some acorn gravy, coffee, and tortillas for us. The woman said that the sergeant's wife was camped over at a place near Bear Canyon and that he would find them there. We went there but only found their tracks going towards Black River. Just before we got to Black River there was a heavy rain. We covered up with our blankets but it didn't do much good. We hurried to get across the river before it would get too high with the rain. From the top of the hill we could see a lot of smoke and knew that there must be many camps down there. When we got in, we went to the sergeant's brother's camp and left the mule there, borrowing a horse in its place. This brother said that the sergeant's family left for Fort Apache yesterday.

Just about sundown we got to Fort Apache. My family was camped above there, and I went to stay with my brother who was a chief. The day after this a young boy who was of my clan went out hunting and killed a little deer. On his way back he met an old medicine man. This medicine man was no good and he said, "Give me that little deer." But the boy would not and went on home with it. That night this boy started to vomit blood and also he bled at the nose. They could not stop him and he died that night.[49] They came and notified me. The next morning I went over and took all my new clothes I was wearing—shirt, vest, drawers, hat, and all—and gave it to the family to dress the boy up in to be buried.[50]

Now the sergeant said to me, "Let's go and get some rations at the agency." So we went there and asked for rations, as all scouts if they had a ticket of leave could draw rations. But the agent would not give us rations. He telegraphed back to Fort Thomas that we had drawn no rations before leaving, and to give us ten days rations. So we drew meat, flour, coffee, sugar, bacon,

Courtesy Arizona Pioneers' Historical Society

Fort Apache circa 1872

and some canned fruit. In nine days we started back for Fort Thomas, we two scouts and my younger brother. The first night we got to Soldier's Hole. The next day we crossed over Hooker Mesa and arrived at Fort Thomas.

The following day the officer said we would all move up to Fort Apache. Some of us went on horse, some on foot. We on horses went up by the mountains and camped. The next morning we crossed Hooker Mesa and saw where the other bunch of scouts had gone on foot. That night we camped near where ash flat ranch is now. The following day we went by the Old Summit Road and on over the mountain to north of Old Summit. From here we could see no camps up on East Fork where our people always camped. This looked funny and we thought maybe there had been trouble and they had gone on the warpath. Even if they had gone on the warpath, we were still scouts and would have to fight for the White men. There was a stump down in a little open place below us, and we said "Let's shoot at it and practice and see who is best."

When we got near Fort Apache, we met an Indian who told us that one of our chiefs, *haškɛha ʔyila* ['Angry, He Takes It Away'], had been killed by the *čačidn* [a clan: 'red rock strata people']. He also said the reason our people were not camped on East Fork was because they had moved their camps to the foot of the hill near the fort. Our pack mules were at the fort, so we went there.

The next day our relatives gave us hide for our moccasin soles. Notice was sent out among the camps that they wanted twenty more men to enlist as scouts and join our company. The first day only fifteen joined, but the next day five more joined and we were filled out. Then we started out for Fort Thomas, making the first camp by Ash Creek. The next day we got to near Hooker Mesa. From here on to Fort Thomas I loaned my horse to another scout and walked. When I got in, my knee was in bad shape. The sergeant went to the officer and tried to get him to send me back but the officer said that the one that could give orders to that effect was at Fort Grant. He wired to Fort Grant about it and got word back to let me ride along with my company. We had brought some boys down with us from Fort Apache to take our horses back from Fort Thomas and this they did. The morning after they gave me a mule to ride with an army saddle.

We camped that night at Cedar Springs. On the way we had passed a lot of prickly pear plants. The fruit was ripe on them and one old scout with us, *haškɛyina'ła'* ('Angry, He Stares At It'), ate quite a lot of this fruit. That night he got sick and started to belch. He had bad breath and his stomach was hurting. The next day they took him to a Chiricahua camp where they were gathering yucca fruit and asked if they had any medicine for him. They had none at all. We went on by the north end of Graham Mountain. The sick man was a good way ahead of us other scouts and a few scouts were with him. He was riding a horse. Pretty soon he could ride the horse no longer and slipped off, lying at the side of the road. He said it was as if something was cutting his insides up with knives. Two scouts came back and met us to get help.

When we got there two men who knew coyote medicine went to him and cured him up right away.[51] What had happened was that he had eaten some fruit which a coyote had urinated on and became sick that way. That is the way it is. If you eat anything or touch anything that a coyote has urinated on and then touch your mouth, you get coyote sickness. This man was pretty near dead, but the two medicine men cured him right away. This all happened near Cedar Springs. Even if a coyote only bites the fruit, it is just as bad.

The day we got into Fort Grant the officer said for the medicine man to take the sick man back to Fort Apache, but the sick man said, "I am all right now." The medicine man said, "What's the matter, you didn't go back and give me a chance to visit in Fort Apache."

They issued the twenty new scouts their rifles and outfits here. Then we moved on south to 'Antelope's Water,' past where Willcox now is, to some springs and then to Fort Bowie. Here we stopped three days to fix our moccasins and get ready. The night before we left Fort Bowie we held a war dance. The officers came down to watch us. About midnight they went back and then we had a social dance. There were no women with us, but some of the men acted as women and we danced with them as partners. This is the way they always used to do for a good time on the warpath. After a war dance the social dance always had to be given, so if there were no women some of the men acted as women.[52]

Now we went on to near where Bowie Station now is,[53] then south up the San Simon Valley, then towards Cave Creek, then Cave Creek, then to the southeast end of the Chiricahua Mountains, then to the northeast end of the Sierra Espuela, then to the head of Guadalupe Canyon, then Round Mountain in New Mexico. From here we went down a long canyon to the southwest and camped at its end. There were lots of soldiers camped here with us. Now we went to the west side of Hachita Mountain and made camp where there were lots of ash trees growing.

Here a band of the Chiricahuas joined us. Their leader was Chihuahua.[54] They were not real scouts but came along with us to help scout all the same. Chihuahua used to be a good friend of mine. From this place the officer said to send fifteen scouts and ten soldiers ahead to keep a lookout for the enemy Chiricahua. The rest were to follow on behind. We went ahead and kept in touch with the main body by sending notes back and forth. We came to lots of black, rocky hills. Here there were many deer which we shot at. One was killed right there. Another got wounded

Chihuahua, Chiricahua war leader and friend of John Rope

and fell dead near me so I claimed it. This deer was fat and we butchered it. I got the hide and one hind quarter and tied the meat up in the hide. Pretty soon we came to some rock tanks where there was water. Here we stopped and the officer with us wrote a letter back to the main column. I left my deer hide and meat on top of a yucca plant right beside the trail with a sign on it that it was mine. The friendly Chiricahua did the same with their deer on the other side of the trail. This way the meat and hides would be put on the pack mules when they came along.

From here we could see a big long mountain range and between us and it was a long, open valley. We started out to cross this valley and struck the old road to Janos, Chihuahua, which we followed, finally coming to a big river where we ate our supper. It made a loop right around the mountains which we had seen from across the valley. After supper we crossed a river. This river was one like we had never seen before. You could not tell which way it ran. We went up on top of the mountain and made camp there. That night, way late, I woke up and could hear Apaches talking some place. We thought it might be the enemy Chiricahuas, but it turned out to be some scouts who had been sent to catch up with us from the main column. We called to them and gave them some food to eat.

The next morning we went on down the other side of the mountain and struck the same river again. It ran over some rocks here so we could tell which way it was going. We made camp at this place to wait for the main column to catch up. They never showed up, so two scouts were sent back to the mountain to see where they were. The troops had come to the river, then taken the wrong canyon to the left and had gone way off that way. Now we all went back, cutting across country to where we thought the troops should be. Pretty soon there was a lot of dust away off. We watched to see if it might be Mexican soldiers but it was our own troops and we went to them. As soon as camp was made we unpacked our mule, got the grub out and cooked, as we had had no food for a long time. At that place we all stayed two days. One of the White soldiers who wore a buckskin shirt shot himself in the arm here. The doctor had to take the bullet out and he got all right again. Now the officer said we would go back to where the river was first struck. The scouts were sent out ahead to look for sign. We ran across a lot of deer and killed some, getting into camp after the soldiers.

Nagutline ['He Is Building Something'] was sergeant of our company. He and I are the only ones still alive from that scout. From this camp we started back the way we had come over the old Janos road. Twelve of us scouts got permission to go and hunt deer over near Little Hachita Mountain. The officer told us that if we twelve were needed back because of trouble, a big fire would be built to signal us to come. We went on over to the mountain and there killed a lot of deer. They were all fat. I packed one into camp and a boy carried the other. That night we watched for a signal fire. The next morning we could see lots of smoke but we waited for a while to see what would happen. If we got lost from the soldiers we would go back to Fort Bowie. Pretty soon we could see the soldiers and scouts coming our way, making lots of dust, so we started out to hunt again.

We killed more deer and also some mountain sheep. There were lots of them there. They ran together like burros and could go up or come down a steep place just as if they were walking on the level. The old-timers used to say that when you were out hunting mountain sheep if you hid behind brush or grass, they could not see you, but that if you hid behind any kind of rock, they could see you right through the rock. The soldiers passed right at the foot of the mountain and started to make camp. We waited up on the mountain till all the unpacking and cooking was done, and then we went down to them, carrying our game. The scouts with the soldiers had killed lots of deer also.

Two canvases were spread, one for the friendly Chiricahuas, the other for us White Mountain scouts. All the game was put on each canvas. Our sergeant saw us and told us to come over and put our meat on the White Mountain canvas, which we did. Then the White soldiers and officers came over to the meat and started taking it all from us and the friendly Chiricahuas as well. Chihuahua got mad and called over 'He Is Building Something,' our sergeant. He said, "They are doing the same with your meat as well as ours. This is not fair. The soldiers did not shoot this meat. They ride horses and we go on foot, and now they want all the meat. These White soldiers are like nothing to us. If they keep this up, we will kill them and take all their horses."

The lieutenant came to the sergeant and said, "Don't hold back this meat now from the soldiers or you will get discharged." I guess the head officer did not know what was going on. Now the top sergeant of my company, to whom the lieutenant was talking, *nabidntel* ['He Is Wide'], got mad and said, "All right, I'll quit now." He threw his gun and cartridge belt down on the ground.

About this time the White interpreter whom we had with us went to the head officer and told him what was going on. The head officer came back down to where the meat was. He brought the other officers with him. He asked 'He Is Wide' what was going on. "I don't know about this taking away of the meat," he said, "it was not my orders." He asked if this had been going on before in the other camps. The sergeant said no, that they had only made a present of the hind quarters of the deer and antelope to the soldiers and kept the front part themselves. The captain told him to pick up his gun and belt, saying that he was a scout and he had not ordered him to quit that way, that the lieutenant had no right to fire him by himself. The captain said, "You scouts travel only on foot and have a hard time of it, work hard to kill meat. From this time on, the meat that you kill is entirely for you." Then we cooked up our meat and ate it.

At this place we stayed two days, then moved to the side of Round Mountain in New Mexico. There were lots of antelope here. When we first jumped them, they scattered, but then they all came together and ran in a long line. We moved on around Round Mountain, keeping five men out ahead to look for sign of enemy Chiricahuas. Now we went on to Guadalupe Canyon, then Cave Creek. There was lots of water this time. The soldiers camped above us. We didn't know it, but they washed their clothes that day. The next morning when we boiled the water for our coffee, it tasted of soap. We only ate bread and meat. Then we moved northward, then to Turkey Creek, and then to Fort Bowie.

There were lots of scouts at Fort Bowie now and we played hoop-and-poles. I played with one Chiricahua man. The first game I won his moccasins, the second his new saddle, the third his new lot of calico and then we quit. I used to play hoop-and-poles a lot and always had good luck. Some Indians threw the pole too soon, but I used to wait till the hoop was just about to fall and then threw the pole under it. It was as if I knew where the hoop was going to fall every time. The other Indians knew this about me.

Now our time was about up so they took our outfits and rifles away from us and we set out for home. The first day we got to some springs, then 'Antelope's Water,' then Fort Grant, then Cottonwood Wash, and then Fort Thomas. Here we stayed two days and drew forty dollars pay. Then we set out for Fort Apache. Here at the end of ten days we were discharged and drew seventy-nine dollars pay. Some scouts used to like to draw their full uniforms and others didn't. The ones that did not were refunded.

My youngest brother was waiting for me at Fort Apache with horses to take me home. Our family was camped right above Rice, and we found them there. From here we all moved to the Gila River. Then we moved to Dewey Flats. In a couple of days a lot of our people camped on the mesa near us. There the Whites were taking the number of people in each family, and the sub-agent from the sub-agency was giving out ration tickets to every man.[55] Some were red and some were green. I rode over near there, but did not go in to get my ticket as there were lots of girls I knew there. I was bashful so I just stood behind my horse. Some of my relatives got my ticket for me.

Mickey Free was raised by my father.[56] He was given to him by the San Carlos people when a little boy. Mickey and I were brought up together, so we called each other brothers. He is dead now, but his son Willie Free is still living at San Carlos and I call him my nephew. Mickey used to have long red hair.

After I had been back at the reservation quite awhile, they enlisted twenty-five reservation police. I joined up as a policeman this time and was on duty quite awhile. The Cibecue people over at Cibecue had been making trouble and killed some American soldiers awhile back [1881].[57] The men who had done this were now renegades, and it was our duty to catch them. Some we caught and turned them over to 'Crooked Nose,' our sub-agent, and others we let go to give them another chance. Finally all that we were after were rounded up and held at Fort Apache, then sent

Mickey Free, Army scout, interpreter, and "brother" of John Rope

on to San Carlos. 'Metal Tooth,' called Sanchez by the Whites, was among these and he was a Carrizo chief. There were about forty of the prisoners altogether. They were loaded into big wagons and taken off to Tucson and put in jail. About six months after this they brought them back from Tucson through the sub-agency. There was an officer who rode in front, then 'Metal Tooth' dressed up in an officer's coat, then the rest of them in column of two's. They took them on up to San Carlos, where all their wives had come to meet them.

There were still lots of renegades out even after this. A White Mountain man was one of them. He had killed one White man and two Indians. A man and the uncle of one of these Indians who had been killed by this renegade caught him. They started out on horseback to take him to San Carlos. The renegade thought sure they would kill him on the way because they were relatives of the men he had killed. He tied a piece of calico around his eyes and rode that way so he would not see them reach for their guns to shoot him. When they finally got to the river crossing and San Carlos lay right across where he could see it, he knew that they were not going to kill him and it was as if he started to live again. They put him in the jail there.

When this renegade had been in jail about a day, he asked one of the two police who were guarding him to let him out to urinate. They did so and he went to the corner and went back all right. They used to keep ten soldiers and ten police always on guard at nights at San Carlos. They ought to have put chains on this renegade in the jail, but they didn't do it. In the early morning he asked again to be let out to urinate. They let him out and he went to the corner of a building as before. From here he ran fast, around by an adobe wall, put his hands up on it, jumped over and ran for the arroyo. The guards shouted that he had got away. It was still dark and they could only see his G-string, which was white. They shot at this but missed. The two men who had brought him in heard what had happened when the news was telegraphed to the sub-agency.

Right across from the sub-agency on the high mesa lots of White Mountain people were camped. The renegade's relatives were there too. 'Crooked Nose,' the sub-agent, sent word for two men, both relatives of the renegade, to come into this sub-

Courtesy Arizona Pioneers' Historical Society

The Apache Kid, renegade

agency. They came in and had a talk. 'Crooked Nose' said to
one that he wanted him to go out and kill this renegade, that if he
did so he would become a chief among his people, and he would
also get paid for it. Also, if he got this renegade they would stop
hunting down the other renegades who were his relatives.[58] "All
right," he said, "we will get him." So the agent gave him a rifle,
five boxes of cartridges, matches, tobacco and some grub, a good
belt, and a black-handled butcher knife like the men used to
carry in those days. These two men got on their horses now and
rode back to their camp. The next day they saw the renegade near

the camp, riding on a buckskin horse which he had found hobbled and taken. His wife was riding behind him. They were going up a wash. One of these men stood about three hundred yards from them, and so when he shot he missed the man but hit the horse's hind legs. The woman ran down the wash and hid. The renegade got off the horse and started to run up the side of a hill, out of sight.

The man who had shot started after him on foot and the other pursuer rode around the side of the hill to head the renegade off. On the top of the hill the renegade hid behind a creosote bush. The first man ran up the hill where he had seen him go. When he got to the top he was out of breath. The renegade had a knife and he jumped out at him. He got scared and instead of shooting the renegade as he should have done, he turned and ran down the hill. The renegade ran after him and as he came he made medicine on him with jaguar power, saying, "Now, I'll jump on you and kill you like jaguar would do." The other man couldn't do anything.[59] He got cut in the belly, but his guts didn't come out. He got slashed on the head too. The renegade's wife was standing right there. There was one man watching all this from a little hill, but he was too weak and lazy and did not even shoot. He was afraid he would get killed.

The White Mountain people came over and reported to the sub-agency what was going on. We police ran to cross the river. It was high and so we took off our moccasins and left them on the bank, thinking that the fight was not far off. The people were shouting to us to hurry from across the river. We thought it was the renegade who got killed, but when we got there we found čałheł ['He Goes Out At Night'] dead. The renegade had taken the rifle and cartridges off him and had run up the arroyo into a small canyon. He had his hand cut badly with the knife and had run up into a cave under the bluff with his wife. Here he stopped to bandage the hand. We trailed him by the blood on the ground and when we got up into the canyon and saw that he had not stopped yet, we turned back. When we got back to the sub-agency lots of people were around the agency building.

That same day a boy called gušhujn ['Wrinkled Neck'] was up at Indian Springs looking for horses. He met the renegade up there. The renegade came over to him and said, "Today I killed

'He Goes Out At Night' down there. I made jaguar medicine on him and grabbed him like a jaguar and killed him. I was like jaguar. This belt and gun I took from him. From now on I am going to kill everyone I meet, no matter if they are my relatives or not. But I know about you, boy, you have always been very poor and have never had much. You have had a hard time. I don't want to kill you, so go on home. But if I meet you again after this, look out for yourself, because I will kill you."[60] 'Wrinkled Neck' came back to the sub-agency and told what had happened to him. 'Crooked Nose' heard about it and sent for the boy. When he got there he made him tell all about what the renegade had said.

ᚷᚷ

Not long after this the Chiricahua came up from the Sierra Madre with Geronimo. They went to San Carlos and there got the Warm Springs people and took them back to Mexico [1882]. The Warm Springs people were camped just east of San Carlos on a high bluff by the river. The other people who ran off were the people of Nachise, Chato, and Chihuahua. The Chiricahuas in Mexico had heard somehow about the killing of the White soldiers over at Cibecue [1881] and thought that now would be a good time to get their friends, the Warm Springs people, to run off to Mexico.

On their way up from Mexico to San Carlos this time they passed near where San Simon now is. Here two of them stole four good horses from some cowboys at a ranch. These two men said they were going to take their horses back to Mexico first before they went to San Carlos, and so they started back. They went by Sierra del Tigre, then north of Carretas, near Bavispe [Sonora], and a little over towards Janos where there is a high mountain with pine trees on it. Some Mexicans were up on this and saw the two Chiricahuas coming with the horses. The Mexicans lay for them and managed to surround and capture both men. They took the two Chiricahuas in to a Mexican fort near there in a canyon. Here the Mexican officer questioned them. He wanted to know where the rest of the Chiricahuas were and where these two were coming from. The two Chiricahuas said

The Chiricahua renegade Nachise (Natchez) and wife

(Above) Bylas, Western Apache chief

(Right) Geronimo

Courtesy Arizona Pioneers' Historical Society

that the rest had gone up to San Carlos and that they had left them two days ago. The Mexican wanted to know how long the others would be gone. The two Chiricahuas said it would take them about four days to get up to San Carlos and that they would probably be back in about twelve days. The Mexican officer said that if these two Chiricahuas were telling the truth they would let them go unhurt, but if they were lying they would be killed. Now all the Mexicans were notified to get ready. It was this time that they killed so many of the Warm Springs people.[61]

The rest of the Chiricahuas had kept on their way to San Carlos. All their women had been left behind in Mexico. They came up near Eagle Creek. Then on down to Ash Flat where Stevens' old ranch was.[62] Richard Bylas's father, called Bylas, was camped there as well as other White Mountain men working for Stevens, helping take care of his sheep.[63] The Chiricahuas came up to one of them who was herding some wether lambs. They asked him if there were many Indians living here. He told them no, just a few. Then the Chiricahuas killed all the lambs and started to cook them. These Chiricahuas got all of our people who were there and put them under guard. Stevens had nine Mexicans working for him here also. There were three Mexican women with them. The Chiricahuas went to where they were and on by, towards Bylas's camp. Bylas saw them coming and drank down a part of a bottle of whiskey he had before they got there.[64]

Geronimo came into Bylas's camp and sat down. Bylas's partner and this man's son were there also. Geronimo saw that Bylas had been drinking just lately. "I know you," he said. "You always have some whiskey around. Give me a bottle." Bylas said he had none but Geronimo kept on asking him for some whiskey. Finally the boy got mad. He said to Geronimo, "This man Bylas is not a boy for you to talk to this way and keep on asking for whiskey.[65] He won't give you any whiskey." Now Geronimo said to bring all the Mexicans here.

The Mexican foreman who worked for Stevens had married a White Mountain woman who had a boy there who was about twenty-five years old. Geronimo said, "This boy is a full-blood Mexican. He is no Apache." The other White Mountain man there said, "No, he is not a Mexican. He is a full-blood White Mountain and his mother is of the 'black water' clan, so he is of that clan

San Carlos in 1887

also."[66] Then the Chiricahuas asked Bylas what the boy was and he answered he was a White Mountain. After this talk the Chiricahuas tied all the Mexicans up together. Right there they killed the nine men and two Mexican women. A third woman got away and ran to the foot of the hill, but they killed her there.[67] The boy of the foreman they did not kill. Now the Chiricahuas left two men behind to guard the White Mountain women lest they should get to San Carlos and report what was happening. All the White Mountain men they took along with them under guard.

At first they had taken Bylas's horse away from him, but now they gave it back to him and let him ride it. They made their next camp on the south side of Ash Flat. Here Geronimo said he would make medicine and find out what was going on at San Carlos.[68] He sang only four songs. The medicine told him that all was going to be well on their way to San Carlos. The Chiricahuas used to have good war medicine and this was why all the people, both Whites and Apaches, slept so soundly that night.[69] From this camp they traveled all night, going near the Gila

River and stopping to rest on the river opposite the sub-agency. Then they started on again keeping four men ahead, crossed the river and went on over Dewey Flat to the old Wagon Road.

At this time there were forty police on the San Carlos Reservation scattered among the camps. Geronimo said he was going to send three men into every camp to kill all these police. It was still night and just east of San Carlos they stopped in the brush along the river. Here it was starting to get light. One of them threw a pebble up in the air and they could see it so they knew it would soon be dawn. This is the way the old-timers always used to do to tell if it was near dawn. Now one of the headmen of the Chiricahuas said to Geronimo, "I thought you were going to send three men into all the camps to kill all those police." But Geronimo would not answer him at all. They stayed there till day, then crossed the river to the Warm Springs camp. The Warm Springs people must have known somehow that the Chiricahua had come that night, for they kept all their horses tied up at their camp. Now Geronimo and the others went among the Warm Springs people and they all got ready to leave.

A man named Sterling was head of police at San Carlos then. If any shot was fired, he always used to get on his horse and

Courtesy Arizona Pioneers' Historical Society

Guardhouse at San Carlos

run right down to the place he had heard it. Just as the Chiricahuas were leaving with the Warm Springs people, they fired two shots for Sterling to come. Sterling heard and got on his horse to come over. The Apache chief of police got on a horse and came with him. One of the Chiricahuas hid on the trail and shot and killed Sterling when he came up. Sterling had on a pair of beaded moccasins so the Chiricahua pulled these off and took them for himself. They told the Apache chief of police to go back as they did not want to shoot him, but he kept following them, so they shot him also.

The Chiricahuas had already cut the telegraph wires from San Carlos to Globe and the sub-agency. Now they turned loose all the White Mountain men that they had brought from Ash Flat. Bylas knew what was happening and went to the sub-agency. Both 'Crooked Nose,' the sub-agent, and the other White man there were gone. But their wives were there. They thought Bylas was drunk and would not believe what he said. By this time they had sent men out and tied the wires up where they had been cut and now they got the news through. All of us police from San Carlos followed after the Chiricahuas and the Warm Springs people. We found the body of the chief of police where he had been shot and then we all turned back to San Carlos.

At the sub-agency they heard that the Chiricahuas and the Warm Springs people were on their way through and everybody ran away up toward Turnbull Mountain, except twenty-five scouts and a White man who cooked for them called Navajo Bill. These stayed behind at the sub-agency. The sergeant opened five boxes of cartridges and told the scouts to fill their belts. The rest of the cartridges were put down in a pit. Around this pit they all gathered so they could get in if fighting started. Their relatives told them they would get captured for sure but that they would be watching them from Turnbull Mountain, and if they did get in trouble they would come and help them. When the Chiricahuas came through they said they didn't want to fight, but had only come to take their relatives away, so there was no trouble.

There was a long line of the Chiricahuas and Warm Springs people going along the north side of the Gila River. Right below Dewey Flat they had held up some freighters. The White men got away by running, but there was a lot of whiskey and some clothes in the wagons. The Chiricahuas and Warm Springs people helped themselves to these. My father and some other men came up to the Chiricahuas and got some liquor to drink from them. The river was high here and the Chiricahuas and Warm Springs started to cross it. My father was a chief and he wanted to shoot the Chiricahuas while they were crossing the river, but the other men with him said no. The Chiricahuas had taken some of our horses but had said they would give them back in a little while. That is why the men were following them and why they did not want to start fighting. Some troops had come up from Fort Thomas to the sub-agency to get the Chiricahuas and Warm Springs people. When they got there and saw them, they turned around and went back, after following them a little way.[70] The Chiricahuas and Warm Springs people went on.

The men who had been following the Chiricahuas and Warm Springs people with my father turned back with him when these people crossed the river. They all went back to where the freighters were and started drinking whiskey and pulling out the goods. They just dipped the whiskey right out of the barrel and drank down lots of it. That night my father never came back to camp. The next day they found him dead. He had drunk too much. That same night one of my relatives also died from drinking and another man got very sick from the same thing.

Twelve of us police were sent to follow the Chiricahuas and Warm Springs people to see which way they went. We tracked them to Yellow Jacket. Here they had left one colt and killed a horse. I got the colt. Their next stop was east of Yellow Jacket, where they could look back over their trail for a long way. Then they went on to the east. We followed them this far and then turned back and reported. The next day I heard of my father's death.

Some time after this we heard that some Chiricahuas had killed some of our people at Fort Apache. It was at that time that they issued a gun and belt to me and put me on special duty. I no longer was a policeman. I was just carrying arms to shoot the Chiricahuas if they should come. Al Sieber said that the Chiricahuas had killed some of my relatives and so he was giving me this rifle to guard myself with.[71] Later on he said he was going to make me a scout.

When they started enlisting scouts again, I joined. They kept us at San Carlos for one month while they were getting together a hundred Indians for scouts. There were two sergeants for us White Mountain scouts and two for the San Carlos scouts and Tontos. The officer made some of the scouts practice shooting at this time. Before we left we put up a big dance. First we had the war dance and then the social dance. There were lots of White Mountain and San Carlos people there and lots of girls and women. We danced all night.

We started out next day and went to the sub-agency, then towards Eagle Creek, then Eagle Creek, then south to the Gila River. There were lots of soldiers with us and Yavapai and Tonto scouts. We went on to Apache Pass, then Bowie Depot, then to another camp. From this place all the pack mules were sent into Fort Bowie to load up with provisions. In two days they were back. We stayed five days here and then went on south to 'Red Rocks Standing,' then near where San Simon now is, then towards the north end of the Sierra Espuela, then Guadalupe Canyon. We stayed here for a while. Our sergeant was riding a horse and still wearing that belt the officer gave to him. We also had with us two Chiricahua women who had left the Chiricahuas in Mexico and come back to San Carlos. From this place they sent twenty of us off for three days to Round Mountain to look for sign of the Chiricahuas.

The first night we left, we stopped and made camp. We had a medicine man with us so we were going to find out if we would see the Chiricahuas or find their tracks.[72] The medicine man sat on the opposite side with the other seven men to help him sing. Now he said, "No one must laugh while we are singing—if they do so it will be no good." When they started to sing, we with eagle feathers closed our eyes and listened to the song. Our feathers commenced to get big and strong in our hands and started to move our arms from side to side. It was not we who moved our arms, but the eagle feathers.[73] Then one of the men singing laughed a little. Right away the eagle feathers and our arms dropped straight down to the ground. The medicine man said, "You make fun while we are singing—now we won't know about the Chiricahuas."

The next day we left our grub in this camp and started out to scout. We got back in at noon. There were lots of deer here and we killed some. The next day we started back to Guadalupe Canyon with our meat. About one month later the paymaster came to our camp there at Guadalupe Canyon and we got our pay. There was no store here or any other place to spend our money, but there were a hundred of us scouts and we gambled all the time. Our party had made a hoop-and-pole set while over at Round Mountain looking for the Chiricahuas that time. Now we played hoop-and-pole a lot. We had a good time there and the days passed quickly. They always kept guards out on two places to watch for Chiricahuas.

A while after this we all started out for Sierra Espuela and camped near there four days by San Bernardino. Then we went to Guadalupe Canyon, stopped at two places on the way. The evening we got back to the main camp the officer called us scouts together. He said six of us and the two Chiricahua women were to go out for about one month and see if we could locate the Chiricahuas. If we found them we were to send the two women to them to see if they could not get them to come back to San Carlos and be friends again.

When the Chiricahuas and Warm Springs people had run off from San Carlos, there had been three Western Apache men married and living with women among these people. They had persuaded the three men to go along with them. These three were *tsoɛ* [a Cibecue man whom the Whites called Peaches][74], and a man called *nanodiʔ* ['He Trots'], and another man. All three of these men had left the Chiricahuas and Warm Springs people in Mexico and come on back to San Carlos. Now they were acting as guides down into Mexico. The six scouts who were chosen to go with the two Chiricahua women were two sergeants, *lagudntɛł* ['Flattened Penis'] and *doʔilnada* ['He Consistently Places His Life in Danger'], both White Mountain men, and *jaʔndɛzi* ['Long Ears'] and *baʔitandaʔ* ['For Him They Search'], both San Carlos men, myself and 'He Trots.' They gave a mule each to the women to ride and a mule to 'He Trots' and one pack mule to pack our grub on. We gave the pack mule to the women to take care of and started out on foot across the mesa.

After awhile we got to a canyon where 'He Trots' said the Chiricahuas always passed through. We crossed a place in the

Tsoe ("Peaches"), Western Apache scout, originally from Cibecue

east side of the Sierra Espuela and camped on the other side of it. Here we all started out to hunt deer. 'He Trots' and I went back a way to the place we had crossed and hunted there. 'He Trots' tied his mule up, and we started to hunt. We killed one blacktail deer and wounded another. It lay down behind a big mescal and so we didn't know where it was. I went to the dead deer and from here I could hear something breathing hard. It was the wounded deer and we found him and killed him by hitting him on the head with a rock. This was a female deer without any young and it was fat. 'He Trots' had gone off and killed another deer. Pretty soon he came back with its skin across his shoulder. It was a big skin and touched the ground on both sides of him. I would like that skin, I thought. "Here," I said, "is this deer I have killed and fixed all up for you. There is the skin." "No," 'He Trots' said. "You keep it for yourself and I'll keep this skin for myself." It is the custom among our people to always give away a deer and its skin to the man you are hunting with.[75] We took all the meat of the female deer, but only the hind quarters and skin of the other.

When we got back to camp all the other scouts were already in. They had killed only whitetail deer and the two women were cooking it for them. The Chiricahuas do not eat whitetail deer in summer, but they will eat blacktail deer. As soon as the women saw our blacktail deer, they cut off some meat and started cooking it.

We didn't start out until after sundown. Then the women rode double on one mule and told us to ride double on the other, which we did. We also rode the pack mule double. We tried to get 'He Trots' to let 'Long Ears' ride up behind him, but he would not. We set out along the foot of the hill where there was lots of brush, so as to keep out of the open country. We got talking about 'He Trots' and why he would not let anyone ride double with him. It looked as though he was doing this way so that if we met the Chiricahuas or Mexican troops he could make a run for it and get away. We decided that if he should do this, we would kill him.[76]

We kept on traveling in the brush till it got dark, and then came out on the edge of the open country to cross over to Sierra de Media. 'He Trots' had some field glasses and he looked first with these over the open country to make sure no one was there.

'Flattened Penis' said, "If the Chiricahuas come to us, don't any of you run away, because if you do you will get killed. Go in the rocks right away and hide there and fight." 'Long Ears' was still on foot. We started across the flat. About in the middle of the flat we could see a herd of antelope running along in front of us the same way we were going and this way we could tell that no one had been here lately. After awhile we came to a rocky place with lots of holes in it and 'He Trots' said that the Chiricahuas had a fight here once with the troops. There was an old cartridge belt, all dried up, lying on the ground. A long way off there was some water and towards this we could see the antelope running ahead of us, so we knew things were still safe.[77] There was a canyon ahead of us with a lot of oak trees in it. 'He Trots' said the Mexican troops always camped there and that they might be there now, but we found no one.

That evening we got to water at the foot of a mountain with lots of white rocks on it, cliffs and canyons and peaks. We camped at this place near the foot of a cliff. The way we used to do when we were traveling was to make lots of fire before sundown so there would be plenty of coals. Then after sundown we would have no flames, only a big heap of coals.

That night we were all sitting around. They sent me and another man up on the hill to see if we could see any fire back that way. We had gone only a little way when we could hear a noise plainly. We went to it. It was only some water dripping in a cave, but it sounded just like a bell. When we got back to camp, all the others were saddled up and ready to leave. We told them about where the noise came from and then we all laughed.

It looked like rain that night and the two women said they were going over under the bluff and sleep, as they didn't want to get wet. 'For Him They Search' followed them up there. Pretty soon he came back and told me that the women wanted me up there too. 'Flattened Penis' said, "Don't go over by the women. We don't want to be going over there."[78] 'For Him They Search' came back a second time to get me but I would not go. He stayed with them all night. Next morning they sent four of us up the mountain to look for tracks, and we got back about noon. That night we talked. We decided tomorrow to send the two women to look for the Chiricahua near Carretas. "If you see them," we said, "tell them to go to the White captain at Guadalupe Canyon, as he wants to meet them and make peace."

The next morning we cooked up lots of food for the two women, took them a way and then let them go on on foot. We stood and watched them with the field glasses till they were out of sight. We stayed in this camp eight days waiting for the women to return and keeping watch from the top of the mountain.

On the eighth day we saddled up all the mules and left them tied up on the mountain. Then we went down to where we had left the Chiricahua women and waited. We looked with the glasses. A long way off we could see two people coming. They were on foot so we knew they must be Apaches. We could see them plainly now. We told 'He Trots' to ride down towards them. He started and we watched him with the glasses till he met the two people. There he got off and went on foot, letting them ride, he going in front. They got back to us about sundown and it was the two Chiricahua women. They had looked all over but found no sign of the Chiricahuas. We had been gone from Guadalupe Canyon fifteen days now.

Our party was about to run out of grub now so we started on back to where the troops were, stopping on the way at a place on the east side of the Sierra Espuela and then in a canyon on the edge of a mountain. From here we went on over a big mesa. 'Flattened Penis' said, "We don't want anyone to see us coming back over this open ground," so he made a wind. He knew medicine for wind and prayed for it.[79] Right in the middle of the mesa a big wind came up and there was so much wind we could hardly see each other. When we got into Guadalupe Canyon, we reported to the officers all that we had done. They said we had done well and also that they had received a letter saying that scouts from all over were gathering to meet by San Bernardino at the mouth of Guadalupe Canyon. All our camp moved on to near San Bernardino, where we stayed two days. All the troops and scouts were there. There were about five hundred of us scouts, some from Fort Huachuca and some from all the other forts. General Crook was there in command [1883][80].

There were lots of mules there for packing. Some had their manes roached, others had only hair between the ears and others had their tails cut in different ways. This was so you could tell which company the mules belonged to. There was one bell mule and all the others followed this one wherever it went. They used to unsaddle the mules in a line and each mule always knew where its own pack was when it was time to saddle up again. If the wrong mule got to another mule's pack, he would be kicked away by the right mule. All our clothes were about worn out from the trip we had been on, but there were no new clothes for us. They brought in a lot of thick red cloth for us, though, and divided it up among all the scouts to use as headbands. This way every one of us scouts had a red headband and we could be told from the Chiricahuas.

Now a big meeting was held. They spread a canvas and under this General Crook and all the officers sat. Out in front all the first sergeants of the scouts' companies stood in line and back of them the second sergeants. Then in back of these all the scout companies lined up. There were three or four sergeants from Fort Apache. Alchise was one of these and Peaches another. There were lots of sergeants from San Carlos. Then General Crook said, "What do you scouts think about us catching the Chiricahuas down in Mexico? Do you think we will find them?" The San Carlos sergeant named *tuʔisdlą* ['He Drinks Much Water'] said we could never catch the Chiricahuas because they could hide like coyotes and could smell danger a long way off like wild animals. Crook said, "I think we are going to catch these Chiricahuas, all of them, and we are going to keep after them till we catch them all. We have orders from Washington where the President lives to catch these Chiricahuas. We are all wearing the President's clothes now and eating his grub and so I want you to help him. This way the President will be glad if we catch all the Chiricahuas. I am the man in charge of all this outfit, and now I am going to sign my name on this paper so that even if I get killed, the President will still know about what we all did and the record won't be lost. Thus, no matter if I die or live, the government will know that it must reward you." I think he was telling us the truth all right because all of us scouts are now drawing pensions.

We were scouts in order to help the Whites against the Chiricahuas because they had killed a lot of people. Now General Crook told us to put up a big war dance that night.[81]

General George Crook and the Western Apache chief Alchise

The next morning we started out to travel south. Al Sieber was head of us scouts. What Sieber told us to do we did. When he said that here would be a good place to camp, we made camp. We traveled towards the Sierra Espuela and down along the east side of it till we came to the canyon in which the town of Bavispe lies. Here we made camp. Then we went on to near Bavispe where we saw some wild peach trees growing. We had never seen peaches before and thought that these were some kind of walnuts. There were lots of trails leading to Bavispe from here on. While going along we saw some Mexicans with a burro. When we got in sight of Bavispe we stopped. Sieber said for a hundred of us scouts to go ahead and for all the rest to follow. We went on, right through the streets. The houses were all made of adobe and some of them were falling down in ruins. In these adobe houses the Mexicans were living on both sides of the street. There were a lot of Mexicans looking at us and a lot of old Mexican women were there. We went right on through and then across a little canyon. Here we saw Sieber stop in front and we all made camp there.

Sieber and some of the others went and butchered ten Mexican cattle without permission from the Mexicans. In a little while the mayor of the town, a Mexican, came riding out on a little pony. He rode his horse right up over the rocks to our camp and the pony seemed to climb up in jumps. Then he ran it as fast as he could to the officers' camp. Now he talked some time with the officers and I guess they had to pay him for those ten steers. All of us were here now except four scouts who had been left with some soldiers at a place just east of where Agua Prieta, Sonora, now is.

That night some of the scouts from our camp sneaked into the Mexican town to get liquor. They brought it back with them and got drunk. Mickey Free came over to me and said, "My grandson, don't go over where they are drinking.[82] This is liable to be some trouble." So I didn't go.

The next morning we moved on to the foot of a mountain just to the east of Huachinera and camped there in a canyon. While in this camp we could see Mexicans watching us from a way off. The day after we started for the Sierra Madre to the southwest. There was only one way to get to the top of this mountain and this was up a long, narrow ridge. On the way one mule fell off over a bluff, pack and all. It was so far below that no one went down to get him at all. Finally we got to the top of the mountain and here we saw three very poor cattle which I guess belonged to the Chiricahuas. The three men who escaped from the Chiricahuas and came back to San Carlos were there with us and they knew the country. We made our camp that night near some springs on the mountain. We stayed here four days, cooking up bread and lots of other grub.

Then Sieber said that fifty scouts were to be ahead and that the pack mules and the rest would follow some distance behind. I was one of these fifty. At that time I had never fought with the Chiricahua and did not know how mean they were, so I was always in the front. We crossed over a canyon, going in single line. First

Al Sieber

there would be ten scouts, then a mule, then ten scouts, then a mule, that way. We scouts in front heard someone whistle in the brush. We stopped and listened and could hear the whistle again. We all thought it was the Chiricahuas and started to run back. One man tripped and fell in a water hole. Afterwards the whistle turned out to be only the wind blowing on an acorn with a hole in it, which was on a blue oak tree.

Pretty soon we came to some old tracks. Here the Chiricahuas had left one horse. He was very poor but we butchered him and took out his liver and the meat that was good. The three men who were with us and knew the country said maybe the Chiricahuas were camped back by a rocky mountain we had passed.

In about three days two pack mules were brought up to us from the others behind with lots of grub on them. A message was sent back from here and we went on ahead to another camp at a canyon near the head of Bavispe River. This was the place where Peaches, "He Trots," and the other man had got away from the Chiricahuas. There were lots of pine trees growing there and we could see where the Chiricahuas had been having a dance here. *Tułąn* ['Much Water'], a Warm Springs Chiricahua who had married a White Mountain woman from Fort Apache, was with us now as scout. He said the dance tracks here looked like they had been making a war dance. From this place the tracks of the Chiricahua scattered out on purpose and I guess they had some place where they met up again.[83]

While we were on the edge of the mountain here, one of the scouts, David Longstreet, who was off by himself came back and said he had seen something shining way across on the side of another mountain opposite us. But the others would not believe him and said he had just seen the sun glinting on some crow flying that way. The man said it was not a crow at all. The side of the mountain was thick with brush and we traveled along its slope looking for tracks. Right on top we came to another Chiricahua camp. They had left three pieces of mescal in a tree here and also had covered their fire over with dirt. We could see their tracks plainly now and they were about two days old. They had tried to hide the tracks again, but we followed. There were lots of pine trees here.

The next morning we kept along the side of the mountain till afternoon. Then the sergeant said to cook some grub. While we did this, the others who were ahead looked with the glasses and then came back. They had seen the Chiricahua camp on top of a ridge across the valley on the side of the other mountain.

On a level place near the camp all the horses of the Chiricahuas were grazing. There were lots of them. We all hurried back and there we could see the camp all right. There were quite a few Chiricahuas in it. Sieber sent two scouts back to tell the other soldiers and scouts who were way behind to hurry up here and to come that same night. Some of the scouts were afraid. It was only about a mile across the valley from where we were to the Chiricahua camp. That night we could not sleep but sat and talked in whispers. Later on we slept a little. Early in the morning the troops and other scouts got in there. They told us all to eat and tie the horses up, as it would soon be daylight.

Now we looked at the Chiricahua camp again. There was lots of smoke coming up from over there. We started out, down across and up towards the camp. Part of the soldiers and scouts went on the left side and part on the right. In the middle went Alchise and his scouts. This way we were going to surround the Chiricahua camp before they found out we were here. One of the scouts on our side of the line went off to one side to urinate. Right then he saw two Chiricahua men riding towards the scouts. He told the others and they waited to surround the two Chiricahuas. One sergeant on the other side of us down the canyon had his gun all cocked, ready to fire. The gun went off by accident, but even so the Chiricahuas did not seem to hear and kept right on coming. Then we scouts started shooting at them, but missed. The two men jumped off their mules and beat it off in the rocks and brush, but they did not go back to their camp.

Now we scouts all ran down into the canyon and drank there, dipping the water up with our hands. Some of the scouts started to say their knees hurt them as an excuse to keep in the rear. Some of them were always doing this way because they were afraid. We all started on for the Chiricahua camp, going up over some rocks where there was lots of water. Right above here some of us could see three Chiricahuas herding some horses to a grassy place. They were coming our way, so we waited. Right behind these three a boy and a girl were riding, each leading a horse behind them. We waited, hiding in the brush till the boy and girl were right opposite us.

Then 'Much Water,' who was there, called to them. "Shew," he said, "come here." He was a Warm Springs man so, of course, he talked like them. The two stopped, but did not come. 'Much Water' called again. "Come here. Hurry up," he said. They dropped the ropes of the lead horses and came over, but they could not yet see us. When they were close to us, we made for them. I grabbed the girl and 'Much Water' got the boy. The girl had lots of beads made from the roots of a kind of brush that grows down there. She had four strings of them and I started to take those off her. Then 'Much Water' said, "No, that girl belongs to a friend of mine and I want to trade you this boy for her."[84] I said all right, and he took the girl and I the boy. Now all the rest of us started to shoot at the three Chiricahua men who were driving the horses. The scouts had told the three to stand still, but they started to run off in the pine woods. Only one of them was shot. The boy I had captured saw all the scouts in a line shooting with their red headbands. "What kind of people are these?" he asked. "These are scouts," I told him, "and they are all after your people." Then he started to cry. The girl didn't cry at all. She just stood there quietly. I told the boy, "If you try to run away, I am going to shoot you, so you had better stay with me." The girl spoke to me. "My friend, don't shoot him," she said. I was wearing two belts of fifty cartridges each, but I did not shoot more than three times because I was satisfied with having helped to catch these two Chiricahuas. My brother was there and I told him to go on to the Chiricahua camp, but he did not want to, so I told him to keep my boy for me and I went towards the camp myself.

Near the place where the one Chiricahua had been killed, I saw someone's heels sticking out of a clump of bushes. I grabbed this person by the heels and pulled him out. It was one of the other two Chiricahuas who had been with the one who was killed. This one was only a boy and there was no blood on him, so I thought he was all right. Just then some of the other scouts came along and said they wanted me to give them the boy, but I said no, that I had found him and was going to keep him. I told the boy to run ahead of me to the camp. He was only a little boy, but he ran fast and we got there quickly. I found where the Chiricahuas had been butchering a horse and the front quarters were cut off already. One man had got to the camp before me and had captured a white mule with a saddle on it. I found an old, worn-out Navajo blanket for the boy and put him up with the scout on the white mule to ride double.

This camp was Chihuahua's and he and his brother had just come from the warpath with lots of cattle. The Chiricahuas had been butchering there and there was meat lying all around on the bushes to dry. I found a good thick cowhide and doubled it over, putting a lot of dry meat and grease inside. This I gave to the scout on the white mule also, giving him half of it for himself. There was some mescal spread around to dry on the bushes and some just boiled. We took this also. I found an old Mexican saddle, bridle and a rope and put these all at the side of the camp together, so that the others would know that they were mine.

They yelled now for all the San Carlos scouts to surround the Chiricahua horses, which they did. Two Chiricahua men got up on a high, rocky shoulder above us. They shot down at us a couple of times, then they yelled, "All right, you're doing this way with us now, but some time we will do the same way with you," and then they went off. One of the sergeants called to us to come up where he was and help him surround a bunch of mules. Seven of us went up to him but there were no mules there. There were some pine trees here and a woman had left her little girl at the foot of one. The girl was hiding behind the trunk now, and I went to her and reached around the tree and grabbed her. She was wearing a string of beads around her neck from which hung a Mexican silver cross. I took this silver cross for myself.

I started back and the first man I met was of the scouts. "Here," I said, "I'm giving this little girl to you." He laughed and took her and then he gave her to *nasta* ['He Knows A Lot'], who was riding a horse and who was also a scout. 'He Knows A Lot' took her and started riding down the hill with her, singing the victory dance song as he went. All the other scouts laughed when they heard him singing this song.[85] This is the song of thanks that they used to sing long ago when a successful war party came back and they gave the victory dance in which men and women danced together.

After we got back to the Chiricahua camp again we burnt all the mescal that was left and also a lot of a kind of big juniper berry that grows down in Mexico and which the Chiricahuas had gathered for food. One of the scouts caught five horses and drove them to the camp. There was one fat sorrel mare, and I took her for myself and put the saddle and bridle I had captured on her. One scout came to me and said one of the boys I had caught was the son of the daughter of Nachise, who was a good friend of his. For this reason he wanted to trade me eighty dollars and a horse and saddle for the boy, but I would not do it. One scout called *mba čo* ['Big Coyote'] had also caught a sixteen-year-old girl when she had come down to get water. This girl was taken back to Fort Apache and is still living on North Fork.

Only four of the Chiricahuas had been killed. One of these was an old woman and it was some San Carlos scouts who shot her. She had stood up when they came to her and asked them not to kill her but just to take her captive. The San Carlos scouts had shot her anyway. We White Mountain men talked to the San Carlos scouts and said, "Why did you kill that old woman? You ought not to have killed her."[86] The San Carlos men said they had come after these Chiricahuas and they were going to kill them.

We started out from the Chiricahua camp, General Crook riding in front. I shot my gun off some because I was feeling happy about what I had done in the fight. The others were shooting too, just for fun. Some of the other scouts were joking me about only firing three shots in the fight. I said, "I have done better than you. I caught three Chiricahuas." Pretty soon my horse gave out, so I killed her and gave my saddle to the man who had given me the horse. I also gave him the boy to carry.

After we had gone a way, we stopped and made camp. I took out my dried meat and fat from the hide and divided it up among the others. We cooked and ate. Then the man who had wanted my boy came again to me. "My cousin," he said, "give me that boy like I asked you. I want him and will buy him from you."[87] But I told him no, that I did not want him to do that way. He kept right on asking me. Then Mickey Free came over and spoke to him. "Don't ask for that boy like that. We are on the warpath now and don't know for sure if this boy belongs to the daughter of your friend or not."

That night they put fifteen scouts out to guard on all four sides of the camp we were in. General Crook said to make all our

Chiricahua prisoners lie down together and sleep and for us to watch and see that they didn't get away. That night the oldest Chiricahua girl we had caught said that almost all the Chiricahua men had gone out on a raid that very day. This girl was called *jagε iłči* ['Antelopes Approach Her'] and later married Alchise's brother.

The next morning General Crook said to bring all the captives to his place. There he asked the oldest girl which was the best one of the horses we had captured. She answered that a certain grey one was. General Crook sent for this horse, but a scout had already taken it for his own and would not give it up. General Crook sent again for it and said, "Bring that grey horse to me here right now." The horse was brought and although the scout who had claimed it was there, he said nothing. They saddled this horse for the two oldest Chiricahua girls and gave them food, also tobacco for Chihuahua.[88]

Now General Crook said, "Go to Chihuahua and tell him that we have only come to take his people back to San Carlos and not to make war." They took the girls back to the Chiricahua camp we had attacked and from there the two followed the Chiricahua tracks. The girls had been told to tell the Chiricahua that the raiding of their camp yesterday was an accident and that it had not meant war. Also that our camp would be at the right end of the mountain and that we wanted the Chiricahuas to come in to that place for a talk. 'Much Water' had told the girl to tell his brother and sister to come into our camp right away. Twelve scouts and 'Much Water' took the girls back to the Chiricahua camp. Some of the Chiricahua had been to their camp again, but had gone back up on top of the mountain.

The next day we saw 'Much Water's' sister and a girl relative with her. The girl was all dressed up with lots of beads on and a blanket over her head. She had a white flag in her hand. They came into camp and we gave them food. 'Much Water' talked with his sister. He said, "We have been all over looking for you people, not to kill you, but to bring you back to San Carlos to be friends. Tell this to Chihuahua." That same day Geronimo's sister came into camp. She said we had taken one white horse with a Mexican saddle on which was a pair of black saddle bags. A silver bit and bridle had also been on this horse, she said. If we wanted Chihuahua for our friend, he said that we must give it to her, and she took it back up on the mountain to where the Chiricahuas were.

The next day we could see someone riding that white horse over some rocky places at the foot of the mountain. It was Chihuahua and he rode fast to our camp. On the end of his horse's tail was tied a strip of red cloth and another strip of red cloth hung from under the bridle. In his belt he wore two pistols and in his hand he carried a lance with a strip of red cloth tied around its end. He rode right up to where we were sitting under some oak trees. We all jumped up, not knowing what he intended to do. He asked where the head officer was, and we told him. Then he ran his horse right through us to General Crook's tent. He rode right through soldiers and scouts alike and they had to get out of his way. Mickey Free, who was one of the interpreters, went right over after him to the General's place.

Chihuahua got off his horse right in front of the tent and there he shook hands with General Crook. Then he said, "If you want me for a friend, why did you kill that old woman, my aunt? If I was trying to make friends with someone, I would not go and raid their camp and shoot their relatives. It seems to me that you are lying when you speak about being friends." Now they gave him some tobacco and some food to take back with him. Then he got on his horse and rode off fast, right through us, the way he had come.

'Much Water's' relatives came back later on and said that Chihuahua felt pretty bad about the way things had happened. He was pretty mad. He had said, "It's no good, all these scouts and soldiers here," and he told the women to get ready to move further away. The Chiricahua women didn't want to go away so far and hid out on him. Anyway, Chihuahua moved his camp off a little further.

Now almost all the Chiricahua women started coming into our camp. All the ones we had captured came in but that one little girl I had found still had no mother. Finally, about sundown the mother came into our camp. She was crying as she came and talking bad about us White Mountain scouts. Mickey Free told her she deserved to have her guts eaten out by a coyote for running off and leaving her baby the way she did. She was a young woman. When she saw the baby, she grabbed it and started crying again.

They gave out lots of rations to the Chiricahua women now. Chihuahua had not shown up yet and we scouts went over to see 'Much Water's' sister to see what she had to say. She said she thought there was going to be more trouble because the other Chiricahua men were due back from their raid in three days, and when they found out what had happened, they would want to fight us sure. She said we had better all look out. The next day we moved the whole camp a little further down by the mountain in a small park there.

Chihuahua was not in yet and we thought he would probably go to join the other Chiricahua men. There was only one day left till their war party was due back and so now the Chiricahua women tore up some flour sacks and tied the white pieces of cloth on poles, which they set up all around our camp. This was to let the Chiricahuas know we didn't want to fight. The women said for us scouts to look out for ourselves. "When the men get back, they may start shooting," they said. We piled rocks and pine logs up to lie behind.

That night the Chiricahua women called towards the brush up on the sides of the ridges where they thought their men now were and told them not to shoot. They called the names of *ka?edine* ['Cartridges All Gone'] and Geronimo and told them why we had come here for the Chiricahuas.[89] The Chiricahua men up on the ridges heard all right. When it started to get light in the morning the women started calling again and telling the Chiricahua chiefs that they, the women, did not want any fighting but only that the Chiricahuas make friends with us. The women told us scouts not to get up till sunrise so that the Chiricahuas would not start to shoot.

We got all ready, put on our belts and loaded our rifles. We lay down that night but we could not sleep, so we just lay there till sunrise. Early that morning *jetikine* ['Pine Pitch House'] from the Chiricahuas crawled close to our camp. He was a man who had been captured while still a boy by some White Mountain people and had been raised among them. On account of this he was like one of us. Now he was living with the Chiricahuas and was just like one of them so he wanted to stay with them. He listened to the different scouts talking and could tell which were the San Carlos and Tonto scouts and which were White Mountain men because we talked differently.[90]

Kaidine ("Cartridges All Gone"), notorious Chiricahua warrior

After sunrise, when we had eaten, we heard some Chiricahuas calling to us from the mountain. We could see lots of men up there together. Geronimo's sister went to them. She came back and said that they wanted some of us scouts to go to them. *Nabijintaha* ['He Is Given Tests'], a White Mountain scout, went up to the Chiricahuas but he didn't talk plainly, so they told him to go back and get some other scouts. He came back and got *dastine* ['Crouched and Ready'], who was related to 'Pine Pitch House' and also a Cibecue scout. 'Pine Pitch House' called 'Crouched and Ready' aside when they got up there. This 'Pine Pitch House' was Geronimo's father-in-law, and he was a chief because he was about the best fighter of any of them. He was a little man and not as tall as an old-fashioned long musket, but even so, the Chiricahua chiefs were like nothing to him and they usually did what he advised.

The Cibecue scout, who was called *haškehagola* ['Angry, He Starts Fights'], talked with his brother-in-law, Chato. After the talk was over, the scouts came back to our camp. Then 'Much Water's' brother gave a yell and started to run into our camp. When he got there, he threw his gun and belt on the ground. Then he said to 'Much Water,' "My brother, you have been looking for me and now I am with you again and as if I belonged to you." Then the two embraced each other. This was the first man to come in. Pretty soon all the rest of the Chiricahua men came in, all except the chiefs, who stayed apart by themselves.

We were camped on a little knoll and all around in the open place below was lots of tall yellow grass. General Crook was off at one side of this hunting birds with a shotgun by himself. When he was there all the Chiricahua chiefs came to him.[91] They grabbed his gun away and took the birds he had shot also. They said he had been shooting towards them. Mickey Free went over there. They all sat on the ground and talked. After about two hours the General came back with all the Chiricahua chiefs to camp.

Some time after the Chiricahuas were all in, three Mexican women and a baby came into camp. They had been captured by the Chiricahuas on their raid. An officer who talked Spanish went to them. All of us scouts and soldiers gathered around to look at them. The officer asked them what their names were and

where they came from. This he put down in a book. The women
said they were traveling along with two Mexican men and some
burros over on the other side of the mountains. The Chiricahuas
had come then, killed the two men and taken the three women
and the baby back here. They did not know at what place they
had been captured. The Chiricahuas said that the reason they had
captured these Mexican women was so that they might take
them to Janos and trade them to the Mexican soldiers there for
some Chiricahua women who had been captured in the Corralitas
fight,[92] and who were now held at Janos. This way the Chiricahuas hoped to get their women back and make friends with the
Mexicans at the same time. They never did this, though, and I
guess it was because we had come and captured them. The three
Mexican women were taken over to the cookfire and fed.[93]
They were wearing old sandals on their feet and these they took
off and threw away, as the officers had given them tall army
boots to wear.

Now we all mixed with the Chiricahuas like friends. About
noon the Chiricahuas went apart and started in to make a victory
dance. Sieber told all us scouts to stay away from the dance and
so only the Chiricahuas themselves were there. But all the same,
one scout went over to the dance that night and danced. A
Chiricahua woman made him pay her twenty cartridges.[94] Some
White Mountain scouts reported on this man and the officer
made him go back and get the cartridges from that woman. The
Chiricahuas had driven in the cattle they had captured. They gave
three head to us White Mountain men. One they gave to 'Angry,
He Starts Fights,' the Cibecue scout, and one they gave to a
San Carlos scout. They butchered lots for themselves.

The next day we started back for San Carlos and made our
first camp on the head of Bavispe River. They let the three
Mexican women ride on pack mules. One scout was leading a
mule on which one of the Mexican women was riding. Some of the
other scouts joked to him, "There you are traveling with your
wife, we see." He got mad and dropped the rope and the mule
went loose. Pretty soon that Mexican woman fell off. We held a
social dance with the Chiricahua every night now and had lots of
good times.

We traveled on from here across where the ground was
yellow and made a camp at some water. In this camp they started

to play hoop-and-poles. *Dajĭdĭl* ['He Moves Lightly and Quickly'], a scout, and 'Cartridges All Gone,' the Warm Springs chief, played together. Before these two started to play they took off their cartridge belts and laid them together. Later on the Chiricahuas sent word for 'Cartridges All Gone' to come to their camp right away, so he had to quit.

The Chiricahuas were camped apart from us and 'Cartridges All Gone' went back there to a council they were holding. The Chiricahua chiefs were talking there. They said that this night they were going to put on a social dance for the White Mountain scouts and all the other scouts and let the Chiricahua girls dance with them. Then all the Chiricahua men would get behind and while the scouts were dancing, they would kill them all. It didn't matter if they themselves, the Chiricahuas, got killed, but they would get us scouts anyway. They sent word for 'Pine Pitch House' to come to the council. When he got there they told him what they planned to do and asked him to join in. 'Pine Pitch House' said, "I won't join in this because the White Mountain people are like relatives of mine," and then he went back to his camp.

After awhile the council sent for him again. When he got there Geronimo said to him, "My father-in-law, we mean to do as we told you tonight. That's why we told you. Whenever we have gone to war before, you have gone with us. But now you won't make up your mind to say yes or no."[95] 'Pine Pitch House' answered, "I told you already that I would not help you do this." He was mad and started to walk away. In a moment he turned back and came to the council again. He said, "You chiefs don't mean anything to me. I have been with you many times and helped you kill lots of Mexicans and Whites and that's the way you got the clothes you are wearing now. I am the one who has killed these people for you and you have just followed behind me. I don't want to hear you talking this way with me again." Then he walked off. That night they started to hold the dance anyway. But one of the scouts, *jaʔndɛzi* ['Long Ears'], had died that day and Sieber sent word for them to stop the dance on account of this, so they did.[96]

The next morning some of the Chiricahuas asked for permits to go and gather up a lot of horses from the Mexicans before they left Mexico. General Crook gave them permission and told them to meet us back at the mouth of Guadalupe Canyon, near San

Bernardino. Lots of the Chiricahuas and their chiefs went, but General Crook didn't try to stop them. He just let them go. They did not like the little San Carlos ponies and wanted to get some good horses before going back. 'Pine Pitch House' went with them also. We made our next camp in a canyon. Some of the Chiricahuas had not come in yet. These were *tudnči ʔlɛsa ʔan* ['Red Water Resting'] and his family, another man, and a White Mountain boy and his mother who were with them. The White Mountain boy and his mother had been captured by the Chiricahuas up on Eagle Creek some time ago. One of the scouts was related to this White Mountain captive woman and her boy and so he was sent out to bring in 'Red Water Resting' and his bunch.[97] He brought them in and they were issued rations.

Whenever I was cooking in camp, that little Chiricahua girl I had captured would come over and eat with me. Her mother would tell her, "There is your friend. Go over and eat with him." Everytime I cooked, she would come over and eat and then go back. The son of a Chiricahua who was one of my father's friends was there with us. He knew who I was and came to me. He told me that his mother had been killed some time ago and that he was now just living with this old aunt. He had no way to get food, he said. I went out and killed a deer and brought it to his camp for him and his aunt and he thanked me.

Now we moved our camp to some springs just north of Carretas that 'Red Water Resting' knew of. This was quite a ways from Janos, but it was near the place where the Mexicans had killed so many of the Chiricahuas and Warm Springs people.[98] We scouts, just some of us, went over to see the battleground. There were lots of bleached-out bones there and pieces of women's dresses lying around and lots of beads scattered around on the ground. Lots of Chiricahuas and Warm Springs people had been killed there. We shouldn't have gone to look at this place, but we did it anyway.[99]

Our next camp was to the north, near Sierra Espuela. We had already moved on past Bavispe. Near Bavispe we saw a sorrel mare with a bell on her. We took this along and kept up along the side of the Sierra Espuela, finally stopping to camp in a canyon where lots of pine trees were. About sundown we saw lots of dust coming up, way back. We thought maybe this was Mexican soldiers coming to fight us and we cleaned our guns and got ready for them. After awhile we could see through glasses that it was the Chiricahua men coming back, driving a big bunch of horses and mules they had taken from the Mexicans.

The next morning we started up along the edge of the Sierra Espuela and made camp at some springs. Then we moved on to near San Bernardino. Here some of us hunted deer. I killed one deer and right then a Chiricahua rode up to where I was. He said they had heard us shooting deer and followed us, as they had no cartridges to kill deer with themselves. I gave him the deer. "Come on, and we will ride double back to camp." "No," I said, "I am going to hunt some more." When I got back that Chiricahua gave me a hind quarter of the deer. Mickey Free was given three horses and mules by some of his Chiricahua friends. One of these, a buckskin mule, he gave to me. We left this place for the springs east of where Agua Prieta now is. A lot of the Chiricahua girls were on foot, so Mickey took one up on front of him and I took another up in front of me also. When we got to the springs there were some soldiers camped there. They had seen us coming and had the grub all cooked up for us. One of the White Mountain sergeants had been stationed there with his company of scouts but he was the only one left. One after another they had gone off and not told him where they were going. Now he was alone. We all laid our guns and belts aside and lined up to get our food; soldiers, scouts and Chiricahuas alike. After one bunch got through eating, then another bunch would eat. This way they did till all were fed. It took almost all the rest of the day and even then some didn't get any food. The next day we moved on to another camp where there were a lot of oaks growing. Here two buggies drove up, each drawn by four mules. These were for General Crook. He and some of the officers and three Mexican women got in and were driven to Tucson. Before he left he said to us that all was done now and for us to go on to San Carlos and keep watch on the Chiricahuas. "You said you thought you would never catch the Chiricahuas, but now you see we have got them all," he said.

Our next camp was near Willcox. Beyond Willcox a citizen met us with a big wagonload of clothes to sell to us; shirts, pants, shoes, hats. We bought some clothes from him and swiped some more because all our clothes were in rags. The Chiricahuas still had some of their cattle and every time we camped they butchered.

'Pine Pitch House' was with them no longer. The Chiricahuas said that while he was getting the horses with them down in Mexico, they had come near some Mexicans. 'Pine Pitch House' had stood up to look at them and the Mexicans had shot him right in the head from a distance of about three hundred yards. We White Mountain men did not believe this because 'Pine Pitch House' had been on the warpath too many times to get killed this way. We think that the Chiricahuas shot him because he would not join them that time they had planned to kill us all at the dance.

It was at the camp we made near the head of Arivaipa Valley that we got our clothes from the citizen. From here we moved by the Winchester Mountains, then to the west of Stanley Butte. Here the Chiricahuas killed their last three cattle. This place is in a narrow canyon and there were so many of us that we filled the canyon right up, from end to end and side to side. The next day we started for San Carlos. All the people there knew that we were coming that day and were waiting for us. We could see lots of looking glasses shining to us in signals from San Carlos. At every camp all of us scouts and the Chiricahuas were counted.

Now they put one hundred of us scouts in front, then all the Chiricahuas, and then the rest of the scouts, then the soldiers, and last of all the pack train. This way we marched to the edge of the Gila River, took off our moccasins (those of us that were on foot), and went across. Sieber rode in front. There was a crowd of Indians on both sides, watching us. Sieber led us straight to the old school building and there stopped. All the scouts went to the right and camped. All the Chiricahuas went to the left and the pack mules were brought into the center. We cooked in eight lots. All our relations came to see us. The next day Alchise and his scouts went on back to Fort Apache. The day after that all of us scouts were discharged and got our pay. The officer said that they wanted forty scouts to enlist again, but lots of the men had had enough of scouting. Soon some cowboys brought up a big bunch of horses to sell to us. I guess General Crook must have told them to bring those horses to sell. I bought one sorrel mare for forty dollars. General Crook had told us we should get good horses and start to raise them.

ᚼᚱ

Many of the Chiricahuas and Warm Springs people were now living at Fort Apache.[100] In about two months I received notice that the officer at San Carlos wanted me to come and join as a scout. The Apache Kid was sergeant and I went and joined up under him.[101] They kept us scouts on the Reservation for quite a while. Then the army paymaster came to San Carlos to pay off the troops, and Sieber sent word to me that I was to ride up with the paymaster and his guards to Fort Apache. I went up to San Carlos and reported. The paymaster was ready to start. They had two buggies and one wagon for the grub and outfit. The paymaster rode in the front buggy and I rode my mule in front of all. Where it was smooth we travelled fast, but if it was rough and rocky, we went slower.

The first night we got to Ash Flat. When they made camp, the first thing they did was set up a little tent, even before unhitching. Then they carried a cashbox out of the buggy and into the tent. Now they unhitched the mules. I was just beginning to understand a little English then. The paymaster went right in the tent where the cashbox was and stayed. They had soldiers on guard around the tent all night long.

The next day we passed by Old Summit and came to Black River. The water was high here, but anyway I rode my mule in and swam across. The others followed where I had crossed. We camped on the further bank. The officer built a little pile of stones on the edge of the river to show where we had crossed. Then we traveled on fast towards Fort Apache, making camp near Turkey Creek where the road comes up on the hill. The next day the paymaster told me to tie my mule up behind the wagon and put my saddle in and to get in myself. We passed by the forks of the White River and went up the canyon. At the fort we could see lots of scouts and some soldiers drilling. We drove right past the soldiers and up to the commissary where the iron box was unloaded. Then we took the mules to the stable. That day we paid off the soldiers.

Mickey Free was living here now and was a scout with Chato.[102] They were living together. Also most of my relatives were here. That day my uncle came to me and said that my brother wanted to see me and for me to come over to his camp. I got the paymaster's sergeant to get me leave for one day, so it was

Chato

all right. I stayed with my brother-in-law that night and he gave
me a Navajo blanket which I tied up behind my saddle. The
sergeant came to the camp and told me we were to start back for
San Carlos tomorrow.

That day I went to Mickey Free's house, where he was living
with Chato. It was a lumber house. I stayed there that night. The
next day we started back with the paymaster, but when we got to
Black River the water was very high and the stone monument the
officer had made was under water, so we turned around and went
back to Fort Apache again. I went back to Mickey's camp. In
the morning the sergeant came and said that the paymaster was
going out by way of Holbrook, so I needn't come any further.

That day Mickey went to his lieutenant and got him to wire
Sieber at San Carlos for orders for me. Sieber wired back for me
to come when the river got low enough to cross. I stayed for some
time with Mickey. We used to go down to Canyon Day where my
relatives were and go to their social parties. I heard that there was
still lots of water in the river, so I stayed on for about ten days.
Some Navajos came down from their country with a lot of
blankets to trade to us.[103] I had no money so I asked a chief
down at Canyon Day to lend me the money to buy a blanket, and
he did. I got a good Navajo blanket. In about fifteen days I
started back for San Carlos. On the way I met a relative who
gave me another Navajo blanket. I had three now.

At this time the Chiricahua 'Red Water Resting' was living
at San Carlos with a woman whom he had not married. He was
getting pretty mean. One day when he was drunk he started
shooting and said he was going to kill some of the Apaches and
then run off in the mountains and turn renegade. They sent the
second sergeant of scouts, *dušdoẹ* ['Flies In His Soup'], for him
but he refused to come in and the sergeant came back without
him. That night his wife came in, though. Now they sent word
out among the camps to get the scouts together to arrest 'Red
Water Resting.' I was up visiting among the camps at the springs
on the mesa to the south and did not get back till late.

That evening they got eight of us scouts together. One of them claimed to be the best medicine man around. But there was one other medicine man who got killed at Fort Grant and he was better. The eight of us started out. We decided to kill 'Red Water Resting' right there if he talked back to us [i.e., if he refused to surrender]. We went to where his camp was, near Peridot. Some medicine men had made a wind for us so there was a lot of dust in the air. We stopped in at the camp of a man named Archie, and he gave us a whole olla of something to drink.[104]

We found out here that 'Red Water Resting' was drinking with some San Carlos people in the camp of a man called *nyugi* ['Something Furry']. A man came to us. He was a secret agent known only to the head officer at San Carlos.[105] We went with him to 'Red Water Resting's' camp, but we didn't find him there. From here the secret agent went and told the headmen around here that if they heard any gunshots to stay right in their camps.

Soon the man came back and we all started for 'Something Furry's' camp where 'Red Water Resting' was. 'Flies In His Soup' had a pistol, one man had a rope, and the rest of us had rifles. The door of 'Something Furry's' camp faced the river and we got there all right. Out in front of the door, on both sides of it, were two men lying on the ground. We made a run at one of those men and grabbed him. A woman yelled to us that that was the wrong man and to get the other one. We let him go and jumped on the other one. I grabbed his hair and banged his head hard on the ground. 'Flies In His Soup' sat on his stomach and another man tied his feet up. When 'Red Water Resting' had come to this camp, he was after a rifle to start out as a renegade. But the people in the camp hid the rifles they had; they hid them under the bed, and some women lay on them.

We kept him there till early morning and then a chief by the name of Casador drove up in his wagon on the way to San Carlos.[106] We loaded 'Red Water Resting' in the wagon and got in ourselves. The chief tried to start his horses, but they would not go and just balked and kept backing up. I think that 'Red Water Resting' must have made some medicine on them so

Casador (and wife), chief of the San Carlos subtribal group

they would not go.[107] We got down and I pushed the horses and whipped them, but they would not go. Then they started to buck and jump around and finally started. We ran after the wagon and jumped in. This was near Peridot, just below the missionary's house. That day was ration day and all the people were going in to San Carlos, which was not far from here.

'Flies In His Soup' said that we had caught this man we were after and that he felt like shooting. So he shot three times with his pistol. *Hastin nabaha* ['Old Man He Searches About'], one of the scouts, said he wanted to shoot also, and asked 'Flies In His Soup' to loan him his pistol. But he had a rifle already loaded and 'Flies In His Soup' asked why he didn't use that. All the same 'Old Man He Searches About' kept on asking for this pistol, which 'Flies In His Soup' would not let him have. Pretty soon they started to fight about it and took their knives out, right in the wagon. Another man and I got off the wagon. 'Red Water Resting' said, "What's the matter with you fellows? This is ration day and they will be butchering and issuing meat. I want you to hurry up and get there in time for these people to get some for me." They quit fighting and we all went to San Carlos.

We drove by the officer's house and Sieber saw us. "Ha ha, ha ha, here is 'Red Water Resting,'" he said, and came over to put leg irons on him. He had no shoes on and was going barefoot at the time we caught him. Sieber told us to take him to the jail. I started out with him to the jail. When we were pretty near there, he stopped, as the irons were chafing his legs. He asked for his blanket so that he might tear it up and put it around his ankles to protect them from the irons. Sieber said to us, "Don't stop there. Hurry up and take him to the jail," and I did. 'Red Water Resting' said to me, "A man like me, you might just as well cut off my head and kill me right away. I have done nothing to get punished like this."

Soldiers and scouts were set outside the jail to guard it. They kept the chains on 'Red Water Resting' for about two months and then they took them off. We were not so careful with him now, and he might have run away. But we had decided that if he should talk mean, or fight, or try to run away, we should kill him right away. After awhile they took him and a lot of other prisoners down to a place where they made a sweat bath. We watched them close then. We had caught 'Red Water Resting' in the fall and kept him in jail till spring.

Then a telegram was sent down from Fort Apache saying that they wanted troops and scouts up there right away. I was on night duty at the telegraph office then to carry messages. I used to stay on till the morning star started to come up. The time the wire was sent I did not know about it, but later the officer said that they were going to move the Chiricahuas and Warm Springs people living at Fort Apache out to Holbrook and off east someplace.[108] He told me not to tell the other Indians as they did not want the news spread around yet. The next day the scouts set out for Fort Apache, taking 'Red Water Resting' with them. When they got there the troops surrounded all the Chiricahuas and Warm Springs people, loaded them into army wagons and took them out to Holbrook where they were put on a train. A lot of Chiricahuas and Warm Springs people rode their ponies out to Holbrook and had to leave them there. After the Chiricahuas and Warm Springs people were sent away, the scouts came back to San Carlos.

$$\zeta$$

I had been scout for quite a while at San Carlos after the Chiricahuas and Warm Springs were sent away. There was lots of trouble going on then on account of all the renegades who were out.[109] The soldiers had a big glass on Graham Mountain, on Turnbull Mountain at Fort Apache, and at another place near which they kept some soldiers and scouts camped.[110]

One day two scouts set out from San Carlos for Turnbull Mountain. When they got to the foot of Turnbull Mountain, they tied their horses up and went up the mountain on foot. When they got back down their horses were gone. Some renegade had taken them. The tracks led towards the Graham Mountains. The two scouts walked back to San Carlos and got in about sundown and reported. The next morning they loaned two horses to these scouts and along with thirteen other scouts and twenty soldiers we started out to the foot of Turnbull Mountain to the place where the horses had been stolen. We scouts always went mounted now.[111] When we got there we took the trail up and followed it along the foot of the mountain, then eastward up onto a spur and around to the south. The tracks showed that there was only one renegade and he was leading one horse and riding the other. I felt pretty sick and had a bad cold. Right on top of a ridge that man had left one of the horses and then gone on to a place at the east end of Turnbull Mountain. When we got to this place, we camped.

The next morning we started on the trail again and found where the man had made camp right near us at the foot of a hill about one night ago. From here he went to a point on Goodwin Wash and then circled around, took a canyon for a way and then climbed out on a ridge where he could see his back trail. There was a lot of ripe prickly-pear fruit here and he had eaten some while he watched. The next day he went by the foot of a place on the head of Goodwin Wash, then to a point just east of Fort Thomas. At this place he had killed a cow with a calf inside her and cut out some of the ribs and the tenderloin with the hide still on it.

Pretty soon we came to where he had found a White man's horse with a bell on it. He had left the other horse here and taken the bell horse but the bell was still lying there on the ground. We couldn't find the scout's horse here, though. The renegade's trail went on to the river where we made camp. The next morning the officer said that this bell horse the renegade now had should be easy to follow as he had bigger feet than most horses around here. So he sent us scouts out to trail him. We followed him a way, but lost the trail in a bunch of other horse tracks and got it mixed up, so we came back to the soldiers and all started for Fort Thomas.

Right above Fort Thomas they used to have an old grist mill. Near this there was a lot of mesquite growing through which the trail led. As we rode along we were talking and making lots of noise. Right here we heard a horse whinny. Pretty soon we heard him whinny again and then the horse came right to us. It was the scout's stolen horse we had missed. We laughed about it and hollered to the soldiers about what had happened.

When we got into Fort Thomas I went to see the army doctor at the hospital with our sergeant. I was sick and could not eat. The doctor looked me over and then weighed out some medicine on a little scale and mixed up some of this for me to

drink. He gave me some more to take along. That night some of
the scouts got hold of a lot of whiskey. One of them brought a
bottle to me and said to drink it. But I didn't want to as I had just
taken the medicine. He said to go on and drink it, that this was
just as good as medicine. But I drank no whiskey that night. I
slept good all night from that medicine. That was the best medicine
yet. The next morning I went to the doctor and got some more.

We left Fort Thomas that day and got back to San Carlos. I
had found the renegade's quirt right where he had dropped it
while changing to the bell horse. The officer had borrowed it
from me, and when we got home he never gave it back. When we
had started out I had felt pretty sick, but now I felt fine. I got sick
from eating too many watermelons.

One day after we had been back at San Carlos for some time,
some of us were playing hoop-and-poles. *Jiyɛˀ* ['He Knows
Hardship'] was playing for cartridges piled up on a big rock. We
asked what he was doing this way for, as it was a funny way to
do. He said that he was getting these to give as a wedding present,
but this was a lie. A short time ago the brother of 'He Knows
Hardship' had died. The head man had had a wagon issued to him
just before this death, but when he died his father burnt it up as
was the custom.[112] One Indian had reported this to the agent
and the father had been put in jail.[113] Now 'He Knows Hardship'
was mad about this and that is why he wanted the cartridges. He
knew who it was who had reported his father.

Now 'He Knows Hardship' saddled up his horse and tied
something up in his blanket behind his saddle. Then he got on
and rode to the store to get something and then rode fast after
the scouts. He was riding a black horse, his best. His brother was
with him. In a little they came to the camp of the man who had
informed on their father. He was lying inside his wickiup. They
called in to him to ask if he had anything to drink. He answered
back that he wished he could give them something, but he had
none. Now 'He Knows Hardship' got down with his rifle loaded
and shot the man in the wickiup. Then he got back on his horse,
and with his brother, rode after the scouts.

They caught up with another man pretty soon and 'He Knows Hardship' said, "Come on, I know where we can get something to drink." "All right," the man said. "Then take this trail here," 'He Knows Hardship' told him, and he motioned the man to ride in front of him. When he got in front he shot him in the back and killed him. He did this because he had already killed the one man and from now on he would kill everyone he met.[114] This happened a little way below Peridot where the San Carlos bridge now is. One man came in and reported the killing of the man near the bridge, and later another man came in and reported the man who had been killed in his wickiup. They sent an army team and wagon to get the bodies. That night we scouts were set at the place where the scout got killed, and also around the other camps in case the renegades should come back.

The next morning a lot of Tontos came to San Carlos, all mounted and with their rifles. A man called Smiley was with them.[115] Four of them got off and came into the agency and talked with the agent. The rest stayed on their horses. We scouts were there with our rifles also. Smiley said to the agent that his relatives were the ones who had been killed yesterday and that after this meeting was over he was going out and kill everyone he met. The agent said that this was not the way to do, that only the ones who had made the trouble should get punished, and that we scouts would arrest those men who had done the killing for him. Those Tontos were pretty mad about their relatives having been killed. The man who had done the killing and his brother turned renegade now and went off in the hills. I heard later that they got caught and the one who did the killing was sent off to some prison. He never came back. I heard he died there. Now our time was up and we scouts were discharged.

We were kept at San Carlos for quite some time. There was one man who had joined the scouts about a month ago. He was a good fellow and not married. He was riding along by Peridot one day and some Indians killed him. Some time later a lot of the head scout's relatives were living below where the steel bridge on the San Carlos River is now. They saw three men riding along the road who were relatives of the people that had killed the scout. Two of them were old men. They made the three men stop, and right there they killed the two old men. The other got away and made it to San Carlos where he reported what had happened. One of the murdered men's horses followed him in all the way. Right away they sent all the scouts up the river to that place, all except myself and another scout whom they kept to ride in front of the soldiers. We two had to wait around while they made the soldiers drill before they could start.[116]

Finally we got under way up the San Carlos River. Later the officer asked where the killing had been done, and the man who had got away and reported said, "Right over that brush there on the other side." The officer said for everyone to wait here while he took eight soldiers over to see that place.

Later on the rest of us went over. A dead man was lying right in the middle of the road. Another had crawled off in the brush and tried to hide. Here they heard him grunting and went to him. He could not talk and only grunted. There were four men who

Courtesy Arizona Pioneers' Historical Society

Ration lines at San Carlos in 1887

had done the killing. These had gone in an old adobe house nearby with their women and children. They had their rifles with them. The officer told these four men to come out and go in to San Carlos right away. But they would not do it. Some of the scouts went over to near Salt Wash to bring in the horses of these four, but they could not find them over there.

A lot of relations of the dead men came down to where we were. They had their rifles and were gathered all around us. Some of their women went to the dead bodies and started to cry and yell.[117] This made their men madder yet, and it looked as though they were going to shoot us scouts. The sergeant said to stay in close, and we did. We told them not to try and shoot. The four men in the adobe house had their rifles ready to shoot. Pretty soon four army wagons drove up, went right around all the people, and stopped by the adobe house. They had been sent for to San Carlos.

Now the four men and their women and children were loaded in with their bedding and started off for San Carlos.[118] The soldiers rode in front and on each side. We scouts rode in back. All that crowd of people followed after us. They wanted to kill those four men. We told them not to follow and make trouble, but they kept right on coming all the same. Right above San Carlos where there is a cliff and lots of catclaw growing, the crowd stopped following us, as we were pretty near to the agency. When we got the people in the wagons to the jail, we took the rifles and belts from the men and put them in jail. Their women and children stayed outside. The next day they sent the whole lot off someplace. They were returned in about a year. In those days the people were always killing each other like this.

9

Not long after this we were lined up for inspection, all with clean clothes on and our rifles shined up. This way we knew that our time was pretty near up and we soon would get paid off. In a couple of days we were discharged. Sieber, who knew me well and whom I like a lot, asked me three times to rejoin the scouts, but I would not do it. Those long scouts we used to make at first, down to the southeast and around Fort Bowie, were good and we could save some money. But this being stationed at San Carlos all the time was no good, as there was always somebody killing someone else, and we were having to go out after them.[119] Then, too, we could never save our pay because we had our families to care for. I am still caring for my family, as my sons have no work.

Since that last scout I have lived at Dewey Flat, then at Calva, and finally at Bylas, here, where I am still living. You see me here still alive and well. That is because I have been good and minded my own business. Lots of the other scouts did not, and they are dead.

David Longstreet

5

DAVID LONGSTREET

In 1931 David Longstreet was an old man living on the San Carlos Reservation. He was born about 1855. According to Goodwin's notes, "Longstreet's real name was naɫte, meaning 'disgruntled' or 'dissatisfied,' which did not apply to him at all—at least not in his late years when he was a most contented and friendly old person." Longstreet's recollections begin around 1865, shortly after the establishment of Camp Goodwin. However, the central events in his narrative deal with the capture of his mother by troops stationed at Tucson and his own experiences as a scout on Crook's famous 1883 expedition into Sonora, Mexico.

I was born near where Fort Apache now is. There I lived with my father, mother and grandfather off and on for nine years. We used to plant our corn there.

While I was still a very small boy, my grandfather, father, a man called Coon-Can, his son-in-law, and three boys all moved to near Yellow Jacket in the Gila Mountains and camped there in a canyon. There were other people there and quite a lot of girls.

All the men went hunting near that place and one man killed a bear. He packed the meat back into camp on foot as we had no horses with us. That evening a coyote came to where the man had

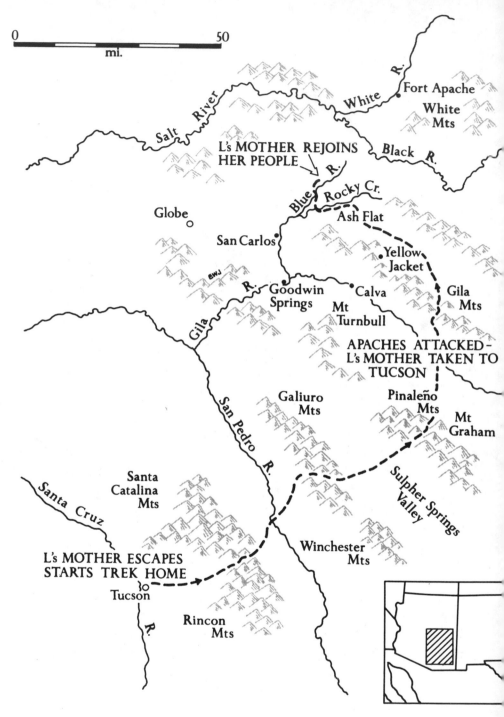

0   50
mi.

Salt River

White R.

Fort Apache

White Mts

Black R.

L's MOTHER REJOINS HER PEOPLE

Blue R.

Rocky Cr.

Ash Flat

Globe

San Carlos

Yellow Jacket

Gila R.

Goodwin Springs

Calva

Gila Mts

Mt Turnbull

APACHES ATTACKED– L's MOTHER TAKEN TO TUCSON

Gila

San Pedro R.

Galiuro Mts

Pinaleño Mts

Mt Graham

Santa Catalina Mts

Sulpher Springs Valley

Santa Cruz

L's MOTHER ESCAPES STARTS TREK HOME

Tucson

Winchester Mts

Rincon Mts

R.

David Longstreet Narrative

butchered the bear and followed his tracks back to the camp. There was a girl sleeping inside the wickiup, and outside it were the three boys. They were lying down sleeping.

The coyote went right in the wickiup where the girl was and grabbed her upper arm and tore off a long piece of skin. The girl woke up and called for help. Then that coyote ran out the door and away. One of the boys shot at him, even though it was dark, and hit him. The girl's mother was off in another camp someplace, gathering grass seeds for food.

Now the boys yelled to the other people and told them what had happened, so they all came to the wickiup. This coyote was mad and when coyotes or foxes get this way, they run around with their mouths open and are like crazy people. The people built a big fire, and no one slept the rest of that night except the children. They were afraid that the coyote or another one like him might come back. Next morning they trailed that coyote to where he was shot and found him lying with his mouth still open.

The whole camp was now moved to a place nearby where a coyote medicine man was camped. When we got there they set up the camps and then went to talk to the medicine man, who was taking a sweat bath.

They told him what had happened and he agreed to work on the girl and try to cure her.[1] This medicine man told us to notify all the Indians to come and help sing.[2] They would start singing that night. It was fall then and the nights were long.

That evening when lots of people had come, the medicine man made each person tie an eagle feather in his hair, even the little children. He told them that this meant they would see a big eagle sitting in a juniper tree near there at the next sunrise. If they saw the eagle it meant that the girl was going to get well.

They sang all that night and were still singing at sunrise when they saw the eagle in the juniper tree. He sat there for a while and then flew off someplace. The medicine man said that now the eagle had gone to tell the other eagles about this sing for the girl, and that it was a sign. He said the eagle had told him before he left to put up a *gan* ['mountain spirit'] dance for this girl.[3] That night a *gan* dance was put up, and the girl danced with the *gan* all night long until sunrise. They all kept the eagle feather tied to the tops of their heads.

Now the medicine man said he would put up another dance at a place about opposite Calva, so we all moved to this place and the girl danced there all night with the *gan* again. The medicine man said that the eagle had told him to keep on making a *gan* dance every night till he got word to stop. The next camp was near Geronimo, and they danced with the *gan* here also.

Then we moved to Goodwin Springs. Here in the afternoon we saw a lot of *gan* up on the ridge. These came down to the camp and danced with the girl that afternoon. In the evening they started the *gan* dance again and held it through the night.

There were lots of American soldiers camped there at Goodwin Springs, and they came down to watch the dance. The American captain then said, "Why do you make this girl dance? She is too sick." One relative of the girl told him that this was to make her well—this was the best medicine.

Now the medicine man sent the people out to gather up a lot of coyote dung. This they put in a basket and stirred up with water till it was soft. Then the medicine man gave a little to each person there.

While the medicine man sang, he was praying. He said, "I know that I am to do this way I am doing from a voice I cannot see.[4] That's why I make this kind of medicine, because I am told to."

From Goodwin Springs the dance was moved to another place. When the dance was over, the medicine man said that the next night they would sing. They did and made the sing all night to finish off the cure. The medicine man said that a coyote who bit people was no good and crazy. The people were still with their eagle feather tied in their hair, and now the medicine man told them to watch for eagles.

In the morning they saw two eagles sitting in a mesquite tree. Now that girl's arm was all healed up and she was well. The medicine man told the girl, "I have worked and sung on you a long time now. From now on I don't want you to step on a coyote track. If you do, you are liable to go crazy. Coyotes are always traveling on trails, so don't walk in a trail but walk on the side of it."[5]

This is the end.

One time our people came from Fort Apache to gather mescal on the south side of Turnbull Mountain. There were quite a lot of us camped there. It was about two days later that something happened.

My uncle was taking care of two boys down at that place. Early in the morning he sent the two boys out to run up a hill nearby to see if everything was all right. When the boys got up on the hill, they could see that their camp had been surrounded in the night by White soldiers, along with some Papago scouts and some Indians that we called *bači* ['Apaches Mansos'] who lived near Tucson.[6]

The two boys had run right through the enemy, and now they started back to the camp, which was completely surrounded. The enemy shot at the boys then, but missed them and they ran off. Now they started shooting into the camp.

All the Apaches in the camp ran down the canyon and tried to get out the other side. One old woman in the camp got shot right in the shoulder. The Papago scouts went to her. She was scared and so she said that she thought they would find a lot of our women hiding in the brush or in the rocks across the canyon and up on the side of the hill. She told them to go over there and look. They did, and what the old woman said was true -they found a lot of women hiding there.

I was still a little boy then, and I got scared and ran off a long way and hid. My mother was taking care of my dead aunt's little girl, and she and this little girl both got caught. One woman was trying to run away, carrying a little boy on her back. The enemy shot at her and hit the little boy so that the bullet passed right through him and killed his mother also. This woman was my mother's sister-in-law and she was the wife of a chief.

One boy and his sister were trying to get away from there. The girl gave out, and the boy was packing her on his back when the enemy shot and killed both him and his sister with one bullet. They captured a lot of women and children that time.

When they had gone my father started looking for me and calling, but I was too scared and did not come to him for a long time. When he finally found me, he told me that my mother was captured. My father wanted to go to the enemy's camp and get my mother and the other women back and fight with the soldiers and Papago scouts, but the chief whose wife was killed said, "No, my brother-in-law, don't go back there. I don't want you to get killed too. Your wife will come back, I think."

The enemy took all their captives to a place on the San Pedro River. They gave them some kind of round cakes to eat. The soldiers kept them here for two days and then took them along towards Tucson. One Apache Manso chief knew my father, and he went to my mother and said, "The old woman who got shot in the shoulder was the one who told us where you women were hiding."

Near Tucson they put all the captives in a big open shade house and stationed three men on each side of it to guard. These guards were White men.

Now the Papagos and the Apaches Mansos set up a victory dance, and a lot of the Papagos and Apache Manso women danced also.[7] While the White guards were watching this dance, my mother got out and went to the officer's tent. This White officer had taken the little girl away from my mother for himself. When my mother went to him, he told her to stay away from the little girl, so my mother had to do as he said. I think this little girl must still be living with the White people someplace.

The Apache Manso chief who had spoken to my mother about the old woman had for a wife a White Mountain woman, the sister of the wife of Stevens. This Stevens used to live in the Arivaipa Valley with his wife, and the Apache Manso chief used to go there to visit him often. They used to keep a lot of Papago and Apache Manso scouts with the troops at Goodwin Springs, and it was here that this chief married his White Mountain wife.

Now his wife went to see my mother. She came and talked to my mother. She said, "I think it is in your mind to run away." My mother said no, that she would not run away, as all her children were killed and now there was nothing left for her, but she was fooling when she said this. This woman told my mother that she did not think that her boy (me) was killed because the scouts had seen four boys running up out of the canyon near the camp. These four boys all got away.

While the chief's wife was talking to my mother, all the guards and the White people and the scouts had gone close to the victory dance to watch. This woman told my mother that she had hidden some corn pudding in a bundle back of the shade house in the brush and that it was there for her whenever she wanted it. She also said her husband had a good horse that she could have too. Then the woman left.

It was dark now and my mother slipped out behind in the brush and took the corn pudding. She thought she was alone, but pretty soon she saw ahead of her a woman carrying a baby. This was another one of the captives. Soon she caught up to her.

Then they saw behind them the old woman who had been shot in the shoulder. She had followed, and now she said, "I am glad to get out of that place, and please go slow so I can keep up." But the woman with the baby said, "This old woman told the enemy where we were hiding. She is no good and we don't want her with us." So they started walking fast and left the old woman behind.

My mother was crying about having to leave her aunt's child behind. The other woman said, "Don't cry. Your sister-in-law and your nephew got killed—you should feel sorry for them. But that little girl will be raised just like a White person."

My mother and the other woman climbed up on the Santa Catalina foothills, and from there they could still hear the drums down at the dance. "They are still dancing and don't know we have gotten away yet," they thought. The other captives were still sleeping down there. They stayed on the Santa Catalinas that night and the next day traveled toward the Galiuro Mountains, making camp about halfway to them.

The next day they got to the Galiuro Mountains. Here they saw some tracks but they said, "These tracks are of the Arivaipa Apaches and they are no good, so we will stay away from them."[8] But these tracks had been made by their own people, who were camped by the Galiuro Mountains, and it would have been all right if they had followed these tracks.

My mother and the other woman camped at some springs in a rocky place here. That Apache Manso chief's wife had also given my mother a knife and some matches, so here they cooked some mescal stalk to eat. Then they moved to the west end of the Graham Mountains and then to Red Knolls. Next day they got to the Gila River where they stayed and took a bath. Now they went down the river, crossed over here and took an old trail that goes up by Gila Peak. It was here that the other said, "Your relatives are living here somewhere around Ash Flat, so you go to them. I am going by Mount Triplet and then on to Cibecue." My mother tried to get her to stay, but she would not, and so she set off by herself.

From there my mother went on alone by some springs and then to the north side of Ash Flat, across Ash Creek, where she looked for tracks. At that place there was a woman gathering sourberries by herself. She and my mother saw each other both at the same time. The woman asked who she was and she told her. Then they came together and embraced. Both were crying. They were sisters.

This woman said that everyone had gone north to Blue River. She gave my mother some mescal to eat and water to drink. Then she said, "Your child is over at Blue River and your husband left to go on the warpath to Mexico about one month ago. He is not back yet. I will get my horse and we will ride double to where your child is."

They started off and went by Rocky Creek and then over the old trail to Blue River. When my mother got there and saw her people again, she started to cry. She had brought back some cloth from where she had been captive, and now she made some clothes for herself and my sister.

My uncle (the one whose wife and boy had been killed together) now butchered a fat mule to celebrate my mother's return. He said, "You have come back to your two children here. That's why I am killing this mule for you." In two days they moved the camp over near Chiricahua Butte, a little above it.

A little while after my mother came back to us, my father was coming from Mexico, riding one horse and driving another in front of him. Right along Rocky Creek he ran into some White troops. There were Pima scouts with them, and also one man who had been captive among the White Mountain people and who spoke their language. He was called *inda dikiyε* ['White Man, Comes To A Point'].

They took after my father, and so he shot the horse he was driving in the shoulder and killed him so they wouldn't capture him. Then he rode on. 'White Man, Comes To A Point' called to him and said, "You are like a coyote and run away from us and kill your horse." My father turned around and rode at the troops. He shouted, "That is my horse and it is no business of yours what I do with it!"

Now the soldiers all shot at him, but he did not get hit and got away. He rode up the creek and got on a hill with lots of rocks on it, just below Rocky Creek on the east side. Soon he could see the officer and 'White Man, Comes To A Point' coming. He called to them to come up, that he was in a good place to fight and was ready for them. He only had a bow and arrows to fight them with.

The officer spoke back through 'White Man, Comes To A Point' and said, "It seems to me that you are not born from a woman. You must have been created from something else when you were a child. If you were a real man you would be dead now. We are going now to Goodwin Springs."

He watched them to see if they were really going to Goodwin Springs, and stayed on the hill till he could see their dust coming up way over by Warm Springs at the head of San Carlos River. Then he came down and went to see about his dead horse. He butchered it and took all the meat with him and got in to our camp where he found my mother had come back all right. From here we moved up to White River and planted our corn at the farms. There were no White people here then.

When the corn was planted we all went down to Goodwin Springs where there were lots of White soldiers. My mother was a good-looking woman then, and lots of the soldiers kept looking at her as if they had seen her before. "Maybe they remember me from the time I was captured," she thought.

Then the officer said he wanted to make a count of all our people, so we lined up for this count. When the soldiers came to my mother, one of the sergeants recognized her and told the officer that this was the woman who had run away near Tucson.

The officer came over and said to her that the Apache Manso chief had come and told him later that her mind was made up to run away. My mother said, "I didn't mean to run away, but that chief's wife got some food and a horse all ready for me, so I came." The officer shook hands with her. He wanted to know how she got home and said she must be strong. My mother said that her legs had been like her horses. She asked about the little girl that the officer had taken from her. The sergeant told her that she was still with that officer and his family and that she no longer spoke Apache, but only English.

The officer gave my mother a paper on which was an order so that she could draw rations. She went over to the commissary and drew a sack of flour, some coffee, and sugar, and also three blankets. The rest of the White Mountain people there didn't understand why my mother should draw more rations than they.

Later on the head officer of the soldiers at Goodwin Springs wanted to put a post on White River near our farms.[9] He asked our chief, Diablo, about it and this chief said it was all right.

We all started back to White River and the soldiers started for this place too, building a road as they came.[10] When the corn was ripe, the soldiers had gotten to White River. We gave them our cornstalks to feed their horses with because they asked for them.

5

I was a government scout several times.[11] Later on when I was older I went down to Mexico to fight against the Chiricahuas with other scouts and soldiers.

The first time I enlisted at San Carlos, my sergeant was a Tonto Apache. The packer was a White man. I don't remember what the name of our officer was. We started off and went by Solomonville, then around the east side of Graham Mountain and on to Fort Grant. From Fort Grant we scouted down to Fort Huachuca where my six months ran out.

The second time I enlisted was at San Carlos again. My sergeant was a Tonto, and the packer was the same man as before. We went down to Fort Bowie and then on to near where Douglas now is. We camped here for a while and then went on to 'round mountain' in what is now New Mexico.[12] From there we turned back and went to Fort Bowie where my six months ran out.

I enlisted a third time at San Carlos. My sergeant was Bylas and the officer was Captain Crawford.[13] We started out and went to Ash Flat, then down to the east, then to Solomonville, and to the southeast over a mountain, then to Fort Bowie. From here we went to near San Bernardino and from there to where we camped on a mesa and reconnoitered. We were sent out to scout from this place for two or three days at a time. Then we went back to Fort Bowie where the six months ran out.

The fourth time I enlisted at San Carlos. Our officer was Captain Crawford. We went up the Gila Valley, then up the San Simon Valley towards Fort Bowie. At one camp Captain Crawford gave me one gallon of whiskey all for myself. He was a good friend of mine and joked with me sometimes. "If you get drunk, I am going to whip you," he said. We went on to Douglas and camped there to reconnoiter. When six months were up we went back to Fort Bowie and then home.

The fifth time I enlisted at San Carlos under a Tonto sergeant. There were two officers for us that time. We started off and went over past Stanley Butte and on up the Arivaipa Valley and then across to Fort Bowie. From here we went to near San Bernardino. To that place came an officer and along with him came more soldiers and lots of scouts. *Tsajn* [Alchise] and his scouts came there also. We had no girls there, but all the same we used to have social dances.

Then the head officer said we were going into Mexico to look for the Chiricahuas and bring them back.[14] "Don't shoot any of them, only round them up," he said. So we started into Old Mexico. I don't know the names of the places we went in that country now because I have forgotten them. We passed through a Mexican town [Bavispe, Sonora] and marched right through the streets which were very narrow. Not far beyond the town we camped.

We got along all right with the Mexicans. Some of the Mexican officers came to tell us that there was lots of mescal liquor in town. "If you want any, go to the town and get it. We are glad you are here looking for these Chiricahuas because they have killed lots of us Mexicans. We don't like them for this. We don't want you scouts and soldiers here in our land, but if you are after the Chiricahuas, it is all right," they said.

From that place we went up on the mountains where there were lots of pines growing [the Sierra Madres, southeast of Huachinera, Sonora]. It was a bad trail and some of the pack mules fell off into the canyon far below. No one bothered to go after them. We kept on and got to where some Chiricahuas had been camping. They had left lots of juniper berries in this camp

piled by their beds. Further on we saw where Mexicans and
Chiricahuas had been fighting each other. No one had been
killed. We only saw the signs. From there we started along the
mountain. There were a lot of scouts ahead of us. A scout called
šəš ['Bear'] and I were just ahead of the soldiers and pack train.

As we were going along I went apart from 'Bear' a way and
there saw across on another mountain the glint of a mirror,
though it might have been a crow's wing in the sun. But I didn't
think it was a crow because it flashed four or five times. I asked
'Bear' if he saw it, but he said he didn't. "Did you see a flash?"
he asked. "Yes," I answered.

Now the soldiers ahead of us stopped to rest and eat. I went
to the officers—there were three of them—and reported about the
mirror. But they said, "You must have seen a crow's wing." "No,
I don't think so," I said. "There must be a camp over there."
"All right, get ready, and we will go over there tomorrow. We
will leave the packs here to follow us in two days," the officers
said.

So the next day we went on the mountain with six scouts out
ahead. There the six men located an old Chiricahua camp. At
this place the Chiricahuas had been making a war dance and
right there the six scouts waited for us to come up.

When we got there we saw where they had danced in a
semicircle, with the open side towards a Mexican town.[15] They
had shot lots of cartridges toward this town, and we found many
empty ones lying on the ground. We tried to find which way they
had gone from here, but they had scattered as if to come together
at some other place.

We moved on, again with six scouts out ahead. After a while
two of these came back to us and said they had located the
Chiricahua camp sure enough, just about where I had seen that
mirror flashing yesterday. Then the officer patted me on the back
and said, "You are right."

Before we got to the camp we saw two Chiricahuas coming
toward us riding mules. There was one girl with them also. Now
we made a line on each side so that they would ride between us
because we wanted to catch them. I was a second sergeant then.
One of our sergeants, just as we were about to close in on the two
Chiricahuas, set his gun off by mistake, and when he did this the

three turned and made a run back into their camp. Now we all got up and started after them. We wanted to catch them and arrest them all, but instead of that they got away. We had orders to shoot the Chiricahuas if they wouldn't let us catch them.

Tułanɛ ['Much Water'] was with us, and he saw two Chiricahua boys coming on horseback. He didn't show himself, but called them over to him and captured them. It was John Rope who really caught them. When they were caught, the boys started to cry. We asked where the boys were going with the horses, and they said they were going to take them to butcher. A way further on we saw a boy herding horses. We called to him, but he left the horses and started to run so the scouts shot at him and killed him.

Later on we saw a lot of Chiricahua women going up the mountain. Some of these women had left their children where the fight had started. There was only one man in the camp and he got away up the mountain. There he stopped and hollered back to us, but we couldn't hear what he said.

In the camp we captured all the Chiricahua belongings. Some of the San Carlos scouts caught one Chiricahua girl. She was a chief's girl, the daughter of *ni ?dagoǰa* ['He Stirs Up Earth']. This way we cleared the camp. Alchise and his scouts never got to that camp. He asked for some of the plunder, but we wouldn't give him any.

They asked that girl they had caught where the Chiricahua men had all gone from that old camp we had found where they had held the war dance. She said that the men had danced for four nights there and then gone on the warpath to try and catch some Mexican girls, because some of their own had been caught by the Mexicans. They wanted to be able to exchange prisoners.

Now we made camp near the Chiricahua camp we had just raided. 'Much Water' tried to make the San Carlos men give back to him that Chiricahua girl they had captured. He said her father was his friend. The San Carlos scouts got mad about this and wouldn't give her up. So 'Much Water' went to see the officers about it, and the officers made the San Carlos men give up the girl. After that the two Chiricahua boys we had captured were sent out with a horse, riding double, to try and bring in the rest of the Chiricahua.

Later on some Chiricahua women came near with a white flag and asked for 'Much Water.' Then they asked where the head officer was because they wanted to shake his hand and get lots of rations from him.

After that more Chiricahuas came in. The officer told them that we had come to take them back to San Carlos. In that fight at the camp we had killed one old woman, one boy and one girl.

In four days most of the Chiricahuas were back and called to us from the sides of the mountain to come to them. But some of the scouts were afraid to go to the Chiricahuas. The officer and the White packer, as interpreter, went off to one side of camp to meet the Chiricahuas. There the Chiricahua men came to them and talked and made peace. After that they fed all the Chiricahuas and spread canvasses from here as far as this railroad [about fifty yards] for them to eat off. This is the way we took the Chiricahuas back to San Carlos. Now my six months were up.

There is one story I want to tell you about the last time that I was a scout up at San Carlos. This is the way it was:

I was a sergeant of scouts at San Carlos. Near Peridot there were living Casador and his band.[16] They were San Carlos people. Casador had killed one woman and shot one man in the nose, crossways, so that he cut a nick out. After this he took his people out on the warpath in the hills.

At the time there had been a bunch of cattle brought in for the Indians to start raising, and I with some other scouts was herding these cattle up the valley by Rice and up the San Carlos River. We passed above with nothing happening and went on with the cattle to a place about ten miles beyond. There were twelve of us driving and we started up onto the mesa.

I was pretty far in the front. We got almost to the top when we saw right on the top in a lot of rocks there, Casador and his people. They had rifles and started to shoot at the four of us who were in front. We turned around and tried to go back, but the trail was narrow and the cattle were crowded. This way it took us some time to get under cover. One of the scouts got shot through the chest and the bullet came out his back. One Yavapai scout was shot in the shoulder, and another scout's horse got killed. We could not see to shoot back at them as they were above us.

Another scout and I got in under a ledge in a rocky place. The renegades called down to this man with me and told him to come up to them. He answered that he would not come up. "Here we are taking care of cattle that your children will own someday, and now you shoot at us," he said. The renegades said, "We know that, but we are on the warpath now and we want you to come up here to us." So the scout said, "All right," and he went up to them.

When he got there they wanted to know who had been with him down below. This was me. The scout said, "That is a certain man's son," and he called my father's name. "You all know about him and that he is doing the right way." The renegades said that they knew this, but now they were on the warpath. They said they were going to kill the scout right there. One of the renegades was this scout's relative-in-law and he would not let them kill him, but they kept him captive all the same.

While they were talking I could not see them, but I could hear all they were saying. Now I got up and ran down the hill, across a little level place and then into a gully. The renegades shot at me and their bullets were hitting the ground all around me as I ran, kicking up lots of dust. If that gully hadn't been there I would have been killed sure. I lay there in the gully and piled some rocks up in front of me for protection.

The renegades were talking again on the hill and I could hear them. They said they were going to where that sergeant was lying in the gully (me) and then pull him out by hair and cut him up in little pieces. "We have killed our own relatives, but we can't help that as we are on the warpath," they said. I was not afraid and pointed my rifle to where they were, ready to shoot. I could not hear that scout whom they had captured now, as they had taken him a way off. I thought he must be killed.

Just then a man called Navajo Bill rode up on a horse with two scouts. He was like a stockman and in charge of the cattle. He had been drinking down in the camps, and for that reason he was not afraid of the renegades. The scout with the renegades was his son-in-law, and as he rode along he called, "Where is my son-in-law? If you kill my son-in-law, I am going to kill every one of you." He told the scouts to give him a gun—that he was going up and shoot the renegades. But they would not give him one.

Now I went over to where the other scouts were. Up on the bluff the renegades had told the scout whom they held that he had to go down and get my horse, which was still standing under the bluff where I had left him. He was a good horse, and my saddle that was on him was good also. That scout said, "Wait awhile," as he was afraid that when he started for the horse the renegades would shoot him in the back.

Navajo Bill came to me now and said that two of our men had been shot in the fight, one horse killed, and that one scout had dropped his gun and run off. Now Navajo Bill started up the trail to the renegades. He shouted to them, "Where are you all going; why don't you come back here and cut that sergeant up in little pieces as you said you were going to do?"

The scout who had been shot through the chest came to me and said, "Those people have killed me. I just want to lie down now," and he did.

They had sent word from Rice to San Carlos about what was happening and now the soldiers got to us with more scouts. One scout came to me and said to stay there with the wounded man, that the rest of them would follow the renegades. The officer left two soldiers to help me also, but they never came near us all night.

That day the soldiers and scouts came back, as they could not find the renegades. We made a stretcher out of yucca poles, laid grass over it, and carried the wounded scout back to the foot of the big bluff above Rice where there was an Army wagon into which we loaded him, and this way started back to San Carlos. When we got him home his relatives could take care of him. We did not get in until after dark and then they kept us standing in line while the officers held a meeting about what had happened.

My father, down at Dewey Flats, had heard that I had been killed. He was a chief, and he came up to ask the head officer about me. The head officer told him that I was not hurt. My father was glad to hear that. He said, "If those people had killed my son, I would have followed them and kept killing them till I got killed myself."

Lots of people had come up from Dewey Flats, as they heard that five of us had been killed. A lot of girls came up because they wanted to see me again before I was buried. When they saw I was still alive, they were glad.

In about six days the renegades came into Globe and gave up because they were hungry. Some soldiers were sent up and they brought the renegades back. They put them all in the jail at San Carlos and we scouts were sent to guard them. I was on guard there and had the keys. After awhile I unlocked the jail and let them out for air; they said it was too hot inside. Now I talked with them about the fight. I told them that I wished I had shot them all right there. They laughed and said they didn't know I was there in the fight.

These renegades had a good song they were singing and it made them feel happy. I said, "I don't think you will get punished for what you have done. If you had killed me, that would be different; I think you would have been killed then.[17] I heard how you were talking about me, about pulling me out by the hair and cutting me in little pieces."

They said it was too hot in the jail, but I told them to get back in there right away and not complain, because they had good homes with sun-shades and cool wickiups, but had left them of their own accord and it was all their fault. About noon I let them out again. I wasn't mad at them because I had not been hurt.

My father told me that when my enlistment ran out he wanted me to quit the scouts, as there were too many Indians about who wanted to kill me. So when my enlistment ran out, I stopped scouting.

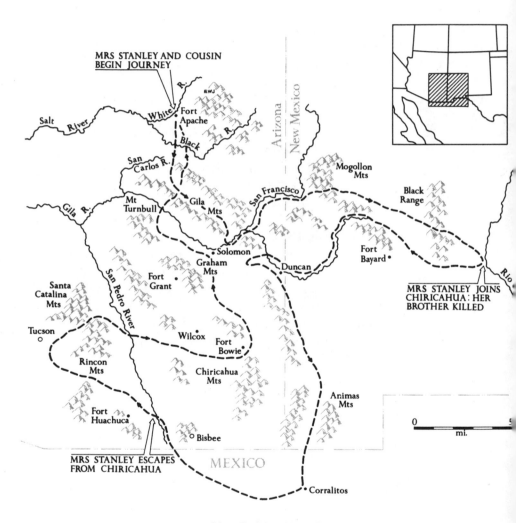

MRS STANLEY AND COUSIN
BEGIN JOURNEY

Salt   River

White   R.

B.W.J

Fort
Apache

Black   R

San
Carlos R.

Arizona
New Mexico

Gila

Mogollon
Mts

San Francisco

Black
Range

Gila R.

Mt
Turnbull

Gila
Mts

Solomon

Duncan

Fort
Bayard

Santa
Catalina
Mts

San Pedro River

Fort
Grant

Graham
Mts

Rio

Tucson

MRS STANLEY JOINS
CHIRICAHUA: HER
BROTHER KILLED

Wilcox

Fort
Bowie

Rincon
Mts

Chiricahua
Mts

Animas
Mts

0   5
mi.

Fort
Huachuca

Bisbee

MEXICO

MRS STANLEY ESCAPES
FROM CHIRICAHUA

Corralitos

Mrs. Stanley Narrative

6

MRS. ANDREW STANLEY

A White Mountain Apache, Mrs. Andrew Stanley was approximately sixty-five years old in 1931. She had led an unusually tumultuous life and was considered extremely well-traveled for a woman. Her narrative begins some time around 1880 when, as a young widow, she left Fort Apache with a female cousin and embarked upon a remarkable journey that ended in a camp of renegade Chiricahuas on the Rio Grande River in New Mexico. In what follows, Mrs. Stanley describes her escape from the Chiricahuas and how, after a series of thoroughly extraordinary adventures, she finally found her way back to her own people.

From the first remembrance I have, the soldiers were at Fort Apache [1868–1870]. I don't remember or know about the first time the soldiers came to Goodwin Springs [1864].

We lived quite awhile at Fort Apache. Then some of our people killed some White people and so we were enemies with them. For this reason we scattered out all over the country, down this way in the Graham Mountains.

Now we started out from there and headed for Cibecue. On our way through Fort Apache, the soldiers followed us. We got to Cibecue after awhile. We stayed for five days at Cibecue. One chief went about among the people talking about us. After awhile the people came together to talk about what they were going to do. Then a lot of them started out to make peace with the Whites at Fort Apache.[1] They made a flag of white cloth and held it up on their way. This way we made peace with the Whites again there.

Now trouble came up again there; A Chiricahua chief killed *itladndijolɛ* ['Round Son'], one of the White Mountain men living there. But that chief had not really done it, we found later. This 'Round Son' had gone to a camp where there was *tułpai* and wanted some, but a brother of his there, the owner of the drink, said, "No, this is not for your mouth," so the man went home crying. He got a gun there and shot himself in the forehead. About the same time that chief rode away. So they thought he did it. His brother who had *tułpai* came running out and stabbed the Chiricahua chief with a knife because he thought he killed his brother.

After that someone came over from where the Chiricahua were, saying that there was to be a great dance there. So our chief told us all to go and see the dance.

When we got there my husband had one brother there. I made cans of *tułpai* and gave it to my husband there. He drank it up. Then he said to his brother, "Let's go and fill this bottle up for the girl at my camp." So they went there, but his brother said, "No, you should not be fooling with girls like that."

So my husband got mad and kicked over the cans of *tułpai*. My husband had a pistol, but didn't use it. Then his brother went for him. He jumped over the brush wall around our camp, but a stick caught in his moccasin and he fell. His brother jumped on him and stuck a knife into his side. His guts stuck out, but he walked all the same. A little later I felt something hard there. So a medicine man was sent for. He cut off the hard piece of dried guts that stuck out.

The dance kept up all that night, then ended. It was to have kept up three or four days, but on account of the trouble they cut it short. Then some Chiricahua women there used witchcraft on my husband, and in four days he died. The Chiricahua must not have liked us being there.[2]

ㄫㅅ

After a long time my mother's younger sister heard that an old man was going to try to marry me. So she said to me, "You had a good husband, but this old man is not the kind that would suit you, so let's get my horse and yours and pull out," she said. So we did. No one was there, so we got horses, put a sack of stuff on each horse, and I told the other girl, "Well, we will go any way you want."

So we started. On the other side of Graham Mountain by Solomonville we went. We stopped on the Gila River, where it starts, way over to the east. Then we went on past the Mogollon Mountains in New Mexico and in ten days we got over to the Rio Grande River—way east. I thought she had meant to go to where other Apaches were, but she had gone the opposite way instead. On our way we stopped often to feed our horses, so they would not give out. I asked that girl, "How long is it till we get there?" "It's far off yet," she said. So we kept on. We met one White man leading a pack horse, but we saw him first and so we hid. He didn't see us.

We went not straight, but in curves, all over, once as if back towards the Gila River. That girl had been there before but had forgotten the trail. We went on. I didn't know that country. On the way one bear jumped out of the brush at us. We ran our horses fast and got away. We sort of headed back to the Mogollon Mountains. We were afraid of animals now. The other girl said, "Do you think we will see more of these animals?" So that night we made camp under a big juniper tree so we could make our bed in the branches.

The next day, we went out in the morning. After a ways we stopped for the night. That girl wanted to do as we did before— make our bed in the tree—but I said, "No, we'll sleep on the ground." So we did. We went on the next day and I told her, "Let's stop here one night and day to rest our horses. They are almost given out." So she said all right. I was kind of mad. I was tired.

Now we got to where we were going and from on top of a mountain we looked down. Below were a lot of Chiricahuas.[3] They ran their horses about. We got off and sat there and watched them. They looked up at us and said, "I wonder why those girls are there." But they knew the horse of the girl with me; it had a stripe of white on one side. Then we would hear them say, "Well, the other must be the woman whose husband was killed at that dance." Then we went down there and some women ran to me and took me off my horse and cried over me. They knew me well. "A Western Apache killed her husband," they said.

Now they unsaddled our horses and put them in the field. They had some boiled meat all ready there and fed us. They said that soon they would have a drink there. I had a brother among those Chiricahuas. He came and took me back to his camp. We had only been there two days when I heard that the girl I had come with married a Chiricahua man there. I guess the two loved each other well—that's why she went all that way to him. This place was right on the Rio Grande River.

After I had lived for about one year there, my brother had a bad dream. He had a pistol and he dreamed that someone had shot him with this pistol. The next day there was to be a dance, and so on account of this dream he gave it away to another man. But in the dance there, while he was dancing, the man who he had given it to shot him in the back, and the bullet came out through the front of his belly. That's the way he got killed. My brother's wife and I were the only ones who buried my brother. There were a lot of Chiricahua there, but they did not offer to help us. It was summer then and my brother had swelled up pretty bad, so he was heavy. On the way we had to drop the body once, but we buried him. He had been a rich man and had lots of blankets, spotted ones, so we cut these up and buried them with him.

It was from that time on that I was a captive to the Chiricahua.[4] We headed back west again and, near Solomon, one of the men with us killed a Mexican—shot him. The horse the Mexican was riding was wild and started to run with the Mexican's foot caught in the stirrup. Those Chiricahua were pretty mean all right and always killed a Mexican when they came on one.

Then they told me, "Go catch that horse," so I did. Then they said, "Take the dead man's foot out of the stirrup," so I did. Then they said, "Get up on him and ride him," so I did. The horse reared up with me at first, but then I rode him all right. I had to do just as the Chiricahua told me now, as I was just as if a captive to them.

We went on from there on horseback, then on this side of the big mountain east of Duncan we stopped there two days and two nights, and there killed that horse of the Mexican. Then we ate the meat there and then started on. We went up another big mountain again, and the men left us there to go someplace again. Those men were pretty mean all right. There were no Whites here then—only Mexicans. They went off and killed a lot of Mexicans someplace and brought back some dresses and food to us.

We stayed there for four days after they got back, because those men were not afraid that anyone would follow them because they thought they were great fighters, and so they never looked back. Now it was like all the women there were like slaves to these men. We ate up all the meat there in the four days and then started on.

On the way we saw two men riding along. These were White men this time—Americans—and they did not see us. So we women hid behind the brush and the men we were with stopped on each side of the trail. They said, "One of us will shoot them, and then we can run to the horses and catch them right away." So we waited to see what would happen. Then they came along and one man shot one and he fell off, and then the other was shot and fell off. Then they caught the horses. They told me to get on one of the horses, a big white one, but I think that he must never have been ridden by a woman before, because he reared up and pawed the air, and I had a hard time.

Right there I was crying and thinking about my mother's sister who had taken me over to the Rio Grande in the first place, and how she had gotten me into all this trouble. If she had not told me to go along in the first place, I would not be in all this trouble that I was. I had a lot of *nadotsusn* [a clan: 'slender peak standing up people'] kin up at Fort Apache, and it was on account of me that a great many of them enlisted as scouts, so as to bring me back from the Chiricahua, but they never got me.

We started on, and on a big mountain further on they killed this white horse. We ate his meat, after butchering him, and stayed there. We went on from there and on over towards Round Mountain near Animas Valley in New Mexico, and the men left us there and went off someplace. They killed two Mexicans and brought back two horses, a sorrel and a black. The meat did not last us long—we ate a lot of it. We stayed there and then killed the black horse and made jerky out of it.

"Maybe the Western Apache will pass through here on their way to fight us," one of the Chiricahua said. It was true that my people as scouts did come through there. The men used to go off and leave us and go on top of a high hill and keep watch. Those people were smart all right. They did not stay in one place all night, but would move out to another place, so this way they did not get caught.

Then the men saw some scouts from San Carlos pass through there looking for the Chiricahua and so they watched to see where they would stop. Then the men came back and told us, "Well, those scouts are camped down there below us." We stayed on top of the hill above. The men went on and circled about the scout camp, but they were not seen at all. They heard the scouts talking about me down there.

My maternal uncle, who was a chief, was talking to the rest. "If you shoot some Chiricahua, be sure and call the name of that woman (me). She might be around there and be sure not to shoot her, please," they heard him say. Then the men came back from there. They told me what they had heard down there and said, "When those scouts shoot us, then you will be shot by us first, so you will have to die." So I said to them, "All right, kill me right now." I told them that because I thought to myself, "I am not afraid to go right now."

One man said, "She is pretty good all right. We did not think that she would say like this, but she is not afraid of anything at all," he said to me.

There were some people living in Mexico, and we thought of going there, but did not, and instead remained about Round Mountain for a long time. If we had gone down to the other place, we would have been killed sure, for all those Chiricahua were killed down there. When we finally did go there, they were all gone. We passed through there where those people had been killed.[5] Their clothes were still piled up there. The men said that they wanted to see the place where all the people had been killed, so they told us to go to one side while they went there. When they got back they told us, "There are a lot of dead people still lying there." They told us this when they got in to where we had made camp.

They called the names of the dead ones and said this man, and that man, and so on. Then while we camped there, two men went back over there to where the place was and buried just their own kin, taking them up in the crevices of the rock and laying them there, but the rest—not kin to them—they just let lay the way they were. If those men had wanted us to go over there and help, we could have, but they did not want us to go over there.

We stayed there about six days, but those two men spent most of the time down where the dead people were and cried there. It could have been the scouts from San Carlos that had done this killing, and I don't know why those Chiricahua there did not kill me right there. But I had two revolvers in a belt on my waist, one on each side, and a lot of cartridges in the belt, and the revolvers loaded, and I told the women that if the men made a move to kill that I would kill one of them first. Those women had the same also, revolvers.

One time I went out and tried practicing shooting at a stump, and when I shot I hit right in the center of it. When I shot, one of the men ran out to me and said, "What do you shoot about camp like that for?" "Well, you told me to practice, so I have to do it," I said. Then he took me back to camp there.

When I got there they said, "Well, we know your mind all right. I guess someday that you think you will shoot us just like that." "No, not that way. I just want to practice." "I guess you just try to shoot so you can help these wild animals about here, so they will know that we are here and our enemies will come and get us," they said. "No, not that way," I said. "I have just tried to help you people out."

Then we left that place and went over towards Fort Huachuca on the east side of the mountain there. We lived there for about one month. It was about June then and soon the acorns would be ripe. There were a lot of White people and Mexicans in that country, but they did not bother them any more because they did not want to start trouble. They just went for meat all the time, sometimes killing a horse and other times killing a cow.

After a month we moved over onto the west side of the mountain and lived there on meat alone. Then we moved back to the east again. We went from one place to another living on tops of mountains, zigzagging back and forth. It was not good that way.

Then one of the women bore a little baby, a boy. As soon as it was born, the men threw it in the canyon there. They were afraid that it would cry at night. That woman all swelled up, way down on her thighs. They ought to have sung over her, but they did not. Instead they waited there for a long time and she got well again.

Then we moved over to the west side of the mountain there. We came to a place called *łiłqha ʔitin* ['Many Horses Seen From Above'] where war parties had gone through long ago with lots of raided horses. The men left us camped there for a long time, and I thought that they had gone off to make war some place, but they did not get anything—just brought back meat. There those men said, "It will be better if we are not on the move all the time. We should stay in one place about a month. If we move about too much, we might run into trouble, so we will stay in one place for one month."

We stayed about that mountain for about one month. The men with us went nowhere, but stayed right there. While we were at this place, I commenced to think that if I had a chance to get a ways off from these people that I would beat it and get away from them. I thought that they would probably kill me if I stayed, so I was scared of that. Those people knew what was in my mind, I guess, for they said to me, "You are homesick, aren't you?" But I told them, "No I am not homesick. I am satisfied to stay here with you. I don't want to go. That's what I want; I went with my relatives to the Rio Grande and then I went off with you. That's what I wanted and now I have it." But I must have shown that I felt bad, for they knew it. Wherever we had gone with those people they had always made me ride right in the middle of them, so that I would not try to escape.

Then those men said that we had been there long enough, so one evening they told us all to saddle up and that we would move from there. As they said this, I was making up my mind what I would do. I had a brown mule there, and I had saddled him up and got all ready. Then we started out and on the way as I rode between them, we came to a tree so that we had to split to get around. I held my mule in and remained on the other side of it from them. They rode on. I don't know how they could have missed their minds that way, but they must have thought that I was still between them and went right on.

As soon as they had gone on, I started to ride west. I did not know just where. Long after, when I had come home, I saw those people I had been with. They told me that they had stayed there at that place for five days and searched all over for me, but could not find me.

I traveled at night, and in the daytime I would get in under a bluff and stay there all day. Traveling this way I got lost and instead of striking up this way (north), I hit pretty near by Tucson but did not know it.[6] I came to a good place in a canyon where there were some cottonwoods and it looked as if there would be water, so I unsaddled my mule and hid the stuff I had with me up in a niche in the bluff, and then I led the mule to water. But I could not find water, so I kept on leading the mule. Then all of a sudden, someone—a Mexican— called out to me, "Hey, Caballo," and I let the mule go and started to run. I had the two revolvers on my belt and as I ran I loaded them, for I thought that if they shot at me, I would shoot back at them and try to get them. But I ran around in back of the hill there, and they did not get me. Now I had lost the mule and was afoot and did not know how I was going to get along. I went up on the hill there and sat there all that day. Then at evening I went back to the place where I had cached my meat and ate some. Then I went to sleep there till the moon came up.

Now I started out and came to where there were a lot of Mexican houses. I could see some White men down there standing, so I turned back. The thing I was after was a horse, and I thought to myself, "Well, you have to have a horse, for without one there is no chance for you to get home. So you may just as well throw your life away trying to get one."

So now I started out around the other side and came down to where there were a lot of houses. I had gone back and left for a little while first. Then I came to a corral there. There were two gates to the corral, one on each side, and inside were lots of horses. But in one gate there was a Mexican sleeping with a yellow dog, and in the other gate was a Mexican sleeping with a black dog, guarding the horses. But I chanced it anyway and got inside somehow and there was my mule.

He knew me for he came up and smelled of me. But I did not take him for there was a big white horse in there with a halter on. I cut this free and led him out. I did not think I was going to be able to do it, but I did. Then I got on the horse and he reared up with me a couple of times, but we started off and that's the way I got home. If one of those dogs had ever waked up and barked at me, I would have been lost.

I rode the horse back to where I had my food and saddle. There I saddled him up and put my things on him. He was a good horse, and I started out and rode to the east. He was a pretty good horse. I sort of headed back the way I had come, but when morning came I found this out and got headed right. I was riding down a hill there into a canyon. Below, a White man was driving a wagon, and I thought that sure he had seen me and was going to shoot me and take the horse from me. So I got in the brush and hid there. But he did not see me and went right on past. Then I came out.

I was nearly dead from thirst and I got down on the road and saw where a trickle of water came out from a big rock that stood up, black. So I went to it and got off and drank. But I was so thirsty that I drank too much. A person who has not had water for a long time should only drink a little. On account of this, I almost died right there and vomited out everything and started to swell up. Then I lost consciouness and lay there for I don't know how long. But somehow I managed to hold to the bridle reins in one hand and the horse standing there finally moved his head so that it moved my hand and brought me to.

I tried to get up, but fell down, then got up and staggered about as if I was drunk. Then I got on the horse and rode up the road, the way the White man had come. I don't know why I was not afraid and rode right up the middle of that road. Then the road came out on a little mesa, and there was a house there. There didn't seem to be anyone there, and I rode my horse all about it, and then got off and went in.

There I found lots of things, sugar and coffee. I had never seen coffee before and did not know what it was. The sugar I stuck my finger in and tasted it. It was sweet, so I took some more.

Then I mixed it up with the coffee and drank it. There were some matches there and I struck them against something, and they caught fire, so I took some of them, a big tin of coffee and sugar, and outside a saddle blanket hanging there, and also a pot. Up till that time I had just had a fire drill to start fires with; now I had the matches.

Then I started off and rode all that night, but got lost again and came too far east, but when the moon came up I got righted again. It was on account of having to travel at night that it took me so long to get home. Then I came to the east side of a big mountain, and I stayed there for five days. I thought to myself that if I did not stop and rest the horse, he would give out and I could not get home. So I stopped there and everyday took the horse out to where there was good grass and let him graze, but I kept hold of the rope on him all the time and did not turn him loose.

Then one evening I left. I headed wrong again. Then at middle of night I thought that I might as well sleep, so I got off and unsaddled and slept all night there. In the morning I went up on top of a big hill and stayed there all day. I went on from there and started on again, and this time I got to the big mountain at Fort Huachuca and went up on top of it. I rested there for two days.

Now about sundown I wanted to go down in a canyon there. I found a lot of acorns and walnuts there. I gathered a lot of them up and put them on a buckskin that I had there. But the horse could not stand it there. I did not know what was the matter with him. He smelled something and kept jumping about. Then in a little while I looked down from there to the north. There I saw a bear running towards me. He was a big, yellow one. Then I thought, well just let him come here to me. Then I got on my horse and started to run off, but he ran after me. I ran him over a little ridge and then a second one and then a third ridge, but there he still followed me. But now he stopped and sat up on his hind legs and let his arms drop at his sides. There he hollered like a bull almost. But from here on he did not chase me at all.

I started on from there again. I traveled all night, every night. Now I got up to *tsɛya ʔdɨdzuk* ['Rocks Pointed Below'], and now I knew where I was.[7] I knew that the Chiricahua had lived there, and that I lived there with them, that we had had a good place there, and that I had lived with my husband there. I sat and thought about it and cried. Up till this time I had not known the country that I had come through. From there at night I started on this way again and came to the Graham Mountains on the south side.

From this place on I traveled in the daytime. I went on towards where Solomon is now, where the road comes from Bowie and joined the other here. There I met someone with a wagon, and driving it were a Tonto Apache and his wife who was a Tonto Apache also. These two had been captured as children by the Mexicans and raised as captives by them. They used to live at Solomon, and I had known them when I was around there with my husband before. They had told me their story, and I had got good friends with them and had given them a horse of mine.

Now this wagon coming along, I recognized that horse I had given them, and by it I knew them and so right there we met. As soon as they saw me, they got off the wagon and both cried and put their arms about me. We used to be good friends, all right. They told me, "We have two Mexicans staying there with us." So I took all the things off my horse and put them in the wagon and went back with them to their camp. They told me to stay there with them for a while.

They said that some Chiricahua had gone again from San Carlos two days ago—had run off. So those two told me, "Let them get far away first, and then you can go home. If you go too soon, they might catch you again." So I stayed there with them and they hid me and told me not to let the Mexicans see me or the horse, so whenever the Mexicans came they always hid me, and the horse also. They also bought some calico there and made a dress for me there. I stayed there for six days. The saddle I had and two blankets I had I gave to those people I stayed with there.

At the end of six days I told them, "Well, I am going to leave you now." I had long hair then and so they braided it up like the Mexican women do, and also I wore beads about my wrists and rings on the fingers, and hair pins. I had never worn them before. The horse I had was tied behind the wagon. They took me to a place north of where they were living. We stopped there for the night. They told me now the trail went on from there. They pointed out how it went through a gap in the Gila Mountains. So the next morning I started off when they turned back over the river to the foot of Mount Turnbull and stopped there, because I was afraid that there might be Chiricahua ahead of me.

I stayed up there three days and nights. Long ago when we used to come down here, my sister had put some mescal up in a tree. I thought about it and wondered if it was still there. When I got there I found it still there. I took some down and filled up a sack of it there. I cried there as I thought of my sister. I put the rest back where it had been.

I started north again, crossed the Gila and over to the Gila Mountains. In the wash on the way up to the mountains, there was water, and I saw where someone had chewed mescal and spat it out just a little while ago, and I did not know who it was. I saw the tracks but just kept on anyway. I did not care if I was killed or not.

Then I came out on a flat place above. While I was there I saw a long black line spread out there. It was soldiers. There was a low place, so I rode down to it. I thought at first they were Chiricahua. I stayed there all day and got very thirsty. I had a white horse and anyone could see it from far off, so I could not travel over any open place during the day.

At evening I started on from there again and saw their tracks where they had gone by. Now I got up on the big mountain and unsaddled my horse and stayed there. Then, that evening, I heard a drum and a dance was going on there. It was some scouts and soldiers from San Carlos and the White Mountain people who had captured some Chiricahua and were taking them back to San Carlos. They had the dance there.

I don't know what put it into my head; I guess I must have been crazy, for I decided to go to the dance. So I dressed up in the new dress that my friends at Solomon had made for me and walked down there. I left my horse behind as I was afraid they would find me out if I took him. When I got there I went in and danced. Then soon two Chiricahua girls came up and danced beside me there. I danced that way two times and then walked off. I went back to where my horse was tied. I slept there that night and still heard the drum.

Then in the morning I heard the bugle blow. Those Chiricahua women were feeling good. I could hear them laugh. Now they were gone, but I stayed there four days and nights. I did not want to go right among the people, as I had been by myself for so long, so I stopped there again. I stayed here five days and then went on and crossed Black River. I was too wild, like a deer; that is why I didn't like to go right among my people.

This side of Fort Apache where there is a mountain and a little pond of water, I stayed. There was lots of feed for the horse. Below there was a camp of our people, but I stayed there alone for six days again. Then I let the horse go and put hobbles on him. Then I started to walk down to that camp. A little further on I thought about the Chiricahua that I had been with so long and cried about them, for they were far off.

As I still cried I walked on to the camp. I got to the river. Right there I met my maternal uncle watering a pinto horse. He talked to me in the Chiricahua language and asked me where I came from. I spoke back to him in the same language. I asked him how his daughter was and called her by name. He had not known me before that. Then he knew me and ran to me and caught me there.

Then he called to his daughter and said, "Your cousin has come home again," so she came running to me also. Then a lot of people gathered about me. But I had been so long alone that they all smelt bad to me, and I could not stand it. I vomited because of it. They gave me food to eat, but I could not swallow it. I was not used to this. I slept a ways apart from the rest, so as to avoid being too close to them.[8]

Then the next day I went up on the hill to get my horse and things. I packed them all on him and came back down to the camps there, but the people had all moved away. They thought that I had gone to bring the Chiricahua to where they were to kill them all. I had told them just how I had been with the Chiricahua and how I had escaped from them, but they would not believe me and so had all moved over close to where the agency was.

Now there was no one there where they had been, only one old woman who was sick that they had just abandoned.[9] When I got down there, I unsaddled the horse. Then I saw this old woman and went to her. She told me, "While you went away, those people said that you had gone after the Chiricahua, so they left here right away." I told the old woman, no, that I was all alone and all right and that I had traveled two months to get here. I told the old woman, "If they don't come back here, I am going to stay two days and then take my horse up on top where I was again." But the old woman said, "Don't go away again, and it was as if you were dead. But now you have come back, so stay."

Those people thought that I was dead long ago, and now when I came back, it was like a ghost coming back to them. But the next day my maternal uncle came back here to see how things were and saw my horse there now. So all the rest came back to their camps now. That's the way it used to be in the old days; whenever a person returned who had been captive to the enemy, their relatives were always afraid that he would lead the enemy to them. This had happened before.

Part II

SELECTED ASPECTS OF RAIDING AND WARFARE

In addition to the autobiographical material presented in Part I, Grenville Goodwin collected a large amount of information on specific aspects of raiding and warfare. The topics treated in Part II are those he considered among the most important and on which his field notes are most complete. Once again, the data are in the form of statements from Western Apaches. Each section is devoted to a single topic and is composed of statements from a number of informants. Selections were made with the double aim of avoiding unnecessary redundancy and giving full representation to differences in informant opinion and interpretation. The first section deals with the manufacture and handling of weapons, poison, and 'war charms' (bahazdɨʔ).

7

WEAPONS

BOWS

Nowadays some of these Indians make their bows out of Wright's willow to sell to the White people, but long ago we only used the wood of wild mulberry for bows, as it was the strongest. We had to get a piece that was straight and had no knots. We worked the bow down into shape while the wood was still green and then hung it up to dry out in our wickiups for about five days to a week.

Then we made the bowstring. A piece of sinew about one and
a half feet long and one and one-quarter inches wide was soaked
up and torn in about six strips. Then the ends of these strips were
spliced together so as to form one long string. Now this was
doubled over and the two parts twisted tightly together and then
the bowstring was finished.

We used to make our bows in two shapes, the single arc
bow and the double arc bow. The double arc bow you get into that
shape when it is still green.

The double arc bow we had before the single arc bow. But
later we learned that the single arc bow was better because there
was more room to string and draw an arrow on it, there being no
hump in the middle.

Bowstrings we made out of sinew from the back of a deer, or
from the muscle on the back of his hind legs. We peeled off several
long strips and let them dry. Then you wet the ends of these and
join them together in one long string, just stuck together. You
have to judge from your bow how long to make the string. It
would have to be a little longer to allow for the twisting.

Now you take your sinew strips, all joined together, and
double the string over and put a stick through the loop at the end
and start to twist, while the sinew is still damp and soft. If there
are any bumpy places on the string as you twist it, you will have
to chew them down even. Before you get finished, you will have
to call a boy to come over and help you hold it.

When it is all made, you put it on your bow and make it just
a little tight and let it dry like that. Then you tie it a little tighter
again. Later on you string it tighter again. When it is all set, then
you string it up well and pull your bow with it to test it. Now it is
finished.

When you shot a bow you had to wear a guard around your
wrist of leather or tanned hide to keep your wrist from being cut

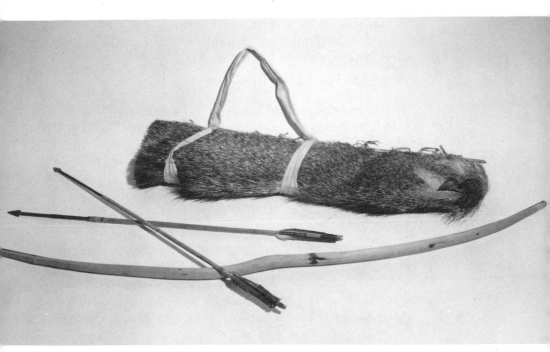

Grenville Goodwin Collection, courtesy Arizona State Museum, Helga Teiwes, photographer
Western Apache bow, javelina-hide quiver, and arrows

by the bowstring. Some men used to make theirs look nice with notches cut in the sides.

When you used a bow you had to use a wrist guard to keep the string from cutting your wrist. They used to either make one of leather or just wrap some rags around their wrists.

You hold the bow in the middle with your thumb braced up against it. The arrow goes to the left side of the bow and rests on the side of your thumb. With your right hand you hold the nock of the arrow to the bowstring with your first, second, and third fingers, the first finger above the nock, the other two below it. With these three fingers you pull the bowstring back and aim right along the arrow, from your eye, and then let it go.

When you shoot a bow and arrow, if you want to make a long shot you hold the bow crossways. If you make a close shot you hold it vertical.

The oldest man would teach his relatives how to make bows, and they would make them the way he told them. If a man started to make his own bow he could not make it the way it should be. They made a string for it and tied the string to it. The old man would test the bow. He would draw it. If it drew too hard, he would look at it and if he found it was too thick on one place, so it drew hard, he would tell them to make this place a little lower.

If there was an old man who was your relative, he would make arrows for you for nothing. But if he was not a relative you would pay him for it. You would give him a shirt or something. The old man who could make good arrows you would hire, who knew about the making of them and straightening them.

After the arrow is all finished, they go and practice shooting. They tear off cedar bark and roll it up in a ball and throw it away so many yards and shoot at it. That's the way they practiced, not every day, but just once in a while. Some would hit it, some would miss it. For a long distance shot we used the bow crossways; it made the arrow shoot higher. If it was a near distance shot we held the bow straight up and down.

If a man hired an old man to make a bow, arrows, a bowstring or a quiver for him, he might give him a buckskin. But if he was his relative he would not give him anything. But he would expect you to help him out when you killed a deer; if you killed a deer with arrows he made, you would give him part. Or if you went out on a raid when you got back if you had a bunch of horses you would give him one or two, without him asking for it.

My grandfather used to make bows to trade. He made the bows well and put bowstrings on them. Then a man would come to him and say, "I have arrows at my camp but no bow at all, so I want to get one from you." They would give him a big buckskin for it.

ARROWS

Long ago, they got reeds for arrows. They went to the place where they were growing, and cut them off with knives of white chert or flint. Then they made bows of wild mulberry, cutting off the wood with white flint knives, and shaping them down so that they were flat on one side. Then they made their bowstring of strands of buckskin twisted together. Now they shot the arrow. It had no feathers and wobbled as it went. So they killed a small bird, and used its feathers—three—to put on the arrow. They used to use the feathers of any bird, any kind of small birds—that was good enough. Now the arrow shot better, and they killed a turkey and put three turkey feathers on the arrow. Then they shot Red-tailed Hawk and took two of his wing feathers and one of his tail feathers and put them on the arrow. The first time they had arrows they had no points, only the wood for the shaft was sharpened. This wasn't much good, so they split the end of the shaft and set in an arrow point made of white flint with pitch and bound it with sinew. Now they went out in the mountains and hunted deer and killed them.

Their arrows were not powerful enough, so the first time they killed a deer, they took some of its blood and part of its guts and mixed in with them parts of plants that have thorns and briars— the kind that stick into your foot. Then they set this up to rot. When it was ready, they put it on the arrowpoints. Now, when they shot a deer, even if he was only a little wounded, he would fall over dead before he went far.

Arrows were made out of cane found growing in camp places in the mountains or along the river bottoms. Bows were made of wild mulberry.

The best canes for arrows have always grown on the Gila River a little below where Coolidge Dam is now. The ones that grow along the river here are too soft. Down in Mexico there are good arrow canes growing, and they used to bring them back from down there when they were on the warpath.

Western Apache arrows with metal and flint points

We used to smooth our arrow-shafts down by using a stone arrow-smoother.[1] We straightened them in the fire. We used to get the stone for these arrow-smoothers at Bear Canyon. It is a whitish, soft stone, and there is lots of it there. The stone was smoothed down and a groove cut in it. When we got ready to straighten arrows, we heated this stone smoother in the fire, and then took it out and rolled the joints of the cane arrows in it, and then ran the shafts back and forth to smooth them. Later on when we had an iron skillet we used to heat it and run the arrow shafts over it.

We used the feathers of red-tailed hawk, turkey, dove, quail, flicker and all kinds of birds that had good feathers. Right where the feathering is we used to paint the arrows in different colors so that we could tell our arrows apart. We could also tell by the make of an arrow to which band or tribe it belonged.

Long ago, when they first got arrows, they tried the first arrow with two feathers. It flew crooked, so they put two more feathers on it—four all together—but when they shot it, it still went in a curve. Now they took one of the feathers off so the arrow only had three. This time they shot it and it flew straight and fast. From that time on we always used three feathers on an arrow.

Arrow foreshafts were made of hard woods. These were worked while green and straightened by fire. They were set into the main shaft with pitch. They either put a stone point on the foreshaft or just left it plain and very sharp. Both kinds were used for deer and other game. A strong shooter at fairly close range could send an arrow right through a man or deer and almost through a man standing sideways.

We made all-wooden arrows out of desert broom [*Baccharis sarothroides*], also, fixed up and painted just like the others, except they had no hard wood foreshaft and the stone points were set right into their ends. Right where the foreshaft would be set into a cane arrow, they bound sinew around the wood shaft so it looked the same. The Chiricahua used to make lots of these kinds of arrows.

Cane arrows are the oldest kind. We learned the all-wooden arrows from the Navajo.

The points of all-wooden arrows are made of catclaw and are set into the cane shaft with pitch. This way we used to do to make them so they wouldn't come out. Sometimes we used to rub pitch into the inner side of a bow also to make it stronger.

The feathers are made on these arrows from red-tailed hawk feathers. You have to scrape down your feathers pretty flat so they fit well onto the shaft. Then you take and start tying them on with sinew. But first you paint the part of the arrow where the feathers go in red and black. The red is hematite, the black is charcoal. Over the paint you put piñon pitch to keep it on.

Then you take some pieces of yucca leaves and double them around the painted part of the shaft and roll it back and forth to polish it. Now when you put your feathers on, you get the sinew wet and soft. First you tie on one or two feathers at a time at their upper ends by the nock. You hold them on with your fingers and start the sinew around once or twice, and then hold one end of it in your teeth and wrap it on the shaft by rolling the shaft.

When you have two feathers held on, then you put the third one on and wrap it the same way, holding one end with your teeth. When they are all tied on, then you make a half-hitch with the sinew, break it off and press the end down so it doesn't show. Now you tie the lower ends of the feathers to the shaft the same way, but all three at once. After you get your feathers all tied on, then you trim them down to the right size.

You must never use more than one part of a feather on the same arrow. You must take the three parts for an arrow all from different feathers, so that they will all face the same way. Like going sunwise. If you don't you will get two facing each other and the arrow will not shoot so well.

In the old days the clans used to paint all their arrows the same way, except the dɛsčidn [a clan: 'horizontally red people'], who painted theirs all red.

We used to use four kinds of arrowpoints; one was a stone point, one was a steel point, one was just the wooden foreshaft sharpened up, and one was with a four crosspiece rig for shooting quail.

The first two kinds, we have to cut a notch in the end of the foreshaft to fit the arrowhead into. Then we tie it on with sinew.

The fourth kind had crosspieces made of hard wood. You cut two shallow notches on opposite sides of the foreshaft about three and a half inches from the point, and in each of these you fit and tie one crosspiece with sinew. Then you tie on the other two crosspieces on top of these.

This rig is for shooting birds so that if you just happen to graze them, you will kill them with these crosspieces.

The old men used to go around to ruins and pick up pieces of white flint there until they had enough to fill a small buckskin sack.[2] Then when they got ready to make arrowpoints, they laid a blanket down and on this spread out their pieces of white flint. Then they picked whichever one they wanted to work on. When they worked on a point, they held a piece of buckskin in the palm of the hand and gripped the flint in this. Then with a piece of deer horn about five inches long they flaked down and worked the point into shape.

We used to tip our arrow foreshafts. The Pimas didn't. They used a great long arrow pointed only with a wooden tip, which was shaped to have four sides. One time they fought with our people and used these arrows and also wooden clubs.

Long ago we couldn't get any iron to tip our arrows with, so we used only flint.

ARROW POISON

Our people used to use poison on their arrows, both in war and in hunting. This poison was made from a deer's spleen. This was dried first, then ground up fine and mixed in with the ground roots or stalk of nettles and also some plant which has a burning taste, like chili. The mixture is put all in a little sack made from a part of the deer's big intestine.

Then when all is ready, the maker spits into the bag and ties it up tightly and quickly so that none of the bad air will escape.

The bag is hung from a tree for about three to five days till good and rotten and in liquid form. Then it is taken out and painted on the points of the arrows.

If the poison gets dry and hard it can be ground up and mixed on a stone with spit, just as paint is.

This is a bad poison, and if you just have a scratch and get this in it, you will swell up all over. When a poison arrow is shot into a deer, no matter if it merely scratches him, he will die in about eighty yards.

Our people used to make a poison to put on the ends of arrows, and later on to paint on those old-fashioned musket balls. I never used this myself, but I have seen the old men making it. I can remember once they had an old Tonto in jail at San Carlos. He knew all about this poison. One officer there went down to see him with the interpreter and offered to give him five dollars, or turn him loose from jail, if he would tell how to make the poison. But he would not tell.

It is made with a deer's spleen, also the leaves of nettles ground up fine, and *tsɛkɔʔ* ['lichen'] which grows on heavy rocks, and this is why they used it.[3] These are all mixed together when the spleen is getting rotten and mixed on a rock. A man, while he is making this, keeps all the boys away from him and also the dogs. If a dog should smell this stuff, then it would be no good. When he is through he puts the rock on which the stuff has been mixed up in a tree, so no one can get hold of it.

This poison is used in hunting and in war also. It doesn't spoil meat, except right around the wound. I remember one time my uncle shot a deer with a poisoned arrow. The arrow stuck in the deer's head and did not come out. The deer ran off though. Next day my uncle and some others went to trail the deer. There was no blood sign at all, but my uncle said he knew he hit that deer. Pretty soon they found him where he had dropped dead while running.

This poison is bad, and if you just get scratched with it, it will kill you. It is called *ɛʔɛstluš*.

In the old days we used to make arrow poison to put on our arrow tips. If you just grazed a deer with a poison arrow, he would die. It was very poisonous.

You take the spleen of a deer and bury it in the ground and let it rot there for about twelve days. Then you get certain kinds of plants and squeeze their juices into the rotten spleen. Also, I used to put in sand because it is rough. Now you take it all out and grind it.

While you work on poison, dogs must not smell of it because if they do then it will be no good. When a man had poison other men living within about a mile of him would come to get some for their own use also.

I have made poison for arrows this way lots of times. They used to say that if a pregnant woman farted into the poison, then it would surely be deadly. But they never did this; it was only a joke.

An old man who was making the poison used to go every day to see how it was getting along on the tree. As long as it smelled very strong, it was not ready. When it didn't smell so much, then it was not ready. When it didn't smell so much, then it was ready and hard like a rock. He would take it down and paint arrows with it now, grind it a little on a rock.

When they moved camp, they used to wrap the poison bag up in a thick bundle of yucca leaves so it wouldn't smell or get touched. When not in use it was hung in a tree. An old man told me about this poison. He used to make it.

The points of arrows were poisoned by a concoction made from a kind of bug. This was put in the ground for three days or so and, when taken out, was ready for use.

I never heard of using snake poison in arrow poison. That would be bad. If a man ate game killed with snake poison it would not be right. It would be bad.

ARROW QUIVERS AND BOW CASES

We used to make arrow quivers out of different kinds of hides
—horse, steer, deer, wolf, wildcat, and mountain lion. When the
hide had a nice tail on it, we would leave that hanging on too, and
decorate the quiver with red flannel. Mountain lion made the
nicest quiver of all. We used to decorate them with brass studs
too. Sometimes if there was a buckskin on them, we would make
painted designs on it.

We also made a quiver with a bow case attached so as to
keep the bow dry. A quiver held about thirty or forty arrows. It
was slung on the back with its shoulder strap going over the right
shoulder and under the left arm. This way you had only to reach
over your right shoulder and draw an arrow out.

Of the two kinds of quivers, the plain quiver without a bow
case is the kind we used first. The quivers with bow cases we saw
the Chiricahua using and so we copied it from them.

My grandfather used to make quivers, good ones. He made
them with mountain lion skins, or gray fox skins, with the tail
hanging down and fringes at the bottom and a red cloth down the
sides. He would make about two of these and trade them for one
horse or one gun. They used to call my grandfather "Blue Fox"
because he was always making sacks and quivers of gray fox
skins.

SPEARS

Our people used to make lances for weapons. We made the
handles sometimes eight or nine feet long, out of the dry, dead
stalks of sotol. We straightened these handles in the fire and made
them smooth. We used sotol stalks because they were good and
light.

Long ago we used to make the lance points out of mountain
mahogany, fairly flat and sharp-pointed. Later on we used
bayonet and saber blades of steel. The lance points were stuck
into the end of the handle, and a piece of a cow's tail about eight
inches long and not cut open was slipped over the point and over
the place where the hafting was, and then allowed to stay there
until dry. Stone spear points were not used.

Western Apache lance, this one approximately four and a half feet long

The shaft of the spear was usually painted: the upper half to the point was usually painted blue, or black if they had no blue; the lower half, butt end, was usually painted red, or sometimes left plain. Right at the point end of the handle were tied two eagle feathers.

Anyone could make a lance at any time as there was no medicine to it. They were used either on foot or on horse. They were never left out of the hands, though, and if one was thrust into a horse or cow it was pulled out right away. They either thrust with it single-handed and underhand, or with both hands near the butt and overhead, stabbing down. Sometimes if the hafting got soaked with blood, it got soft and the point would not come out.

Lance handles were made from the sotol stalk. This was done while the stalk was still a little green, so that it might be bent straight and allowed to dry in that way. These handles were made about two yards long, and the steel point was fastened on their ends. Points were also made of hard wood and of stone.

In use, the spear was held with part of the shaft under the elbow and sticking out behind. The point was waved around in a circular motion, and the thrust made at the last moment so that the enemy might not be able to dodge.

The way they fought with spears was to hold them in their hands all the time and fence with them. They did not throw them. If you threw them then you were lost and had no spear. Two men fought each other with them, and the man who was the fastest won and killed the other. If one was just a little slow and left himself open any place, then the other would lance him. We never threw spears at all, nor did we have any loop on the handle to hold on to it with.

A man who was a good fighter and who could run fast was the one to use a spear.

We used to make our spears about eight to ten feet long in all.

The handles we made of the stalk of sotol. We just used the straightest ones and only the stalks of the hardest sotol. If they were not straight enough, then we heated them near the fire and bent them straight in the crotch of a tree.

Then we fitted in a steel spearhead and pulled over it the tail of a burro, still green and not cut except at the end. When this dried, it held the spear point in tight. Then around this again we bound thick buckskin.

There were two kinds of spear points: a short, broad one, and a long one called *espada*.

The half of the handle from the middle to the point we coated with pitch and then rubbed black charcoal paint on it to make it all black. Around the head of the spear—only when we went to war with it—we tied a piece of red cloth. The rest of the time it did not have this cloth. In the old days I think they used to make the spear points of obsidian.

Long ago there was an old man about whom there is a story. He had a wooden-pointed spear, and I saw this spear myself, though I never saw what he did with it. He was in a battle with some Mexicans, and he was about to spear one Mexican. This Mexican ducked down low, and when the man thrust with his spear, the point hit the crown of the Mexican's head and went clear through his skull and killed him.

WARCLUBS

We used to make warclubs out of rawhide. A round piece of hide was cut out and a round stone sewed up inside it. The handle was made of a cow's tail, peeled off and not cut. Inside this was put a long stick. Then the tail was allowed to dry. The hair was kept on it so that it hung down long.

You had to hit a man on the head with one of these to kill him. I think we learned this kind of club from the Pimas, as one time they killed some of our people and some Tonto Apaches when they were sleeping, with clubs like these.

Grenville Goodwin Collection, courtesy Arizona State Museum, Helga Teiwes, photographer

Western Apache warclub

Our people used to use warclubs a lot to fight with and protect themselves from bear, mountain lion and other wild animals in the mountains. The war parties used to make nice ones while they were down in Mexico and bring them back. You have to hit on the head with them to kill. They were carried hung from the belt.

They took a peeled cow's tail and shoved a hardwood stick down inside it. At the end they sewed a round rock inside the rawhide. Sometimes they sewed the tail up along the stick also. They put a thong in the handle so that you could slip your wrist through it. I have never seen or heard of one of these being painted.

SHIELDS

Long ago our people did not use shields. We learned how to make them from the Mexicans. I guess one time they caught a Mexican who showed them how.

Our people used to make their shields of horsehide or cowhide. The hide from the middle of the back was used. They used to peg the hide out when it was wet and peg it so that it was about three or four inches above the ground. Then they would put a weight in the center to weight that part of the hide down. It was allowed to dry this way.

When dry, it was taken off the pegs and the center part of the hide cut out in a square. Later the corners were trimmed so as to make it all round. Only one thickness of hide is used in a shield. A loop for a handle is put right in the center of the back of the shield. This handle is made thick and hard like the crupper of a harness.

The front of the shield is painted in figures of snakes, bears, and other animals. Around the top edge of the shield and halfway down it, they used to tie eagle feathers on with buckskin, and at each side were more feathers than on the top. Later on when we got red cloth, we used to put this where the eagle feathers were, and the feathers on top of it.

They used to make a cover of buckskin or cloth to fit over the shield.

Only a man who knew about making these shields and *inda kɛʔhoʔndi* ['enemies-against power'] could make one of the

Western Apache war shield

shields.[4] The other men would go to him and get him to make them one. Only rich men who knew about war medicine used these shields. They had to pay the equivalent of about thirty or forty dollars to the maker.

On a war party they usually carried only one of these shields. When they were going into battle with the Mexicans, the war medicine man with his shield would go out in front of the rest of the warriors. With him would go three other men who were trying to be brave. They all four would walk out in front in an even line abreast. The medicine man would hold the shield up so that it covered the middle of his body. No arrow or bullet could pass through this shield.

When the owner of a shield died, the shield was not burned but was passed on to someone of his relatives.

I have never seen but one of these shields, and that was when I was a little boy.

A shield was used by the White Mountain Apaches in war. It was round, made of two thicknesses of rawhide sewn together, painted with a design on the front and with a handle on the back side. The shield had a strip of cloth halfway round the edge, with each end hanging down a little. On the cloth was sewn a fringe of eagle feathers.

In battle the shield tilted one way and then another to present a glancing surface from which arrows and even bullets at times could be deflected.

We have used shields for a very long time. Long ago we learned to use them from the Navajo, I think.

Before we were able to get cowhides or horsehide we didn't have any shields. Deerskin was too thin for shields.

Not everyone could make a shield; it had to be a man who understood about these things, who knew war medicine. An ordinary man might be in danger from painting a shield. In the middle of a shield and around on it are painted pictures as a prayer to make the shield strong so the owner will not get hurt.

A shield, called *nan ʔidi ʔ* or *nastaži ʔ*, was only used by a man who understood about war and who was a fast runner and good fighter. When a man who knew about shields used one of them, then you couldn't see anything behind the shield at all; it just looked as if only the shield was there.

Sam Dushey's father had one of these shields. He is dead now. He was a short man. Long ago one time, they were getting ready to go on the warpath together with the Chiricahua. The Chiricahua said they wanted to see how the Eastern White Mountain Apache danced with the shield. Sam's father went out and started to dance with his shield when they called his name at the war dance. He held his shield out in front of him with his left hand, and in his other hand he held a spear. He did well and pretended to be in battle. You couldn't see him at all behind the shield. It was as if he was invisible. Only you could see the shield there. When he got through the Chiricahua said: "There, there is the man who understands about war; there is the man you will follow no matter what kind of men the rest of you are."

I have only seen one or two shields ever, at the times when they danced with them. War parties going down into Mexico used to take along one or sometimes two shields. In battle, a man with a shield didn't have to go out in front; he could go anyplace he wanted. Only the chief and the very bravest and best fighting men had to stay out in front.

These shields had eagle feathers hung around the upper half of them, and right where they ended on each side was hung one crow feather. This was like a prayer to the crow for some reason. When a man took his shield out on the warpath down to Mexico, he would take all the feathers off it and carry it on his back on his way. When he got to Mexico, then he would put the feathers on it again. They kept these shields in a buckskin case.

On the inner side of his shield a man would draw a figure of some kind very faintly so you could hardly see it. This was only for himself to see and meant that he would be successful in war. On the outer side they used to paint the shield up well.

A man learned to use one of these shields from some old man, usually his father, his uncle, or his grandfather, who knew war medicine. If he wanted a shield, this old man used to get it made for him as a gift. He would hire four men to work on the shield. The old man wouldn't work on it, but he would be right there all the time to supervise the work. The man for whom the shield was made wouldn't have to pay for it, but the old man would keep it in his mind that sometime when he came back from the warpath, he would make a present of some horses or cattle to the old man and his four helpers.

They used to make shields of horse or cowhide from the thick part right over the hips on the back. They pegged the hide out and let it dry. Then they cut a round piece out of it the size of the shield when it was dry. This piece they had to trim down so it was just round. They had to make it very tight and strong so no bullet or arrows would go through it.

I once saw an old man show how the shield was used. There were some of us sitting on the ground and he started to come toward us, holding the shield. I couldn't see his body at all, only the shield. A bullet, if it hits one of these shields, will glance off. It can't go through.

WAR CHARMS

The only kind of man who can make a *bahazdi?* ['war charm'] is a man who has 'enemies-against power.' He is the only man who makes these. He can make one for himself, and if anyone else wants one he can make one for them also. He gets paid for this. When he has made it, then he prays over it and teaches the man for whom it is, about everything that is on it and how to pray to it also.

Yes, in the old days I saw war charms, and some had little hoops of wood on them and some had a little cross of wood on them. They used them to go to war with, and they were holy— respected. When they were at home they put them away in a sack in the camp and did not wear them about at all. But if, for instance, a man went from here to Fort Apache just on a trip, he would wear it all right, even though he was not going to war. This was to keep all danger from him.

Western Apache war charm

These charms keep bullets off from you. They are taken to war all right, but not worn in sight by the owner till he goes into battle; then he wears it on the outside where it can be seen. The chiefs always had them and wore them in battle as they went in front of their men. A chief prayed that the bullets might be held back from his men, and that is the way that he would take them into battle, and none of them would get hurt behind him. The missiles could not get past him on account of his charm.

Chiefs always knew about 'enemies-against power,' and if a man came to them and asked for one of these war charms to be made, if he was a good brave man, he could make it for him all right; but if the man was not a brave man, did not get in the thick of the fight, he would not be willing to make one for him. He would know all his men.

These charms were not good for gambling or hunting or crops—just for war. Some men did not like these charms, for if you had one, it took your luck away from hunting and gambling, spoiled your chances in these for you, as it sort of held your life over there where war was, and you had already lots of good luck from it for war, so it held luck back from other things. You already had all that was coming to you. But men who like to go to war like to have these.

SLINGS

Only boys used to make and use slings. The men never used them in war as they were not powerful enough. The pocket part was cut of buckskin in a diamond shape about four inches long. Sometimes there were four holes cut in this piece. At each end of it was attached with sinew a long strip of buckskin. One of these had a lap on its end which the finger was put through. Stones—round ones—were used to throw. Only one whirl was given before release.

8

WAR DANCE

Prior to the departure of a war party, the men who had been invited to participate gathered together and took part in a major ceremonial which, following Goodwin, has been glossed here as 'war dance.' This ceremonial was divided into several discrete parts or phases and began shortly after dark. In the first phase, called 'going to war,' the warriors of each clan were called forth to dance and demonstrate how they would fight the enemy. The second phase was termed 'cowhide, picked up' and involved the singing of chants that described the acquisition of enemy property. In the third phase, labelled 'invite by touching,' women of all ages were encouraged to choose a male partner and engage in social dancing. The fourth and final phase was performed at dawn the following day. Twelve of the bravest and most experienced warriors stood in a line and, one after the other, sang one song about a personal success in war. After the last song, the warriors staged mock attacks on several camps, indicating in this fashion how they intended to surprise and defeat the enemy. This concluded the war dance, and shortly thereafter the expedition made ready to depart.

When they were going to give a war dance they would notify all the people, so that they would come to the dance. Then near where the dance was to be, they set up a great sweat lodge big

enough for forty men to go in at once. Also they would kill two
horses for these men who were taking sweat baths to eat. In the
sweat lodge they placed hot rocks in five different places—to the
east, to the west and north, and also in the middle.

That same day they would tell all the women to go with their
burden baskets and bring in lots of wood to where the dance was
to be. In the evening the dance would start.

The man who instigated a war dance, who sent out word
inviting other people to participate, was called *ba ʔsi ʔan* or *ba ʔsi ʔa*.
When word was sent out it was sent just to the chiefs of each clan—
no others. Then the chief would talk to his clansmen, and if they
wanted to join the war party they would set off along with their
chief. When the dance started, all the different clans would be
grouped about in a big circle about the dance place. Each clan's
men were with their leader in the war dance. This leader was their
chief. When the singing started, the first clan on the list—its
chief—was called, and he led his men out in the dance. His name
was called in the song. There he danced with his men. When their
turn was through, they went back to their position and it was the
next clan's turn. The chief would leave his men and maybe go
to where his family sat and join them. But it was always the clan
chief who led them out the first time.

When each clan had had its turn and its chief had led it out,
then they would have gone all the way about the circle. Only
men danced. Then they would start the rounds again, giving each
clan its turn. But this time they did not call the chief's name.
Instead they called the bravest man's name, and he led them out.
The chief did not dance with them. Thus each clan had its turn
again, all the way about the circle. When it got around twice this
way it was the end. Then they danced with a cowhide about the
fire four times. When this was done it was the sign that it was time
to start the social dance.

First they had the real war dance, called *ʔikałsɨtaʔ* ['going to
war']. Chiricahuas call it *haškɛgojitał* ['angriness dance']. When
they start a dance like this they divide up the men into their clans.

Each one of these clan groups has a leader appointed from them. This man is usually the one who has the most property or who has the most knowledge of all of them, usually an old man; he may be the clan chief or just an appointed head man, but he is chosen for the occasion.

All the men carry their spears, or bows and arrows, or shields, etc. When they start the first song everyone listens carefully. In the song they will call the name of one of those head men and say, for instance, "You are a brave man. Let's see you come out before these people and show them how you can do." Then that leader will step out and all his men will follow him and they will dance. Those with spears will pretend to lance; those with bows will draw them back to show how far they can draw; those with shields will use them also.

When one song is over, then the ones who have been dancing stop, and it is another clan's turn. Now they call the leader's name again and he leads his bunch out.

They sing different songs because they want to give one to every different clan and give them a chance to show off and dance so they will be satisfied. If one clan was left out they would feel bad, because it was as if the others said they were not good fighters—were weak, left out.

When this series of dances of clan leaders and men were over, all those men picked up a cowhide and danced four times about the fire with it. This is called *ʔikałnadita* ['hide picked up'; 'cowhide dance']. If one of the women or girls wanted to go in and dance now they could. The men would be shouting. While they sang they would be singing about enemy's property and things. When the cowhide dance was over they gathered up in a bunch. They had their guns, firearms, all weapons, and picked out the best men to sing. Then the relatives of the family who was giving the dance would go out among the camps and talk to all the people, "Loan me your wife tonight. She can dance with a man, but she will return to you just as she left you. She can dance all night, even if she is dancing with another man and talking with him, it means nothing. The same way with the girls. They will come back in the morning."[1] This social dance, called *łeda ʔjičuš*, lasted all night until sunrise.

Then in the morning they pick out twelve of the bravest men, ones who in a fight would never hold themselves back in their minds, always think brave and go right into the fight. These twelve men were right there at the dance place. All the people gathered about them in a circle and the twelve men would be standing right in the middle of them. Everyone kept absolute silence and listened to the twelve men. While they did this, all twelve lined up. Then one man from the line would step out in front and dance, and while he danced he sang maybe about one time when he was in a fight, how his enemy ran after him and almost killed him, but he was brave and fought and came out all right. That was one time he had a hard time and showed how brave he was.

At the end of the song, one man in the circle of people about the twelve would have a drum and he would sound it three or four times. This meant that the people were satisfied about what they had heard and approved of this. There was no drum sounded while the men sang though. Each one of the twelve had his turn at this to sing his own song. They each sang different. One would say, "I was attacked by a bear one time and had a hard time to go by, but got by all right."

When it was the turn of the last man of these twelve to sing, he sings a song that means, "There is death everywhere. You cannot go anywhere without death. There are different kinds of death. Death comes to everyone sometime." When he finishes his song all the people standing about the twelve call out, "You will not die. You will come back all right."

When this dance is over everyone goes back to their camp. Then they pick out twelve men, different ones from the other twelve, ones who have come from far off because they were invited to help in war. These twelve men paint their bodies. They have their bows and spears in their hands. Then they go about from place to place, to the ones who set up the dance, and to the whole tribe and sing as they go. They sing only two songs. They go to four camps without songs. As they go to the camps these twelve destroy the clay pots and dishes and if the family has a dog they shoot it with arrows and kill it. Then they cut off the tail or one of the legs and thrust in the end of a stick and carry it about raised up above them. The people know they are coming and if they have pots they hide them or hide their dog.

When the dance is all over one of the chiefs says, "The dance is over now. If a woman wishes to talk she can. If an old woman wishes to talk she can walk among us. Tomorrow we will be ready to go. Everything was ready and packed when the dance was going on."

While the dance was going on the chief who set up the dance would talk to other chiefs or headmen. He would tell them, "I picked you out. I depend on you. I depend on your hands. I depend on your ribs. You are brave so I picked you. You are my mind—just like my mind. You think as I do. I picked you out because I want to kill one of my enemies. If we go there and one of you gets killed there will be one more man among us here, for there will be one woman here who will bear a boy baby who will grow to be a man. So it will make no difference if you are killed." On that same day they distributed all the food they had among the men who were going. They gave them all mescal, ground seeds, and corn so that no one was left out.

When the men were ready to go they picked out two old men who were going to stay at home. Then they gave these two men the number of days they would be gone. They might say forty or thirty days. Then one of the chiefs would give these two old men a long buckskin cord. They would tell these old men that each day they should tie a knot in the string like a calendar. When they had reached within ten days of the said return, from then on they were to be expected to return any time. Then one of the chiefs going to war would put these two men in charge of the whole camp. They would tell them, "You shall take these women and children over to a certain place where there is a spring and we will return to you there."

After 'going to war,' the men picked up a cowhide and started to dance with it. This was called 'hide picked up.' They danced about the fire with the hide four times. They only beat the hide on one side of the fire, the south, when going to Mexico; facing opposite when going north to Navajo. They didn't beat it on four sides of the fire. They didn't throw the hide away; the man who owned it would just pick it up and take it to his home.

In the social dance after 'hide picked up' they sang *bɨłeda ʔji-čuššɨ* ['invite by touching him song'].[2] The social dance songs sung after the war dance were the same social dance songs as sung at any social dance. They were just regular social dance songs. But they are different from the ones of today.

The man who sang the social dance songs after the war dance would be given a present by the returned warriors.

At sunrise, the day after the war dance, twelve men dance. The drum is beaten just once. Everyone is in silence. The last of the twelve sings about death. This same man sings this song when the war party gets near the enemy, so that they will not be afraid. In these twelve men there must be a representative from each clan; they may pick out two men from the same clan to fill out the quota of twelve though. The twelfth man, picked to sing the song about death, would be picked not by clan, or because he was the war-dance sponsor, but because he was the bravest man and knew that song.

This song he sings is not a *basɨ* ['war song']. It is *ndɛbɨjɨʔi jɛsɨ* ['death song']. When he sings that he makes the men's hearts strong, so that they will not run from the enemy. This is the only death song there is, there are no others. They sing it going into battle. The man who sang this song would have 'enemies-against power,' and by this he would make the other men brave.

Then, after that, twelve other men raid the camp of the war-dance sponsor and the camps of the members of his clan. This was done because these were the people they were going on the warpath for. They made a picture this way of what they were going to do for them against the enemy. These twelve men had to be all from different clans.

The songs we used in the war dance were sung as sort of prayers. They were only used at the war dance. We never sang these on the warpath, just at the dance. We sang them nowhere else. The songs we sing at the war dance are called *basɨ*.

There were certain men who knew these songs well, and always sang them. I don't know where they learned them or how.

These war songs were not for curing at all—just for bravery. Some might still think they can sing these, but all that knew them well have all died off. But there are quite a few who still know the songs for social dances.

They did not pay a man to sing at a war dance. He was glad to do it, and help his people. They would request him to. But when the war party got back, if successful, they would give him half a beef or something, but would never say what it was for.

Men wanted to know war songs so they could sing them and make up a war dance. They would not want them to pass out of use. These songs started from the beginning of things. They don't sing them at all nowadays. Lots of men would help the men to sing at the war dance, just like a social dance.

A war dance lasts two days. During this time the people must not do evil things. Women and men should not have arguments or quarrels. No bad words should be spoken. The chief would talk to his people and tell them what to do. A man would talk. He might be head of the men going to war. "We have lots of women here, they can bring more children to birth." By saying this he meant to ask everyone to help make the men brave, so they would go along. If a man got killed a woman would bear another boy to replace him, so they would not be out another man.

There would be many clans represented at a war dance, possibly some outside group's clans. The chief would talk to them and say "the boys of one clan must talk polite to girls of another clan and not touch them. The boys of this clan must not touch girls of that clan." This was to stop all trouble between peoples gathered there.

9

LEADERSHIP

The following selections give some indication of the qualities that the Western Apache considered necessary for leadership in raiding and war. Among the most highly prized were fearlessness, previous experience, a record of past successes, and the possession of 'enemies-against power,' a potent supernatural force that was believed to weaken the enemy and make them vulnerable to attack. The statements in this section also provide valuable information about the rights and duties of chiefs when at war or on a raid.

The chief of a raiding party or a war party was always a man who knew about war, had gone many times, and who was brave. He did not have to be a clan chief. He was only a chief on a raid or when the men went to war. Most of those war chiefs had 'enemies-against power' and could use it to help their men. That way they were protected and would have good luck. That's why the other men would always want someone like that to lead them.

The man who was chief of a war party was in charge of it. Sometimes he was a chief of a clan. But even if he wasn't, and even if clan chiefs were along, they had to obey him. He was in charge.

The war chief was the leader of a war party. He was in charge, even if a clan chief was along. At a war dance a war chief talked to all the men. He told them what he wanted of them. He would mention all his kin; he would mention all his relatives. "We are going out to war against Whites. They killed my relatives some time ago, that's why I have invited you here to help me. So we will get even, that's why I have invited you," he would say. "If your wife wants to dance, let her dance, she won't be hurt at all. Even if she pretends not to want to, let her; she will have a good time. Also bring out all your girls and big girls. Let them have a good time."

After this man got through, maybe another chief would speak. "Listen to what this man said. You heard it, you all have got good ears." After that an old man would get up, "Boys, we need your help. Help us any way he wants you to. Listen to him whatever he says to you. Do whatever he says to you wherever you are at."

Then a grown woman would get up and talk, "That way it's good, that way it's good. Listen boys, that man wants your help. You can go along. You married men turn out your wives, your girls, and big girls all to join in the dance. At one time one of his kin got killed, and he wants you to go down with him to get even. White men are born from women also, they are not hard, they are not like rock, they are born from us also. You will not turn to rock, so go along with him."

§

A war chief on the warpath never hauled wood or water, and never did camp work. They wanted him to keep quiet. But he was always in the lead. He would talk to the men while they were on the way, how they should attack the enemy, how they should look out for snakes. While he was in the lead, they called him 'he destroys dew,' because he walked ahead and shook off the dew first. Whenever they stopped to camp, he would talk to the older men, tell them why they were out there, what they wanted. They would all listen to what he said because he was brave and knew things. They used to think that a man like this was equal to twelve men.

If they found cattle they could kill a beef, but this man would not help butcher it or cut pieces of flesh or cook meat for himself. All the other men along would cook and as soon as it was done would give it to him. That's the way they respected him. While at camp he would talk to men. "You were at the war dance. You went around with other men's girls. While we are out here we want to get even. If we kill one of those Mexicans like they killed one of us, we will all be talked about and praised. Don't be scared—be brave like men. Don't run away from fights. If they kill you as you go, the bullet will enter your back. That would not be right. Be brave, stand up to fight, try to kill your enemy. If the bullet enters your chest and comes out your back, that will be a lot better, even if you are killed. That will show your people that you are brave. People who run off are not good."

When a war party was going south to raid the White people or Mexicans, they appointed one of the chiefs to lead it. So this chief would take his men along. If they captured any horses or cattle, they would drive them home. When they got there, the chief of the party would take as many stones as there were horses or cattle. His men would gather then, and he would give so many stones to each man. This meant that the number of stones a man got was the number of animals he would get. When all the stones were divided out, what was left over the chief would take for himself.

In peace times a war chief did not have any duties at all. He was just a common man. He went out hunting deer just like any other man did. He did not take charge of any deer hunts or anything at all.

10

PREPARATIONS AND CONDUCT

This section begins with several brief statements about the preparation of supplies for a raid or war party and the manner in which warriors decorated their bodies. The remaining selections describe some of the tactics and strategies that were customarily employed within enemy territory.

They used to notify eight or ten men who wanted to go to raid in Mexico, to get ready. Now they fixed their moccasin soles. Also they used to skin the neck of a deer out without cutting it and from this they would cut around and around, and make one long strand of rawhide for making ropes later on. When they had everything finished—each man for himself—then they made up their packs with the rawhide and buckskin and mescal and dry seeds.

On the warpath, when we started out, we always got food ready to take along. We used to pack mescal on our backs, also buckskin sacks filled with ground corn. They used to pound the fruit of prickly pear up into dry cakes and let it harden for us to take along. These cakes were about eight inches in diameter. Also we had ground berries in buckskin sacks. Whenever we stopped to camp we would mix these berries with mescal and water and eat it.

In the old times when the Western Apache went to war, the men used to paint a white, black, or red stripe across their faces, over the nose and under the eyes. Their hair they used to tie up in a bunch on the top of their heads. They wore a G-string that came down to about the middle of their thighs.

In the old days when our men went to war, just before they went into battle, they used to paint two white bands across their chests. They also used to tie their hair around with a red cloth, so that they could tell each other from the Mexicans with whom they would be fighting.

When a man went on the warpath he used to make four pairs of moccasins to take along with him for use.

They used to paint the whole body all over red, for war, even the face. Around the mouth and on the cheeks they put little white dots.

In the morning the war party started out. We would send two men ahead to keep watch. Then we would go on down to the foot of the mountains and wait there for evening. When sunset came, then we would start out and cross the Gila Valley to the south. After this we never traveled in open country, but always traveled along the mountains.

From the mountains we could always watch for Mexicans. This is the way we traveled clear down into Mexico.

Every war party always had a chief along, and what he said, the others had to do—all of them. This chief didn't have to pack anything, as the other men packed for him. Also he never had to get any wood or water or do any work of that kind. The other men could not talk back to him.

When we had to cross open country we always waited for evening, and even then we were very careful not to leave any tracks. Sometimes we used to walk just on our toes to leave a small track. And sometimes we kept a man out behind to brush over our tracks with some bushes. Our old war parties used to travel far into Mexico this way. Sometimes we went close to the ocean, way to the southwest.

When the party got near a Mexican town we would go up on a high mountain and make camp. Here the chief would say he wanted us to stay and keep a lookout for any Mexicans traveling out of or into the town. Or sometimes he would tell us to look out for horses in the Mexican pastures to see which ones were the fattest, because we always sort of looked over horses before we took them.[1]

If the men that were sent out from here found any wagon tracks, they would come back to the mountain camp and report it to the rest. They would say, "We saw some wagons pass; they must have clothes and other property in them, so we might as well go ahead and hold them up."

The chief would send some men who understood about war and explain to them just what to do. They had to go to some narrow place where the wagons would pass through, and there hide themselves at different places for quite a ways along the side of the road. We had to lie down and cover ourselves over with dry grass so no one could see us. Then we had to wait until the teams and wagons got in the gap, till the last wagon was opposite the first of us. Then we would start to shoot. This was the way we always had to start to fight all at the same time.

Now we would kill all the Mexicans and butcher the horses or mules or oxen for meat. Then we got all the clothes and calico in the wagons to take home for our people.

When the fight was over we used to take the dead Mexicans off and put them where they would not be found. Then we would burn the wagons and hide everything as much as possible so none of the other Mexicans would get word that we were in the country. Now we would go some other place, and so the same way.

Sometimes we would go near a Mexican town where they had Mexican soldiers garrisoned. This was when some of our relatives had been killed by the Mexicans on another raid before and we had come back to avenge them. This time we would be looking for a fight.

When we got near the garrison town, the chief would send four men together who were real strong men—fearless and knowing about war—to the outskirts of the town. The rest of us would wait off on some hill or canyon. We would try to get a canyon or gap of some kind to wait in, hiding ourselves along both sides.

Those four men would go right up to the outside of the town where the Mexican soldiers were herding their horses. Here they would show themselves to the Mexicans.

As soon as the Mexicans saw them, they would leave their horses and make a run for the town. When they got in there they would tell their officer that the Apaches had run off their stock. Those four men hadn't come to run the horses off, but the Mexicans thought that way.

We wouldn't know how many soldiers there were, but out they would come to chase those four men. These four would pretend to run away, but they would lead the Mexicans over to that place where the rest of us were waiting. When all the Mexicans were led in between us, then we would show ourselves and start fighting. The Mexicans had guns and we only had bows and arrows and spears, but this made no difference. We killed all the Mexicans. One man with just a spear killed four Mexicans.

Now we all went to the town because all the soldiers were killed. When we got there we pulled the women out of the houses by their hair and killed everyone in the town.

Now the chief would tell us to look for horses and cattle. We would have lots of calves, saddles, ropes, everything we wanted. From the mountains we would start about sundown and round up what horses and cattle we wanted.

Then we would start on our way back home, herding all our stock and packing the rest of the things we had captured. We kept two good men out in front, and two other men way out behind as guards. The rest of us herded the stock along in the middle. If the men out in front saw danger ahead, then they would come back and tell us and we would change our direction. This way we traveled, never sleeping at night, and going fast until we were out of the Mexican country and close to home. We had to watch all the springs on our way, as there were likely to be Mexicans living near them. This way sometimes we only got water once a day, sometimes once in two or three days.

Every war party always had a medicine man along to cure any man who might get wounded or sick. They could cure a man right away. Also they would be able to tell what was going to happen ahead of time, and we would know what way the Mexicans were going to act.[2] If Mexican troops were ahead of us, and the medicine man said it was all right to go through where they were, then we would go.

As soon as we started, the medicine man would make a big wind so that it would blow brush around and raise so much dust that we couldn't see each other.[3] He would pray. Sometimes he would make a big hail come down so that it would hit the Mexicans and knock them down. This way we would travel past the Mexican troops as they would be all wet, and their things would be washed away, and by the time they got ready again we would be a long ways past. Now the chief would tell us to travel a little faster. What stock gave out we would butcher for eating.

When we got safely out of the Mexican country, then we stopped and sent two men back a long ways to stay and guard. Then we would make camp for a couple of days and rest up. Now we would fix all our moccasins up, and our ropes, and cook up lots of beef and make grub up into a pack. Just as we had done before when we started out from home. This way we wouldn't have to make a fire again. Now we set off again.

When we got pretty near home, up towards our mountains, the chief would send a man ahead to tell all our relatives that we would get back on a certain day, and to meet us at a certain place and to get ready for us. Then our relatives would be happy when they heard what we had done. When we got in, everything we brought back we divided among our people. "Good, thank you," they would say. Then all those people whose relatives had been killed before in Mexico would come and would be thankful to us for avenging them. Now they could rest easily in their minds.

When a war party started out they always left some old man behind to take care of the women. They usually allowed about thirty to forty-five days to be gone, and would tell their people when they expected to be back. One of the old men who stayed behind would have a cord of buckskin about two feet long, and for every day that the war party was away they would tie a knot in it. This way he could tell when they were due back, and the others could come to him to find out also.

A war party figured on carrying just enough food with them

to last until they got to Mexico, as when they got there they could get cattle, horses, mules, or burros. When they got down into Mexico, they would make camp on some big, rocky mountain where it was safe. In this camp the boys and older men of the party were left.[4]

The other men went out from here to near some Mexican town. They would go to the town and steal the stock that was in the pastures, as they knew this would be gentle stuff and what they wanted. When they got the stock, they would drive it back to where the others were waiting for them in the mountain camp. This way they were usually away three days.

Now they would talk and say, "Here we have what we came for—lots of horses and mules—so we might as well go back," so they would all start back, traveling always at night and never sleeping until they got out of the Mexican country. Then they would travel slower. They always kept two men way out behind and two men way out in front to watch for the Mexicans. The rest would drive the captured stock in the middle.

When they got near home they would send the two men way ahead to the home camp where all their relatives were to notify them that they were coming with lots of stock.

When on the warpath, a man wore nothing but his moccasins, a G-string, and his headband.

Our people used to use smoke signals to warn each other when they knew the Mexicans or White people were on the warpath and coming to fight. That's the only way I know of.

The times war or raiding parties used to pick to go to Mexico were in the spring and in August and in the fall. At these times there was lots of water. On a raiding party they usually took from twelve to thirty men, and on a war party about forty men. When they got down into Mexico they used to wait for the moon to get nearly full before they captured the Mexican stock. This was so they could travel at night.

ᒐ

In old times they used to figure on getting to the enemy country when the moon was full. They would set the time so that they would arrive there just about the day that the moon would come up in the evening—full.

On the raid if they saw any enemies coming, they would try to meet them at the narrowest place, maybe where a road is narrow. Our men could hide in bushes, or dig little holes and lie in them. Then when the enemy got by, the men with spears would jump out first and spear them down. They would not have time to shoot them. The spearmen were always the best runners.

Four or five or six or ten men who were good friends together would go out raiding. We used to do this in order to get horses from the Mexicans. We used to go to where the Mexicans were living and capture lots of their ponies. When we brought these back to our country we butchered them to eat. The horsehides we used for making our moccasin soles with. The sinew from along both sides of the backbone, we took out and used to sew our moccasins with.

We never got on well with the Pima and Papago, and we always used to go down to their country and steal lots of horses and burros from them. After that we made war against the White people because we found them coming into our country and living there.

Just as we had raided the Mexicans and Pima and Papago before, now we raided the White people. We took their horses and cattle, and drove them back to our country and used them. Cowhides we used to make moccasin soles of. We also made some into buckskin.

This way, our people and the Americans didn't like to see each other, because when they did there was always a fight. We killed lots of Americans, and they killed lots of us also. They had rifles, caps, powder, and bullets, and we captured these for ourselves. We kept on fighting the Americans with these.

Now when we killed them we took their shoes and pants and shirts and coats and boots, and used them for ourselves, and dressed like Americans we had seen. If we saw some Americans in big wagons, we would go to them and capture their outfit. In these wagons we found lots of flour, blankets and calico, and all other things. Sometimes there would be five, seven, or ten wagons. We took what we wanted out of them and used it for ourselves.

Out of the calico we started making dresses for the women. Now we were wearing clothes all over our bodies. Before that we went about almost naked.

One time there was the son of a chief. For some reason he had never married. Lots of the people had wanted him to marry their daughters, but he did not want to marry.

One time he started to Mexico, leading a raiding party. Down there his party captured a lot of cattle, and they started home, driving them in three separate herds. All the men had spears, and on their spear handles, running down them, were painted zigzag lines, like snakes.

There was one gap they had to go through on their way, and at this place the Mexicans always used to try and cut the war parties off and attack them. So that chief's son, the leader of the party, rode on ahead to find out if there were any Mexicans there.

When he got near he could see there were Mexicans there, but he had a good horse and a good spear, and he kept right on. When he got there the Mexicans attacked him, but he fought them off. Finally they killed him, but by that time the others had gone on with the cattle and got away.[5]

11

TABOOS AND
WARPATH LANGUAGE

The members of raiding and war expeditions observed a set of ritual proscriptions, or taboos, that were believed to protect them from danger and confer important advantages over the enemy. The most striking of these proscriptions was the use of a warpath language in which a set of special nouns and noun compounds were employed in place of conventional forms. Besides nouns, the Western Apache warpath language included a small set of lengthier constructions which substituted at the level of the phrase. For a description and analysis of the Chiricahua warpath lexicon see Opler and Hoijer (1940).

Husbands of pregnant women cannot go to war. It makes them too heavy.

A man whose wife is pregnant shouldn't go to war. It makes him heavy. A man might not know it and arrange to go, but he later finds out and goes to the men and says, "I can't go now. I find my wife is no good."

From the time the war party started until it got back, the men in the party had all kinds of *gudnɬsi* ['taboos'] to observe. Mostly, these were about how they had to talk. There were sacred names

for many things, and a man had to know these and use them, for
if he didn't something bad would happen to him and to all the
other men that were with him.

ᐱᐱ

Yes, it is true that on the warpath there were special words
that had to be used; a horse was called by a different word; a
woman was; a Mexican was also. Also men could not scratch
themselves with fingers. They had to do it with a stick.

Bitsi ꞌyaditaš ['shakes his tail'] was the name for burro and
mule. Old women were called *istsanɑdlɛhɛ* ['Changing Woman,' a
prominent mythological figure]; all women and girls were called
this. There was no special name for man at all. *Tlo bɛ ꞌo ꞌise* ['grass,
it catches on your toes'] we called going down to Mexico. When
we came back it was called *tlo bɛna ꞌiči* ['grass blown, swayed by
the wind']. *Hai ꞌgohɛ* when played down there we called it *še*, not
by its real name.[1] We used to bet dry meat to gamble. There was
no special name for cattle. Wind had no special name at all. Earth
and sky, trees, had no special name. No special name for spear,
bow, shield, arrow. We called Mexicans *naidlɛhɑ*.[2] These are about
all the names there are that we used; if you don't use them, then
something bad will happen to you.

⑤

On the warpath there were special terms and words for everything, not the regular speech. On starting south from White River,
on the way the men used just regular speech till they crossed the
Gila River, but from there on till they recrossed it on the way back
they had to use this special speech. A boy going on a raid for the
first time knew these words all right, for he was instructed in them
by an old man before he left, his instructor who told him how to
say each thing. For instance, when they came on the fresh trail of
the enemy, instead of saying, "Here is where the enemy passed
by," they will say, *čidoɫjok* ['something has been dragged by
here'], and another way is *jɛhotlɛk* ['here it has hopped along like
a frog']. They call a White man *nančin*. Water was called *nahina ꞌ*
['it keeps moving']. One time a man almost fought his wife over
this. He asked her to bring him water by this term by mistake,
and she, not knowing what it meant, brought some tops off some

bushes and brought them to him. He got mad. These are all the names that I know, only these four.

One time on a raid, one man in the bunch, while they camped, was a little scared I guess. While they stood about the fire one night, this man said, "What are you men scared of?" They found out it was a mountain lion sneaking about in the bush. So they moved far off and made another camp, and stood about the fire. Then that same man said again, "What are you men scared for?" Right then a mountain lion jumped out, grabbed him, and dragged him off. This is the one reason why a man has to watch taboos on the warpath. If he doesn't something like this will happen to him. This happened, so that's why we respect everything. As soon as we got across the Gila River, we called it White man's country, and from then on they respected everything. The reason the lion killed that man was because he said they were scared—made fun of them. They went back the next day and found him all eaten up.

Just as soon as he gets back to camp after a war party, a man can do anything he wants to. There are no longer taboos that he must observe. He can eat anything he wants, sleep with his wife, gamble at cards, play hoop-and-pole, say any kind of words.

It is only on the warpath that there are taboos a man must observe.

A man who has taken a scalp may do anything as soon as he gets home, even before taking a sweat bath. He could eat anything, say anything, sleep with his wife.

I never heard of any man getting sick from going to war and killing or touching a dead enemy or being touched by one. We never got sickness from that at all.

If only two or three men went to raid, then it was the same way as if a lot of them went. They observed taboos and they had a leader just the same. They had to use the warpath words and every other taboo was observed, even if there were only two or three men.

12

TABOOS FOR WOMEN

In one sense, the success of a war party or raiding expedition did not depend completely on the men who composed it. Through the observance of certain taboos, women who stayed at home could help contribute to the success of the enterprise and, equally important, take steps to assure the party's safe return.

Taboos for a wife while her husband is gone on a raid or to war: She prays every morning for four days after he goes; every time she pulls a pot of meat off the fire, she prays that he may get what he wants. She must only use one end of the fire poker to poke the fire till he gets back. This applies also to grown daughters in the same wickiup. In the case of a single man whose mother and grown sisters live in his wickiup, they do the same.

A woman can pray for the safety or success of her husband on the warpath by stirring ashes as she takes the pot off the fire, or putting charcoal on the tortillas, and saying, "Good luck, go with him."

Pregnant women, touching or stepping over gun, rifle, arrows, cartridges, will cause the owner of them to miss aim with them.

A woman whose husband had gone to war prays that no harm will come to him. The mother of a man will do the same. Some pray for just four days, but others pray all the time during his absence. They can pray two times, once in the morning and also again at noon, if they want.

A woman while she was having her monthly could handle her husband's bow and arrow all right. But a pregnant woman could not handle them. If a pregnant woman handled them, then when he shot the arrow wouldn't go straight at all. If a man kills a deer, and if his wife is in a family way, she must not eat any guts or the calves of the deer's legs. If she does, the arrow will not go straight. There is no danger from it; it is just because she might give him bad luck that she does not eat that.

A woman who is pregnant cannot handle a rifle, and a bow and arrow for the same reason, nor can she even step over it. But a menstruating woman can. She can step over it or handle it. Pregnant women can't even handle the cartridges for a gun.

Any woman could handle a spear, whether pregnant or not. This was because it just depended on a man being a good runner for him being successful with a spear. But with arrow and bow you had to shoot straight.

A woman could handle her husband's shield if he had one, even if she was pregnant, or menstruating, because it belonged to him. But I don't think any other women could touch it. Any man could touch it though. It had no danger for them. It was made with a lot of power in it, so that's why other women would not dare to touch it. It was dangerous. The man's wife could touch it all right because he could protect her from the power that he threw into the shield.[1]

If you had a war club anyone could handle it. It was not very important, only stone. Any woman could handle it, whether pregnant or not.

Yes, it is true that in old times when a woman's husband went to war there was a taboo for her that she could not use the poker for the fire except on one end—the right end—just as in pregnancy. If she used the other end, then it meant that something bad would happen to her husband. But it was not all women who were careful to observe this taboo or ones like it, for some just did not think about it and were not careful. It was women who were careful and religious who did it.

A woman can wash her hair all right, but she cannot look in her clothes or body for lice. When a man goes hunting his wife has to observe taboos. It is the same when he goes to war. That's all the taboos I know of. She must not talk bad words either. Some women were not good and while their man was off to war they would run about with some other man.

For a man's wife at home while he was on a raid there were no taboos on sex. There would not have been a taboo about women having intercourse because I have heard of some women doing this with another man while their husband was gone. When the husband got back he would be mad, sometimes he would quit her, sometimes not. The women at home could eat any food they wanted while men were on the warpath. Also they could use any words. Only men on the warpath had to be careful.

Grown men on the warpath could eat anything. Only boys could not eat certain parts of animals on their first time.

I have never heard that a man must not sleep with his wife for four nights before he goes to war. It is all right if a man cohabits with his wife the night before he leaves to go to war.

13

THE USE OF 'POWER'

The Western Apache term diyi? *('supernatural power') was used to refer to one or all of a set of abstract and invisible forces which were believed to derive from certain classes of animals, plants, meteorological phenomena, and mythological figures within the Western Apache universe. Any of the 'powers' could be acquired by man— although this was by no means easy—and if properly handled used for a variety of purposes. 'Powers' were controlled and manipulated with prayers and the singing of appropriate chants. The following statements describe the types of 'power' that were most closely associated with raiding and warfare and some of the uses to which they were put.*

The most important power for war is *inda kɛ ʔho ʔndi* ['enemies-against power']. It is the real war power. This power comes from *nayanɛzganɛ* ['Killer of Monsters'], for in the beginning he was the one who went all over the earth doing things and killing monsters, and he was the first one to use his power in doing this, so it all comes from him. But this power was given to *nayanɛzganɛ* by his father, the sun, and was given in like manner to *tubačɨsčɨnɛ* ['Born of Water']. Also, 'Changing Woman' has power for war.[1] She and

[270]

the two brothers got it from the sun. She did not have her own war power; hers came from the sun. But of these three *nayanɛzganɛ* has the most of this power.

If you have this power ['enemies-against power'] and you only have a knife and another man attacks you with a gun, then you can win out and kill him if you use the power and liken yourself to mountain lion. Also, if you use this and call yourself mountain lion, and a man shoots you with a gun, even then you will get him and kill him, even if you have nothing.

'Enemies-against power' is a power related to 'wind power.' When on the warpath men painted wind tracks along the outside of their moccasins to make them light.

Some chiefs had plenty of 'enemies-against power,' and they would say their own words over themselves [i.e., bless and protect themselves] when about to go to a war. But other chiefs used to have to hire a medicine man to sing over them so that no harm would come to them on the warpath.

My maternal grandfather, an old man, used to take a little piece of cottontail rabbit skin and tuck it in each man's moccasins, right over the top. This way the moccasins never wore out. It was a charm. This same man sang over my father half a night, the night before he started to war. He sang over him only, but there was a crowd in there, but no women were allowed in. This song was to protect him from being shot or wounded. Women were not allowed in there because they walked too heavy, and the men might get the same way on the warpath and walk too heavy. I don't know the song. It was a hard one. Women can't sing it.

One time I was on the trail going to Chiricahua Butte. I tied one of my horses up and hobbled the other. I fell asleep there. It

was night. Close to daylight I had a dream. I dreamed that someone talked to me, "Tomorrow a man wearing a long beard and a
mustache will take the rope away from you," [i.e. attack you and
steal your horses]. The only place where there were any White
people was at Fort Apache, so I thought it must be that the people
at Fort Apache would take my horses away from me tomorrow.

I got up then. Then at sunrise I put my saddle on. While I was
riding I looked back over the canyon to the south and saw some
people coming slowly on big horses. Then I looked in front to thick
growing trees of oak and juniper and saw the White men lined up
all ready for ambush. They must have seen me coming. I ran my
horse in a hurry to the thick brush to see which way those fellows
were coming. When I got close to the thick brush, all at once I
heard a trampling of horses, and saw a bunch of White men coming
out. There was a large hill there, bare, with only a few scattered
trees on it. I started to lead my horse up it and all at once the
Whites ran and made a circle about me.

Now while they shot at me I said a few words to my power.
"Hold their guns up; don't let them shoot at me. Let the bullets go
over."

When I spoke these words not one of my horses got hurt, and
I didn't even hear the sounds of the bullets. In those days we used
to pray in war like this.

There were words to use with a power when you were fighting
against your enemy. These made your enemy's bow break. His
bow would break and he would have nothing to shoot you with.
I don't know any words to make an arrow pass over or to the side
of you.

I have heard of some men using power on the warpath so that
the enemy would not be ready for them, not think we were coming.
This way it was easy to attack them because they were not ready.

The power for making hail and wind on the enemy belongs to
'enemies-against power.'

ς

Warriors are made like bats by a medicine man in a fight so they can't be hit. 'Bat power' makes them elusive.

Na²itluk is a power with songs used to foretell coming events, used on the warpath.

There is a kind of power used in wrestling, in which a man having it can throw a man twice his size if he uses the power on him. He does not do it by his strength at all, but by his power. There is no name for this power at all, except that known to the man who has it.

I have heard that men knowing this when they were going to wrestle, as they approached their opponent, would say, "On my right side is mountain lion holding up my arm, and on my left side is another mountain lion holding up my arm." This is the way that he was strong and could grapple the other man.

Some men had *gałkɛ²ho²ndi* ['running power']. That way they could run fast on the warpath. I never saw anyone use it, just heard of it.

There is a power called 'running power' also. A man who has this power can run long distances, and even on the shortest day could run from Fort Grant to Fort Apache and get there in mid-afternoon.

Medicine men with 'star power' also had power over guns. They usually had one of their own, and in battle would say words over it, and put their power in it. You could also get him to put power in your gun for you, pray over it, so you would never miss anything. This could be done for hunting as well as war. Also if a fight was coming off soon then he would pray over his own gun this way and put his power in it.

One time down here the father-in-law of Harvey Nashkin sang over someone and got paid a cow for it. This was brought down to his camp there at Dewey Flat, and the old man told his son to shoot it. He handed him a bow and arrow. His son took the arrow and spat on the point of it; then he shot it and it went right through the cow and out the other side. Some people saw the arrow come out the other side and go on, and said that he had missed, but pretty soon the cow gave a grunt and blood started to flow from its nose. So I know that a man who can shoot like that must have some words he says when he shoots.

I have heard that in old times, when a raiding party was on the way to Mexico, some man who knew 'horse power' would rope a tree on the way, and then each man there would rope a tree. As he roped it he would call out the kind of horses that he wanted. Then they would stand there as the rope hung on the tree and a horse medicine man would sing horse songs. Then on the way, before they got to the enemy country, they would do this four times in all. This way it made it easy for them to get horses in Mexico. When they got there then they would be roping the kind of horses that they had asked for.

I have heard that some men used to have a power for cattle, and that in driving them back from Mexico they could make them drive easily, so they would not run off. A man who had this power used to ride around a herd in the evening four times, saying words, and then the cattle would bed down and stay there all night.

There are 'leg songs' sung to cure tired legs on the warpath.

'Arrow songs' [kɔsi̧] are used to sing over a man who is injured, whether badly cut, wounded with a bullet or arrow, or with broken bones. They can be sung at night or daytime. The first song of the arrow songs says "It points towards me, arrow," and represents a man shooting at a person. In the second song they say, "Me you strike, with arrow." In the third song they say, "From me, it [the arrow] goes through." They say in the fourth song, "From me, it [the arrow] hits the ground, it can't go any further on." That's the way it is mentioned in the four different songs. It means as if the sick man was shot through by the arrow, and it thus cures him. 'Arrow power' makes it that way.

When men get back from the warpath they would all take a sweat bath. They would be all dirty and would want to wash themselves. They would sing *gožǫsį* ['happiness songs'] and by doing this they would pray.[2] They did not sing all these songs. There were too many of them. We sang about twelve *nantasį* ['chief songs']. After that we sang any songs we wanted to, *diyįsį* ['power songs'] for any power, Snake, Lightning, Deer—any kind —it didn't matter. The twelve chief songs are called chief songs because in them the people are instructed how to live, just as a chief instructs his people in the ways of living when he talks to them early in the morning. We only sing four of these songs at a time in sweat bath, then come out. It takes three times in sweat bath to sing them. Then the fourth time we sing any kind of song. We made the sweat bath big enough to hold eight to twelve men— a big one. The day after we got back the women used to wash our hair out. The second day we took this sweat bath. We did it in daytime, never at night. Not only the men who had been to war went in the sweat bath, but men who had stayed at home also went because they would want to hear the stories of what happened.

On the warpath we used to make sweat baths and sing in them. At these times we used to sing 'happiness songs' and 'horse songs.' That's the only songs we sang at all on the warpath. But when we got back we could sing any kind of songs. On the warpath, if a man knew any 'enemies-against power,' he would go away by himself and talk to his power. This power was never sung to on the war-path in the sweat bath. Nor was it used on a man's return. It was dangerous to use around women and children.

14

SCALPING

Scalping took place shortly after the victim had been slain and only in enemy territory. Judging from Goodwin's notes, the taking of a single scalp was usually considered sufficient, probably because no more were needed for the short ceremonial that followed. The decision to scalp rested solely with individual warriors, but it is noteworthy that those who lacked 'enemies-against power' may have had special motives for engaging in this practice. No other form of mutilation is reported, and there is no evidence to suggest that captives were scalped.

 It is called *bɨtsaʔha dogɨž* ['his head top cut off']. We used to scalp our enemy in the enemy's country, but our men never brought the scalps home. I never saw this done; I just heard about it. They may have done this to gain 'enemies-against power.' Also they might do it to show how much they hated their enemy. They used to spear a man three or four times through the body after he was dead, just to show how much they hated him. After the battle they would get together and cut scalps off the enemy and carry them about on the end of a pole. They may have had some ways of praying to them I think. I think they would only keep them one day. They would not keep them during a night. They would be scared of them—of ghosts. When they cut the scalp off, they put it on the end of a pole and danced about with it.

It doesn't have to be the man who killed the enemy that scalps him, and dances about with it. Anyone can do it. All have a right to, the man who killed the enemy also.

A man who knows 'enemies-against power,' after he cuts the scalp off the enemy, he might talk words to it from his power. This way he makes the White people weaker by it, not so strong and able to look out for themselves. When he cuts the scalp off he might mention all the Whites, Mexicans, Navajos, all Indian enemies, any enemy. When he talks to the scalp, whatever race it belongs to is made weaker by his talking to it. That is why this is done. I think that they must have done it for that purpose.

When they were through with the scalp they would put it up in a big tree, so no coyote could get it. They would just throw it up in a big bush or tree, just so it would not fall on the ground. Nothing was wrapped about it; it would not be taken care of just because it was an enemy's scalp.

They would never scalp enemies among their own people, among their own group. Only real enemies like Navajo, Mexicans, Whites. Even then they didn't do this scalping every time—just sometimes on occasions.

I never heard of taking any other part of an enemy but his scalp. Never his fingers or ears.

We never heard of eating any part of our enemies. We never did anything like that. This almost makes me sick to my stomach, it is so terrible to think about.

When they scalped an enemy they sang one song over it, a special song. The song goes on about—"I will get a piece of the enemy's ribs, and I will get a piece of the enemy's backbone for me." It goes on and tells about that. That is all there is to it. They did not take a scalp and bring it home, but the way they did was to capture prisoners and take them back home.

Yes, I have heard that they used to scalp one man if they killed enemies down in Mexico. They took this scalp right there and danced with it right there in a circle about the dead man they had scalped. They tied the scalp to the end of a spear and held it aloft and danced all in a circle about the dead one.

When the scalp is taken off there is no taboo or respect to it. It is taken off any way because the man doing it is mad and does not have to treat it gently. I don't know if he talks to the scalp as if he were talking to his enemy or not. I have not heard if he said any words.

15

THE VICTORY CELEBRATION

The return of a successful raiding expedition — or war party if it came back with livestock — was celebrated with a performance of 'enemies their property dance.' The primary purpose of this dance was to provide women who were not relatives of the raiders, or who had no man to look after them, with a share of the spoils. This they could obtain simply by singing for a raider or by choosing him for social dancing. A truly festive event with few (if any) ritual overtones, 'enemies their property dance' was accompanied by high spirits, clowning, and the relaxation of normal sanctions against sexual promiscuity.

When a war party came back, the warriors there used to dress just in a G-string, and paint themselves up also like they had done before they went to fight. The warriors used to paint a white band across the chest, over the right shoulder, and under the left arm. This was all spotted with black. Over the left shoulder and under the right arm they painted a white band also. Sometimes they spotted this band with red, and sometimes left it plain. Different clans, among our people, didn't use to paint themselves differently at this time.

When they got back they would butcher their horses and cattle and give away the meat to all the people. Some they would give away alive for use.

Now, that night, they would send out notice that there was to be a dance so that all the people would come. Before the dance men used to go around in a bunch with their rifles. They would sneak up on the camp of one of the men who had killed some Mexicans on the warpath this time. They would be careful not to let that man see them.

When they had surrounded his camp, then they would start shooting and yelling and make believe to attack his camp. The man would run out and pretend to be scared and surprised. Then right there, those men who had surrounded his camp would start to sing and dance.

The man from the camp would go to where they were dancing. When he came they would holler loudly and sing about how they had won it [meat]. "Yes, you have won it," the man would say. And he would tell them what they had won; maybe a horse of such-and-such a description, or a cow. "Tomorrow I will butcher it for you," he would say.[1]

In the evening, when they held the real dance, they built a big fire and danced around it in a big circle, men and women, young men and girls together. They had a man there who knew the right songs, and drums also.

Sometimes one or two *bɨžan* ['widow'; 'divorcee'] would get out there all fixed up and dance for the man who was giving the dance, or someone of the men who had been on the warpath this time. These women would not go back to their regular clothes till the man they had danced for had paid them a horse, or steer, or something. Then when they had been paid, they would take off this rig and go back to regular clothes. You had to pay any woman or girl you danced with at one of these dances.

During the dance the man who was leading the songs would call out for them to stop dancing. Then he would say the man's name who was giving the dance. "That horse of yours, spotted with White man's or Mexican's blood, I want it for myself," he would say; "I sing for it," and he would describe the horse he meant. Then the man would have to give him that horse the next day.

The regular dance lasted either one or two nights till the man who gave the dance paid up the dancers. The man who gave the dance had to be someone who was rich and who had just killed some enemy on the warpath. A poor man, even though he had killed some of the enemy, could not afford it.

After coming back from a raid or the warpath with lots of horses and American cattle, they would hold a dance, for the women, called *inda bigidɛgojitał* ['enemies their property dance']. There would be lots of people there. The women didn't dance for nothing. When they were singing, the women would call out and ask for a horse, or blanket, or calico—all kinds of things. The men did this also, and those who had captured these things would have to give them to the people who asked this way for them.

At a victory dance grown women without husbands danced without clothes, in their G-strings. Girls and maidens did not.

Women did not paint themselves in the victory dance to look like a man on the warpath. They danced without clothes because they wanted to get something from him. It was doing him an honor to dance this way for him, and it was a pretty thing, all painted up on body. They would thank him in this way for killing an enemy who had killed their relatives some time before. Also they would ask for gifts. About midnight he would go out and dance with these women just once. Then the women would leave, and he would go back into his camp. The women would say we have what we came after now that we have danced with him. He would know what they wanted.

At a victory dance, *bɨžan* ['widow'; 'divorcee'] only danced without clothes. Sometimes they danced in small G-strings and with a handkerchief tied around their breasts. Young girls and married women would not do this.

During the victory dance things sort of opened up and there was license, but only in regard to the *bɨžan*, not married women or girls. It was all right for men to go off with *bižan* the nights of dance. But other times this license did not exist.

One time at a victory dance, one woman took all her clothes off and cut a piece of stomach out of a horse, and put it between her legs. She went and danced by some girls. They all ran off, and youths also, because they were ashamed.[2]

One time at a victory dance an old man stripped and danced naked, without a G-string. But he tied a piece of bear hide between his legs; it had a hole in it. Through the hole he ran a throat of a cow so it hung down between his legs and swung back and forth as he danced. Some maidens and youths would not go there to dance, because they were ashamed. He kept it on all day and the next night. Some people said, "Don't do that any more. No boys or girls came to the dance on account of it last night."

They used to have some great war parties in the old days. I remember one time when a war party came back, and they set up a dance. One of the men gave a horse he had captured to be butchered. They killed the horse and started to cut it up before they had stopped hiding. They never bothered to skin it, just cut the meat out in chunks, with the hide on it. That's the way they used to do.

They got all the guts out, and there was a hole cut in the side of the horse. One man in the crowd went there and was reaching in the hole trying to get some of the meat. Someone pushed him and he fell right inside, and got smeared all over with blood. When he climbed out he had nothing at all, and everyone laughed at him.

The man I heard singing most at victory dances was a little short man called *hastin diłhił* ['Old Man Black']. He used to wear an owl-feather cap. He knew those songs the best. But I don't know who made the songs in the beginning. They came down from the beginning of Earth I guess. I think he didn't make any of these himself, but learned them at the dances when he was a boy. I wanted to know where these songs came from so I asked my mother's mother one time, "Is this your song?" "No, I did not make these. They come from long, long ago," she said. No one ever taught a man these songs. He just picked them up at dances. He never paid to learn them.

The little old man who used to sing at victory dances didn't get paid. But he was given a piece of meat. He was old and used a cane to get about with.

One time we asked the old man, "Why do you wear that owl cap on your head?" "Well, when you walk alone at night and wear it, nothing bothers you. You can't hear any owls at all," he said.[3]

16

CAPTIVES

It is impossible to determine from Goodwin's notes how often Western Apache war parties returned home with captives or under what circumstances this was considered a primary objective. It is clear, however, that adult captives were not taken for economic purposes (i.e. to become slaves), but rather so they could be killed by female relatives of the men whose death the war party had been sent to avenge. A sister or close maternal cousin was generally given the privilege of striking the final blow, and was thereby afforded the satisfaction of personally compensating for the death of her kinsmen.

The women were given a captive to be killed I think because it made him suffer a little longer. Men could put him out of his misery quicker; it would take longer for women to, as they were not as skilled. But the real reason is that if a woman's relative was killed in Mexico then the woman relative closest to that man, maybe his sister, would be avenged by a war party sent down to Mexico. If any prisoner was brought back she would be the one in charge of killing him. But the women who helped her do it would not have to be all of the same clan. They could be of any clan.

The woman in charge had the first shot, I think; then after her each woman had her chance shooting, or with a spear, to see who would finally kill him. But they never scalped the captive. They just buried the body, because if they didn't it would stink.

One time I heard that they captured a Mexican on a raid and brought him back. They had a victory dance. They turned this man over to the women to kill. They shot him with bows and arrows. Some of the women shot the man pretty good, and the arrows stuck into his body, but others did not pull the string hard enough, and the arrows bounced back and fell on the ground.

One time they captured two Mexicans and brought them back here. One of them was a Mexican captain, and these two men were made to dance with two women. Then as they danced, the chief under whom the dance was given rode up to them and said to the captain: "You know that these two women you are dancing with here will be the ones to kill you in a little while?" "No, there is never a woman who will kill me at all. I am not a woman, I am a man," the captain said.

But pretty soon they took these two men and bound their hands behind their backs and led them over to the foot of a hill. Some of the women went with rifles, and it was these who shot and killed them. Pretty soon they came back bearing the arms and legs of the two men. They danced with these.

It was when the captive was killed that they scalped him and danced with his scalp as I told you. They sometimes scalped on the warpath, but they did not dance over it—just threw it away and never brought it back home.

⑤

This is how it happened. This side of Phoenix a war party went. My father was along. He had a spear and later fought with it there. When the party got near the Pimas' home that night, a chief with them called *tlanagudε* ['Big Hips, Heavy'] made a drum right there from cowhide, and got it all ready for the time when they would start the fight in the morning.

When it got early morning he threw a rock up in the air and kept on doing this every so often till he could see it all right. Then he knew it was time to start the attack because it would also be light enough to be able to see arrows and dodge them. "Now let's go," he said, "but first let's sing once more, and then we will go into the fight, as we may get killed." So they sang one more song and then started for the Pima village.

They set fire to the Pima tipis. 'Big Hips, Heavy' Started to hit his drum, and kept on hitting it while the men went into the fight. They killed lots of Pima men and only one Pima man got away. He saved his life by fleeing to the top of a high sharp point down towards Phoenix. I saw it one time when I was in the scouts over that way.

Well, they got all the Pima women and girls in one bunch and then killed all the older ones, just saving the good, younger ones to take back with them.

Captives that they brought home and let live were called *yodasčin*, which means 'born outside' [i.e. not in the Apache country]. There are lots of them at Cibecue.

Sometimes when they brought back a Mexican captive that they didn't want to keep, they would make him dance all night with them. Then in the morning they would kill him.

One time the Chiricahua captured a boy who was a relation of mine. They took this boy off to their own country. When they got home, they started a dance that night, and they made this boy dance all night with them also. The boy didn't know what was going to happen; he thought this was all for fun.

In the morning the medicine man said he was going to sing four songs, and then they were to kill the boy. He made the men lay their guns on the ground, all in a row. The medicine man started in to sing four songs. In between each song they would stop and make a prayer. When the fourth song was sung they shot the boy, but his body was still shaking, so they shot him again and killed him.

One time, my relatives had an Apache Manso captive. He was captured and raised among our people. He was a boy about twelve or fifteen years old, old enough to know his own mind.

Then he ran off back to his own people in Tucson. When this boy ran off to Tucson he saw all Whites and Mexicans in Tucson. He knew now where our people lived most of the time. So they appointed him a leader for the Mexicans. From that time on there were a lot of attacks on our people because this captive knew where our people would be at different times of year. He knew where all the springs were and where our people camped.

If an Apache was captured for one day or one year or more, when he escaped and got back he did not have to have any ceremony performed over him at all. He was not unclean from that. He just came back and started in where he left off. Nothing was ever done over him.

17

THE NOVICE COMPLEX

In most Apachean cultures, the training of adolescent boys in pre-reservation times was directed towards attaining proficiency in activities connected with raiding and warfare. It is not surprising, therefore, that in several of these tribes, including the Western Apache, the nearest thing to a formal initiation ceremony took place on the occasion of a youth's first raiding expedition. During the entire expedition, the youth's behavior was regulated by a set of ritual proscriptions which, if properly observed, were believed to assure him and his party of safety and success. These proscriptions, together with the training which prepared a boy to observe them, comprise what other writers on the Southern Athabascans have called the "novice complex" (c.f. Opler and Hoijer 1940).

Strictly speaking, the novice complex began four days before a Western Apache youth departed for his first raid. At this time, he was introduced to the taboos he would be required to observe, instructed in the men's warpath language, and given several important items of ritual paraphernalia. The novice's instruction ended the night before he left for enemy territory, and early the following morning, just prior to his departure, a short ceremonial was performed to protect him against adversity or mishap.

A novice on his first raid did not take part in the actual stealing of livestock. He was taken within a mile or so of the enemy's camp and told to search for a high point of land from which he could study all that went on. Usually, an older man remained behind with him to comment on matters of tactics and strategy. In this way, the boy was able to acquire much valuable knowledge without risking injury or death.

As soon as it became apparent that the raid was a success, the novice left his vantage point, rejoined his comrades, and prepared to help them drive the livestock home. At regular intervals along the way—and especially if the enemy was following close behind—he was called upon to protect his party by performing ritual acts. No ceremonial was held to celebrate a novice's return home. He might be given a horse or two by the man who had led the raid, but this was not mandatory.

When a boy was from fifteen to seventeen years old he was old enough to go on a raid. The first time he went he could not be just like the real warriors, but had to act sort of as a servant to the others. He was advised what to do by his father or nearest male kin. He had to be careful how he acted.

When a boy is old enough to go on the warpath for the first time, he goes to some man who understands about war, a person not his relative. This man teaches the boy how to act and speak on the warpath, and all how he must do, so he will know about it.

For four days before the boy went on his first raid he was instructed by an old man about how he had to do. Then at the end of this instruction a drinking tube and scratcher were made for him. Then just before he left with the other men for Mexico, these were placed on him and they sang four songs over him. The man that they will get to instruct him will sometimes be his kin, sometimes not. If he is not, then he is regularly hired and paid for it.

He teaches the boy for a little while each of the four days, not all day, and he does not teach him any 'power' or medicine at all. He just teaches him practical things that he should do on different emergencies on the raid path, and all the taboos that he must observe and that a man must observe on the raid path. The man that they get to teach the boy is some man who is a good raider, and has been to Mexico many times.

My maternal grandfather taught one boy he should act this way. It was his maternal grandson. The boy is instructed not to look back towards home for four days after he leaves to go to raid.

When you eat don't open your mouth wide; a boy is taught this. Also he is told not to drink before others on the raid path, but to wait.

My grandfather taught the boy for four days before he left. He taught him in the daytime only, by himself in a wickiup. This lasted only about half the day, this teaching. It was not at night. They let no one in while he taught him. I heard what I did from outside.

It was my maternal grandfather, the same one, who made the scratcher and the drinking tube and war cap for the boy and put them on him. When they tied the feathers on top of the hat he used Gambel quail feathers. "White Man will be scared of that," my maternal grandfather said. "You know how quail jump right out from under you and scare you."

The war cap of a novice was different from that of a warrior. A man's war cap was made plain, just a cap with large eagle feathers on it. There were no words said over it. But a novice's cap had hummingbird pinfeathers from each wing, the first front feathers. Also he had little breast feathers from oriole tied about the base of the larger feathers.[1] Also small quail breast feathers, and downy eagle feathers.[2] This made four. The hummingbird feathers in there were to make him run fast, so no one could see him, just like hummingbird. But there was no painting on the cap at all. The boy wore no abalone like a puberty girl does.[3]

The war cap of a boy novice is different from that of a man. There is no power in the former's, but it has four different feathers

in it, quail, eagle down, oriole down, and two wing pinfeathers of
hummingbird for speed.

Before a boy went on his first warpath he didn't go to any
medicine man to learn about 'enemies-against power,' because he
was only a young boy and not experienced enough to learn such
things.[4] It would be dangerous for him to fool with anything
like that.

Only after he had become a successful warrior and had luck
and had minded what the other men had told him, then only
would he be able to learn about 'enemies-against power' from the
men who knew it. If he was not a successful warrior, or didn't
do as he had been ordered, then he would never learn about such
things, for they would not tell him.

That's the reason why among all our people there are only a
few men who understand war medicine, and because they did
understand it they were successful. That's why they are always
the ones who had lots of cattle and horses, and property. The
majority of men do not know this medicine.

Such a man who knows this medicine, the rest would follow
anywhere on the warpath. He fought only with a shield and spear.
With them he would ride right into Mexican and American soldiers
and stay there, killing them with his spear. He never could get
scared and run.

Just before the raiding party starts in the morning, the novice
boy stands there, and men, women and children will each take
pollen and form in a line and put pollen on the boy, praying to
him as they do.[5] They pray for lots of spoils, cows and horses,
and that the raiders will bring back many and that no White man
will see them. Praying to him that way, all those things will come
easy. At this same time they put the drinking tube and scratcher
on him. They also sing four *gožǫsi* ['happiness songs'] over him
there, and while they sing he has to dance there.[6] But I don't know
which four songs these are. He has a stripe of pollen painted
across his face. Sometimes they will hold this ceremony for two

boys at the same time who are going, just as they do for two girls sometimes.

When the party leaves they put pollen over him and pray, "Let everything be easy for you." A whole line of women and men do just as they do at *nai?ɛs* ['girls' puberty ceremonial'] and put pollen on him one by one. "We all feel good and laugh on our way," they get him to say. This means nothing will happen to him. Some say, "It will never wear out, what we are wearing." They tell the boy to say this for them. This way his moccasins will never wear out.

Also when he leaves they tell him to come back in thirty days, so the boy has to say, "I will come back in thirty days." Then if he says it, it comes true. Also they make him say, "These two things I must have in my mind—horses and cattle—so I would like to have these," and he makes a gathering motion with his arms to gather them up. But they don't pray to kill lots of enemies at all. That is different; that is 'enemies-against power.' Just cattle and horses they ask for from the boy.

A boy on his first raiding party could not take a shield and say, "Let no bullets go through this." He has no power for that. Everyone thinks well, not about war or fighting or death. They think only about the cattle they will bring home.

A boy at this time is called *sanbitigiše* ['old age beckoning to him.'] They say to him, "You are the same as a puberty girl today.[7] You have a drinking tube and scratcher, so you must not look around, and do just as you are supposed to do."

The men all have a bag in which they pack food, but the boy novice carried nothing but a bow and four arrows. Each of these is a bird arrow, with a wooden point. The reason for taking these arrows is that they are not for war—just for hunting. If there are flint points on the arrows, it means war, angriness, trouble, and death. They don't want the boy to think about this kind of thing at all. They want to keep his mind straight and his thoughts good.

A boy novice's parents and siblings pray for him while he is gone. His mother has to pray for him every morning for four days after he leaves. She prays, "Let my son have everything easy." Horses and cattle she means.

A novice boy must only drink through his cane tube, for if water touched his lips he would get a mustache. He must only scratch himself with the wooden scratcher, which can be made from any piece of wood. He must not eat the insides of animals, but only the plain meat.

He had to pack mescal and rawhide for moccasin soles for himself as well as the others. He also carried arms for the others, as well as himself sometimes. He often carried extra arrows in a quiver for the others. He had to get firewood in camp and do the cooking, as well as all other camp work.

If he was not closely observing the rules about drinking, scratching, and eating of meat, he would get blisters on his feet and his muscles would get sore, and in this way the others would find out about it.

The first time a youth goes on a raiding party he has to work hard and act as sort of servant to the older men. He also must carry a little stick to scratch himself with and a short section of cane to suck water through, as he must not let his lips touch water. If he does, hair will grow on his upper lip. While on the raid path he must call all things by their sacred names.

A novice boy cannot swim or wash his face for four days before he starts on his first two raids until he gets back. Also he cannot cross a river unless he has to on the raid path. The reason that he must keep away from water is that a big rain will come if he gets wet. The second time he has the same water taboo.[8]

A boy novice also has to sleep on a mano for four days before he goes, and on a rock when on the raid path for four days, the same way, so he won't go to sleep. Also he has to sleep with his head to the east for the whole duration till he gets home. Also he must be the first to get up in the morning. When he gets home he can sleep any way and can bathe and do all. All taboos are lifted.

Before he goes on his first raid, a boy sleeps with his head on a rock or mano. Bathing or having water on him causes a rainstorm. His mind is especially kept off evil, violent things like war.

The first time he goes they tell him he must not drink water from a pool or river, but he must drink it from a drinking tube made for him of cane. To this is tied a stick with which he scratches himself if he itches.

The second time he goes on the raid path he is told that he must not sleep at night, but get up every so often and run around in the dark. Then in the early morning he does this. There will be a hill with a tree on top of it close to the camp, and he has to run up the hill to that tree and urinate on it. Then he scratches dirt over where he urinated, like a coyote does, and then hollers like a coyote does. This way they tell him to do so that he will be like a coyote and always be able to steer clear of trouble and be smart when he goes to war.

Also on his second raiding party they will never let him eat hot food, only cold food. "If you eat hot food, then later on your teeth will drop out," they tell him. After the second war party, he can eat hot food, and do just as a regular raider.

Wherever they go to raid this boy has to go in front, at the head, for four days. He must not look back or look around. He must look straight ahead where he goes. They stop at noon; then, after they eat, they start on again. They stop again at night. But after four days a boy can look anywhere he wants.

On the warpath a boy is always at the front for four days. No one must ever pass him when he sits down. They all stay behind. It is this way till they get to the Mexican towns. On the way back it is not this way.

All the way, from the time they leave till they get back, this boy does not go right in front—the chief does that—but wherever he does go, if he should stop in the line, then all the other men have to, and if he should sit down, then all the other men have to do the same way. But if he should sit down this way they will tell him right there that he should not do this way any more. The reason is that if the boy does this he is likely to keep on being this way—sort of heavy—and the men tell him that if he does that it will make them heavy also.

Also each morning on the way down and back, the boy must make a run for a way and then back again. This is so that he will be a good runner. It is only for the first two times that he goes to war that he has these taboos. The third time he goes he will be like a regular man.

The men along with him would tell the boy to exercise, run, in the early morning around the camp. At night they would tell him he must learn not to sleep hard, and to make himself a pillow of sharp rocks, so that if he should fall asleep, his head would roll off it and wake him up.

Yes, it is true that the first time a boy went on a raid he had certain taboos to observe; he could eat no guts. But he could eat the lungs of animals, and such a boy had to eat the lungs while out this way, so that he and all the men with him would be light and swift. His doing it stood for all the others.

On the way and after they get to the land where they are going to raid, they will get this boy to say: "We are going to get lots of horses," or "There will be lots of cattle for us," and this way it will come true. Also, after they get the horses or cattle, then if that boy eats any of the guts of these animals, the cattle will go dead on the way home.

⟨⟨⟨

It is true though that a boy, the first time that he goes on a raid, must not take a bath or have water poured on him at all. If he does there will come a great rainstorm—a bad one—so they are taught about this. None of the other men going along can take a bath either down there, but if they did nothing would come of it like a rainstorm. But as soon as they arrive home, the day after, they will all take a sweat bath, and from then on the boy can swim all he likes and no harm will come of it. He takes the sweat bath also.

Down in Mexico, when they finally get their horses and cattle together and are ready to drive them home, they ask the boy to say for them, "Don't let *nančin* [the warpath term for Mexicans and Whites] think about their cattle and horses. Don't let them miss them. Let us take them home easily."

On the raid, on their way home, a boy like this would some-times be told to draw four lines across their trail so no enemy could follow them at all. Men knowing 'enemies-against power' did the same thing also.

Down in Mexico when they start to drive cattle home, then they tell the boy to draw a line on the ground and say, "Let no one pass over this." A little farther on they do this again, till they have done it four times. That way no enemies will follow and catch them.

They never mention enemies right out on the warpath. They always said *nančin*. "Now we have what we want, so we might as well go," the men say. Lots of our people believe that luck happened from a novice boy.

When a boy gets back he gives his drinking tube and scratcher and hat to his mother, and she puts them away in a buckskin sack for him till he goes the second time. They are then taken out again and he uses them in just the same way. He does the same things, has the same powers, and is taught for four days by his instructor before he leaves. Then when he gets back the second time, it is all over.

From then on there are no more taboos for him. He gives the scratcher and tube with the oriole feathers tied to it to his mother again. She will put it away for another son to use in the same way later on, sometime, when he is ready.

On his return the drinking tube and scratcher are never saved but are always put away up a tree someplace, and prayed to in the doing of it. All pray to this: "May we always be lucky as we were with him [the boy] this time. May no one ever get killed as no one was this time."

If anything happened to the original owner of the cap and scratcher and drinking tube, the set was all put away and never used. But if he was a lucky warrior and killed enemies, got lots of cattle, they would want to keep them and use them, and thus other users would be like him.

When a boy who has been on a raid the first time gets home he will take his scratcher and drinking tube and hang them up in a tree somewhere. But I don't know if he prays at this time or not. He just does all this for himself, out of respect for his life, for he has never been to war before and does not know what it means or what goes on down there. The other people respect him for this also.

When they had a war dance to avenge killed relatives, novice boys never got in there. Only the men who had been to Mexico before—never novice boys. It was only after our people had been to war that they had the victory dance. For just a plain cattle raid there was no war dance or victory dance at all. It was plain cattle raids that novices went on only. They went when everything was happy, never when men's hearts were mad or when they intended to fight. When a novice boy got home there was nothing done for him, nor was he sung over, or any ceremony for him. But sometimes they would give him four cattle and three horses first of all, even before the chief, and he got more than the others. This was because he had been sort of the head of things.

REFERENCE MATERIAL

NOTES TO THE TEXT

Pages 32–43

PART I

1   ANNA PRICE

1   The Western Apache made horseshoes from pieces of cowhide softened in water. They were fitted over the hoof like a low boot and gave protection against thorns and sharp stones.

2   Prior to a raid, it was customary for the men who were going to take part to meet in a sweat bath and discuss their plans.

3   For descriptions of the 'war dance' that preceded the departure of war parties see Part II of this volume, Chapter 8.

4   The manufacture and use of war shields are described in Part II of this volume, Chapter 7.

5   Diablo is alluding to the fact that the Navajo and White Mountain Apache often traded peacefully with one another and, on such occasions, displayed the friendliness and goodwill characteristic of persons who share food.

6   The events recounted in Anna Price's narrative probably took place between 1855 and 1865, when the Navajo were warring with U.S. troops in New Mexico.

2   PALMER VALOR

1   Canyon Day, a long-time Western Apache (White Mountain band) settlement, is located approximately five miles west of Fort Apache.

2   Prior to the establishment of U.S. military control in Arizona Territory, the Western Apache raided deep into Mexico. It is difficult to determine precisely where they went, but many of their thrusts were aimed at villages along the coast of Sonora. Hence their knowledge of the "sea," i.e., the Gulf of California.

3   Even today the Western Apache maintain strong taboos against eating or handling 'things that come from water' (*tudnde ?yo*).

4   The Mogollon Mountain Valor referred to in this passage is a prominent peak in the Mogollon Mountains of west-central New Mexico.

5   At an early age, Apache boys were encouraged to prepare themselves for raiding and warfare. They practiced constantly with bow and arrow, ran overland for long distances, and swam regularly in mountain streams. For further information see Goodwin's *The Social Organization of the Western Apache*, pp. 428–521.

6   Palmer Valor's mother may have been recalling a meteoric shower, visible throughout Arizona, which occurred November 13, 1833. See also Leslie Spier (1933) *Yuman Tribes of the Gila River*, pp. 138–39.

7   The leaves and stems of wild daisies were believed by the Western Apache to have medicinal properties and were used in a variety of curing ceremonials.

8   In the early and middle 1800s, the Western Apache regularly embarked on raids on foot, leaving behind what horses they had to provide food for women and children.

9   For detailed descriptions of the 'victory dance' that was held to celebrate the return of successful war parties see Part II of this volume, Chapter 15.

10   The "enemies" Valor refers to here could have been Navajos, but more likely they were Pimas or Papagos. Navajo forays into Western Apache territory appear to have been relatively infrequent, but there is evidence to suggest that the Pima and Papago mounted attacks against the Apache as often as two or three times a year (Underhill 1938, 1939; Ezell 1961). At the time Valor is referring to, presumably the period between 1850 and 1860, Mexican troops stationed at Tucson rarely went north of the Gila River. Regardless of who the "enemies" were, it is noteworthy that they chose to attack when the men of the local group were absent.

11   Persons with 'horse power' were believed to be able to control the actions of the animals and make them docile and easy to handle. In addition, 'horse power' could be used to locate herds and, on raiding expeditions, lure them to places where they could be easily surrounded and driven off. For additional information on supernatural power and its uses see Part II of this volume, Chapter 13.

12   Apaches claim that the acquisition of supernatural power precipitates noticeable changes in an individual's personality. Among other things, a man becomes less fearful and makes no attempt to avoid dangerous situations.

13   The Western Apache took sweat baths for cleanliness as well as to cure certain types of sickness. The sweat lodge had a dome-shaped framework of sticks, bent over and tied in place, which was covered with several layers of blankets. Stones were heated and taken inside where water was thrown over them to make steam.

14   This passage is difficult to interpret. At the time Palmer Valor is speaking of, presumably between 1850 and 1865, there were no U.S. troops in the vicinity of Turkey Creek. It is possible that the officer he mentions was Col. E. A. Rigg, who established Camp Goodwin in 1864, but this seems unlikely. Perhaps Valor meant that a message was sent to his people by an officer far away. This would make the most sense in view of the events that follow.

15   In a note to the original typescript of Palmer Valor's narrative, Grenville Goodwin wrote: "The soldiers whom the Apaches joined on their way to Fort Wingate were almost certainly not Mexicans. They were probably New Mexico militia composed of several companies of Ute Indians. The time of the event was

during the campaign against the Navajos, 1864–1865, which was led by Kit Carson. The White officer might well have been Carson himself." In view of these remarks, I have taken the liberty of replacing the term "Mexican(s)" with "New Mexican(s)," a change Goodwin probably would have made himself.

16   The Apaches went after the horses to prevent the Navajo from escaping. The New Mexican soldiers, apparently over-anxious for blood, neglected this tactic with the result that many of the Navajo got away.

17   This meeting probably occurred in either 1858 or 1859 at a place called 'urinating toward the water' in Canyon del Oro on the west side of the Santa Catalina Mountains near Tucson. For additional details see Goodwin 1942:22.

18   Located near a spring on the south bank of the Gila River, Camp Goodwin was established June 12, 1864 by Colonel E. A. Rigg and Lt. Colonel Nelson Davis with California Volunteers. The "White officer" Valor refers to was probably Colonel Rigg. For further information about Camp Goodwin see the narrative of John Rope.

19   Speeches of this sort were made prior to battle in an attempt to dispel fear and fire confidence. The enemy is typically portrayed as having developed from a weak and defenseless condition (infancy) and this, in turn, is held up as a sign of his vulnerability.

20   Men who hid during battle or who ran from the enemy were subjected to biting ridicule, especially from the women of their clan and local group.

3   JOSEPH HOFFMAN

1   A camp site in the territory of the Canyon Creek band (Cibecue subtribal group), this settlement was apparently located near some prehistoric cliff dwellings.

2   Canyon Creek rises under the Mogollon Rim, flows southeast through the Fort Apache Indian Reservation, and finally joins the Salt River in Gila County.

3   A farm site of the Canyon Creek band (Cibecue subtribal group), 'cottonwoods growing out' was located somewhere along Canyon Creek itself, probably a few miles south of the present site of Chediskai Farms.

4   Hoffman is describing here a segment of the 'victory dance' which was held to celebrate the return of successful war parties. The women who stripped down to their G-strings and ambushed the war chief were widows and/or divorcees. For a fuller description of this and other aspects of the 'victory dance' see Part II of this volume, Chapter 15.

5   For descriptions of war shields and how they were manufactured see Part II of this volume, Chapter 7.

6   The woman's comment to the war chief has been given a literal translation in the text and, for this reason, may be difficult to understand. It may be re-phrased as follows: "For a man, young and strong, there are few better ways to die than in the killing of a White enemy."

7   The two clans mentioned in this passage belonged to the same phratry and were considered "closely related." It was on this basis that their members sought each other's help. For a detailed description of the Western Apache phratry system see Goodwin (1942) and Kaut (1957).

8   In this instance, the kinship term probably denotes the speaker's father's matrilateral parallel cousins.

9   Because Hoffman's father had given his young relatives permission to go raiding, he felt directly responsible for their deaths. Having mourned alone for many months, he was now ready to seek revenge.

10   If Hoffman's account of the Navajo campaign is factually correct, the predictions of 'Hears Like Coyote' give ample support to the belief that men with 'war power' could predict future events with extraordinary accuracy. There is a strong possibility, however, that Hoffman related his story with the aim of portraying medicine men as infallible. If so, predictions that turned out to be false would be overlooked or purposely excluded. In any event, the narrative as a whole illustrates with unusual clarity and detail the manner in which an influential medicine man could affect the organization and direction of war parties.

11   By permitting a woman to sing or dance with him at a victory celebration, a man obligated himself to present her with a substantial gift. For additional details on this practice see Part II of this volume, Chapter 15.

4   JOHN ROPE

1   Detailed information on Western Apache irrigation systems, which at certain farm sites were quite extensive, may be found in Buskirk (1949).

2   A staple food of the Western Apache, the acorns of Emory's oak were gathered in July and August and stored away in sacks. In the winter, the acorns were shelled, and the meats mashed on a stone to produce a coarse meal. This was mixed with cooked meat and other foods.

3   Another Apache staple, juniper berries were gathered in the late fall. They were allowed to dry and were then boiled in water until soft. Next, they were ground into a pulp and molded into balls which could be stored for future use. Prepared in this way, the food has a sweet flavor and is quite palatable.

4   At the time of these events—probably around 1860—the White Mountain Apache had not yet acquired canvas, matches, etc., from the Whites.

5   Cedar bark torches were used as slow matches to carry fire from camp to camp.

6   Located on the south bank of the Gila River six miles below Camp Thomas, Camp Goodwin was established June 12, 1864 by Col. Edwin A. Rigg and Lt. Colonel Nelson Davis with California Volunteers. It was abandoned due to malaria March 14, 1871. Before Rigg relinquished his command on August 11, 1864, he apparently succeeded in persuading several influential Apaches, Diablo among them, that the White soldiers were anxious for peace. In the years that followed, the White Mountain bands, together with those from the Cibecue region, did relatively little raiding and, after General George Crook assumed command of the Department of Arizona on May 2, 1871, provided him with many skilled and trustworthy scouts.

7   The hay was used as fodder for the soldiers' horses.

8   This firearm was probably the Model 1855 or 1861 Springfield rifled musket (calibre .58).

9   Known to Whites as Diablo, 'He is Constantly Angry' was chief of the *nadostusn* clan ('slender peak standing up people') as well as the entire eastern White Mountain band. In pre-reservation times, his influence extended well beyond Apache country where he maintained alliances with the Hopi and Zuni. Apparently

an earnest seeker of peace, Diablo dealt honestly with Whites and urged his followers to abide by reservation regulations. Anna Price, one of Goodwin's most competent informants, was Diablo's daughter.

10 Presumably, the White officer called 'Wrinkled Neck' was either Colonel Edwin Rigg or Major Joseph Smith (5th California Infantry) who replaced Rigg in August of 1864.

11 In the spring of 1870, a road was built into the White Mountains of Arizona under the supervision of Major John Green (First Infantry). On May 16, a post was established at its terminus, near the present town of Whiteriver. Known briefly as Camp Ord, Mogollon, and Thomas, it was renamed Camp Apache on February 2, 1871. In September of the same year, Vincent Colyer, secretary to the Board of Peace Commissioners for the management of Indian affairs, visited Camp Apache and officially designated the surrounding area as a reservation.

In 1871–72 General George Crook—now commander of the Department of Arizona—journeyed to Camp Apache and there recruited his first company of Indian scouts. This post was of singular importance during Crook's subsequent campaigns into the Tonto Basin region, and gained added significance in the years following 1873 when, in accordance with Washington's ill-fated centralization policy, virtually all the mountain tribes of Arizona and New Mexico were concentrated on the San Carlos Reservation. Camp Apache was renamed Fort Apache on April 5, 1879 and in 1924 was turned over to the Indian Service for use as a boarding school.

12 In pre-reservation times, the five Western Apache subtribal groups were politically autonomous and operated independently of each other. Amicable relations prevailed most of the time but, as the events described above illustrate so well, this did not preclude the possibility of one group fighting against another.

13 Colorful, humane, and articulate, John P. Clum was appointed Indian Agent for the San Carlos Reservation in March, 1874. An outspoken critic of the military, he respected his Apache charges and was anxious to give them greater control over their own affairs. Accordingly, he created a four-man Indian police force and organized a court to try infractions of law and discipline. After the government's removal policy went into effect in 1875, it became Clum's duty to supervise the nearly four thousand Indians that were gathered at San Carlos. Unable to do so without interference from the military, which he considered both unnecessary and incendiary, Clum resigned in disgust on July 1, 1877.

14 The 'red rock strata people' were limited almost exclusively to the Carrizo band of the Cibecue group. They moved to the vicinity of Whiteriver in 1869, and were the only people on the Fort Apache Reservation who were not forced to go to San Carlos in 1875.

15 On this point, John Rope's chronology is incorrect. The first Apache scouts were recruited at Camp Apache in 1871–72. Rope is probably referring here to Clum's newly organized Indian police force. It should be noted, however, that many of the policemen at San Carlos in 1875 had been (or later became) scouts. Also, there is linguistic evidence which suggests that the Apache did not distinguish between the two. Scouts and police alike were designated by the borrowed Spanish term *salada*.

Goodwin notes that "eventually Apaches acquired the status of regular enlisted men. They were enlisted in companies of 25 men, and all non-coms were Apaches. The companies were commanded by a White officer. The pay for enlisted men was thirteen dollars a month, and the term of enlistment was for six months. The scouts were furnished with rifle, cartridge belt, canteen and blanket by the Government and could draw uniforms if they wished."

16   Situated in the heart of Chiricahua territory (a few miles south of the modern town of Bowie in Cochise County), Camp Bowie was established on July 28, 1862. During the two decades that followed, troops from this post were involved in numerous skirmishes with hostile Apaches. Camp Bowie was renamed Fort Bowie in 1879 and, in the early eighties, served as a vital en route camp for U.S. forces entering Mexico in pursuit of renegades. On April 2, 1886, the Chiricahua chief Chihuahua was brought to Fort Bowie, as were Geronimo and Nachez following their surrender a few months later. After Apache threats had ended in the Southwest, the fort lost its usefulness and was officially abandoned on October 17, 1894.

17   On May 3, 1876, Clum received orders to escort to San Carlos the Chiricahuas (mostly members of the central and southern bands) who had come to the reservation at Apache Pass. He arrived there on June 5, together with fifty-six of his Indian police. Two weeks later he returned to San Carlos with 325 Indians. Approximately four hundred others, under the recalcitrants Juh and Geronimo, eluded Clum and fled into Sonora.

18   Having completed the removal of the Chiricahuas at Fort Bowie, Clum's next assignment was to bring to San Carlos those camped at Ojo Caliente. Most of these people were members of the eastern (Warm Springs) Chiricahua band, at the time headed by Victorio. Clum arrived at Ojo Caliente with 102 Indian police on April 21, 1877, only to discover that Geronimo, with a force of between eighty and a hundred, was camped nearby. The next day, after concealing his police in the agency's commissary building, Clum persuaded Geronimo and several of his followers to come in for a talk. At a given signal, the commissary doors swung open and the renegades, taken completely by surprise, were easily captured. Victorio, who was not involved in this incident, agreed to go to San Carlos, and May 1 was set as a departure date. On that day there was an outbreak of smallpox, and it was not until May 20 that Clum, with 453 Chiricahuas, Victorio and Geronimo among them, reached his destination.

19   Camp Thomas was established on August 12, 1876, as a replacement for Camp Goodwin (located seven miles southwest), which had been abandoned because of malaria. Often described as the worst Army post in the southwest, Thomas served as an important supply station throughout the Chiricahua campaigns. It was renamed Fort Thomas in 1882, and was given over to the Department of the Interior ten years later.

20   Established in 1860, Camp Grant was first known as Fort Arivaypa. It was located on the Gila River near the mouth of the San Pedro, in the territory of the Western White Mountain Apache. To prevent capture by Confederate troops, Union officials had it destroyed on July 10, 1861. A year later, under the name Camp Stanford, the post was reestablished by California Volunteers. It became Camp Grant on November 1, 1865.

In 1871, a large area of land around Camp Grant was set aside as a reservation, and a group of some 300 Apaches (Arivaipa band; San Carlos group) settled peacefully nearby. Depredations on White settlements continued, however, and certain high-ranking citizens of Tucson charged that the Camp Grant Indians were responsible. On April 30, an enraged mob of 140 private citizens and Papago

Indians advanced on Camp Grant and killed over 100 Apaches. All but eight were women and children. This incident came to be known as the Camp Grant Massacre.

Due to an increase of malarial infections among resident troops, Camp Grant was moved on December 19, 1872, to the west side of Mount Graham, twenty-five miles north of Willcox. Two months later, approximately 1500 Pinal and Arivaipa Apaches (San Carlos group) were taken from Grant and moved to San Carlos. On April 5, 1879, the post name was altered to Fort Grant. It was officially abandoned in 1895.

21 Situated in the heart of Chiricahua Apache territory (central band) just south of the Dos Cabezas Mountains, the Chiricahua Mountains run north-south for a distance of about thirty miles. Throughout the 1870s, this rugged range provided a refuge and stronghold for renegade forces.

22 Rucker Canyon was formerly the site of Camp Powers, a small military post established in 1878 at the juncture of the north and south forks of the White River. On January 1, 1879, it was renamed for Lt. John A. Rucker of the Twelfth Infantry. Brandes (1960:63) writes: "Rucker drowned on July 11, 1878, in a mountain stream after trying unsuccessfully to rescue a fellow officer, Lt. Austin Henely, who had been caught in a flash flood." Almost certainly this was the drowning described by John Rope in the following pages.

23 Located in the Guadalupe Mountains, Guadalupe Canyon is a deep ravine in the extreme southeast corner of Arizona. It enters Sonora near the town of Estes, and was a favorite runway for Apache raiders with stolen livestock.

24 Among the Western Apache, older male relatives—especially siblings, maternal uncles, and maternal parallel cousins—possessed considerable authority over their younger kinsmen and regularly instructed them in matters of importance.

25 If they chose not to draw uniforms, Apache scouts were entitled to a refund at the end of their enlistment.

26 Unmarried Western Apache girls arranged their hair in a long hourglass shape which was fastened at the back of the neck with a piece of buckskin decorated with red cloth, beads and brass tacks.

27 "From this time on," Goodwin observes in a footnote, "Chiricahua scouts enlisted in campaigns against their own people, apparently because of sharply divided opinions."

28 The Winchester Mountains are located in southeast Arizona, northwest of Willcox, in Cochise County. Like the Chiricahua Mountains to the southeast and the Graham Mountains to the north, they served as a virtually impregnable retreat for renegade Chiricahuas.

29 It was not until General Crook's expedition into Mexico in 1883 (which John Rope later describes) that the Mexican government allowed U.S. troops to cross the international boundary in pursuit of hostile Apaches.

30 Cave Creek rises on the eastern slope of the Chiricahua Mountains and flows northeast into Sulphur Springs Valley.

31 Geronimo, together with several other noted warriors, had fled San Carlos April 4, 1878, for the Sierra Madre in Mexico. There he joined forces with Juh, leader of the southern Chiricahua band and probably the Apache referred to by Rope as 'He Brings Many Things With Him'. Shortly thereafter, Ogle (1940: 198) reports, they "established a heavy traffic in stolen goods with the citizens of

Janos." By July, 1879, it was learned where they were, and by early December they were anxious to surrender, at least for the winter. Thrapp (1967:189) notes that Juh and Geronimo spent the winter months near Fort Apache, but it is entirely likely that they made initial contact at Fort Bowie, the post nearest their homeland in Sonora.

32   The White man called 'Pine Pitch House' had been captured as a boy by the White Mountain Apache and raised among them. Later, he married a Chiricahua woman and went to live with her people. As one who understood the White Mountain Apache and their language, 'Pine Pitch House' figured prominently in the negotiations General Crook had with the Chiricahuas in Sonora in 1883.

33   The Chiricahua term which translates literally as 'brainless people' was used by all three bands of Chiricahua to designate the Western Apache. The latter did not seem to resent it.

34   The Western Apache claim that the very best acorns grow around Ash Flat and Rocky Creek. The former is an open valley in the southeast corner of the San Carlos Reservation; the latter is a small stream that flows through a shallow valley to the northeast.

35   This is an expression used by Western Apaches to indicate that a dance is about to be given. The drum is used in the dance.

36   The social dance of the Western Apache differs somewhat from that of the Chiricahua. Among the former, partners are not required to put their heads on each other's shoulder.

37   At social dances it is the woman's privilege to select a partner.

38   Hoop-and-poles was a favorite gambling game. Two men played. Each had a long pole, and one rolled a small hoop along the ground. The object was to throw the pole in such a way that the hoop would fall on top of it. The game required a great deal of skill. It is not played at the present time.

39   Victorio fled the reservation at San Carlos on September 1, 1877, taking with him over 300 men, women, and children. In the fall of 1879, after a few quiet months at Ojo Caliente, he bolted once again and embarked immediately upon a series of raids and killings that threw the residents of New Mexico and northern Mexico into a state of panic. In early May, 1880, Victorio re-entered Arizona with a small force and moved towards San Carlos. "Their exact purpose was not clear," says Thrapp (1967:199), "and they may have intended to reach relatives living on the Arizona reservation. Apparently they skirmished with peaceful Indians . . ." In light of Rope's account, it seems likely that the skirmish involved members of the eastern White Mountain group, and was prompted by Victorio's wish to avenge the death of one of his followers, probably a close relative.

40   For more information about the Western Apache 'war dance' see Part II of this volume, Chapter 8.

41   The Western Apache considered it dangerous for religious reasons to sever the head of a deer prior to the removal of its hide and innards.

42   Hair was removed so that the skins might later be made into buckskin.

43   The fact that none of the scouts in John Rope's company knew English well enough to act as an interpreter suggests that gestures occupied a prominent place in the Apache-White soldier communication system. Note, for example, that the two soldiers out of water could not transmit this message verbally but were forced to convey it by upending their empty canteens.

44   The *gan* are a group of supernatural beings who, impersonated by masked dancers, manifest themselves in certain types of curing ceremonials.

45   The Negro soldiers were probably stationed at Fort Bayrd, which was located approximately ten miles east of Silver City in New Mexico.

46   At this point in the original manuscript, Goodwin notes: "It was not the custom for a man to claim a deer he had shot, but to allow one of his companions to do so."

47   This may have been the first time that John Rope and his fellow Apache scouts tasted butter.

48   Warm Springs (not to be confused with Ojo Caliente in New Mexico) is located on Ash Creek, a narrow stream in the southeast corner of the San Carlos Reservation which joins the San Carlos River northeast of the present settlement of San Carlos. Bear Canyon is located approximately ten miles to the northwest.

49   The medicine man had used witchcraft on the boy and caused him to die. For an analysis of Western Apache witchcraft as it operates today see Basso 1969.

50   It was the custom in Rope's time, as it is today, for relatives of the deceased to see that the body was decently dressed for burial, preferably in a new set of clothes.

51   Among the Western Apache there were (and are today) various types of medicine men. Each type specialized in the treatment of a particular set of disease causes. Any illness diagnosed as having been contracted from a member of the canine family was handled by a medicine man who possessed 'coyote power.' For additional details on the diagnosis of disease and its treatment in the context of ritual see Goodwin 1937 and Basso 1968, 1969.

52   On a variety of occasions, the Western Apache performed different types of ceremonials as components in a fixed sequence. Failure to follow out the sequence— for example, omitting the social dance after the war dance—was believed to nullify the effectiveness of all its components (including those already performed) and was considered extremely dangerous.

53   Bowie Station (S.P.R.R.) was located at the junction of the Globe branch line, approximately fourteen miles from Fort Bowie.

54   A principal chief of the central Chiricahua band, Chihuahua was among the most cunning and intractable of Apache war leaders. His reasons for joining the expedition of which John Rope was a member are not made clear but, almost certainly, he had no intention of leading the soldiers to the renegade Chiricahuas they were searching for. Probably, he was curious to determine the strength of Rope's company and learn what he could of the Army's future plans. Chihuahua's contempt for the Whites comes through clearly in these pages, as when he observes: "These White soldiers are like nothing to us. If they keep this up, we will kill them and take all their horses." With Chato, Nachise, and Geronimo, Chihuahua helped perpetrate the San Carlos outbreak of 1882. Four years later, his forces depleted and weary of war, he surrendered at Fort Bowie.

55   In order to obtain weekly rations, the Apaches were required to present tickets to an agency official. The tickets were punched and retained by their owners for use the following week.

56   Of Mexican-Irish descent, Mickey Free was captured by Western Apaches as a small boy and raised by John Rope's father, probably in the vicinity of Fort Apache. As an adult, he became famous as a government interpreter and scout.

57　The so-called "Cibecue Massacre" occurred on August 30, 1881, when troops stationed at Fort Apache went to Cibecue and attempted to arrest a medicine man, the leader of a nascent nativistic movement. In the fight that ensued a number of U.S. soldiers were killed. Several troop companies were rushed to the Fort Apache area, and within a few weeks many of the Apaches who had been involved in the affair surrendered voluntarily. Most were ultimately released (Sánchez included) but three, who had been scouts, were court-martialed for mutiny and later hanged at Fort Grant. The Cibecue incident created much unrest among the Chiricahuas living at San Carlos and was undoubtedly an important factor in their decision to flee the reservation in 1882.

58　Under all but the most extreme circumstances, the Western Apache refrained from killing relatives. In this case, the two men probably agreed to hunt down the renegade in hopes that other of their relatives would be spared a similar fate.

59　When used against human beings, 'jaguar' or 'mountain lion power' was believed to render them immobile with fright. Concomitantly, the person who employed the power was able to fight with unusual ferocity.

60　The story of the renegade and the poor boy is familiar to many Apaches living today. It is usually interpreted to mean that even the most hardened and desperate men may retain a sense of justice.

61　In September of 1881, over seventy Chiricahuas led by Juh (southern band) and Nachise (central band; a son of Cochise) fled from San Carlos and joined forces with Chato, Chihuahua, and Geronimo in the Sierra Madre. Seven hundred Chiricahuas, mostly of the central and eastern bands, stayed behind under the steadying influence of Loco, a respected leader of the eastern band who thought it best to remain at peace. In need of reinforcements and anxious to see their relatives, the renegades left Mexico in January, 1882, and headed for San Carlos, eager to persuade Loco and his followers that the time was right for a break. They were successful. On April 18 the Chiricahuas bolted. Raiding and killing as they went, most of them reached Mexico. There, on April 27, near Corralitas in Sonora, Lorenzo García of the Sixth Mexican Infantry ambushed a large body of the eastern (Warm Springs) Chiricahuas, killing seventy-eight and capturing thirty-three (Thrapp 1964:239).

62　George H. Stevens was born in Massachusetts and came to Arizona in 1866. He married a White Mountain Apache woman, served as a scout under General Crook, started several ranches, and eventually served as a member of the territorial legislature.

63　Bylas was an eastern White Mountain chief for whom the present settlement of Bylas (San Carlos Reservation) is named.

64　The implication here is that Bylas disliked Geronimo and did not wish to share the whiskey with him.

65　Especially when speaking to someone who merits respect, such as Bylas, who was a chief, the Western Apache consider it extremely improper to voice a request more than once. Hence the boy's admonition to Geronimo.

66　The Western Apache were strongly matrilineal, and a child, regardless of who his father was, automatically belonged to the clan of his mother. Under these circumstances, it was quite natural for the White Mountain people to consider the foreman's son an Apache. The Chiricahua reckoned descent bilaterally, and Geronimo obviously thought less in unilineal terms.

67 The Chiricahuas disliked Mexicans intensely and rarely showed them mercy. According to Thrapp's (1967:232) account of the Stevens's Ranch massacre, Geronimo's men roasted one child alive and threw another into a nest of needle-crowned cactus.

68 In the original manuscript of John Rope's narrative, Goodwin notes at this point that "Geronimo was really a medicine-man, and it was from this power that he gained most of his influence among his people." Goodwin also notes that, by singing four songs, "Geronimo was putting himself in a state that would give him second sight."

69 It was believed that war medicine, if used effectively, made an adversary sleep soundly, thus rendering him more vulnerable to early morning attack.

70 Why the soldiers did not attack is a mystery. Perhaps they were too greatly outnumbered.

71 A White man, Al Sieber was chief of scouts for many years at San Carlos. He was admired and respected by Apaches and Whites alike. For additional information see Thrapp's excellent biography, *Al Sieber: Chief of Scouts* (1964).

72 Medicine men who accompanied war parties were frequently called upon to use their 'power' to look into the future. On such occasions, it was essential that everyone be serious; otherwise, the medicine man's 'power,' offended by what it considered disrespectful behavior, would refuse to cooperate. This is what happened in the incident described by John Rope.

73 Even today, older Western Apaches maintain that eagle feathers, activated by 'power,' become animate and move by themselves.

74 Peaches was a member of the Canyon Creek band, Cibecue group. His name was bestowed upon him by White soldiers because of his light complexion and rosy cheeks.

75 John Rope tried to use a little diplomacy here, hoping that the other man would give him the bigger deerskin.

76 Among the Western Apache, the penalty for failing to aid one's comrades in battle was ostracism or, in exceptional cases, death.

77 If other people had been ahead of the antelope, the herd would have swerved and run in some other direction.

78 Ordinarily, the members of war parties abstained from sexual intercourse because, they believed, it sapped their strength and made them sluggish.

79 There was almost always some man among the members of a war party who possessed 'wind power.' This was used to create dust storms which hid the movements of the party from the enemy.

80 General George Crook was relieved of command of the Department of Arizona in 1875, but after the Chiricahua outbreaks in 1882 he assumed the position once again. He reviewed the conditions at San Carlos and, finding them deplorable, set about making improvements. He then turned his attention to the renegades in Mexico. Reports of hostilities below the border filled the air, and Crook was worried that the raiders might return to Arizona. He wanted to seek out and, if necessary, destroy the Apaches in the Sierra Madre, but he lacked official permission to campaign below the international boundary. Permission came in the spring of 1883,

and on May 1, having established a base camp at San Bernardino, Crook headed into Sonora with a force of nearly 250 men. Of these, 193 were Indian scouts (Thrapp 1967:277).

As related here, John Rope gives a thoroughly unique account of Crook's famous campaign. Besides relating a series of incidents which to my knowledge are not recorded elsewhere, Rope's narrative shows clearly how Crook's acute understanding of Apaches enabled him to deal effectively with the hostile Chiricahua chiefs. For another account of Crook's famous expedition, see John G. Bourke's *An Apache Campaign in the Sierra Madre.*

81   The Apache attached great importance to ritual preparation for warfare, and Crook was aware that forbidding a war dance might create ill-feeling among his scouts. By suggesting that the dance be held, he avoided this possibility and, at the same time, demonstrated his respect for Apache custom.

82   When speaking to a close friend, either in giving advice or seeking it, Western Apaches often use grandchild-grandparent terms to gain attention and show respect.

83   To befuddle anyone that might be following them, the Chiricahua made it appear as though all the participants in the war dance had departed in different directions.

84   Children taken in war belonged to the person who captured them and, like stolen livestock, could be sold, traded, or given away.

85   Compared to the stealing of livestock, which was the aim of every seasoned raider, the capture of children was not considered an impressive feat. By singing a victory chant, the scout 'He Knows A Lot' was calling attention to this fact and, at the same time, poking fun at himself. The other scouts found his actions amusing.

86   The scouts knew that killing the old woman, who was defenseless and anxious to give herself up, could only serve to antagonize the Chiricahua further.

87   The scout who wanted the boy captive may not have been John Rope's relative. Cousin terms were often applied to non-relatives as an expression of solidarity and good will.

88   This incident is a fine example of Crook's diplomatic skill. If he had sent his emissaries to Chihuahua on anything but the finest mount, the Chiricahua chief could have construed it as a personal insult and, on these grounds, refused to negotiate.

89   Known in the historical literature as *Kaya Venne, Kayetene,* etc., 'Cartridges All Gone' was given his name because he fought so hard that he soon used his supply of cartridges. After returning from Mexico, he was sent to Fort Apache where he became the focus of considerable unrest. He was arrested after an unsuccessful attempt to ambush Lt. Britton Davis (whom Crook had placed in command of scouts), tried by an Indian jury at San Carlos, and sentenced to three years imprisonment at Alcatraz. In 1886, he was released at Crook's request and, together with Alchise, helped secure the final surrender of Chihuahua, Nana, and other notable Chiricahua leaders (c.f. Thrapp 1967:344–5).

90   There were distinct dialect differences between the several Western Apache subtribal groups.

91   Crook's apparent nonchalance at this critical moment was calculated to impress the Chiricahuas. The General's willingness to separate himself from his

troops showed that he was not preparing for a fight. It also gave the appearance of confidence and fearlessness, qualities he knew the Chiricahuas admired.

92   This is a reference to the fight with the Mexican Colonel García in 1882 in which a large number of Warm Springs Apaches were killed.

93   Goodwin notes that "These three Mexican women were later returned to their relatives."

94   As noted previously, a man by dancing with a woman obligated himself to present her with a gift, in this case ammunition.

95   In Chiricahua society a man was under the direct authority of his father-in-law and refrained from doing anything that might incur his displeasure. This probably explains why Geronimo was reluctant to carry out his plan without 'Pine Pitch House's' approval. Under normal circumstances an avoidance relationship would have existed between these two men, but apparently the urgency of the situation caused them to ignore it.

96   The Western Apache considered it dangerous to hold ceremonials immediately after a death. Sieber was acting on this knowledge.

97   Throughout John Rope's narrative, there is abundant evidence that kinship ties played an important role in the instigation and negotiation of peaceful surrenders. This incident is an excellent case in point.

98   Again the reference is to the García ambush in 1882.

99   Owing to a very real fear of ghosts and the belief that witches made poison from the flesh of exhumed corpses, the Western Apache were reluctant to visit graves or places where people had been killed.

100   A number of the Chiricahuas who returned from Mexico in 1883 were sent to live at Fort Apache. Most of them, according to Rope, were members of the eastern and central bands. In 1886, General Nelson A. Miles, who had succeeded General Crook, arrested these people and ordered them shipped to Florida as prisoners of war.

101   A trusted scout when John Rope knew him, the Apache Kid, whom Goodwin describes simply as "a San Carlos man," turned renegade in 1887. Charged with many murders in the years that followed, he was widely hunted but never captured. The last clue to his whereabouts came from an Apache woman who, in 1894, reported that he was critically ill with tuberculosis in the Sierra Madre. For an excellent résumé of the Apache Kid's career see Thrapp 1963:320–350.

102   After surrendering to Crook in Mexico, Chato went to live with his wife's people at Fort Apache. He was made a scout and, according to Goodwin, quickly advanced to the rank of sergeant.

103   As late as 1910, Navajos traveled to San Carlos and Fort Apache on trading expeditions. In exchange for blankets, which the Apache prized for their warmth and durability, the Navajo received buckskins and woven baskets.

104   The man called Archie may have been Archie MacIntosh, a half-blood Chippewa scout who served Crook in the Northwest, later accompanied him to Arizona, and rendered invaluable assistance throughout the Apache campaigns. For further details see Thrapp 1964:88–89.

105   Goodwin notes that on certain reservations, notably San Carlos and Fort Apache, "Spy systems were in operation whereby certain Apaches were paid to keep the commanding officer informed of all suspicious activity."

106   Casador was, at the time he turned renegade, the main chief of the San Carlos band.

107   Today, as in John Rope's time, a number of Western Apaches are believed to have 'power' which enables them to control the actions of horses.

108   The Chiricahuas were shipped to Florida via Holbrook, Arizona. They left Fort Apache on September 7, 1886.

109   As Goodwin explains in a note, John Rope is referring here not to Chiricahuas but to "Western Apaches, themselves turned renegade, who were out in the hills around San Carlos."

110   To facilitate rapid communications, General Miles had ordered the installation of thirty heliograph stations atop peaks in Arizona, New Mexico, and Mexico. The signal system was designed to keep all forces constantly informed about the movements of troops and Indians. It was completed by the end of 1886 and is said to have worked effectively.

111   During the early years and through most of the Chiricahua campaigns, the Apache scouts traveled on foot. Later, they went mounted.

112   Immediately after burial, it was customary to destroy the deceased's personal possessions. In part a gesture of respect, this activity was also believed to protect the living against 'ghost sickness.'

113   The man who informed on 'He Knows Hardship's' father may well have been one of the spies, or "secret agents," mentioned earlier. See note 105.

114   It is evident from Rope's narrative that, having committed the act of murder, a renegade expected neither mercy nor forgiveness. Knowing that if scouts did not capture or kill him the relatives of his victim would, he viewed his plight as hopeless. Under these conditions, many renegades "went crazy" and, abandoning all caution and judgment, began to kill indiscriminately.

115   Smiley was a chief among the Tontos at Fort Apache.

116   With a trace of humor, Goodwin notes at this point: "The scouts could never see why the soldiers had to go through all the maneuvers of formation before they went somewhere."

117   When mourning over a corpse, it is customary for Western Apache women to keen in long, drawn-out wails.

118   It should be noted that the murderers did not leave the adobe house until they were certain of military protection. Without it, they would have been killed instantly.

119   The desperation of renegades, coupled with their willingness to kill, made the task of capturing them extremely difficult. By comparison, the scouts considered the earlier, long-distance campaigns less dangerous.

5   DAVID LONGSTREET

1   The medicine man was obligated not only to cure the girl who had been bitten but to rid the entire camp of "coyote fear"—a generalized apprehension that sets in whenever a coyote comes too close or performs an "unnatural" act.

2   It was customary to notify everyone in the immediate vicinity of an impending ceremonial, especially the patient's matrilineal kinsmen. The latter stood

to benefit from the ceremonial as much as the patient himself and were expected to make substantial contributions of food and labor.

3   The *gan* are a set of supernaturals who, impersonated by masked dancers, manifest themselves in a type of curing ceremonial. The *gan* dance is frequently referred to in the popular literature as the "devil dance," but this is a misnomer. Neither the ceremonial nor the dancers have any connection with the devil, a concept which the Western Apache probably borrowed from the Mexicans.

4   The voice to which the medicine man refers in this passage is his supernatural 'power,' an invisible but potent force that instructs him in the performance of ritual and aids him in curing the sick.

5   Having contracted illness from a known or diagnosed source—in this case coyotes—Apaches were advised to avoid all contact with it (or anything it had touched) in the future. In this way, it was believed, the chances of the illness recurring were significantly reduced.

6   The Apaches Mansos ('mild' or 'tame' Apache), were a small band of Athapaskan speakers who lived in the vicinity of San Xavier, a few miles south of Tucson. On friendly terms with the Papago, they frequently led Mexican and White soldiers on raids against the Western Apache. (See, for example, Underhill 1938:22). The ambush described by Longstreet probably occurred after 1860. Goodwin notes explicitly that it was not the famous Camp Grant Massacre.

7   For a description of the Papago victory dance and the purification rituals that accompanied it see Underhill (1939).

8   At this point, Goodwin notes: "Between bands of different Western Apache groups there was often enmity and mistrust. Hence the reluctance of the two women, who belonged to the eastern White Mountain band, to go to the Arivaipa people for help."

9   The "head officer" Longstreet mentions was probably Col. E. A. Rigg, who established a military post (Camp Goodwin) near Goodwin Springs in 1864. The meeting with Diablo, at which Rigg secured permission to build a road to the present site of Fort Apache, is described in the narrative of John Rope.

10   The old military road went from Calva on the Gila River, across Ash Flat, north to the Black River, and finally to Fort Apache.

11   From 1872 on, Western Apache scouts enlisted with U.S. troops and gave indispensible assistance in bringing hostile Apaches to terms. For further details see the narrative of John Rope.

12   The peak that the Western Apache called 'round' or 'squat mountain' was located near Cloverdale, New Mexico.

13   The military career of John Emmet Crawford was as notable as it was brief. Captain Crawford achieved prominence in 1882 when he assumed military control of all Indian reservations in the Department of Arizona. In 1883, having rendered outstanding service as a member of Crook's famous expedition into Mexico, he was assigned to supervise the Chiricahuas at San Carlos. Transferred to Texas in 1884, Crawford was recalled to Arizona immediately after Geronimo's outbreak in May of 1885. A few months later, in pursuit of the renegade, he was mortally wounded when his company of scouts, mistaken for hostile Apaches, was ambushed by Mexican troops.

14   The "head officer" was General George Crook and the time was April, 1883, shortly before the start of his campaign into the Sierra Madre. Longstreet's

account of this campaign is less complete than the one given in the narrative of John Rope and differs from it on several minor points.

15   The Chiricahua had conducted the war ceremony facing the town they were planning to attack.

16   There is some evidence to suggest that Casador was, philosophically at least, a pacifist. However, once branded a murderer, he had no choice but to turn "renegade" and face the consequences of having broken reservation law.

17   Longstreet is alluding here to the fact that, since he was the son of a chief, his death—had it occurred—would have been avenged with unusual swiftness.

6   MRS. ANDREW STANLEY

1   Mrs. Stanley is probably referring here to the Apaches who surrendered voluntarily after the so-called "Cibecue Massacre" of 1881. For additional information about this event see the narrative of John Rope, note 57.

2   From 1878 on, there were large numbers of captive Chiricahuas living at or around Fort Apache. Although they appear to have mixed freely with the White Mountain Apache on certain occasions, it is clear from Mrs. Stanley's account that hostilities between the two groups were not uncommon.

3   These were hostile Chiricahuas, probably a remnant of the eastern (Warm Springs) band. They were camped on the Rio Grande, but precisely where is uncertain.

4   Without her brother—the only person she could count on for support and protection—Mrs. Stanley found herself at the complete disposal of the Chiricahua. The latter saw that she was virtually defenseless and treated her accordingly—like a "captive."

5   Evidently, Mrs. Stanley and her party passed by the spot near Corralitos, Sonora, where, in April, 1882, Mexican troops led by Lorenzo García ambushed a large body of Warm Springs Apaches. For additional details see the narrative of John Rope.

6   Unlike men, whose raiding activities regularly took them far from home, Apache women were unfamiliar with distant territories and experienced serious difficulty when forced to navigate them alone. Hence Mrs. Stanley's tendency to get lost.

7   This was a group of low, rocky hills just south of Fort Bowie.

8   The feeling persists among Apaches today that persons who have lived alone for long periods of time will have difficulty readjusting to the conditions of social life. It is said that such individuals have lived "too long inside themselves" and, initially at least, "don't know how to act" with others. One of the most interesting—and moving—aspects of Mrs. Stanley's narrative is the trepidation and apprehension that grips her when she finally returns home. Aware that her recent experiences have made her "wild like a deer," she is anxious and uncertain about how her relatives will accept her.

9   The aged and the dying were sometimes abandoned under the threat of enemy attack. Unable to travel and no longer useful, they were a burden to others and knew it. There are one or two cases on record in which old people, tired of living this way, demanded to be left behind.

PART II

7   WEAPONS

1   The stone from which most arrow straighteners were fashioned was pumice.

2   The territory of the Western Apache is dotted with the remains of prehistoric dwellings, and it was to these that the old men went in search of flint.

3   The use of lichens in arrow poison was predicated on the belief that whatever was wounded with the poison would become as "heavy" (i.e. immobile) as the rocks on which lichens grow.

4   A man who made a shield without full knowledge of 'enemies-against power' ran the risk of angering this 'power' and, as a result, falling seriously ill. For additional information see Part II of this volume, Chapter 13.

8   THE WAR DANCE

1   The members of the family sponsoring the war dance were saying, in effect, that they were seeking women and girls for social purposes only—to dance—and not with the intention of promoting or engaging in illicit sexual relations.

2   Women wishing to participate in the social dance selected partners by tapping them on the arm or shoulder. Hence the name given to the songs sung at social dances: 'invite by touching him.'

10   PREPARATIONS AND CONDUCT

1   Fat horses were preferred because they made the best eating and were easier to herd.

2   Medicine men with 'star power' were especially adept at looking into the future. As members of raiding and war parties, they used their 'power' to anticipate the actions of enemies.

3   The dust storms created by medicine men served the primary purpose of obscuring war parties from would-be attackers.

4   The men and boys who stayed behind served as lookouts and, if livestock was stolen, helped drive it home.

5   The Apache were mightily impressed with individual acts of bravery, especially when they were instrumental in saving the lives of others. The story of the "lonesome chief's son" (lonesome because he did not marry) is a famous one and is told to this day.

11   TABOOS AND WARPATH LANGUAGE

1   A gambling game, *hai?gohɛ* is played with four flat sticks, each one specially marked. The sticks were thrown much like dice and points awarded according to how they fell.

2   The regular terms for these objects are as follows: 'burro' [*tuɫkaiye*]; 'mule' [*tsandezi*]; 'old women' [*san*]; 'Mexican' [*nɛkaiyɛ?*].

12   TABOOS FOR WOMEN

1   Any object in which large amounts of 'power' resided was considered dangerous for women to touch. This was especially true of shields and ritual paraphernalia which had been used in ceremonials.

13   THE USE OF 'POWER'

1   After the world was created, according to myth, Changing Woman was impregnated by Sun and gave birth to 'Killer of Monsters,' the foremost Western Apache culture hero. A short time later, Changing Woman gave birth to 'Born of Water.' Having first been instructed in all things by Changing Woman, the two half-brothers left home and rid the world of much that was evil, thus making it a suitable place for Apaches to live. For an excellent collection of Western Apache myths see Goodwin.

2   'Happiness songs' were sung on the warpath, at the girls' puberty ceremonial, during sweat bath, and on a variety of non-ceremonial occasions. Unlike 'power songs' they were not used in curing rituals.

15   THE VICTORY CELEBRATION

1   A warrior whose camp was honored by a mock attack was obligated to present his attackers with a substantial gift, usually in the form of livestock.

2   In the context of a victory dance, obscene acts of this sort were interpreted by adults as an expression of high spirits. However, young people, lacking in sophistication, found them very embarrassing.

3   Owls were closely associated with ghosts. Hearing an owl was interpreted to mean that the ghost of a deceased relative—possibly bent upon causing sickness—was close at hand.

17   THE NOVICE COMPLEX

1   The oriole feathers symbolized clear-headedness, a quality that Apaches deemed essential to success in battle.

2   The eagle feathers on the boy's war cap were believed to give protection against injury, sickness, and misfortune.

3   During the girls' puberty ceremonial, and for four days following, the pubescent girl wears a piece of abalone shell on a rawhide thong tied round her head. The shell identifies her with Changing Woman, a mythological figure whom she personifies during the ceremony.

4   The Apache viewed experience and maturity as prerequisites for the acquisition of 'power.' Persons lacking these qualities were liable to use 'power' incorrectly and bring misfortune to themselves and to others. Judging from Goodwin's material, Apache men acquired 'enemies-against power' only after they had been to war a number of times.

5   At the close of the girls' puberty ceremonial, anyone in attendance may bless the pubescent girl by sprinkling a pinch of cattail pollen on her head and shoulders. At the same time, he may request the girl to grant him personal good fortune. Novice boys were blessed with pollen for the same reason.

6   Songs from the same corpus, i.e. 'happiness songs,' were sung for the girls' puberty ceremonial.

7   This term is also applied to maidens who are going through the girls' puberty rite. During this ceremonial, and for four days thereafter, the girl may drink only through a section of hollow reed (the drinking tube) and touch herself only with a small wooden "scratching stick." The same restrictions applied to boys taking part in their first raid. For a detailed description of the girls' puberty ceremonial as it is performed today see Basso 1966.

8   A taboo against washing and bathing was also applied to pubescent girls.

REFERENCES

BASSO, KEITH H.

1966   The Gift of Changing Woman. Bulletin of the Bureau of American Ethnology, No. 196. Smithsonian Institution, Washington, D.C.

1969   Western Apache Witchcraft. Anthropological Papers of the University of Arizona, No. 15. University of Arizona Press, Tucson.

BETZINEZ, JASON

1959   I Fought with Geronimo. Stackpole Company, Harrisburg, Pennsylvania.

BIGELOW, LT. JOHN JR.

1958   On the Bloody Trail of Geronimo. Edited by Arthur Woodward. Westernlore Press, Los Angeles.

BOURKE, JOHN G.

1886   An Apache Campaign in the Sierra Madre. Charles Scribner's Sons, New York.

1891   On the Border with Crook. Charles Scribner's Sons, New York.

BRANDES, RAY

1960   Frontier Military Posts of Arizona. Dale Stuart King, Globe, Arizona.

BUSKIRK, WINIFRED

1949   Western Apache Subsistence Economy. Unpublished doctoral dissertation, University of New Mexico, Albuquerque.

CLUM, WOODWORTH
   1936   Apache Agent. Houghton Mifflin, Boston.

CROOK, GEORGE
   1946   General George Crook: His Autobiography. Edited by Martin
          F. Schmitt. University of Oklahoma Press, Norman.

CRUSE, THOMAS
   1941   Apache Days and After. The Caxton Press, Caldwell, Idaho.

DAVIS, BRITTON
   1929   The Truth About Geronimo. Yale University Press, New
          Haven.

EZELL, PAUL
   1961   The Hispanic Acculturation of the Gila River Pimas. American
          Anthropological Association, Memoir 90, Menasha, Wisconsin.

FONTANA, BERNARD L.
   1968   *Review* of Dan L. Thrapp, The Conquest of Apacheria (The
          University of Oklahoma Press, Norman). *In* Ethnohistory
          15:446–47.

FORBES, JACK D.
   1960   Apache, Navaho, and Spaniard. The University of Oklahoma
          Press, Norman.

GETTY, HARRY T.
   1964   Changes in Land Use among the Western Apaches. *In* Indian
          and Spanish American Adjustments to Arid and Semi-arid
          Environments. Edited by Clark Knowlton, The Committee on
          Desert and Arid Zone Research, No. 7, Lubbock, Texas.

GOODWIN, GRENVILLE
   1935   The Social Divisions and Economic Life of the Western
          Apache. American Anthropologist 37:55–64.
   1936   Experiences of An Indian Scout: Excerpts from the Life of
          John Rope, an Old-Timer of the White Mountain Apaches.
          Arizona Historical Review, Vol. 7, Nos. 1 and 2.
   1937   The Characteristics and Function of Clan in a Southern
          Athapascan Culture. American Anthropologist 39:394–407.
   1938   White Mountain Apache Religion. American Anthropologist
          40:24–37.
   1942   The Social Organization of the Western Apache. University of
          Chicago Press, Chicago.

HALL, EDWARD T.
   1944   Recent Clues to Athapascan Prehistory. American Anthropol-
          ogist 46:98–105.

KAUT, CHARLES R.
   1957   The Western Apache Clan System: Its Origins and Develop-
          ment. University of New Mexico Publications in Anthropology
          No. 9, Albuquerque.

KROEBER, ALFRED L.
   1939   Cultural and Natural Areas of Native North America. Univer-
          sity of California Publications in American Archaeology and
          Ethnology, Vol. 38, Berkeley.

MOORHEAD, MAX L.
   1968   The Apache Frontier: Jacobo Ugarte and Spanish-Indian
          Relations in Northern New Spain, 1769–1791. The University
          of Oklahoma Press, Norman.

OGLE, RALPH HEDRICK
   1940   Federal Control of the Western Apaches: 1848–1886. Univer-
          sity of New Mexico Press, Albuquerque.

OPLER, MORRIS E.
   1941   An Apache Life-Way. University of Chicago Press, Chicago.

OPLER, MORRIS E. AND HARRY HOIJER
   1940   The Raid and Warpath Language of the Chiricahua Apache.
          American Anthropologist 42:617–34.

SPIER, LESLIE
   1933   Yuman Tribes of the Gila River. University of Chicago Press,
          Chicago.

SPICER, EDWARD H.
   1967   Cycles of Conquest. University of Arizona Press, Tucson
          (Second Printing).

THRAPP, DAN L.
   1964   Al Sieber: Chief of Scouts. University of Oklahoma Press,
          Norman.
   1967   The Conquest of Apachería. University of Oklahoma Press,
          Norman.

UNDERHILL, RUTH
   1938   A Papago Calendar Record. University of New Mexico
          Anthropological Series, No. 2, Albuquerque.
   1939   Social Organization of the Papago Indians. Columbia Univer-
          sity Contributions to Anthropology, No. 30, New York.

INDEX

Acorns, 308 *n*; Emory's Oak, 304 *n*
Agua Prieta, 110, 156, 171
Alchise, 154, 159, 163, 172, 197; 155 *ill*;
  312 *n*
'Angry, He Is Agitated,' 112
'Angry, He Stares At It,' 129
'Angry, He Starts Fights,' 167–68
'Angry, He Takes It Away,' 129
Animas Valley, 209
'Antelopes Approach Her,' 163
'Antelope's Water,' 104, 108, 115, 130, 135
Apache Kid, The, 173; 138 ill; 313 *n*
'Apache Mansos,' 12, 191–93, 195, 286,
  315 *n*
Apache Pass, 148
Apache Peaks, 82–83; band, 85
Arivaipa, Apaches, 78–79, 85–86, 193,
  306 *n*; Valley, 192, 197
Arrows, 227–31; all-wooden, 229–30;
  desert broom, 224; cane, 227, 230; reeds,
  227; stone smoother, 229; Western
  Apache, 228 *ill*
Arrow decorations, charcoal, 230;
  hematite, 230
Arrowpoints, catclaw, 230; flint, 231, 317 *n*;
  four crosspiece rig, 231; steel point, 231;
  stone point, 231
Ash Creek, 127, 129, 194, 309 *n*
Ash Flat, 46, 110, 143–44, 146, 173, 194,
  196, 308 *n*, 315 *n*

Bači. See 'Apache Mansos'
Baʔitandaʔ. See 'For Him They Search'
Bavispe, Sonora, 140, 155, 170, 197; river,
  158, 168
Bear, 198
Bear Canyon, 127, 229, 309 *n*
Bešn. See 'metal knife'
'Big Coyote,' 162
'Big, Hips Heavy,' 285–86

Bitsaʔha dogiž ['his head top cut off'] *See*
  Scalping
'Black rope,' 93
Blue Range, 31
Blue River, 98, 100, 194
'Born of Water,' 270
Bows, 223–26; double arc, 224; mulberry,
  223; single arc, 224; Western Apache,
  225 *ill*; Wrights willow, 223; wristguard
  for, 224–25
Bowstrings, deer sinew, 224
Bourke, Captain John C., 3
'Brainless people,' 110, 308 *n*
Bureau of Indian Affairs, 6, 22
Bylas, Arizona, 3–4, 93, 310 *n*; Richard,
  143–44, 146, 185, 196, 310 *n*; uncle of
  Richard (Bylas), 103, 116, 123, 142 *ill*

Čačidn. See 'red rock strata people'
Ča daʔizkan. See 'Hat, Soft and Floppy'
Całhčł. See 'He Goes Out At Night'
California Volunteers, 303 *n*
Calva, 45, 98, 103–04, 108, 185, 190, 315 *n*
Camp Ord, 305 *n*
Camp Powers, 307 *n*
Camp Stanford, 306 *n*
Camp Verde, 21–22, 24
Canyon Creek, 73, 303 *n*, 311 *n*
Canyon Day, 5, 41, 175
Canyon del Oro, 303 *n*
Captives, 284–87; *yodasčin*, ['born
  outside'], 286; killed by women, 284–86
Carretas, 140, 152
Carrizo, 137
Carson, Kit, 308 *n*
'Cartridges All Gone,' 165, 169; 166 *ill*;
  312 *n*
Casador, 200; 177 *ill*; 314 *n*, 316 *n*
Cave Creek, 109, 130, 134, 307 *n*
Cedar Creek, 93, 96, 98, 104, 115, 129–30

[325]